AREA 7 & CONTEST

At only 27 years of age, Matthew Reilly is the international bestselling author of four novels, *Contest*, *Ice Station*, *Temple* and now *Area 7*. He wrote his first two books while studying Law at the University of New South Wales, and now spends his time writing novels and screenplays.

Contest, *Ice Station* and *Temple* were all runaway bestsellers both in Australia and overseas, and rights to Matthew's novels have now been sold to over twelve countries including the UK, US and Germany. Film rights to *Contest* have been optioned.

A keen fan of Hollywood action blockbusters, Matthew hopes to direct one of his own action-adventure screenplays sometime in the near future. He lives in Sydney.

For more information on Matthew and his books, visit his website: www.matthewreilly.com

Also by Matthew Reilly

ICE STATION

TEMPLE

MATTHEW REILLY

AREA 7
&
CONTEST

PAN BOOKS

Area 7 first published in Great Britain 2001 by Macmillan.
First published in paperback 2002 by Pan Books.
Contest first published 1996 by Karanadon Entertainment.
This edition first published 2000 by Pan Macmillan Australia.
First published in Great Britain 2001 by Pan Books.

This omnibus first published 2005 by Pan Books
an imprint of Pan Macmillan, a division of Macmillan Publishers Limited
Pan Macmillan, 20 New Wharf Road, London N1 9RR
Basingstoke and Oxford
Associated companies throughout the world
www.panmacmillan.com

ISBN 978-0-330-44374-6

3 5 7 9 8 6 4 2

A CIP catalogue record for this book is available from
the British Library.

Printed and bound by CPI Group (UK) Ltd, Croydon, CR0 4YY

AREA 7

For John Schrooten, my friend

Acknowledgements

I'll try to be quick. Sincere thanks once again to:

Natalie Freer—who gets to see (and put up with) my creative eccentricities up close. Her patience and generosity know no bounds;

My brother, Stephen Reilly—tortured writer, constructive and creative critic, and good friend; and to his wife, Rebecca Ryan, because they come as a package;

My wonderful parents—Ray and Denise Reilly—for encouraging me to build miniature movie sets for my *Star Wars* action-figures when I was a kid; my creativity comes directly from them;

My good friends, John Schrooten, Nik and Simon Kozlina, the whole Kay clan (notably Don, who made me shrink the size of the cats in *Temple*) and to Paul Whyte for accompanying me on an extraordinary trip to Utah while researching this book.

A special mention to two American friends—Captain Paul M. Woods, US Army, and Gunnery Sergeant Kris Hankinson, USMC (retired), who generously gave of their time and assisted me with the military details of this book. Any mistakes are mine, and were made over their objections.

And finally, once again, thanks to everyone at Pan Macmillan. This is our fourth outing together and it still rocks. Thanks to Cate Paterson (legend publisher), Jane Novak (legend publicist), Sarina Rowell (legend editor), and Paul Kenny (legend). And, of course, as always, to the sales reps at Pan for the countless hours they spend on the road between bookshops.

To anyone who knows a writer, never underestimate the power of your encouragement.

All right! Now on with the show . . .

UNITED STATES AIR FORCE
SPECIAL AREA (RESTRICTED) NO. 7

GROUND LEVEL: Main Hangar

LEVEL 1: Hangar Bay

LEVEL 2: Hangar Bay

LEVEL 3: Living Quarters

LEVEL 4: Laboratories

LEVEL 5: Confinement

LEVEL 6: X-rail platform

GROUND LEVEL: MAIN HANGAR

The 'top door' exit

Regular elevator

Northern office

Hangar Doors

Helicopters

Aircraft elevator platform

Control centre

Detachable mini-elevator platform

Storage closet

Armoured door

Southern office

LEVEL 1: UNDERGROUND HANGAR BAY

Water tanks

Regular elevator

Air vent

Aircraft elevator Shaft

Ramp

LEVEL 2: UNDERGROUND HANGAR BAY

Regular elevator

Stairwell opening in floor

Air vent

Aircraft elevator Shaft

Ramp

LEVEL 3: LIVING QUARTERS

Regular elevator

Air vent

Aircraft elevator shaft

Library, study/office area

7th Squadron living quarters

Officers' quarters

Common room area

Stairwell

Scientific staff living quarters

Gym

LEVEL 4: LABORATORIES AND QUARANTINE

Regular elevator

Dividing wall

Elevator catwalk

Air vent

Aircraft elevator shaft

Laboratory and observation areas (upper level)

Test chambers

Ramp from Level 5

Door

Stairwell

Cube

Bench

Decompression chamber

LEVEL 5: CONFINEMENT

Regular elevator

Ramp to Level 4

Ante-room (transition area)

Air vent

Aircraft elevator shaft

Prisoner cells

Animal cells

Stairwell

Closet

LEVEL 6: X-RAIL PLATFORM

Regular
elevator

Emergency
Exit Vent

Air vent

Pylons

Central platform

Stairwell

X-rail tracks

Tunnel
blast doors

X-rail engines

Maintenance
vehicle

The single greatest fear that America faces today is that its military forces no longer tolerate the continuing incompetence of its civilian leadership.

Mr George K. Suskind,
Defense Intelligence Agency,
Evidence given before the House
Sub-committee on the Armed Forces,
22 July 1996

The difference between a republic and an empire is the loyalty of one's army.

Julius Caesar

INTRODUCTION

From: Katz, Caleb
The C.B. Powell Memorial Address: 'The Presidency'
**(Speech delivered at the School of Politics,
Harvard University, 26 February 1999)**

'There is no other institution in the world quite like the President of the United States.

All at once, the person who holds this title becomes the leader of the fourth most populous nation on earth, the commander-in-chief of its armed forces, and the chief executive officer of what Harry Truman called "the largest going concern in the world".

The use of the term "chief executive" has made comparisons with company structures inevitable, and to a certain extent, they are appropriate—although, what other corporate leaders in the world have 2 trillion dollar budgets at their fingertips, a licence to use the 82nd Airborne Division to enforce their will, and briefcases at their sides that can unleash an arsenal of thermonuclear devastation against their competitors?

Among modern political systems, however, the American

President is unique—for the simple reason that he is both head of government *and* head of state.

Most nations separate these two functions. In the United Kingdom, for instance, the head of state is the Queen; the head of *government* is the Prime Minister. It is a separation born out of a history of tyrants—kings who wore the crown, but who also governed at their often erratic pleasure.

But in the US, the man who runs the country is also the *symbol* of the country. In his words and his deeds, the President's every act is a barometer for the glory of the nation. For his strength is the people's strength.

John F. Kennedy staring down the Soviets over Cuba in 1962.

Harry Truman's nerves-of-steel decision to drop the atomic bomb on Japan in 1945.

Or Ronald Reagan's confident smile.

His strength is the people's strength.

But there are dangers in this arrangement of things. For if the President is the embodiment of America, what happens when things go wrong?

The assassination of John F. Kennedy.

The resignation of Richard Nixon.

The humiliation of William Jefferson Clinton.

The death of Kennedy was the death of America's innocence. Nixon's resignation drove a knife into the heart of America's optimism. And the humiliation of Clinton was the global humiliation of America—at peace summits and press conferences around the world, the first question asked of Clinton was invariably directed at his sexcapades in a study adjoining the Oval Office.

Be it in death or disgrace, decisiveness or courage, the President of the United States is more than just a man. He is an institution—a symbol—the walking, talking embodiment of a nation. On his back ride the hopes and dreams of 276 million people . . .' [pp.1–2]

From: Farmer, J.T.
'Coincidence or Co-ordinated Murder?
The Death of Senator Jeremiah Woolf'
Article from: *The Conspiracy Theorist Monthly*
[circulation: 152 copies]
(Delva Press, April issue, 2001)

'. . . The body was found in the woods surrounding the senator's isolated hunting cabin in the Kuskokwim Mountains in Alaska.

Truth be told, at the time of his death Jerry Woolf was no longer a senator, having retired abruptly from Congress only ten months earlier, surprising all the pundits, citing family reasons for the unexpected move.

He was still alive when they found him—no mean feat considering the high-velocity hunting bullet lodged in his chest. Woolf was immediately taken by helicopter to Blaine County Hospital, one hundred and fifty miles away, where emergency residents tried in vain to stem the bloodflow.

But the damage was too severe. After forty-five minutes of emergency treatment, former United States Senator Jeremiah K. Woolf died.

Sounds simple, doesn't it? A terrible hunting accident. Like so many others that happen every year in this country.

That's what your government would have you believe.

Consider this: Blaine County Hospital records show that a patient named Jeremiah K. Woolf was declared dead in the emergency ward at 4:35 p.m. on the afternoon of February 6, 2001.

That is the only record of the incident that exists. All other records of Woolf's examination at the hospital were confiscated by the FBI.

Now consider this: *on that very same day*—February 6, 2001—on the other side of the country, at exactly 9:35 p.m., Jeremiah Woolf's Washington townhouse was destroyed in an explosion, an explosion that killed his wife and only daughter. Investigators would later claim that this blast was caused by a gas leak.

The FBI believes Woolf—previously a vibrant young senator, crusader against organised crime, and potential presidential candidate—was the victim of an extortion racket: leave us alone, or we'll kill your family.

This is, without a doubt, a government smokescreen.

If Woolf was being blackmailed, well, one has to ask: *why?* He had retired from the Senate ten months previously. And if he was killed in a routine hunting accident, why were the records of his emergency room procedures at Blaine County Hospital taken by the FBI?

What *really* happened to Jerry Woolf? At the moment, we just don't know.

But consider this final point: owing to the time difference, 9:35 p.m. in Washington DC is 4:35 p.m. in Alaska.

So at the end of the day, after all the talk of hunting accidents and Mafia blackmail and faulty gas valves is cast aside, one fact remains: at the *exact* same moment that former United States Senator Jerry Woolf's heart stopped beating in an emergency room in Alaska, his home on the other side of the country exploded in a gigantic ball of flames . . .'

AREA 7

PROLOGUE

It had been his last request.

To watch the inauguration ceremony on television.

Sure, it had delayed the trip to Terre Haute by an hour, but then—so the powers-that-be at Leavenworth had reckoned—if the condemned man's last request was reasonable, who were they to refuse him.

The television threw a flickering strobe-like glow onto the concrete walls of the holding cell. Tinny voices came from its speakers:

'. . . do solemnly swear . . .'

'. . . do solemnly swear . . .'

'. . . that I will faithfully execute the office of President of the United States . . .'

'. . . that I will faithfully execute the office of President of the United States . . .'

The condemned prisoner watched the television intently.

9

And then—despite the fact that he had less than two hours to live—a smile began to spread across his face.

The number on his prison shirt read: 'T-77'.

He was an older man, fifty-nine, with a round, weather-beaten face and slicked-down black hair. Despite his age, he was a big man, powerfully built—with a bull neck and broad shoulders. His eyes were a bottomless unreadable black and they glistened with intelligence. He'd been born in Baton Rouge, Louisiana, and when he spoke, his accent was strong.

Until recently, he had been a resident of T-Wing—that section of Leavenworth devoted to inmates who are not safe among the general prison population.

Two weeks ago, however, he had been moved from T-Wing to Pre-Transit—otherwise known as the Departure Lounge—another special wing where those awaiting execution stayed before they were flown out to Terre Haute Federal Penitentiary in Indiana for execution by lethal injection.

A former Civil War fort, Leavenworth is a maximum-security federal prison. This means it receives only those offenders who break *federal* laws—a class of individuals that variously includes violent criminals, foreign spies or terrorists, organised crime bosses, and members of the US armed forces who sell secrets, commit crimes or desert.

It is also perhaps the most brutal penitentiary in America.

But in that peculiar way of prisons the world over, its inhabitants—men who have themselves killed or raped—

have, over the years, developed a strange sense of justice.

Serial rapists are themselves violated on a daily basis. Army deserters are beaten regularly, or worse, branded on their foreheads with the letter 'D'. Foreign spies, such as the four Middle Eastern terrorists convicted of the World Trade Centre bombing in 1993, have been known to lose body parts.

But by far the most ferocious treatment of all is reserved for one particular class of prisoner: traitors.

It seems that despite all their own crimes, all their own atrocities, the American inmates of Leavenworth—many of them disgraced soldiers—still profess a deep love of their country. Traitors are usually killed within their first three days in the pen.

William Anson Cole, the former CIA analyst who sold information to the Chinese government about an impending Navy SEAL mission to the Xichang Launch Centre, the epicentre of China's space operations—information which led to the capture, torture and death of all six SEAL team members—was found dead in his cell two days after he had arrived at the prison. His rectum had been torn from repeated violations with a pool cue and he had been strangled, hog-style, with a bed leg tied across his throat—a crude simulation of the Chinese torture method of strangulation by bamboo pole.

Ostensibly, prisoner T-77 was in Leavenworth for murder—or more precisely, for *ordering* the murder of two senior Navy officers—a crime which in the US military carried the death sentence. However, the fact that the two Navy officers he'd had killed *had been advisers to the Joint Chiefs of Staff* elevated his crime to treason. High treason.

11

That—and his own previous high ranking—had earned him a place in T-Wing.

But even in T-Wing a man isn't entirely safe. T-77 had been beaten several times during his short residency there—on two occasions, so severely that he'd required blood transfusions.

In his former life, his name had been Charles Samson Russell and he had been a three-star Lieutenant General in the United States Air Force. Call-sign: *Caesar*.

He had a certified IQ of 182, genius level, and as such he had been a brilliant officer. Methodical and razor-sharp, he'd been the ultimate commander, hence his call-sign.

But most of all . . . *patient*, Caesar thought now as he watched the flickering television screen in front of him.

The two men on the screen—the Chief Justice of the Supreme Court and the President-Elect—were finishing their duet. They stood in grey, wintry sunshine, on the West Portico of the Capitol Building. The new President had his hand on a Bible.

'. . . and will to the best of my ability . . .'

'. . . and will to the best of my ability . . .'

'. . . preserve, protect, and defend the Constitution of the United States, so help me God.'

'. . . preserve, protect, and defend the Constitution of the United States, so help me God.'

Fifteen years, Caesar thought.

Fifteen years, he had waited.

And now, at last, it had happened.

It hadn't been easy. There had been several false starts—including one who had made it to the election as a

12

vice-presidential candidate, only to lose in a landslide. Four others had made it to the New Hampshire primary, but then failed to secure their parties' candidacy.

And of course, you always had some—like that Woolf fellow—who would quit politics before they had even begun to truly explore their presidential potential. It was an extra expense, but no matter. Even Senator Woolf had served a useful purpose.

But now . . .

Now, it was different . . .

Now, he had one . . .

His theory had been borne out of a very simple fact.

For the last forty years, every American president bar two has hailed from two very elite clubs: state governors and federal senators.

Kennedy, Johnson and Nixon were all senators before they became President. Carter, Reagan and Clinton were all state governors. The only exceptions were George Bush Snr and Gerald Ford – Bush was a member of the House of Representatives, not the Senate and Ford's rise to the Presidency stands in a category of its own.

But, as General Charles Russell had *also* discovered, men of influence were also men of extremely unpredictable health.

The ravages of their political lifestyles—high stress, constant travel, chronic lack of exercise—often took a great toll on their bodies.

And while getting the transmitter onto the heart of a sitting President was nigh on impossible, given the narrow source of American Presidents—senators and governors—

getting it onto a man's coronary muscle *before* he became President wasn't out of the question.

Because, after all, a man is just a man before he becomes President.

The statistics for the next fifteen years spoke for themselves.

Forty-two per cent of US senators had had gall bladder surgery during their time in office, gallstones being a common problem for overweight middle-aged men.

Of the remaining fifty-eight per cent, only four would avoid some sort of surgical procedure during their political careers.

Kidney and liver operations were very common. Several heart bypasses—they were the easiest operations during which to plant the device—and not a few prostate problems.

And then there had been this one.

Halfway through his second term as governor of a large south-western state, he had complained of chest pains and laboured breathing. An exploratory procedure performed by a staff surgeon at the Air Force base just outside Houston had revealed an obstruction in the Governor's left lung, detritus from excessive smoking.

Through a deft procedure involving state-of-the-art fibre-optic cameras and ultra-small wire-controlled surgical instruments called nanotechnology, the obstruction was removed and the Governor told to quit smoking.

What the Governor did not know, however, was that during that operation the Air Force surgeon had attached a *second* piece of nanotechnology—a microscopic radio transmitter the size of a pin-head—to the outer wall of the Governor's heart.

Constructed of evanescent plastic—a semi-organic material which, over time, would partially dissolve into the outer tissue of the Governor's heart—the transmitter would ultimately take on a distorted shape, giving it the appearance of a harmless blood clot, thus masking it from discovery by any observation techniques such as X-rays. Anything larger or more regularly shaped would be detected on an incoming President's first physical, and that just couldn't be allowed to happen.

As a final precaution, it was inserted into the Governor's body 'cold'—unactivated. The White House's AXS-7 anti-bugging system would detect an unauthorised radio signal in an instant.

No.

Activation would occur later, when the time was right.

As usual, at the end of the procedure, one final operation was performed: a fine-grained plaster mould of the Governor's right hand was made.

It would also be necessary, when the time came.

The guards came for him ten minutes later.

Cuffed and chained, General Charles 'Caesar' Russell was escorted from his cell and taken to the waiting plane.

The trip to Indiana passed without incident, as did the sombre walk to the injection room.

The record would later show that as he lay spread-eagled on the injection table like a horizontal Christ, his arms and legs bound with worn leather straps, the prisoner refused to take the last rites. He had no last words, no final expression of remorse for his crimes. In fact, throughout the whole pre-injection ritual, he never

15

said a word at all. This was consistent with Russell's post-trial actions—indeed, his execution had been fast-tracked because he had lodged no appeals of any kind.

The military tribunal that had sentenced him to death had said that so heinous was his crime, he could never be allowed to leave federal custody alive.

They had been right.

At 3:37 p.m. on 20 January, the grim procedure took place. Fifty milligrams of sodium thiopental—to induce unconsciousness—was followed by ten of pancuronium bromide—to stop respiration—and then, finally, twenty milligrams of potassium chloride to stop Russell's heart.

At 3:40 p.m., three minutes later, Lieutenant General Charles Samson Russell was declared dead by the Terre Haute county coroner.

Since the General had no living relatives, his body was taken from the prison by members of the United States Air Force for immediate cremation.

At 3:52 p.m.—twelve minutes after he had been declared officially dead—as his body was being rushed through the streets of Terre Haute, Indiana, in the back of an Air Force ambulance, two electro-shock defibrillator paddles were applied to the dead General's chest and charged.

'*Clear!*' one of the Air Force medical personnel yelled.

The General's body convulsed violently as a wave of raw electric current shot through his vascular system.

It happened on the third applicaton of the paddles.

On the electro-cardiogram monitor on the wall, a small spike appeared.

The General's heartbeat had resumed.

Within moments, it was pulsing at a regular rhythm.

As General Russell well knew, death occurs when the heart is no longer able to deliver oxygen to the body. The act of respiration—breathing—oxygenates a person's blood, and then the person's heart delivers that oxygenated blood to the body.

It was the supply of *hyper*oxygenated blood coursing through Russell's arteries that had kept him alive for that crucial twelve minutes—blood that had been biogenetically crammed with oxygen-rich red cells; blood which during that twelve-minute period had continued to supply Russell's brain and vital organs with oxygen, even though his heart had stopped beating—blood which had been supplied to the General during the two transfusions that had been required after his unfortunate beatings at Leavenworth.

The military tribunal had said that he would never leave federal custody alive.

They had been right.

While all this was happening, in a stark empty cell in the Departure Lounge at Leavenworth Federal Penitentiary, the rickety old television remained on.

On it, the newly-crowned President—smiling, ecstatic, elated—waved to the cheering crowds.

O'Hare International Airport,
Chicago, Illinois
3 July (Six months later)

They found the first one at O'Hare in Chicago, sitting inside an empty hangar at the farthest reaches of the airfield.

A regulation early-morning sweep with an electromagnetic reader had revealed a weak magnetic signal emanating from the suspect hangar.

The hangar had been completely deserted, except for the warhead standing in the exact centre of the cavernous interior space.

From a distance, it looked like a large silver cone about five feet tall mounted on a cargo pallet. Up close, one would recognise it more easily as a conical warhead designed to be inserted into a cruise missile.

Wires sprang out from its sides, connecting the warhead to a small upwardly-pointed satellite dish. Through a clear rectangular window set into the warhead's side, there could be seen a luminous purple liquid.

Plasma.

Type-240 blast plasma. An extremely volatile quasi-nuclear liquid explosive.

Enough to level a city.

Further investigations revealed that the magnetic signal that had been detected inside the hangar was part of a complex proximity sensor array surrounding the warhead. If anyone stepped within fifty feet of the bomb, a red warning light began to flash, indicating that the device had been armed.

*

Lease records revealed that the empty hangar belonged to the United States Air Force.

Then it was discovered that according to the airfield's log books, no Air Force personnel had set foot inside that hangar for at least six weeks.

A call was made to USAF Transportation Command at Scott Air Force Base.

The Air Force was vague, non-committal. It knew nothing about any plasma-based warheads at its civilian hangars. It would check with its people and get back to O'Hare ASAP.

It was then that reports came flooding in from around the country.

Identical warheads—all of them surrounded by magnetic proximity sensors; all with fold-out satellite dishes pointing up into the sky—had been found inside empty Air Force hangars at all three of New York's major airports: JFK, La Guardia and Newark.

And then Dulles in Washington called.

Then LAX.

San Francisco. San Diego.

Boston. Philadelphia.

St Louis. Denver.

Seattle. Detroit.

Fourteen devices in all, at fourteen airports across the country.

All armed. All set. All ready to go off.

All they were waiting for now was the signal.

FIRST CONFRONTATION

3 July, 0600 Hours

The three helicopters thundered over the arid desert plain, booming through the early morning silence.

They flew in tight formation—like they always did—shooting low over the tumbleweeds, kicking up a tornado of sand behind them, their freshly waxed sides glinting in the dawn light.

The giant Sikorsky VH-60N flew out in front—again, like it always did—flanked on either side by two menacing CH-53E Super Stallions.

With its pristine white roof and hand-polished dark-green flanks, the VH-60N is unique among American military helicopters. It is built for the United States government in a high security 'caged' section at the Sikorsky Aircraft plant in Connecticut. It is non-deployable—meaning that it is never used in any operational capacity by the United States Marine Corps, the branch of the military charged with its upkeep.

It is used for one thing, and one thing only. And it has no replicas on active duty—and for good reason, for no-one but a few highly-cleared Marine engineers and executives at Sikorsky can know all of its special features.

Paradoxically, for all this secrecy, the VH-60N is without a doubt the most recognised helicopter in the Western world.

On air traffic control displays, it is designated 'HMX-1', Marine Helicopter Squadron One, and its official radio call-sign is 'Nighthawk'. But over the years, the helicopter that ferries the President of the United States over short-to-medium distances has come to be known by a simpler name—Marine One.

Known as 'M1' to those who fly in it, it is rarely observed in flight, and when it is, it is usually in the most demure of circumstances—taking off from the manicured South Lawn of the White House or arriving at Camp David.

But not today.

Today it roared over the desert, transporting its famous passenger between two remote Air Force bases located in the barren Utah landscape.

Captain Shane M. Schofield, USMC, dressed in his full blue dress 'A' uniform—white peaked hat; navy-blue coat with gold buttons; medium-blue trousers with red stripe; spit-polished boots; white patent leather belt with matching white holster, inside of which resided an ornamental nickel-plated M9 pistol—stood in the cockpit of the Presidential helicopter, behind its two pilots, peering out through the chopper's reinforced forward windshield.

At five-ten, Schofield was lean and muscular, with a handsome narrow face and spiky black hair. And although they were not standard attire for Marines in full dress uniform, he also wore sunglasses—a pair of wraparound anti-flash glasses with reflective silver lenses.

The glasses covered a pair of prominent vertical scars

24

that cut down across both of Schofield's eyes. They were wounds from a previous mission and the reason for his operational call-sign, 'Scarecrow'.

The flat desert plain stretched out before him, dull yellow against the morning sky. The dusty desert floor rushed by beneath the bow of the speeding helicopter.

In the near distance, Schofield saw a low mountain—their destination.

A cluster of buildings lay nestled at the base of the rocky hill, at the end of a long concrete runway, their tiny lights just visible in the early light. The main building of the complex appeared to be a large aeroplane hangar, half-buried in the side of the mountain.

It was United States Air Force Special Area (Restricted) 7, the second Air Force base they were to visit that day.

'Advance Team Two, this is Nighthawk One, we are on final approach to Area 7. Please confirm venue status,' the pilot of M1, Marine Colonel Michael 'Gunman' Grier said into his helmet mike.

There was no reply.

'I say again, Advance Team Two. Report.'

Still no reply.

'It's the jamming system,' Grier's co-pilot, Lieutenant Colonel Michelle Dallas, said. 'The radio guys at 8 said to expect it. These bases are all Level-7 classified, so they're covered at all times by a satellite-generated radiosphere. Short-range transmissions only, to stop anybody transmitting information out.'

Earlier that morning, the President had visited Area 8, a similarly isolated Air Force base about twenty miles to the east of Area 7. There, accompanied by his nine-man Secret Service Detail, he had been taken on a brief tour of the facility, to inspect some new aircraft stationed in its hangars.

While he had done so, Schofield and the other thirteen Marines stationed aboard Marine One and its two escort choppers had waited outside, twiddling their thumbs underneath Air Force One, the President's massive Boeing 747.

While they waited, some of the Marines had started arguing over why they hadn't been allowed inside the main hangar of Area 8. The general consensus—based solely on wild unsubstantiated gossip—had been that it was because the facility housed some of the Air Force's top secret new aeroplanes.

One soldier, a big-smiling, loud-talking African–American sergeant named Wendall 'Elvis' Haynes, said that he'd heard they had the *Aurora* in there, the legendary low-orbit spy plane capable of speeds over Mach 9. The current fastest plane in the world, the SR-71 Blackbird, could only reach Mach 3.

Others had proffered that a whole squadron of F-44s—ultra-nimble, wedged-shaped fighters based on the flying-wing shape of the B-2 stealth bomber—were stationed there.

Others still—perhaps inspired by the launch of a Chinese space shuttle two days previously—suggested that Area 8 housed the X-38, a sleek 747-launched offensive space shuttle. A black project run by the Air Force in association with NASA, the X-38 was reputedly the world's first fight-capable space vehicle, an attack shuttle.

Schofield ignored their speculation.

He didn't have to guess that Area 8 had something to do with top-secret aeroplane development, probably space-based. He could tell it from one simple fact.

Although the Air Force engineers had concealed it well, the regulation-size black bitumen runway of Area 8 actually *extended* another thousand yards in both directions—as a pale concrete landing strip hidden beneath a thin layer of sand and carefully-placed tumbleweeds.

It was an elongated runway, designed to launch and receive aircraft that needed an extra-long landing strip, which meant aircraft like space shuttles or—

And then suddenly the President had emerged from the main hangar and they were on the move again.

Originally, the Boss had intended to fly to Area 7 on Air Force One. It would be faster than Marine One, even though the distance was short.

But there had been a problem on Air Force One. An unexpected leak in the left wing's fuel tank.

And so the Boss had taken Marine One—always on stand-by for precisely this situation.

Which was why Schofield was now gazing at Area 7, lit up like a Christmas tree in the dim morning light.

As he peered at the distant hangar complex, however, Schofield had a strange thought. Curiously, none of his colleagues on HMX-1 knew any stories about Area 7, not even wild unsubstantiated rumours.

No-one, it seemed, knew what went on at Area 7.

Life in the immediate vicinity of the President of the United States was a world unto itself.

It was at the same time both thrilling and frightening, Schofield thought.

Thrilling because you were so close to one with so much power, and frightening because that man was surrounded by a great number of people who claimed his influence as their own.

Indeed, even in his short time on board Marine One, Schofield had observed that at any one time, there were at least three competing power clusters vying for the President's attention.

First was the President's own staff, those people—largely self-important Harvard types—whom the President had appointed to aid him on a range of matters: from national security and domestic policy; to the management of the press corps or the management of his political life.

No matter what their field of expertise, at least insofar as Schofield could see, each of the President's personal staff seemed to have one all-encompassing goal: to get the

President outside, onto the streets, and into the public eye.

In direct contrast to this objective—indeed, in direct opposition to it—was the second group vying for the President's ear: his protectors, the United States Secret Service.

Led by the stoic, no-nonsense and completely impassive Special Agent Francis X. Cutler, the Presidential Detail was constantly at loggerheads with the White House staff.

Cutler—officially known as 'Chief of the Detail', but known to the President merely as Frank—was renowned for his coolness under pressure and his complete intransigence to pleas from political ass-kissers. With his narrow grey eyes and matching crew-cut hair, Frank Cutler could stare down any member of the President's staff and rebuff them with a single word, 'No'.

The third and last group pressing for presidential attention was the crew of Marine One itself.

Not only were they also subjected to the inflated egos of the presidential staff—Schofield would never forget his first flight on Marine One, when the President's Domestic Policy Adviser, a pompous twenty-nine-year-old lawyer from New York, had ordered Schofield to get him a double latte, and to 'make it quick'—they were also often at odds with the Secret Service.

Securing the President's safety may have been the job of the Secret Service, but when he was on HMX-1, so the Marine Corps reasoned, the Boss had at least six United States Marines on board with him at any given time.

An uneasy truce had been brokered.

While on board Marine One, the President's safety would be in Marine hands. As such, only key members of

his Secret Service Detail—Frank Cutler and a few others—
would fly with him. The rest of his personal Detail would
fly in the two chase helicopters.

As soon as the President stepped off Marine One,
however, his well-being was once again the exclusive
responsibility of the United States Secret Service.

Gunman Grier spoke into his helmet mike. 'Nighthawk
Three, this is Nighthawk One. Go and check on Advance
Team Two for me. This radiosphere is screwing up our
long-range comms. I'm picking up their All-Clear beacon,
but I can't get any voice contact. They should be over at
the exit vent. And if you get close enough, see if you can
raise Area 8 again. Find out what's happening with Air
Force One.'

'*Copy that, Nighthawk One,*' a voice replied over the
short-wave. '*On our way.*'

From his position behind Grier and Dallas, Schofield
saw the Super Stallion to their right peel away from the
group and head off over the desert.

The two remaining choppers of Marine Helicopter
Squadron-1 continued on their way.

In a darkened room somewhere, a blue-uniformed man
wearing a radio headset and seated in front of an illuminated computer display spoke quietly into his wraparound
microphone.

'—Initiating primary satellite signal test . . . *now*—'

He pressed a button on his console.

*

30

'What the hell—?' Dallas said, touching her earpiece.

'What is it?' Gunman Grier asked.

'I don't know,' Dallas said, swivelling in her seat. 'I just picked up a spike on the microwave band.'

She looked at the microwave display screen—it depicted a series of jagged spikes and troughs—then shook her head. 'Strange. Looks like an incoming microwave signal just hit us and then bounced away.'

'Anti-bugging was done this morning,' Grier said. 'Twice.'

Comprehensive sweeps for listening devices planted on Marine One—and her passengers—were done with rigorous regularity. It was nigh on impossible to plant a transmitting or receiving device on the President's helicopter.

Dallas peered at her screen, shrugging. 'The signal's too small to be a location beacon. Ditto, speech or computer data. It didn't send or take any information—it's as if it was just, well, checking to see if we were here.' She turned to Grier questioningly.

The Presidential Helicopter Pilot frowned. 'Most probably it's just a surge in the radiosphere, a deflected microwave signal. But let's not take any chances.' He turned to Schofield. 'Captain, if you wouldn't mind, would you please do a sweep of the aircraft with the magic wand.'

'—Return signal received,' the console operator in the darkened room said. 'Primary signal test successful. The device is operational. Repeat. *The device is operational.* Switching back to dormant mode. All right. Commencing test of secondary signal—'

Schofield stepped into the main cabin of Marine One, waving a AXS-9 digital spectrum analyser over the walls, seats, ceiling and floor, searching for anything that was emitting an outgoing signal.

As one would expect of the President's helicopter, the interior of M1 was plush. Indeed, with its deep maroon carpet and widely-spaced seats, it looked more like the first-class section of a commercial airliner than the hold of a military aircraft.

Twelve beige leather seats took up most of the main cabin. Each seat had the Seal of the President of the United States embroidered on it, as did the oversized armrests that adjoined each chair and the scotch glasses and coffee mugs, just in case anyone forgot in whose presence they were travelling.

At the rear of the central area, guarded at all times by a Marine in full dress uniform, was a polished mahogany door that led to the aft-most section of the helicopter.

It was the President's private office.

Small but elegantly appointed—and featuring an amazingly compact arrangement of phones, faxes, computers and televisions—Marine One's office allowed the Boss to monitor the nation's business wherever he happened to be.

At the very rear of the President's office, behind a small pressure-sealed door, was one final feature of Marine One which was reserved for use in only the most dire of circumstances—a small one-man ejection unit, the Presidential escape pod.

Schofield waved his spectrum analyser over the seats in the first-class section, searching for bugs.

Seated there were Frank Cutler and five of his Secret Service people. They peered out the windows, ignoring Schofield as he did his sweep around them.

Also there were a couple of the President's advisers— his Deputy Chief of Staff, his Communications Director— both of whom flicked through thick manila folders.

Standing above them, manning the two exit doors at either end of the main cabin, were a pair of straight-backed United States Marines.

There was one more person seated in the main cabin.

A stocky no-necked man dressed in an olive US Army uniform, sitting quietly at the back of the cabin, in the first-class seat closest to the President's office.

To look at him, with his carrot-red hair and bushy orange moustache, he didn't seem like anyone special, and truth be told, he wasn't anyone special.

He was an Army warrant officer named Carl Webster, and he followed the President wherever he went—not because of any special expertise or knowledge he possessed, but because of the extremely important object handcuffed to his right wrist: a stainless-steel briefcase that contained the codes and the activation switches to America's nuclear arsenal, a briefcase known as 'the Football'.

Schofield finished his sweep, including a short 'excuse me' check of the President's office.

Nothing.

There was not a single bug to be found on the helicopter.

He returned to the cockpit, just in time to hear Gunman Grier say into his mike: 'Copy that, Nighthawk Three, thank you. Continue on to the vent.'

Grier turned to his co-pilot. 'Air Force One's back on

33

deck. It was just a valve leak. It'll stay at Area 8. We'll bring the Boss back after our little visit to Area 7. Scarecrow?'

'Nothing,' Schofield said. 'The helicopter's clean.'

Grier shrugged. 'Must have been the radiosphere. Thanks, Scarecrow.'

Suddenly Grier touched his helmet as another message came through.

He sighed wearily as the voice at the other end nattered into his ear.

'We'll do our best, Colonel,' he said, 'but I make no promises.' Grier switched off his mike and shook his head. 'Fucking Ramrod.'

He turned to Schofield and Dallas. 'Ladies and gentlemen, our esteemed White House Liaison Officer has asked us to pick up the pace a little. Apparently, the Boss has an afternoon tea with the Washington Ladies' Auxiliary to get to, and Liaison Officer Hagerty thinks we're not going fast enough to meet his schedule.'

Dallas snuffed a laugh. 'Good ol' Ramrod.'

When it came to the use of Marine One, all White House–Marine Corps correspondence went through a Marine colonel called the White House Liaison Officer, a position which for the last three years had been held by Colonel Rodney Hagerty, USMC.

Unfortunately, Hagerty, forty-one years old, tall and lanky, with a pencil-thin moustache and a far too proper manner, was regarded by many in HMX-1 as the worst kind of soldier—a ladder climber, but also a ruthless expert in office politics, someone more interested in getting stars on his shoulders than actually being a United States Marine. But as so often happens, the upper echelons of the Corps didn't see this and kept promoting him nonetheless.

Even Schofield disliked him. Hagerty was a bureaucrat—a bureaucrat who had obviously come to enjoy his proximity to power. Although his official call-sign was 'Hot Rod', his rigid adherence to procedure and protocol, even when it was patently impractical, had earned him an alternate call-sign among the troops: 'Ramrod'.

At that very same moment, the lone Super Stallion chopper that was Nighthawk Three was landing in a cloud of dust on the sandy desert plain. About half a mile to the west stood the low rocky mountain that housed Area 7.

As the big chopper's tyres hit the ground, four Marines dressed in full combat attire leaped out from it and ran over to a small trench carved into the rock-hard desert floor.

The trench housed Area 7's EEV—Emergency Escape Vent—the well-concealed exit point of a long underground tunnel that provided emergency egress from Area 7. Today it was the primary escape route from the complex, in the unlikely event that the President encountered any trouble there.

The lead Marine, a lieutenant named Corbin 'Colt' Hendricks, approached the dusty earthen hole, accompanied by his three subordinates, MP-5/10—sometimes called the MP-10, they were 10 mm versions of the Heckler & Koch MP-5—in hand.

A steady *beep*-pause-*beep* warbled in Hendricks' earpiece: Advance Team 2's All-Clear beacon. The A-C beacon couldn't transmit voice messages, but its powerful digital signal still provided a worthwhile service: if

Advance Team 2 encountered any kind of ambush or disturbance, its lead agent simply flicked off the All-Clear beacon and everyone else in the presidential entourage would know that danger was afoot. Its presence now was reassuring.

Hendricks and his squad came to the edge of the trench and looked down into it.

'Oh *shit . . .*' Hendricks breathed.

The other two Presidential helicopters raced toward Restricted Area 7.

'Hey, Scarecrow?' Gunman Grier turned in his seat to face Schofield. 'Where's your harem?'

Through his reflective silver sunglasses, Schofield offered a crooked smile to the Presidential Helicopter Pilot.

'They're over on Nighthawk Two today, sir,' he said.

Grier was referring to the two female members of Schofield's former unit who had joined him on his tour on board Marine Helicopter Squadron-1—Staff Sergeant Elizabeth 'Fox' Gant and Gunnery Sergeant Gena 'Mother' Newman.

As a former commander of a Marine Force Reconnaissance Unit, Schofield was something of a rarity on board Marine One.

Owing to the largely ceremonial duties associated with working on the President's helicopter and to the fact that time spent on board the helicopter is *not* counted as 'active deployed airtime', many Marines choose to avoid HMX-1 duty. Indeed, with few exceptions, most of the troops assigned to HMX-1 are relatively junior soldiers who won't miss any promotional opportunities.

So to have a former Recon commander on board was highly unusual, but something which Gunman Grier welcomed.

He liked Schofield. He'd heard on the grapevine that he was a gifted field commander—a man who looked out for his men, and as a result, got the very best out of them.

Grier had also heard about what had happened to Schofield on his last mission and he respected the young captain for it.

He also liked both Mother and Gant—admired their attitudes to their work and their fierce loyalty to their former commander—and his labelling of them as Schofield's 'harem' was a sign of affection from a man who rarely showed it.

Schofield, however, was used to being considered unusual.

Indeed, that was why he was stationed aboard Marine One.

About eighteen months previously, as a lieutenant, he'd been in command of a Marine Reconnaissance Unit that had been sent to a remote ice station in Antarctica, to investigate the discovery of a possible alien spacecraft.

In a word, the mission had gone to hell on an express elevator.

Including himself, only four of his twelve Marines had survived the nightmare, during which they had been forced to defend the station against two foreign military forces and infiltrators from within their own unit. To top it off, Schofield himself had been declared dead by some corrupt members of the Marine Corps hierarchy, men who had been prepared to make that lie a reality.

His eventual return to America—alive and well—had sparked a media frenzy.

His face appeared on every major newspaper in the nation. Wherever he went, even after the initial frenzy, tabloid journalists and photographers tried to snap his picture or coax information out of him. After all, he was a walking talking monument to the corruption of the United States military—the good soldier who had been targeted for extermination by the faceless generals of his own military leadership.

Which left the Marine Corps with a serious problem: *where to put him?*

In the end, the answer had been rather inventive.

The safest place to hide Schofield was right in front of the world's media, but in the one place where they wouldn't be able to touch him.

He would be assigned to Marine One.

The chopper was based at the Marine Corps Air Facility at Quantico, Virginia, so Schofield could live on the base, making access to him all but impossible. And he would work on board the President's VH-60N, which was only really ever seen landing at the White House, and even then, always at a safe distance from the press.

When the transfer was made, Mother and Gant had elected to go with Schofield. The fourth survivor of their Antarctic disaster, a private named Rebound Simmons, had decided to leave the Marine Corps after their ill-fated mission.

That had been a year ago.

In that time, Schofield—quiet at the best of times and not given to small talk—had made only a handful of friends in the White House: mainly people among the Secret Service and the domestic staff; the ordinary people. With his reflective silver anti-flash glasses, however, he was popular with the President's playful grandkids. As such, to their delight, he was nearly always assigned to guard them whenever they visited. And yet, despite this, he had never actually spoken conversationally with the President.

Area 7 loomed large in front of Marine One. Schofield could see the massive doors of the complex's enormous hangar slowly opening, revealing bright electric lighting inside.

Grier spoke into his helmet mike: 'Nighthawk Two, this is Nighthawk One, beginning descent now.'

In the belly of Nighthawk Two, Sergeant Elizabeth 'Fox' Gant sat hunched in a canvas jumpseat, trying vainly to read from a folder perched on her knees.

Unlike Marine One, the rotor noise inside Nighthawk Two was absolutely deafening. And since it never carried the President, its interior decor was about a thousand times more utilitarian. No upholstered seats or embroidered armrests here.

Now a staff sergeant, Libby Gant was twenty-eight years old, well, as of six hours ago.

Compact and fit, she had short blonde hair and sky-blue eyes, and in regular battle dress—fatigues, body armour and MP-10—she cut a smart figure. In full dress uniform—peaked hat, dress coat and trousers—she looked spectacular.

Since they were flying in restricted Air Force airspace,

the mood on board Nighthawk Two was relaxed. The usual tensions of co-ordinating Marine One's flight path with those of civilian air traffic weren't an issue, so Gant—studying part-time for entry into Officer Candidate School—took the opportunity to brush up on some of her notes.

She was just getting to Course 9405, Advanced Tactical Command, when a soft voice invaded her consciousness.

'Happy birthday to you . . .

Happy birthday to you . . .

Happy birthday, dear Staff Sergeant Ga-ant . . .

Happy birthday to you.'

She looked up from her work and sighed.

Sliding into the empty seat beside her was Nicholas Tate III, the President's Domestic Policy Adviser. Tate was handsome in a European sort of way—with dark eyebrows, olive skin and a male model's jawline—and confident in the extreme. Today he wore a three-thousand-dollar Armani suit and matching Armani cologne. Apparently it was the latest thing.

Tate held out a small neatly-wrapped package for Gant to take.

'Twenty-eight, if I'm not mistaken,' he said.

'That's right, sir,' Gant said.

'Please, call me Nick.' He nodded at the gift. 'Well, go on. Open it.'

Reluctantly, Gant unwrapped the small package, unveiling an aqua-green box. She popped the lid, revealing an absolutely gorgeous silver necklace.

Small and thin, it looked like a length of the finest silver thread, its polished surface sparkling. A small but stylish diamond dangled like a teardrop from the front of the necklace.

41

'It's from Tiffany's,' Tate said.

Gant looked up at him. 'I'm not allowed to wear jewellery in uniform, Mr Tate.'

'I know. I was hoping you could wear it when I took you to dinner at Nino's next Saturday.'

Nino's was a restaurant in Georgetown, popular among Washington socialites and arguably the most expensive eatery in town.

Gant sighed. 'I'm seeing someone.'

It was kind of true. Only last weekend, after a tentative start, she and Shane Schofield had gone out on something resembling a date.

'Now, now, now,' Tate said, 'I heard about that. One date does not a relationship make.'

This was getting difficult. Gant held the necklace up to the light of the window. 'You know, this looks a lot like a necklace I saw in Paris once.'

'Oh, really?'

At Gant's mention of the word 'Paris', however, one of the other Marines sitting nearby cocked her head to the side. Tate never saw it.

'Yes,' Gant said. 'We were there a couple of months ago with the Boss, and I had a day off, so I—'

'Jesus H. Christ, would you take a look at *that*!' a lusty woman's voice cut Gant off.

'Hey there, Mother,' Gant said, as Gunnery Sergeant Gena 'Mother' Newman appeared in the narrow aisle next to her.

'How you doin' there, Birthday Babe?' Mother said with a knowing smile.

The 'Paris' code was one they had used several times before. When either of them encountered an unwanted

42

male admirer, she would slip the word 'Paris' into the conversation and the other, hearing the signal, would come to the rescue. It was a common trick used by girl-friends worldwide.

Granted, at six feet four inches and an even 200 pounds, Mother rarely had to use it. With her dark, heavyset features, fully shaved head and gruff no-nonsense manner, she was almost the perfect antithesis of Libby Gant. Her call-sign, 'Mother', said it all, really. It wasn't indicative of any extraordinary maternal qualities. It was short for *motherfucker*. A gifted warrior, adept at all kinds of heavy weaponry and guncraft, she'd been pro-moted to the highly-respected rank of gunnery sergeant a year ago.

In addition to this—thanks to a close encounter with a killer whale during the disastrous mission to Antarctica—Mother had one other, highly unusual physical feature.

A prosthetic lower left leg.

The nasty incident with the killer whale had deprived her of everything below the left knee. That said, she'd done better than the killer had. It had received a bullet to its brain.

What Mother now had in place of her natural left foot and shin was a state-of-the-art prosthetic limb which, so its makers claimed, guaranteed total and undiminished body movement. Featuring titanium-alloy 'bones', fully rotating joints and hydraulic muscle simulators, its operation was so sophisticated—involving nerve impulse reception and automatic weight-shifting—that it required an internal prologic computer chip to control it.

Mother was gazing at the glistening Tiffany's necklace. 'Whoa, that is one mighty fine piece of jewellery,' she gawped. She turned to Nick Tate: 'That piece of string must have cost you a pretty penny, sonny Jim.'

'It was within my price range,' Tate said coolly.

'Probably cost more than I make in a *year*.'

'Probably did.'

Mother ignored him, turned to Gant. 'Sorry to rain on your parade, Birthday Babe, but the skipper sent me back to get you. He wants you up front for the landing.'

'Oh, okay.'

Gant stood, and as she did, she handed Tate back his necklace. 'I'm sorry, Nicholas, but I can't accept this. I'm *seeing* someone else.'

And with that she headed up front.

Over at the Emergency Escape Vent, Colt Hendricks just stood with his mouth agape, staring down into the trench.

The sight before him was nothing short of horrific.

All nine members of the Secret Service's secondary advance team lay on the sand-covered floor of the trench, their bodies twisted at all angles, riddled with bullet holes. The size of the wounds indicated hollow-point ammunition had been used—bullets that expanded once they entered the wound, guaranteeing a kill. A few of the agents had been shot in the face—their heads had been all but blown off. Blood was everywhere, drying in the sand.

Hendricks saw the agent-in-charge of the Secret Service team, a man named Baker—mouth open, eyes wide, bullet hole in the forehead. In Agent Baker's out-stretched hand was the Advance Team's All-Clear beacon switch. The attack must have happened so quickly that he hadn't even had time to flick the switch.

Beyond Baker, Hendricks saw a solid-looking steel door set into the dirt wall of the trench—the escape vent itself. It just stood there, resolutely closed.

Hendricks spun on his heel, yanked out his radio, headed back toward Nighthawk Three.

'Nighthawk One!'

Radio static.

'*Goddamn it!* Nighthawk One! This is—'

It was as if the desert just came alive.

The dusty desert floor parted—sand falling off canvas ambush covers—and suddenly, from *both* sides of Hendricks, about a dozen man-sized shapes rose from the sand, sub-machine guns raised and firing.

A second later, a 9-millimetre Silvertip bullet entered Hendricks's brain from the side. The subsequent gaseous expansion of the hollow-pointed projectile caused his head to explode.

Hendricks never saw the man who killed him.

Never saw the dark team of desert wraiths take down the rest of his men with clinical, ruthless efficiency.

And he never saw them take his helicopter and fly it back toward Area 7.

The two remaining Presidential helicopters descended together, landing in a whirlwind of sand in front of the massive main hangar of United States Air Force Special Area (Restricted) No. 7.

The giant hangar's enormous twin doors yawned wide, its interior brightly illuminated. The low mountain into which the hangar had been carved loomed over the squat four-building complex.

No sooner had the two choppers touched the ground than the Secret Service people from Nighthawk Two were dashing to their positions around Marine One.

A welcoming party stood on the runway in front of the hangar, standing silently in the cool morning air, silhouetted by the hangar light behind them.

Two Air Force officers—one colonel and one major—stood at the head of the welcoming unit.

Behind the two officers stood four rows of fully-armed commandos, ten men to a row. All of them were dressed in full combat gear—black battledress uniforms, black body armour, black helmets—and they all held high-tech Belgian-made P-90 assault rifles rigidly across their chests.

Looking out through Marine One's cockpit windshield, Schofield recognised their insignia patches at once. They were members of a unit rarely seen at US military exercises, a unit which was shrouded in secrecy, a unit which many believed was used only in the most critical of missions.

It was the elite ground unit in the United States Air Force, the famous 7th Special Operations Squadron.

Based in West Germany for much of the Cold War, its official task during that time was the defence of US airfields against the elite Soviet Spetsnaz units. Its unofficial achievements, though, were far more spectacular.

Masterminding the defection of five senior Soviet nuclear missile specialists from a secret base in the Ukraine mountains. The assassination of KGB operations chief Vladimir Nakov in Moscow in 1990, before Nakov could himself assassinate Mikhail Gorbachev. And, finally, in 1997, the daring rescue of the CIA's captured Far Eastern Bureau Chief, Fred Conway, from the dreaded Xiangi Prison—the all but impregnable maze of grim cells and torture chambers belonging to the notorious Chinese External Intelligence Service.

Each man in the formation wore a special combat mask around his throat—an ERG-6 gas-mask. Black and hard, it looked like the lower half of a hockey mask, and it covered its wearer's mouth and nose in much the same way Jesse James's mask had covered his face in the old days.

Three other men stood out in front of the detachment of 7th Squadron members on the deserted runway. All three wore starched white labcoats. Scientists.

Once the Marine and Secret Service people from

Nighthawk Two were in place, a set of Airstairs folded down from the forward left-hand side of Marine One.

Two Marines emerged from the helicopter first and took up their positions at the base of the stairs, backs straight, eyes forward.

A moment later, Special Agent Frank Cutler stepped out of the chopper, hand on his holster, eyes watchful. The Secret Service trusts nobody. Not even the United States Air Force. Even it could have a disgruntled soldier who might take a shot at the President.

The President came out next, followed by his staff.

Schofield and a young Marine corporal emerged last of all.

As usual, Marine One's two pilots, Gunman and Dallas, stayed on board just in case a rapid departure was called for.

The two parties faced each other on the runway in the early morning light—the Air Force detachment stationed at the complex; the President and his entourage.

Twisting coils of windswept sand swirled around their bodies. A sandstorm was due later in the day.

A young Air Force captain guided the President over to the colonel at the head of the Air Force formation—a severe-looking man with grey hair and eyebrows. As the President came closer, the colonel stepped forward and crisply saluted his Commander-in-Chief.

'Good morning, Mister President,' he said. 'My name is Colonel Jerome T. Harper, United States Air Force Medical and Surgical Command, and commanding officer of United States Air Force Special Area (Restricted) 7. This is Major Kurt Logan, commander of the 7th Squadron forces here at the base. Your two Secret Service advance teams are waiting for you inside. We're honoured to have you, sir. Welcome to Area 7.'

'Thank you, Colonel,' the President replied. 'It's a pleasure to be here. Lead the way.'

As soon as the President was taken away, disappearing inside the enormous main hangar with his highest-level entourage in tow, the major in charge of the 7th Squadron detachment came up to Schofield.

Major Kurt Logan was about six-one, with closely shaved hair and heavily pockmarked skin. Schofield had actually met him before, although he doubted Logan would remember him.

It had been at a special command and leadership course run by the Navy at their SEAL compound in Fort Lauderdale in 1997. Through a combination of smart tactics and ruthless follow-through, the softly-spoken Logan had come first in the class by a clear forty points. He could assess any battlefield situation in an instant, and when it came to engaging the enemy, he was uncompromising. Schofield, then just a budding Recon Unit commander, had come tenth in a class of sixteen.

From the looks of things, Logan hadn't changed much. His whole bearing—hands clasped firmly behind his back, steely level gaze—indicated a powerful, confident inner strength. Battle-hardened strength.

'Excuse me, Captain,' Logan said in a soft Southern drawl. He offered Schofield a sheet of paper. 'Our personnel list for your records.'

Schofield took the list, then gave one of his own to Logan in return.

It was common practice at presidential inspections for both sides to swap personnel lists, since the President's people wanted to know who was at the base they were inspecting, and the base people wanted to know exactly who was in the presidential convoy.

Schofield glanced at the Area 7 list. Columns of meaningless names ran down it.

UNITED STATES AIR FORCE
SPECIAL AREA (RESTRICTED) 07
ON-SITE PERSONNEL
CLASSIFICATION: TOP SECRET

NAME	UNIT	NAME	UNIT
COMMAND UNIT			
Harper, JT (CO)			
7TH SQUADRON			
Alvarez, MJ	A	Golding, DK	D
Arthurs, RT	C	Goldman, WE	A
Atlock, FD	B	Grayson, SR	E
Baines, AW	A	Hughes, R	A
Bennett, B	E	Ingliss, WA	B
Biggs, NM	C	Johnson, SW	D
Boland, CS	B	Jones, M	D
Boyce, LW	D	Kincaid, R	B
Calvert, ET	E	Littleton, SO	E
Carney, LE	E	Logan, KW (MAJ)	A

Christian, FC	A	McConnell, BA	B
Coleman, GK	E	Messick, K	E
Coles, M	B	Milbourn, SK	D
Crick, DT	D	Morton, IN	C
Criece, TW	A	Nance, GF	D
Davis, LR	C	Nystrom, JJ	D
Dayton, AM	E	Oliver, PK	E
Dillan, ST	D	Price, AL	C
Doheny, FG	A	Rawson, MJ	C
Egan, RR	B	Sayles, MT	B
Fraser, MS	C	Sommers, SR	C
Fredericks, GH	A	Stone, JK	C
Frommer, SN	E	Taylor, AS	B
Gale, A	D	Willis, LS	C
Giggs, RE	B	Wolfson, HT	A

CIVILIAN STAFF

Botha, GW	MED
Franklin, HS	MED
Shaw, DE	MED

He did notice something, though.

There were more names here than there were 7th Squadron men on the tarmac. While there had been forty commandos out on the tarmac, there were fifty 7th Squadron members on the list. He figured there must be another ten-man unit inside the base somewhere.

As Schofield looked at the list, Logan said, 'Captain, if you wouldn't mind, we'd like you to move your—'

'What appears to be the problem, Major?' a voice said from behind Schofield. 'Don't bother with Captain Schofield. *I* am in command here.'

It was Ramrod Hagerty, the White House Liaison Officer. With his Englishman's moustache and distinctly *un*battle-hardened posture, Hagerty was everything Kurt Logan was not.

Before he answered him, Logan looked Hagerty up and down. What he saw obviously didn't impress him.

'I was led to believe that Colonel Grier was in ultimate command of Marine One,' Logan said coolly—and correctly.

'Well, ah, yes . . . yes, *technically*, he is,' Hagerty said. 'But, as White House Liaison, anything to do with the movement of these helicopters must go through me first.'

Logan looked at Hagerty in stony silence.

Then he said, 'I was about to ask the captain here if he wouldn't mind rolling your helicopters into the main hangar while the President is at the base. We wouldn't want enemy satellites knowing that we had the Boss visiting, now would we?'

'No, no, of course not. Of course not,' Ramrod said. 'Schofield. Make it happen.'

'Yes, sir,' Schofield said drily.

The giant double doors of the hangar closed with a resounding *boom*.

The two lead helicopters of Marine Helicopter Squadron-1 were now parked inside the main hangar of Area 7, their rotors and tail booms folded into their stowed positions. Despite their own considerable size, the two Presidential helicopters were dwarfed by the cavernous hangar.

Having supervised the roll-in of the choppers, Schofield now stood in the middle of the massive interior space, alone, scanning it silently.

The rest of the Marine, White House and Secret Service

contingent—those who hadn't been senior enough to go with the President, about twenty people—variously milled about the helicopters or drank coffee in the two glass-walled offices that flanked the main doors.

The size of the hangar stunned Schofield.

It was *gigantic*.

Completely illuminated by brilliant white halogen lights, it must have stretched at least a hundred yards into the mountain. A ceiling-mounted rail system ran for its entire length. At the moment, two large wooden crates hung from the rails at either end of the hangar.

At the far end of the vast space—facing the doors that led out to the runway—stood a two-storey, completely *internal* building that ran for the full width of the hangar. This building's upper floor had angled glass windows that looked out over the hangar floor.

A small unobtrusive personnel elevator sat quietly underneath the overhang created by the building's upper level, sunk in the hangar's northern wall.

Apart from the Presidential helicopters, there were no other aircraft in the hangar at present. Some large white-painted towing vehicles not unlike those seen at airports lay scattered around the hangar floor—indeed, Schofield had used two of them to bring in the choppers.

By far the most striking feature of the immense hangar, however, was the massive aircraft elevator platform that lay in its centre.

It was *huge*, unbelievably huge, like the enormous hydraulic elevators that hang off the sides of aircraft carriers—a giant square-shaped platform in the very centre of the hangar.

At 200 feet by 200 feet, the platform was large enough

to hold an entire AWACS Boeing 707—the Air Force's famous radar-detecting aeroplanes, known for the thirty-foot flying-saucer-like rotodomes mounted on their backs.

Supported by an unseen hydraulic lift system, the giant platform took up nearly the whole of the central area of the hangar. As with similar aircraft elevators, to maximise efficiency, on the north-eastern corner of the platform was a small *detachable* section which was itself a working elevator, capable of operating independently of the larger platform. To do this it ran on rails attached to the wall of the elevator shaft rather than on the main platform's telescoping hydraulic strut—a kind of 'platform within a platform', so to speak.

Today, however, the Air Force personnel at Area 7 were putting on the whole show.

As he stood at the edge of the enormous elevator shaft, Schofield could see the President—with his nine-man Secret Service Detail and his high-ranking Air Force tour guides—standing on the full-sized platform, getting smaller and smaller as they descended the wide concrete shaft on it.

At that very same moment, as Shane Schofield stood in the centre of the vast hangar bay, looking down into the wide elevator shaft, someone else was watching *him*.

The watcher stood in Area 7's darkened control room, on the upper floor of the internal building that formed the eastern wall of the hangar. Around him, four uniformed radio operators spoke softly into headset microphones:

'—Alpha Unit, cover the Level 3 common room—'

'—Echo Unit advises that the Marine investigatory team from Nighthawk Three had to be neutralised out at the EEV. They found the secondary advance team. Echo is parking their chopper in one of the outside hangars now. Returning to the main hangar when they're done—'

'—Bravo and Charlie Units are to remain in main hangar—'

'—Delta Unit reports that it is now in position—'

'—the Secret Service are trying to contact their primary advance team on Level 6. The simulated All-Clear signal, however, appears to be working—'

Major Kurt Logan arrived at the side of the shadowy figure. 'Sir. The President and his Detail just arrived on Level 4. All units are in position.'

'Good.'

'Shall we move now?'

'No. Let him take the tour,' the faceless man said. 'There is still one more thing that has to be taken care of before we can begin.'

'Good morning.'

Schofield turned, and saw the smiling faces of Libby Gant and Mother Newman.

'Hey there,' he said.

'Ralph's still pissed at you,' Mother said. 'He wants a rematch.'

Ralph was Mother's husband. A short nugget of a man with a moon-shaped smiling face and a limitless ability to put up with Mother's eccentricities, he was a trucker, owning his own Mack eighteen-wheeler. It had a painting of an arrow-struck heart on its side with the word '*Mother*' flowing over it. With his short stature and ready smile, Ralph was widely regarded in the Marine community as a bona fide legend.

He was also the proud owner of a new barbecue, and at the obligatory Sunday afternoon lunch at Mother's place a few weeks ago, he'd challenged Schofield to a shoot-off on the garage basketball hoop. Schofield had let him win and Ralph knew it.

'Maybe next weekend?' Schofield said. 'How about you? How'd that check-up on the leg go yesterday?'

'In a word, Scarecrow, sen-*fucking*-sational,' Mother said. 'I got full movement and I can run just as fast as I used to. That seemed to satisfy the docs. Hell, I told 'em that just last week I bowled 275, but that didn't seem to mean much. Either way, since I'm now part machine, I want a new nickname: Darth Fucking Vader.'

Schofield laughed. 'Okay, Darth.'

'You having trouble with Ramrod again?' Gant asked seriously.

'The usual,' Schofield said. 'Hey, happy birthday.'

Gant smiled. 'Thanks.'

'I got you something.' Schofield reached into his dress coat pocket. 'It's not huge or anything, but . . .' he frowned, patted his other pockets. 'Damn, it's here somewhere. Maybe it's back on the chopper . . .'

'Don't worry about it.'

'Can I give it to you later?'

'Sure.'

Mother gazed at the enormous hangar around them. 'What the fuck is this place? Looks like Fort Knox.'

'More than that,' Schofield said.

'What do you mean?'

'Look at the floor just inside the hangar doors.'

Mother and Gant did. A series of box-shaped indentations ran in a line across the concrete floor in front of the doors. Each indentation was at least a yard square and deep.

'Now look up.'

They did, and saw a series of thick, tooth-like metal protrusions—protrusions which, when lowered, would fit perfectly into the box-shaped indentations on the floor.

'Piston-driven armoured door,' Schofield said, 'like the

ones they have on Nimitz-class carriers. They're used to divide the ship's hangar bays into self-contained zones in case of fire or explosion. But, you'll notice that there aren't any other armoured doors in this hangar. That's the only one, which means it's the only exit.'

'So what are you saying?' Mother asked.

'I'm saying,' Schofield said, 'that whatever they're doing in this complex is more important than you or I could possibly imagine.'

The wide elevator platform holding the President of the United States jolted to a halt in front of a giant steel door marked with an enormous black-painted '4'.

The wide concrete elevator shaft stretched up into the air above the President and his Secret Service Detail like an oversized vertical tunnel. The bright artificial light of the ground-level hangar was but a small square of white now—three hundred feet straight up.

No sooner had the elevator stopped than the massive steel door in front of it rumbled upward. Colonel Jerome Harper led the way, walking and talking quickly:

'This facility was once the headquarters for the North American Air Defence Command—NORAD—before NORAD was moved to a more modern facility built underneath Cheyenne Mountain in Colorado in 1975.

'The complex is surrounded by a two-foot-thick titanium outer wall, which is itself buried beneath one hundred feet of solid granite. Like the Cheyenne Mountain complex, it is designed to withstand a direct hit from a thermonuclear missile.'

Harper handed the President a sheet of paper, on

which was a schematic diagram of the subterranean structure.

The hangar appeared at the top of the diagram—at ground level, capped by the low mountain—then the wide aircraft elevator shaft led downwards, until it met a multi-levelled structure built deep within the earth.

Harper said, 'The underground complex contains six levels, the first two of which—Levels 1 and 2—are storage hangars for high-risk aircraft, much like the ones you saw at Area 8 earlier this morning. Level 3 houses communications and staff living quarters. Level 5 is confinement. And Level 6 is the X-Rail system.

'Each level is completely sealable to both radiation and airborne contagions, and the whole facility, if locked down, is capable of living off a self-contained supply of oxygen for thirty days. Food supplies are kept in a storage area on Level 3. Water supply is kept in a 100-millon-gallon tank in the Level 1 hangar.'

Their group came to a short upwardly-sloping corridor, at the end of which sat a squat solid-looking door that looked like a gigantic safe. An Air Force man hurriedly began opening it.

'Project Fortune was stationed here four years ago, after the first viable embryo reached maturity,' Harper said. 'Now, at last, it has reached a stage where it can be put to use.'

The President waited patiently while the three-foot-thick door was pulled open.

Frank Cutler and the eight other members of the President's personal Detail stood behind him—silent, impassive, invisible. At three-minute intervals, Cutler would silently check his earpiece for the All-Clear beacons from both of his advance teams. The beacons came in loud and clear.

Then, finally, the door swung open, and the President looked casually beyond it.

And his jaw dropped.

'Oh . . . my . . . *God* . . .'

'My money's on the superbomb,' Elvis Haynes said as he leaned back in his chair.

Elvis, Schofield, Gant and Mother were sitting in one of the glass-walled offices by the main doors of the hangar. With them were Colonels Grier and Dallas, all the other Marines stationed on board the Presidential helicopters, as well as the three remaining Secret Service agents.

In a not-so-subtle division of management and labour, all the White House people who had remained up in the hangar either sat in the *other* glass-walled office on the southern side of the hangar or worked inside their helicopters, which, they said, were more suited to their rank than the spartan Air Force offices.

They also—so Nicholas Tate had said to Gant when he had invited her to stay on Marine One with him—had better coffee, plunger stuff.

Gant went with Schofield and the others.

Ramrod Hagerty, on the other hand, sat over with the White House people.

'No way, man,' a small bespectacled corporal named Gus Gorman said. 'The superbomb doesn't exist.'

Gorman was a thin, nerdy-looking individual, with thick glasses, a big nose and a narrow scrawny neck. Not even full dress uniform could make him look sexy. Popular with the other troops for his almost-photographic memory and sharp wit, his call-sign 'Brainiac' was a compliment, not an insult.

'Bullshit,' Elvis said, 'DARPA made it in the nineties, in conjunction with the Navy—'

'But they could never make it *work*. Thing depended on some element only found in meteorites and they could never find a live specimen of it.'

'You guys'll believe anything,' a softly-spoken voice said from the other side of the office.

Everybody turned, Schofield included.

The speaker was a new sergeant to the unit—an intense young man with a heavy-browed face, pug nose and deep brown eyes. He didn't talk much, so when he did it was something of a special occasion for the team. At first, it had been a trait which some had mistaken for contempt. But soon it was discovered that Sergeant Buck Riley Jnr just didn't like to talk unnecessarily.

Riley Jnr was the son of a highly-regarded Marine staff sergeant. His father, Buck Riley Snr, had also been a man Shane Schofield had known better than most.

They had met under fire—back when Schofield had been in a god-almighty mess in Bosnia and Riley Snr had been on the rescue team. They had become good friends and Riley Snr had become Schofield's loyal staff sergeant. Sadly, he had also been on that fateful mission to Antarctica—where he had been murdered in the most brutal fashion by an enemy whose name Schofield had been forbidden to mention by the Official Secrets Act.

Sergeant Buck Riley Jnr—silent, intense and serious—bore his father's call-sign with pride. He was known throughout the unit simply as 'Book II'.

Book II looked at Elvis and Brainiac. 'Do you guys seriously believe that DARPA has built a bomb that can destroy a third of the earth's mass?'

'Yes,' Elvis said.

'No,' Brainiac said.

'Well, they haven't. The superbomb is an urban myth,' Book II said, 'designed to keep the conspiracy theorists on the Internet and the gossipy old women in the United States Marine Corps happy. Want me to give you a couple more examples? That the FBI sends agents into prisons as deep cover operatives. That the United States Air Force has nuclear bombers stationed in commercial hangars at every major airport in the United States for use in the event of a sudden outbreak of war. That USAMRIID has developed a cure for AIDS but hasn't been allowed to release it. That the Air Force has developed a magnetic-propulsion system that allows vehicles to float on air. That the *losing* tenderer in the bid to build the stealth bomber proposed a supersonic plane that could attain complete invisibility through the use of nuclear-powered air refraction—and built the plane anyway, even after they *lost* the bid. Heard any of those?'

'No,' Elvis said, 'but they're *way* cool.'

'What about you, Captain?' Book II turned to Schofield. 'You heard any of those before?'

Schofield held the young sergeant's gaze. 'I've heard about the last one, but not the others.'

He turned away from the debate, scanning the office around him.

He frowned. Someone was missing.

And then it hit him.

'Hey, where's Warrant Officer Webster?' he said.

The President of the United States stared out through the slanted observation windows, his mouth agape.

Through the windows, in the middle of a high-ceilinged, hall-like room, he saw a large freestanding *cube* made of a clear glass-like substance.

It just sat there in the middle of the hall, not quite reaching the ceiling, not quite reaching the walls, a glass cube the size of a large living room, bounded on two sides by the elevated L-shaped observation structure.

It was what lay *inside* the glass cube, however, that seized the President's attention.

Indeed, he couldn't take his eyes off it.

'The cube is made of high-tensile polyfibre, and has its own separate oxygen supply. It is completely airtight,' Colonel Harper said. 'Should its structural integrity be compromised, the cube's internal air pressure is automatically raised, so that no contagions can enter it.'

Harper gestured to one of the three scientists who had been up on the tarmac earlier. 'Mr President, I'd like you to meet Doctor Gunther Botha, the guiding force behind Project Fortune.'

The President shook Botha's hand. Botha was a fat, wide-faced, balding man of fifty-eight, and he spoke with a guttural South African accent: 'It's a pleasure to meet you, Mister President.'

'Doctor Botha is from—'

'I know where Doctor Botha is from,' the President

said, a trace of disapproval in his voice. 'I saw his file yesterday.'

Gunther Botha was a former member of the South African Defence Force's notorious Medical Battalion. Though not widely known, throughout the 1980s South Africa was second only to the Soviet Union in the creation and stockpiling of biological weapons, principally for use against the black majority.

But with the fall of the apartheid regime, Gunther Botha quickly found himself out of a job and directly in the firing line of the Truth and Reconciliation Commission. His clandestine hiring by the United States government in 1996 was not unlike its harbouring of Nazi scientists after World War II. Specialists in Botha's chosen field of expertise were exceedingly hard to come by.

The President turned back to look out through the observation windows. 'So this is the vaccine . . .' he said, gazing down at the clear fibreglass cube.

'Yes, sir, it is,' Botha said.

'Tested?' The President didn't turn as he spoke.

'Yes.'

'In serum-hydrate form?'

'Yes.'

'Against the latest strain?'

'We tested it against 9.1 yesterday afternoon, as soon as it arrived.'

'Mister President,' Colonel Harper said, 'if you'd like, we can give you a demonstration.'

A pause.

'All right,' the President said. 'Do so.'

*

'Where did he go?' Schofield asked as he stood in the middle of the wide main hangar of Area 7 with Libby Gant.

Warrant Officer Carl Webster—the man in charge of the Football—wasn't in either of the two Presidential helicopters, nor was he in the hangar's two offices. And a quick check with the Secret Service people had revealed that he hadn't gone with the President on the tour of the facility.

Warrant Officer Webster was nowhere to be found.

It was cause for concern because there were strict rules of protocol as to Webster's movements. If he wasn't with the President, he was supposed to stay close to Marine One at all times.

'Take a look at the welcoming committee, the famous 7th Squadron,' Gant said, eyeing the three groups of P-90-armed commandos stationed at various points around the hangar bay. The crack Air Force troops just watched Schofield and Gant impassively.

'They look pretty mean to me,' Schofield said.

'They're jacked up,' Gant said.

'What?'

'Yellow tinges to their eyes.'

'Steroids?'

'Uh-huh,' Gant said.

'No wonder they look so edgy,' Schofield said.

'Elvis doesn't like them,' Gant said. 'Says he heard somewhere that they're, quote, "unofficially racist". You'll notice that there are no black members in these squads.'

It was true. Apart from a couple of Asian–American members scattered among them, the 7th Squadron units in the hangar were absolutely lily-white.

'Yes, I've heard those rumours, too,' Schofield said. Although no-one liked to admit it, in some sections of the armed forces, racism—particularly against black soldiers— was still a problem. And with their brutal selection courses, special forces units like the 7th Squadron could easily wield subtle discriminatory powers.

Schofield nodded at the leaders of the three ten-man groups, distinguished from the others by the fact that they didn't have to hold their P-90s in their hands. Their machine guns were secured behind their shoulderblades, in back-mounted holsters. 'You know what they call the five 7th Squadron unit commanders at exercises?'

'What?'

'The Five Snakes. As the overall squadron leader, Kurt Logan commands one ten-man team, the first one, Alpha Unit. The other four units are run by four captains— McConnell, Willis, Stone and Carney. And they're good. When they've cared to show up at the inter-service combat exercises at Bragg, they've always come in at number one. One time, a lone 7th Squadron unit took out three SEAL defensive teams all by itself—and that was *without* Logan.'

'Why do they call them the Five Snakes?' Gant asked.

'It started out as a jealous joke among the other field commanders. Three reasons. One, because tactically they resemble snakes: they strike quickly and with maximum force, and with a total lack of mercy. Two, because, personally, they're all very cold individuals. They would never mix with their counterparts in the other services. Always stuck together.'

'And the third reason?'

'Because each of their call-signs is a variety of aggressive snake.'

'Nice,' Gant said wryly.

They kept walking. Gant changed the subject: 'You know, I had a good time last Saturday night.'

'You did?' Schofield turned to face her.

'Yeah. Did you?'

'Oh, *yeah*.'

Gant said, 'I was just wondering, you know, because, well, you didn't . . .'

'Wait a second,' Schofield said suddenly. 'Something's wrong here.'

'What?'

Schofield looked at the three 7th Squadron units stationed around the hangar again.

One squad stood guard over by the regular elevator. The second group of ten men stood beside the wide aircraft elevator shaft. The third unit stood on the south-eastern side of the hangar, over by a door that led into the two-storey control building.

It was at that moment that Schofield saw the sign on the door behind the third group of 7th Squadron men.

And then, in his mind's eye, he saw it.

'Come on,' he said, heading back toward the offices. 'Quickly.'

'The arming codes have been entered, sir,' Logan said. 'The Football is ready. Warrant Officer Webster was most . . . forthcoming.'

The radio operators inside the control room continued their verbal updates:

'—emergency sealing system ready—'

'—self-contained oxygen supply ready—'

'Major Logan,' one of them said, 'I'm still picking up those trace heat signatures in sector nine outside, out by the EEV.'

'Size?'

'Same as before. Between twelve and seventeen inches. I'm not sure, sir, but I'd swear they've moved closer to the vent since the last time I looked.'

Logan looked at the satellite image. A zoomed-in black-and-white shot of the desert to the east of the main complex showed about twenty-four rod-shaped white blobs arrayed in a wide three-hundred-yard circle around the Emergency Escape Vent.

'Twelve to seventeen inches.' Logan peered closely at the image. 'Too small to be men. Probably just a pack of desert rats. Get an enhanced image from the satellite, just to be sure. Keep an eye on them.'

The shadowy figure turned to face Logan. 'Where is the President now?'

'He's down in the testing lab on Level 4.'

'Contact Harper. Give him the green light. Tell him we're ready. Tell him the mission is go.'

'Subject One has *not* been immunised with the vaccine,' Dr Gunther Botha said in a neutral scientific voice.

The President now stood in near darkness, in another area of Level 4, facing two brightly-lit test chambers.

Inside each chamber stood a completely naked man. Both men, in perverse contrast to their nakedness, wore gas-masks and a series of electrodes attached to their chests.

'Subject One is a white, Caucasian male, five foot seven inches, one hundred and sixty pounds, age thirty-six. Subject is wearing a standard-issue anti-contagion gas-mask. Releasing the agent now.'

There was a soft hissing sound as a light mist of mustard-yellow aerosol particles was released into the first man's chamber. He was a thin man, gangly. He looked about himself fearfully as the gas entered his air-tight room.

The President said, 'Where did you get the virus?'

'Changchun,' Botha said.

The President nodded.

Changchun was a remote town in northern Manchuria. Although the Chinese government denied it, Changchun was the Chinese Army's chief biological weapons testing facility. It was said that political prisoners and captured foreign spies were sent there and used as guinea pigs for virus and nerve agent testing.

The naked man in the gas chamber was still standing, still looking nervously about himself.

'Secondary infection occurs via indirect ingestion through dermatological orifices—hair follicles in the skin, open cuts,' Botha said blandly. 'Without administration of an effective vaccine, death will occur approximately thirty minutes after contact. For indirectly ingested nerve agents, this is a relatively fast kill-rate.

'But,' Botha held up a finger, 'when compared with the effects of *direct* inhalation of this agent, it is highly *in*efficient.'

He pressed an intercom switch and addressed the man in the chamber. 'Would you please remove your mask.'

In response, the man gave Botha the finger—firmly.

Botha just sighed and pressed a button on a nearby console. Subject One received a severe shock through his chest electrodes.

'I said, would you please remove your gas-mask.'

Subject One slowly took off his mask.

And immediately—*violently*—the virus took effect.

The man clutched his stomach and coughed a deep, hacking cough.

'As I said, *far* more efficient,' Botha said.

The man doubled over, started wheezing.

'Gastrointestinal irritation begins within approximately ten seconds of onset.'

The man vomited explosively, splatting brown-green vomit all over the test booth's floor.

73

'Stomach liquefication within thirty seconds . . .'

The man dropped to his knees, gasping for air. A chunky liquid dribbled down his chin. He clutched at the booth's glass wall, right in front of Botha.

'Liver and kidney liquefication within a minute . . .'

The subject puked a bloody black sludge all over the window. Then he fell to the ground, shuddering and shivering.

'Total organ failure within ninety seconds. Death within two minutes.'

Soon, the naked man inside the chamber—coiled in the foetal position—lay still.

The President watched, trying to hide his revulsion.

It was beyond cruel, this method of death, even for a man such as this.

Nevertheless, he tried to justify Subject One's grisly death in the light of what Subject One had done during his life. With a friend, Leon Roy Hailey had tortured nine women in the back of his van, laughing at them as they begged for mercy. The two men had recorded the girls' death throes on a video recorder for later gratification. The President had seen those tapes.

He also knew that Leon Roy Hailey had been sentenced to four hundred and fifty-two years in prison for his crimes. He was never to leave prison alive. And so, after five brutal years in jail, he—like every other test subject at Area 7, all of them serving multiple life sentences—had elected to submit himself to scientific testing.

'Subject Two,' Botha said tonelessly, 'has been given the vaccine in serum-hydrate form. Serum was mixed into a glass of water he drank exactly thirty minutes ago.

74

Subject is a white, Caucasian male, six feet eight inches, two hundred and fifteen pounds, age thirty-two. Releasing the agent now.'

Again, the hissing came, followed by the sudden puff of mustard-yellow aerosol mist.

The man in the second chamber saw the gas enter his booth, but unlike the first test subject, he didn't do anything in response. He was much bigger than the first man—a massive six-eight—broadchested, too, with bulging biceps, enormous fists and a small elliptical head that seemed way too tiny for his body.

With his gas-mask on and the yellow mist falling all around him, he just stared out through the one-way glass of the test chamber, as if a painful agonised death didn't worry him in the slightest.

No coughing. No spasming. With the gas-mask on, the virus hadn't affected him yet.

Botha flicked the intercom switch: 'Take off your mask, please.'

Subject Two obeyed Botha's command without objection, removed his mask.

The President saw the man's face, and this time he caught his breath.

It was a face he had seen many times before—on television, in the newspapers. It was the evil tattooed face of Lucifer James Leary, the serial killer known across America as 'the Surgeon of Phoenix'.

He was the man who had killed thirty-two hitch-hikers, most of them young backpackers, whom he had picked up on the interstate between Las Vegas and Phoenix between 1991 and 1998. In every case, Leary had left his trademark—a piece of the victim's jewellery, usually a ring or necklace, lying on the roadway at the spot where the victim had been abducted.

A disgraced former medical student, Leary would take his victims to his home in Phoenix, amputate their limbs and then *eat* those limbs in front of them. The discovery of his house by FBI agents—complete with blood-smeared basement and two live but partially-eaten victims—had horrified America.

Even now, Lucifer Leary looked like the picture of evil. The entire left-hand side of his face was covered by a black tattoo depicting five vertical claw marks, as if Freddy Krueger himself had slashed his razor-tipped fingers viciously down Leary's cheek. The tattooed slash-marks were impressive in their detail—torn ragged skin, imitation blood—designed to evoke maximum revulsion.

At that moment, to the President's horror, Leary *smiled* at the observation window, revealing hideous yellow teeth.

It was then that it hit the President.

Even though his gas-mask was off, Leary didn't seem to be affected by the airborne virus.

'As you will see,' Botha said proudly, 'even when the virus is inhaled *directly* into the lungs from the air, an orally-administered vaccine delivered in serum-hydrate form is effective in preventing infection. The vaccine neutralises the invading virus by restricting the release of the protein diethylpropanase by the virus, a protein which attacks the pigmentation enzyme metahydro-genase and the blood group protein, DB—'

'In English, please,' the President said tersely.

Botha said, 'Mr President, what you have just seen is a quantum leap forward in biotechnological warfare. It is the world's first genetically-engineered biological weapon, a completely synthetic agent, so there are no natural cures. And it works with a degree of efficiency the likes of which I have never seen before. It is a purely *constructed* virus, and make no mistake, it has been constructed in a very particular way.

'It is an ethnic bullet, designed to kill only *certain* races of people, people possessed of certain ethnically exclusive genes. In this case, it attacks only those people who are possessed of the enzyme metahydrogenase and DB blood protein. These are the enzymes which cause white skin pigmentation, the characteristic enzymes of Caucasian people.

'Mister President, the same enzyme that makes our skin white makes us susceptible to this virus. It is extraordinary. I don't know how the Chinese did it. My government in South Africa tried for years to develop a virus that it could put in the water supply which would make only black people sterile, but we never succeeded.

'But from the look of this agent, it would not be difficult to adapt the genetic make-up of the virus so that it would also attack African–Americans, since their pigmentation enzyme is a variant of metahydrogenase—'

'Bottom line,' the President said.

'The bottom line is simple, Mister President,' Botha said. 'The only people safe from this virus are people of Asian origin, because they do not possess these pigmentation enzymes *at all*. As such, they would be immune from the agent while Caucasians and African–Americans everywhere would die.

'Mister President. Allow me to introduce you to the latest Chinese biological weapon. Meet the Sinovirus.'

'I'm telling you, there's something not right here,' Schofield said.

'Bullshit, Captain,' Ramrod Hagerty waved his hand dismissively. 'You've been reading too many comic books.'

'What about Webster, then? I can't find him anywhere. He's not allowed to just disappear.'

'Probably in the john.'

'No, I checked there,' Schofield said. 'And Nighthawk Three? Where are they? Why hasn't Hendricks called in?'

Hagerty just stared at him blankly.

Schofield said, 'Sir, with all due respect, if you would just look at where these 7th Squadron guys are standing . . .'

Hagerty turned in his chair. He, Schofield and Gant were in the southern office of the main hangar, with the small group of White House people. Hagerty casually looked out through the office's windows at the 7th Squadron commandos spaced around the hangar outside.

'Looks like they're guarding every entrance,' Hagerty shrugged. 'To stop us going into areas we're not supposed to.'

'No, sir, they're not. Look *closely*. The group to the north are guarding the regular elevator. The middle group are guarding the aircraft elevator. They're both fine. But look at the group over by the control building, the group in front of the door.'

'Yeah, so . . .'

'Sir, they're guarding a storage closet.'

Hagerty looked from Schofield to the Air Force commandos. It was true. They were standing in front of a door marked 'STORAGE'.

'That's very nice, Captain. I'll put your observations in my report.' Hagerty resumed his paperwork.

'But sir . . .'

'I *said*, I'll put your observations in my report, Captain Schofield. That will be all.'

Schofield straightened.

'With respect, sir, have you ever been in combat?' he said.

Hagerty froze, looked up. 'I'm not sure if I like your tone, Captain.'

'*Have you ever been in combat?*'

'I was in Saudi during Desert Storm.'

'Fighting?'

'No. Embassy staff.'

'Sir, if you'd ever been in combat, you'd know that those three groups of Air Force commandos are not standing in defensive positions. Those are *offensive* positions. More than that, those men are perfectly placed to rout *these two offices*—'

'Rubbish.'

Schofield grabbed the sheet of paper Hagerty had been writing on and scribbled a quick map of the hangar:

79

'This is where they are now,' Schofield tapped the three big black dots on the diagram. 'Twelve o'clock, ten o'clock and four o'clock. But when they move like this . . .' Schofield added some arrows to his diagram:

'. . . we've got serious trouble. All the Marines and Secret Service people over in the northern office will face the full force of the attack, while the White House people here in the southern office will naturally run the other way—right into the the third unit of 7th Squadron soldiers.'

Hagerty looked at Schofield's diagram for a long moment.

Then he said, 'That has got to be the stupidest thing I've ever heard, Captain. These are *American* servicemen.'

'For Christ's sake, just *listen* to me—'

'No, you listen to me,' Hagerty spat. 'Don't think for a moment that I don't know who you are. I know all about Wilkes Ice Station. I know what happened there. But just because you were some kind of hero once doesn't give you a licence to spout out fucking conspiracy theories and expect to be believed. I've been in this Corps for twenty-two years and I have risen to where I am by—'

'—what? Pushing pencils,' Schofield said.

Hagerty fell silent. His face grew beetroot red.

'That's it, Schofield. For the sake of the Corps, I won't make a scene here, but when we get back to Quantico, as soon as we touch down, you will be taken into custody and held for court martial on charges of gross insubordination. Now get *the fuck* out of my sight.'

Schofield just shook his head in exasperation and left.

'And these, sir, are the men who brought back the Sinovirus,' Colonel Harper said, guiding the President around the test booths on Level 4.

A giant thirty-foot-long quarantine chamber stood before them. Through a small glass window set into the side of the reinforced chamber, the President saw four men, all seated on sofas watching a television and bathed in blue ultra-violet light. All of them, he noted, were of Asian extraction.

As soon as they saw the President, two of the men inside the chamber rose to their feet and stood to attention.

81

'Mister President, meet Captain Robert Wu and Lieutenant Chet Li from the 7th Squadron—'

Just then Harper's cell phone buzzed.

The colonel excused himself and stepped away to take the call.

'It's a pleasure to meet you both, gentlemen,' the President said, stepping forward. 'Your country owes you a debt of gratitude.'

'Thank you, sir.'

'Thank you.'

'How long do you have to stay in there for?' the President inquired, asking the obligatory personal question.

'Another couple of hours, I think, sir,' the one named Wu said. 'We got back yesterday with the new strain, but we have to stay in here for twenty-four hours. The chamber is operated on a time-lock. Can't be opened until 0900 hours. So they can be sure there are no other bugs on us.'

'Well, I won't be here come nine o'clock,' the President said, 'but rest assured, you'll be receiving something from me in the very near future.'

'Thank you, sir.'

'Thank you, sir.'

Having finished his call, Colonel Harper returned.

'And that concludes our tour, Mister President,' he said. 'Now, if you'll come this way, I have one last thing to show you.'

Schofield and Gant stood inside Marine One, behind Brainiac.

Brainiac was seated at the helicopter's communications console, typing quickly on a keyboard.

'Anything from Nighthawk Three or the two advance teams?' Schofield asked.

'Nada from Nighthawk Three,' Brainiac said. 'And just the beacons from the Secret Service teams.'

Schofield thought for a moment. 'Are we plugged into Area 7's local network?'

'Yep. So the President can collect secure transmissions by the landline.'

'Okay then, can you bring up the complex's security camera system for me?'

'Sure.'

The President was led up a set of firestairs to Level 3, the living quarters of Area 7.

With his nine-man Secret Service Detail he was brought into a wide low-ceilinged common room—couches, coffee tables, kitchenette and, taking pride of place over by the wall, a big-screen Panasonic TV.

'If you would just wait here for a moment, Mister President,' Colonel Harper said, 'I'll send someone down in a minute.'

And then he left the room, leaving the President and his Detail alone.

A series of black-and-white monitors flickered to life in the communications bay of Marine One.

Each monitor depicted a grid of views from the multitude of security cameras around Area 7.

'We have contact,' Brainiac said.

From various angles, Schofield saw empty stairwells—

the main hangar—something that looked like a subway station—the interiors of the glass-walled offices in the main hangar, one of them filled with Marines and Secret Service people, the other containing White House staff members—and, in grainy black-and-white, the inside of an elevator—

Schofield froze at the final image.

The elevator was packed with ten fully-armed 7th Squadron commandos.

And then suddenly movement from one of the other monitors caught his eye.

It was the view from one of the stairwell cameras.

A whole stream of armed 7th Squadron commandos were storming down the stairwell.

'This is going to be very painful,' he said flatly.

Schofield stepped out of Marine One onto the hangar floor, Gant and Brainiac close behind him.

Although nothing *physical* about it had changed, somehow the hangar now looked very different.

Now it looked menacing.

Dangerous.

Schofield saw the three groups of 7th Squadron commandos arrayed around the enormous interior space—saw the commander of one of the groups touch his ear as he caught a radio transmission.

'Stay here,' Schofield said.

'Okay,' Brainiac said.

'Hey,' Gant said.

'What?'

'Try not to look so spooked.'

'I'll do my best,' Schofield said as he stepped out from the cover of Marine One and started walking casually across the hangar floor, toward the northern glass-walled office.

He was about halfway there when it happened.

Loud and sudden.

Boom!

Like a curtain falling at the end of a stage show, a giant piston-driven titanium door thundered down in front of the hangar's main doors. Its leading edge—lined with nasty-looking tooth-like protrusions—lodged firmly into the series of box-like indentations that ran across the entry to the hangar.

And with the falling of the massive armoured door, Schofield gave up any pretence of trying to appear calm.

He broke into a run just as the two nearest groups of 7th Squadron commandos—the ones at twelve o'clock and ten o'clock—raised their P-90s and the air around him became awash with sizzling bullets.

It had been five minutes now and nobody had come for them and the President of the United States was not accustomed to waiting.

The President and his protective Detail just stood in the common room on Level 3, looking about themselves, waiting in the silence.

'Frank,' the President said to the Chief of the Detail, 'see what's going on—'

The big-screen television came on.

The President and his Detail whirled around.

'What the fuck . . .' somebody said.

On the screen, large and bold, was the bright yellow insignia of the Emergency Broadcast System—the special all-spectrum broadcast network that was capable of cutting off regular broadcasting in the event of a national emergency.

Then, abruptly, the EBS symbol disappeared, and a face appeared in its place.

'What the hell . . .' this time it was the President who spoke.

The face on the screen was that of a dead man.

It was the face of Lieutenant General Charles Samson Russell, USAF, call-sign: 'Caesar.'

On every television screen in Area 7—and, it appeared, every television in the United States—the round, heavy-browed face of Charles Russell began to speak.

'Mister President. People of America. Welcome to Area 7. My name is General Charles Russell, United States Air Force. For too long, I have watched this country eat itself. I will do so no longer.' His tone was measured, his Louisiana accent thick.

'Our representatives at both federal and state levels are incapable of genuine leadership. Our free press is no longer the tool for controlling government that it was intended to be. To every man who has ever fought or died for this country, this state of affairs is a disgrace. It can no longer be allowed to continue.'

In the common room, the President just stared at the big-screen television.

'And so I propose a challenge, Mister President—both to you and to the system you represent.

'Implanted on your heart is a radio device. It was attached to the outer tissue of your cardiac muscle during an operation on your left lung four years ago.'

Frank Cutler spun to face the President, a look of horror spreading across his face.

'I will initiate its signal now,' Caesar said. He pressed some buttons on a small red unit that he held in his hand. The compact unit had a black stub antenna sticking out from its top.

Frank Cutler pulled a debugging wand from his coat—a spectrum analyser used to detect any signal-emitting device—and waved it over the President's body.

Feet and legs . . . okay.

Waist and stomach . . . okay.

Chest . . .

The wand went crazy.

'My challenge to you, Mister President, is simple.' Russell's voice echoed throughout the underground base.

'As you well know, at every major airport in the United States there are at least three hangars devoted to the storage of United States Air Force bombers, fighters and ordnance.

'Right now, inside fourteen of those hangars, sit fourteen Type-240 blast plasma warheads. The airports include John F. Kennedy, Newark and La Guardia in New York, Dulles in Washington, O'Hare in Chicago, LAX in Los Angeles, and airports in San Francisco, San Diego, Seattle, Boston, Philadelphia and Detroit. Each plasma warhead, as you know, has a blast radius of sixteen miles and a detonation yield of ninety megatons. All are armed.'

In the common room on Level 3, everyone was silent.

'The only thing that will stop the detonation of these warheads, Mister President,' Charles Russell said with a smile, 'is the continued beating of your heart.'

Russell went on.

'All the devices at the airports are patched in to a single satellite in geosynchronous orbit above this base. That satellite, Mister President, emits a high-powered microwave signal which is picked up and bounced back to it by the transmitter placed on your heart.

'But the radio transmitter on your heart, once started, is kinetically operated. If your heart should stop beating, the transmitter will cease to operate, and the satellite's signal will *not* be bounced back to it—in which case, the satellite will instruct the bombs in the airports to detonate.

'Mister President. If your heart should stop, America as we know it dies. If your heart keeps beating, America lives.

'You are the symbol of a bankrupt culture, sir: a *politician*, a man who seeks power for power's sake, but, like the people you represent, one who lives safe in the knowledge that he will never ever be called upon to stand up and fight for the system that gives him that power.

'Well, you have lived safely for too long, Mister President. Now you have been called to account. Now you have been called to fight.

'I, on the other hand, am a warrior. I have spilled my blood for this country. What blood have you spilt? What sacrifices have you made? None. *Coward*.

'But like an honest patriot, I will give you and the system you represent a final chance to prove your worth. For the people of this country need proof. They need to see you flounder—see you fall—see you *sell them out* to save your skin. They elected you to represent them. Now you shall do that—literally. If you die, they die with you.

'This facility has been completely sealed. It is designed to withstand the full force of a nuclear blast, so there is no way out of it. Inside it with you is a fifty-man detachment of the best ground force this country has to offer, the 7th Special Operations Squadron. These men have orders to kill you, Mister President.

'With your Secret Service Detail, you will face them in a fight to the death. Whoever wins, gets the country. Whoever loses, dies.

'Of course, the American people must be kept appraised of the score in this challenge,' Caesar said. 'Therefore, every hour on the hour, I shall address them via the Emergency Broadcast System and give them an update on the pursuit.'

The President looked up at the nearest security camera. 'This is ridiculous! You couldn't *possibly* have put a—'

'Jeremiah K. Woolf, Mister President,' Caesar Russell said from the TV screen. The President immediately fell silent.

No-one else spoke.

'I will assume from your silence that you have seen the FBI file.'

Of course the President had seen the file—the peculiarities

90

of the ex-senator's death had demanded it.

At the exact moment that Jeremiah Woolf had died in Alaska, his home in Washington DC had exploded. No culprit—for either incident—had ever been found. It was a coincidence too bizarre to ignore, but in the absence of any evidence to explain it, to the mass media it had remained simply that, a tragic coincidence.

As the President knew, however, one particular aspect of the ex-senator's death had never been made public: namely, the elevated levels of red blood cell production in his bloodstream, plus extremely low alveolar and arterial phosphate pressures. All of these symptoms indicated a prolonged period of hyperventilation *before* Woolf had been shot—a period during which the ex-senator had experienced a heightened state of 'fight or flight' physiology.

In other words, the ex-senator had been running from someone when he'd been shot. He had been hunted.

And now it made sense.

Woolf had been implanted with a transmitter . . .

. . . and then in Alaska he had been hunted and shot, and when, finally, his heart had stopped, his home on the other side of the country had been destroyed.

Caesar Russell's voice invaded his thoughts. 'Former Senator Woolf's unexpected retirement from government left me with an extra transmitting device. And so he became a guinea pig, a test run. A test run for today.'

The President exchanged a look with Frank Cutler.

Caesar said, 'Oh, and just in case you're harbouring ambitions of escaping this facility . . .' He lifted an object into view.

It was a stainless steel briefcase.

Warrant Officer Carl Webster's steel briefcase.

The case's handle still had the pair of handcuffs attached to it—only now the open-ended cuff was no longer attached to anything. It was splattered all over with blood.

It was the Football.

And it was open.

The President saw the briefcase's flat-glass palm-print analyser and keypad. The palm-print analyser was an identification feature programmed to recognise the President's palm-print, so that only he could activate—and de-activate—America's thermonuclear arsenal.

Somehow, though, Russell had managed to falsify the President's palm-print and enter the arming codes. But how could he have got a copy of the President's *hand*?

'In addition to the transmitter on your heart, Mister President,' Russell said, 'all the devices in the airports have been networked to a recycling timer of exactly ninety minutes, as is shown on the Football's display screen. Only the application of *your palm-print* to the analyser—once every ninety minutes—will reset that timer and stop the plasma warheads from going off, so don't think of leaving. The Football, for your information, will be kept up here in the main hangar.

'This is a great day in the history of the nation, Mister President, a day of reckoning. Come the dawn of tomorrow, the glorious Fourth of July, we shall see if we all awake in a new, reborn America. Good luck, Mister President, and may God have mercy on your soul.'

At that moment, as if right on cue, the main doors to the common room burst open and a team of 7th Squadron commandos—led by Major Kurt Logan and wearing their fearsome ERG-6 gas-masks—rushed into the room, their devastating P-90 machine guns blazing.

The challenge had begun.

SECOND CONFRONTATION

3 July, 0700 Hours

UNITED STATES AIR FORCE
SPECIAL AREA (RESTRICTED) NO. 7
0700 HOURS

GROUND LEVEL: Main Hangar

LEVEL 1: Hangar Bay

LEVEL 2: Hangar Bay

LEVEL 3: Living Quarters
LEVEL 4: Laboratories
LEVEL 5: Confinement

LEVEL 6: X-rail platform

The main hangar had become a battlefield.

Bulletholes raked the floor at Shane Schofield's feet as he raced for the doorway to the northern glass-walled office.

He poked his head around the doorway: 'Marines! *Scatter!*'

But that was all he could say before the window next to him shattered into a thousand fragments and he dived away, crawling for the cover of the two Presidential helicopters and their towing vehicles.

He looked back just in time to see a couple of full-dress-uniformed Marines burst out through the windows of the office a moment before the small structure was hit by a Predator shoulder-launched missile and its walls blasted outwards in a shower of glass and billowing fire.

Schofield slid under Marine One, and found himself lying next to Libby Gant and Brainiac.

Gunfire echoed out all around them. And then bizarrely, above the gunshots, Schofield heard a voice booming out from the hangar's loudspeaker system: '—*ood luck, Mister President, and may God have mercy on your soul.*'

'Holy *shit!*' Brainiac yelled.

'This way!' Schofield said, crawling on his stomach underneath the big helicopter.

He arrived at a wide grille in the floor. It came away easily. An air vent opened up beneath it. The steel-walled vent plunged down into the earth, disappearing into darkness.

'Let's go!' Schofield yelled above the gunfire.

Abruptly, a metal panel in the bottom of Marine One burst open—almost decapitating Schofield—and a figure with an M-16 dropped down behind him, the gun levelled at his forehead.

'*Fuck!* It's you,' Mother said as she lowered herself out of the helicopter's emergency escape hatch onto the ground.

'Here, happy birthday,' she said, tossing an MP-10 machine pistol to Gant. 'Sorry, Scarecrow, nothing for you. That was all I could find in the basic arms cabinet on board. There's more in the forward armoury, but Gunman's got the key to that.'

'Never mind,' Schofield said, 'the first thing we've got to do is get out of here and regroup. Then we have to figure out a way of taking these bastards down. This way.'

'Did you catch any of that shit on the television?' Mother said as she crawled over to the vent.

Gant and Brainiac climbed down into the vent first, bracing their legs against its walls, shimmying themselves down into it.

'No,' Schofield said, 'I was too busy dodging bullets.'

'Then I've got a lot to tell you,' Mother said as they lowered themselves into the shaft.

*

The President of the United States was moving faster than he had ever moved before. In fact, his feet barely even touched the ground.

At the first sight of the 7th Squadron commandos storming the common room, his nine-man Protective Detail had thrown itself into action.

Four men immediately took up defensive positions in between the President and the oncoming assault troops, throwing their coats open to reveal Uzi sub-machine guns. The Uzis buzzed as they unleashed a brutal wave of gunfire at a crushing 600 rounds per minute.

The other five members of the Detail crash-tackled the President out into the nearby fire escape, practically lifting him off his feet as they gang-rushed him out of the room, covering his body with their own.

The door to the fire stairs slammed shut behind them, but not before they saw the 7th Squadron troops clinically take up covering positions behind couches, doors and cupboards and leap-frog each other and tear to shreds the four Secret Service men who had remained behind—drowning out the buzz of their Uzis with the whirring drone of their P-90 assault rifles.

The Uzis might have fired at 600 rounds per minute. But the P-90, made by the FN Herstal company in Belgium, fired at an astonishing 900 rounds per minute. Indeed, with its rounded hand guard, internal blowback system, and incredible hundred-round magazine mounted above the barrel, it looked like something out of a science fiction movie.

'Down the stairs! *Now!*' Frank Cutler yelled as bullets slammed into the other side of the firedoor. 'Head for the alternate exit!'

The President and what was left of his Detail flew down the stairs, taking them four at a time, hurling themselves around every turn. Every one of them had a weapon in his or her hand now—Uzis, SIG-Sauers, anything.

The President himself could do nothing but run with them, so tightly was he flanked by his bodyguards.

'Advance Team One! Come in!' Cutler yelled into his wrist microphone as he ran.

No reply.

'Advance Team One! Come in! We are approaching Exit Point One with Patriot and we need to know if it is open!'

He received no reply.

Up in the main hangar, Book II was in hell.

Bullets strafed the floor all around him, glass rained down on his head.

He was tucked up against the outside of the northern office with Elvis—in the tiny gap between it and the hangar's armoured door—the two of them having dived out through the office's bullet-shattered windows a moment before it had been blasted to smithereens by the Predator missile.

The three ten-man teams of 7th Squadron men were everywhere, moving with precision and speed, racing around the helicopters, leaping over dead men, their guns pressed against their shoulders, eyes looking straight down the barrels.

On the other side of the hangar, Book saw the White House people come streaming out of the southern glass-walled office—about ten people in total—screaming, looking about themselves, only to be met by the 7th

Squadron unit that had been stationed on the eastern side of the floor.

The White House men and women were cut down where they stood, hit head-on by a wave of merciless fire. Their bodies convulsed and shuddered under the weight of the brutal onslaught.

And then suddenly Book II heard a shout and he looked up and saw Gunman Grier burst out of the remains of the northern office, yelling with rage, his nickel-plated Beretta up and firing.

No sooner had he appeared, however, than Grier's chest literally *exploded* in a gout of red as two 7th Squadron troopers blasted him at the same time.

The force of their fire pummelled Grier's body, keeping him standing long after he was dead—sending him staggering backwards, reeling with each impact, until he slammed into a wall and fell to the ground in a heap.

'This is a real fucked-up situation!' Elvis yelled above the gunfire. 'There's no way out of here!'

'Over there!' Book II pointed at the regular elevator on the northern side of the hangar. 'That's the only way out I can see!'

'But how do we get there?'

'We drive!' Book II shouted, nodding at one of the big towing vehicles attached to the tail boom of Nighthawk Two, ten yards away.

The four radio men inside the control room spoke rapidly into their headsets.

'—Bravo Unit, close down all remaining hostile agents inside that northern office—'

'—Alpha Unit is in pursuit of Presidential Detail down the eastern fire stairs—'

'—Charlie Unit, break off from the main hangar, I have visual on four Marines heading down the primary air vent—'

'—Delta Unit, be patient, maintain your position—'

'What do you mean, they attached a radio transmitter to his heart?' Schofield said as he made his way down the vertical ventilation shaft, his feet splayed wide, pressed against its silver steel walls.

Gant and Brainiac were further down, shimmying their way quickly down the vent, a seemingly bottomless drop beneath them.

'If his heart stops, the bombs go off, in every major airport, in every major city,' Mother said.

'Jesus,' Schofield said.

'And he's got to report in every ninety minutes, to reset a timer on the Football. Again, if he doesn't, *boom*.'

'Every ninety minutes?' Schofield pressed a button on his old digital watch, starting a timer of his own. He gave it a few minutes head-start. It started ticking down from 85:00 minutes—85:00 . . . 84:59 . . . 84:58—when abruptly, he heard a clattering noise from somewhere above him and he snapped his head up—

Bullets sprayed everywhere.

Peppering the metal walls all around him and Mother.

Schofield saw a P-90 rifle sticking over the rim of the ventilation shaft—held by someone out of sight—firing wildly down into it.

'*Scarecrow!*' Gant called from ten feet below them. She

was crouched inside a small horizontal tunnel that branched off the main vertical shaft. 'Down here!'

'Go, Mother! Go!' Schofield yelled.

Both he and Mother released their footholds on the shaft's walls and let themselves slide down the vertical vent.

Whooosh!

They shot down the narrow vertical tunnel, sizzling-hot bullets impacting all around them, before—*reeeech!*—they dug their heels into the shaft's walls just short of the horizontal tunnel.

Mother came to a perfect halt right in front of it. Schofield, however, overshot the cross-vent, but somehow managed to throw his hands out and grip it with his fingertips, a split second before he fell several hundred feet to his death.

Mother stepped inside the cross-vent first, then hauled Schofield into it after her, not a moment before a long abseiling rope dropped down the vertical shaft above them.

The 7th Squadron were coming.

Up ahead, Gant ran in the lead, closely followed by Brainiac. The silver-walled tunnel was about five feet square, so they all had to crouch slightly to run through it.

Gant came around a slight bend on the tunnel and saw light up ahead. She sped up—and then lurched to a sudden halt, clutching desperately for a handhold.

She stopped so suddenly that Brainiac almost bowled right into her. It was lucky he pulled up in time. A collision would have sent both of them falling a hundred and eighty feet straight down.

'Fuck me . . . ' Brainiac said.

'What's the hold-up—?' Mother said as she and Schofield arrived on the scene. 'Oh . . .'

Their tunnel ended at the main elevator shaft.

The giant concrete-walled chasm, two hundred feet across, yawned before them.

On the other side of it, directly opposite them, they saw an enormous heavy steel door with a black-painted '1' on it. It looked like a hangar door of some sort.

And nearly two hundred feet *below* them—parked at the fourth underground level—they saw the wide hydraulic elevator platform.

'You know, it's at times like this I wish I had a Maghook,' Schofield said. A Maghook was a combined grappling hook and high-powered magnet—the signature weapon of Marine Recon Units.

'There are a couple upstairs in Nighthawk Two,' Mother said.

'Wouldn't do us any good,' Gant said. 'Distance is too far. A Maghook has a maximum rope length of a hundred and fifty feet. This is at least two hundred.'

'Well, we better think of something,' Brainiac said, looking back down the cross-vent, listening to the whizzing sounds of the 7th Squadron men abseiling down the main vertical shaft beyond it.

Schofield looked at the wide concrete chasm in front of them. It was clearly well used—covered in grime and grease.

Indented at regular intervals on its walls, however, were a series of thin rectangular conduits—small horizontal gutters cut into the shaft's concrete walls. Each gutter was about six inches deep and ran right around the enormous elevator shaft, circling it. They were designed, it seemed, to house wires and cabling without hindering the elevator platform's upward and downward movement.

But right now, they afforded Schofield no escape.

Boom!

He spun. It was the sound of heavy boots clanging on metal.

The 7th Squadron men had arrived at the other end of the horizontal tunnel.

The Air Force men moved fast, racing half-crouched down the cross-vent, guns up.

There were four of them—all wearing black combat gear: helmets, gas-masks, body armour. Unsure of which cross-tunnel Schofield's group had taken, the others in their unit had gone further down the vertical vent to check the other levels.

The two lead men rounded the bend in the tunnel—and stopped.

They had come to the end of the horizontal cross-vent, to the point where it met the massive elevator shaft.

But there was no-one here.

The end of the tunnel was empty.

When the President of the United States visits a certain venue, the Secret Service has always plotted in advance at least three alternate exit routes, in case of emergency.

In big city hotels, this usually comprises a back entrance, a service entrance—say, through the kitchen—and the roof, for lift-out via helicopter.

At Area 7, the Secret Service had sent two advance teams to secure and then guard the alternate exit points that they had chosen.

Alternate Exit Point 1 was on the lowest level of Area 7—Level 6. The exit itself was the eight-hundred-yard-long Emergency Exit Vent that opened onto the desert floor about half a mile from the low mountain that covered the base. The first Secret Service advance team was stationed down on Level 6, the second up at the Vent's exit on the desert floor itself.

The President and his five-man Detail charged down the fire stairs, a hailstorm of bullets sizzling past their cheeks, shooting right through their flailing coats. The 7th Squadron's first unit—Alpha Unit, led by Major Kurt Logan—was close behind them.

They came to a firedoor that read: 'LEVEL 4: LABORATORY FACILITIES'. Dashed past it.

More stairs, another landing, another door. This one had a larger sign on it:

LEVEL 5: ANIMAL CONTAINMENT AREA

NO ENTRY

THIS DOOR FOR EMERGENCY USE ONLY

ENTER VIA ELEVATORS AT OTHER END OF FLOOR

The President ran right past it.

They arrived at the bottom of the stairwell—at a door marked: 'LEVEL 6: X-RAIL STATION'.

Frank Cutler was running in the lead. He came to the door, yanked it open—

—and was immediately assaulted by a ferocious barrage of automatic gunfire.

Cutler's face and chest became a ragged bloody mess as a relentless wave of bullets rammed into it. The Chief of the Detail went flying back into the stairwell, skidding across the floor, the man immediately behind him *also* going down.

Another agent—a young female agent named Juliet Janson—dived forward and slammed the door shut again, but before she did she got a fleeting, horrifying glimpse of the area beyond it.

The sixth and lowest level of Area 7 looked like an underground subway station—with a flat, raised platform sitting in between two sets of extra-wide railway tracks. The door to the Emergency Exit Vent—their goal— lay buried in the concrete wall of the right-hand track.

Positioned on the train tracks in front of that door, however, and covered by the station's chest-high platform, was a whole *other* unit of 7th Squadron soldiers, all with their P-90s trained on the fire escape.

In front of the 7th Squadron men, lying face-down in their own blood, lay the bullet-riddled bodies of the nine members of the Secret Service's Advance Team One.

The door slammed shut and Special Agent Juliet Janson turned.

'Quickly!' she shouted. 'Back up the stairs! Now!'

'—All units, be aware, Delta Unit has engaged the enemy—'one of the radio men in the control room said. 'Repeat, Delta Unit has engaged the enemy—'

Shane Schofield tried not to breathe, tried not to make a sound.

All they had to do was look over the edge.

He was hanging by his fingertips from one of the horizontal cabling gutters carved into the concrete wall of the elevator shaft, a bare three feet below the mouth of the cross-vent he had been standing in only moments before.

Standing in that cross-vent right now were the four heavily-armed 7th Squadron men who had stormed it only seconds earlier.

Beside him, Mother, Gant and Brainiac were also clinging to the cabling gutter with their fingers.

Above them, they could hear one of the 7th Squadron men speaking into his helmet mike.

'Charlie Six, this is Charlie One, they're not in the Level 1 cross-vent. Copy that, we're on our way.'

Heavy footsteps, then nothing.

Schofield sighed with relief.

'Where to now?' Brainiac asked.

'There,' Schofield said, jerking his chin at the giant steel hangar door on the opposite side of the wide elevator shaft.

'You ready?' Book II yelled to Elvis.

'Ready!' Elvis shouted back.

Book II looked out at the big white-painted Volvo towing vehicle attached to the tail boom of Nighthawk Two ten yards away. With its oversized tyres, low-slung body and small two-man driver's cabin, it looked like either a brick on wheels or a giant cockroach. Indeed, it was this resemblance that had earned the towing vehicle the nickname 'cockroach' among airport workers around the world.

At the moment, Nighthawk Two's cockroach was facing outwards, pointed at the armour-plated titanium door that had thundered down into place only minutes earlier, sealing the hangar.

Book II was now holding two nickel-plated Berettas in his hands, one his own, the other pilfered from a dead Marine nearby. He shouted to Elvis: 'You take the wheel! I'll go for the other side!'

'You got it!'

'Okay! *Now!*'

The two of them leapt to their feet and dashed out into the open together, their legs moving in time.

Almost instantly, a line of bullets raced across the ground behind them, nipping at their heels.

Elvis flung himself into the driver's seat, slammed the

door shut behind him. Book II made for the passenger side, but he was met with a brutal volley of gunfire, so instead he just dived onto the towing vehicle's flat steel roof and yelled, 'Elvis! *Punch it!*'

Elvis keyed the ignition. The Volvo's big 600-horse-power engine roared to life. Then Elvis jammed it into gear and floored it.

The towing vehicle's tyres squealed as they shot off the mark, heading straight for the armoured door that cut the hangar off from the outside world, taking Nighthawk Two, a full-sized CH-53E Super Stallion transport helicopter, with it!

The two remaining units of 7th Squadron men in the hangar—twenty men in total—swept across the hangar on foot, pursuing the speeding cockroach with their guns.

A wave of supercharged bullets pummelled the big Volvo's sides.

Elvis yanked on the steering wheel and the big cockroach swung around, rocketing toward the southern glass-walled office.

On its roof, Book II raised himself on one knee and fired both his pistols at the oncoming 7th Squadron commandos.

It didn't do much good—the Air Force assassins had him outgunned. It was like attacking a battery of Patriot missiles with a pea-shooter. He ducked back behind the cockroach's cabin amid a flurry of return fire.

'*Oh, crap!*' Elvis shouted from the driver's cabin.

Book II looked up.

A lone 7th Squadron commando stood about thirty yards in front of them—*right in their path*—on the southern side of the central elevator shaft, with a Predator anti-tank rocket launcher hefted onto his shoulder!

The commando pulled the trigger.

There was a puff of smoke before a small cylindrical object came blasting out of the launcher, shooting toward the speeding cockroach at phenomenal speed, leaving a dead-straight vapor-trail in the air behind it.

Elvis reacted quickly, did the only thing he could think to do.

He yanked his steering wheel hard to the left.

The massive Volvo towing vehicle rose onto two wheels as it swung violently left—and for a moment it looked like it was going to drive straight into the yawning chasm that was the elevator shaft.

But it just kept turning . . . turning . . . wheels screeching . . . until suddenly it was heading north, along the narrow section of floor *in between* Marine One and the elevator shaft.

Nighthawk Two wasn't so lucky.

Since it was bouncing along—in reverse—behind the runaway cockroach, Elvis's sudden turn had brought it directly into the missile's line of fire.

The Predator hit it, slamming into Nighthawk Two's reinforced glass cockpit at tremendous speed.

The result was nothing short of spectacular.

The whole front section of the CH-53E Super Stallion exploded magnificently—blasting out in an instant, showering the area behind the quickly moving helicopter with glass and twisted metal, leaving the chopper with a jagged metal *hole* where the glass bubble of its cockpit was supposed to be!

The impact of the missile had also destroyed the landing wheels under the nose of the chopper. So now the giant helicopter was being hauled behind Elvis's towing vehicle with its nose—or what was left of it—dragging wildly on the floor, kicking up sparks.

'Elvis!' Book II yelled. 'Go for the elevator! The regular elevator!'

7th Squadron soldiers dived out of the way as the speeding cockroach thundered in amongst them, wildly out of control.

Elvis saw the elevator doors off to his right, and yanked the steering wheel hard over. The cockroach responded, swinging right, cutting the corner of the aircraft elevator shaft—so that for the briefest of moments, Book II, partially hanging off the roof of the vehicle, saw nothing but a wide chasm of emptiness falling away beneath him.

Three seconds later, the cockroach—with the semi-destroyed helicopter behind it—skidded to a squealing halt right in front of the elevator doors on the northern side of the hangar.

Book II leapt off the top of the big Volvo and hit the call button, Elvis joining him, when suddenly two armed men leapt over the big towing vehicle behind them.

Book II spun, snapping his guns up, triggers half-pulled.

'Whoa! Whoa! Whoa!' one of the armed men said, holding his pistol up.

'Easy, Sergeant,' the other one said calmly. 'We're with you.'

Book II eased back on his triggers.

They were Marines.

The first was Sergeant Ashley Lewicky, an extra-ordinarily ugly career sergeant with a thick monobrow, battered pug nose, and mile-wide grin. Short and stout, his call-sign was a slam-dunk: 'Love Machine'. Of roughly equal age and rank, he and Elvis had been buddies for years.

The second Marine, however, couldn't have been more different from Love Machine. Tall and handsome in a clean-cut kind of way, he was a twenty-nine-year-old captain named Tom Reeves. A promising young officer, he'd been tagged for rapid promotion. Indeed, he'd already been promoted over several more-experienced lieutenants. Despite his obvious skills, the men called him 'Calvin', because he looked like a Calvin Klein underwear model.

'Jesus H. Christ, Elvis,' Love Machine said, 'where the hell did you learn to drive! A demolition derby?'

'Why? Where have you two been?' Elvis asked.

'Where do you think, knucklehead? Inside Nighthawk Two. We both dived in there when the shit hit the fan. And we *were* kinda happy there until you guys drove us into the sights of that rocket laun–'

Just then, a volley of bullets smacked into the wall above their heads.

Ten 7th Squadron men—Bravo Unit—were charging across the wide hangar after them.

'I presume you had a plan when you drove over here, Sergeant,' Calvin Reeves said to Book II.

At that moment, the elevator pinged and its metal doors slid open. Thankfully, it was empty.

'This was it, sir,' Book II said.

'I approve,' Calvin said and they all rushed inside. Book II went straight to the control panel and hit 'DOOR CLOSE'.

The doors began to close. A bullet sizzled inside, smacked against the back wall of the lift.

'Hurry *up* . . . ' Elvis urged.

The doors kept closing.

They heard boots thud onto the roof of the cockroach outside, heard machine-gun bolts cock—

The doors came together . . .

. . . a bare second before they erupted with dome-like welts from the barrage of bullets outside.

It had taken them a while, but moving hand over hand, hanging by their fingertips from the cabling gutter that ran all the way around the elevator shaft, they had eventually made it to the wide hangar door on the other side.

Hanging one-handed from the horizontal gutter, Schofield hit a button on a control panel beside the hangar door. Instantly, the massive steel door began to rumble upward.

Schofield climbed up onto level ground first, made sure there were no enemy troops around, then turned to help the others up behind him.

When they were all up, they gazed at the area before them.

'Whoa, *mama* . . . ' Mother breathed.

A cavernous—completely *underground*—aircraft hangar stretched away from them.

In the control room overlooking the main ground-level hangar, the wall of black-and-white television monitors flashed an array of images from the underground complex:

Juliet Janson and the President running up the stairwell.

Book II, Calvin Reeves, Elvis and Love Machine inside the regular elevator, punching out the ceiling hatch and climbing up through it.

Schofield and the others stepping up into the doorway of the underground hangar.

'—okay, Charlie Unit, I have them. The ones who were in the ventilation shaft. Level 1 hangar bay. Four Marines: two male, two female. They're all yours—'

'—Bravo Unit, your targets have just exited the personnel elevator through the ceiling hatch. About to lose visual contact. But they're in the shaft. Sealing all elevator shaft doors except yours. Okay, they're shut in. Take them out—'

'—sir, Echo Unit has cleaned out the rest of the main hangar. Awaiting further instructions—'

'Send them to help Charlie,' Caesar Russell said, eyeing the monitor with Shane Schofield on it.

'—Echo, this is Control, proceed to Level 1 hangar bay for rendezvous with Charlie Unit—'

'—Alpha Unit, Presidential Detail is climbing the stairs. Coming right for you. Delta Unit, the Level 6 fire door is unguarded. You are free to enter the stairwell and engage—'

It was absolutely gigantic.

An enormous subterranean hangar, roughly the same size as the one up at ground level, perhaps even larger.

It had several aircraft in it, too.

One converted Boeing 707 AWACS plane, with the characteristic flying-saucer-like rotodome mounted on its back. Two sinister-looking B-2 stealth bombers, with their black radar-absorbent paint, futuristic flying-wing design, and angry furrowed-brow cockpit windows. And parked directly in front of the stealth bombers, one Lockheed SR-71 Blackbird, the world's fastest operational aircraft, with its sleek super-elongated fuselage and twin rear thrusters.

The massive aeroplanes towered above Schofield and his team, dominating the cavernous space.

'What do we do now?' Mother asked.

Schofield was momentarily silent.

He was staring intently at the AWACS plane. It just stood there silently, pointing towards the wide aircraft elevator shaft.

Then he said, 'We find out if what they're saying about the President's heart is true.'

The air in the fire stairs was filled with flying bullets.

The Presidential Detail, down to three now, guided their charge up the stairs, leading with their guns, a makeshift array of Uzis, SIG-Sauers and spare ankle revolvers.

A young male agent named Julio Ramondo led the way, spraying the stairs above them with his Uzi, despite a bullet wound to his shoulder.

Special Agent Juliet Janson came after him, having assumed command of the Detail more by action than protocol. She guided the President along behind her.

The third and last surviving agent of the Detail—his name was Curtis—covered their rear, firing down the stairs behind them as they moved.

At twenty-eight, Juliet Janson was the most junior member of the President's Detail, but that didn't seem to matter now.

She had degrees in criminology and psychology, could run a hundred metres in 13.8 seconds and was an excellent marksman. The daughter of an American businessman father and a Taiwanese university lecturer mother, she had a flawless Eurasian complexion—smooth olive skin, a sharply defined jawline, beautiful almond-brown eyes and shoulder-length jet-black hair.

'Ramondo! Can you see it!' she shouted above the gunfire.

After the horror of their attempt to get to Level 6 and the bloody death of Frank Cutler, the President and his Detail had been left in the middle of a 7th Squadron sandwich.

The unit down on Level 6 was coming up after them, while the unit that had chased them out of the common room on Level 3 was closing in on them from above.

What that had left them with was a race—a race to get to one of the floors *in between* Level 6 and Level 3 before they faced fire from both above and below.

'Yes! I see it!' Ramondo yelled back. 'Come on!'

Juliet Janson arrived on the landing next to Ramondo, with the President beside her. Thumping footfalls echoed down the stairwell above them, bullets ripped apart the walls all around them.

Janson saw the nearest door, saw the sign on it:

LEVEL 5: ANIMAL CONTAINMENT AREA

NO ENTRY

THIS DOOR FOR EMERGENCY USE ONLY

ENTER VIA ELEVATORS AT OTHER END OF FLOOR

'I think this qualifies as an emergency,' she said, before blasting the door's locks with three shots from her SIG-Sauer.

Then she kicked open the door and hauled the President into Level 5.

Book II looked up into the darkness of the regular elevator shaft, saw the outer doors that led to the ground-level hangar about fifty feet above him.

He was standing on top of the personnel elevator—now stopped midway down the shaft—with Calvin, Elvis and Love Machine. A few widely-spaced fluorescent lights illuminated the enclosed concrete elevator well.

'Why did we have to get out of the elevator?' Elvis asked.

'Cameras,' Book II said. 'We couldn't stay—'

'We'd have been sitting ducks if we'd stayed inside it,' Calvin Reeves said, cutting in. 'Gentlemen, as the ranking officer here, I am taking command.'

'So what's the plan then, Captain America?' Love Machine asked.

'We keep moving—'Calvin began, but that was all he got out, because at that moment, the outer doors above them burst open and almost immediately three P-90 gun-barrels appeared, bright yellow flashes bursting forth from their muzzles.

A flurry of ricochets impacted all around the elevator.

Book II ducked and spun—and saw a series of vertical counterweight cables running down the wall of the shaft, disappearing down the side of the stationary elevator.

'The cables!' he yelled, scampering over to the wall, not caring for the chain of command. 'Everybody down! *Now!*'

Shane Schofield burst into the forward cabin of the AWACS plane in the hangar on Level 1.

'Brainiac.'

'Already on it,' Brainiac headed aft, disappearing inside the main cabin of the aircraft.

'Close the door,' Schofield said to Mother, who had come in last.

Schofield charged aft. The interior of the AWACS was very similar to that of a commercial airliner—albeit a commercial airliner that had had all its seats ripped out and replaced by large flat-topped surveillance consoles.

Brainiac was already at one of the consoles. It was whirring to life as Schofield took a seat beside him. Mother and Gant went straight for the plane's two door-windows, peered out through them.

Brainiac started typing at the console.

'Mother said it was a microwave signal,' Schofield said. 'The satellite beams it down and then the radio chip on the President's heart bounces the signal back up.'

Brainiac typed some more. 'Makes sense. Only a micro-wave signal could penetrate the radiosphere over this base—and then only if it knew the trapdoor frequency.'

'Trapdoor frequency?'

Brainiac kept typing. 'The radiosphere over this base is like an umbrella, a giant hemispherical dome of scrambled electromagnetic energy. Basically, this umbrella of garbled energy stops all unauthorised signals from either entering or escaping the base. But, like all good jamming systems, it has a designated frequency for use by *authorised* trans-missions. This is the trapdoor frequency—a microwave bandwidth that wends its way through the radiosphere, avoiding the jamming signatures. Kind of like a secret path through a minefield.'

'So this satellite signal is coming in on the trapdoor frequency?' Schofield said.

'That's my guess,' Brainiac said. 'What I'm doing now is using the AWACS' rotodome to search all the micro-wave frequencies *inside* this base. These birds have the best bandwidth detection systems around, so it shouldn't take—bingo. Got it.'

He slammed his finger down on the 'ENTER' key and a new screen came up.

'Okay, you looking at this?' Brainiac printed out the screen. 'It's a standard rebounding signature. The satellite sends down a search signal—they're the tall spikes on the positive side, about 10 gigahertz—and then, soon after, the receiver on the ground, the President, bounces that signal back. Those are the deep spikes on the negative side.'

Brainiac circled the spikes on the printout.

121

'Search and return,' he said. 'Interference aside, the rebounding signature seems to repeat itself once every twenty-five seconds. Captain, that Air Force general ain't lying. There's something down here bouncing back a secure satellite microwave signal.'

'How do we know it isn't just a beacon or something?' Schofield said.

'The irregularity of it,' Brainiac said. 'See how it isn't quite a perfectly replicating sequence? See how, every now and then, there's a medium-sized spike in between the search and the return signals?' Brainiac tapped the mid-sized spikes inside two of the circles.

'So what does that mean?'

'It's an interference signature. It means that the source of the return signal is moving.'

'Jesus,' Schofield said. 'It's real.'

'And it just got worse,' Gant said from the window set into the escape door on the left-hand side of the cabin. 'Have a look at this.'

Schofield came over to the small window, looked out through it.

And his blood went cold.

There must have been at least twenty of them.

Twenty 7th Squadron soldiers running quickly across the hangar outside—P-90 assault rifles in their hands, ERG-6 masks covering their faces—forming a wide circle around the AWACS plane, surrounding it.

It was the smell that hit them first.

It smelled like a zoo—that peculiar mix of animal excrement and sawdust in a confined space.

Juliet Janson led the way into Level 5, pulling the President along behind her. The other two Secret Service agents hurried in after them, jamming the stairwell door shut behind them.

They were standing in a wide, dark room, lined on three sides with grim-looking cages—forged steel bars set into walls of solid concrete. On the fourth side of the room were some more modern-looking cages: these cages had clear, floor-to-ceiling fibreglass walls and were filled with inky black water. Janson couldn't see what lurked inside the sloshing opaque water.

A sudden grunting sound made her spin.

There was something very large inside one of the steel cages to her right. In the dim light of the dungeon, she could make out a big, hairy, lumbering shape moving behind the thick black bars.

There came an ominous scratching sound from the cage—like someone dragging a fingernail slowly and deliberately down a chalkboard.

Special Agent Curtis went over to the cell, peered into the darkness beyond the bars.

'Don't get too close,' Janson warned.

Too late.

A hideous bloodcurdling roar filled the dungeon as an enormous black head—a blurred combination of matted hair, wild eyes and flashing six-inch teeth—burst out from behind the bars and lunged at the hapless agent.

Curtis fell back from the cage, landing on his butt as the animal—enraged, ferocious, frenzied—reached in vain for him with a long hairy claw, held back only by the superstrong bars of the cell.

The would-be ambush over, Janson now got a better look at the creature.

It was huge, at least nine feet tall, and covered in shaggy black fur—and it looked completely out of place in a concrete underground cell.

Janson couldn't believe it.

It was a *bear*.

And it didn't seem to be a very happy bear either. Its fur was matted and stringy, sweat-stained, growing in clumps. The animal's own faeces clung to the fur on its hindquarters, making the world's largest living land carnivore look like some deranged horror movie monster.

The three other cages on the northern side of the dungeon held more bears—four females and two cubs.

'Jesus . . . ' the President breathed.

'What the hell is going on in this place?' Julio Ramondo whispered.

'I don't care,' Janson said, pulling the President toward a heavy-looking door on the far side of the dungeon. 'Whatever it is, we can't stay here.'

The hangar bay on Level 1 was silent.

The giant AWACS plane stood in the centre of the vast hangar, surrounded by the ring of 7th Squadron commandos.

'This isn't the situation I was hoping for,' Schofield said.

'How do they keep knowing where we are?' Mother asked.

Gant looked at Schofield. 'I would imagine a base like this is wired up the kazoo.'

'Agreed,' Schofield said.

'What are you talking about?' Mother said.

'Cameras,' Schofield said. 'Surveillance cameras. Somewhere in this base, someone's in a room watching a bank of monitors and telling these guys where we—'

Whump!

There came a heavy thump from somewhere outside.

Gant peered out through the window in the escape door. 'Shit! They're on the wing!'

'Oh, *Christ*,' Schofield said, 'they're going for the doors . . .'

He exchanged a look with Gant.

'They're going to storm the plane,' he said.

They looked like ants crawling over a toy aeroplane. Eight 7th Squadron men—four to each side—stalking along the wings of the giant Boeing 707.

Captain Luther 'Python' Willis, commander of the 7th Squadron's third sub-unit, Charlie Unit, stood on the hangar floor, watching his men move along the wings of the stationary plane.

'The Avengers are on the way up,' his master sergeant said.

Python said nothing, just nodded coldly.

Inside the AWACS plane, Schofield was charging down the central aisle, checking the plane's rear entry points. Gant and Brainiac manned the two side windows.

'There's nobody back here!' Schofield called from the aft section of the plane, where there were two emergency doors. 'Fox!'

'I got four on the left wing!' Gant yelled.

'I got four on the right!' Brainiac said.

'Mother!' Schofield called.

No answer.

'Mother!'

Schofield strode quickly through the main cabin, moving forward.

There was no sign of Mother anywhere. She was supposed to be checking the plane's forward entrances—the bail-out door in the floor of the forward cabin, and the roof hatches in the cockpit above the pilots' ejection seats.

As he hurried forward, Schofield looked out through the nearest window, saw the armed commandos on the left-hand wing.

He frowned: *what were they doing out there?*

They couldn't just burst in through the wing doors. Even with their nickel-plated pistols, Schofield and his Marines could easily repel a single-file entry through such a small entrance.

It was at that moment, however—out through the

window in the side door of the Boeing 707—that he saw the Avengers.

There were two of them and they entered the hangar bay from the vehicle access ramp at the far eastern end of the floor.

The Avenger air-defence vehicle is a modified Humvee. It has the basic wide-bodied chassis of a Humvee, but mounted on its back are two square-shaped pods, which each hold four Stinger surface-to-air missiles. Attached to the underside of these missile launchers is a pair of powerful fifty-calibre machine guns. It is basically a highly-efficient, highly-mobile aeroplane killer.

'Okay, now I know what they're going to do,' Schofield said aloud.

They were going to blast the plane with the Stingers and then, in the smoke and confusion that followed, make a forced entry.

Good plan, Schofield thought. And very painful for him and his three Marines.

The two Avengers split up as they raced across the wide-open floor of the hangar, one heading for the right flank of the AWACS, the other heading for the left.

Schofield saw them go, disappearing from his limited field of vision.

Shit.

He had to do something, and fast—

VROOOM!

The wing-mounted engines of the AWACS plane thundered to life. In the enclosed space of the hangar, their roar was positively deafening.

Schofield spun where he stood. 'Mother,' he said.

The Avengers skidded to a halt on either side of the AWACS plane just as the massive Boeing 707 began to roll forward, its engines filling the hangar with the thunderous roar of blasting air.

At the sudden movement of the plane, the eight men on its wings were jolted off balance.

Schofield charged into the cockpit of the AWACS.

Mother was sitting in the captain's seat.

'Hey there, Scarecrow!' she yelled above the din. 'Want to join me for a Sunday drive!'

'You ever driven a plane before, Mother?'

'I saw Kurt Russell drive one in a movie once! Hell, it can't be much different from driving Ralph's eighteen-wheel—'

Whack-whack-whack-whack-whack!

A volley of bullets assaulted the windshield of the cockpit, shattering it, sending glass flying all over Mother and Schofield, the upwardly-directed shots punching into the ceiling.

And then Schofield saw one of the Avengers skid to a halt off to the left of the AWACS plane, saw its twin missile pods tilt upward on their hinges, getting ready to fire at the cockpit.

'Mother! Quickly! Go left!' he shouted.

'What?' Going left would put them on a collision course with the Avenger.

'Just do it!' Schofield leapt into the right-hand co-pilot's seat and using the plane's pedal-operated steering controls, brought her hard to port, at the same time as he pushed forward on the plane's thrusters.

The giant AWACS plane responded immediately.

It picked up speed, moving quickly inside the confines of the enormous hangar, swinging sharply to the left— *heading directly for the Avenger!*

The 7th Squadron men on the Avenger saw what was going to happen.

Abandoning their efforts to get a lock on the plane with their Stingers, they dived from the missile-mounted Humvee a bare second before the enormous forward wheels of the Boeing thundered right over the top of the Avenger, crushing it like a tin can, rolling over its crumpled remains like a monster truck at a car rally.

'Yee-hah!' Mother yelled as the aeroplane bounced wildly over what was left of the Humvee.

'It's not over yet,' Schofield said. 'There's still another one out there. *Fox!* Where's that other Avenger!'

Gant and Brainiac were still in the main cabin of the AWACS, covering the wing-entry doors on either side of the plane—Gant with her MP-10, Brainiac with his Beretta.

'It's behind us to the left!' Gant yelled. Out her window, she saw the Humvee on the hangar floor outside, over by the northern wall, its missile pods raised and ready. Then, without warning, there came a puff of smoke from one of the pods.

'Bracing positions!' she called. 'Missile away!'

There came a sudden *monstrous* explosion and abruptly the whole AWACS plane shuddered violently as its rear wheels were lifted clear off the ground.

Billowing smoke rushed into the main cabin, shooting forward from the rear as the giant plane came back down to earth, jouncing on its suspension.

'They've hit our tail!' Gant yelled.

It was worse than that.

The second Avenger had reduced the entire tail section of their 707 to a smoking, gaping hole. The high tail fin of the plane lay bent and broken on the floor of the hangar, completely detached from the plane.

The AWACS continued to turn in a wide circle, its massive wheels rolling quickly, at the same time as it was pummelled by a continuous rain of fire from the 7th Squadron soldiers on the ground.

In the enormous space of the underground hangar, the plane's movement seemed almost comical—for something so big and so heavy to move so quickly and so recklessly was a sight to behold.

The plane came around 180 degrees—the tip of its right wing bouncing off the flank of the parked SR-71 Blackbird—so that now it was facing the *opposite* direction from which it had started, its open rear end now exposed to the withering fire of the 7th Squadron men on the ground.

Bullets raked the interior of the central cabin, smashing into the ceiling and walls. Gant and Brainiac hit the deck as fragments of plastic and plaster rained down all around them.

'Fuck!' Brainiac yelled. 'They don't teach *this* at Parris Island!'

Book II was also moving fast.

He slid quickly down one of the vertical counterweight cables that ran up the side of the regular elevator shaft. Calvin, Elvis and Love Machine slid down the cables after him, lowering themselves down the shaft.

After avoiding the barrage of fire up on the roof of the elevator, they now had to find a way out of the shaft, before the 7th Squadron men up there got around the elevator that now formed an obstacle between them.

Book II stopped at a pair of outer doors marked with a large black-painted '1', and immediately heard the muffled sounds of a firefight—clattering automatic gun-fire, booming explosions, squealing tyres.

'Not this one,' Calvin Reeves said as he came alongside Book II. 'Let's try the next one.'

They slid further down the shaft.

Inside the hangar bay, Python Willis watched the AWACS plane as it sped in a wild circle around the enormous hangar.

He spoke without emotion into his headset mike: 'Avenger Two. Go for the cockpit. Two missiles.'

In the cockpit of the AWACS plane, Schofield pumped on the steering pedals.

'Mother!' he yelled. 'Get back in the main cabin! Cover

the tail! Make sure no-one gets in through there! I'll take care of the driving up here!'

Mother grabbed her M-16 and headed aft.

As she left, Schofield saw the second Humvee appear in front of him, over by the northern wall. It swung around quickly, taking up a new position, getting ready to fire again.

He keyed the plane's intercom.

'*Brainiac!*' Schofield's voice boomed over the plane's speaker system. '*Engage electronic countermeasures!*'

Back in the main cabin, Brainiac looked up at the sound of Schofield's voice. 'Oh, yeah. Of course!'

'What is he talking about?' Gant yelled as Mother joined them in the main cabin.

But Brainiac was already clambering toward one of the consoles. He slid into the seat, began typing quickly.

Gant peered out her door-window—saw the walls of the hangar streaking by outside—saw the surviving Humvee skid to a halt over by the wall, preparing to fire another of its missiles.

'It's going to hit us again!' she called.

'*Brainiac . . .*' Schofield's voice said expectantly over the speakers.

Brainiac typed fast. The words 'ENGAGE MF SCRAMBLER' appeared on his screen.

'Bracing positions!' Gant yelled.

Two clouds of smoke puffed out from the Humvee's missile pods—

—at exactly the same moment as Brainiac slammed his finger down on the 'ENTER' key.

A pair of Stinger missiles shot out from the pods on the back of the Humvee, twin smoke-trails zooming out behind them. They were heading directly for the forward section of the AWACS plane, flying in perfect formation.

And then, all of a sudden, the Stingers went crazy.

Despite the fact that the missiles were heat-seekers, the AWACS's powerful anti-missile countermeasures still affected them—disrupting their chip-to-chip electronics, scrambling their internal-logic systems. It was as if a tidal wave of electronic noise, blasting invisibly outward from the AWACS's enormous rotodome, had slammed into the two Stingers.

The two missiles responded accordingly.

They went haywire.

They broke formation in an instant, parting in a looping Y-shape—one rolling wildly to the right, the other swinging left. The right-hand one shot quickly *underneath* the rolling AWACS plane, while the left-hand one sailed clear *over* it.

From the cockpit of the AWACS Schofield watched in amazement as one of the missiles shot across his bow and then—bizarrely—headed *back toward* the Humvee that had launched it!

A second later the missile *slammed* into the concrete wall above the Humvee—thundering at tremendous speed right into a ten-foot-high box-shaped compartment mounted above the floor of the hangar.

The missile detonated—sending an enormous gout of concrete spraying out from the wall all around the compartment. The compartment's wide steel door was blasted off its hinges by the stunning impact and went bouncing across the hangar, a twisted metal wreck. Large chunks of concrete rained down on the very Humvee that had fired the missile.

Whatever that compartment was, Schofield thought, it was toast now.

But there was still one more out-of-control missile swooping around the hangar.

This second missile swung around the destroyed rear section of the moving AWACS plane, rolling wildly through the air, before it too doubled back and hit the hangar's northern wall, right alongside the regular elevator's doors.

A hailstorm of concrete blasted out from the wall, showering chunks everywhere.

This blast of concrete, however, was followed by a most peculiar sight.

A shockingly powerful geyser of water—yes, *water*—began to shoot out from the newly formed hole in the wall, jetting outward with tremendous force.

Schofield frowned. 'What the hell . . . ?'

An ominous explosion shook the walls of the regular elevator shaft.

Book II, now hanging with his group next to the outer doors of Level 3—the doors to Level 2 had also been locked, so they'd moved down to the next floor—looked up sharply at the sound.

The sight that met him was as terrifying as it was unexpected.

A whole section of the concrete wall alongside the Level 1 doorway sixty feet above them just blasted outward, showering the shaft with chunks of concrete.

And then, right behind the concrete, came the water.

It rained down on Book II and the others like spray from a goddamned firehose.

Torrents and torrents of pouring water, roaring like a waterfall down the narrow elevator shaft, gushing out of the hole in the wall on Level 1, pounding down against their bodies.

It was all they could do to hold on to their cables.

But as soon as he felt the surging weight of the waterfall, Book II saw the future: the wall of water was just too strong.

They were going to fall.

'—All units, be aware. We have rupture of the long-term water tanks on Level 1. Repeat: integrity of water tanks on Level 1 has been broken—'

'—Water from the tanks is entering the regular elevator shaft—'

'Initiate airtight countermeasures,' Caesar Russell said calmly. 'Seal off the shaft. Keep that water contained. Let it flood the shaft.'

'Yes, sir.'

Love Machine fell first.

In the face of the powerful waterfall, he lost his grip on the counterweight cable and dropped straight past Book.

He fell fast—falling away from Book II in a kind of nightmarish slow motion; eyes wide, mouth open, his shout drowned out by the roar of the waterfall—before he disappeared into the inky darkness of the shaft.

Book II swore. 'Damn it!'

And then he did the only thing he could think to do.

'Sergeant! *No!*' Calvin yelled, but it was too late.

Book II loosened his grip on his cable and slid like a bullet down the shaft after Love Machine, disappearing into the darkness.

Book II dropped into blackness.

He slid for a long time, whizzing down the counter-weight cable, sliding fast, the heat from the cable burning through his white formal gloves.

Then suddenly, with a splash, he entered water—*deep* water—at the bottom of the shaft.

Just as he had hoped.

The elevator shaft was approximately ten feet square and if all its exit doors were sealed, then with the monumental quantities of water rushing out of the hole on Level 1, he'd figured it wouldn't take long for it to accumulate at the bottom and fill to a reasonable depth.

Sure enough, Love Machine hovered in the pool of water next to him, gasping for air, coughing water. But alive.

'You okay!' Book II yelled.

'Uh-huh!'

Calvin and Elvis arrived at the base of the shaft a few moments later, sliding down the counterweight cables. The roaring waterfall thundered into the pool all around them, kicking up spray.

'Okay, Captain Fantastic,' Elvis said to Calvin, 'our nice safe elevator shaft is now filling with water! What do you suggest we do now?'

Calvin hesitated.

Book II didn't. He nodded at the pair of outer doors a few feet above them. 'Simple. We bust out!'

'Mother*fucker* . . . ' Brainiac said as he peered out from the rear of the AWACS plane's main cabin.

A high-pressure geyser of water was now shooting out of the hole in the wall over by the personnel elevator, throwing a carpet of water all over the concrete floor of the hangar. 'What the hell is this ride?'

'Just another day of mayhem and destruction with the Scarecrow,' Mother said.

'Hey,' Gant said, looking out through her door-window. 'What happened to the guys on the wings?'

Mother and Brainiac spun to look out at the plane's wings.

The AWACS's wings were bare.

The 7th Squadron men who had been out there before were nowhere to be seen.

It was only then that they heard the ominous sound of thumping footsteps on the roof.

The AWACS plane continued on its rampaging circuit of the hangar, now travelling through a layer of water one inch deep.

It had almost come full circle—so that now it was facing the empty section of the hangar that led to the wide-open doorway of the aircraft elevator shaft.

Schofield pumped on the steering pedals, trying to keep the enormous surveillance plane under control.

He saw the doorway to the aircraft elevator shaft directly in front of him. At the moment, a shallow film of water cascaded over it like Niagara Falls, dropping out of sight into the shaft.

The big hydraulic elevator platform was almost certainly the best way out of this jam, but the last he had seen, it was stopped down on one of the lower levels—

And then, more suddenly than Schofield could possibly have anticipated, the roof above him exploded in a shower of sparks.

In actual fact, it wasn't the roof—it was one of the blast hatches *set into* the roof of the cockpit, one of the hatches that blew open when the pilot's ejection seat was activated.

No sooner had the hatch blasted open than a veritable *hailstorm* of gunfire flooded down through it, smashing into the aeroplane's dashboard, shattering all its gauges and dials.

This torrent of bullets was quickly followed by a second volley which ripped through the empty pilot's seat—the left-hand seat; the seat Mother had been sitting in before—tearing it to shreds.

Schofield saw what was going to happen next and he quickly dived out of his seat, rolling forward into the tiny section of floorspace in front of it.

Not a moment later, a pair of combat boots landed with a thump on the pilot's seat—boots that belonged to a fearsome-looking 7th Squadron commando.

The masked commando spun quickly, his P-90 assault rifle pressed firmly against his shoulder, searching for enemies at the rear of the cockpit. Then he turned to look forward, and downward—where, to his complete surprise, he saw Schofield lying curled up on the floor.

Gunless and defenceless, Schofield saw the masked commando's black-gloved trigger finger begin to squeeze—

And so he lashed out with his foot.

Not at the man's legs, but at the lever that ran alongside the flight seat underneath him—the ejection lever.

Schofield's kick connected.

The lever snapped backward.

And with a loud, blasting *whoosh!* the pilot's ejection seat shot up through the hole in the cockpit's roof—taking the 7th Squadron commando with it!

Python Willis watched in complete and utter astonishment as one of his men went rocketing up at incredible

139

speed *out* of the cockpit of the AWACS and past his shocked colleagues on the roof of the plane, on top of an ejection seat!

The man shot into the air like a bullet, before smashing—violently, concussively—into the concrete ceiling of the hangar.

The crack of the man's neck echoed sickeningly throughout the underground hangar bay—it was distinct even above the roar of the AWACS's engines, so hard did his body hit the ceiling. He was killed instantly, the force of the three-hundred-pound ejection seat snapping his spine like a twig as it squashed him against the concrete roof.

In the meantime, Schofield had got his own Beretta pistol out and, sliding on his back onto the floor behind the pilots' seats, was firing it up at the roof of the cockpit—trying to deter anyone else from following their comrade into the flight deck.

In seconds, his gun went dry and he stood up and looked out through the forward windshield—

—and saw that the plane was heading directly for the massive doorway leading to the elevator shaft!

'Oh, this just keeps getting better and better,' he said.

In a fleeting second, he tried to find a solution to the situation.

The plane was heading for the shaft.

The 7th Squadron were all over its roof—all over the hangar for that matter.

And he and Gant and Mother and Brainiac were stuck inside the plane.

What was the solution?

Simple.

Get out of the hangar.

But there is no way out. We're stuck in this plane, and if we leave it, we're dead.

Unless, of course, we get out of the hangar while we're still on board the plane . . .

Oh, yeah . . .

And with that Schofield climbed back into the co-pilot's seat and took control of the plane again. Despite the bullet damage, the controls still worked.

He pushed forward on the collective, speeding up the big Boeing 707, keeping it pointed directly at the enormous steel doorway that led out to the elevator shaft.

'What the hell is he doing . . . ?' Python said.

The giant AWACS plane was picking up speed, rumbling across the wide expanse of the hangar, heading straight for the open elevator doorway.

The commandos on the roof of the plane felt it surge forward, gaining momentum.

They looked forward, saw where it was heading, and their eyes widened.

'He can't be serious,' Python breathed, as he watched his men leap off the roof of the moving aeroplane as it careered toward the open doorway.

In the cockpit of the speeding plane, Schofield was strapping on his seatbelt. As he did so, he keyed the intercom switch.

'Ladies and gentlemen, this is your captain speaking. Find a chair and buckle up tight, because we're about to take off.'

Back in the main cabin, Gant and the other two Marines spun to look forward.

Through the AWACS's cabin, they could see all the way through to the cockpit—could see the open elevator shaft looming ahead of them, rapidly approaching.

'Is he thinking what I think he's thinking?' Gant said to Mother.

Mother paused before she spoke. 'Yes, he is.'

They leapt as one for the nearest available seats and clutched desperately for the seatbelts.

The converted Boeing 707—deprived of its entire tail section—thundered across the wide subterranean hangar bay, the wet concrete floor rushing by beneath it, heading straight for the open elevator shaft.

And then, before anyone could even hope to stop it, the plane shot through the doorway and tipped off the edge and fell down into the shaft, disappearing from view.

The AWACS plane soared down the elevator shaft fast—nose-first—looking like a crazed kamikaze fighter.

Down the wide concrete shaft it went—down, down, down—before it crashed, loudly, on the massive hydraulic elevator platform resting on Level 4, one hundred and eighty feet below.

The nose of the AWACS plane crumpled instantly as it thundered into the elevator platform. Loose parts flew everywhere, blasting outward like shrapnel. Two of the plane's jet engines bounced high into the air as they smashed into the platform.

The plane itself, however, seemed to teeter on its broken nose for an eternity. And then, with a loud metal-on-metal groan, like a slow-falling California redwood, it fell, landing with a colossal thump on its left-hand wing, snapping the wing in an instant, before the whole ruined aircraft slammed down against the elevator platform with a resounding *boom*.

Inside the AWACS plane, the world was tilted forty-five degrees to the left.

Mother, Gant and Brainiac all sat comically in their seats, strapped in, but hanging dramatically to the side. They were starting to unbuckle themselves from their seatbelts when Schofield hurried into the main cabin from the cockpit.

'Come on,' he said, helping Mother with her belt, 'we can't stay here. They'll be down soon.'

'Where are we going?' Gant asked, as she dropped out of her seat and stood up.

Schofield pursed his lips. 'We have to find the President.'

'—Jesus! He just drove the plane off the fucking edge—'

'—Charlie and Echo Units, initiate pursuit—'

'—President is on Level 5, heading into the confinement area. Delta Unit, you are free to enter the animal quarters—'

'—Copy that, Bravo leader. Yes, they're in the water at the bottom of the shaft. Good idea—'

'What's Boa doing?' Caesar Russell asked. Captain Bruno 'Boa' McConnell was in command of Bravo Unit, one of the Five Snakes.

'He's on top of the personnel elevator, sir. He's going to lower the elevator down the shaft. Drown the bastards. And if they try to crawl up the sides, shoot them dead.'

Book II and the others hovered in the ever-deepening pool of water at the base of the regular elevator shaft.

The super-heavy rain of water blasted down all around them. It showed no sign of stopping and the elevator shaft was flooding rapidly, the water level rising fast, lifting them to the nearest pair of outer doors.

And then abruptly, above the roar of falling water, a loud clunking noise echoed down the shaft, followed by the hum of mechanical movement.

Book II looked upwards—just as the rain of water stopped.

Well, sort of stopped. Now it started raining down the *sides* of the shaft, covering the counterweight cables with a curtain of gushing water.

'What's happening?' Love Machine said.

And then Book II saw it.

Saw a shadow superimposed on the darkness above them—a *box-shaped* shadow, growing larger and larger as it came closer and closer.

'What is *that*?' Calvin Reeves said.

'Oh, damn . . . ' Book II breathed. 'It's the elevator.'

The personnel elevator edged its way down the shaft, water pounding onto its roof and cascading off its sides.

High above it, in the open doorway up on ground level, two 7th Squadron snipers lay with night-scoped rifles at the ready, aimed down into the shaft.

Their guns were trained on the roof of the elevator, waiting for anyone to emerge from the gaps on either side of the lift, the only points where the enemy could climb out from underneath the downward-moving elevator.

'Not nice,' Book II said flatly. 'Not nice.'

Either they drowned as the elevator pushed them under the surface, or they climbed up the sides of the lift, where no doubt, the bad guys would be waiting . . .

He looked quickly at the pair of outer doors two feet above him. They had a large '5' painted on them.

Level 5.

He wondered what was on this level, then decided he didn't care. These doors were the only way out. Period.

He hauled himself out of the water, stood on his toes on the edge of the doorway. A curtain of water poured down onto his head.

Like all the other outer doors in this elevator shaft, he saw, these two were closed tight, air-sealed.

The elevator above him continued its descent, moving slowly and steadily downward.

The rising water reached the base of the doorway, splashed against his boots, moving equally steadily upward.

Calvin Reeves appeared at his side. 'How the hell do we open these doors, Sergeant!'

Book guessed that the doors' release mechanism was contained somewhere within the wall.

'I can't see it!' he shouted back. 'It must be hidden inside the wall!'

The elevator was close now, looming one floor above them, grinding inexorably downward.

Water continued to pour.

And then Book II saw it—a thick insulated cable running out from the concrete wall to the right of the doors and *down* into the pool of water beneath him.

'Of course!' he yelled. An emergency release lever wouldn't be on this level. It would be situated either *above* or *below* the floor, so that the doors could be opened when the elevator was stopped here.

Without so much as a second thought, Book II took a deep breath and dropped into the pool of water beneath him.

Silence.

The eerie quiet of the underwater world.

Book II swam downwards, his fingers feeling their way along the thick black cable attached to the concrete wall.

After about nine feet, he came to a steel utility box sunk into the wall. He opened it, felt for a lever, found a row of six, and yanked the fifth one.

He immediately heard a sharp *shoosh!* from somewhere above him—the sound of a pressure door being released.

He swam upward, fast. Came to the surface, broke it—

'—Book! *Quickly!* Come on!' were the first words he heard.

He'd come up a few feet away from the now-opened doors and immediately saw Calvin Reeves and Elvis standing up on level ground. Love Machine clung to the edge of the doorway, reaching out for Book II with an outstretched hand.

Then Book II looked up.

The descending elevator was barely three feet above his head and coming down fast!

He threw out a hand and Love Machine grabbed it, and hauled him over to the doorway, pulling him through the water. Then Elvis and Calvin grabbed them both and yanked them out of the water, *just as* the elevator slid past the edge of the doorway and abruptly came to a halt— right in front of the doorway.

Everybody froze.

Water began to ooze up around the floor of the lift,

rising up from beneath it, hungrily searching for an escape from the shaft. It immediately began to spread out across the concrete floor of Level 5.

Book II waited tensely for the elevator's doors to open—waited for a phalanx of 7th Squadron men to burst out from it with their guns blazing.

But none did.

The lift was empty.

They were safe, for the moment.

Book II turned to face the room around him. A layer of expanding water had already started filling it.

It was a wide anteroom of some sort. Some wooden desks, a Lexan glass cabinet full of shotguns and riot gear. Plus a couple of holding cells.

Book II frowned.

It was almost as if he was standing in the reception room of a *jail*.

'What in God's name is this place?' he said aloud.

At that very same moment, on the other side of Level 5, Juliet Janson and the President of the United States found themselves standing in a whole new kind of hell.

Juliet had thought the animal cage room had been bad.

This was worse.

After bursting through the heavy-looking door on the western side of the animal cage room, she now found herself staring at a far more frightening part of Area 7.

A wide, dark, low-ceilinged room stretched away from her. It was sparsely lit, with only one in every three lights turned on, a policy which had the effect of leaving small patches of the vast room hidden in perfect blackness.

But the low light couldn't hide the true nature of this level.

It was *filled* with cells.

Old rusty concrete cages—thick-walled, with anodised black bars sunk deep into concrete dividers. The cells were quite obviously aged, and in the half-light of Level 5, they took on a positively Gothic appearance.

It was, however, the groans and hoarse whispers coming from the darkness behind the bars that betrayed the nature of their occupants.

These were not animal cells, Juliet realised in horror. They were *human* cells.

The prisoners heard the heavy door burst open—heard Juliet and the President and the other two Secret Service agents charge through it—and they rushed as one to the doors of their cells to see what the commotion was.

'Oh, hey, *baby*!' one toothless individual cried as Juliet, striking and purposeful as she held her silver SIG-Sauer pistol in her hand, charged past his cell, pulling the President behind her.

'Ramondo!' she yelled. 'Block that door behind us!'

A row of steel lockers lined the wall near the door leading back to the animal cage room. Ramondo yanked the first three of them down from their upright positions, strewing the lockers in front of the door.

The prisoners began to shout and cry out.

Like all lifers, they could sense fear instantly, and they took pleasure in heightening it. Some yelled obscenities, others rattled their bars with enamel drinking mugs, others still just wailed a constant ear-piercing '*Ahhhhhhhhh!*'

Juliet bolted through the nightmare, grim-faced and determined.

She saw a gently-sloping ramp off to her right—fenced off by a big barred gate. The ramp seemed to lead up to the next level. She made for it.

'Hey, baby! You wanna go for a spin . . . on top of my flagpole!'

The President stared wide-eyed at the chaos all around him. Prisoners in blue denim uniforms, unshaven and crazed, leaned out from their cages, trying to grab him.

'Hey, old man. I bet you got a *nice* soft marshmallow ass—'

'Come on,' Juliet yanked the President away from the voices.

They came to the barred gate.

As one would expect on a cell block, its lock was thick and strong. They couldn't shoot through it.

'Curtis,' Juliet said crisply. 'Lock.'

Special Agent Curtis slid to his knees in front of the gate and pulled a high-tech-looking lock-picking device from his coat pocket.

As Curtis unfolded his lock-picker, Janson scanned the area around them.

There was movement and noise everywhere. Arms flailed out of cell doors. Snarling faces tried to squeeze through the bars. And the shouting, the constant shouting.

'*Ahhhhhhhh!*'

None of the prioners seemed to recognise the President. They all just seemed to enjoy making noise, inciting fear—

Then abruptly, there came a loud *boom* from somewhere behind them.

Juliet spun, pistol up.

She was met by the sight of a Marine, his full dress uniform completely saturated, charging toward her with a Remington pump-action shotgun raised.

Behind the first man were three more Marines, also soaked to the skin.

The lead Marine lowered his shotgun when he saw Juliet and the President.

'It's okay! It's okay!' Book II said, coming closer,

lowering the shotgun he had pilfered from the arms cabinet in the anteroom. 'It's us!'

Calvin Reeves stepped forward, spoke seriously. 'What's happened down here?'

Juliet said, 'We've lost six people already, and those Air Force bastards are in the next room, right on our asses.'

Behind her, Special Agent Curtis inserted his lock-picker into the gate's lock, pressed a button.

Zzzzzzzzz!

The lock-picking device emitted a shrill dentist-drill-like buzz. The lock clicked loudly and the gate swung open.

'What's your plan from here, Agent Janson?' Calvin asked.

'To be where the bad guys aren't,' Juliet said. 'First of all, by going up this ramp. Let's move.'

Special Agents Curtis and Ramondo headed up the ramp first, followed by Calvin. Juliet pushed the President after them. Love Machine and Elvis went next. Book II fell into step beside Juliet, covering the rear.

Just as they were about to head up the ramp, however, they both heard a voice above the din.

'—not a prisoner—a scientist!—*know this facility*—can help you!'

Juliet and Book II spun.

It took them a second to locate the owner of the voice.

Three cells down from the ramp, in the cell closest to the animal cage room.

The owner of the voice was standing up against the bars of his cell—which in the surrounding chaos had only made him look just like all the other prisoners.

But upon closer inspection, he looked considerably different from the others.

He wasn't wearing a blue denim inmate uniform. Rather, he wore a white labcoat over shirtsleeves and a loosened tie.

Nor did he look deranged or menacing. Quite the opposite, in fact. He was short, with glasses and thinning blond hair that looked like it had been combed every day of his life.

Juliet and Book came to his cell.

'Who are you?' Juliet shouted above the din.

'My name is Herbert Franklin!' he replied quickly. 'I'm a doctor, an immunologist! Until this morning, I was working on the vaccine! But then the Air Force people locked me in here!'

'You know this facility?' Book II yelled. Beside him, Juliet stole a glance at the heavy door leading back to the animal cage room. It was banging from the other side.

'Yes!' the man named Franklin said.

'What do you think?' Book II asked Juliet.

She pondered it for a moment.

Then she shouted up the ramp: 'Curtis! Quickly! Get back here! I got another lock I need opened!'

Two minutes later, they were all heading up the ramp, now with a new member added to their group.

As they raced up the sloping walkway, however, making for the next floor, none of them noticed the layer of expanding water that lapped up against the bottom of the ramp.

When Schofield's runaway AWACS plane had crashed down onto it, the massive aircraft elevator platform had been parked on Level 4—at the spot where the President's entourage had left it nearly an hour earlier.

Now, the crumpled remains of the Boeing 707 lay sprawled across the width of the elevator platform.

Gnarled pieces of metal lay everywhere. A couple of tyres had been thrown clear with the impact. The plane itself lay pointed downwards, tilted over on its side, its nose dented sharply inwards, its left-hand wing broken in half, crushed beneath the plane's tremendous weight. Miraculously, the AWACS plane's thirty-foot flying-saucer-like rotodome had survived the fall completely intact.

Shane Schofield stepped out of the wreck of the plane, followed by Gant, Mother and Brainiac. They jumped over the debris as they ran for the giant steel door that led to Level 4.

A smaller door set into the base of the gigantic door opened easily.

No sooner had they opened it than Schofield raised his

gun and fired. The shot smashed into a wall-mounted security camera, blasting it to oblivion in a shower of sparks.

'No cameras,' he said as he walked. 'That's how they're following us.'

The four of them made their way up a short upwardly-sloping corridor. A squat solid-looking door loomed at the end of it.

Mother spun the flywheel on it and the big door swung open.

Schofield stepped through the doorway first, his nickel-plated pistol leading the way.

He emerged inside a laboratory of some sort. Super-computers lined the walls, their lights blinking. Keyboard terminals and data screens and clear-plastic experiment boxes occupied the remaining bench space.

Otherwise, the lab was deserted—

Blam!

Gunshot.

Blam!

Another.

It was Gant, exterminating a couple of security cameras.

Schofield continued to scan the wide room.

The most dominant feature of the laboratory was a line of slanted glass windows that lay directly opposite the entrance.

He stepped up to the observation windows and peered out through them—

—and found himself looking out over a wide, high-ceilinged room, in the centre of which stood a gigantic glass cube.

The cube was freestanding, occupying the centre of the hall-like room, but without touching its ceiling or walls.

The wall on the far side of the cube—a wall which divided this level in two—didn't quite reach the ceiling. Rather, it stopped about seven feet short of it, replaced by thick glass. Through that glass, Schofield saw a series of criss-crossing catwalks suspended above whatever was on the other side of the floor.

But it was the cube in front of him that held his immediate attention.

It was about the size of a large living room. Such a conclusion was easy to come to, given that the glass cube was filled with regular household furniture—a couch, a table, chairs, a TV with Playstation 2 and, most strangely of all, a single bed draped with a Jar Jar Binks doona cover.

Some toys lay strewn about the glass-enclosed living room. Matchbox cars. A bright yellow *Episode I* spaceship. Some picture books.

Schofield shook his head.

It looked like the bedroom of a little boy.

It was at that precise moment that the occupant of the glass cube ambled casually out from a discreetly curtained-off corner of the cube—the toilet.

Schofield's jaw dropped.

'What on earth is going on here?' he breathed.

There was a set of stairs on the northern side of the elevated lab leading down to the cube.

When he reached the base of the stairs, Schofield walked alongside the dividing wall that sealed this section off from the eastern side of the floor. Gant walked with him. Mother and Brainiac stayed up in the observation lab.

Schofield and Gant came to a halt before the giant freestanding cube, gazed into it.

The occupant of the glass cube saw them coming, and casually walked over to the edge of the completely sealed structure.

The occupant arrived at the clear glass barrier in front of Schofield, cocked his head to one side.

'Hey, mister,' the little boy said.

'—Sir, I have complete visual blackout in the labs on Level 4. They've started shooting the surveillance cameras—'

'I'm surprised it took them this long,' Caesar Russell said. 'Where is the President?'

'Level 5, moving up the ramp to Level 4.'

'And our people?'

'Alpha Unit is in position, waiting in the decompression area on Level 4. Delta Unit has been stopped in the animal containment area on Level 5.'

Caesar smiled.

Although Delta was momentarily halted, the theory behind its movements was sound. Delta was forcing the President up through the complex—to where Alpha was waiting . . .

'Tell Delta to get through that doorway and push up the ramp, and cut off the President's retreat.'

He couldn't have been more than six years old.

And with a bowl-shaped shock of brown hair that came down to his eyes, Disneyland T-shirt and Converse sneakers, he looked like any of a million American kids.

Only this kid lived inside a glass cube, in the belly of a top-secret United States Air Force base.

'Hey there,' Schofield said warily.

'Why are you frightened?' the boy asked suddenly.

'Frightened?'

'Yes, you're frightened. What are you scared of?'

'How do you know I'm frightened?'

'I just know,' the boy said cryptically. He spoke with such a serene, even voice that Schofield felt like he was in some kind of dream. 'What's your name?' the boy asked.

'Shane. But most people call me Scarecrow.'

'Scarecrow? That's a funny name.'

'What about you?' Schofield said. 'What's your name?'

'Kevin.'

'And your last name?'

'What's a last name?' the boy asked.

Schofield paused.

'Where are you from, Kevin?'

The boy shrugged. 'Here, I guess. I've never been any-where else. Hey, do you want to know something?'

'Sure.'

'Did you know that Twinkies give kids half their daily glucose requirement as well as giving them a tasty snack?'

'Uh, no, I didn't know that,' Schofield said.

'And that reptiles are so sensitive to variations in the earth's magnetic field that some scientists say they can predict earthquakes? Oh, and *nobody* knows news like NBC,' the boy said earnestly.

'Is that so?' Schofield exchanged a glance with Gant.

Just then, a loud mechanical noise echoed out from the other side of the dividing wall.

Schofield and Gant spun, and through the glass section at the top of the wall, saw the lights on the other side of Level 4 suddenly and unexpectedly go out.

The President of the United States moved cautiously up the ramp that linked Level 5 to Level 4, surrounded by three Secret Service agents, four United States Marines and a lone bookish scientist.

At the top of the ramp was a large retractable grill—kind of like a garage door mounted horizontally.

Juliet Janson hit a switch on the wall and the horizontal door began to slide open, revealing ominous darkness above it.

'Ramp door is opening . . . ' one of the ten 7th Squadron commandos inside the Level 4 decompression area whispered into his radio mike.

The other nine members of Alpha Unit were arrayed around the eastern section of the floor in various hiding places—their guns focused on the ramp in the centre of the room. With their half gas-masks and night-vision goggles they looked like a gang of insects waiting for the kill.

The horizontal door slid slowly open, casting a wide beam of light up into the darkened room. The only other light in the area came through the section of glass at the top of the wall which divided this level in two.

'Stay out of sight until they're all up on level ground,' Kurt Logan said from his position. 'No-one gets out alive.'

*

160

The two Secret Service agents Curtis and Ramondo stepped up into the semi-darkness first, armed with their Uzis. They were followed by Calvin Reeves and Elvis.

The President came next, with Juliet Janson by his side. He held a small SIG-Sauer P-228 pistol awkwardly in his hand. Juliet had given it to him, just in case.

Behind them came the scientist, Herbert Franklin, and bringing up the rear, Book II and Love Machine, both armed with pump-action shotguns.

As soon as he stepped up into the semi-darkness, Book II didn't like it.

Various structures loomed around them. To his immediate right, on the southern side of the enormous room, was a long hexagonal chamber. To his left, shrouded in deep shadow, he saw eight telephone-booth-sized chambers. In the hazy light filtering through from the other side of the floor, he could just make out a series of catwalks high up near the ceiling, twenty feet above the floor.

As soon as Book II stepped clear of the floor-level doorway, its horizontal door slid smoothly back into place near his feet, sealing the exit.

Calvin had hit a switch in the floor nearby, closing it.

Book II swallowed. He would have preferred to keep that door open.

He flicked on a heavy police flashlight he had taken from the Level 5 anteroom. Holding it under the barrel of his shotgun, he played its beam over the room around them.

Calvin Reeves assumed command of strategy.

'You two,' he whispered to Curtis and Ramondo, 'check behind those telephone booths, then take the stairwell door. Haynes, Lewicky, Riley'—he said, using

Elvis's, Love Machine's and Book II's surnames—'the area behind this decompression chamber, then secure that other door,' he pointed toward the dividing wall. 'Janson. You and I stay with the Boss.'

Curtis and Ramondo disappeared in amongst the test chambers, then, moments later, reappeared at the stairwell end.

'No-one back there,' Ramondo said.

Book II, Elvis and Love Machine entered the darkness behind the decompression chamber. A narrow, empty section of floor greeted them. Nothing.

'Clear back here,' Book II said, as the three Marines emerged from behind the long hexagonal chamber. They headed for the door in the dividing wall.

Reeves was following standard tactics in close-quarter, indoor engagements—where there is no sign of the enemy, secure all exits, then consolidate your position.

It was his biggest mistake.

Not only because it limited his options for retreat, but because it was exactly what Kurt Logan—already *inside* the room—was expecting him to do.

While Elvis and Love Machine headed for the dividing wall, Book II played his flashlight over the thirty-foot-long decompression chamber. It was absolutely huge.

At the end of the elongated chamber, he found a small glass porthole, and shone his light in through it.

What he saw made him jump.

An Asian face stared back at him, a man's face, pressed up against the glass.

The Asian man was smiling cheerfully.

162

And then he pointed up—toward the roof of the de-compression chamber.

Book II followed the man's finger with his flashlight and peered up at the top of the decompression chamber—

—and found himself staring into the mantis-like face of a 7th Squadron commando wearing night-vision goggles and a gas-mask!

The flashlight was the only thing that saved Book II's life.

Primarily because it blinded the man hiding on top of the decompression chamber, if only for a moment. The man shied away from the light as his night-vision goggles magnified its beam by a factor of 150.

That was all the time Book II needed.

His shotgun boomed, blasting the commando's goggles to pieces, sending him flying off the top of the chamber.

It was a small victory, for at that exact moment, gunfire erupted around the darkened room as a legion of dark figures emerged from their positions *on top of* the decom-pression chamber and *inside* the telephone-booth-like test chambers and rained hell on Book's hapless group in the centre of the floor.

Over by the stairwell door, Curtis and Ramondo were assaulted by a barrage of P-90 gunfire from both flanks. They were cut down where they stood, their bodies riddled with bloody wounds.

Juliet Janson crash-tackled the President, hurling him to the floor at the base of the decompression chamber, just as a volley of rounds whistled past their heads.

Calvin Reeves wasn't so lucky.

The crossfire of bullets ripped into the back of his head, and he jolted suddenly upright, then dropped to his knees, a look of stunned dismay on his face—as though he had done everything right, and still lost. Then his face smacked down hard against the floor, right next to the spot where Herbert Franklin lay with his head in his hands.

Bullets sizzled through the air.

Juliet yanked the President to his feet, firing with her free hand, dragging him toward the cover of the lab benches over by the dividing wall, when suddenly she saw a 7th Squadron commando rise up from the roof of the decompression chamber and take aim at the President's head.

She brought her gun around. Not fast enough—

Blam!

The 7th Squadron man's head exploded, his neck snapping backwards. His body tumbled off the decompression chamber.

Juliet spun to see who had fired the killing shot, but strangely she saw no-one.

Book II, Elvis and Love Machine all dived together behind a lab bench just as the benchtop was raked with gunfire. They returned fire, aiming at three Air Force commandos taking cover among the test booths.

But it quickly became clear that the Marines' makeshift assortment of shotguns and pistols was going to be no match for the rapid-fire P-90 machine guns of the 7th Squadron troops. The shelves around them shattered and splintered under the phenomenal weight of enemy fire.

Elvis ducked for cover. 'Goddamn!' he yelled. 'This is seriously *fucked up*!'

'No kidding,' Book II shouted. He shucked his pump-action and snapped up to fire, but when he appeared above the benchtop and loosed a couple of shots, he saw a very strange thing happen: he saw all three of the shadowy 7th Squadron shooters get yanked clean off their feet from behind.

Their guns went silent, and Book II found himself staring at an empty area of the battlefield.

'What the . . . ?'

From his own position near the stairwell door, Alpha Unit's leader, Kurt Logan, saw what was happening.

'Fuck! There's someone else in here!' he yelled angrily into his microphone. 'Somebody's picking us off!'

Suddenly the trooper beside Logan took a hit to the side of the head and half his skull exploded, spraying blood and brains everywhere.

'*Fuck!*' Logan had expected to lose maybe two of his men in the shootout—but now he had lost six. 'Alpha Unit, pull out! Everybody back to the stairwell now! Take emergency evac measures!'

He threw open the stairwell door, just as a line of bullets punctured the wall all around it, almost taking his head off. His remaining men dashed past him, out through the door, into the shelter of the eastern stair-well—but not before they had brutally fired down at their fallen comrades' bodies, peppering the corpses and the floor all around them with bullets.

Logan himself mercilessly strafed the body of a dead 7th Squadron man on the ground beside him. Then, when he was done, he disappeared through the doorway after the others and abruptly there was silence.

Book II was still crouched behind his lab bench with Elvis and Love Machine, acrid gunsmoke rising into the air all around them.

Silence.

Deafening silence.

Juliet Janson and the President lay on the floor five feet away from Book and the others, shielded by another bench, covered in dust and broken bits of plastic. Juliet still had her gun raised—

Whump!

A pair of boots landed with a loud thud on the bench-top above them.

They all snapped to look up—and found themselves staring at Captain Shane M. Schofield, USMC, dressed in full dress uniform, with two nickel-plated Berettas gripped in his hands.

He smiled at them. 'Hey there.'

Meanwhile, in bars and offices and homes around America and the world, people sat glued to their television sets.

Because there was so little footage, CNN and the overseas news networks just kept broadcasting the existing few minutes' worth of tape over and over again. Experts were brought in to give their opinions.

Government people sprang into action, although no-one could really do anything substantive, since the exact location of the nightmarish affair was known only to a select few.

In any case, in a few minutes it would be eight o'clock Mountain Daylight Time and the people of the world tensely awaited the next hourly update.

THIRD CONFRONTATION

3 July, 0800 Hours

UNITED STATES AIR FORCE
SPECIAL AREA (RESTRICTED) NO. 7
0800 HOURS

GROUND LEVEL: Main Hangar

LEVEL 1: Hangar Bay

LEVEL 2: Hangar Bay

LEVEL 3: Living Quarters

LEVEL 4: Laboratories

LEVEL 5: Confinement

Rising water level

LEVEL 6: X-rail platform

Space Division, that part of the Defense Intelligence Agency which deals with foreign powers' space capabilities, is located on the second-to-bottom floor of the Pentagon, three storeys directly below the famous Pentagon Situation Room.

And although its title may sound exotic and exciting, as David Fairfax knew such a perception couldn't have been farther from the truth.

In short, you got sent to Space Division as punishment, because nothing ever happened in Space Division.

It was nearly 10.00 a.m. on the East Coast as Fairfax— oblivious to any commotion going on in the outside world—tapped away on his computer keyboard, trying to decipher a collection of phone taps that the DIA had picked up over the past few months. Whoever had been using the phones in question had fitted them with sophisticated encoders, masking their content. It was up to Fairfax to crack that code.

It's funny how times change, he thought.

David Theodore Fairfax was a cryptanalyst, a code-breaker. Of medium height, lean, with floppy brown hair and thin wireframe glasses, he didn't look like a genius. In fact, in his Mooks T-shirt, jeans and sneakers, he looked more like a gawky university student than a government analyst.

It was, however, his brilliant undergraduate thesis on theoretical non-linear computing that had brought him to the attention of the Defense Intelligence Agency, the Department of Defense's chief intelligence-gathering organisation. The DIA worked in close consultation with the NSA, America's chief signals gatherer and code-breaker. But that didn't prevent it from running its own team of codecrackers—who often spied *on* the NSA—of which Dave Fairfax was a part.

Fairfax had taken to cryptanalysis immediately. He loved the challenge of it, the battle between two minds: one which hopes to conceal, the other which hopes to reveal. He lived by the maxim: *No code is unbreakable*.

It didn't take him long to get noticed.

In the early 1990s, US authorities were confounded by a man named Phil Zimmerman and his unbreakable encryption software, 'PGP'. In 1991, Zimmerman had posted PGP on the Internet, to the great consternation of the US government—principally because the government couldn't crack it.

PGP employed a cryptographic system known as the 'public key system,' which involved the multiplication of very large prime numbers to obtain the code's all-important 'key'. In this case 'very large prime numbers' meant numbers with over 130 digits.

It was unbreakable.

It was claimed that it would take all the supercomputers in the world twelve times the age of the universe to check all the possible values for a single message.

The government was annoyed. It became known that certain terrorist groups and foreign governments had started using PGP to encrypt their messages. In 1993, a grand jury investigation into Zimmerman was initiated on the basis that by uploading PGP onto the Internet, he had exported a *weapon* out of the United States, since encryption software came under the government's definition of a 'munition'.

And then strangely, in 1996, after hounding Zimmerman for three years, the US Attorney General's office dropped the case.

Just like that.

They claimed that the horse had bolted and the case was no longer worth pursuing, so they closed the file.

What the Attorney General never mentioned was the call she had received from the Director of the DIA on the morning she dropped the case, saying that PGP had been cracked.

And as anyone in cryptography knows, once you crack your enemy's code, you don't let them know you've cracked it.

And the man who cracked PGP: an unknown twenty-five-year-old DIA mathematician by the name of David Fairfax.

It turned out that Fairfax's theoretical non-linear computer was no longer theoretical. A prototype version of it was built for the express purpose of breaking PGP, and as it turned out, the computer, with its unimaginable calculative abilities, could factor extremely large numbers with considerable ease.

No code is unbreakable.

History, however, is tough on cryptanalysts—for the simple fact that they cannot talk about their greatest victories.

And so it was with Dave Fairfax. He might have cracked PGP, but he could never talk about it, and in the great maze of government work, he had simply been given a small pay rise and then moved on to the next job.

And so here he was in Space Division, analysing a series of unauthorised phone transmissions coming into and out of some remote Air Force base in Utah.

In a similarly isolated room across the hall from him, however, was where all the good stuff was happening today. A joint taskforce of DIA and NSA cryptanalysts were tracking the encrypted signals coming out of the Chinese space shuttle that had launched from Xichang a few days earlier.

Now that was interesting, Fairfax thought. Better than decrypting some phone calls from a stupid Air Force base in the desert.

The recorded phone calls appeared on Fairfax's computer screen as a waterfall of cascading numbers—the mathematical representation of a series of telephone conversations that had taken place in Utah over the last couple of months.

A huge pair of headphones covered Fairfax's ears, emitting a steady stream of garbled static. His eyes were fixed on the screen.

One thing was clear: whoever had made these calls had encrypted them well. Fairfax had been at this for the last two days.

He tried a few older algorithms.

Nothing.

He tried a few newer ones.

Nothing.

He could do this all month if he had to.

He tried a program he had developed to crack Vodafone's newest encryption system—

'—*Kan bevestig dat in-enting plaasvind*—'

For a brief second, a strange guttural language materialised in his ears.

Fairfax's eyes glowed to life.

Gotcha . . .

He tried the program on some of the other telephone conversations.

And in a miraculous instant, formless static suddenly became clear voices speaking in a foreign tongue, interspersed with the odd sentence of English.

'—*Toetse op laaste poging word op die vier-en-twientigste verwag. Wat van die onttrekkings eenheid?*—'

'—*Reccondo span is alreeds weggestuur*—'

'—*Voorbereidings onderweg. Vroeg oggend. Beste tyd vir onttrekking*—'

'—*everything is in place. Confirm that it's the third*—'

'—*Ontrekking kan 'n probleem wees. Gestel ons gebruik die Hoeb land hier naby. Verstaan hy is 'n lid van Die Organisasie*—'

'—*Sal die instruksies oordra*—'

'—*mission is a go*—'

'—*Die Reccondos is gereed. Verwagte aankoms by beplande bestemming binne nege dae*—'

Fairfax's eyes gleamed as he gazed at the screen.

No code is unbreakable.

He reached for his phone.

After the short battle in the decompression area, Schofield and the others retreated to the opposite side of Level 4, to the observation lab overlooking the giant cube—locking the doors behind them and then blasting the security keypads with gunshots.

Of all the places Schofield had seen so far, this area was the most easily defended.

Barring the regular personnel elevator, it had only two entrances: the short ramp leading back to the aircraft elevator and the doorway leading to the staircase that went down to the cube.

Juliet Janson flopped to the floor of the lab, exhausted.

The President did the same.

The Marines—Book II, Elvis, Love Machine, Mother and Brainiac—formed a huddle and quickly told each other of their respective adventures inside flooding elevator shafts and runaway AWACS planes.

The last member of their rag-tag group—the labcoat-wearing scientist, Herbert Franklin—took a seat in the corner.

Schofield and Gant remained standing.

They had a few weapons now, gear that they had scavenged from the bodies of the 7th Squadron men in the decompression area—guns, a few radio headsets, three extremely high-powered grenades made of RDX compound, and two thumbtack-sized lock-destroying explosives known as Lock-Blasters.

Logan's men, however, had spoiled well.

The brutal gunfire that they had directed at their own fallen men *hadn't* been intended as kill shots—it had been intended to destroy any weapons the dead men might offer their enemy. Consequently, only one P-90 assault rifle had been salvaged from the battlefield. All the others had been shattered, as had many of the fallen men's semi-automatic pistols.

'Mother,' Schofield said, tossing the P-90 to her, 'keep an eye on the ramp entrance. Elvis, the stairs going down to the cube.'

Mother and Elvis dashed off.

Although just about everyone else in the world would have gone straight over to the President at that time, Schofield didn't. He could see that the President hadn't been injured—still had all his fingers and toes—and so long as his heart was still beating, he was all right.

Instead, Schofield went over to Juliet Janson.

'Update,' was all he said.

Janson glanced up at Schofield, looked into the reflective silver lenses of his wraparound anti-flash glasses.

She'd seen him around the Presidential helicopters before, but had never really talked to him. She'd heard about him from the other agents, though. He was the one from that thing in Antarctica.

'They ambushed us in the Level 3 common room, just

after the message came over the Emergency Broadcast System,' she said. 'Been right on our tails ever since. We hit the stairwell, made for the Emergency Exit Vent down on Level 6, but they were waiting for us. We came back *up* the stairs—they were waiting for us again. We diverted through 5 and came up the ramp to 4—and they were waiting for us again.'

'Casualties?'

'Eight agents from the President's Personal Detail killed. Plus the whole Advance Team down on Level 6. That makes seventeen in total.'

'Frank Cutler?'

'Gone.'

'Anything else?'

Janson nodded at the little labcoated man. 'We picked him up on 5, before we walked into that ambush in the decompression room. Says he's a scientist working here.'

Schofield glanced over at Herbert Franklin. Small and bespectacled, the little man just bowed his head in silence.

'What about you?' Janson asked.

Schofield shrugged. 'We were up in the main hangar when it went down. Scrambled down the ventilation shaft, arrived in one of the underground hangars, destroyed a Humvee, crashed an AWACS plane.'

'The usual,' Gant added.

'How did you know about the ambush next door?' Janson asked.

Schofield shrugged. 'We were down next to the cube when the lights went out in the decompression area. We were hoping it was someone friendly, trying to hide from the security cameras. So we checked it out from above, from the catwalks. When we saw who it was, saw them

178

surrounding that ramp in the middle of the room, we figured they were waiting for the big score'—he nodded at the President—'so we set up a little counter-ambush of our own.'

On the other side of the room, Brainiac sat down next to the President.

'Mister President,' he said with deference.

'Hello,' the President replied.

'How you feelin', sir?'

'Well, I'm still alive, which is a good start, considering the circumstances. What's your name, son?'

'Gorman, sir. Corporal Gus Gorman, but most of the guys just call me Brainiac.'

'Brainiac?'

'That's right, sir,' Brainiac hesitated. 'Sir, if you don't mind, I was wondering, if it wasn't too much trouble, if I could ask you a question.'

'Why not?' the President said.

'Okay, then. Okay. Well, you bein' President and all, you'd know certain things, right?'

'Yes . . . '

'Right. Cool. Because what I always wanted to know was this: is Puerto Rico a United States protectorate because it has the highest number of UFO sightings in the world per annum?'

'*What?*'

'Well, think about it, why the hell else would we want to hold onto Puerto-fucking-Rico, there ain't nothing there—'

'*Brainiac,*' Schofield said from across the room. 'Leave

the President alone. Mister President, you better come and see this. It's almost eight o'clock and Caesar will be giving his hourly update any second.'

The President went over to join Schofield—but not before he gave Brainiac a strange look.

At the tick of eight o'clock, Caesar Russell's face appeared on every television set in Area 7.

'My fellow Americans,' he boomed, 'after one hour's play, the President is still alive. His cause, however, is not looking good.

'His personal Secret Service Detail has been decimated, with eight of its nine members already confirmed dead. Two more Secret Service units—advance teams, one stationed down in the lowest floor of this facility, another at one of the exterior exits, consisting of nine men each— were also eliminated, bringing the total of presidential losses to twenty-six men. On both occasions, no losses were sustained by my 7th Squadron men.

'That said, some knights in shining armour *have* arrived on the scene. A small band of United States Marines— members of the President's ornamental helicopter crew, looking very pretty in their dress uniforms—have come to his defen—'

Just then, completely without warning, the television sets throughout Area 7 abruptly died, their screens shrinking to black.

At the same moment, all the lights in the complex blinked out, plunging Area 7 into darkness.

Inside the lab on Level 4, everybody looked up at the sudden loss of power.

'Uh-oh . . . ' Gant said, eyeing the ceiling.

Then, a second later, the lights whirred back to life and the TV system rebooted, Caesar's face still looming large, still talking.

'—which leaves us with five 7th Squadron units versus a handful of United States Marines. Such is the state of play at eight o'clock. I shall see you again for another update at 0900 hours.'

The TV screens cut to black.

'Liar,' Juliet Janson said. 'That son of a bitch is distorting the truth. The advance team down on Level 6 was already dead when we got there. They were killed before all this started.'

'He also lied about his losses,' Brainiac said. 'Sneaky bastard.'

'So what do we do?' Gant asked Schofield. 'They have us outnumbered, outflanked and outgunned. Plus, this is their turf.'

Schofield was wondering exactly the same thing.

The 7th Squadron had them completely on the run. They had all the leverage, and more importantly, he thought, looking down at his formal full dress uniform, they had come prepared to fight.

'Okay,' he said, thinking aloud. 'Know your enemy.'

'What?'

'First principles. We have to even things up, but to do

that, we need knowledge. Rule Number One: know your enemy. Okay. So who are they?'

Janson shrugged. 'The 7th Squadron. The Air Force's crack ground unit. The best in the country. Well trained, well armed—'

'And on steroids,' Gant added.

'More than just steroids,' another voice said.

Everyone turned.

It was the scientist, Herbert Franklin.

'Who are you?' Schofield said.

The little man shuffled nervously. 'My name is Herbie Franklin. Until this morning, I was an immunologist on Project Fortune. But they locked me up just before you all arrived.'

Schofield said, 'What did you mean, "more than just steroids"?'

'Well, what I meant was that the 7th Squadron men at this base have been . . . *augmented* . . . for want of a better word.'

'Augmented?'

'Enhanced. *Improved* for better performance. Ever wondered why the 7th Squadron do so well at inter-service battle competitions? Ever wondered why they can keep fighting while everyone else is falling over with exhaustion?'

'Yes . . .'

Franklin spoke quickly: 'Anabolic steroids to enhance muscle and fitness levels. Artificial erythropoietin injections for increased blood oxygenation.'

'Artificial erythropoietin?' Gant repeated.

'EPO for short,' Herbie said. 'It's a hormone that stimulates production of red blood cells by the bone

183

marrow, thus increasing the supply of oxygen in the bloodstream. Endurance athletes, mainly cyclists, have been using it for years.

'The 7th Squadron are stronger than you, and they can run all day long,' Herbie said. 'Hell, Captain, these men were tough when they got here, but since their arrival they have been augmented by the latest pharmacological technology to fight harder, better and longer than anybody else.'

'Okay, okay,' Schofield said, 'I think we get the picture.'

He was thinking, however, of a small boy named Kevin, living fifty feet away, inside a glass cube. 'So is that what you do here? Is that what this base is all about? Enhancing elite soldiers?'

'No . . . ' Herbie said, casting a wary glance over at the President. 'The augmentation of the 7th Squadron troopers is only performed as an ancillary task, since they guard the base.'

'So what the hell *is* this place?'

Again Herbie looked at the President. Then he took a deep breath before answering—

It was another voice, however, that spoke.

'This base houses the most important vaccine ever developed in the history of America,' it said.

Schofield spun.

It was the President.

Schofield appraised him. The President was still wearing his charcoal-coloured suit and tie. With his neatly-combed light-grey hair and familiar wrinkled face, he looked like a middle-aged country businessman—albeit a businessman who had been sweating hard for the last hour.

'A vaccine?' Schofield said.

'Yes. A vaccine against the latest Chinese genetic virus. A virus that targets Caucasian people by way of their pigmentation DNA. An agent known as the Sinovirus.'

'And the source of this vaccine . . . ?' Schofield said.

' . . . is a genetically-constructed human being,' the President said.

'A *what?*'

'A person, Captain Schofield, who since the embryonic stage of his existence has been *purpose-built* to withstand the Sinovirus, whose very blood can be harvested to produce antibodies for the rest of the American population. A human vaccine. The world's first genetically-tailored human being, Captain, a boy named Kevin.'

Schofield's eyes narrowed.

It explained a lot—the tight security surrounding the complex, the presidential visit, and a boy living inside a glass cube. He was also struck by one other aspect of what the President had just said: the President knew his name.

'You *created* a boy to use as a vaccine?' Schofield said. 'With respect, sir, but doesn't that bother you?'

The President grimaced. 'My job is not made up of black and whites, Captain. Just grey, infinite grey. And in that world of grey, I have to make decisions—often difficult ones. Sure, Kevin existed long before I became President, but once I knew about him, I had to make the call to continue the project. I made that call. I may not like it, but in the face of an agent like the Sinovirus, tough decisions are necessary.'

There was a short silence.

Book spoke. 'What about the prisoners downstairs?

'And the animals. What are they used for?' Juliet said.

Schofield frowned. He hadn't seen Level 5, so he didn't know about any animals or prisoners.

Herbie Franklin answered. 'The animals are used for

both projects, the vaccine and the 7th Squadron augmentation. The Kodiak bears are utilised for their blood toxins. All bears have extremely high blood-oxygen levels for use when they hibernate. The blood enhancement research for the 7th Squadron came from them.'

'So what about the other cages, the water-filled ones?' Janson asked. 'What's in them?'

Herbie paused. 'A rare breed of monitor lizard known as the Komodo dragon. The largest lizard in the world, about thirteen feet long, as big as a regular crocodile. We have six of them.'

'And what are they used for?' Schofield asked.

'Komodos are the most ancient reptilian species on earth, found only on the scattered middle islands in Indonesia. They're great swimmers—been known to swim between islands—but they're equally fast on land, easily capable of running down a man, which they do regularly. Their internal antibiotic system, however, is extraordinarily robust. They are all but impervious to illness. Their lymph nodes produce a highly-concentrated antibacterial serum that has protected them against disease for thousands of years.'

The President said, 'The Komodo dragons' blood by-products have been reconfigured to match the structure of human blood, and as such form the basis of Kevin's immune system. We then harvest Kevin's genetically-constructed blood plasma to produce a serum that can be inserted into America's water supply—a serum-hydrate solution—thereby immunising the general population against the Sinovirus.'

'You spike the water supply?' Schofield said.

'Oh, it's been done before,' Herbie said. 'In 1989,

against botulinum toxin, and in 1990—because of Iraq—against anthrax. Although Americans don't know it, they're resistant to all the world's major biological weapons.'

'What about the human prisoners?' Book II asked. 'What are they here for?'

Herbie looked to the President, who nodded silently.

The little scientist shrugged. 'The human prisoners are another story altogether. They're not here to provide any sort of blood by-product or serum. Their role is simple. They're guinea pigs for the testing of the vaccine.'

'Jesus Christ,' Gant breathed when she saw the list of prisoner names.

After Herbie had told them the purpose of the prisoners downstairs, he had brought up a list of their names on one of the laboratory's computer terminals.

There were forty-two of them in total, all multiple lifers or death-row candidates who had somehow escaped the chair.

'The worst of the worst,' Herbie said, nodding at the list of names.

Schofield had heard of many of them.

Sylvester McLean—the child-murderer from Atlanta. Ronald Noonan—the Houston baker turned clock-tower sniper. Lucifer Leary—the serial killer from Phoenix. Seth Grimshaw—the notorious leader of the Black League, an ultra-violent terrorist organisation that believed the US government was preparing America for a United Nations takeover.

'Seth Grimshaw?' Gant said, seeing the name. She turned to Juliet Janson. 'Wasn't he the one who –?'

'Yes,' Janson said, glancing nervously at the President over on the far side of the lab. 'In early February. Just after the inauguration. He's a genuine 18-84.'

Gant said, 'Oh, man, do I hope their cages are sturdy.'

'All right. Great,' Schofield said, bringing everyone back to the present. 'Which brings us back to the here and now. We're shut in here. They want to kill the President. And because of the radio transmitter on his heart, if he dies, fourteen major cities go up in smoke.'

'And all right in front of the people of America,' Janson said.

'Not necessarily,' the President said, 'because Caesar wouldn't know about the LBJ Directive.'

'What's the LBJ Directive?' Schofield asked.

'It's a feature of the Emergency Broadcast System, but known only to the President and the Vice-President. It's essentially a safety valve, brought in by Lyndon Johnson in 1967, to stop the EBS from being used too soon.'

'So what does it do?'

'It provides for a forty-five-minute delay of any broadcast sent over the system, unless a presidential override code is entered. In other words, except in the most urgent circumstances, it stops a panic broadcast from being sent out, effectively allowing for a forty-five-minute cooling-off period.

'Now, since it's 8:09, Caesar's initial broadcast has got out there, but if we were to find the EBS transmission box inside this complex, we could stop all his subsequent transmissions.'

Schofield pursed his lips, thinking. 'That has to be a

secondary consideration. Something to do only if we happen to be in the right place at the right time.'

He turned to Herbie. 'Tell us about this complex.'

Herbie shrugged. 'What's there to know? It's a fortress. Used to be NORAD headquarters. When it shuts down, it *shuts down*. The thing is, I don't think anyone ever expected it to be used to keep someone locked *in*.'

'But even a total lockdown must have a release procedure,' Schofield said. 'Something which opens the doors when the crisis is over.'

Herbie nodded. 'The time-lock.'

'Time-lock?'

'In the event of total lockdown, a timer-controlled security system is activated. Every hour on the hour, those people still alive inside the base have a five-minute window period to enter one of three possible codes.'

'What kind of codes?' Gant asked.

'Remember,' Herbie said, 'this facility was intended for use in a full-scale US–Soviet nuclear exchange. The codes reflect that. As such, there are three possible entry codes.

'The *first* code simply continues the lockdown. The nuclear crisis is still going, so the facility remains locked down. The *second* code assumes the crisis has been resolved. It calls an end to the lockdown—armoured blast doors are retracted and all entrances and exits are re-opened.'

'And the third code?' Gant asked.

'The *third* code is a halfway measure—it allows for messenger escape. It authorises the opening of individual exits and entrances for messengers to leave the facility.'

Schofield was listening to Herbie carefully.

'What happens when *no code* is entered during the hourly window period?' he asked.

'You're fast, Captain. You see, that's the kicker, isn't it. If no code is entered, the complex's computer is warned that the facility may have been taken by the enemy. It then gives you one chance to re-enter one of the other codes at the *next* hourly window period. If no code is entered at that time, then the computer assumes that the facility has been taken by the enemy, at which point the facility's self-destruct mechanism is activated.'

'*Self-destruct mechanism*,' Brainiac blurted. 'What the fuck is that?'

'A one-hundred-megaton thermonuclear warhead buried beneath the complex,' Herbie said simply.

'Oh, Christ . . . ' Brainiac said.

Gant said, 'Surely they removed that when the Soviet Union collapsed.'

'I'm afraid not,' Herbie said. 'When this base was re-configured as a chemical weapons facility, it was decided that the self-destruct device still had value. If there was an accident and a virus spread throughout the facility, the whole contaminated complex—virus included—could be destroyed by a superheated nuclear blast.'

'Okay,' Schofield said, 'so if we want to leave, we have to wait for the hourly window period, find a computer connected to the central network, and then enter the correct code.'

'That's right,' Herbie said.

'So what are the codes?' Schofield asked.

Herbie shrugged helplessly. 'That I don't know. I can initiate a lockdown if there's been an outbreak, but I don't have clearance to undo one. Only the Air Force guys can do that—'

'Uh, excuse me,' Juliet Janson said, 'but aren't we forgetting something?

'Like what?' Brainiac said.

'Like the Football,' Janson said. 'The President's brief-case. The one that's been rigged to *stop* him from escaping this complex. He has to press his palm against the analyser plate on the Football once every ninety minutes, other-wise the plasma bombs in the cities go off.'

'Damn it,' Schofield said. He had forgotten all about that. He looked at his watch.

It was 8:12 a.m.

This had all started at 7:00 a.m. Which meant they had to get the President's hand onto the Football by 8:30.

He looked up at the others. 'Where are they keeping the Football?'

'Russell said it would be kept in the main hangar, up on ground level,' the President said.

'What do you think?' Gant said to Schofield.

'I don't think we have much choice. Somehow, we have to get his hand onto the Football.'

'But we can't keep doing that forever.'

'No,' Schofield said, 'we can't. At some point, we'll have to come up with a more long-term solution. But until then, we deal with the short-term ones.'

Janson said, 'It'd be suicide to bring the President out into the open upstairs, they'll almost certainly be waiting.'

'That's right,' Schofield stood up. 'Which is why we don't do that. What we do is quite straightforward. We bring the Football to him.'

'The first thing we have to do,' Schofield said, rounding everyone up, 'is take care of those security cameras. While they're still operating, we're screwed.' He turned to Herbie Franklin. 'Where's the central junction box in this place?'

'In the Level 1 hangar bay, I think, on the northern wall.'

'Okay,' Schofield said. 'Mother, Brainiac, I want you guys to take care of those cameras. Cut the power if you have to, I don't care, just shut down the camera system. You got me?'

'Got it,' Mother said.

'And take Doctor Franklin with you. If he's lying, shoot him.'

'Got it,' Mother said, eyeing Herbie suspiciously. Herbie gulped.

'What about the rest of us?' Juliet asked.

Schofield headed toward the short ramp that led to the wide aircraft elevator shaft.

'The rest of us are going upstairs to play some football.'

*

193

'—System reboot is complete—'

'Status?' Caesar Russell asked.

Ten minutes previously, during Caesar's second EBS broadcast, the entire complex had experienced an abrupt power shutdown, causing all its interior systems to switch off.

'—Confirm: main power supply has been cut,' one of the radio operators said. 'We're running on auxiliary power now. All systems operational.'

'—We lost that enhanced satellite image of the EEV that was coming through. Renewing contact with the satellite now—'

Another operator: 'Copy that. Main power supply was switched off at the Level 1 junction box at exactly 0800 hours, by operator 008-72—'

'8-72?' Caesar frowned, thinking.

'—Sir, we have no visual feed. All cameras went down with the cutting of the main power supply—'

Caesar's eyes narrowed. 'All units, report in.'

'—*This is Alpha*,' Kurt Logan's voice said. '*Initiate frequency swap. Possibility that enemy has obtained some of our radio equipment—*'

'—Frequency swap complete,' the senior operator said. 'Go ahead, Alpha Leader—'

'—*We are in the Level 2 hangar bay. Heading for the personnel elevator for rendezvous up in the main hangar. Report six dead—*'

'—*This is Bravo Leader, we're up in the main hangar, covering the Football. All men present and accounted for. No casualties—*'

'—*This is Charlie Leader. We are moving in tandem with Echo through the common room area on Level 3. We have one*

194

dead, two wounded from that AWACS shit before. Understand targets were last sighted on Level 4. Preparing for joint assault through floor-to-ceiling hatches between 3 and 4. Please advise—'

'—Charlie, Echo, this is Control. We have lost all visual contact on the Level 4 lab area—'

'Engage at will, Charlie and Echo,' Caesar Russell cut in sharply. 'Keep them moving. They can't run forever.'

'—This is Delta. We are still on 5. No casualties. By the time we broke down that door on 5, the targets had already gone up the ramp to Level 4. Be advised, there is substantial flooding in the Level 5 confinement area. Awaiting instructions—'

'—Delta, this is Caesar,' Russell said coolly, 'head back down to Level 6. Cover the X-rail exits.'

'—Affirmative, that, sir—'

Twenty black-clad 7th Squadron commandos hurried down one of the corridors of the Level 3 living area, their boots thundering on the floor—the men of Charlie and Echo Units.

They came to a pressure-sealed manhole in the carpet. A code was entered and the circular hatch came free with a sharp hiss, revealing a crawlspace between the floor of Level 3 and the ceiling of Level 4. Another pressure hatch lay directly beneath this one—the entry to Level 4.

One of the commandos lowered himself through the manhole.

'Control, this is Charlie Leader,' Python Willis said into his headset mike. 'We are at the manhole leading to the observation lab on Level 4. Preparing to storm the floor from above.'

'*Do it*,' Caesar's voice replied.

Python nodded to his man in the crawlspace.

The commando released the pressure valve and let the hatch drop to the floor ten feet below him. Then he jumped down to the ground after it, three others close behind him, their P-90s aimed and ready.

Nothing.

The lab around them was empty.

There came a loud mechanical rumbling from within the walls.

The 7th Squadron men whirled around as one.

It was the sound of the hydraulic aircraft elevator platform.

The commandos of Charlie and Echo Units hurried down the short sloping walkway that led from the observation lab to the aircraft elevator shaft.

They got there just in time to see the underside of the giant elevator platform rising up into the shaft above them, heading for the main hangar.

Python Willis spoke into his helmet mike. 'Control, this is Charlie Leader. They're going for the Football.'

The gigantic aircraft elevator groaned loudly as it lumbered up the wide concrete shaft.

It moved slowly, carrying the crumpled remains of the crashed AWACS plane on its back.

The plane lay tilted forward, like a wounded bird, its nose lower than its destroyed rear section, its broken wings splayed wide. The plane's rotodome—still intact—towered high above the whole sorry image.

The massive elevator rumbled up the greasy concrete shaft.

As it passed the open doorway to the Level 1 hangar bay, however, three tiny figures quickly leapt off it, hustling into the underground hangar.

It was Mother and Brainiac and, puffing along behind them, Herbie Franklin.

They were heading for the central junction box that Franklin had said was located in the Level 1 hangar bay, to disable Area 7's camera system.

The hangar was deserted now, the 7th Squadron men

long gone. The two stealth bombers and the lone SR-71 Blackbird still stood silently in the cavernous space, like a trio of sleeping sentinels.

Mother checked her watch as she skirted the left-hand wall of the hangar.

8:20.

Ten minutes to get the President to the Football.

As she moved along the concrete wall, watchful for enemy soldiers, she saw a large box-shaped compartment at the far end of it. The compartment's ten-foot-tall steel door was twisted and bent, partially destroyed.

'Oh, yeah,' she said.

'What?' Herbie asked from behind her.

'Our little run-in with the 7th Squadron up here earlier,' Mother said. 'They got a couple of Stingers off— one hit that compartment, the other punctured some water tanks inside the wall over by the personnel elevator.'

'Oh,' Herbie said.

'Let's see what's left,' Mother said.

Upstairs, the giant elevator platform rose slowly into the main hangar.

The remains of the AWACS plane appeared first, rising above the rim of the square-shaped shaft.

Then the exploded rear section of the fuselage . . .

. . . followed by the intact rotodome . . .

. . . then the snapped wings . . .

The rest of the battered plane rose slowly into view and then, with a loud *boom!*, the platform came level with the hangar floor and stopped.

There was a long silence.

The ground-level hangar bore the scars of the battle that had taken place there nearly an hour and a half before.

Marine One—still attached to its towing vehicle—stood on the western side of the elevator platform, while its semi-destroyed sister chopper, Nighthawk Two, and its cockroach stood on the northern side of the platform, over by the personnel elevator.

On the eastern side of the AWACS plane, however, stood something entirely new: a team of ten 7th Squadron commandos—Bravo Unit—positioned in between the elevator platform and the internal building, standing inside a semi-circular barricade of wooden crates and Samsonite containers.

On a chair in the centre of the barricade sat a familiar stainless-steel briefcase, folded open, revealing a series of red and green lights, a keypad, and a flat-glass analyser plate.

The Football.

Captain Bruno 'Boa' McConnell—the grey-eyed leader of Bravo Unit—gazed at the crumpled AWACS plane suspiciously.

The broken plane just sat there in the centre of the enormous hangar—silent, unmoving—a great big pile of junk.

More silence.

'*How's it going down there, Mother?*' Schofield's voice whispered in Mother's earpiece, borrowed from one of the dead Secret Service agents.

Down on Level 1, Mother surveyed the damaged electricity junction box in front of her. Fully half the switchboard had been destroyed by the missile impact. The other half was a mixed bag—some parts were intact, others were just mounds of melted wires. At the moment, Herbie Franklin was tapping the keys on a computer terminal that had survived the impact.

'Just a second,' she said into her wrist microphone. 'Yo, Poindexter. What's the story?'

Franklin frowned. 'It doesn't make sense. Somebody's been here already, about twenty minutes ago at eight o'clock. They cut the main power. The whole base is running on auxiliary power . . . '

'Can you cut the cameras?' Mother asked.

'Don't have to. They were shut down when the main power was disabled.' Herbie turned to face Mother. 'They're already off.'

Up in the main hangar, the regular elevator's doors opened.

Out of the lift stepped Kurt Logan and the three other survivors from Alpha Unit. They met up with Boa McConnell and the men of Bravo Unit.

'What's happening?' Logan asked.

'Nothing . . . ' Boa replied. 'Yet.'

'—*Control, this is Charlie Leader,*' Python Willis's voice said over the control room's speakers. '*There's no-one down here on Level 4.*'

'—Copy, Charlie Leader. Bring your team up to the

main hangar in the personnel lift. Echo, stay down there. Caesar wants you roving around the lower levels. We've lost all camera visuals and we need some eyes down there—'

On Level 1, Mother keyed her wrist mike. 'Scarecrow, this is Mother. Cameras are down. Repeat: Cameras are down. We're heading for the aircraft elevator shaft.'

'Thanks, Mother.'

'All right, we're in business,' Schofield said, turning to the President, Book II and Juliet. They were in a dark place.

He looked at his watch:

8:25:59

8:26:00

This was going to be close.

'Fox, Elvis, Love Machine, get ready. On my mark. In three . . . '

The main hangar was silent.

'Two . . . '

Marine One stood about thirty feet away from the wreck of the AWACS plane, shining in the harsh artificial light.

'One . . . '

The men of Bravo Unit eyed the shattered AWACS bird cautiously, guns up, trigger fingers tensed.

' . . . mark.'

Schofield pressed a button on a small hand-held unit—

it was the remote detonation switch for one of the RDX-based grenades that he had found on the 7th Squadron men in the decompression room. Pound for pound, aluminised RDX is about six times more powerful than C4—it blows big and it blows wide, a *super*blasting charge.

As soon as he hit the button, the RDX charge that he had left in the cockpit of the AWACS plane exploded—blasting outwards, showering the hangar with a star-shaped rain of glass and shrapnel.

And then everything happened at once.

The men of Bravo Unit dived away from the explosion.

Sizzling-hot pieces of the plane's cockpit shot low over their heads, lodging in the barricade all around them like darts smacking into a corkboard.

As they clambered back to their feet, they saw movement, saw three shadows climb out from the air vent *underneath* Marine One.

'*There!*' Boa pointed.

One of the shadows ran out from beneath the President's helicopter, while the other two slithered up through a hatch in its underbelly.

A moment later, Marine One's engines roared to life.

Its tail boom folded into place from its stowed position, as did its rotor blades. No sooner were the rotor blades extended than they began to rotate, despite the fact that the President's helicopter was still attached to its towing vehicle.

Gunfire erupted as the lone Marine who had dashed out from underneath the chopper—Love Machine—*disengaged* the cockroach attached to its tail and climbed inside the towing vehicle's tiny driver's cabin.

'What the fuck . . . ?' Kurt Logan said as the cockroach skidded out from behind Marine One and swung *around* the elevator platform, heading directly for the 7th Squadron men guarding the Football.

'Open fire,' Logan said to Boa and his men. 'Open fire now.'

They did.

A barrage of P-90 fire assaulted the speeding towing vehicle's windscreen, shattering it.

Inside the driver's cabin, Love Machine ducked below the dashboard. Bullets tore into the seatback behind him, sending the fluffy innards of the seat showering everywhere.

The cockroach careered across the hangar, bouncing wildly, taking fire.

Then suddenly, behind it, Marine One rose into the air—inside the hangar—the deafening *thump-thump-thump* of its rotor blades reverberating off the walls, drowning out all other sound.

Inside its cockpit, Gant worked the controls while Elvis hit switches everywhere.

'Elvis! Give me missiles!' she shouted. 'And whatever you do, don't hit the Football, okay!'

Elvis slammed his finger down on a launch button.

Shoom!

A Hellfire missile shot out from a pod mounted on the side of the Presidential helicopter, a finger of smoke extending through the air behind it, the missile shooting at tremendous speed toward the internal building on the eastern side of the hangar.

The missile hit the exact centre of the building—right above the Bravo troops guarding the Football—and detonated.

The middle section of the internal building blasted outwards in a shower of glass and plasterboard. A section of the glassed-in upper level collapsed to the ground behind the Bravo men guarding the Football.

The 7th Squadron commandos leapt clear of the falling debris—only to have to roll again a split-second later to avoid a second source of danger: the oncoming cockroach driven by Love Machine.

It was chaos.

Mayhem.

Pandemonium.

Exactly as Schofield had planned.

Schofield watched the confusion from his position inside the destroyed AWACS plane. His watch read:

8:27:50

8:27:51

Two minutes left.

'Okay, Book, let's go.' He turned to Juliet and the President. 'You two stay here until we've checked the status of the Football. If we can get it, we'll bring it back to you. If not, you'll have to come out.'

And with that Schofield and Book II leapt down from the gaping hole at the rear of the AWACS plane and ran out into the open.

At exactly the same moment, a six-barrelled Vulcan mini-gun popped out from a compartment underneath the nose of Marine One and began spewing out a devastating stream of supermachine-gun fire.

The 7th Squadron men—already scattered every-where—were dispersed even more. Some dived behind their barricade for cover, others found shelter among the ruins of the AWACS plane and fired up at the President's helicopter.

Gant sat at the controls of Marine One as her enemy's bullets left scratches on the Lexan windshield. And the armour-plated walls of the big Sikorsky were built to withstand missile impacts, so gunfire wasn't a problem.

Beside her, Elvis was yelling, '*Yee-ha!*' as he rained hell on the 7th Squadron men with the mini-gun.

Schofield and Book II ran eastward, sidestepping quickly toward the 7th Squadron men guarding the Football.

They moved in tandem, guns up, firing—*bizarrely*—at Love Machine's runaway cockroach and up at Marine One.

The fact that they were firing at their own people was probably best explained by the fact that they were dressed in the black fatigues, black body armour and half-face gas-masks of the 7th Squadron—slightly damaged uniforms they had pilfered from the dead Air Force commandos in the decompression area down on Level 4.

Schofield and Book danced sideways, edging toward the barricade in front of the Football, firing hard at their own men—but missing woefully.

They reached the barricade, and Schofield immediately saw the Football on the chair.

Then he saw the tether.

'Damn it!'

The presidential briefcase was anchored to a tie-down

stud on the floor by a thick metal cord. It looked like titanium thread.

Watch.

8:28:59

8:29:00

'Shit,' Schofield keyed his wrist mike. 'Janson! The Football's tethered to the floor. We can't move it. You're going to have to bring the President out into the open.'

'*Okay,*' came the reply.

'Fox! Love Machine! I need another thirty seconds of mayhem! Then you know what to do.'

Fox's voice: '*Whatever you say, Scarecrow!*'

Love Machine: '*Roger that, Boss!*'

And then Schofield saw Janson and the President leap out from the rear section of the AWACS plane—also dressed in full 7th Squadron attire and brandishing pistols, which they fired determinedly at Love Machine's cockroach.

Janson fired her SIG-Sauer with a firm two-handed grip. The President wasn't as fluid, but he did all right for a guy who'd never served in the military.

Marine One banked in a wide circle around the enormous hangar, drawing fire, the roar of its speed-blurred rotor blades thunderous in the enclosed space.

Love Machine's towing vehicle swung past the barricade protecting the Football, then veered left, heading north, *smashing* through some broken pieces of the AWACS plane and then disappearing behind it.

From the first-floor control room of the internal building, Caesar Russell watched the chaos unfolding below him.

He saw the Presidential helicopter performing death-defying passes *inside the enclosed hangar!* He saw the speeding cockroach blasting through the remains of the AWACS plane on the elevator platform.

And he saw his own men—scattered and dispersed— firing wildly at both of these two crazy threats, as if they had been prepared for any ordered attack but not a totally insane one.

'Goddamn it!' he roared. 'Where is Charlie?'

'Still coming up in the personnel elevator, sir.'

And then, in an instant of total clarity, as he watched his men down on the hangar floor, Caesar saw him, and his jaw dropped.

'No . . .'

Caesar watched in stunned amazement as one of his own men raced over to the Football—which, of course, was still *surrounded* by a few men from Bravo Unit, all of them facing outwards—pulled off one of his black leather gloves, and under the watchful eye of three other black-clad impostors, moved his hand toward the palm-print analyser inside the steel briefcase.

Schofield's watch ticked ever forward.

8:29:31

8:29:32

Amid the roar of the rampaging helicopter and the cacophony of gunfire all around him, and guarded by Schofield, Book II and Juliet Janson, the President stepped up to the Football.

He yanked off his glove, took a final look around himself, and then, as he strode past the Football, he inconspicuously placed his hand on the palm-print analyser, just as the countdown timer on its display hit 0:24.

The briefcase beeped and the timer instantly ticked over from 0:24 to 90:00 and started counting down again.

When Schofield saw that the deed was done, he and Book II fell into step alongside Juliet and the President.

'Remember, guns up and firing,' he said. He held his wrist mike to his lips, 'Fox, Elvis, Love Machine: get out of here. We'll meet you downstairs. Mother, the platform. *Now*.'

Mother stood inside the enormous hangar doorway down on Level 1, looking up into the elevator shaft.

Two hundred feet above her, she could see the underside of the massive aircraft platform, beyond which she could hear the sounds of the battle.

She hit the call button, and immediately the giant elevator platform high above her jolted sharply and slowly began to descend.

Up in the main hangar, the shattered remains of the AWACS plane—and the platform on which they stood—began to disappear into the floor.

The elevator was going down.

Schofield, Book II, Juliet and the President charged toward it, firing up at Marine One as they did so—acting like good 7th Squadron soldiers.

In the control room overlooking the hangar, Caesar grabbed a microphone.

'Boa! Logan! The President is there! He walked right in

among you and hit the analyser and now he's heading for the elevator platform. For Christ's sake, he's wearing one of *our own goddamn uniforms!*'

In the main hangar, Kurt Logan spun around where he stood, and he saw them—saw four 7th Squadron people leaping down onto the slowly descending elevator platform, now completely ignoring Marine One and the runaway cockroach.

'The platform!' he yelled. 'Bravo Unit! Converge on the platform! Alpha, take out the helicopter and kill that fucking cockroach!'

Marine One was already swooping toward the ground again—her diversionary mission accomplished.

Gant landed the big chopper right where she had found it—over the air vent in the floor on the western side of the elevator shaft—and with Elvis's help, she manoeuvred the big bird around so that her floor hatch stopped directly above the ventilation shaft.

Once the helicopter was stopped, she leapt out of the pilot's seat and headed for the floor hatch, while Elvis dashed for the rear left-hand door and threw it open for Love Machine.

Love Machine was in a world of pain.

His Volvo towing vehicle wasn't as bulletproof as Marine One and he was taking all kinds of shit from the 7th Squadron men.

Tyres squealed, bullets impacted, glass shattered.

And now he had to get over to Marine One.

His biggest problem, however, was that he had just swung his cockroach around for another pass at the 7th Squadron men on the *eastern* side of the platform when Schofield's call had come in.

He was now on the *other* side of the shaft from Marine One, heading northward, and the elevator platform—now sinking slowly into the shaft—was no longer there to drive on.

He'd have to go around.

More bullets hit his cockroach as three 7th Squadron commandos appeared right in front of him and assailed his vehicle with a harrowing wave of gunfire.

Bullets riddled the driver's compartment.

Two slugs slammed into Love Machine's left shoulder, spraying blood.

Love Machine roared.

A separate volley hit both of his front tyres and they punctured loudly, and suddenly he was skidding out of control, sliding precariously close to the edge of the elevator shaft and the now ten-foot drop to the slowly descending platform.

Somehow, he didn't fall into the shaft. Instead, he bounced across the north-eastern corner of the great square hole, shooting past the 7th Squadron men who had hammered him with gunfire, and slammed at tremendous speed into the remains of Nighthawk Two, which still sat near the northern wall of the hangar—attached to its own towing vehicle, its cockpit blasted open—right where Book II had left it ninety minutes earlier.

*

Elvis saw the crash from his position inside Marine One, saw Love Machine's cockroach plough into Nighthawk Two and lurch to a thunderous halt, the brick-like towing vehicle half-buried in the helicopter's crumpled side.

And then he saw the three 7th Squadron men rushing toward the crashed cockroach.

'Oh, no . . . ' he breathed.

Meanwhile, Schofield, Book II, Juliet and the President—still dressed in their black 7th Squadron uniforms—were fighting their own unique kind of battle.

Since it was now descending into the square-shaped shaft, the aircraft elevator platform had effectively become a great walled pit, the four walls of the shaft bounding it on every side. And with the remains of the AWACS plane still strewn about the platform, it was also now a twisted steel maze.

Seven members of Bravo Unit moved among the pieces of the plane, searching for them, hunting them.

Schofield guided his people along the eastern edge of the platform, leading the way, hurdling broken pieces of plane, eyes watchful for the enemy, but searching the floor for something else, something he had planted—

There.

The broken section of wing was right where he had left it.

Schofield hurried over to it. It was resting on the ground at the corner of the moving elevator platform, up against the northern and eastern walls. With Book II's help, he lifted the portion of wing off the elevator's floor, revealing a wide square hole in the platform.

The hole was about ten feet square. It was that part of the platform that usually housed the detachable mini-elevator.

Right now, the detachable section of the elevator platform lay about fifteen feet *below* them, further down the shaft—nestled in the corner, unmoving, waiting for them.

By placing the broken section of wing over the top of it earlier, Schofield had ensured that the 7th Squadron didn't know this exit existed.

It was their escape route.

'Love Machine! You still alive?' Elvis yelled into his mike from the cockpit of Marine One.

'Aw, fuck . . .' came the pained reply.

'Can you move?'

'Get out of here, man. I'm gone. I'm hit and my ankle was busted in the crash—'

'We don't leave anyone behind,' another voice said firmly over the same frequency.

It was Schofield's voice.

'Elvis. You and Fox get clear. I'm closer—I'll take care of Love Machine. Love Machine, sit tight. I'm coming for you.'

On the downward-moving elevator platform, Schofield spun and looked upwards.

'What are you doing?' Book II asked.

'I'm going to get Love Machine,' he said, eyeing the destroyed fuselage of the AWACS plane above him. It was still tilted sharply forward—nose down, ass up. The elevated rear section of the plane was still above the rim of the hangar floor. But not for long. Soon the downward movement of the platform would bring it below the rim.

'Take the President down,' he said to Book II and Juliet.

'What are you going to do?' Juliet said.

'I'm going to get my man,' Schofield said. 'I'll meet you downstairs.'

With that he took off into the twisted metal forest around them.

Book II and Juliet could only watch him go. And then they set about their own task of leaping down to the detachable mini-elevator in the shaft below them.

Schofield ran.

Up the steeply sloping left-hand wing of the destroyed AWACS plane.

He reached the top of the wing, then used some dents in the side of the fuselage to climb up onto the battered plane's roof. It was then that he was spotted by two of the Bravo Unit men on the platform below him.

Their P-90 assault rifles erupted.

But Schofield never stopped moving. He just kept running, dancing up the slanted roof of the plane, heading aft—toward the point where the rear section of the downward-moving plane was about to swing past the rim of the shaft.

He hit the rear edge of the plane's roof *just as* it swooped past the rim and he jumped—diving forward, leaping full-stretch—and landed with a thud, face-first, out of the line of fire, on the main hangar's shiny concrete floor, twenty feet away from Love Machine's crashed cockroach.

He looked up just in time to see the three 7th Squadron commandos arrive at the cockroach's door.

Love Machine sighed as he saw the muzzle of a P-90 assault rifle appear a few inches in front of his face.

The features of the 7th Squadron commando holding the gun were obscured by the soldier's half-faced gas-mask, but the man's eyes weren't covered. They glinted with satisfaction.

Love Machine closed his eyes, waited for the end.

Blam!

No end.

Confused, he opened his eyes again—to see his executioner, now with only half a head, sway unsteadily on his feet, and then fall in a kind of stunned slow motion to the ground.

The other two commandos spun instantly, only to be cut down by a ferocious volley of semi-automatic pistol fire. They were hurled out of view and then to Love Machine's complete surprise, he saw, standing in their place—

The Scarecrow.

Dressed in his black 7th Squadron clothing.

'Come on,' Schofield said. 'Let's get you out of here.'

Book II landed on the non-skid deck of the mini-elevator, next to Juliet and the President, eight feet below the downward-moving main platform.

It was dark down here, in the shadow of the principal platform.

As soon as they were all on the detachable deck, Juliet hit a button on a small console built into its floor.

The detachable deck began to glide quickly down the side of the shaft, travelling on its own set of wall-mounted rails, moving faster than the gigantic main platform above it.

Pulling away.

Schofield began to haul Love Machine out of the cockroach.

As he did so, he saw several weapons strewn about the exploded-open cockpit of Nighthawk Two—a couple of MP-10s, some grenades, a chunky .44 calibre 'Desert Eagle' semi-automatic pistol, and, most pleasing of all for Schofield, two gun-like weapons, still in their black-leather back-holsters, that must have spilled out of

Nighthawk Two's weapons cabinet when it had been blown apart earlier.

They looked like high-tech Tommy guns, each possessed of a short stubby barrel and two handgrips. Sticking out of each gun's barrel, however, was a chrome grappling hook with a bulbous magnetic head.

It was the famous Armalite MH-12 Maghook, a grappling hook which also contained a high-powered magnet for adhesion to sheer metallic surfaces.

'Oh, *yes* . . . ' Schofield said, grabbing the two Maghooks and handing one of them to Love Machine. He also grabbed an MP-10, and the big Desert Eagle pistol, which he shoved into his belt—

Ping!

At that moment, the doors to the nearby personnel elevator abruptly opened—

—*revealing ten fully-armed 7th Squadron men!*

Python Willis and the men of Charlie Unit.

Python's eyes nearly popped out of his head when he saw Schofield standing so close and dressed in 7th Squadron attire.

His men raised their P-90s instantly.

'Oh, *shit*,' Schofield said as he shoved Love Machine back into the cockroach's driver's compartment and clambered in there with him as a volley of bullets slammed into the cockroach's frame.

Schofield jammed the stick into reverse—hoped to God it would still go—and planted the gas pedal to the floor.

The cockroach squealed off the mark, its rear tyres smoking, shooting backwards out of the wreck of Nighthawk Two, impact sparks chasing it across the floor.

The cockroach rushed across the hangar floor in

reverse, narrowly missing the edge of the elevator shaft as it rocketed toward the now-abandoned barricade on the eastern side of the shaft.

Schofield turned in his seat as he drove—saw the barricade rushing toward him a second too late.

He hit the brakes and the big three-ton towing vehicle did a wild 180-degree spin. The front end of the cockroach came swinging around like a baseball bat and took out the barricade with one devastating swipe, sending crates and Samsonite containers flying everywhere.

The cockroach jolted to a halt.

In its driver's compartment, Schofield lurched forward. When he looked up to see where he was, he was surprised to see that, right next to his door, not three feet away, stood the chair upon which sat the President's briefcase—the Football.

Holy shit.

The briefcase's handgrip was still tethered to the floor by the length of superstrong titanium cord, but now, since the President had successfully reset its ninety-minute timer, it had been abandoned by the 7th Squadron men, rightfully assuming that the President's sole objective was now to get out.

So now the Football just sat there, alone, completely unguarded.

Schofield saw the opportunity, and took it.

He leapt out of the driver's compartment and slid to the floor beside the Football.

The men of Charlie Unit were charging across the hangar, guns blazing, pummelling the exposed rump of the cockroach with a million rounds of lead.

Sheltered by the big towing vehicle, Schofield brought

one of the tiny 7th Squadron Lock-Blasters out of his pocket, attached it to the tie-down stud in the floor that held the Football to the ground, hit the activate button, and dived away.

One, one-thousand . . .

Two, one-thousand . . .

Three—

The blast was short and sharp.

With a loud *crack!* the tie-down stud broke free from the floor, and suddenly the Football—with the length of titanium cord still attached to it—was free.

Schofield scooped it up and dived back into the cab of the cockroach, just as the first 7th Squadron men arrived.

Two of them leapt up onto the back of the cockroach, landing on it at the exact same moment that Schofield floored the accelerator and the cockroach took off, the sudden lurch of motion sending one of the commandos falling ass-over-head off the back of the towing vehicle.

The second man had better reflexes. He discarded his P-90, giving himself an extra hand, and somehow managed to hang on to the roof of the speeding vehicle.

Schofield swung the cockroach around the southern side of the enormous elevator shaft—tyres squealing, engine roaring, and now with an extra passenger on its back.

He saw Marine One up ahead, standing on the western side of the shaft, its rotor blades still turning.

That was where he wanted to go. Pull alongside Marine One, race inside it and then leap down into its floor hatch and escape into the ventilation shaft below it.

But his hopes were dashed when he saw the three black-clad men from Alpha Unit appear from the other side of the Presidential helicopter, guns up.

Ready for him.

But for some reason, they didn't fire.

Why weren't they fi—?

With shocking suddenness, the small rear window of the driver's compartment behind Schofield's head exploded all around him, showering Schofield and Love Machine with glass, and a pair of black-gloved hands appeared on either side of Schofield's head, one of them brandishing a knife!

It was the 7th Squadron commando on the back of the cockroach. With his head held above the driver's compartment, he was reaching in with his hands to kill Schofield.

On a reflex, Schofield grabbed the man's knife-hand, while the assassin's other hand clutched madly at his face.

They were still rushing toward Marine One, the cockroach—its two front tyres punctured, its driver fighting for his life—carooming wildly across the shiny hangar floor.

Grappling with the commando behind him, Schofield saw Marine One ahead of them, saw its rapidly spinning vertical tail rotor, a blurring circle of motion about six feet off the ground, a few inches higher than the roof of the cockroach . . .

Schofield didn't miss a beat.

He threw the fast-moving cockroach into a skid, fishtailing the big vehicle sideways—sliding it *underneath* the tail rotor of Marine One, so that the buzz-saw-like blades of the vertical rotor passed low over the cockroach's roof.

Then he heard the commando behind him scream in terror before—abruptly—the yell was cut short as the tail rotor sheared the commando's head clean off his body and a shocking waterfall of blood gushed down from the roof of the driver's compartment.

The three men of Alpha Unit standing near Marine One hurled themselves clear of the sliding towing vehicle as it shot beneath the tail boom of the President's helicopter.

The cockroach emerged on the other side of the chopper, skidding to a sideways halt, so that now the bullet-battered towing vehicle was facing the great square hole that was the elevator shaft.

Schofield saw the yawning shaft before him—with its wide hydraulic platform inside it, still making its ponderous descent; saw the AWACS plane's flying-saucer-like rotodome about ten feet below the floorline.

He revved the engine.

Love Machine saw what he was thinking.

'You are *out* of your *mind*, Captain.'

'Whatever works,' Schofield said. 'Hang on.'

He gunned it.

The cockroach shot forward, rear tyres squealing, rushed toward the edge of the shaft.

Speed is everything, Schofield thought as he drove. He needed enough forward velocity so that the cockroach would reach the . . .

The cockroach rushed toward the rim.

Bullet sparks exploded all around it.

Schofield drove hard.

Then the cockroach hit the edge of the elevator shaft and launched itself out into the air . . .

The cockroach soared—wheels spinning, nose high.

Then, as it fell, its forward bumper began to droop and it resumed the appearance of three tons of steel that was never intended to fly.

By this time, the elevator platform had descended about thirty feet below floor-line, but the body of the destroyed AWACS plane—and its intact rotodome— made the fall for the soaring cockroach only about ten feet.

The cockroach landed—*smash!*—right on top of the AWACS plane's downward-slanted rotodome.

The rotodome, titanium-based and very rigid, resisted the downward energy of the falling vehicle valiantly.

Its support struts, however, did not.

They buckled instantly, snapping like twigs, as did the body of the aeroplane underneath the rotodome.

The AWACS's cylindrical fuselage just *crumpled* like an aluminium can under the weight of the falling towing vehicle, effectively cushioning the roach's fall.

The rotodome was driven down into the fuselage, creating a ramp-like effect which allowed Schofield's cockroach to skip off the other side of the plane and bounce down onto its destroyed left-hand wing.

Schofield and Love Machine were thrown about like rag dolls as the cockroach bounced and jounced and thundered forward.

Somehow, Schofield managed to hit the brakes and the cockroach skidded and spun, before slamming to an abrupt halt against the far wall of the shaft, right next to the square-shaped hole that normally housed the detachable mini-elevator.

Schofield was already moving when the cockroach stopped, helping Love Machine out of the driver's cabin just as the first 7th Squadron men emerged from the twisted steel forest around them and opened fire.

But their bullets were too slow.

Indeed, they could only watch in stunned amazement as Schofield handed Love Machine the Football, draped the wounded man's arms over his shoulders, and without even a blink, jumped with Love Machine down into the hole in the platform, disappearing into the blackness beneath it.

Like a pair of tandem skydivers, Schofield and Love Machine dropped down the side of the massive elevator shaft, dwarfed by its immense size.

As instructed, Love Machine gripped Schofield's shoulders as hard as he could—holding onto the Football as he did so. That didn't stop him screaming '*Arrrrrgghh!!!*' all the way down.

The grey concrete wall rushed past them as they freefell down the side of the shaft.

As he dropped, Schofield looked down and saw a square of white light stretching out from the hangar on Level 1, illuminating the tiny mini-elevator platform stopped there—two hundred feet below.

He unholstered his newly-acquired Maghook, snapped open its grappling hook.

He couldn't fire it up at the underside of the main platform. Maghooks only had one hundred and fifty feet of rope. It wouldn't be long enough.

No, he had to wait until they dropped about fifty feet, and then—

As he dropped past it, Schofield lodged the Maghook's grappling hook into a metal bracket sticking out from the greasy concrete wall. The bracket kept a series of thick cables running down the side of the shaft bundled together.

As the Maghook gripped the bracket, Schofield and Love Machine continued to fall, the hook's rope playing out above them, unspooling rapidly, wobbling through the air.

The mini-elevator's deck rushed up toward them at shocking speed.

Faster, faster, faster . . .

Jolt.

And they stopped, *three feet* above the mini-elevator's deck, in front of the massive doorway that led into the Level 1 hangar bay.

Schofield released his grip on a black button on the Maghook's forward grip—it was a trigger that initiated a clamping mechanism that bit into the Maghook's unspooling rope. He'd hit it just in time. He and Love Machine were lowered the final three feet.

Their boots touched the ground and they turned to find that they had company.

Standing in front of them just inside the hangar bay doors were Book II, Juliet and the President. With them were Mother, Brainiac and the scientist, Herbie Franklin.

'If anybody makes a joke about "dropping in",' Mother said, 'I will personally rip that person's throat out.'

'We have to keep moving,' Schofield said when he'd reeled in his Maghook. The giant aircraft elevator was still lumbering down the shaft above them—with its cargo of 7th Squadron commandos.

Schofield's group headed for the vehicle ramp at the far end of the enormous underground hangar bay, Book II and Mother carrying the wounded Love Machine between them.

Juliet Janson came alongside Schofield. 'So, now what?'

'We've got the President,' he said. 'And we've got the Football. Since the Football was the only thing keeping the President here, I say we ditch this party. That means finding a networked terminal. We use the computer to open up an exit during the next hourly window period and then we get out of Dodge.

'Doctor Franklin,' he turned as they all started down the circular vehicle access ramp. 'Where's the nearest security computer? Something that will open up an exit during the next window period.'

Herbie said, 'There are two on this level—one in the hangar's office, the other in the junction box.'

'Not here,' Schofield said. 'The bad guys'll be here any minute.'

'Then the nearest one is on 4, in the decompression area down there.'

'Then that's where we're going.'

A woman's voice came through Schofield's earpiece as he moved: *'Scarecrow, this is Fox. We are at the bottom of the ventilation shaft. What do you want us to do?'*

'Can you cut across the bottom of the aircraft elevator shaft?'

'Yeah, I think so.'

'Meet us in the Level 4 lab,' Schofield said into his wrist mike.

'Got it. Oh, and Scarecrow, we—uh—picked up a couple of new passengers.'

'Wonderful,' Schofield said. 'See you soon.'

They raced down the vehicle ramp to Level 2, where they came to an opening in the floor that accessed the emergency stairwell. The eight of them hurried down the stairs until they arrived at the heavy firedoor that led to the decompression area on Level 4.

Brainiac tested the door.

It opened easily.

Schofield was immediately worried. This was one of the doors they had locked and then disabled earlier. Now it was unlocked. He made a hand signal: 'Proceed with caution.'

Brainiac nodded.

He quickly and silently swung the door open as Book II and Mother slipped inside, an M-16 and a P-90 pressed against their respective shoulders.

No fire was necessary.

227

Aside from the bodies on the floor—from their previous encounter with the 7th Squadron here—the decompression area was empty.

Juliet and the President went in next, stepping over the bodies. Schofield followed, with Love Machine draped over his shoulder.

A couple of computer terminals sat sunk into the wall on their right, partially hidden behind the telephone-booth-sized test chambers.

'Doctor Franklin, pick a terminal,' Schofield said. 'Brainiac, go with him. Find out what we have to do to get out of this rat-maze. Book, take Love Machine. Mother, check the lab next door for a first-aid kit.'

Mother headed for the doorway leading to the other side of the floor.

Book II lowered the grimacing Love Machine to the ground, then made to shut the door behind them.

'What the hell . . . ?' he said as he looked at the door.

Schofield came over. 'What is it?'

'Look at the lock.'

Schofield did so, and his eyes narrowed.

The door's bolt mechanism—the thick rectangular part of the lock that extended out from the door and secured itself inside a matching slot in the doorframe—had been sheared off.

Cleanly.

Perfectly.

Indeed, the cut was so clean that it could only have been done by some sort of *laser* . . .

Schofield frowned.

Somebody had been through here since the battle.

'Scarecrow,' someone said.

It was Mother.

She was standing in the doorway leading to the western side of Level 4. Standing with her was Libby Gant, who had appeared from the other side of the floor.

'Scarecrow. You better see this,' Mother said.

Schofield went over to the doorway set into the white wall that divided Level 4.

He checked the lock on the door as he met Gant and Mother. Its bolt had also been sheared off with a laser cutting device.

'What is it?' he said.

He looked up and was surprised to see, standing with Gant, Colonel Hot Rod Hagerty and Nicholas Tate III, the President's slick Domestic Policy Adviser. Gant's new passengers.

Gant jerked her thumb at the area behind her—the high-ceilinged hall-like space that housed the great glass cube.

Schofield looked into it . . .

. . . and immediately felt his blood run cold.

The cube looked like a bomb had hit it.

Its clear walls lay at all angles, shattered and broken. Entire sections of glass had fallen in on the bedroom inside it, exposing the room to the outside air. Toys lay on their sides. The colourful furniture had been overturned, hurled roughly aside.

There was no sign of the boy, Kevin.

'Looks like they took a whole bunch of stuff from up in the lab, too,' Gant said. 'The entire area has been ransacked.'

Schofield bit his lip in thought as he looked at the scene before him.

He didn't want to say it. Didn't even want to think it. But there was no denying it now.

'There's someone else in here,' he said.

The language was Afrikaans.

The official language of the white regime that had ruled South Africa up until 1994, but which now, for obvious reasons, was no longer the country's official language.

After consulting with the DIA's two African language specialists, Dave Fairfax now had all of his recorded conversations translated and ready for presentation to the Director.

He looked at the transcript again and smiled. It read:

COMM-SAT SECURE WIRE TRACE E/13A-2
DIA-SPACEDIV-PENT-DC
OPERATOR: T16-009
SOURCE: USAF-SA(R)07

29-MAY	**22:10:56**	**AFRIKAANS – ENGLISH**

VOICE 1: Kan bevestig dat in-enting plaasvind.   *Can confirm that vaccine is operational.*

VOICE 1: Toetse op laaste poging word   *Test on latest strain expected*
op die vier-en-twientigste   *on the third. What about*
verwag. Wat van die   *the extraction unit?*
onttrekkings eenheid?

VOICE 2: Reccondo span is   *Reccondo team has already*
alreeds weggestuur.   *been dispatched.*

VOICE 1: Voorbereidings onderweg.   *Preparations under way.*
Vroeg oggend. Beste tyd vir   *Early morning. Optimal time*
onttrekking.   *for extraction.*

VOICE 3: Everything is in place.   *Everything is in place.*
Confirm that it's the third.   *Confirm that it's the third.*

VOICE 1: Ontrekking kan 'n   *Extraction is the biggest*
probleem wees. Gestel ons   *problem.*
gebruik die Hoeb land   *Plan is to use the Hoeb land*
hier naby. Verstaan hy is 'n lid   *nearby. Member of Die*
van Die Organisasie.   *Organisasie.*

VOICE 2: Sal die instruksies oordra.   *Will pass on those instructions.*

VOICE 3: Mission is a go.   *Mission is a go.*

23-JUN   01:18:22   AFRIKAANS – ENGLISH

VOICE 1: Die Reccondos is gereed. *Reccondos are in place.*
          Verwagte aankoms by beplande *Estimate arrival at target*
          bestemming binne nege dae. *destination in nine days.*

'That is some seriously weird shit, my friend,' one of the African language experts said as he was putting on his jacket to leave. He was a short, pleasant fellow named Lew Alvy. 'I mean, Reccondo Units. Die Organisasie. Jesus.'

'What do you mean?' Fairfax asked. 'What are they?'

Alvy took a quick look around himself.

'The Reccondos,' he said, 'are the baddest of the bad when it comes to elite units. They're the South African Reconnaissance Commandos. Before Mandela, they were *the* crack assassination squad of the white regime. Specialists in cross-border raids, covert hits—usually on black resistance leaders—*trained* to be ghosts. They would never leave a trace of their presence, but you'd know they'd been there because of all the cut throats.

'Tough bastards, too. I heard once, in Zimbabwe, a squad of Reccondos lay in ambush for nineteen *days*, not moving, hiding in the veldt under heat-deflecting dirt covers, until their target arrived. The target came by, thinking the area was secure, and—*boom*—they nailed him. Some say that in the eighties they bolstered their numbers by enlisting Angolan mercenaries, but the argument became academic in 1994 when Mandela took power and the unit was disbanded in light of its previous missions. Suddenly they all became mercenaries, a crack hit squad for hire.'

'*Shit*,' Fairfax breathed. 'And Die Organisasie? What's that?'

Alvy said, 'Part myth, part reality. No-one's really sure. But MI6 has a file, so does the CIA. It's an underground organisation of exiled white South Africans who actively plot the demise of the ANC government in the hope of returning South Africa to the bad old days. Rich bastards—rich, racist bastards. Also known as the "Third Force", or the "Spider Network". Hell, it was listed last year on Interpol as an active terrorist organisation.'

Fairfax frowned as Alvy departed.

What could an ultra-rich right-wing South African organisation and an elite light commando unit possibly want with a remote US Air Force base?

Typically, Hot Rod Hagerty and Nicholas Tate went straight over to the President. Elvis, on the other hand, rushed over to check on his wounded buddy, Love Machine.

Schofield stood in the centre of the decompression area on Level 4, with Gant at his side.

Gant nodded at Hagerty and Tate. 'We found them inside Marine One, holed up inside the Presidential escape pod. Hiding.'

'He'll take command,' Schofield said.

'He *is* the ranking officer,' Gant said.

'He's never been under fire.'

'Shit.'

A few yards to their left, over by the test chambers, Brainiac and Herbie Franklin sat before a computer terminal.

Schofield stepped up behind them. 'So, what's the story?

'This is very odd,' Herbie said. 'Here, look,' he pointed at the screen. It read:

TIME	KEY ACTION	OPERATOR	SYSTEM RESPONSE
06:30:00	System status check	070-67	All systems operational
06:58:34	Lockdown command	105-02	Lockdown enacted
07:00:00	System status check	070-67	All systems operational (lockdown mode)
07:30:00	System status check	070-67	All systems operational (lockdown mode)
07:37:56	WARNING: Auxiliary power malfunction	System	Malfunction located at terminal 1-A2 Receiving no response from systems: TRACS; AUX SYS-1; RAD COM-SPHERE; MBN; EXT FAN
07:38:00	WARNING: Auxiliary power capacity: 50%	System	Terminal 1-A2 not responding
08:00:15	Main power shutdown command (terminal 3-A1)	008-72	Main power disabled
08:00:18	Auxiliary power enabled	Aux System	Auxiliary power start up
08:00:19	WARNING: Auxiliary power operational. Low power protocol enabled	Aux System	Low power protocol in effect: non-essential systems disabled
08:01:02	Lockdown special release command entered (terminal 3-A1)	008-72	Door 003-V opened

08:04:34	Lockdown special release command entered (terminal 3-A1)	008-72	Door 062-W opened
08:04:55	Lockdown special release command entered (terminal 3-A1)	008-72	Door 100-W opened
08:18:00	WARNING: Auxiliary power capacity: 35%	Aux System	Terminal 1-A2 not responding
08:21:30	Security camera system shutdown command (terminal 1-A1)	008-93	SYSTEM ERROR: Security camera system already disabled per low power protocol

'Okay,' Herbie said. 'Well, it starts out all right. Standard system checks by a local operator. Probably one of the console operators up in the main hangar on ground level. Then comes the lockdown at 6:58, keyed in by operator number 105-02. That's someone high up. A 105 prefix indicates a colonel or above. Probably Colonel Harper.

'But *then*, at 7:37, something must have happened up on Level 1. At that time nearly half the complex's auxiliary power supply went up in smoke.'

'A missile hit the junction box,' Schofield said, recalling his battle with the missile-mounted Humvees up in the Level 1 hangar bay earlier. His tone made it sound like this sort of thing happened every day.

'O-*kay*,' Herbie said. 'That would explain it. That junction box housed the auxiliary power generators. The unfortunate consequence of that, however, happened here,' he pointed at another line:

08:00:15	Main power shutdown command (terminal 3-A1)	008-72	Main power disabled

'Somebody turned off the main power supply,' Herbie said. 'That was why I couldn't disable the cameras before. See here, you can see my entry at 8:21. I'm operator 008-93.

'The problem was *somebody else*—operator number 008-72—had already turned the cameras off by shutting down the main power supply. As soon as anyone shuts off the main power, the system switches over to auxiliary power—but now, because of your missile impact, this place only has *half* its auxiliary power remaining, which as you can see, is draining fast.

'But . . . when the auxiliary power supply kicks in, the system switches off all non-essential power drains—things like excess lighting and the security camera network. That's the low power protocol that keeps getting mentioned.'

'So by cutting the power, he cut the cameras . . .' Schofield thought aloud.

'Yes.'

'He didn't want to be seen . . .'

'More than that,' Herbie said. 'Look at what he did next. He keyed in three special lockdown release codes—once at 8:01 and twice at 8:04—opening three exit doors.'

'The five-minute window period,' Schofield said.

'That's right.'

'So which doors did he open?'

'Just a second, I'll find out. ' Herbie tapped some keys. 'Now, the first one was 003-V.' A schematic diagram of the Area 7 complex came up on his screen. 'There it is. The Emergency Exit Vent.'

'And the other two?'

'062-W and 100-W . . . ' Herbie said aloud, scanning the screen. 'Door 062-W stands for door sixty-two/west. But that would mean it was part of the . . . '

'What?' Schofield said.

Herbie said, '62-West is the blast door that seals off the westward X-rail tunnel down on Level 6.'

'And the other one? 100-West?'

'It's where that X-rail tunnel ends, over by Lake Powell, about forty miles west of here. 100-West is the security door leading out to the lake.'

Brainiac asked, 'Why would he open those three doors?'

'You open the Emergency Exit Vent to let your companions in. To help you steal the booty,' Schofield said.

'And the other two doors?'

'You open them so all of you can get out.'

'So why cut the power?' Gant asked.

'To disable the security cameras,' Schofield said. 'Whoever did this didn't want the Air Force people to see him doing it.'

'See him doing what?' Brainiac said.

Schofield exchanged a look with Gant.

'See him taking the boy,' he said.

'Quickly,' Schofield said to Herbie, 'can you find out who operator number 008-72 is?'

'Sure.' Herbie began typing fast.

A moment later, he said, 'Got it.' A list appeared on his screen. Schofield scanned the list until he found the entry he was looking for:

008-72 BOTHA, Gunther W.

'Who's Gunther Botha?' Schofield asked.

'Son of a bitch,' a voice said from behind them.

It was the President. He stepped up behind Schofield's shoulder.

'Botha,' he spat. 'I should have known.'

'South African scientist, working here on the vaccine,' the President said. 'You make a deal with the Devil, and it comes back to bite you in the ass.'

'Why would he want to take the boy?'

'The Sinovirus kills both white people *and* black people, Captain,' the President said. 'Only people of Asian origin are safe from it. That boy, however, has been genetically designed to be a universal vaccine, for *both* blacks and whites. But if only white people are given the vaccine, then only white people would survive an outbreak of the Sinovirus. And if Botha is working for who I think he's working for . . . '

'So what do we do now?' Herbie said.

'We go after the boy,' Schofield said instantly. 'And we—'

'*No, you do not*, Captain,' Hot Rod Hagerty said, appearing suddenly behind Schofield. 'You will stay here and you will guard the President.'

'But . . . '

'In case you haven't been paying attention, if the President dies, so does America. One little boy can wait. I think it's time you got your priorities straight, Captain Schofield.'

'But we can't just leave him—'

'Yes, we can, and yes we will,' Hagerty said, his face reddening. 'In case you have forgotten, *Captain*, I am your superior officer, and I am now ordering you to obey me. The United States government pays me to do the thinking for you. So this is what you will think: your country is more important than the life of one little boy.'

Schofield didn't move a muscle. 'I wouldn't want to

240

live in a country that leaves a little boy to die . . . '

Hagerty's eyes blazed. '*No. From now on, you will do as I say, how I say, and when I say*—'

The President himself seemed about to interfere when Schofield stepped forward, right in front of Hagerty.

'No, *sir*,' he said firmly, 'I will not follow you. Because if you'd waited for me to finish what I was going to say earlier, you would have heard me say: "We go after the boy, *and we take the President with us*". Because in case *you* haven't been paying attention, that Botha guy and whoever's with him opened up an *exit* to this place! They've given us a way out.'

Hagerty fell silent, grinding his teeth.

'Now, if you don't mind,' Schofield said, 'and if nobody else has any better ideas, what do you say we all get the hell out of this place.'

Up in the control room overlooking the main hangar, Caesar Russell's four radio operators were working overtime.

'—main power's down, no cameras operational at all. All systems running on auxiliary power supply—'

'—Sir, someone's initiated the lockdown release codes. The western X-rail door has been opened—'

'Who?' Caesar Russell asked pointedly.

The console operator frowned. 'It looks like it was Professor Botha, sir.'

'Botha,' Caesar said quietly. 'How predictable.'

'Sir,' another operator said, 'I have movement on the X-rail system. Someone heading westward toward the canyons—'

'Oh, Gunther. You couldn't help yourself, could you? You're trying to snatch the boy,' Caesar smiled sadly. 'What's the ETA on that X-rail train at the lake?'

'Forty miles of track at one hundred and seventy miles per hour. About fourteen minutes, sir.'

'Get Bravo down to Level 6 on the double, to pursue Botha on the X-rail. Then open the top door and send

Charlie out in the AH-77s to cut him off at the lake—we'll get him from in front and behind. Now go. Go. Although Gunther could never know it, we *need* that boy. This will all be for nothing if we don't have that child.'

Schofield, Mother, Gant and Book II flew down the fire stairs at full speed.

Schofield ran with his Desert Eagle held out in front of him. The Football now dangled from his waist, its hand-grip attached to a clip on his 7th Squadron combat webbing.

Behind them came the President and Juliet, Herbie the scientist, Hot Rod Hagerty and Nicholas Tate. Bringing up the rear were Elvis and Brainiac, carrying Love Machine between them.

They came to the Level 6 doorway. Frank Cutler's bloodied and broken body still lay on the floor beside it.

'Be careful,' Juliet said to Schofield as he put his hand on the doorknob. 'This was where they got us before.'

Schofield nodded.

Then—quickly, silently—he whipped open the door, and took cover.

There was no sound.

No gunshots went off.

No bullets whistled into the stairwell.

'Holy *Christ*!' Mother said, as she looked beyond the doorway.

The massive aircraft elevator lumbered down the shaft.

On its back, amid the pieces of the destroyed AWACS plane, stood the ten men of Bravo Unit. They were moving down through the complex, heading for Level 6, in pursuit of Gunther Botha and the boy.

The gigantic elevator platform rumbled down the shaft, the dirty grey concrete walls sliding past the Beta Unit men.

They swung by Level 3, moving downward . . . then Level 4 . . . then—

—the elevator platform *plunged into water*!

As it came to Level 5, the cell block level, the elevator platform rushed down into a wide body of water that had formed at the bottom of the shaft. Several tons of water immediately gushed onto the platform, slithering in amongst the pieces of the crumpled AWACS plane.

'Goddamn!' the leader of Bravo Unit, Boa McConnell, exclaimed as the water rushed up to his waist.

He reached for his radio mike.

*

'—Bravo Unit reports substantial flooding on Level 5. It's starting to fill the main elevator shaft. Only access to Level 6 is via the eastern firestairs or the western ventilation shaft. Bravo is going for the ventilation shaft—'

'—Sir. That enhanced satellite image of the Emergency Escape Vent is coming through now.'

A sheet of high-gloss paper edged out of a nearby printer. A radio operator tore it clear, checked the timecode at the top. 'This one's from ten minutes ago. Another one coming through—*what the fuck*—?'

'What is it?' Caesar Russell said, taking the printout from the operator. Russell recalled the subject of the satellite scans: the twenty-four rod-like objects that had been picked up on the infra-red satellite earlier, the ones that had been fanned out in a wide circle around the EEV.

Caesar's eyes narrowed.

The enhanced satellite image showed a few of the 'rods' very clearly. They weren't rods at all.

They were combat boots—sticking out from underneath heat-deflecting covers.

The second satellite scan came through. Caesar grabbed it. It was more recent than the first. Only a minute old.

It showed the same image as the first scan: the Emergency Exit Vent and the desert floor around it.

Only now the cluster of combat boots surrounding the Vent was nowhere in sight.

They were gone.

'Mmmm, *very* clever, Gunther,' Caesar said softly. 'You brought the Reccondos with you.'

There were bodies everywhere.

Christ, Schofield thought. *It looked like a war had been fought down here.*

He wasn't far wrong.

Level 6 resembled a subway station—with a central elevated concrete platform, flanked on either side by train tracks. Like a regular train station, at both ends of the extremely elongated space were a pair of train tunnels that disappeared into darkness. Unlike a regular train station, however, three of those four tunnels were sealed off by heavy grey-steel blast doors.

On the central platform lay nine corpses, all dressed in suits.

The nine members of the Secret Service's Primary Advance Team.

Their bodies lay at all angles, bathed in blood, their suits ripped to shreds by the penetration of countless bullets.

Beyond them, however, lay *another* set of bodies—ten of them—all dressed in black combat clothing.

7th Squadron men.

All dead.

Three of them lay spread-eagled on the platform, with enormous star-shaped holes in their chests. Exit wounds. It seemed that these men had been shot in their backs as they'd clambered up onto the platform from the right-hand railway track, their ribcages exploding outwards with the sudden gaseous expansion of the hollow-pointed bullets that had hit them.

More 7th Squadron men lay sprawled on the track itself, in various states of bloodiness. Three of them, Schofield saw, bore very precise bullet holes in their foreheads.

Four of the 7th Squadron commandos, however, had not been shot.

They lay slumped next to a steel door sunk into the wall of the right-hand track—the entrance to the Emergency Exit Vent.

Their throats had been slit from ear to ear.

They had been the first to die, Schofield thought, *when their assailants had emerged from the vent behind them.*

Schofield stepped out from the stairwell doorway, onto the platform.

The underground station was empty.

It was then that he saw them.

They sat on either side of the central platform, one to each track: X-rail engines.

'Whoa,' he breathed.

X-rail systems are high-speed underground railway systems used by the US military for equipment delivery and transport. X-rail engines—or 'railcars' as they are known—move so fast that they require *four* railway tracks for stability: two tracks on the ground and two fastened to the ceiling above the railcar.

The X-railcars that Schofield saw now *exuded* power and speed.

They were about sixty feet long—about the size of regular subway carriages—but their sleek curves and sharp pointed noses were quite clearly designed for one purpose: to slice through the air at tremendous speed.

Each train's design was based on that of the most well-known high-speed train in the world, the Japanese Bullet Train. A steeply slanted nose, aerodynamically grooved sides, even a couple of wing-like canards jutting out from the bow of each train were all included as part of the relentless pursuit of speed.

The X-rail train to Schofield's left was actually made up of *two* carriages connected by way of an accordion-like passageway. The two railcars were positioned back-to-back, their sharpened noses pointed in opposite directions. Both engines were painted glistening white, so that they looked like a pair of space shuttles connected tail-to-tail.

It was only when Schofield saw their struts, however, that he realised why the system was called an 'X'-rail.

Jutting out from both the front and rear edges of each engine, swept back like the wings of a fast-flying bird, were four elongated struts, which when seen from head-on would look like an 'X'. The lower struts reached down to the wide railway-like tracks beneath the railcar, while the upper struts reached up to an identical pair of tracks attached to the ceiling of the tunnel. All the struts, top and bottom, were contoured like aeroplane wings to allow for maximum speed.

Nestled up against the blast door behind the double-engined train was a smaller type of X-rail vehicle—a kind of miniature car that was barely a third the size of the longer engines. It was little more than a round two-person cockpit mounted in the centre of a set of four struts.

'Maintenance vehicle,' Herbie said. 'Used for tunnel upkeep and cleaning. Faster than the bigger engines, but it only holds two.'

'Now why don't they have *these* on the New York subway?' Elvis said, eyeing the double-engined X-rail train.

'Hey, over there,' Brainiac said, pointing at the open tunnel door at the far end of the left-hand railway track. It was the only tunnel that wasn't sealed off by a blast door.

'That's door 62-West,' Herbie Franklin said. 'That's how they got out.'

'Then that's where we're going,' Schofield said.

They all hurried for the twin-engined X-rail train, dashing out into the open, halfway down the length of the station's platform.

Schofield reached the forward engine's side door and hit a button. With a soft *shoosh*, all the side doors of the two railcars—two doors per car—slid open.

Schofield stood inside the lead railcar's forward doorway, the Football hanging from his waist, as he ushered the others inside. Book II dashed in first, headed straight for the driver's cabin, Herbie close behind him.

The President and Juliet came next, rushing in through the lead car's rear doorway. They were flanked by Gant and Mother, and followed by Hot Rod Hagerty and Nick Tate—always keen to stay close to the President.

Trailing last of all, still making their way across the platform, were Elvis and Brainiac with the wounded Love Machine draped between them.

'Elvis! Brainiac! Pick it up! Come on!'

Schofield looked back into the interior of the railcar. The inside of the car looked like a cross between a standard subway carriage and a freight car. It had a few rows of passenger seats near the back, and a wide open empty space near the front for cargo boxes and the like to be stored.

Schofield saw the President over by the rear door, about forty feet away, slumping into a passenger seat in exhaustion.

And then it happened.

Completely without warning.

One moment, Schofield was looking down the interior of the railcar, looking at the seated figure of the President; the next, *every single window* on the platform side of the railcar just exploded, glass spraying inwards under the weight of a shocking amount of automatic gunfire, blasting tiny shards of glass all over the inside of the carriage.

More gunfire followed—loud, relentless, booming. It impacted hard against the right-hand flank of the X-rail engine, so hard in fact that it caused the entire carriage to shudder violently.

Schofield ducked, shielding his face from the rain of flying glass. Then he spun and peered out through the shattered window beside him—

—and saw a phalanx of 7th Squadron commandos come leaping out of the air vent at the far *western* end of the platform, armed with P-90 rifles and a couple of devastating six-barrelled mini-guns.

The mini-guns whirred, spewing out an unbelievable storm of bullets, pummelling the side of the railcar.

'You okay?' Schofield yelled to Juliet and the President, his voice barely audible above the thunderous gunfire.

The President, now lying face-down on the floor, nodded feebly in reply.

'Stay down!' Schofield called.

Abruptly, the X-rail engine beneath them roared to life.

Schofield snapped around to see Book II and Herbie in the driver's compartment, flicking switches, pushing throttles. The railcar's power system thrummed loudly, warming up.

Let's go, Schofield thought anxiously. *Let's go . . .*

And then suddenly a voice exploded in his earpiece: '*Hey!* Wait for us!'

It was Elvis.

Elvis, Brainiac and Love Machine were still out on the platform.

Lagging behind the others under Love Machine's weight, they hadn't been able to make it to the two connected railcars by the time the 7th Squadron commandos had appeared at the other end of the underground station.

Now they were pinned down behind a concrete pillar, only ten feet away from the rearmost door of the second railcar, the area all around them shredded by the 7th Squadron's brutal mini-gun fire.

'All right! We have to move! Get ready!' Elvis yelled. 'Okay, now!'

They burst out from their position. Bullets slammed into the pillars all around them. Chunks of concrete flew everywhere. Two bullets blasted clean through Elvis's left shoulder.

251

'Come on, Love Machine, stay with us!' he yelled.

They reached the rear door of the second railcar, began to shove Love Machine inside it when—

Smack!

Love Machine's head jolted violently to the left, snapping at an unnatural angle, smacking hard against the side of Elvis's shoulder.

'Oh, man,' Brainiac said, seeing it. 'No.'

Elvis turned.

Love Machine's head lolled lifelessly against his shoulder, a goopy syrup of brains and blood dripping slowly out of a bullet hole in the back of it.

Love Machine was gone.

Elvis just froze, oblivious to his own wounds.

Brainiac said, 'Elvis, come on. Get him inside. The train's about to go.'

Elvis didn't reply. He just looked at the lifeless body of Love Machine, slumped against his shoulder.

'Elvis . . .'

'Go,' Elvis said softly, as bullets hit all around them. He lowered Love Machine's body to the ground beside the X-railcar. Then he looked Brainiac square in the eyes: 'Go. Now.'

'What are you doing?' Brainiac said.

'I'm staying here with my friend.'

And then Brainiac saw the sadness in Elvis's eyes— saw Elvis look lethally over at the 7th Squadron men sidestepping their way toward them from the far end of the platform.

Brainiac nodded. 'Take care of yourself, Elvis.'

'Never,' Elvis said.

'*Brainiac!*' Schofield yelled, gun in hand, trying to see what was happening at the back of the train without getting his head blown off. 'What's going on back there!'

Brainiac's voice said, '*We lost Love Machine, sir, and Elvis has—oh, fuck!*'

Just then, two loud puncture-like booms echoed out through the underground station.

Thawump!

Thawump!

Schofield turned—

—just in time to see two black baseball-sized grenades come rocketing through the air toward him and the X-railcar!

They had been shot from a pair of M-203 grenade launchers held by the 7th Squadron commandos.

The two high explosive rounds shot in through the blasted-open windows of the lead X-railcar—one entering near the front of the car, right next to Schofield; the other rocketing in through a broken window near the rear of the car, near Gant and Mother and the President.

The grenade near Schofield bounced off the far wall

and spun to a halt on the floor a couple of yards away from him.

Schofield didn't waste a second.

He dived forward—*toward* the grenade, sliding across the floor on his chest—and swiped the charge back out through the open door of the railcar with his hand. The grenade whipped across the hard floor of the carriage and disappeared through the door. Schofield then ducked back behind the wall as the grenade detonated outside, sending a vicious ball of flames rushing in through the doorway.

At the other end of the carriage, Gant and Mother weren't so lucky.

Their grenade had landed in among the passenger seats that occupied the rear half of the carriage. There was no way anyone could get to it before it detonated.

'Everybody! This way!' Gant said, yanking the President to his feet and shoving him toward the accordion-like tunnel that connected the two X-railcars.

A glass door slid sideways as Gant pushed the President through the passageway. Mother, Juliet, Hot Rod and Tate clambered through behind them.

The glass door slid shut as a second connecting door opened and Gant and the President dived through it—entering the second railcar—and threw themselves sprawling to the floor, closely followed by the others, just as the grenade in the first railcar exploded brilliantly, spreading fire in every direction, shattering the first connecting door, but only cracking the second one, its flaming claws left to scratch hungrily at the glass.

Schofield was thrown to the ground by the blast of the second grenade.

He staggered to his feet, spoke into his radio-mike: 'Fox! Mother! You guys all right?'

Gant's voice: *'We're still here, and we've still got the President. We're in the second carriage now.'*

'Brainiac,' Schofield said. 'Are you on board?'

'Yeah, I'm in the back of the second car . . .'

'Book!' Schofield yelled forward. 'Have you figured out how to drive this thing yet?'

'I think so!'

'Then punch it!'

A moment later, the X-rail train began to move forward on its tracks, heading toward the oncoming 7th Squadron soldiers.

'Sir,' it was Brainiac's voice. *'I have to tell you something. We lost Love Machine . . .'*

'Ah, shit,' Schofield said sadly.

' . . . and we're about to lose Elvis.'

'What?' Schofield said, perplexed and horrified at the same ti–

But he didn't get to discuss it further, for at that moment, three more puncture-like whumps reverberated through the underground station.

Thwump!

Thwump!

Thwump!

Three rocket-launched grenades sped across the width of the station, zeroing in on the slow-moving X-rail train, three thin lines of smoke cutting through the air behind them, before suddenly—*swoop!-swoop!-swoop!*—one after the other they shot in through the shattered windows of the second X-railcar.

The X-railcar that held the President.

As if on cue, Schofield heard Mother's voice roar over his earpiece: '*Oh, fuck me!*'

The twin-engined X-rail train began to pick up speed, heading for the tunnel.

In the second railcar, Gant couldn't believe what was happening.

Three grenades!

All in her carriage.

She saw the options in a nanosecond: *If we stay, we die for sure. If we get out, we take our chances with the 7th Squadron. In that case, death is probable, but not certain.*

'We can't stay here!' she yelled instantly. 'Out! *Out!*'

She and Juliet immediately grabbed the President by his coat and hauled him toward the door. They didn't miss a step as they ran through the doorway and dived out of the moving train onto the platform, rolling quickly as they landed.

Hot Rod Hagerty and Nicholas Tate jumped nervously from the moving railcar, landing awkwardly.

A split second later, the figure of Mother—obviously not wanting to wait in line behind Hagerty and Tate—came flying out through one of the broken windows next to the doorway. She somersaulted as she hit the platform, gun tucked up against her chest, rolled to her feet.

A moment later, the three grenades went off—three consecutive blasts, *booming* out from the second railcar.

A trio of brilliant fireballs expanded laterally through-out the interior of the railcar—illuminating the entire

256

carriage like a spectacular elongated light-bulb—consuming every available inch of space within it.

Angry flames billowed out from the windows of the carriage, snapping the window-frames like twigs, cracking the car's walls.

The fireballs fanned out over the underground platform, expanding over Gant and the others' heads as they scurried behind the station's concrete pillars to avoid the fire of the advancing 7th Squadron men.

The entire X-rail train rocked with the triple grenade explosion, but it kept on going, picking up speed with every yard.

In the front carriage, Schofield was almost knocked off his feet by the blast. When he managed to regain his balance and look back down the track, he felt a rush of horror sweep through him.

He saw the President—flanked by Gant and Mother and Juliet—taking cover on the underground station's platform.

Damn it!

The President was off the train!

The accelerating X-rail train was now approaching the western end of the station, coming alongside the 7th Squadron commandos positioned there. Schofield saw the 7th Squadron men, right alongside his carriage, but they paid him no heed.

They only had eyes for the President.

And suddenly Schofield had a decision to make.

Leap off the train and stay with the President—the President on whose back the fate of the country rested.

Or go after the boy . . .

Then, in a fleeting instant, just as the train was about to

disappear into the tunnel, Schofield saw *him*, and he knew then that the President would get away—at least away from the Level 6 station. And he knew that Gant and Mother would see it, too.

And with that, he made his decision to go after Kevin.

A second later, Schofield's view of the X-rail station—the image of the ten 7th Squadron commandos leapfrogging their way down the platform toward the President of the United States and his last few guardians—was replaced with that of the impenetrable black wall of the tunnel.

Gant ducked, covering her head from the chunks of concrete that were raining down all around her.

They were screwed.

The 7th Squadron had them.

There was nowhere they could go, nowhere they could run. They were stuck out in the very middle of the platform, outnumbered, outgunned and out of goddamned luck.

And then she saw Elvis.

Walking like a robot—an automaton, completely out in the open—*toward* the advancing 7th Squadron men, despite the raging gunbattle going on all around him.

He had no weapon in his hands. Indeed, his massive fists were clenched firmly on either side of his body as he walked. His face was entirely devoid of emotion—his eyes fixed, his jaw set.

Elvis, it seemed, had his own mission now.

'Oh, Jesus,' Gant breathed. 'Take care, Elvis.'

Then she turned to the others, 'Get ready, people. We're leaving.'

'*What?*' Hot Rod Hagerty blurted. '*How?*'

'Elvis is going to buy us some time. Take cover and get ready to move.'

Sergeant Wendall 'Elvis' Haynes, USMC, strode purpose-fully toward the oncoming 7th Squadron commandos, *in between* them and the President's group.

The 7th Squadron men slowed slightly, if only because this was such an odd thing for Elvis to do. He was quite obviously unarmed and yet he just kept moving slowly forward—twenty yards from them, twenty yards from the President—completely calm.

The 7th Squadron commandos never heard the mantra he was repeating softly to himself as he walked. 'You killed my friend. You killed my friend. You killed my friend . . . '

Quickly and efficiently, one of the 7th Squadron men raised his P-90 and fired a short burst. The volley ripped Elvis's chest to shreds and he fell, and the 7th Squadron men resumed their advance.

It was only when they reached Elvis that they heard him speaking, gurgling through his own blood: 'You killed my friend . . . '

And then they saw his bear-like right hand open like a flower—

—to reveal, resting in his palm, a high-powered RDX hand grenade.

'You killed my . . . '

Elvis drew his final breath.

And his hand relaxed completely—releasing the grenade's spoon—and to the utter horror of the men of Bravo Unit standing close around it, the powerful RDX grenade went off with all its terrible force.

The X-rail train rocketed through the tunnel system.

Sleek and streamlined, with its bullet-shaped nose and its flat X-framed fuselage, the twin-carriage train whipped through the wide tunnel at a cool two hundred miles per hour—and this despite its blasted-out windows and bullet-battered walls.

It moved with little noise and surprising smoothness. This was because it was propelled not by an engine, but rather by a state-of-the-art magnetic propulsion system that had been developed to replace the ageing steam-operated catapults on the Navy's aircraft carriers. Magnetic propulsion required few moving parts yet yielded pheno-menal ground speeds, making it very popular among engineers who lived by the rule that the more parts a piece of machinery has, the more parts it has that can break.

Book II sat in the driver's compartment, hands on the controls. Herbie sat beside him. The driver's compart-ment was the only part of the X-railcar that hadn't had all its windows blasted to pieces.

'Aw, *shit*!' Schofield's voice yelled from behind them. '*Shit! Shit! Shit!*'

Schofield strode into the driver's compartment.

'What's wrong?' Book II asked.

'This is what's wrong,' Schofield said, indicating the silver Samsonite briefcase dangling from his combat webbing. The Football. 'Damn it! Everything was happening too fast. I never even thought about it when the President dived off the train. What time is it?'

It was 8:55.

'Great,' he said. 'We now have just over an hour to get this suitcase *back* to the President.'

'Should we turn around?' Book II asked.

Schofield paused, thinking fast, a thousand thoughts swirling through his head.

Then he said decisively: 'No. I'm not leaving that boy. We can get back in time.'

'Uh, but what about *the country*?' Book II said.

Schofield offered him a crooked smile. 'I've never lost to a countdown yet, and I'm not about to start today.' He turned to Herbie. 'All right, Herbie. Twenty-five words or less: tell me about this X-rail system. Where does it go?'

'Well, it's not exactly my area of expertise,' Herbie said, 'but I've travelled on it a few times. So far as I know, it's actually made up of *two* systems. One heads west from Area 7, taking you to Lake Powell. The other heads east, taking you to Area 8.'

As Herbie explained, they were on the system that extended forty miles to the west, out to Lake Powell.

Schofield had heard of Lake Powell before. Truth be told, it was not so much a lake as a vast one hundred-and-ninety-mile-long maze-like network of twisting water-filled canyons.

Situated right on the Utah–Arizona border, Lake Powell

had once looked like the Grand Canyon, an enormous system of gorges and canyons that had been carved into the earth by the mighty Colorado River, the same river that would create the Grand Canyon further downstream.

Unlike the Grand Canyon, however, Lake Powell had been dammed by the US government in 1963 to generate hydroelectric power—thus backing up the river, creating the lake, and turning what was already a striking vista of rock formations into a spectacular desert canyonland *that was half-filled with water*.

Now giant sand-yellow mesas rose majestically out of the lake's sparkling blue waters, while towering temple-like buttes lorded over its flat blue horizon. And, of course, there were the chasms and canyons, now with canals at their bases instead of dusty rocky paths.

Kind of like a cross between the Grand Canyon and Venice, really.

Like any large project, the damming of the Colorado River in 1963 had raised howls of protest. Environmentalists claimed that the dam raised silt levels and threatened the ecosystem of a two-centimetre-long variety of tadpole. This seemed like nothing, however, to the owner of a tiny rest-stop gas station, who would see his store—built on the site of an old western trading post—covered by a hundred feet of water. He was compensated by the government.

In any case, with its ninety-three named gorges and God-only-knew how many others, for a few years Lake Powell became a popular tourist destination for houseboaters. But times had changed, and the tourist trade had slackened off. Now it lay largely silent, a ghost-like network of winding chasms and ultra-narrow 'slot canyons', in which there was to be found no flat ground, only sheer vertical rock and water, endless water.

'This X-rail tunnel meets the lake at an underground loading bay,' Herbie said. 'The system was built for two reasons. First, so that the construction of Areas 7 and 8 could be kept absolutely secret. Materials would be hauled on barges up the lake and then delivered forty miles underground to the building site. We still use it occasionally as a back-door entrance for supplies and prisoner delivery.'

'Okay,' Schofield said. 'And the second reason?'

'To act as an escape route in the event of an emergency,' Herbie said.

Schofield looked forward.

X-rail tracks rushed by beneath him—and *above* him—at incredible speed. The wide rectangular tunnel in front of the train bent away into darkness.

A sudden noise made him spin, pistol up.

Brainiac froze in the doorway to the driver's compartment, his hands snapping into the air.

'Whoa-whoa-whoa! It's me!'

Schofield lowered his gun. 'Knock next time, will you.'

'Sure thing, boss.' Brainiac sat down in a spare seat.

'Where have you been?'

'In the back of the second carriage. I got separated from the others when those rocket grenades came flying in. Dived into a storage compartment just as the three grenades went off.'

'Well, it's good to have you here,' Schofield said. 'We need all the help we can get.' He turned to Herbie. 'Can we get telemetry on any of the other trains on this system?'

'I think so,' Herbie said. 'Just give me a second here . . . '

He punched some keys on the driver's console. A computer monitor on the dashboard came to life. In a few seconds, Herbie brought up an image of the X-rail system.

Schofield saw an elongated S-bend that stretched horizontally from Area 7 to the network of canyons that was Lake Powell. He also saw two blinking red dots moving along the track-line toward the lake.

'The dots are X-rail trains,' Herbie said. 'That's us closer to Area 7. The other one must have left about ten minutes ahead of us.'

Schofield stared at the first blinking dot as it arrived at the loading bay and stopped.

'So, Herbie,' he said, 'since we've got a bit of time, this Botha character. Who is he?'

No sooner had Elvis's hand grenade gone off than Gant and Mother and Juliet were up on their feet and firing their guns hard, covering the President as they all ran back toward the fire stairwell from which they had entered Level 6.

The blast of Elvis's RDX grenade had killed five of the 7th Squadron men instantly. Their bloodied limbs now lay splayed across the X-rail tracks on either side of the central platform.

The five remaining members of Bravo Unit had been further away from the grenade when it had gone off. They had been knocked over by the concussion wave, and were now scrambling to find cover—behind pillars and down on the X-rail tracks—in the face of Gant and the others' retreating fire.

Into the firestairs.

Gant led the President up the stairwell. She was breathing hard, legs pumping, heart pounding, Mother, Juliet, Hagerty and Tate close behind her.

The group came to the Level 5 firedoor.

Gant reached for the door's handle—then pulled her hand back sharply.

Small jets of water spurted out from the edges of its frame. The jets of water shot out from the door's rubber seal, mainly from down near the floor, losing intensity as they moved higher. No water sprayed out from the top of the door.

It was as if there was a waist-high body of water behind the fireproof door, just waiting to break through.

And then, from behind the door, Gant heard some of the most hideous shrieking sounds she had ever heard in her life. It was horrific—pained, desperate. The cries of trapped animals . . .

'Oh, no . . . the bears,' Juliet Janson said as she came

alongside Gant and saw the firedoor. 'I don't think we want to go in there.'

'Agreed,' Gant said.

They raced up the stairs and came to Level 4. After checking the decompression area beyond the door, Gant gave the all-clear.

The six of them entered, fanned out.

'*Hello again!*' a voice boomed out suddenly from above them.

Everyone spun. Gant snapped her gun up fast, and found herself drawing a bead on a wall-mounted television set.

Caesar's face was on it, grinning.

'*People of America, it is now 9:04, and thus time for your hourly update.*'

Caesar gave his report smugly.

'*—and your Marines, inept and foolish, have yet to inflict any losses on my men. They do little but run. Indeed, His Highness was last seen making a desperate bid for freedom down on the lowest level of this facility. I am informed that a firefight has just taken place down there, but await a report on the result of that exchange . . .*'

As far as Gant was concerned, it was all bullshit. Whatever Caesar said, whatever lies he told, it didn't affect their situation. And it certainly didn't help to watch him gloat.

So while Caesar spoke on the television and the others watched him, Gant investigated the sliding door set into the floor that led down to Level 5.

She could just make out muffled shouts coming from the other side of it. People yelling.

She hit the 'DOOR OPEN' switch, raised her gun. The horizontal door slid away.

The shouts became screams as the prisoners down on Level 5 heard the door grind open.

Gant peered down the ramp.

'Good God,' she breathed.

She saw the water immediately, saw it lapping against the ramp below her. In fact, the ramp simply disappeared into it.

While Caesar's voice continued to boom, she edged down the sloping walkway, until her spit-polished dress shoes stepped ankle-deep into the water.

She crouched down on the ramp, looked out over Level 5.

What she saw shook her.

The entire level was flooded.

Easily to chest height.

It was terribly dark as well, which only served to make the flooded cell block look all the more frightening.

The inky-black indoor lake stretched away from her, to the far end of the floor, its liquid form slipping in through the bars of all the cells—cells which held an assortment of the most wretched-looking individuals Gant had ever seen.

And then the prisoners saw her.

Screams, shrieks, wails. They shook the bars of their cells, cells that they would ultimately drown in if the water level continued to rise.

Like Schofield, Gant hadn't seen the cell bay before. She had only heard the President talk about it when he'd told them about the Sinovirus and its vaccine, Kevin.

'We'd better go.' Juliet appeared at her shoulder. Caesar's broadcast, it seemed, had concluded.

'They're going to drown . . . ' Gant said, as Janson pulled her gently back up the ramp to Level 4.

'Believe me, drowning's too good for the likes of them,' the Secret Service agent said. 'Come on. Let's find some-where to hole up. I don't know about you, but I sure as hell need a rest.'

She hit the 'DOOR CLOSE' button and the horizontal door slid shut, cutting off the prisoners' pained shouts.

Then, with the President and Mother and Hot Rod and Tate in tow behind them, Gant and Juliet headed for the western side of the floor.

None of them noticed the long decompression chamber as they departed.

Although from a distance it appeared normal, had they looked at it more closely, they would have seen that the timer-activated lock on its pressurised door had timed out and unlocked itself.

The door was no longer fully closed.

The decompression chamber was now empty.

It was 9:06 a.m.

'—Bravo Leader, come in. Report —' one of the radio operators said into his microphone.

'—*Control, this is Bravo Leader. We have suffered serious casualties on the X-rail platform. Five dead, two wounded. One of their guys had an RDX grenade and did a fucking kamikaze—*'

'—What about the President?' the radio man cut in.

'—*The President is still in the complex. I repeat: The President is still in the complex. Last seen heading back up the firestairs. Some of his Marine bodyguards, though, took off down the tunnel in the second X-rail train—*'

'—And the Football?'

'—*No longer with the President. One of my boys swears that he saw that Schofield guy with it on the train—*'

'—Thank you, Bravo Leader. Bring your wounded up to the main hangar for treatment. We'll get Echo to flush the lower floors for the President now—'

'Gunther Botha used to be a colonel in South Africa's Medical Battalion,' Herbie said, as the X-railcar hurtled down the tunnel toward the desert lake.

'The Meds,' Schofield said distastefully.

'You've heard of them?'

'Yes. Not a very nice group to be involved with. They were an *offensive* bio-medical unit, a specialised subdivision of the Reccondos. Elite troops who used biological weapons in the field.'

'That's right,' Herbie said. 'See, before Mandela, the South Africans were the world leaders in bio-warfare. And, boy, did we love them. Ever wondered why we didn't do all that much about defeating apartheid? Do you know who brought us the Soviet flesh-eating bug, necrotising fasciitis? The South Africans.

'But as good as they were, one thing still eluded them. They'd been trying for years to develop a virus that would kill blacks but not whites, but they never found it. Botha was one of their leading lights and apparently he was on the verge of a breakthrough when the apartheid regime was overthrown.

'As it turned out,' Herbie said, 'Botha's core research could be adapted for use on something the American government was working on—a vaccine against the Sinovirus, a virus that distinguishes between races.'

'So we brought him here,' Schofield said.

'That's right,' Herbie said.

'And now it seems we're discovering that Professor Botha isn't all that trustworthy.'

'It would seem so.'

Schofield paused for a moment, thinking.

'And he's not working alone,' he said.

'How do you know?'

Schofield said, 'All those dead 7th Squadron men we saw when we arrived on Level 6 earlier. I've never met

270

Gunther Botha before, but I'm pretty sure he couldn't wipe out an entire 7th Squadron unit all by himself. Remember, Botha opened three doors, the two X-rail doors and the Emergency Escape Vent—which opens onto Level 6.

'He let a team of men in through that vent. They were the ones who killed the 7th Squadron men there. Judging by the bullet wounds in their backs and the amount of slashed throats, I presume Botha's friends caught the 7th Squadron men from behind.' Schofield bit his lip. 'But that still doesn't tell me what I want to know.'

'And what is that?'

Schofield looked up. 'If Botha is selling us out, what I want to know is: who is he selling us out *to*?'

'It was a security risk from the start, but we couldn't have done it without him,' the President said.

He and the others were sitting in the observation lab overlooking the smashed glass cube on Level 4, catching their breath.

When they'd arrived moments earlier, they'd been confronted by the sight of a thick circular ceiling hatch lying on the floor of the lab.

The 7th Squadron had been through here.

Which hopefully meant they wouldn't be coming back soon. It would be a good place to hide, for a while.

Libby Gant was the only one who stood—still on edge—gazing down at the destroyed cube. The underground complex had grown strangely silent since Caesar's last update, as if the 7th Squadron weren't prowling around it anymore, as if they had stopped hounding the President, at least for the moment.

Gant didn't like it.

It meant something was up.

And so she had just asked the President about Gunther Botha, the man who had taken Kevin.

'Botha knew more about racially-targeted viruses than all of our scientists put together,' the President went on. 'But he had a history.'

'With the apartheid regime?'

'Yes, and beyond that. What we feared the most were his links with a group called Die Organisasie, or the Organisation. It's an underground network comprising former apartheid ministers, wealthy South African land-owners, former elite troops from the South African armed forces, and ousted military leaders who fled the country when apartheid collapsed, rightfully fearing that the new government would have their heads for past crimes. Most intelligence agencies believe that Die Organisasie only wants to retake South Africa, but we're not so sure.'

'What do you mean?' Gant asked.

The President sighed. 'You have to realise what's at stake here. Ethnically-selective bio-weapons like the Sinovirus are like no other weapon in the history of mankind. They are the ultimate bargaining tool, because they have the power to sentence a *defined population* to death while absolutely, without question, protecting another.

'Our fears about Die Organisasie don't just relate to what they'd do to the Republic of South Africa. It's what they'd do to *the entire African continent* that frightens us.'

'Yes . . .'

'Die Organisasie is a racist organisation, pure and simple. They actually *believe* white people are genetically superior to black people. They *believe* that black people should be slaves to whites. They don't just hate South African black people, they hate *all* black people.

'Now, if Die Organisasie has the Sinovirus *and* the vaccine to it, they could release it Africa-wide, and give the cure only to those white groups who supported them. Black Africa would die, and the rest of the world wouldn't be able to do a thing about it, because we wouldn't have the vaccine to the Sinovirus.

'Do you remember in 1999 when Ghaddafi spoke of uniting Africa like never before. He spoke of creating "the United States of Africa", but it was regarded as a joke. Ghaddafi could never have made that happen. There are far too many tribal issues to overcome to unite the various black-African nations. But,' the President said, 'an organisation that had the Sinovirus *and* its cure in its possession could rule Africa with an iron fist. It could turn Africa— resource-rich Africa, complete with a billion-strong black slave workforce—into its own private empire.'

Schofield's battered X-railcar raced through the underground tunnel.

They had been travelling for ten minutes now and Schofield was beginning to feel anxious. They would be arriving at the loading dock adjoining the lake soon and he didn't know what to expect.

One question about Area 7, however, was still bothering him. 'Herbie, how did the Air Force get a sample of the Sinovirus?'

'Good question,' Herbie said, nodding. 'It took a while, but eventually we managed to turn two Chinese lab workers at the biowarfare facility in Changchun. In return for a one-way trip to America and twenty million US dollars each, they agreed to smuggle several vials of the virus out of China.'

'The guys in the decompression chamber,' Schofield said, recalling the Asian faces he had seen inside the chamber on Level 4 earlier.

'Yes.'

'But there were *four* men inside the chamber.'

'That's right,' Herbie said. 'As you'd probably under-stand, in China, top-secret government lab workers can't just up and leave the country that easily. We had to get them out. The other two men inside that quarantine chamber were the two 7th Squadron soldiers who extracted them from China—two Chinese–American officers named Robert Wu and Chet Li. Wu and Li used to be a part of Echo Unit, one of the five 7th Squadron teams based at Area 7, which was why they were chosen—'

Abruptly, Schofield held up his hand, moved to the front windshield.

'Sorry, Doctor Franklin,' he said, 'but I'm afraid that'll have to do for the moment. I have a funny feeling that things are about to get a little hairy.'

He nodded at the tunnel ahead of them.

At the end of the long concrete tunnel, beyond its rapidly streaking grey walls, was a tiny luminous speck of light—growing larger as they approached it—the familiar glow of artificial fluorescent lighting.

It was the loading dock.

They had arrived at the end of the tunnel.

'Don't go in,' Schofield said to Book. 'They could be waiting for us inside. Stop in the tunnel. We'll walk the rest of the way.'

The bullet-riddled X-rail train slowed to a halt in the darkness of the tunnel, a hundred yards short of the illuminated loading dock.

Schofield was out of it in an instant—Desert Eagle in one hand, the Football flailing from his waist—leaping down to the concrete next to the tracks. Brainiac, Book II and Herbie followed close behind him.

They ran down the tunnel toward the light, guns up.

Schofield came to the end of the tunnel, peered around the concrete corner.

Brilliant white light assaulted his eyes. He found himself staring at a giant rocky cavern that had been converted into a modern loading dock—a curious mix of flat concrete and uneven rocky surfaces.

Two sets of X-rail tracks lay on either side of a long central platform. The track on Schofield's side of the platform was empty, while the track on the other side was occupied by another X-rail train—Botha's.

It lay still, unmoving.

Some black steel cranes ran on wall-mounted rails, leading from the X-rail tracks to a wide pool of water at the far end of the enormous rocky cavern.

The water in the pool glowed a brilliant aquamarine green, enriched by the minerals of Lake Powell. The pool itself disappeared to the west, winding its way into a twisting black cave that Schofield could only assume led out to the lake. Three ordinary-looking houseboats and a couple of strange-looking sand-coloured speedboats bobbed on its surface, tied to the loading bay's concrete dock.

There was one other thing that Schofield noticed about the immense underground loading bay.

It was empty.

Completely and utterly empty.

Deserted.

Schofield stepped cautiously out from the tunnel, and climbed up onto the central platform between the two X-rail tracks, dwarfed by the sheer size of the cavern.

And then he saw it.

Standing at the other end of the platform, over by the pool of water leading out to the lake.

It looked like some bizarre kind of supermarket display: a small chest-high 'pyramid' of yellow ten-gallon barrels, in front of which sat a chunky Samsonite trunk—black and solid and high-tech. The trunk's lid was open.

As he approached them, Schofield saw that the yellow barrels had words stencilled on their sides.

'Oh, *damn* . . .' he said as he read them.

AFX-708: EXPLOSIVE FILLER.

AFX-708 was a shockingly powerful explosive epoxy,

276

used in the famous BLU-109 bombs that had ripped Saddam Hussein's bunkers to shreds in the Gulf War. A 109's superhardened nose would drive down into a solid concrete bunker and then the AFX-708 warhead inside it would detonate—hard—and blow the bunker up from the inside.

With Book II, Brainiac and Herbie behind him, Schofield looked inside the open Samsonite trunk that sat in front of the collection of AFX barrels.

A timer display stared back up at him.

00:19

00:18

00:17

'Mother of God . . .' he breathed. Then he turned to the others, 'Gentlemen! *Run!*'

Seventeen seconds later, a bone-crunching explosion ripped through the loading bay.

The cluster of AFX-708 barrels sent a devastating ball of white-hot light shooting out in every direction, expanding radially.

The rock-and-concrete walls of the loading bay cracked under the weight of the explosion, blasting outwards in a million lethal chunks, one entire wall just disintegrating to powder in the blink of an eye. Gunther Botha's X-rail train— so close to the source of the blast—was simply vapourised.

Schofield never saw it.

Because by the time the explosives went off, he and the others were no longer inside the loading bay.

They were outside.

FOURTH CONFRONTATION

3 July, 0912 Hours

NORTH-EASTERN POWELL,
UTAH, USA

Loading dock

X-rail
tunnel

N

W — E

S

Mesa
Canyon

Desert plain

The heat hit them like a blast furnace.

Blistering desert heat.

It was everywhere. In the air. In the rock. Against your skin. Enveloping you, surrounding you, as if you were standing in an oven. The complete opposite of the subterranean cool of Area 7 and the X-rail tunnel.

Out here, the blazing desert sun ruled.

Shane Schofield sped down a narrow water-filled canyon at breakneck speed, blasting through the heat, sitting at the controls of a very odd-looking—but very fast—speedboat.

With him in the boat was Book II, while behind them, in a similar craft of their own, were Brainiac and Herbie.

Technically, Schofield's boat was called a PCR-2—patrol-craft, river, two-man—but it was more commonly known as a 'bipod', a small two-man jet-propelled rivercraft built by the Lockheed Shipbuilding Company for the US Navy. The bipod was known for its unique design configuration. Basically, it looked as if someone had joined two small bullet-shaped jet-boats with a thin seven-foot crossbeam, in effect creating a catamaran-type vehicle with two pods at either end of the beam. Since both open-topped pods were possessed of powerful two-hundred-horsepower Yamaha pump-jet engines, it made for an extremely fast—and extremely stable—boatframe.

Schofield's bipod was painted in desert camouflage colours—brown blobs on a sandy yellow background—and it shot over the water at incredible speed, kicking up twin ten-foot sprays of water behind it. Schofield sat in the left-hand pod, driving, while Book II sat in the right-hand one, manning the boat's sinister bow-mounted 7.62 mm machine gun.

The sun shone—burning hot.

It was already 100 degrees in the shade.

'How you guys doing over there?' Schofield said into his wrist mike as he looked back at the other bipod behind him—Brainiac was driving, Herbie sat in the gunner's pod.

Brainiac's voice: '*I'm okay, but I think our scientist friend here is turning green.*'

They were speeding down a twenty-foot-wide slot canyon that wended its way southward, toward the main body of Lake Powell.

The pool of water at the far end of the loading bay had indeed led out to the lake, a tight, dark, winding cave whose exterior door—a brilliantly camouflaged plate-steel gate designed to look like a wall of rock—had been left open by the escaping thieves.

Schofield and his men had emerged from the cave at the end of a dead-end canyon and powered off not a moment before the entire wall of rock behind them had been blasted outward by the monstrous AFX explosion.

The two bipods sped around a wide bend in the water-filled canyon.

When viewed from above, this canyon resembled a race-car track, a never-ending series of twists, turns and full 180-degree bends.

That wasn't so bad.

The trouble started when it met up with all the *other* narrow canyons of Lake Powell—then the canyon system resembled a giant high-walled maze of interconnecting natural canals.

They came to an intersection of three canyons, arriving at it from the north-east.

At first Schofield didn't know what to do.

Two rock-walled canals stretched away from him—a fork in the watery road. And he didn't know *where* Botha was going. Presumably the South African scientist had a plan—but what?

And then Schofield saw the waves. Saw a collection of ripples lapping against the sheer stone walls of the canyon branching away to the left—barely perceptible, but definitely there—the residual waves of a motorboat's wash.

Schofield gunned it, swinging left, heading south.

As he travelled down the canyonways, banking with the bends, he looked upward. The rocky walls of these canyons rose at least two hundred feet above the water level. At their rims, Schofield saw clouds of billowing sand, blowing viciously, offering sporadic relief from the blazing sun.

It was the sandstorm.

The sandstorm that had been forecast to occur that

morning, but which the members of HMX-1 had expected to miss.

It was absolutely *raging* up there, Schofield saw, but down here, in the shelter of the canyons, it was relatively calm—a kind of meteorological haven below the canyon system's high rocky rim.

Relatively calm, Schofield emphasised.

Because at that moment, he rounded a final corner and, completely unexpectedly, burst out into wide open space— into an enormous crater-like formation with a giant flat-topped mesa rising out of the water in its centre.

Although the crater was bounded by magnificent sheer rock walls, it was too wide to offer total protection from the wild sandstorm above. Flurries of sand whipped down into the vast expanse of open water, swirling maniacally.

It was then that through the veil of wind-hurled sand, Schofield saw them.

They were rounding the right-hand base of the mesa, speeding away.

Five boats.

One large white powerboat that looked like a hydro-foil, and four nimble bipods, also painted sand-yellow.

To Schofield's horror, at least a half-dozen slot canyons branched out from the walls of this circular crater, like the points on a clock, offering a multitude of escape routes.

He hit the gas, charged into the sandstorm, heading for the southern end of the central mesa, hoping to take the South Africans by surprise on the other side.

His bipod skipped over the water at incredible speed, propelled by its powerful mini-jet engines. Brainiac and Herbie's bipod bounced along beside it, kicking up spray, jouncing wildly through the horizontal rain of flying sand.

They rounded the left-hand end of the mesa—and saw the five South African boats heading for a wide vertical canyon that burrowed into the western wall of the crater.

They gave chase.

The South Africans must have seen them, because right then two of their bipods peeled away from the main hydrofoil, turning in a wide 180-degree arc, angling menacingly toward Schofield's boats, their 7.62 mm machine guns flaring to life.

Then suddenly—*shockingly*—the left-hand South African bipod exploded.

It just blew out of the water, consumed in a geyser of spray. One second it was there, the next it was replaced by a ring of foaming water and a rain of falling fibreglass.

For its part, the *right-hand* South African bipod just wheeled around instantly, abandoning this confrontation, and took off after the other South African boats.

Schofield spun. *What the—?*

SHOOOOOM!!

Without warning, three black helicopters came bursting out of the sandstorm above the crater and plunged into the canyon system from behind him!

The three choppers swung into the relative shelter of the crater like World War II divebombers, banking sharply before righting themselves without any loss of speed. They thundered over Schofield and his team, powering toward the South African boats as they disappeared inside the slot canyon to the west.

The choppers just shot into the narrow canyon after them.

Schofield's jaw dropped.

In a word, the three helicopters looked *awesome*. Sleek

and mean and fast. They looked like nothing he had ever seen before.

They were each painted gunmetal black and looked like a cross between an attack helicopter and a fighter jet. Each helicopter had a regular helicopter rotor and a sharply pointed nose, but they were also possessed of downwardly canted *wings* that extended out from their frames.

They were AH-77 Penetrators—medium-sized attack choppers; a new kind of fighter-chopper hybrid that combined the hovering mobility of a helicopter with the superior straight-line speed of a fighter jet. With their black radar-absorbent paint, swept-back wings and severe-looking cockpits, they looked like a pack of angry airborne sharks.

The three Penetrators shot forward, banking into the narrow canyon after the four South African speedboats, completely ignoring Schofield and his men.

And in a fleeting instant, Schofield had a strange thought. *What the hell were the Air Force people doing out here? Weren't they after the President? What did they care about Kevin?*

In any case, this was now a three-way chase.

'*Sir!*' Brainiac's voice came in. '*What do we do?*'

Schofield paused. Decision time. A tornado of thoughts whizzed through his mind—Kevin, Botha, the Air Force, the President, and the unstoppable countdown on the Football that at some point would force him to give up on this chase and turn back . . .

He made the call.

'We go in after them,' he said.

Schofield's bipod roared into the canyon the South Africans and the Penetrators had taken, Brainiac and Herbie's bipod close behind it.

It was a particularly winding canyon, this one—left then right, twisting and turning—but, thankfully, sheltered from the sandstorm.

About a hundred yards in, however, it forked into two sub-canyons, one heading left, the other right. Little did any of them know that the sub-canyons of Lake Powell have a habit of swinging back on each other, like interweaving pieces of string, forming multiple intersections . . .

Schofield saw the three Air Force choppers split up at the fork—one going left, two going right. The four South African rivercraft up ahead of them must have already split up.

'Brainiac!' he yelled. 'Go left! We'll take the right! Remember, all we want is the boy! We get him and then we high-tail it out of here, okay!'

'*Got it, Scarecrow.*'

The two bipods parted—taking separate canyons— Schofield peeling right, Brainiac banking left.

*

For Schofield, it was like entering a fireworks show—a spectacular display of tracer bullets, missiles and dangerously exploding rock.

He saw the two black choppers eighty yards up ahead—trailing the lead hydrofoil and one of the South African bipods. The two speeding helicopters stayed below the canyon's rim—the raging sandstorm above the canyon system preventing them from going any higher—banking and turning with the bends of the winding canyon, their rotor blades thumping.

Tracer bullets streamed out from their nose-mounted Vulcan cannons. Air-to-ground missiles streaked out from their wings and *blasted* into the rocky walls of the canyon all around the two South African speedboats.

For their part, the South Africans weren't exactly shy either.

The men in the bipod had come prepared to protect the lead hydrofoil—they had a shoulder-mounted Stinger missile launcher. While one man drove the bipod, the gunner thrust the Stinger onto his shoulder and fired it up at the trailing Penetrators.

But the Penetrators must have had the same ultra-powerful electronic countermeasures that the AWACs planes inside Area 7 had, because the Stingers just shot past them, spiralling wildly, careering into the walls of the canyon where they detonated, sending showers of car-sized boulders splashing down into the canal below—boulders which Schofield had to swerve to avoid.

And then suddenly Schofield saw a long, white object drop out of a hatch in the belly of one of the black choppers and, dangling from a small drogue parachute, splash down into the water.

A second later, the water beneath the chopper churned into a froth and he saw a finger of bubbles stretch out from the roiling section of water, *heading straight for the South African bipod*.

It was a torpedo!

Five seconds later, completely without warning, the speeding bipod exploded violently.

The force of the blast was so strong that it lifted the fast-moving bipod clear off the water's surface. Indeed, such was the bipod's velocity that it tumbled end over end, totally out of control, bouncing across the water's surface like a skimming stone until it *slammed*—top-first—into the hard rock wall of the canyon and blew apart.

Schofield drove hard, closing in, now fifty yards behind the action. He needed to catch up, but the South Africans had had too much of a head-start.

And then abruptly the canyon turned . . .

. . . and intersected with its twin from the left—the sub-canyon that Brainiac and Herbie had taken in pursuit of the other two South African bipods—so that now the two canyons formed a giant X-shaped junction.

And it happened.

The white South African hydrofoil shot into the inter-section from the top-right-hand corner of the X—*at exactly the same time* as one of its own bipods entered the junction from the bottom-right.

Speeding rivercraft shot every which way.

The hydrofoil and the bipod swerved to avoid each other. Both fishtailed wildly on the water, sending a wall of spray flying into the air—and losing all of their forward momentum in an instant.

The second South African bipod from Brainiac's canyon never even had a chance to slow down.

It just shot straight through the X-shaped junction like a bullet—*between* the two boats that had been forced to stop, blasting spectacularly through their spray—before zooming off down the canyon ahead of it, heading west.

The three Air Force Penetrators—two from Schofield's canyon, one from the other canyon—were also thrown into chaos. One managed to haul itself to a halt, while the other two whipped through the airspace *above* the junction, crossing paths, missing each other by inches, and overshooting the momentarily stalled boats below.

It was all Schofield needed.

Now he could catch up.

In his bipod, Brainiac was still eighty yards short of the X-junction.

He saw the mayhem in front of him—saw the restarting hydrofoil, and the stalled South African bipod.

His gaze fell instantly on the hydrofoil, which was now rotating laterally in the water, preparing to resume its run down the canyon to the bottom-left of the X.

Brainiac cut a beeline for it.

Schofield arrived at the junction just as the hydrofoil peeled away to the south and Brainiac's bipod swooped into the narrow canyon fast behind it.

'*I'm going after the hydrofoil, sir!*'

'I see you!' Schofield yelled.

He was about to follow when some movement to his right caught his eye. He spun to look down the long high-walled canyonway that stretched away from him to the west.

He saw one of the South African bipods disappearing down the elongated canyonway—all on its own.

It was the bipod that had shot straight through the intersection, from the bottom-right corner to the top-left. Curiously, it was not even *trying* to return to give aid to the hydrofoil.

Then, in a blink, the tiny bipod was gone, vanishing down a narrow side canyon at the far end of the larger canyonway.

And it hit Schofield.

The boy wasn't in the hydrofoil.

He was in the bipod.

That bipod.

'Oh, no,' Schofield breathed as he snapped round and saw Brainiac's speeding bipod disappear around a bend in the southern canyon in pursuit of the hydrofoil. 'Brainiac . . .'

Brainiac's sand-coloured bipod was moving fast.

Really, really fast.

It came alongside the speeding South African hydrofoil, the two rivercraft hurtling down the narrow rock-walled canal like a pair of runaway stock cars, with two of the Air Force Penetrators firing wildly down on them as they did so.

'*Brainiac, can—you hear—e—?*' Schofield's garbled voice

291

said in Brainiac's ears, but in the roar of bullets, engines and helicopter rotors, the young Marine couldn't make out Schofield's words.

Brainiac got Herbie to use his pod's controls and bring the bipod in close to the speeding hydrofoil while Brainiac himself climbed out of his seat.

He watched the hydrofoil as they sped alongside it—saw its two strut-like bow-mounted skids carving through the water—but he couldn't see inside the big speedboat's smoked-glass windows.

Then, with a deep breath, he jumped—across the gap between the two speeding boats—landing on his feet, on the foot-wide side decking of the moving hydrofoil.

'—ainiac—out—of there!—'

Schofield's voice was a blur.

Brainiac grabbed a handhold on the roof of the speeding hydrofoil. He wasn't sure what he expected to happen next. Perhaps some resistance—like someone throwing open one of the hydrofoil's side doors and firing on him. But no resistance came.

Brainiac didn't care. He just dive-rolled onto the hydrofoil's forward deck and blasted out the vehicle's windshield. Glass flew everywhere and a second later, when the smoke cleared, he saw the inside of the boat's cabin.

And he frowned.

The hydrofoil's cabin was empty.

Brainiac climbed inside—

—and saw the hydrofoil's steering controls moving of their own accord, guided by some kind of computer-controlled navigation system, an anti-impedance system that directed the vehicle away from all other objects, rock walls and boats alike.

Then suddenly, in the silence of the cabin, Schofield's voice was loud and alive in Brainiac's ear.

'*For God's sake, Brainiac! Get out of there! The hydrofoil is a decoy! The hydrofoil is a decoy!*'

And at that moment, to his absolute horror, Brainiac heard a shrill *beep* that would signal the end of his life.

A second later, the entire hydrofoil blew, its windows blasting outwards in a shockingly violent explosion.

The force of the blast flipped Herbie's bipod, too, causing the little speedboat to flip over onto its top and skid in a gigantic spraying mess across the surface of the canal, before it smashed into the wall of the canyon and stopped.

After the impact, the crumpled bipod just lay still, droplets of water raining down all around it.

Back at the X-intersection, Schofield was about to take off after the rogue South African bipod that had skulked away from the fight when, from completely out of nowhere, a line of bullet geysers shattered the water all around his boat.

It was the fourth and last South African bipod firing on him.

It had started up again and was now heading eastward, *back* into the canyon that led to the crater with the mesa in its middle.

Before Schofield could even think of a response, two parallel lines of much bigger bullet-geysers erupted all around his sand-coloured bipod. They hit so close, their spray spattered his face.

This barrage of fire came from the third Penetrator helicopter, which still hovered above the X-shaped junction, turning laterally in mid-air, searching for Kevin. The black chopper's six-barrelled Vulcan cannon roared loudly as it spewed forth a long tongue of bright yellow flames.

Schofield gunned the engine of his bipod, wheeling it around to the left, *away* from the Penetrator's gunfire—

but also, unfortunately, away from the rogue bipod that he was sure contained Kevin—instead taking off after the *other* South African bipod that had headed back east, toward the crater with the mesa in it.

The Penetrator gave chase, lowering its nose, powering forward like a charging T-rex, its thrusters igniting.

Schofield's bipod skimmed across the surface of the water, its hull barely even touching the waves, trailing the South African bipod through the winding rock-walled canyon, the shark-like Penetrator looming in the air behind it.

'Any ideas?' Book II yelled from the gunner's pod.

'Yeah!' Schofield called. 'Don't die!'

The Penetrator opened fire and two more lines of geysers hit the water all around their speeding bipod.

Schofield banked left—hard—so hard that the boat's left-hand pod lifted clear out of the water, just as a line of bullets ripped up the choppy surface beneath it.

And then, just then, two torpedoes dropped out of the bottom of the Penetrator.

Schofield saw them and his eyes widened.

'Oh, man.'

One after the other, the torpedoes splashed down into the water and a second later two identical fingers of bubbles took off after the two bipods, charging up the water-filled canyon behind them.

One torpedo immediately zeroed in on Schofield's boat.

Schofield cut right, angling for an oddly shaped boulder that jutted out from the right-hand wall of the canyon. The gently sloping boulder looked remarkably like a ramp . . .

The torpedo closed in.

Schofield's bipod whipped across the water. Book II saw what Schofield was aiming for—the boulder . . .

The bipod hit the rock ramp, just as the torpedo swung in underneath its jet engines and—

—the bipod shot up out of the water, its exposed twin hulls rocketing up the length of the rock—scratching, shrieking, screeching—and then suddenly, *whoosh!*, like a stunt car leaping up into the sky, it shot off the end of the sloping boulder, *just as* the torpedo detonated against the base of the ramp, shattering it into a thousand fragments that went showering upwards in a glorious flower-shaped formation behind the soaring bipod.

The double-hulled boat landed in the water with a splash, still moving fast.

Schofield looked forward just in time to see the South African bipod up ahead of him veering left, heading for a semi-circular tunnel burrowed into the left-hand wall of the canyon.

He took off after it, the remaining torpedo charging through the water behind him like a hungry crocodile.

The South African bipod shot into the tunnel.

A second later, Schofield's twin-hulled boat whipped into the darkness behind it.

The torpedo swung in after them.

Their headlamps blazing, the two bipods zoomed down the length of the narrow tunnel at almost a hundred miles an hour, the dark wet walls of the passageway streaking past them in a blur, like some ultra-fast indoor roller-coaster ride.

Schofield concentrated hard as he drove.

It was so *fast*!

The tunnel itself was about twenty feet wide and roughly cylindrical in shape, with its walls curving slightly as they touched the shallow water surface. About two hundred yards ahead of him, he saw a small point of light—the end of the tunnel.

Suddenly Book II yelled, 'It's closing!'

'What!'

'That other torpedo!'

Schofield spun.

The torpedo behind them was indeed moving in quickly, closing the gap fast.

He snapped to look forward—saw the water-blasting jet engines of the South African bipod five yards in front of him. *Damn it.* Since each bipod was about thirteen feet wide, the tunnel wasn't wide enough to pass.

Schofield gunned it left—but the South African bipod cut him off. Tried right. Same deal.

'What do we do?' Book II called.

'I don't—' Schofield cut himself off. 'Hang on!'

'*What?*'

'Just hold on tight!'

The torpedo weaved its way under the surface of the shallow water like a slithering snake, edging dangerously close to Schofield's stern.

Schofield hit his thrusters, pulled *closer* to the South African bipod in front of him—so that now the two sleek twin-hulled boats were whipping along at a hundred miles an hour in the tightly enclosed space *barely a foot apart*.

Schofield saw the South African driver turn quickly in his seat and see them.

'Hello!' Schofield gave the man a wave. 'Good-bye!'

And with that, just as the torpedo began to disappear underneath the stern of Schofield's boat, Schofield jammed his thrusters as far forward as they would go and yanked his steering yoke hard to the right.

His speeding bipod swung quickly right, the whole twin-hulled boat lifting completely out of the water as it ran *up* the curving right-hand wall of the tunnel. The bipod bounced so high up the wall that for a moment it was actually travelling at right angles to the earth.

The torpedo didn't care. With its original target lost, it quickly overtook Schofield's wall-skimming boat and zeroed in on the only other object in the vicinity—the South African bipod.

The explosion in the narrow confines of the tunnel was huge.

The South African bipod was blasted to bits—bits that were flung all around the tunnel, followed by a rolling, roaring fireball that filled the narrow cylindrical passage-way.

Still moving fast, Schofield's twin-hulled boat swooped down off the sloping wall and blasted right through the charred remains of the South African bipod, exploding through the billowing wall of fire that now filled the tunnel before—suddenly, gloriously—it burst into the bright open space of the awaiting canyon at the end of the passageway.

Schofield eased back on the throttle and his bipod ground to a halt in the middle of this new canyon.

His face and body were soaking wet, covered in spray. Book II was the same.

He looked at this new high-walled canyon around them, trying to get a bearing on where they were, and quickly realised that this wasn't a new canyon at all—it was the same sub-canyon he had taken earlier when he and Book II had separated from Brainiac. Indeed, as he now saw, he and Book weren't far from the fork in the canyon where they had split up from Brainiac.

Schofield revved the engine, started to swing around, to continue his pursuit of the rogue South African bipod, when suddenly he heard a strange thumping noise to his right.

He snapped around.

And saw *another* helicopter—a fourth helicopter—half-obscured by the vertical wall of the canyon, hovering fifty feet above the water at the fork of the two sub-canyons.

One thing about this helicopter struck him straight away.

It wasn't a Penetrator. It was far too chunky, not nearly sleek enough.

As he saw it swing around in mid-air, Schofield recognised the chopper to be a CH-53E Super Stallion, a powerful heavy-lift transport bird like the two that usually accompanied Marine One. The Super Stallion was renowned for its toughness and strength—with its lower-able rear loading ramp, it could hold fifty-five fully-equipped men and carry them into hell and back.

The Air Force men must have brought this Super Stallion along to carry the boy back in, as the attack-configured Penetrators only had room for three crew members.

Judging by the way it hovered at the fork of the two canyons, however, slowly turning laterally, Schofield figured that this chopper was more than just a prisoner transport—it was providing support of some kind.

Schofield spun his bipod around, headed slowly and cautiously toward the Super Stallion.

'What are you doing?' Book II asked. 'The kid is *that* way.'

'I know,' Schofield said, 'but the way I see it, we're not going to catch that boy on the water. It's time we got into the air.'

The three 7th Squadron commandos inside the Super Stallion all wore headsets. One flew the chopper while the other two spoke into microphones, speaking quickly amid the roar of the helicopter's rotor noise.

They, too, were searching for the rogue South African bipod that had slipped away after the near collision in the X-intersection.

'—Penetrator One, this is Looking Glass,' one of them said. 'There's a canyon coming up on your right, take that. It might have gone down that way—'

The other radioman said, 'Penetrator Two. Cut back to the north and check that slot canyon on your left—'

A map of the canyon system glowed green on each of the men's computer screens.

The three illuminated dots on the left—P-1, P-2 and P-3—indicated the three Penetrators prowling the canyons for the rogue bipod. The stationary dot near the mesa crater, 'L-G', depicted the Super Stallion, call-sign 'Looking Glass'. The black line indicated the path of the chase so far.

While the two radiomen continued to issue instructions, the pilot peered forward through the bubble-like canopy of the helicopter, his eyes searching the canyon in front of them.

Amid the roar of the rotor blades and the sound of their

301

own voices in their headsets, none of the crew heard the dull *thunk!* of a Maghook hitting the underside of their mighty chopper.

Schofield's bipod sat in the water directly beneath the Super Stallion—bucking and bouncing on the churning wash generated by the helicopter's downdraft—having approached the big transport bird from behind.

A thin thread-like rope connected the bipod to the underside of the Super Stallion fifty feet above it—the black Kevlar fibre rope of Schofield's Maghook.

And then suddenly a tiny figure whizzed up into the air toward the chopper, reeled upward by the Maghook's internal spooler.

Schofield.

In a second, he was hanging from the Super Stallion's underbelly—fifty feet above the water's surface, right next to an emergency access hatch built into the big helicopter's floor—gripping the Maghook as it clung to the helicopter's underside by virtue of its bulbous magnetic head.

The noise was shocking up here, deafening. The windblast from the rotors made his 7th Squadron clothes press against his skin, made the Football hanging from his webbing twist and flap wildly.

Super Stallions have fully retractable landing gear, so Schofield grabbed a fat cable eyehole as a handhold. Then he hit a button on the Maghook, allowing it to unspool down to Book.

Within seconds, Book II was beside him, hanging from the Maghook on the underside of the Super Stallion.

Schofield grabbed the access hatch's pressure-release handle. 'You ready?' he yelled.

Book II nodded.

Then, with a firm twist, Schofield turned the handle and the emergency hatch above them dropped out of its slot.

The men inside the Super Stallion felt the blast of wind first.

A gale of fast-moving air rushed into the rear cabin of the Super Stallion a second before Schofield swung up through the hatch in its floor, closely followed by Book II.

They came up inside the chopper's rear troop compartment, a wide cargo hold separated from the cockpit by a small steel doorway.

The two radiomen in the cockpit both spun at once, looking back into the hold. They went for their guns.

But Schofield and Book II were already moving fast, guns up, mirroring each other's movements perfectly. One shot from Schofield and the first radioman went down. Another from Book and the second guy was history.

The chopper's pilot saw what was happening, and realised quickly that a gun wasn't his best way out of this situation.

He pushed forward on the Super Stallion's control stick, causing the entire helicopter to lurch dramatically.

Book II lost his balance immediately, and fell.

Schofield, already dancing quickly toward the cockpit, dived to the floor and slid—forward, *fast*, on his chest—toward the open cockpit door.

The pilot tried to kick the door shut and seal off the cockpit, but Schofield was too quick.

He slid head-first—rolling onto his back as he did so—sliding in through the doorway, into the cockpit, and jolting to a perfect halt inside the threshold—one hand propping open the door, the other gripping his .44 calibre Desert Eagle, aimed directly up at the bridge of the pilot's nose.

'Don't make me do it,' he said from the floor, his eyes looking up the barrel of his gun, his finger poised on the trigger.

The pilot was stunned, his mouth open. He just glared down at Schofield—on the floor, with his gun held unwaveringly in the firing position.

'Don't make me,' Schofield said again.

The pilot went for the Glock in his shoulder holster.

Blam!

Schofield put a bullet in his brain.

'Damn it,' he said, shoving the dead pilot out of his seat and taking the controls. 'I *told* you, you asshole.'

Schofield and Book's Super Stallion roared down the narrow canyonway, banking with each bend, heading for the X-intersection where all the rivercraft had nearly collided earlier.

In his mind's eye, Schofield remembered seeing the rogue bipod sneaking off down the western branch of that intersection and then disappearing off to the right, into a narrow slot canyon at the far end.

With the help of the Super Stallion's map of the canyon system, he now saw that slot canyon—it snaked its way to the north, opening onto another lake-like crater with a small mesa in it.

That was where the rogue bipod had been heading.

But what was waiting in that crater? Schofield thought.

Why were the South Africans heading there?

The Super Stallion thundered down its narrow rock-walled canyon, heading for the X-intersection, rounded a bend—

—and came face to face with one of the Air Force Penetrators.

Schofield yanked on the control stick, reining the Super Stallion to a lurching halt in mid-air.

The Penetrator was hovering above the X-intersection, turning laterally in the air, looking down each of the four rock-walled alleyways that met there. It looked like a gigantic flying shark, searching for its prey.

It saw them.

'Looking Glass, this is Penetrator Three,' a voice said sharply over Schofield's cockpit intercom. *'Got any real-time imagery from the satellite yet?'*

Schofield froze.

Shit.

'Book, quickly. Weapons check.'

The Penetrator turned in the air to face the Super Stallion.

'Looking Glass? You listening?'

Book II said, 'We got a nose-mounted Gatling gun. That's it.'

'Nothing else?'

The two helicopters faced each other, hovering above the intersection like a pair of eagles squaring off, a hundred yards apart.

'Nothing.'

'Looking Glass,' the voice on the intercom became cautious. *'Please respond immediately with your authentication code.'*

Schofield saw the Penetrator's downturned wings—saw the missiles hanging from them.

They looked like Sidewinders.

Sidewinders . . . Schofield thought.

Then, abruptly, he hit the 'TALK' button on his console. 'Penetrator gunship, this is Captain Shane Schofield, United States Marine Corps, Presidential Detachment. I am now in command of this helicopter. I've only got one word to say to you.'

'*And what is that?*'

'Draw,' Schofield said flatly.

Silence.

Then: '*Okay . . .*'

'What the hell are you doing?' Book II said.

Schofield didn't reply. He just kept his eyes locked on the Penetrator's wings.

A moment later, with a flash of light, an AIM-9M Sidewinder missile blasted forward from the left-hand wing of the Penetrator.

'Oh, *shit . . .*' Book II breathed.

Schofield saw the charging missile from head-on—saw its domed nose, saw the star-shaped outline of its stabilising fins, saw the looping smoketrail issuing out behind it as it rolled through the air *heading straight for them*!

'What are you *doing*?' Book II exclaimed. 'Are you just going to sit there—?'

And then Schofield did the strangest thing.

He jammed his finger down on his control stick's trigger.

With the Sidewinder missile hurtling toward it—and only a bare second away from impact—the Super Stallion's nose-mounted Gatling gun came to life, spewing forth a line of glowing orange tracer bullets.

Schofield angled the line of laser-like bullets toward the oncoming missile, and just as the missile came within twenty yards of his helicopter—*boom!*—his bullets hit the Sidewinder *right on its forward dome*, causing it to explode in mid-air, fifteen yards short of the hovering Super Stallion.

'What the—?' Book II said.

But Schofield wasn't finished.

Now that the Sidewinder was out of the way, he swung his line of tracer bullets back up toward the Penetrator.

In the near distance, he could see the Perpetrator's two pilots fumbling to launch another missile, but it was too late.

Schofield's tracer bullets rammed into the canopy of the Penetrator—one after the other after the other—pummelling it, pounding it, causing the entire attack helicopter to recoil helplessly in the air.

Schofield's relentless stream of bullets must have gone right *through* the Penetrator's cockpit, because an instant later, one of the chopper's fuel tanks ignited and the whole attack helicopter spontaneously exploded, bursting into a billowing ball of flames before the entire flaming chopper just *dropped* out of the sky and crashed into the water below.

With the Penetrator out of the way, Schofield gunned his Super Stallion down the western canyonway, heading for the narrow slot canyon into which the rogue bipod had disappeared.

'What the hell did you do back there?' Book II asked.

'Huh?'

'I didn't know you could shoot down a missile with tracer bullets.'

'Only Sidewinders,' Schofield said. 'Sidewinders are heat-seekers—they use an infra-red system to lock in on their targets. But to accomplish that, the forward seeker dome on the missile has to allow infra-red radiation to *pass through* it. That means using a material *other* than plate steel. The seeker dome of a Sidewinder is actually made of a very fragile transparent plastic. It's a weak point on the missile.'

'You shot it at its weak point?'

'I did.'

'Pretty risky strategy.'

'I saw it coming. Not many people get to see a Sidewinder from head-on. It was worth taking the chance.'

'Are you always this risky?' Book II asked evenly.

Schofield turned at the question.

He paused before answering, appraised the young sergeant beside him.

'I try not to be,' he said. 'But sometimes . . . it's unavoidable.'

They came to the narrow slot canyon into which the South African bipod had fled.

The little canyon was cloaked in shadow, and it was a lot narrower than Schofield thought it would be. His Super Stallion's whizzing rotor blades only just fitted between its high rock walls.

The giant helicopter roared along the narrow canyon, moving through the shadows, before abruptly it burst out into brilliant sunshine, out into a wide crater-like lake bounded by three-hundred-foot-high vertical rock walls and with a small mesa at its northern end.

As with the other crater, the sandstorm up above the canyon system invaded this open stretch of water. The wind-hurled sand fell like rain, in slanting wave-like sheets. It assaulted Schofield's windshield, drummed against it.

'You see anything?' Schofield yelled.

'Over there!' Book II pointed off to their left, at the

vertical outer wall of the crater opposite the mesa, at a point where a particularly wide canyon branched westward, away from the circular mini-lake.

There, Schofield saw a tiny rivercraft sitting on the water's surface, bucking with the medium-sized waves generated by the sandstorm.

It was the rogue South African bipod.

And it was alone.

Schofield's Super Stallion zoomed over the water-filled desert crater, flying low and fast, its rotors thumping.

Schofield stared at the bipod as they came closer.

It appeared to be stationary, as if it were lying at anchor, about twenty yards out from where the sheer rock wall of the crater plunged down into the water.

Schofield swung the Super Stallion to a halt thirty yards away from the bipod, kept it in a hovering pattern ten feet above the choppy surface of the water. Wind-hurled sand pelted the windshield.

He looked at the bipod more closely—a rope of some sort stretched down into the water beneath it.

The bipod *was* at anchor . . .

And then suddenly he saw movement.

On the bipod.

Through the veil of flying sand, he saw a pudgy-looking, bald-headed man in shirtsleeves get to his feet inside the left-hand pod, the driver's pod.

Gunther Botha.

Botha had been bent over in his pod, doing something, when Schofield's chopper had arrived under the cover of the roaring sandstorm.

In the *right-hand* section of the bipod, however, Schofield saw someone else.

It was the tiny figure of Kevin, looking very small and out of place in the fearsomely equipped gunner's pod.

Schofield felt relief wash over his body.

They'd found him.

Schofield's voice boomed out from the exterior speakers of the Super Stallion: *'Doctor Gunther Botha, we are United States Marines! You are now under arrest! Hand over the boy, and give yourself up now!'*

Botha didn't seem to care. He just hurriedly tossed something square and metallic over the side of his bipod. It splashed into the water and sank, disappearing.

What the hell is he doing? Schofield thought.

Inside the Super Stallion's cockpit, he turned to Book. 'Open the loading ramp. Then bring us around, rear-end first.'

The Super Stallion turned laterally, rotating in mid-air as its rear loading ramp folded down, opening.

The giant chopper's rear-end came round toward the stationary bipod, hovering ten feet above the water. Schofield stood on the now-open loading ramp, his Desert Eagle pistol in his hand, a hand-mike in the other, wind-blown sand flying wildly all around him.

He raised the microphone to his lips.

'The boy, Botha,' his amplified voice boomed.

Still Botha didn't seem to care.

Kevin, however, turned in his seat and saw Schofield, standing in the hold of the Super Stallion. A broad smile appeared across the little boy's face. He waved—a child's wave, his arm swatting rapidly from side to side.

311

Schofield waved back briefly.

At the moment, he was more concerned with what Botha was up to, for now he could see the fat South African virologist much more clearly.

Botha had a scuba tank strapped to his back, over his white shirtsleeves. He hurriedly threw a full-face diving mask to Kevin and gesticulated for the little boy to put it on.

Schofield frowned. *Scuba gear?*

Whatever Botha was doing, it was time to stop him.

Schofield raised his gun and was about to fire across Botha's bow to get his attention, when suddenly there came a loud whumping noise from somewhere close above him and completely without warning, he saw the tail rotor of his Super Stallion blast out into a million pieces and *separate completely* from the rest of the chopper!

Like a tree branch snapping, the Super Stallion's tail boom broke free of the chopper's main body and dropped down into the water, causing the entire helicopter to spin wildly and veer away from the bipod.

With its tail rotor gone, the Super Stallion spun out of control—and wheeled down toward the water's surface below.

Book II wrestled with the chopper's control stick, but the Super Stallion was beyond salvation. It rolled sharply in the air, heading nose-first for the water.

In the rear cargo bay, Schofield was hurled against the side wall, somehow managed to get a grip on a canvas seat there.

The Super Stallion hit the lake.

Water flew everywhere, a gigantic whitewater splash.

The big helicopter's nose *drove* down into the water,

going under for a full ten seconds before its buoyancy righted it again, and the massive chopper bobbed slowly on the surface.

Book II hit the kill switch and the chopper's engines died instantly. Its rotor blades began to slow.

Water rushed into the cargo hold.

It didn't come in through the open rear loading ramp just yet—since the ramp was designed to rest just above the water's surface in the event of a water landing—but rather it entered the crashed helicopter via the small access hatch that Schofield and Book II had used to enter it earlier.

A Super Stallion is built to stay afloat for a short while in a water crash, but since Schofield and Book had discarded the chopper's floor access hatch when they'd entered it, this Super Stallion wasn't even going to do that.

It was sinking. Fast.

Schofield ran into the cockpit. 'What the hell was that? Something hit us!'

'I know,' Book II said. He nodded out through the windshield. 'I think it was them.'

Schofield peered out through the forward windshield.

Hovering above the water in front of their sinking helicopter, partially obscured by the veil of wind-hurled sand—and flanking the anchored South African bipod—were the two remaining Air Force Penetrators.

The Super Stallion sank with frightening speed.

Water gurgled up through the access hatch, expanding outward as it rose up into the cargo hold, pulling the rear end of the chopper down into the lake.

As more water rushed into it, the helicopter dropped lower in the water. Within a minute, the rear loading ramp fell below the waterline and from that moment on, water came *flooding* in through the wide rear opening.

Up in the cockpit, Schofield and Book II were standing ankle-deep in water when abruptly the entire chopper tilted sharply skyward.

'Any risky ideas now?' Book II shouted, grabbing for a handhold.

'Not a one.'

The Super Stallion continued to sink slowly, rear-end first.

With the Football still hanging from his side, Schofield looked out through the cockpit's forward windshield.

He saw one of the Penetrators approach Gunther Botha's bipod. It hovered directly in front of the tiny rivercraft, like a gigantic menacing vulture.

Schofield saw Botha stand in his pod and face the black Air Force helicopter—waving. With his arms flailing, he looked like a tiny pathetic figure beseeching an angry bird-god.

Then, without warning, a Stinger missile shot down from the right-hand wing of the Penetrator, trailing a dead-straight finger of white smoke.

The missile hit Botha's pod and *blasted* it out of the water.

One second Botha was there, the next he was gone, replaced by a frothing circle of ripples.

Kevin's pod, however, remained intact—severed cleanly from Botha's by the missile impact.

His pod and the cracked remains of the bipod's crossbeam just bobbed in the water under the steely gaze of the hovering Penetrator.

From his position inside the sinking Super Stallion, Schofield blanched.

They'd just killed Botha!

Holy shit.

His Super Stallion was now three-quarters underwater—its entire rear section underneath the surface. Only its dome-like glass windshield and the tip of one of its rotor blades still protruded above the waterline.

Water began to lap up against the outside of the windshield.

The entire rear cargo hold was now filled with encroaching dark-green liquid—water that wanted to rise into the cockpit, and devour the whole helicopter.

The chopper sank further.

Through the green-tinged waves slapping against the windshield, Schofield saw the Air Force Penetrator swing in above the half-destroyed bipod and lower a rescue harness down to Kevin.

'Ah, damn it,' he said aloud.

But the Super Stallion just continued to sink—down and down—and the last thing Schofield saw before the windshield was completely covered over by lapping green water, was the image of Kevin being hauled up toward the Penetrator on the harness and being pulled into the rear section of the attack helicopter's three-man cockpit.

Then the windshield was covered over completely and Schofield saw nothing but green.

The two Air Force Penetrators were well aware of who was inside the Super Stallion.

Their calls to 'Looking Glass' on a designated alternate frequency had gone unanswered for the last few minutes. Indeed, it was a transponder trace on the Super Stallion that had led them to this crater—where they had found Botha and the boy.

The two Penetrators hovered above the sinking Super Stallion, watching it founder, watching it drown.

Inside the lead Penetrator sat Python Willis, the commander of Charlie Unit. He gazed intently at the sinking Super Stallion, making sure it disappeared beneath the waves.

The Super Stallion's cockpit went under, followed by the tip of its rotor blade—the last remaining part of the helicopter above the waterline.

A legion of bubbles rose instantly to the surface as every ounce of air inside the sinking helicopter was replaced with water.

The two Penetrators waited.

The Super Stallion disappeared into the inky green depths of the lake, trailing multiple lines of bubbles.

Still Python Willis waited—until the bubbles stopped coming, until he was sure that there could be no air whatsoever inside the sunken helicopter.

After a few minutes, the water surface became calm.

Still the two Penetrators waited.

They lingered another ten minutes, just to be absolutely certain that nobody came up. If anyone did, they would finish them off.

Nobody came up.

At last, Python made the decision and the two Penetrators wheeled around in the air and headed back toward Area 7.

No-one could have stayed under that long, not even inside an air pocket. The air in a pocket would have gone bad by now.

No.

Shane Schofield—and whoever else was in that Super Stallion with him—was now, without a doubt, dead.

Gant, Mother, Juliet and the President were still on Level 4, in the semi-darkened observation lab. Hot Rod Hagerty and Nicholas Tate were also still with them.

'We should move,' Gant said.

'What are you thinking?' Mother asked.

'No. What are you *doing*, Sergeant Gant?' Hot Rod demanded.

'We shouldn't stay here,' Gant said.

'But this is a perfectly good hiding place.'

'We should keep moving. If they're searching for us, and we stay in the same place, they'll eventually find us. We should move at least once every twenty minutes.'

'And where exactly did you learn this?' Hagerty asked.

'It's in the training manual for Officer Candidate School,' Gant said. 'Standard evasive techniques. Surely you read it at some point in your career. Besides, there's something else I'd like to check out—'

Hagerty went red. 'I will not be spoken to like that by a *sergeant*—'

'Yes. You will,' Mother stepped up to Hagerty. At six-two, she towered over him. She nodded over at Gant:

'Because that little chickadee is smarter and cooler in a combat situation than you'll ever be. And, for your information, she ain't gonna be a sergeant for long. Soon she's gonna be an officer. And I'll tell *you* something, I'd put my life in her hands before I put it in yours.'

Hagerty pursed his lips. 'Right. That's—'

'Colonel Hagerty,' the President said, stepping forward, 'Sergeant Gant has saved my life twice this morning—on the train downstairs and then on the platform. In both instances, she was decisive and cool-headed in a situation that would have brought many other people unstuck. I am happy to trust my safety to her judgement.'

'Fucking-A,' Mother said. 'The power of estrogen, man.'

'Sergeant Gant,' the President said. 'What are you thinking?'

Gant smiled, her sky-blue eyes gleaming.

'I'm thinking we do something about that transmitter attached to your heart, sir.'

In his sterile windowless room on the second-to-bottom floor of the Pentagon, Dave Fairfax was still hard at work decoding the intercepted telephone conversations that had come out of United States Air Force Special Area (Restricted) No. 7.

Having decrypted the incoming and outgoing messages in Afrikaans, Fairfax was pretty pleased with himself.

There was, however, still one thing that nagged at him. The two messages in English that he had found in amongst the Afrikaans messages.

He played the two messages again, listened intently.

16-JUN	19:56:09	ENGLISH – ENGLISH
VOICE 3: Everything is in place.		*Everything is in place.*
Confirm that it's the third.		*Confirm that it's the third.*

22-JUN	20:51:59	ENGLISH – ENGLISH
VOICE 3: Mission is a go.		*Mission is a go.*

One thing was certain. It was the same voice on both messages.

A man's voice. American. Southern accent. Speaking slowly, deliberately.

Fairfax pushed his glasses up onto his nose, started typing on his keyboard.

He brought up a voice analysis program.

Then he compared the taped voice's digital signature—or 'voiceprint'—with the signatures of every other voice in the DIA's mainframe, every voice the Agency had ever secretly recorded.

Spiked displays whizzed across his screen as the program accessed the Agency's massive database of voiceprints.

And then the computer beeped:

6 MATCHES FOUND
DISPLAY ALL MATCHES?

'Yes, please,' Fairfax said as he hit the 'Y' key.

Six entries appeared on his screen:

No.	DATE	DIVISION	SOURCE FILE
1.	29-May	SPACEDIV-01	SAT-SURV (FILE 034-77A)
2.	07-Jun	SPACEDIV-01	SAT-SURV (FILE 034-77A)
3.	16-Jun	SPACEDIV-02	USAF-SA(R)07 (FILE 009-21D)
4.	22-Jun	SPACEDIV-02	USAF-SA(R)07 (FILE 009-21D)
5.	02-Jul	SPACEDIV-01	SAT-SURV (FILE 034-77A)
6.	03-Jul	SPACEDIV-01	SAT-SURV (FILE 034-77A)

Okay, Fairfax thought.

He discarded the third and the fourth entries—they

were the two messages that he'd just played. Their division designator, SPACEDIV-02, meant his own section, Section 2.

The other four messages, however, were the property of Section 1, the main unit of Space Division located across the hall.

The source file for the Section 1 messages, SAT-SURV, stood for 'Satellite Surveillance'. Section 1, it seemed, had been tapping into foreign satellite transmissions lately.

Fairfax clicked on the first entry:

| 29-MAY | 13:12:00 | SATELLITE INTERCEPT | (ENGLISH) |

VOICE 1: They did the test this morning. The vaccine is operational
against all previous strains. All they need now is a sample of
the latest version.

Fairfax frowned. The messages in Afrikaans had also mentioned a vaccine. And a successful test.

He hit the next entry:

| 7-JUN | 23:47:33 | SATELLITE INTERCEPT | (ENGLISH) |

VOICE 1: Virus snatch team is en route to Changchun. Names are
CAPTAIN ROBERT WU and LIEUTENANT CHET LI. Both can
be trusted. As discussed, the price for delivery of the vaccine
to you will be one hundred and twenty million dollars, ten
million for each of the twelve men involved.

Changchun, Fairfax thought. The Chinese bio-weapons production facility.

And a hundred and twenty million dollars, to be divided among twelve men.

This was getting interesting.

Next:

2-JUL   02:21:57   SATELLITE INTERCEPT (CHINESE–ENGLISH)

VOICE 1: Copy that, Yellow Star. We'll be there.

What is this—? Fairfax thought.

Yellow Star?

But that was the . . .

He clicked on the final message:

3-JUL   04:04:42   SATELLITE INTERCEPT   (ENGLISH)

**VOICE 1: WU and LI have arrived back at Area 7 with the virus. Your
           men are with them. All the money has been accounted for.
           Names of my men who will need to be extracted: BENNETT,
           CALVERT, COLEMAN, DAYTON, FROMMER, GRAYSON,
           LITTLETON, MESSICK, OLIVER and myself.**

Fairfax was looking at the names on the last message when suddenly the door to his subterranean office was flung open and his boss—a tall, bald bureaucrat named Eugene Wisher—stormed into the room, followed by three heavily armed military policemen. Wisher was in charge of the operation going on across the hall—the tracking of the newly launched Chinese space shuttle.

'*Fairfax!*' he bellowed. 'What the hell are you doing in here!'

Fairfax gulped, eyed the MPs' guns fearfully. 'Uh, wha— what are you talking about?'

'Why are you accessing intercepted transmissions from our operation?'

'*Your* operation?' Fairfax said.

'Yes. Our operation. Why are you downloading information from the mainframe that pertains to the classified operation going on in Section 1?'

Fairfax fell silent, deep in thought, while his boss kept yelling at him.

And suddenly it all became very, very clear.

'Oh, Christ,' he breathed.

It took some explaining—at gunpoint—but after five minutes, Dave Fairfax suddenly found himself standing in front of two DIA Assistant Directors in the operations room across the hall from his windowless office.

Monitors glowed all around the room, technicians worked at over a dozen consoles—all of it related to the tracking of the newly launched Chinese Space Shuttle, the *Yellow Star*.

'I need a personnel list for Special Area 7,' the twenty-five-year-old Fairfax said to the two high-ranking DIA chiefs standing before him.

A list came.

Fairfax looked at it. It read:

> **UNITED STATES AIR FORCE**
> **SPECIAL AREA (RESTRICTED) 07**
> **ON-SITE PERSONNEL**
> **CLASSIFICATION: TOP SECRET**

NAME	UNIT	NAME	UNIT

COMMAND UNIT

Harper, JT (CO)

7TH SQUADRON

NAME	UNIT	NAME	UNIT
Alvarez, MJ	A	Golding, DK	D
Arthurs, RT	C	Goldman, WE	A
Atlock, FD	B	Grayson, SR	E
Baines, AW	A	Hughes, R	A
Bennett, B	E	Ingliss, WA	B
Biggs, NM	C	Johnson, SW	D
Boland, CS	B	Jones, M	D
Boyce, LW	D	Kincaid, R	B
Calvert, ET	E	Littleton, SO	E
Carney, LE	E	Logan, KW (MAJ)	A
Christian, FC	A	McConnell, BA	B
Coleman, GK	E	Messick, K	E
Coles, M	B	Milbourn, SK	D
Crick, DT	D	Morton, IN	C
Criece, TW	A	Nance, GF	D
Davis, LR	C	Nystrom, JJ	D
Dayton, AM	E	Oliver, PK	E
Dillan, ST	D	Price, AL	C
Doheny, FG	A	Rawson, MJ	C
Egan, RR	B	Sayles, MT	B
Fraser, MS	C	Sommers, SR	C
Fredericks, GH	A	Stone, JK	C
Frommer, SN	E	Taylor, AS	B
Gale, A	D	Willis, LS	C
Giggs, RE	B	Wolfson, HT	A

CIVILIAN STAFF

Botha, GW	MED
Franklin, HS	MED
Shaw, DE	MED

Fairfax grabbed a printout of the last message he had downloaded earlier.

3-JUL	04:04:42	SATELLITE INTERCEPT	(ENGLISH)

VOICE 1: WU and LI have arrived back at Area 7 with the virus. Your
men are with them. All the money has been accounted for.
Names of my men who will need to be extracted: BENNETT,
CALVERT, COLEMAN, DAYTON, FROMMER, GRAYSON,
LITTLETON, MESSICK, OLIVER and myself.

'Okay,' he pulled a fluorescent pink highlighter from the neck of his Mooks T-shirt. 'Bennett, Calvert, Coleman . . .'

He started highlighting the personnel list. When he was done, it looked like this:

UNITED STATES AIR FORCE
SPECIAL AREA (RESTRICTED) 07
ON-SITE PERSONNEL
CLASSIFICATION: TOP SECRET

NAME	UNIT	NAME	UNIT

COMMAND UNIT
Harper, JT (CO)

7TH SQUADRON

NAME	UNIT	NAME	UNIT
Alvarez, MJ	A	Golding, DK	D
Arthurs, RT	C	Goldman, WE	A
Atlock, FD	B	Grayson, SR	E
Baines, AW	A	Hughes, R	A
Bennett, B	E	Ingliss, WA	B
Biggs, NM	C	Johnson, SW	D
Boland, CS	B	Jones, M	D
Boyce, LW	D	Kincaid, R	B

327

Calvert, ET	E		Littleton, SO	E
Carney, LE	E		Logan, KW (MAJ)	A
Christian, FC	A		McConnell, BA	B
Coleman, GK	E		Messick, K	E
Coles, M	B		Milbourn, SK	D
Crick, DT	D		Morton, IN	C
Criece, TW	A		Nance, GF	D
Davis, LR	C		Nystrom, JJ	D
Dayton, AM	E		Oliver, PK	E
Dillan, ST	D		Price, AL	C
Doheny, FG	A		Rawson, MJ	C
Egan, RR	B		Sayles, MT	B
Fraser, MS	C		Sommers, SR	C
Fredericks, GH	A		Stone, JK	C
Frommer, SN	E		Taylor, AS	B
Gale, A	D		Willis, LS	C
Giggs, RE	B		Wolfson, HT	A

CIVILIAN STAFF

Botha, GW	MED
Franklin, HS	MED
Shaw, DE	MED

'Anybody else see a pattern here?' Fairfax said.

All of the men named in the intercepted transmission were from the unit designated 'E'—or in military parlance 'Echo'.

'The only man in "E" who *isn't* mentioned,' Fairfax said, 'is this one, "Carney, LE". I can only assume that he's the man speaking on the tape.'

Fairfax turned to the two DIA chiefs standing beside him. 'There's a rogue unit at that base. A rogue unit that has been communicating with the Chinese government and its new space shuttle. All the men in Echo Unit.'

'—Echo Unit. Report—'

'—*This is Echo leader*,' the voice of Captain Lee 'Cobra' Carney replied.

Cobra spoke with a slow Southern drawl—measured, icy, dangerous. *'We're in the Level 3 livin' quarters. Just swept the two underground hangar levels. Nothin' there. Workin' our way down through the complex now, coverin' the stairwell as we go.'*

'—Copy that, Echo leader—'

'Sir,' another of the radio operators turned to Caesar Russell, 'Charlie Unit just arrived back from the lake. They're outside, and they have the boy.'

'Good. Losses?'

'Five.'

'Acceptable. And Botha?' Caesar asked.

'Dead.'

'Even better. Let them in through the top door.'

Gant and the others headed for the fire stairwell at the eastern end of Level 4.

'I know this isn't exactly relevant to the present situation,' Mother said as she and Gant walked side-by-side, 'but I've been meaning to ask you about your little date with the Scarecrow last Saturday. You haven't said anything about it.'

Gant gave Mother a crooked grin. 'Not looking for gossip, are we, Mother?'

'Why, hell yes. That's exactly what I'm looking for. Old married hags like me get off hearing about the sexual gymnastics of pretty young things like you. And I was just, you know . . . interested.'

Gant smiled sadly. 'It didn't go as well as I would have liked.'

'How do you mean?'

Gant shrugged, kept walking, gun in hand. 'He didn't kiss me. We had a great dinner at this quiet little restaurant, then we walked along the banks of the Potomac, just talking. God, we talked all evening. And then, when he dropped me home, I was hoping that he'd kiss me. But he . . . just . . . didn't. And so we stood there awkwardly and said we'd see each other later, and the date just . . . ended.'

Mother's eyes narrowed. 'Oooh, Scarecrow. I'll kick your ass . . .'

'Please don't,' Gant said as they came to the door leading to the stairwell. 'And don't tell him I told you anything.'

Mother ground her teeth. 'Mmm, okay . . .'

'In any case, I'd rather not think about it right now,' Gant said. 'We've got work to do.'

She opened the firedoor a crack, peered through it, her gun raised beside her face.

The stairwell was dark and silent.

Empty.

'Stairwell's clear,' she whispered.

She opened the door fully, took a few steps up the stairs.

Mother moved into position behind her, both of their eyes looking up the barrels of their guns.

They came to the Level 3 landing, saw the door leading into the complex's living quarters.

There was no-one here.

That's odd, Gant thought.

There were no soldiers stationed on the landing, not even a sentry left there to block their movement up through the complex.

Very odd, she thought. If she had been in charge of the opposing forces, she would be flushing every floor for the President, and *ensuring* that she blocked off the stairwell while she did so.

Obviously, the 7th Squadron operated differently.

With the stairwell unguarded, Gant and her team made swift progress upwards, came to the Level 2 hangar bay.

The Level 2 hangar—untouched, so far, by the mayhem of the day—was practically identical to the one above it, the only difference being that the collection of planes inside it was far less exotic. While the Level 1 hangar contained its pair of Stealth bombers and the SR-71 Blackbird, this one only held two AWACS surveillance aeroplanes.

Which was exactly what Gant wanted.

Two minutes later, she was inside the lower cargo hold of one of the AWACS planes, unscrewing a heavy lead panel in the floor.

The panel came free, revealing an electronics compartment—and in the middle of that compartment, secured firmly in place, was a very sturdy-looking fluorescent-orange unit, about the size of a small shoebox. The orange box appeared to be made of some superstrong material.

'What's that?' Juliet Janson asked from behind Gant.

The President answered for her. 'It's the plane's flight data recorder. The black box.'

'Doesn't look very black,' Ramrod Hagerty said sourly.

'They never are,' Gant said, extracting the small orange unit from its nook. 'It's just the name they're known by. Black boxes are nearly always painted bright orange, for better visibility in a wreck. That said, they're usually found another way—'

'Oh, *very good* . . .' the President said.

'What?' Hagerty asked. 'What?'

'Ever wondered how they find the black box so fast after an aeroplane crash?' Gant said. 'When a plane goes down, debris is spread all over the place, yet they always find the flight data recorder very quickly, usually within a few hours.'

'Yes . . .'

Gant said, 'That's because all black boxes have a battery-powered transponder inside them. That transponder emits a high-powered microwave signal, giving the box's location to crash investigators.'

'So what are you going to do with it?' Hagerty asked.

Gant called up through the hatch above her. 'Mother!'

'*Yeah?*' Mother's voice floated back.

'You found that signal yet?'

'*I'll have it in two seconds!*'

Gant gave Hagerty a look. 'I'm going to try to impersonate the signal coming from the President's heart.'

*

In the main cabin of the AWACS plane, Mother sat at a computer console.

She pulled up the screen showing the microwave signal coming into Area 7 from the low-orbit satellite. It was the same screen Brainiac had found inside the other AWACS plane earlier, depicting a twenty-five-second rebounding signature.

Gant came up from the cargo hold with the orange-coloured black box. She plugged a cable into a socket on its side, connecting it to Mother's terminal. Immediately, the spike graph appeared on a small illuminated LCD screen on the black box's top.

'Okay,' Gant said to Mother, 'see that search signal, the upward spike? I want you to set it as the "find" frequency on the black box.'

When crash investigators search for a black box, they use a radio transmitter to emit a preset microwave signal called the 'find' frequency. When the black box's transponder detects that signal, it sends out a return signal, revealing its location.

'Okay . . .' Mother said, typing. 'Done.'

'Good,' Gant said. 'Now set that rebounding frequency—the downward spike—as the return signal.'

'Okay, just a minute.'

'Will the signal strength from the black box be powerful enough to reach all the way up to the satellite?' the President asked.

'I think it'll work. They used microwave signals to talk to Armstrong on the moon, and SETI uses them to send messages into outer space.' Gant smiled. 'It's not the size that matters, it's the quality of the signal.'

'All right, done,' Mother said. She turned to Gant. 'So, Fearless Leader, what exactly *have* I just created?'

'Mother, if you've done it right, when we activate the transmitter inside this black box, we'll be mimicking the signal coming out of the President's heart.'

'So what now?' the President asked.

'Yes,' Hagerty said meanly. 'Do we just switch it on?'

'Definitely not. If we turn it on, the satellite will pick up *two* identical signals, and that might cause it to detonate the bombs. We can't risk that. No, we've just laid the groundwork. Now it's time for the hard part. Now we have to *substitute* the black box's signal for the President's.'

'And how do we do *that*?' Hagerty asked. 'Please don't tell me that you're going to perform open-heart surgery on the President of the United States with a pocket knife?'

'Do I look like MacGyver to you?' Gant asked. 'No. My theory is this: somehow Caesar Russell got that transmitter onto the President's heart . . .'

'That's right. He did it during an operation I had a few years ago,' the President said.

'But I'm figuring he didn't turn it on until today,' Gant said. 'The White House's scanners would have picked up an unauthorised signal as soon as it was turned on.'

'Yes, so . . .' Hagerty said.

'So,' Gant said, 'somewhere in this complex, Caesar

Russell has a unit that turns the President's transmitter on and off. I'm guessing that that unit—probably just a hand-held initiate/terminate unit of some kind—is sitting in the same room as Caesar himself.'

'It is,' the President said, recalling the small unit that Caesar Russell had turned on at the very start of the challenge. 'He had it when he appeared on the television sets before, at the beginning of all this. It's red, hand-held, with a black stub antenna.'

'Right then,' Gant said. 'Now all we have to do is find his command centre.' She turned to Juliet. 'Your people have checked out this place. Any ideas?'

Juliet said, 'The main hangar. In the building over-looking the floor. There's a whole command-and-control room up there.'

'Then that's where we're going,' Gant said. 'So what we do now is simple. First, we take Caesar Russell's command centre. Then, *in between* the search signals sent down from the satellite, we use his initiate/terminate unit to turn off the transmitter attached to the President's heart, while a second later, we turn *on* the black box.'

She gave the President a wry smile. 'Like I said. Simple.'

The five remaining members of Charlie Unit were moving quickly through a low concrete tunnel, all running in a half-crouch.

Trotting along with them—and because of his height, not needing to crouch—was Kevin.

Charlie Unit had just returned from Lake Powell, after killing Botha, retrieving Kevin, and watching Schofield's chopper drown.

They had parked their two Penetrators outside and were now re-entering the complex through an entrance that connected the main facility with one of the outside hangars, an entrance known as the 'top door'.

The top door's tunnel opened onto the rear of the personnel elevator shaft, at ground level, by virtue of a foot-thick titanium door.

Charlie Unit came to the heavy silver door.

Python Willis punched in the appropriate override code. The top door was a special entrance to Area 7—if you were senior enough to know the override code, you could open it anytime, even during a lockdown.

The thick titanium door swung open—

—and Python froze.

He saw the roof of the personnel elevator parked just below his feet, sitting right there in front of him.

And standing on top of it, was Cobra Carney and four members of Echo Unit.

The other half of Echo, Python saw through the hatch in the elevator's roof, were down in the car itself.

'Jesus, Cobra,' Python said, 'you scared the shit out of me. Wasn't expecting to see you guys here—'

'Caesar told us to come get you,' Cobra drawled. 'Make sure you all got in okay.'

Python shoved Kevin forward, onto the roof of the stopped elevator. 'We lost five, but we got him.'

'Good,' Cobra said. '*Very* good.'

It was then that—through the roof hatch of the elevator— Python saw *four more men* standing in the elevator car with the Echo men.

Four Asian men.

Python frowned.

They were the four men who had been inside the decompression chamber earlier that morning—7th Squadron Captain Robert Wu and Lieutenant Chet Li, and the two Chinese lab workers. The men who had brought the latest strain of the Sinovirus back to Area 7.

'Cobra, what's going on?' Python said suddenly, looking up.

'Sorry, Python,' Cobra said.

And with that he gave a short nod to his men.

In a flash, the four members of Echo Unit on the elevator's roof raised their P-90s and unleashed a withering storm of fire on Charlie Unit.

Python Willis was hit by about a million rounds. His

337

face and chest were turned instantly to mush. The four Charlie men behind him also dropped like flailing marionettes, one after the other, until the only figure left standing on that side of the elevator's roof was the wide-eyed and terrified Kevin.

Cobra Carney strode forward and grabbed the little boy roughly by the arm.

'Smile, kid, you're coming with me now.'

The control room overlooking the main hangar was quiet.

Boa McConnell and the four other surviving members of Bravo Unit sat slumped in the corner, looking bloodied and dirty. Two of Boa's men were seriously wounded. Colonel Jerome T. Harper—the ostensible CO of Area 7, but in reality a minion of Caesar Russell—tended to their wounds.

Another figure sat at the back of the room, shrouded in shadow—he had been sitting inside the control room for the whole morning, never uttering a word. He just watched silently.

Major Kurt Logan and the remainder of Alpha Unit were also in the control room. Logan now stood with Caesar, whispering in hushed tones. His Alpha Unit had fared little better than Bravo Unit: of his original team of ten men, including himself, there were only four left.

Caesar, however, seemed absolutely unperturbed by their losses.

'Any word from Echo Unit?'

'Cobra reports that they are now on Level 4. No sign of the President yet—'

'Damn it, *shit*!'

It was one of the other radio operators. His computer monitor had just blinked out.

There had been no warning. No dying whine.

'What is it?' the head operator asked.

'*Fuck!*' another radio man yelled as his monitor also crashed.

It spread around the control room like a virus. All around the command centre, one after the other, monitors blinked out.

'—Air-conditioning systems just went down—'

'—Water cooling system is gone—'

'What's going on?' Caesar Russell said calmly.

'—Power to the cell bay is falling rapidly—'

'The complex's power supply is crashing,' the senior operator said to Russell. 'But I don't know why . . .'

He brought up a system display screen.

S.A.(R) 07-A
SECURITY ACCESS LOG
SOURCE POWER HISTORY (3-JUL)
7-3-010223077

TIME	KEY ACTION	OPERATOR	SYSTEM RESPONSE
06:30:00	System status check	070-67	All systems operational
06:58:34	Lockdown command	105-02	Lockdown enacted
07:00:00	System status check	070-67	All systems operational (lockdown mode)
07:30:00	System status check	070-67	All systems operational (lockdown mode)
07:37:56	WARNING: Auxiliary power malfunction	System	Malfunction located at terminal 1-A2

			Receiving no response from systems: TRACS; AUX SYS-1; RAD COMS-SPHERE; MBN; EXT FAN
07:38:00	WARNING: Auxiliary power capacity: 50%	System	Terminal 1-A2 not responding
08:00:15	Main power shutdown command (terminal 3-A1)	008-72	Main power disabled
08:00:18	Auxiliary power enabled	Aux System	Auxiliary power start up
08:00:19	WARNING: Auxiliary power operational. Low power protocol enabled	Aux System	Low power protocol in effect: non-essential systems disabled
08:01:02	Lockdown special release command entered (terminal 3-A1)	008-72	Door 003-V opened
08:04:34	Lockdown special release command entered (terminal 3-A1)	008-72	Door 062-W opened
08:04:55	Lockdown special release command entered (terminal 3-A1)	008-72	Door 100-W opened
08:18:00	WARNING: Auxiliary power capacity: 35%	Aux System	Terminal 1-A2 not responding
08:21:30	Security camera system shutdown command (terminal 1-A1)	008-93	SYSTEM ERROR: Security camera system already disabled per low power protocol
08:38:00	WARNING: Auxiliary power capacity: 25%	Aux System	Terminal 1-A2 not responding

Time	Warning	System	Status
08:58:00	WARNING: Auxiliary power capacity: 15%	Aux System	Terminal 1-A2 not responding
09:04:43	Lockdown special release command entered (terminal 3-A2)	077-01E	Door 62-E opened
09:08:00	WARNING: Auxiliary power capacity: 10%	Aux System	Initiate system reboot?
09:18:00	WARNING: Auxiliary power capacity: 5%	Aux System	Initiate system reboot?
09:28:00	WARNING: Auxiliary power capacity: 0%	Aux System	Commence system shutdown

'Jesus, we've been running on auxiliary power since eight o'clock!' the senior console operator said.

Colonel Harper stepped forward. 'But that should have kept us going for at least three hours, enough time to reboot the main power supply.'

While they spoke, Caesar gazed at the computer screen, at the entry:

Time	Command	Code	Status
09:04:43	Lockdown special release command entered (terminal 3-A2)	077-01E	Door 62-E opened

The '077' prefix indicated a member of the 7th Squadron. 'E' stood for Echo Unit; and '01', its leader, Cobra Carney.

Caesar's eyes narrowed. It appeared that during the last lockdown window period, Cobra Carney had opened Door 62-E—the eastern X-rail blast door down on Level 6 . . .

Jerome Harper and the radio man were still debating the power situation.

'It should have, yes,' the radio man said. 'But it appears the system only had *half* power when it kicked in, so it only lasted an hour and a half—'

The senior man's monitor blinked out. It was the last one to go.

Then, all at once, the overhead lights in the control room went out.

Caesar and the console operators were devoured by darkness.

Caesar spun, turned to look out through the windows overlooking the enormous ground-level hangar. He saw the bright halogen lights running along the length of the hangar shut off in sequence, one after the other after the other.

The hangar—and all its contents: Marine One, the destroyed cockroach towing vehicles, the blasted-open Nighthawk Two, the overhead crane system—was consumed by inky blackness.

'All systems down,' someone said in the darkness. 'The whole complex has lost power.'

Down in the AWACS plane on Level 2, Libby Gant and the others were preparing to head up through the underground base, to locate and take out Caesar Russell's control room, when without warning every single light in the subterranean hangar went out.

The gigantic hangar was plunged into darkness.

Pitch darkness.

Gant flicked on the pencil-sized flashlight attached to the barrel of her MP-10. Its thin beam illuminated her face.

'The power,' Mother whispered. 'Why would they cut the power?'

'Yeah,' Juliet said, 'surely that would only make it *harder* to find us.'

'Maybe they had no choice in the matter,' Gant said.

'What does this mean for us?' the President asked, coming up beside them.

'It doesn't change the plan,' Gant said. 'We're still going for the command centre. What we have to figure out, though, is how it affects this environment.'

At that moment, from somewhere deep within the bowels of the complex, they heard a scream—a wild scream; human, but at the same time, somehow *not* human; the terror-inspiring howl of a seriously deranged individual.

'Oh, Jesus,' Gant breathed. 'The prisoners. They're out.'

FIFTH CONFRONTATION

3 July, 0930 Hours

UNITED STATES AIR FORCE
SPECIAL AREA (RESTRICTED) NO. 7
0930 HOURS

GROUND LEVEL: Main Hangar

LEVEL 1: Hangar Bay

LEVEL 2: Hangar Bay

LEVEL 3: Living Quarters
LEVEL 4: Laboratories
LEVEL 5: Confinement

Rising water
level

LEVEL 6: X-rail platform

About ten minutes *before* the power went off at Area 7, a chunky CH-53E Super Stallion transport helicopter was sinking slowly through the aqua-green water of Lake Powell.

It made for a peculiar sight.

With its tail section completely blown apart, the chopper sank rear-end first, almost vertical, its open loading ramp swallowing water by the ton. Against the hazy green backdrop of the water all around it, it looked as if the Super Stallion was free-falling in silent ultra-slow motion.

Thin streams of bubbles weaved their way to the surface above it—the same bubbles that were being watched by the two Air Force Penetrators hovering above the lake.

Shane Schofield and Buck Riley Jnr stared out through the sinking helicopter's Lexan windshield—looking straight up.

They saw the water's surface high above them, rippling like a glass lens, fifty feet away and getting more and more distant.

Beyond the distorted lens of water they could make out the twin images of the Penetrator attack choppers hovering above the surface, waiting for them to emerge, if they dared.

In the water all around them, a bizarre yet extraordinary underwater landscape revealed itself. Giant boulders rested on the lakebed, desert trails that had once been dry land twisted and turned, there was even a giant submerged cliff that soared upward, disappearing above the water's surface. The submerged desert world appeared as a ghostly pale green.

Book II turned to Schofield. 'If you've got any more magic escape plans, now would be the time to use them.'

'Sorry,' Schofield said. 'I'm all out.'

Behind them—or rather, *below* them—water was flooding up into the cargo bay. It rose quickly through the hold, entering the helicopter via the wide-open loading ramp and any other orifice it could find.

Thankfully, the cockpit was airtight, so at seventy feet down, the still-sinking helicopter reached equilibrium— and an air pocket formed in the upturned cockpit, the same way a drinking cup submerged upside-down in a bathtub will form an air bubble.

The helicopter glided downwards until, at ninety feet, it hit the bottom.

A billowing cloud of silt exploded all around the Super Stallion as its destroyed tail section impacted against the floor of the lake and came to rest—still upright—against a massive submerged boulder.

'We haven't got much time,' Schofield said. 'This air will go bad real fast.'

'What do we do?' Book II said. 'If we stay, we die. If we swim to the surface, we die.'

'There has to be *something* . . .' Schofield said, almost to himself.

'What do you mean?'

'There has to be a *reason* . . .'

'What are you talking about?' Book II said angrily. 'A reason for what?'

Schofield spun to face him. 'A reason why Botha stopped here. In this spot. He didn't stop here for the hell of it. He had a reason to drop anchor here—'

And then Schofield saw it.

'Oh, you cunning bastard . . .' he breathed.

He was staring out over Book II's shoulder, out into the murky green haze of the underwater world.

Book II spun, and he saw it, too.

'Oh my God . . .' he whispered.

There, partially obscured by the aqua-green mist of the water, was a structure—not a boulder or a rock formation, but a distinctly *man-made* structure—a structure which looked totally out of place in the green underwater world of Lake Powell.

Schofield and Book saw a wide flat awning, a small glass-windowed office, and a wide garage door. And underneath the awning: two old-style petrol pumps.

It was a gas station.

An underwater gas station.

It was nestled up against the base of the cliff, at the point where the enormous circular crater containing the small mesa met a wide canyon stretching westward, right on the corner.

It was then that Schofield remembered what this gas station was.

It was the rest-stop petrol station that had been flooded over when Lake Powell had been created in 1963 by the damming of the Colorado River—the old 1950s-era gas station that had been built on the site of an old trading post.

'Let's move,' he said. 'Before we use up all the oxygen in here.'

'To where?' Book II asked incredulously. 'The gas station?'

'Yep,' Schofield said, looking at his watch.

It was 9:26.

Thirty-four minutes to get the Football back to the President.

'Gas stations have air pumps,' he said, 'for inflating tyres. Air that we can breathe until those Penetrators go away. Maybe when the government compensated him, the guy who owned this station just upped and left everything behind.'

'*That's* your magic escape plan? Any air left in those pumps will be forty years old. It could be rancid, or contaminated by God-only-knows what.'

'If it's air-sealed,' Schofield said, 'then some of it may still be good. And right now, we don't have any other options. I'll go first. If I find a hose, I'll signal you to come over.'

'And if you don't?'

Schofield unclipped the Football from his webbing and handed it to Book II. 'Then you'll have to come up with a magic plan of your own.'

The Super Stallion lay on the bottom of the lake, surrounded by the silent underwater world.

Abruptly, a finger of bubbles issued out from its open rear section—trailing the figure of Shane Schofield, still dressed in his black 7th Squadron battle uniform, as he entered the water from within the sunken helicopter.

Schofield hovered in the void for a moment, looked about himself, saw the gas station, but then suddenly he saw something else.

Something resting on the lake-bed directly beneath him, about three feet away.

It was a small silver Samsonite container—heavy-duty; obviously designed to protect its contents from strong impacts; about the size of two video cassettes placed side-by-side. It sat on the silty lake floor, perfectly still, weighed down by a small anchor.

It was the object Gunther Botha had tossed over the side of his bipod when Schofield and Book had interrupted him.

Schofield swam down to it, cut away the anchor with a knife, and then attached the silver container's handle to the clip on his combat webbing.

He'd look at its contents later.

Right now he had other things to do.

He headed for the underwater gas station, pulling himself through the water with long powerful strokes. He covered the distance between the Super Stallion and the gas station quickly, and soon found himself hovering in front of the ghost-like submerged structure.

His lungs began to ache. He had to find an air hose soon—

There.

Beside the open doorway of the gas station's office.

A black hose, connected to a large pressurised drum. Schofield swam for it.

He came to the hose, grabbed it and pressed down on its release valve.

The hose's nozzle sputtered to life, spewing out some pathetically small bubbles.

Not a good sign, Schofield thought.

And then, in a sudden billowing rush, a wash of big fat bubbles came bursting out of the hose.

Schofield quickly put his mouth over it and, without a second thought, breathed in the forty-year-old air.

At first, he gagged, and coughed awfully. It tasted bitter and stale, foul. But then it got cleaner and he began to breathe it in normally. The air was okay—just.

He waved to Book in the helicopter, gave him the thumbs up.

As Book swam over with the Football, Schofield pulled

the air hose into the gas station's little office, so that any stray bubbles got trapped against the office's ceiling rather than rising to the lake's surface and alerting the Penetrators to their new air source.

While he did so, he looked at the submerged gas station all around him.

He was still thinking about Botha.

The South African scientist's escape plan couldn't have involved just coming to this sunken petrol station. It had to be something *more* than that . . .

Schofield looked around the gas station's office and the garage adjoining it. The whole structure was nestled up against the base of the sunken cliff.

Just then, however, through the rear window of the little office, Schofield saw something built into the base of the cliff behind the gas station.

A wide boarded-up doorway.

It was constructed of thick wooden beams, and it appeared to burrow *into* the cliff-face. A pair of mine-car tracks disappeared underneath the planks that sealed its entrance.

A mine.

Botha's plan was beginning to make more sense.

Thirty seconds later, Book II joined him inside the office and gulped in some air from the hose.

Another minute and Schofield leaned outside the office and saw the blurred rippling outlines of the Air Force Penetrators above the surface wheel around in the air and depart, heading back for Area 7.

As soon as they were gone, he got Book's attention and pointed at the mine entrance behind the gas station, signalling, *I'm going there. You wait here.*

Book nodded.

Schofield then flicked on the small barrel-mounted flashlight on his Desert Eagle pistol and swam out through the rear window of the office, heading for the mine entrance at the base of the cliff.

He came to the boarded-up mine, and found that some of its rotting planks had been removed—possibly recently.

He swam inside.

Darkness met him. Impenetrable underwater darkness.

The narrow beam of his flashlight revealed rough rocky walls, submerged support beams, and the pair of mine-car tracks on the floor, disappearing into the shadows.

Schofield swam quickly through the mine tunnel, guided by the beam of his flashlight.

He had to keep track of how far he had gone. There would come a time very soon when he would have to make a choice: go back to Book and get some more air from the hose, or keep going, and hope he made it to a part of the mine that wasn't filled with water.

The only thing that convinced him that he would find such an air source was Botha. The South African scientist wouldn't have come here if he couldn't—

Suddenly Schofield saw a narrow vertical shaft branching off his tunnel. A rung-ladder ran up its length.

He swam over to the shaft, pointed his flashlight up into it. The shaft went both up and down, disappearing into blackness in both directions. It was an access shaft of some sort, allowing quick and easy movement to all levels of the mine.

Schofield was running out of air.

He did the math.

The lake was about ninety feet deep here. Hence, ninety feet up that rung-ladder, the water should level out.

Screw it.

It was the only option.

He turned back to get Book.

Two minutes later, he returned to the mine tunnel, this time with Book II—and the Football—beside him, plus a new lungful of air.

They headed straight for the vertical access shaft, used its rung-ladder to pull themselves up it.

The shaft was a tight cylinder, with earthen doorways opening off it every ten feet or so. Climbing it was like climbing up a very narrow sewer pipe.

Schofield led the way, moving quickly, counting the rungs as he climbed, calculating one foot for every rung.

At fifty rungs, his lungs began to burn.

At seventy, he felt bile crawling up the back of his throat.

At ninety, he still saw no sign of the surface, and he started to worry that he had got it all wrong, that he had made a fatal mistake, that this was the end, that he was about to black out—

—then suddenly, gloriously, Schofield's head exploded out of the water into beautiful cool air.

He immediately swung his body to the side to allow

355

Book II to surface next to him. Book burst out of the water and both of them gulped in the fresh air as they hung from the ladder in the tight vertical well.

The shaft still rose into darkness above them—only now it was no longer filled with water.

Once he had regained his breath, Schofield climbed up out of the water and stepped through the nearest earthen doorway.

He emerged inside a wide flat-floored cavern, an old administration chamber for the mine. What he saw *inside* the chamber, however, stopped him cold.

He saw boxes of provisions—food, water, gas cookers, powdered milk—hundreds of boxes.

Hundreds and hundreds of boxes.

A dozen fold-out cots lined the walls. A table covered with fake passports and drivers' licences stood in one corner.

It's a camp, Schofield thought. *A base camp.*

With enough food to last for weeks, months even—for however long it would take for the United States government to *stop* searching Lake Powell for the men who had stolen the Sinovirus and its prized vaccine source: Kevin.

Then, once the coast was clear, Botha and his men would leave the lake and make their way back to their homeland at their leisure.

Schofield looked at the stacks of boxes. Whoever had done this had been bringing stuff here for a *long* time.

'Geez.' Book II joined Schofield in the chamber. 'Some-body came prepared.'

Schofield looked at his watch.

9:31 a.m.

'Come on. We've got twenty-nine minutes to get this briefcase back to the President,' Schofield said. 'I say we go for the surface, and see if there's a way to get back to Area 7.'

Schofield and Book II climbed.

As fast as they could. Up the vertical access shaft. Schofield with Botha's small Samsonite container. Book II with the Football.

Within a minute, they reached the top of the ladder and stepped up into a wide aluminium building of some sort, kind of like an oversized shed.

A set of mine-car tracks began over on the far side of the shed, disappearing into the earth. They were flanked by a collection of rusty loading trays and old conveyor belts. Everything was covered in dust and cobwebs.

Schofield and Book raced for the external door, kicked it open.

Brilliant sunlight assaulted their eyes, wind-blown sand blasted their faces. The sandstorm was still raging.

The two tiny figures of Schofield and Book II stepped out of the mine shed . . .

. . . and they found themselves standing on a gigantic flat-topped desert peninsula that stretched out into Lake Powell. They looked like ants against the magnificent Utah landscape—the magnitude of the earth around them dwarfing even the large aluminium shed from which they had emerged.

Strangely, though, there was *another* structure on this vast flat-topped peninsula. It stood a bare fifty yards away from the mine shed: a small farmhouse, with a barn attached to its side.

Schofield and Book ran for it through the storm-tossed sand.

The letterbox at the gate read: 'HOEG'.

Schofield bolted past it, into the front yard.

He came to the side of the farmhouse, crouched underneath a window, peered inside, just as the wall beside him exploded with automatic gunfire. He spun to see a man dressed in denim overalls come charging around the corner of the farmhouse with an AK-47 assault rifle in his hands.

Blam!

Another shot rang out above the sandstorm and the farmer dropped to the dusty ground, dead.

Book II appeared at Schofield's side, his M9 pistol smoking.

'What the hell is going on here?' he yelled.

'I'm guessing,' Schofield said, 'that if we live through this, we'll find that Mr Hoeg is a friend of Gunther Botha's. Come on.'

Schofield ran for the barn, threw open its doors, hoping against hope that he would find some kind of transportation inside it . . .

'Well, it's about time we had a bit of luck,' he said. 'Thank you, God. We deserved a break.'

Standing there before him—glistening like a new car in a showroom—was a vehicle common to the farms in these parts: a beautiful lime-green biplane, a cropduster.

Three minutes later, Schofield and Book were shooting through the sky, soaring high over the snake-like canyons of Lake Powell.

It was 9:38 a.m.

This is going to be close, Schofield thought.

The plane was a Tiger Moth—an old World War II biplane often used for cropdusting in the dry south-west. It had two parallel wings, one above the fuselage and one below, that were joined by vertical struts and criss-crossing wires. Two spindly landing wheels stretched down from the forward end of its body, like the elongated legs of a mosquito, and an insecticide sprayer was attached to its tail.

Like most biplanes, it was a two-seater—the pilot sitting in the back seat, the co-pilot up front.

And it was a good plane too, well looked after. Mr Hoeg, it seemed, in addition to being a goddamned spy, was obviously an aeroplane enthusiast.

'What do you think?' Book said into his flight helmet's microphone. 'Do we go for the X-rail?'

'Not now,' Schofield replied. 'There's not enough time. We head straight for Area 7. For the Emergency Exit Vent.'

Dave Fairfax's heart was racing.

This had turned into quite an eventful day.

After he'd heard Dave's assessment of the situation at Area 7 and the presence of a rogue unit there, the DIA assistant director in charge of surveilling the Chinese space shuttle had ordered a blanket tap of a one-hundred-mile circle surrounding Areas 7 and 8. Now, *any* signal coming out of that zone would be picked up by the DIA's surveillance satellites.

Impressed by Fairfax's work on the matter thus far, the assistant director also gave the young cryptanalyst free rein to further pursue the case. 'Do whatever you have to, young man,' he'd said. 'You report directly to me now.'

Fairfax, however, was still puzzled.

Perhaps he was just excited, but something still nagged at him. The pieces still didn't quite add up.

The Chinese had a shuttle up in space, communicating with a rogue unit at a US Air Force base.

Okay.

So there was something at this base that the Chinese

wanted. Fairfax guessed it was the virus vaccine that kept getting mentioned in all the decoded messages.

Okay . . .

And the shuttle was the best way to communicate directly with the men on the ground.

No.

That wasn't right. The Chinese could use any of a dozen different satellites to communicate with men on the ground. You didn't need a whole shuttle to do that.

But what if the shuttle had another purpose . . .

Fairfax turned to one of the Air Force liaison people the DIA had called in. 'What sort of hardware does the Air Force keep at Area 7?'

The Air Force guy shrugged. 'Couple of Stealths, an SR-71 Blackbird, a few AWACS birds. Apart from that, it's mainly used as a biological facility.'

'What about the other complex then? Area 8?'

The Air Force man's eyes narrowed. 'That's another story altogether.'

'Hey. This is need-to-know. Believe me, I *really* need to know.'

The Air Force man hesitated for a moment.

Then he said, 'Area 8 contains two working prototypes of the X-38 space shuttle. It's a satellite killer—a smaller, sleeker version of the standard shuttle that gets launched off the back of a high-flying 747.'

'A satellite killer?'

'Carries special zero-gravity AMRAAM missiles on its wings. It's designed for a quick launch and short target-oriented missions: flying up into a low-earth orbit, knocking out enemy spy satellites or space stations, then coming home.'

'How many people can it hold?' Fairfax asked.

The Air Force man frowned. 'Three command crew. Maybe ten or twelve in the weapons hold, at the very most. Why?'

Now Fairfax was thinking fast.

'Oh, no way . . .' he breathed. 'No *way*!'

He lunged for a nearby printout.

It was the printout of the last message he had decoded, the same one he had used to reveal the men of Echo Unit as traitors. It read:

3-JUL   04:04:42   SATELLITE INTERCEPT   (ENGLISH)

VOICE 1:   WU and LI have arrived back at Area 7 with the virus. Your
**   men are with them. All the money has been accounted for.**
**   Names of my men who will need to be extracted: BENNETT,**
**   CALVERT, COLEMAN, DAYTON, FROMMER, GRAYSON,**
**   LITTLETON, MESSICK, OLIVER and myself.**

Fairfax read the line: 'Names of my men who will need to be extracted.'

'Extracted . . .' he said aloud.

'What are you thinking?' the Air Force liaison man asked.

Fairfax was in a world of his own now. He saw it all clearly.

'If you wanted to get a top-secret vaccine out of a top-secret Air Force base in the middle of the US desert, how would you do it? You couldn't fly it out, because the distance is too far. You'd be shot down before you even made it to California. Same for an overland extraction. You'd never make it to the border before we caught you.

By sea? Same problem. But these Chinese bastards have figured it out.'

'What do you mean?'

'You don't get something out of America by going north, south, east or west,' Fairfax said. 'You get it out by going *up*. Into space.'

Schofield looked at his watch.

9:47 a.m.

Thirteen minutes to get the Football to the President.

He and Book II had been flying for several minutes now, soaring over the desert landscape in their gaudy lime-green biplane at a swift 190 miles an hour.

In the distance ahead of them—rising up out of the flat desert plain—they could just make out the low mountain, the runway, and the small cluster of buildings that was Area 7.

Immediately after they had taken off, Schofield had taken the opportunity to open the silver Samsonite container that he had found on the lake floor.

Inside it, he saw twelve shiny glass ampoules, sitting in foam-lined pockets. Each tiny glass bulb was filled with a strange blue liquid. A white stick-on label on each ampoule read:

I.V. VACCINATION AMPOULE
Measured dose: 55 ml
Tested against SV strain V.9.1
Certified: 3/7 05:24:33

Schofield's eyes widened.

It was a field vaccination kit—measured doses of the vaccine that Kevin's genetically-constructed blood had provided, doses that could be administered by syringe. And created only this morning.

It was Gunther Botha's masterwork.

The antidote to the latest strain of the Sinovirus.

Schofield stuffed six of the little glass ampoules into the thigh pocket of his 7th Squadron fatigues. They might come in handy later.

He tapped Book II on the shoulder, handed him the other six. 'Just in case you catch a cold.'

Still sitting in the forward seat of the biplane, for the whole trip thus far Book II had been staring silently forward.

He took the ampoules Schofield offered him, pocketed them in his stolen 7th Squadron uniform. Then he just resumed his brooding forward gaze.

'Why don't you like me?' Schofield asked suddenly, speaking into his helmet mike.

Book II's head cocked to the side.

A moment later, the young sergeant's voice came through Schofield's helmet. 'There's something I've been wanting to ask you for a long time, Captain.' His voice was low, cold.

'What's that?'

'My father was on that mission to Antarctica with you. But he never came back. How did he die?'

Schofield fell silent.

Book II's father—Buck Riley Snr, the original 'Book' Riley—had died an horrific death during that terrible mission to Wilkes Ice Station. A murderous British SAS

366

commander named Trevor Barnaby had fed him, live, to a pool of ferocious killer whales.

'He was captured by the enemy. And they killed him.'

'How?'

'You don't want to know.'

'*How?*'

Schofield shut his eyes. 'They hung him upside-down over a pool of killer whales and lowered him in.'

'The Marine Corps never tells you how,' Book II said softly, his voice tinny over the radio. 'They just send you a letter, telling you what a patriot your dad was, and informing you that he was killed in action. Do you know, Captain, what happened to my family after my father died?'

Schofield bit his lip. 'No. I don't.'

'My mother used to live on the base at Camp Lejeune, North Carolina. I was in basic training at Parris Island. You know what happens to a Marine's wife when her husband is killed in action, Captain?'

Schofield knew. But he said nothing.

'She gets moved off the base. Seems the wives of living soldiers don't like the presence of newly single widows on the base—widows who might go stealing *their* husbands.

'So my mother, after losing her husband, got moved out of her home. She tried to start over, tried to be strong, but it didn't work. Three months after she was moved off the base, they found her in the bathroom of her new shoebox apartment. She'd taken a whole bottle of sleeping pills.'

Book II turned in his seat, looked Schofield straight in the eye.

'That's why I was asking you about using risky

strategies before. This isn't a *game*, you know. When some-one dies, there are consequences. My father is dead, and my mother killed herself because she couldn't live without him. I just wanted to make sure my father didn't die because of some high-risk tactical manoeuvre of yours.'

Schofield was silent.

He'd never really known Book II's mother.

Book Snr hadn't really socialised with his fellow Marines, preferring to spend his downtime with his family. Sure, Schofield had met Paula Riley at the odd lunch or dinner, but he'd never really got to know her. He'd heard about her death—and at the time he'd wished that he'd done more to help her.

'Your father was the bravest man I have ever known,' Schofield said. 'He died saving another person's life. A little girl fell out of a hovercraft and he dived out after her, shielded her from the fall. That's how they caught him. Then they took him back to the ice station and killed him. I tried to get back in time, but I . . . I didn't make it.'

'I thought you said you'd never lost to a countdown.'

Schofield said nothing.

'He talked about you, you know,' Book II said. 'Said you were one of the finest commanders he'd ever served under. Said he loved you like his own son, like me. I don't apologise for being a little cold toward you, Captain. I just had to get your measure, make my mind up for myself.'

'And your decision?'

'I'm still making up my mind.'

The plane swooped down toward the desert floor.

It was 9:51 when the lime-green Tiger Moth touched down on the dusty desert plain, kicking up a cloud of sand behind it, in the midst of the raging sandstorm.

As soon as the biplane skidded to a halt Schofield and Book II were out of it—Schofield holding the Football and his Desert Eagle pistol, Book with two nickel-plated M9s—charging toward the trench carved into the earth that housed the entrance to the Emergency Exit Vent.

Bodies lay everywhere, half-covered in sand.

Nine Secret Service people, all dressed in suits. And all dead. Members of Advance Team 2.

Four dead Marines littered the ground as well. All in full dress uniform. Colt Hendricks and the men of Nighthawk Three, who had come out here to check on the Escape Vent.

Christ, Schofield thought as he and Book II hurdled the bodies, heading for the Vent's entrance.

All this death . . . and all of it would have consequences.

9:52 a.m.

Schofield and Book hit the entrance to the Emergency Exit Vent on the fly—it was still open from the Reccondos' entry before—and entered a narrow concrete tunnel and the cool shade of the Area 7 complex.

They came to a rung ladder that stretched down into darkness—grabbed it and slid down it for a full *five hundred feet*. There were no lights here, so they slid by the light of Schofield's small barrel-mounted flashlight. Armed with his two ornamental pistols, Book II didn't have a flashlight.

9:53 a.m.

They hit the bottom, and saw a long one-man-wide concrete tunnel stretching away from them, gradually sloping downward—again, no lights.

They took off down it, running hard.

Schofield spoke into his Secret Service wrist mike as he ran: 'Fox! Fox! Can you read me? We're back! We're back inside the complex!'

His earpiece fizzled and crackled.

No reply.

Maybe Secret Service radios weren't designed to withstand long underwater swims.

9:54.

After several hundred yards of running down the ultra-narrow passageway, they burst out through the Emergency Exit Vent's door on Level 6, and found themselves standing on the northern tracks of the X-rail station.

The underground station was pitch-black.

Total darkness.

Frightening.

By the beam of his gunlight, Schofield could make out a score of dead bodies, plus a charred, blasted-open section in the middle of the central platform—the spot where Elvis's RDX grenade had gone off earlier.

'The stairs,' he said, pointing his beam at the door leading to the firestairs on their left. They leapt up onto the platform, charged for the door.

'Fox! Fox! Can you read me?'

Fizzle. Crackle.

They came to the stairwell door. Schofield threw it open—

—and immediately heard the rapid *clang-clang-clang* of more than a dozen pairs of combat boots booming down the stairs . . . and getting louder.

'Quickly, this way,' he said, diving down onto the tracks on the southern side of the platform, taking cover underneath the struts of the small X-rail maintenance vehicle sitting there.

Schofield killed his flashlight as Book II landed on the tracks beside him—not a second before the stairwell door burst open and Cobra Carney and the men of Echo Unit came charging out of it, a gaggle of wobbling flashlight beams moving quickly through the darkness.

Schofield immediately saw Kevin among them, surrounded by four men of Asian extraction.

'What is *this*?' Book II whispered.

Schofield stared at the four men flanking Kevin.

They were the four men he had seen inside the decompression chamber earlier, the ones who had brought the Sinovirus back from China.

His mind raced.

What was going on?

Kevin had only just been returned to Area 7 on the Penetrators. Yet now he was being moved again. Had Caesar instructed this team of commandos to take him to another, more secure location?

371

And yet again the question nagged Schofield: *What did Caesar Russell care for Kevin? Wasn't he after the President?*

Cobra and his men leapt down onto the tracks on the other side of the platform, moving with purpose.

It was then—by the light of Echo Unit's flashlights—that Schofield saw that the blast doors sealing the X-rail tunnel on the other side of the platform were *open*. They were the doors that sealed off the tunnel that led to Area 8.

Cobra and his men, with Kevin and the four Asian men among them, disappeared inside the eastern tunnel, looking behind themselves as they went.

Looking behind themselves . . . Schofield thought.

And then he saw Cobra Carney take one last anxious glance over his shoulder before he entered the tunnel, and suddenly Schofield knew.

These men were *stealing* Kevin . . . *from Caesar*.

Up in the darkened hangar on Level 2, Gant looked nervously at her watch.

9:55 a.m.

Five minutes until the President had to place his palm on the Football's analyser plate.

And still no word from Scarecrow.

Shit.

If he didn't come back soon, this show was over.

Gant and Mother—with Juliet, the President, Hagerty and Tate—had left the AWACS plane on Level 2, and guided by the flashlights on their gunbarrels, had made their way across the underground hangar toward the wide aircraft elevator shaft.

Still carrying the black box that she had pilfered from

the AWACS's belly, Gant was heading for Caesar Russell's command centre up on ground level to carry out her plan.

But if Schofield didn't get back with the Football soon, any plan she had would become academic.

The complex was eerily silent.

When combined with the pitch darkness that now shrouded the underground facility, it made for a very haunting atmosphere.

For a moment, Gant thought she heard her earpiece crackle: ' —*ox? —ead me?*'

Juliet heard it, too. 'Did you hear that—?'

And then so suddenly that it made them all jump, a gunshot echoed up through the elevator shaft.

Loud and booming.

The blast of a pump-action shotgun.

What followed the gunshot, however, was infinitely more terrifying.

A cackle of laughter.

An *insane* cackle that floated up the shaft, cutting through the air like a scythe.

'Nah-ha-*haaaaaaaah! Hellooooo* everybody! *We're coming to get you!*'

This was followed by a man's voice howling like a wolf. 'Arrooooo!'

Even Mother gulped. 'The prisoners . . .'

'They must have found the arms cabinet down in the cell bay,' Juliet said.

Abruptly, a loud mechanical clanking noise reverberated up through the elevator shaft.

Gant looked out over the edge.

The giant aircraft elevator platform lay at the bottom of

the shaft on Level 5, the remains of the destroyed AWACS plane on its back half-submerged in a wide body of water.

At various places on the elevator platform, Gant saw torches—flaming torches, about twenty of them—moving all around, flickering in the darkness. Torches held aloft by men.

The escaped prisoners.

'How many do you see?' Juliet asked.

'I don't know,' Gant said. 'Thirty-five, forty. Why, how many are there?'

'Forty-two.'

'Oh, perfect.'

Then, abruptly, with a great groaning lurch, the elevator platform lifted up out of the lake at the base of the shaft, dripping water.

'I thought the power . . .' Mother began.

Juliet shook her head. 'It has a stand-alone hydraulic engine, for use in a power blackout like this.'

The elevator lumbered up the shaft, its massive form moving steadily through the darkness.

'Quickly. Away from the edge.' Gant pushed the President back behind the landing gear of one of the AWACS planes nearby. She and Mother and Juliet clicked off their barrel-mounted flashlights.

The gigantic elevator platform rumbled past the open doorway of Level 2, continued slowly upward. As it did so, Gant peered around the landing gear of the AWACS.

The scene looked like something out of a horror movie.

They were standing on the rising elevator platform— holding flaming torches above their heads; shotguns and pistols in their spare hands—and they howled like animals, whooping it up, their shrill calls grating like fingernails on a chalkboard in the dark silence of the complex.

The prisoners from the Level 5 cell block.

Half of them were not wearing shirts—their bare chests shone in the firelight of their torches. Others wore bandannas wrapped around their heads and biceps.

All of them, however, wore soaking-wet trousers, caused by the rising water on Level 5.

Then the elevator rose out of Gant's view, and she emerged from her hiding spot to watch its underside climb and climb until it arrived at the main hangar with an ominous, thunderous boom.

Caesar Russell strode purposefully across the control room overlooking the main hangar.

He had just seen the aircraft elevator platform—with its cargo of howling and shotgun-firing prisoners—rise into view. No sooner had it stopped than prisoners bolted off it, scattering in every direction.

'Get on the hand-helds,' Caesar ordered coolly. 'Tell Charlie to wait at the top door and prepare for evacuation to the secondary command post. We'll come to them. Where's Echo?'

'I can't raise them, sir,' the nearest radio man replied.

'Never mind. We'll contact them later. Let's go.'

Everyone started moving. Logan and his three Alpha men. Boa McConnell and his four Bravo men.

Caesar used a keypad to unlock a small pressure-door set into the northern wall of the control room, hurled it open.

A smooth concrete passageway stretched away from him, sloping down and to the left, where it would ultimately connect with the top door's passageway.

The three Alpha men led the way. They charged into the passageway, guns first. Caesar himself went next, followed by Logan.

Colonel Jerome Harper was next in line, but he never got the chance.

For just as Logan disappeared inside the passageway's entrance, the regular door on the *other* side of the control room flew open, revealing five shotgun-toting prisoners!

Boom!

An entire console was blasted to pieces.

In the escape passageway, Logan spun—and saw the intruders, and realised that the others weren't going to make it into the tunnel—and with a look to Harper, he made the call and slammed the escape door shut behind him, sealing off the passageway, sealing Harper and the remaining Air Force men inside the control room.

Eleven men in total were left behind: Harper, Boa McConnell, Boa's four Bravo Unit men, the four radio operators, and the unseen man who had been observing the morning's events from the shadows.

All were left in the control room, at the mercy of the murderous prisoners.

Down in the Level 6 X-rail station, Schofield and Book II hurried out from their hiding spot underneath the compact maintenance vehicle, leapt up onto the platform and dashed for the door to the firestairs.

9:56.

Schofield yanked open the door and instantly heard shotgun fire echoing down the stairwell, followed by a loud '*Arroooo!*'

He shut the door quickly.

'Well, it's official,' he said. 'We have just arrived in hell.'

'Four minutes to find the President,' Book II said.

'I know. I know,' Schofield looked about himself. 'But to do that we have to get up into the complex somehow.'

He stared out into the darkness of the underground railway station.

'Quickly, this way,' he started racing down the platform.

'What?' Book II said, chasing after him.

'There's another way up into the complex. Those 7th Squadron guys used it before—the air vent at the other end of the platform!'

9:57.

The two of them reached the air vent.

Schofield tried his mike again, hoping he hadn't busted it during that swim through Lake Powell.

'Fox! Fox! Can you read me?'

Pop. Fizz. Nothing.

He and Book clambered into the air vent, hurried down its length, their boots reverberating with every step.

They came to the base of the vent's four-hundred-foot-tall vertical shaft.

'Whoa,' Book II said, looking up the shaft. It disappeared into black infinity.

9:58.

Schofield said, 'Quickly, up the air vent. We use the cross-vents to reach the aircraft elevator shaft and then we cut across the platform and see if we can find them.'

Schofield fired his Maghook up into the darkened air vent, delaying the activation of its magnet. The grappling hook boomed up the shaft, flying fast, before Schofield initiated its magnetic charge and immediately—*whump!*— the hook snapped left in mid-air, dragged sideways by its powerful magnetic pull, and attached itself to the vertical wall of the vent.

9:58:20.

Schofield went first, whizzing up into the shaft on the Maghook's rope. Book II came up behind him.

9:58:40.

They hurried into the nearest horizontal cross-vent, charged down it, the Football flailing in Schofield's spare hand.

9:58:50.

They came to the enormous aircraft elevator shaft. It

yawned before them, shrouded in black. The only light: some orange firelight way up at the top of the shaft winking through the tiny square aperture that usually contained the mini-elevator. The main platform, it seemed, was right up at ground level, up in the hangar there.

Schofield and Book II stood at the mouth of the cross-vent. They were on Level 3.

Schofield brought his mike to his lips.

'Fox! Fox! Where are you!'

'*Hey!*' a familiar female voice echoed down through the shaft.

Schofield snapped to look up, brought his gunlight around.

And saw a small white spot—the beam of another barrel-mounted flashlight—blinking back at him *from the other side of the shaft*, but from one level above, from the massive hangar doorway of Level 2.

And above the flashlight, in the glow of its beam, Schofield saw the very anxious face of Libby Gant.

9:59:00.

'Fox!'

'*Scarecrow!*'

Gant's voice came through Schofield's earpiece loud and clear now. The water damage must have only affected its range.

'Damn it!' Schofield said. 'I thought the elevator platform would be here!'

'*The prisoners took it up to the main hangar,*' Gant said.

9:59:05

9:59:06

'Jesus, Scarecrow. What do we do? We only have a minute left . . .'

Schofield was thinking the same thing.

Sixty seconds.

Not enough time to go down to the bottom of the shaft, swim across, and come back up again. And not enough time to shuffle hand-over-hand around the walls of the shaft, either. And they couldn't swing across on a Maghook—it was too far.

Damn, he thought.

Damn-damn-damn-damn-damn-damn-damn-damn.

'What about a Harbour Bridge?' Mother's voice came in over Schofield's earpiece.

The 'Harbour Bridge' was a legendary Maghook trick. Two people fired two oppositely-charged Maghooks in such a way that the two hooks hit in mid-air and stuck together. It was named after the Sydney Harbour Bridge, the famous Australian landmark that was built from opposite sides of Sydney Harbour, two separate arcs that ultimately met in the middle. Schofield had seen a number of Marines try it. None of them had succeeded.

'No,' he said, 'the Harbour Bridge is impossible. I've never seen anyone hit another Maghook in mid-flight. But maybe . . .'

9:59:09

9:59:10

He looked over at the President and Gant standing in the doorway to Level 2, gauged the distance.

Then he looked up—and saw the darkened underside of the aircraft elevator platform, way up at the top of the shaft.

Mother's suggestion, however, had given him an idea.

Maybe with two Maghooks they could . . .

'Fox! Quickly!' he said. 'Where is the mini-elevator?'

'*Where we left it before, up on Level 1,*' Gant said.

'Go up to Level 1. Get on it. Take it up the shaft and stop it a hundred feet below the main elevator platform. Go! *Now!*'

Gant knew not to argue. There was no time. She grabbed the President and dashed out of Schofield's sight.

9:59:14

9:59:15

Schofield dashed past Book II, heading back along the horizontal cross-vent to the main vent.

He came to the vertical ventilation shaft and without even a blink, fired his Maghook up into it again.

This time he waited until the Maghook had played out its entire one hundred and fifty feet of rope before initiating the grappling hook's magnetic pull.

As before, the Maghook's powerful magnetic charge yanked the upwardly-flying hook sideways in mid-air, and it thunked hard against the metal wall of the vent, and held fast.

9:59:22

9:59:23

Schofield whizzed up the shaft again.

This time Book II didn't go with him—Schofield didn't have the time to send the Maghook back down for him. He'd have to do this alone, and besides, he needed the Maghook . . .

Schofield shot up the shaft on the Maghook's rope, the air vent's close steel walls rushing past him on all four sides. He stopped the hook's reeling mechanism as he came to another cross-vent three levels up—but still a hundred feet below the main hangar. He charged into the cross-vent.

9:59:29

9:59:30

Came to the aircraft elevator shaft again. The underside of the giant elevator platform loomed closer now, only a hundred feet above him. He could hear the gunshot blasts and catcalls of the prisoners up in the hangar and wondered for the briefest of moments what on earth they were doing up there.

9:59:34

9:59:35

And then, by the light of his barrel-mounted flashlight, he saw the mini-elevator whizzing up the concrete wall on the other side of the massive elevator shaft. The small figures of Gant, Juliet, Mother and the President were on it.

9:59:37

9:59:38

As the mini-elevator drew level with him, Schofield said, 'Okay! Stop there!'

The mini-elevator jolted to a halt, now diagonally opposite Schofield but separated from him by a sheer concrete chasm two hundred feet wide.

And so they faced each other, from opposite sides of the enormous shaft.

9:59:40

'Okay, Fox,' Schofield said into his radio. 'I want you to fire your Maghook into the underside of the elevator platform.'

'But it's not long enough to swing across on . . .'

'I know. But *two* Maghooks will be,' Schofield said. 'Try and hit the platform about a quarter of the way across. I'll do the same from this side.'

9:59:42

Schofield fired his Maghook. With a loud, puncture-like whump, the hook flew into the air, flying diagonally up into the shaft.

And then—*clunk!*—the magnetic head of the hook affixed itself to the underside of the elevator platform.

9:59:43

Clunk! A similar noise came from the other side of the shaft. Gant had done the same with her Maghook.

9:59:45

9:59:46

Schofield held his Maghook with one hand. Then he opened the Football, revealing the countdown timer inside it—00:00:14 . . . 00:00:13—and held it by its handle, *folded open*.

'Okay, Fox,' he said into his mike. 'Now give the rope to the President. We've got twelve seconds now, so we'll only get one shot at this.'

'*Oh, you have got to be kidding,*' Mother's voice said.

On the other side of the shaft, Gant gave the Maghook's launcher to the President of the United States. 'Good luck, sir.'

Now, Schofield and the President stood on opposite sides of the great concrete elevator shaft, holding onto the diagonally-stretched ropes of their respective Maghooks, looking like a pair of trapeze artists about to perform their act.

9:59:49

9:59:50

'Go!' Schofield said.

*

And they swung.

Out over the shaft.

Two tiny figures, on two equally tiny thread-like ropes.

Indeed, as the two of them swung in mirroring pendulum-like arcs, they *did* look like trapeze artists—swinging toward each other, aiming to meet in the middle, Schofield holding out the open briefcase, the President reaching forward with his outstretched hand.

9:59:52

9:59:53

Schofield reached the base of his arc, started coming up.

In the dim light, he saw the President swooping in toward him, a look of sheer terror plastered across his face. But the chief executive swung well, gripping his rope tightly, reaching forward with his right hand.

9:59:54

9:59:55

And they came close, rising in their pendulum motions, reaching the extremities of their arcs . . .

9:59:56

9:59:57

. . . and, four hundred feet above the base of the elevator shaft, swinging in near total darkness, *they came together*, and the President pressed his outstretched palm against the analyser plate in Schofield's hand.

Beep!

The timer on the Football instantly reset itself.

00:00:02 became 90:00:00 and the clock immediately began counting down once more.

As for Schofield and the President, having briefly shared the same space of air four hundred feet above the world, they now parted, swooping back toward their respective starting points.

The President arrived back at the mini-elevator platform, where he was caught by Gant, Mother and Juliet.

On the other side of the elevator shaft, Schofield swung back to his cross-vent.

He landed lightly on the edge of the tunnel, breathing deeply with relief, the stainless-steel Football hanging open in his hand.

They'd done it. At least for another ninety minutes. Now all he had to do was get himself and Book over to the President. Then they'd be back in business.

Schofield reeled in his Maghook, then turned to head back down the cross-vent to get Book—

Shuck-shuck.

Three men were blocking his way—men wearing blue jeans but no shirts. They also brandished pump-action Remingtons and they variously had tattooed chests, bulging biceps, or no front teeth.

'Reach for the sky, pardner,' one of the shotgun-toting prisoners said.

Caesar Russell charged through the low concrete escape tunnel.

The three remaining men from Alpha Unit ran in front of him. Kurt Logan hurried along behind.

They'd just left Harper and the others in the control room to be captured by the escaped inmates, and were now bolting down the escape passageway, racing for the point where it met the top door exit.

They rounded a bend, came to a heavy steel door half-buried in concrete, keyed the code. The door opened.

The top door's exit tunnel appeared before them, heading right and left.

To the right—freedom, via the exit that opened onto one of the exterior hangars here at Area 7.

To the left, around a bend, the regular elevator shaft, and . . .

. . . something else.

Caesar froze.

He saw a combat boot protruding around the corner that led to the regular elevator shaft.

The black combat boot of a dead commando.

Caesar stepped closer.

And saw that the boot belonged to the horribly bloodied body of Python Willis—the commanding officer of Charlie Unit, the 7th Squadron unit that had been bringing Kevin back to Area 7.

Caesar's face darkened.

Charlie Unit lay dead before him. And Kevin was nowhere to be seen.

Then Caesar saw the mark on the wall next to Python Willis's dead fingers, a symbol scrawled in blood, a final gesture from Charlie Unit's commander before he'd died.

A single capital 'E'.

Caesar just stared at it, pursing his lips.

Logan came up beside him. 'What is it?'

'Let's get to the secondary command post,' Caesar said flatly. 'And when we get there, I want you to find out what's happened to Echo Unit.'

Shane Schofield emerged from the air vent hatch underneath Marine One, flanked by the four heavily-armed prisoners. He no longer carried the Football. One of his captors now held it like a new toy.

As he slid out from underneath the Presidential helicopter, he thought he heard clapping and shouting . . .

. . . and then suddenly—*boom!*—a gunshot made him start. The shot was quickly followed by a loud roar of approval.

Then another booming gunshot—and more cheers and applause.

Schofield felt his blood run cold.

What the hell was he walking into?

He emerged from beneath Marine One and immediately saw about thirty prisoners, their backs to him, gathered around the central aircraft elevator platform.

In the time since his capture in the air vent down below, the massive platform—with the tangled remains of the destroyed AWACS plane still on it—had been lowered about ten feet below the floorline of the hangar and halted, so that now it formed a gigantic square-shaped pit in the centre of the hangar.

The mob of inmates was crowded around the makeshift pit, looking intently down into it like gamblers at a cockfight, shaking their fists, shouting and cat-calling. One shaggy-looking individual was screaming, 'Run, little man! Run! Run! *Ha-haaaaa!*'

They were the most motley crew Schofield had ever seen.

Their angry faces were covered in scars and tattoos. Each prisoner's uniform had been tailored to his own personal tastes—some had ripped off their shirtsleeves and turned them into headbands, others wore their shirts open, others still, wore no shirts at all.

Schofield was marched over to the edge of the pit. He looked down into it.

Amid the maze of AWACS plane pieces that littered the square concrete hole, he saw two blue-uniformed Air Force men—young men and, judging by their perfectly pressed uniforms, office bunnies, radio operators probably—running like frightened animals.

In the pit with them were five burly inmates—all armed with shotguns—prowling through the maze, *hunting* the two hapless radio operators.

Schofield saw the bodies of two more radio men lying

in pools of blood in separate corners of the pit: the cause of the cheers he had heard moments before.

It was then, however, that to Schofield's horror, a small band of prisoners emerged from the *other* side of the hangar.

In the midst of this new group of inmates, Schofield saw Gant, Mother, Juliet . . . and the President of the United States.

'Tell me this isn't happening,' he breathed to himself.

Down in the darkness of the Level 1 hangar, Nicholas Tate III, Domestic Policy Adviser to the President of the United States, gazed nervously up into the elevator shaft.

The President and his three female protectors hadn't returned from their trip up the shaft on the detachable mini-elevator, and now Tate was worried.

'Do you think the inmates got them?' he asked Hot Rod Hagerty.

They could hear the shouts and gunshots from up in the main hangar. It was like standing outside a stadium during a football match.

'I hope not,' Hagerty whispered.

Tate continued to stare up into the shaft, a thousand thoughts flickering through his mind, most of them relating to his own self-preservation. A minute passed.

'So what do you think we should do?' he said at last, without turning around.

There was no reply.

Tate frowned, spun around. 'I said—' He froze.

Hagerty was nowhere to be seen.

The Level 1 hangar stretched away from him, shrouded

in darkness, the only presence, the shadows of the gigantic planes inside it.

Tate's face went blank.

Hagerty was gone.

Vanished—silently, *instantly*—in the space of a single minute.

It was as if he'd just been erased from existence.

A lightning bolt of fear shot through Nicholas Tate. Now he was alone, *down here*, in a locked-down facility filled with treacherous Air Force commandos and the nastiest collection of murderers known to man.

And then he saw it.

Saw a glint of light on the floor a few yards away from him, at the spot where he had last seen Hagerty standing. He went over to it, picked it up.

It was a ring.

A gold officer's ring.

Hagerty's graduation ring from Annapolis.

The last two radio operators didn't last long.

As the final shots rang out from within the pit, Schofield and Gant were shoved together, the others beside them.

'Hey there,' Gant said.

'Hi,' Schofield said.

After Schofield and the President's daring trapeze act, Gant and her team hadn't fared any better than Schofield had.

No sooner had the President swung back onto the mini-elevator than the little platform had jolted suddenly and whizzed up the shaft—called by someone up in the main hangar.

They had risen up into the hangar and found themselves in the middle of a whole new nightmare.

The prisoners—the former test subjects for Gunther Botha's vaccine—were now in charge of Area 7.

Although there was no way she could have hidden their meagre supply of guns, Gant did manage to hide her Maghook on their short ride up the shaft. It now lay clinging magnetically to the *underside* of the detachable mini-elevator.

Unfortunately, when the little platform had arrived up in the ground-level hangar—rising up through the matching square hole in the corner of the main platform—Gant had still had the black box from the AWACS plane in her possession.

But she hadn't wanted to alert any of the prisoners to its significance, so she'd placed it on the floor of the mini-elevator, and as soon as the platform had come flush against the floor of the main hangar, she'd 'accidentally' kicked it clear, sending it tumbling out onto the hangar floor, a short way from the elevator shaft.

With the hunt in the pit now over, the prisoners gathered around the aircraft elevator shaft turned their attention to the President and his guardians.

An older prisoner stepped out of the larger group of inmates, a shotgun held lazily in his hand.

He was a very distinctive-looking individual.

He appeared to be about fifty, and judging from the confidence of his stride, he clearly had the respect of the group. Although the top of his head was bald, long grey-black hair flowed down from its sides, growing past his shoulders. A narrow angular nose, pale white skin, and hollow bloodless cheeks completed his very Gothic appearance.

'Come into my parlour, said the spider to the fly,' the long-haired man said as he stepped in front of the President.

He had a soft silky voice, menacing in its slow articulation.

'Good morning, Mister President,' he said pleasantly. 'How nice of you to join us. Remember me?'

The President said nothing.

'But of course you do,' the prisoner said. 'I'm an 18-84. In one way or another, you've met all nine of the people who during your presidency have been convicted under Title 18, Part I, Chapter 84 of the United States Code. It's that part of the Code that prohibits ordinary Americans from attempting to assassinate their President.

'Grimshaw, Seth Grimshaw,' the long-haired prisoner said, offering his hand. 'We met in February, just a couple of weeks after you became President, as you were leaving the Bonaventure Hotel in LA via its underground kitchen. I was the one who tried to put a bullet in your skull.'

The President said nothing.

And he didn't take Grimshaw's proffered hand.

'You managed to keep that whole incident quiet,' Grimshaw said. 'Very impressive. Especially since all someone like me really wants is publicity. And besides, it's not wise to scare the nation, is it? Better to keep the ignorant masses unaware of these troublesome little attempts on your life. As they say, ignorance is bliss.'

The President said nothing.

Grimshaw looked him up and down, cast a bemused eye over the black combat clothing that the Chief Executive now wore. The President, Juliet and Schofield were all still dressed in their black 7th Squadron combat attire. Gant and Mother, on the other hand, still wore their formal—but now very dirty—Marine dress uniforms.

Grimshaw smiled, a thin, satisfied smile.

Then he strolled over to the inmate holding the Football

and took the silver briefcase from him. He opened it, then glanced from its countdown display screen to the President.

'It would appear that my recently liberated associates and I have intruded upon something rather interesting. A game of cat-and-mouse, it would seem, judging by your clothes and the way you unceremoniously scampered through my cell block earlier.' He clucked his tongue reproachfully. 'Really, Mister President, I must say, this is not at all presidential. Not at all.'

Grimshaw's eyes narrowed.

'But who am I to stop such an imaginative spectacle? The President and his loyal bodyguards versus the treacherous military–industrial complex.' Grimshaw turned. 'Goliath. Bring the other captives over here.'

At that moment, an extraordinarily large prisoner—Goliath, Schofield guessed—stepped out from behind Grimshaw and headed off in the direction of the hangar's internal building. He was an absolute *giant* of a man, with massive tree-trunk-sized biceps and a squared-off head reminiscent of Frankenstein's monster. He even had a flat square bulge that protruded from his forehead—the signature mark, Schofield knew, of someone who'd had a steel plate inserted in his skull. Goliath carried a P-90 assault rifle in one massive fist and Schofield's Maghook in the other.

He returned moments later.

Behind him came the seven Air Force men who—along with the four unfortunate radio operators—had been captured inside the control room earlier:

Colonel Jerome T. Harper.

Boa McConnell and his four Bravo Unit men, two of whom were badly wounded.

And the lone individual who had been observing the

morning's events from the shadows of Caesar Russell's control room.

Schofield recognised him instantly.

So did the President.

'Webster . . .' he said softly.

Warrant Officer Carl Webster, the official guardian of the Football, stood with the Air Force people, looking *very* uncomfortable. Beneath his thick hairy eyebrows, his eyes darted left and right, as if searching for an escape.

'You cocksucking little bastard,' Mother said. '*You* gave the Football to Russell. You sold out the President.'

Webster said nothing.

Schofield watched him. He had wondered whether Webster had been abducted by the 7th Squadron earlier that morning. More than anything else, Caesar Russell had needed the Football to carry out his presidential challenge, and Schofield had speculated as to how he had obtained it from Webster.

Quite clearly, force hadn't been necessary—the blood on the Football's handcuffs had obviously been a ruse. Webster, it seemed, had been bought long before the President had arrived at Area 7.

'Now, now, children,' Seth Grimshaw said, waving the Football in his hand. 'Save your strength. You'll be able to settle all your scores in a moment. But first'—he turned to the Air Force colonel, Harper—'I have a question that needs answering. The exit to this facility. Where is it?'

'There is no exit,' Harper lied. 'The facility is in lock-down. You can't get out.'

Grimshaw raised his shotgun, pointed it at Harper's face, shucked the pump action. 'Perhaps I'm not being specific enough.'

He then turned and fired two booming shots into the two injured Bravo Unit men standing next to Harper. They were blasted off their feet.

Grimshaw turned the gun back to Harper, raised his eyebrows expectantly.

Harper's face went white. He nodded over at the regular elevator: 'There's a door that branches off the personnel elevator shaft. We call it the top door. It leads outside. Keypad code is 5564771.'

'Thank you, Colonel, you really are too kind,' Grimshaw said. 'Now then, we must let you children finish what you've started. As I'm sure you'll understand, once we depart this dreadful place, we can't allow any of *you* to leave it alive. But as a final gesture of goodwill, I am going to offer you all one last favour—albeit one that is more for my entertainment than yours.

'I am going to give you all one last chance to kill each other. Five against five. In the killing pit. So at least the winner will die knowing who won your impromptu civil war.' He turned to Goliath. 'Put the Air Force people in here. Start the President's little posse on the other side.'

Schofield and the others were marched at gunpoint to the far side of the pit, the eastern side.

The five remaining Air Force men—Jerome Harper, Boa McConnell, the last two men from Bravo Unit, and the traitor, Warrant Officer Webster—stood directly opposite them, separated by the two-hundred-foot-wide sunken aircraft elevator platform.

'Let the battle begin,' Seth Grimshaw bared his teeth. 'To the *death*.'

Schofield dropped down into the pit and immediately found himself confronted by a twisted metal maze—the enormous broken pieces of the smashed AWACS plane.

The Boeing 707's wings lay at all angles, snapped and broken and still dripping with water. Its gigantic barrel-like jet engines stood on their ends. And in the very centre of the pit—easily the largest single piece of the destroyed plane—stood the AWACS's horribly broken fuselage. Long and cylindrical, it lay diagonally across the pit, nose down, like a massive dead bird.

The darkness of the main hangar didn't help things.

The only light was the firelight from the inmates' torches—they cast long shadows down into the maze, turning it into a dark metal forest where you couldn't see more than a few feet in front of your face.

How the hell did we get into this? Schofield thought.

He and the others stood on the eastern side of the pit, up against its solid concrete wall, not sure what to do.

Abruptly, a shotgun round blasted into the wall above Schofield's head.

Seth Grimshaw called: 'The two teams will engage

each other immediately! If you do not begin eliminating one another soon, we will start eliminating you from up here!'

'Christ . . .' Juliet Janson gasped.

Schofield turned to face his group. 'Okay, we don't have much time, so listen up. Not only do we have to survive this, but we have to find a way out of here afterwards.'

'The mini-elevator,' Gant nodded to their right, to the north-eastern corner of the pit where the detachable mini-platform now lay flush against the pit's floor, albeit covered by five armed prisoners.

'We're going to need a diversion,' Schofield said, 'something to—'

The flying piece of metal nearly took his head clean off.

Schofield saw it at the very last second and on a reflex, he ducked, just as the jagged piece of steel slammed like an axe into the concrete wall behind him.

He spun, searching for the source of the projectile—and he saw it in the shapes of the two commandos from Bravo Unit, bursting out of the darkness, hurdling the pieces of broken plane, each man holding a length of jagged metal like a sword, and charging at Schofield's group at speed!

'Scatter!' Schofield yelled as the first commando came storming toward him, swinging down hard with his 'sword'.

Schofield blocked the blow by grabbing the man's downward-moving wrist, while Gant engaged the other commando.

'*Go!*' Schofield yelled to Juliet, Mother and the President. 'Get out of here!'

398

Juliet and the President dashed off into the darkness. But Mother hesitated.

Schofield saw her. 'Go! Stay with the President!'

The prisoners cheered with delight as over by the eastern wall of the pit, Schofield fought with the first 7th Squadron commando, while behind him, Gant grappled with the second Bravo Unit man.

The President and Juliet—with Mother a short distance behind them—dashed north through the darkened maze, heading for the mini-elevator at the north-eastern corner.

From above them, however, the chanting prisoners saw what Juliet and the President and Mother could not: three figures closing in on them from their left, moving quickly along the northern wall of the pit—Jerome Harper, Carl Webster, and co-ordinating the assault, Captain Boa McConnell.

Schofield and Gant stood back-to-back, fighting their own separate battles.

Gant had taken up a length of piping from the floor, and was now wielding it like a quarterstaff against the blows of her Bravo Unit commando.

The Bravo man swung his piece of steel viciously, two-fisted, but Gant parried well, holding her length of pipe sideways, blocking the blow.

'How you doing back there?' Schofield asked, between blows with his own enemy.

'Just . . . frigging . . . dandy,' Gant said, gritting her teeth.

'We have to get to the President.'

'I know,' Gant said, 'but first . . . I have to . . . save your ass.'

She glanced over her shoulder at him and smiled, and in a fleeting instant, she saw his opponent move in for another blow and she shouted, 'Scarecrow! *Duck!*'

Schofield dropped like a stone.

His opponent's sword swooshed over his head, and the man overbalanced, and stumbled right toward Gant.

Gant was waiting.

Turning her attention from her own assailant for the briefest of moments, she swung her length of pipe hard, baseball-style.

Shwack!

The sound of her pipe hitting the Bravo Unit man's head was absolutely sickening. The commando collapsed in a heap just as Gant spun again—pirouetting like a ballet dancer—returning just in time to block the next blow from her own attacker.

'Scarecrow! Go!' she yelled. 'Get to the President!'

And with a final look at her, Schofield dashed off into the darkened wreckage.

About twenty yards to the north of Schofield and Gant, Juliet Janson and the President were running hard, weaving their way through the debris-littered maze, heading for the north-eastern corner, but unaware of the three men closing in on them from the left.

They went for Juliet first.

Two figures came bursting out of the darkness, from behind the destroyed rear-end of the AWACS plane—Boa

400

McConnell and Warrant Officer Carl Webster. They crash-tackled Juliet hard, hurling her to the floor.

The President spun to see her hit the floor, held down by Boa and Webster. Then he turned again, and saw Colonel Jerome Harper, standing amid the AWACS wreckage, watching from a distance.

The President was hurrying to help Juliet when—*whoosh*—a large blurring shape came exploding out of the nearby wreckage, missing him by inches.

Mother.

Flying through the air, out of the darkness, linebacker-style.

Crunchhhh!

She shoulder-charged Boa McConnell so hard that she almost snapped his neck. The 7th Squadron commander was thrown off Juliet's body, visibly dazed.

Carl Webster was momentarily startled by the sudden loss of his fellow attacker, and he turned to see what had happened—

—just in time to receive a powerful punch from Mother.

Even though he was a bulky man, Webster was thrown right off Juliet by the blow and went crashing into a collection of plane pieces. Without a pause, he snatched up a wicked-looking four-foot strip of metal and brandished it at Mother.

Mother growled.

Webster charged.

The fight was as brutal as they come.

They couldn't have been more evenly matched—both were experienced in hand-to-hand combat, both were over six feet tall, and they both weighed in at over two hundred pounds.

Webster roared as he swung his makeshift metal sword. Mother ducked, then quickly grabbed a busted piece of the AWACS's wing-flap to use as a shield. Webster's blows clanged down against her shield as he forced her back toward the battered wing of the plane.

As she danced backwards, staving off Webster's slashes, Mother bent down and scooped up a jagged sword of her own.

She tried to strike back, but Webster had all the momentum. He swung again, cutting deep into her shoulder, tearing open the sleeve of her dress coat, drawing blood.

'Arrgh!' Mother shouted, dropping her shield, fending off the next three blows with only her sword.

Damn it, all she needed was one opening, one chance . . .

'Why did you betray the President!' she yelled as she stumbled backwards, trying to distract him.

'There comes a time when a man has to make a decision, Mother!' the Army warrant officer barked back, yelling between blows. 'When he has to choose a side! I have fought for this country! I have had friends who died for it, only to be *fucked over* later by politicians like him! So when the opportunity arose, I decided that I was no longer going to stand by and watch yet another two-bit, whore-banging, draft-dodging *fuck* drive this country into the ground!'

Webster swung—a lusty, sideways swipe.

Mother jumped backwards, avoiding the blow, leaping up onto the wing of the plane, so that she was now three feet off the ground.

But the wing wobbled slightly under her weight, and she lost her balance for a split second and Webster slashed viciously with his sword—once again slicing sideways—

aiming for her now-exposed ankles, way too fast for her to block in time.

And the vicious blow hit home—

Clang!!!

Webster's weapon-hand vibrated monstrously as his jagged metal sword slammed into Mother's dress-uniformed pants leg, just below the knee.

Webster blanched.

'What—?'

Mother smiled.

He'd hit her prosthetic lower leg—her *titanium-alloy* prosthetic lower leg!

Seeing her opponent's confusion, Mother took her one and only opportunity, and swung her own makeshift sword with all her might.

Slash!

A fountain of blood sprayed out from Webster's throat as Mother's blade sliced across his neck, severing his carotid artery.

Webster's blade fell from his hand, and he dropped to his knees, clutching his bleeding throat. He held his hands out in front of him, gazing at the blood on them in disbelief. Then he took one final horrified look up at Mother, after which he fell face-first into a pool of his own blood.

The crowd of inmates roared with delight.

By now, the assembled mob—Seth Grimshaw included—had moved around to the northern side of the pit in an effort to find better spectating positions.

Some of them had started cheering for the President, a happily deranged chant in the tradition of American Olympic supporters: *'U–S–A! U–S–A!'*

On the eastern side of the pit, Gant was still engaged in the fight of her life.

Her 7th Squadron opponent's sword-like length of steel clanged against her own quarterstaff pipe.

They fought amid the wreckage, trading blows, the Bravo Unit commando driving her backwards. As he did so, he began to smile with every raging swing. Clearly, he felt he had the edge.

And so he swung harder, but as Gant saw, this only served to wear him out more with every blow.

So she feigned fatigue, staggered backwards, 'desperately' fended off his swings.

And then her assailant swung—a lunging sloppy effort, the swipe of a tiring man—and quick as a flash, belying her apparent fatigue, Gant ducked beneath the blow and launched herself upward, thrusting her pipe forward—end-first—ramming its solid tip right into the throat of her stunned opponent, crushing his Adam's Apple, ramming it two inches back into his windpipe, stopping him dead in his tracks.

The man's eyes went instantly wide with disbelief. He wobbled unsteadily, wheezing, choking. He may have been standing up, but he was already dead. Staring stupidly at Gant, he crumpled to the ground.

The crowd of prisoners was oddly silent—stunned, it seemed, by Gant's lightning-fast death blow.

Then they *roared* their approval. Wolf whistles rained down on Gant. Claps and cheers.

'Whoa, baby!'

'Now *that* is what I call a *woman*!'

At the northern end of the pit, the President slid to the ground beside Juliet Janson, hauled her up, but when they both got to their feet, they froze.

Before them, standing next to one of the upturned engines of the AWACS plane—alone but closer now—stood Colonel Jerome T. Harper.

On the ground to his left, lying on the floor, was Boa McConnell. He was groaning painfully, still reeling from Mother's crunching shoulder-tackle earlier.

The hoots and hollers from the prisoners enveloped them.

'Come on, Mister Prez! Get some blood on your hands! *Kill the fucker!*'

'Eat shit, Harper!'

'*U–S–A! U–S–A!*'

Harper knew the score. All his men were either dead or useless.

And yet still he seemed strangely confident . . .

It was then that he pulled something out of his pocket.

It looked like a hi-tech grenade of some sort—a small pressurised cylindrical canister with a nozzle on its top and a vertical clear-glass window on its side.

Through the narrow glass window, the President could see the contents of the grenade very clearly.

It was filled with a mustard-yellow liquid.

'Oh, Jesus . . .' he breathed.

It was a biological grenade.

A *Chinese* biological grenade.

A pressure-sealed explosive charge filled with the Sinovirus.

An evil grin cracked Harper's face.

'I was hoping it wouldn't come to this,' he said. 'But fortunately for me, like every Air Force man at this complex, I have already been immunised against the Sinovirus. The same, however, cannot be said for you or your brave Marine guardians.'

Then, without so much as a blink, Harper pulled the pin on the Sinovirus grenade.

Harper didn't see him until it was too late.

As he pulled the pin on the grenade, all he saw was a flashing blur of movement from the wreckage to his immediate left.

The next thing he knew, Shane Schofield was standing beside him, emerging from the darkness, swinging a length of piping upward like a baseball bat.

The pipe struck Harper on the underside of his wrist, causing the Sinovirus grenade to fly out of his hand and go soaring upwards.

The live biological grenade flew up into the air.

It flew in a kind of bizarre slow motion, tumbling end-over-end, high above the northern half of the pit.

Schofield watched it, eyes wide.

The prisoners watched it, mouths agape.

The President watched it, awestruck.

Harper watched it, an evil grin forming on his face.

One, one-thousand . . .

Two, one-thousand . . .

Three . . .

At that moment, at the height of its arc, about thirty feet above the floor of the pit—directly above its northern-most section—the Sinovirus grenade went off.

In the firelight of the prisoners' torches, the aerosol explosion of the grenade inside the hangar was almost beautiful.

It looked like the blast of a water-filled firecracker—a giant star-shaped burst of mist—with multiple fingers of watery yellow particles shooting outwards from a central point, showering laterally, fanning out like a giant umbrella over the sunken aircraft elevator platform, orange fire-light glinting off every single particle.

And then in wondrous slow motion, the whole misty cloud began to *fall*, first at its extremities, then in its centre, down over the pit.

Like slow-falling snow, the Sinovirus particles descended.

Since it had detonated above the floor-line of the hangar, the yellow mist hit the prisoners standing on the rim first.

Their reaction was as sudden as it was violent.

Most of them doubled over where they stood, started hacking, vomiting. Some fell to their knees, dropping their flaming torches, others lapsed instantly into involuntary fits.

Within a minute, all but two were on the floor, writhing in agony, screaming as their insides began to liquefy.

Seth Grimshaw was one of the two.

Along with Goliath, he stood unaffected by the falling yellow mist, while everyone around him lay dying.

Although only they and the now-dead Gunther Botha knew it, Grimshaw and Goliath had been the original test subjects for the vaccine against the Sinovirus the previous afternoon.

Unlike the others, they had Kevin's vaccine coursing through their veins.

They were immune.

The yellow mist fell through the darkness.

It was now about fifteen feet above the lowered elevator platform—five feet above the rim—and still falling steadily.

Alone on the eastern side of the pit, Libby Gant had seen the grenade detonate, had seen the spectacular aerosol explosion high above the pit. She didn't have to be a rocket scientist to guess what it was.

A biological agent.

The Sinovirus.

Move!

Gant spun. She was standing right next to the eastern wall of the pit, ten feet below the rim. The rim itself was now empty, all the inmates having moved around to the northern side earlier.

Gant didn't waste a second.

She was still wearing her full dress uniform, which meant she had no gas-mask—so she definitely didn't want to be here when the Sinovirus descended into the pit.

The particles were fourteen feet off the floor.

And falling . . .

Gant pushed one of the AWACS plane's big black tyres up against the concrete wall, jumped up onto it, hauled herself out of the ten-foot-deep pit.

She rolled up onto the hangar's floor, careful to stay low, beneath the layer of descending Sinovirus particles.

She saw the hangar's internal building about twenty yards away from her, saw the slanted observation windows of its upper level.

The control room, she thought. *Caesar's command centre.*

Staying low but moving fast, Gant hurried for the doorway at the base of the internal building.

The yellow haze continued to fall.

Having consumed the prisoners on the northern edge of the pit, its particles now dipped below the rim, *drifting down into the pit itself.*

Schofield looked anxiously about himself.

In the pandemonium of the grenade blast and the ensuing wails of the dying prisoners—as they fell, they dropped their torches, plunging the pit into even thicker darkness—he had lost sight of Jerome Harper.

After the blast, Harper had dashed off into the darkened forest of the AWACS wreckage, disappearing. Schofield didn't like the idea of him lurking somewhere in the area.

But right now, he had other things to worry about.

The mist was now *inside* the pit—nine feet off the floor—and still falling.

He looked over at the President and Juliet.

Like him, they were still wearing their stolen 7th

Squadron uniforms—complete with ERG-6 half-face gas-masks wrapped around their necks.

'Captain! Your gas-mask! Put it on!' the President yelled, pulling on his own mask. 'If you breathe the virus into your lungs directly, it'll kill you in seconds! With the mask on, it's a lot slower!'

Schofield lifted his mask over his face.

Juliet, however, yanked her mask up and over her head and threw it over to Mother, just back from her fight with Webster. Unlike the other three, Mother was still dressed in her mask-less full dress uniform.

'But what about you—?' she said.

Juliet indicated her Eurasian features. 'Asian blood, remember. It won't hurt me. But it'll kill you if you don't put that on!'

'Thanks!' Mother said as she clamped the mask over her nose and mouth.

'Quickly!' Schofield said. 'This way!'

Gas-mask on, he charged into the darkened maze of wreckage, heading for the north-eastern corner, for the mini-elevator parked there.

The others took off after him, racing into the darkness.

After several seconds of running, Schofield came to the mini-elevator, lying flush against the floor in the corner of the pit.

A flaming torch lay on it. One of the dying prisoners up on the rim must have dropped it into the pit when the virus had struck him down.

Schofield snatched it up and turned to see the President and Mother arrive at his side.

It was only then that any of them noticed.

No Juliet.

Juliet Janson lay sprawled on the ground back near the AWACS's fuselage.

Just as she had been about to charge into the maze after Schofield and the others, a strong hand had appeared from completely out of nowhere and grabbed her ankle, causing her to trip and fall.

The hand belonged to Boa McConnell, lying spread-eagled on the floor, still dazed from Mother's tackle earlier, but alert enough to recognise one of his enemies.

Now, he held onto Juliet's ankle, refusing to let go.

Juliet struggled.

Boa extracted a long K-Bar knife from his boot, raised it. Juliet's eyes went wide as he made to plunge the knife into her ankle . . .

Blam! McConnell's head exploded like a burst balloon, shot from somewhere above them. He flopped to the floor, dead.

Juliet scrambled away from the body. She looked upward, searching the darkness for the source of the gun-shot.

She found it in the shape of a flaming torch over on the southern side of the pit, being waved from side to side, accompanied by a voice that called: 'Janson! Agent Janson!'

Juliet squinted to see the owner of the torch.

In the flickering glow of the torch's flames, she could just make out the man holding it—a man in 7th Squadron clothing brandishing a nickel-plated pistol in his spare hand.

Book II.

'Janson! Where are you?' Schofield said into his radio mike, as he waited impatiently on the detachable mini-elevator.

Book II's voice answered him. *'Scarecrow, it's Book. I've got Janson. You get out of here.'*

'Thanks, Book. Fox, you still alive?'

No reply.

Schofield's whole body froze.

And then: *'I'm here, Scarecrow.'*

He started breathing again. 'Where are you?'

'I'm inside the building at the eastern end of the hangar. Get the President out of here. Don't worry about me.'

'All right . . .' Schofield said. 'Listen, I have to get to Area 8. The bad guys have taken Kevin there. I'm going to take the President with me. Rendezvous with us there when you—oh, shit!'

'What is it?'

'The Football. It's still up in the hangar somewhere. Grimshaw had it.'

'Leave that to me,' Gant said. *'You just get the President out of here. I'll meet you at Area 8 as soon as I can.'*

'Thanks,' Schofield said. 'And Fox . . .'

'Yeah?'

'You be careful.'

There was a pause at the other end. *'You too, Scarecrow.'*

And with that Schofield pressed a button and the mini-elevator whizzed him, Mother and the President swiftly down the shaft.

As they descended quickly, Mother touched Schofield on the shoulder, spoke through her gas-mask.

'Area 8?'

Schofield turned to face her. 'That's right.'

No matter how he looked at it, his mind kept coming back to the same image: the image of the 7th Squadron unit down on the Level 6 platform taking Kevin into the X-rail tunnel, heading for Area 8.

Kevin . . .

The little boy was at the centre of all of this.

Schofield said, 'I want to find out what this whole thing has been about. But to do that, I need two things.'

'What?'

He indicated the President. 'First: *him*.'

'And second?'

'Kevin,' Schofield said firmly. 'Which is why we have to get to Area 8 fast.'

Caesar Russell, Kurt Logan and the three surviving commandos from Logan's Alpha Unit charged across the runway of Area 7 in the glare of the blazing desert sun, raced into the four-storey airfield control tower that stood about a hundred yards from the main complex.

Having emerged from the top door exit inside a small side hangar, they'd made their way to the tower, which doubled as the base's secondary control room.

They hurried into the tower's command centre—it was a replica of the one inside Area 7—and started flicking switches. Television monitors came to life. Console lights flicked on.

Caesar said, 'Get me a fix on Echo Unit's personnel locators.'

It didn't take long for Logan to find Echo. Every 7th Squadron member had an electronic locator surgically implanted beneath the skin on his wrist.

'They're on the X-rail. Arriving at Area 8 right now.'

'Fire up the Penetrators,' Caesar said. 'We're going to Area 8.'

*

Down on Level 1 of the underground complex, Nicholas Tate was wandering around in a terrified daze.

After the sudden and mysterious disappearance of Hot Rod Hagerty, he didn't know what to do.

Flashlight in hand, he walked absently to the far end of the darkened hangar, searching for Hagerty. But he stopped twenty yards short of the ramp there when he saw something emerging from it. Already somewhat muddled, now his mind reeled at the sight that met him.

It was almost surreal.

A family of bears—yes, *bears*—stepped out from the ramp and onto the floor of Level 1.

One gigantic male, a smaller female, and three awkward-looking little cubs ambled out onto the hangar floor. They were all hunched forward, padding along on all fours, sniffing the petrol-soaked air all around them.

Tate wobbled unsteadily.

Then he turned and ran back toward the main elevator shaft.

The detached mini-elevator whipped down the aircraft elevator shaft in near total darkness, with Schofield, Mother and the President on its back, the orange glow from Schofield's torch the only light.

As they descended, Schofield yanked a couple of Gunther Botha's glass ampoules from his thigh pocket—the small glass bulbs containing the antidote to the Sinovirus.

He turned to the President, spoke through his gas-mask: 'How long do we have?'

'Half an hour till the first symptoms set in,' the President said, 'when it invades the body through the skin. Dermal infection is slower than direct inhalation. That antidote, however, will neutralise the virus in its tracks.'

Schofield handed a glass bulb to both Mother and the President, then pulled out another one for himself. 'We need to find some hypodermic needles before we head to Area 8,' he said.

They rode the mini-elevator down to Level 1.

When they arrived there, however, they were met by Nicholas Tate, bursting forth from the darkness wide-eyed and alarmed. He stepped straight *onto* the mini-elevator.

'I ... er ... don't think you want to go that way,' he said.

'Why not?' Schofield asked.

'*Bears*,' Tate said dramatically.

Schofield frowned, looked to the President. Clearly, Tate had lost it.

'Where's Ramrod?' Mother asked.

'Gone,' Tate said. 'Just—*poof*—disappeared. One minute he was standing here behind me, the next he was just *missing*. All he left was this.'

Tate held up Hagerty's Annapolis graduation ring.

Schofield didn't get it.

The President did.

'Oh, *Jesus*,' he said. 'He's out.'

'Who's out?' Mother asked.

'There's only one person in this complex who is known to leave a person's jewellery at the site of an abduction,' the President said. 'The serial killer, Lucifer Leary.'

'The Surgeon of Phoenix . . .' Schofield whispered, recalling the name and the horror that went along with it.

'Oh, super,' Mother spat. 'Just what we need. *Another* fucking wacko running around this place.'

The President turned to Schofield. 'Captain, we don't have time for this. If Caesar Russell's got that boy . . .'

Schofield bit his lip. He didn't like leaving anybody behind, even Ramrod Hagerty.

'Captain,' the President said, his face hard, 'as I said earlier this morning, sometimes in this job I have to make difficult decisions—and I'm going to make one now. If he's still alive, Colonel Hagerty is going to have to look after himself. We can't spend the next hour searching this facility for him. There's something bigger at stake here. Much bigger. We have to get that boy back.'

They took the mini-elevator to the second underground hangar, Level 2, and—now accompanied by the confused Nicholas Tate—dashed down its length.

Thankfully, there were no bears in this hangar.

They hit the fire stairwell at a run and rushed down it, guided by the light of Schofield's flaming torch. Since they had come direct from their fight in the pit, they had no weapons, no flashlights, no nothing.

They came to the bottom of the stairwell, and the door to Level 6.

Cautiously, Schofield opened it.

The Level 6 X-rail platform was completely dark.

No sound. No sign of life.

Schofield edged out onto the platform. Dark shapes littered the area—bodies from the three separate gunfights that had taken place down there over the course of the morning, the charred remains of Elvis's RDX explosion.

Schofield and Mother ran straight over to the bodies of some Bravo Unit men. They grabbed a P-90 assault rifle each, plus SIG-Sauer pistols. Schofield even found a first-aid field kit on one of the men which contained four plastic-wrapped hypodermic needles.

Perfect.

He tossed a SIG to the President, but didn't offer a gun to the unstable Tate.

'This way,' he said.

He hurried along the platform, heading for the X-rail engine that sat on the northern tracks of the underground railway station, pointing toward the open tunnel that led to Area 8.

Up in the main hangar, Book II was pulling Juliet Janson out of the ten-foot-deep pit that was the aircraft elevator platform. He was wearing his uniform's ERG-6 gas-mask.

A thin residual mist hung over the area, the lingering cloud of the Sinovirus.

Juliet came out of the pit, and with a shout, she saw them: Seth Grimshaw and the giant Goliath disappearing inside the personnel elevator. And Grimshaw was still holding the Football.

'Over there!' she pointed. 'They're going for the exit in the elevator shaft. That Air Force guy Harper gave Grimshaw the exit code.'

'Do you know the code?' Book II asked.

'Do I ever,' Juliet leapt to her feet. 'I was there when Harper said it. Come on.'

Libby Gant was on her own.

She was standing in a dark hallway inside the command building at the eastern end of the hangar, at the base of a set of stairs—unarmed but alert as hell.

In the hangar outside, the Sinovirus was loose, and she didn't have a gas-mask.

Okay, she thought, *surely in a facility like this, there would have to be some—*

She found them in a cupboard underneath the stairs: biohazard suits. Great big yellow Chemturions—with large, baggy plastic helmets, balloon-like yellow coveralls, and self-contained air-packs.

In the same cupboard, Gant also found a chunky Maglite flashlight. Very handy.

She slipped into one of the Chemturion suits as fast as she could, pulling its Ziploc zipper shut, turning on its self-contained air-supply. The suit immediately inflated and she started hearing her own breathing as a Darth Vader-like wheeze.

Now safe from the Sinovirus, she had something else she wanted to do.

She recalled her previous plan: find Caesar Russell's command centre—get the initiate/terminate unit that he'd used to start the transmitter on the President's heart—then use the black box that she'd taken from the AWACS plane earlier to impersonate the President's radio signal.

The black box.

So far as she knew, it was still on the floor of the main hangar, in the spot where she had kicked it away from the mini-elevator.

She decided to search the command centre for the I/T unit first. Then she'd go back for the black box.

Guided by the light of her newfound flashlight, she climbed the stairs, came to the command room's doorway.

The door was ajar.

Slowly, Gant pushed it open, to reveal a very battered-looking room.

It looked like a war had been fought in there.

The room's plasterboard walls were shredded with bullet holes. The slanted windows overlooking the main hangar were cracked or completely shattered. Several computer consoles bore fat round holes in their monitors. Others just sat there blank, lacking a power source.

Dressed in her yellow biohazard suit, Gant entered the room, stepping over a pair of dead 7th Squadron men lying all shot up on the floor. Their weapons were gone, presumably taken by the inmates who had stormed through here.

Through the faceplate of her airtight suit, Gant's eyes swept the control room, searching for the—

Yes.

It was sitting on top of one of the computer monitors and it was just as the President had described it: a small red hand-held unit, with a black stub antenna sticking out of its top.

The initiate/terminate unit.

Gant picked it up, examined it. It looked like a miniature mobile phone.

She saw two switches on its face. Beneath each switch was a crude length of tape marked with a handwritten '1' and '2'.

Gant frowned. *Why would Caesar need . . . ?*

She shook the thought away, stuffed the I/T unit into the chest pocket of her biohazard suit.

As she did so, she peered out over the darkened hangar to see if she could spot the black box down by the pit.

The vast hangar floor stretched away from her, veiled by the unearthly mist of the Sinovirus.

Except for the flickering flames of the prisoners' discarded torches, nothing moved.

The area was awash with irregularly-shaped objects: slumped bodies, Marine One, a crashed cockroach, one battered helicopter, even Bravo Unit's busted-open barricade of crates and boxes.

Gant's flashlight had a powerful beam, and in the middle of some bodies and debris on the near side of the pit, it illuminated the bright-orange outline of the AWACS's black box.

Excellent . . .

Gant made to leave, when abruptly, a glint of pale-blue light caught her eye.

She paused. It seemed that not *every* monitor in the control room had been shot or lost power.

Hidden underneath a fallen piece of shredded plasterboard, a lone screen was still glowing.

Gant frowned.

The complex's power was out—which meant this system must be operating on an independent power source. Which meant it must be pretty important . . .

She lifted the broken piece of wall off the screen. The screen read:

423

LOCKDOWN PROTOCOL S.A.(R) 7-A

FAILSAFE SYSTEM HISTORY

7-3-468201103

TIME	KEY ACTION	SYSTEM RESPONSE
0658	AUTHORIZED LOCKDOWN INITIATE CODE ENTERED	LOCKDOWN PROTOCOL ENABLED
0801	AUTHORIZED LOCKDOWN EXTENSION CODE ENTERED	LOCKDOWN PROTOCOL CONTINUED
0900	AUTHORIZED LOCKDOWN EXTENSION CODE ENTERED	LOCKDOWN PROTOCOL CONTINUED
1005	NO AUTHORIZED CODE ENTERED	FACILITY SELF-DESTRUCT MECHANISM ARMED
1005	*********************************WARNING*********************************	

EMERGENCY PROTOCOL ACTIVATED.
IF YOU DO NOT ENTER AN AUTHORIZED LOCKDOWN
EXTENSION OR TERMINATION CODE BY 1105 HOURS,
FACILITY SELF-DESTRUCT SEQUENCE WILL BE ACTIVATED.
SELF-DESTRUCT SEQUENCE DURATION: 10:00 MINUTES.
*********************************WARNING*********************************

Gant's eyes went wide.

Facility self-destruct sequence . . .

No wonder this system operated on an independent power source.

But for whatever reason—presumably the sudden intrusion of the inmates—Caesar Russell's people had failed to enter the appropriate lockdown extension code during the window period after 10:00 a.m.

So now, if no-one entered an extension or termination code before 11:05 a.m., Area 7's self-destruct sequence would begin—a ten-minute procedure that would culminate in the hundred-megaton thermonuclear warhead buried in the earth beneath the complex going off.

'Holy mother of God . . .' Gant breathed. She looked at her watch.

It was 10:15 a.m.

She turned to go—

—at the same moment as a long length of steel piping crashed down against the back of her suit-hooded head.

Gant dropped to the floor, out cold.

She never saw her attacker.

Never saw him heft her onto his shoulder.

Never saw him carry her out of the control room.

The X-rail train boomed through the tunnel system, rocketing along on its quartet of tracks at tremendous speed, heading toward Area 8.

It wouldn't be a long trip. At two hundred miles per hour, they'd cover the twenty miles in about six minutes.

Although he didn't know exactly where Echo Unit was going with Kevin, Schofield at least knew they had come this way.

It was better than nothing.

Having set the train's autopilot, he walked back into the main cabin and sat down with Mother and the President. Nick Tate was off at the other end of the carriage, still somewhat out of it, staring with great concentration at the buttons on his cellular phone.

Schofield sat down. As he did so, he pulled out his newfound syringe and the antidote to the Sinovirus, and set about injecting himself with it. Mother and the President did the same.

As he jabbed the needle into his arm, Schofield looked up at the President. 'Now, sir, if you don't mind, would you *please* tell me what the hell is going on at this base.'

The President pursed his lips.

'You could start,' Schofield prompted, 'with why an Air Force Lieutenant General wants to kill you in front of the nation. Then you could tell me why he *also* wants to keep his hands on a genetically-engineered boy who is the vaccine to an ethnic bullet.'

The President bowed his head, and nodded.

Then he said, 'Technically, Caesar Russell is no longer a lieutenant general in the Air Force. Technically, he is *dead*. On the twentieth of January this year, the day of my inauguration, Charles Samson Russell was executed by lethal injection at Terre Haute Federal Penitentiary for the crime of high treason.

'What he *wants*,' the President said, 'is what he wanted before he was executed. To radically change the face of this country. Forever. And the two things he needs to do to effect that are: one, kill me, in a highly visible, highly embarrassing way. And two, to retain control of the Sinovirus vaccine.

'To understand why he's doing this, however, you have to understand Russell's history, in particular his links with a clandestine Air Force society known as the Brotherhood.'

'Yes . . .' Schofield said cautiously.

The President leaned forward. 'Over the past thirty years, various Congressional Armed Services Committees have heard about the existence of certain *undesirable* societies within the branches of our armed forces; informal underground organisations with less-than-acceptable common interests. Hate societies.'

'For example?'

'In the eighties there was a secret group of men in the Army known as the Bitch Killers. They opposed the presence of women in the Army, so they engaged in activities to drive them out of the service. More than eighteen sexual assaults in the Army were attributed to members of this group, even if actual proof was difficult to establish. The extent of its membership was never fully ascertained, but then, that's the problem with these sorts of societies: there is *never* any physical proof of their existence. They're like ghosts, existing in non-tangible ways—a knowing look during a salute, a nod in a hall-way, a subtle promotion over a non-member.'

Schofield was silent.

While he had never been approached by anyone linked with such a group in his career, he had heard of them. They were like hardcore college fraternities, small groups with their own secret handshakes, their own 'codes', their own disgusting initiation ceremonies. For officers, they started at places like West Point and Annapolis; for enlisted men, at training camps around the country.

The President said, 'They form for various reasons: some have religious skews—for example, anti-Semitic groups like the old 'Jewboy League' in the Navy. Or the sexist ones, like the Bitch Killers. The formation of groups like this in high-risk occupations is well-documented— even police forces like the L.A.P.D. are known to have secret hate societies within their ranks.

'But in terms of sheer violence, the worst groups were always the racist societies. There used to be one in every service. In the Navy, it was the Order of White America. In the Army, the Black Death. In the Air Force, it was a group known only as the Brotherhood. All three displayed a particular hostility toward black Americans in their ranks.

'But the thing is,' the President said, 'they were all thought to have been wiped out during a Department of Defence-initiated purge in the late 1980s. Now while we haven't heard about a resurgence of racist elements in either the Army or the Navy, it was discovered recently that the Brotherhood is indeed alive and well, and one of its key figures was none other than General Charles "Caesar" Russell.'

Schofield said nothing.

The President shifted in his seat. 'Charles Russell was tried and convicted for ordering the murder of two Navy admirals, advisers to the Joint Chiefs of Staff. Turned out, Russell had approached them shortly after my announcement to run for President and asked them to join him in some kind of treasonable endeavour that would change America forever. The only details he told them were that the plan would involve the removal of the President, and that it would rid America of its "human waste products". The two admirals refused his offer, so Caesar had them eliminated. What he didn't know was that one of those admirals had secretly taped his offer and tipped off the FBI and the Secret Service.

'Russell was arrested and tried for murder and treason. Since it was a military proceeding, the trial was held immediately, albeit in closed session. During the case the question as to what America's "human waste products" actually were was debated at length. Equivocal evidence was brought that Russell was a member of the Brotherhood—a secret cabal of high-ranking USAF officers, mainly from the Southern belt, who intentionally hinder

429

the rise of black Americans through the ranks of the Air Force. It didn't help that the military prosecutor was black, but in any case the issue was never resolved. On the basis of the taped evidence, Russell was found guilty and sentenced to death. When he decided not to lodge any appeals whatsoever, his execution was fast-tracked—and he was "executed" in January of this year. And that was that. Or so we thought.'

Schofield said, 'I get the feeling that you knew what Caesar was planning, even if it didn't come out in the court case.'

The President nodded.

'Over the past ten years, Caesar Russell has been in charge of every major United States Air Force base between Florida and Nevada. The 20th at Warren in Wyoming, which looks after our ICBM stockpile. Space Warfare at Falcon, Colorado, which controls defence satellites and space missions. Area 7, of course. Hell, he even spent a year at AFSOC at Hurlbut Field in Florida, supervising the Air Force's crack special ops teams, including the 7th Squadron. He has loyal followers at each of those bases, senior officers who owe their positions to him, a small but powerful clique of base-commanders who we now suspect are also members of the Brotherhood.

'What Russell also knows, however, is what's inside every one of our most secret bases. He knew of the Sinovirus from its earliest development phases, knew of its potential uses, and he knew of our response to it—a genetically-constructed virus-resistant human being— right from the very beginning.

'The thing is, Charles Russell is smart, very smart. He thought of *other* possibilities for the one person in the world in possession of the ultimate ethnic bullet and its vaccine. Judging by this transmitter attached to my heart, it looks like he's been planning a revolution for some time now, but it's only the advent of the Sinovirus that makes it totally perfect for him.'

'How so?'

'Because Caesar Russell wants to take America back to its pre-Civil War state,' the President said simply.

There was a silence.

'Did you hear the names of the cities he's put his plasma bombs in? Fourteen devices, in fourteen airports, all around the country. Not true. They're not placed *all* around the country. They're only placed in *northern* cities. New York, Washington DC, Chicago, LA, San Francisco, Seattle. The farthest south those bombs get is St Louis. No Atlanta, no Houston, no Miami even. Nothing below the Tennessee–Kentucky state line.'

'Why those cities, then?' Schofield asked slowly.

The President said, 'Because they represent the North, the liberals, the dandies of America who talk a lot, produce nothing, and yet consume everything. And Caesar wants an America *without the North*.

'For with the Sinovirus and its cure in his possession, he will have what's left of the nation at his mercy. Every man, woman and child—black and white—will owe their life to him and his precious vaccine.'

The President winced.

'I imagine the black population would be eliminated first, with the vaccine being administered only to white Americans. Considering Caesar's racist tendencies, I assume it was the black population he was talking about when he mentioned "human waste products".

431

'But remember what I said before: he has to do two things to get what he wants: he has to have Kevin in his possession, *and he also has to kill me*. For no revolution—no true revolution—can take place without the visible and humiliating destruction of the previous regime. The execution of Louis XVI and Marie Antoinette in France; the imprisonment of the Czar in Russia in 1918; Hitler's complete "Nazification" of Germany in the thirties.

'Anybody can kill a President, if they are determined enough. A revolutionary, however, has to do it *in front of the people he desires to rule*—showing them that the previous ruling system no longer deserves their respect.

'And don't be mistaken, Caesar Russell isn't doing this in front of America. He's doing it in front of the most extreme elements of America—the Timothy McVeighs of the country; the poor, the angry, the disenfranchised, the white supremacists, the white trash, the anti-federal militias—those parts of the nation, located mainly in the southern states, that wouldn't give two shits if the cappuccino-drinking liberals in New York, Chicago and San Francisco were blasted off the face of the earth.'

'But the country would be decimated . . .' Schofield said. 'Why would he want to rule a destroyed country?'

'Yes, but you see, Caesar doesn't see it that way,' the President said. 'To his mind, the country wouldn't be destroyed. It would merely be purified, renewed, *cleansed*. It would be a new beginning. The southern city centres would be intact. The Mid-West would still be largely intact, able to provide sustenance.'

Schofield asked, 'What about the other armed forces? What would he do about them?'

'Captain, as you would well know, the US Air Force

receives more funding than all the other armed services combined. Sure, it may have only 385,000 personnel, but it has more missiles and strike capability than all the other services combined. If, by virtue of the Brotherhood and his previous commands, Caesar has even a *fiftieth* of the Air Force behind him, he could scramble his bombers and take out every key Army and Navy installation in this country—plus every Air Force base that was not allied with him—before they could even raise a small counter-offensive effort.

'Foreign defence would be the same. With its stealth bombers, strike fighters and a stockpile of nuclear missiles greater than that of any other *country* in the world, Caesar's new Air Force, acting alone, would be more than capable of handling any hostile foreign incursion.

'Captain, make no mistake, to Caesar's warped mind, this scenario would be perfect: America would be isolationist once again, completely self-sufficient, and governed by an absolutely lily-white regime. Back to its pre-Civil War state.'

'Mother*fucker* . . .' Mother breathed.

Schofield frowned.

'Okay, then,' he said, 'so what if Russell *can't* pull this off? What if he fails? Surely he isn't just going to accept defeat and walk away. I can't see him simply disarming his bombs if he loses and saying, "Oh well, I was wrong, you win."'

'No,' the President said seriously. 'That worries me, too. Because if by some miracle we do survive all this, the question becomes: what has Caesar got in store for us then?'

After prising apart the personnel elevator's exterior doors, Book II and Juliet Janson came to the 'top door' exit.

Juliet entered the code Harper had revealed earlier: 5564771.

With a sharp hiss, the heavy titanium door opened.

They raced down the concrete corridor beyond it, each holding one of Book's pistols.

They ran for about forty yards before, abruptly, they burst through another door and found themselves standing inside an ordinary-looking aircraft hangar. Shafts of brilliant sunlight slanted in through the hangar's wide-open doors. The hangar was completely empty: no planes, no cars, no—

Goliath must have been waiting behind the door.

Juliet stepped out first, only to feel the barrel of a P-90 press up against the side of her head.

'Bang-bang, you're dead,' Goliath said oafishly.

He squeezed the trigger *just as* Book II—whom Goliath hadn't seen yet—lunged forward and with lightning speed swiped back the P-90's charging handle, *ejecting* the round that was in its chamber.

Click!

The gun against Juliet's head fired nothing.

'Wha—?' Goliath snapped to look at Book II.

And then everything happened very fast.

In one movement, Juliet grabbed the barrel of Goliath's P-90 and whipped up her own gun, at the same moment as Goliath's *other* enormous fist—which still held Schofield's Maghook—came rushing at her face. The Maghook hit Juliet on the side of the head, and she and the P-90 went sprawling to the floor. Juliet hit the ground hard. The P-90 clattered away.

Book raised his Beretta—but not fast enough. Goliath caught his gunhand . . . and growled at him.

Now the two men were holding the same gun.

Goliath thrust his Frankensteinian chin right up close to Book II's face as he began depressing Book's own trigger finger.

Blam!-Blam!-Blam!-Blam!-Blam!-Blam!-Blam!-Blam!

As the gun boomed, Goliath brought it round in a wide arc, angling it so that in a few shots' time, it would be pointed at Book's head.

It was like an arm wrestle.

Book II tried with all his might to stop the movement of the gun, but Goliath was far too strong.

Blam!-Blam!-Blam!

The gun was now pointed at Book's left arm—

Blam!

Book's left bicep exploded. Blood sprayed all over his head. He roared with pain.

Then before he knew it, the gunbarrel was pointing directly at his face and—

Click.

Out of ammo.

'That's better,' Goliath grinned. 'Now we can have a fair fight.'

He discarded the gun and—one-handed—grabbed Book by the throat and thrust him up against the wall.

Book's feet dangled twelve inches off the ground.

He struggled uselessly in Goliath's grip, his wounded arm burning. He let fly with a weak punch that hit Goliath square on the forehead.

The big man didn't even seem to feel the blow. Indeed, Book's fist seemed to just bounce off his skull.

Goliath chuckled stupidly. 'Steel plate. May not make me too bright, but it sure makes me tough.'

Goliath brought up the Maghook in his spare hand, so that it was now pointed at Book's eyes.

'What about you, soldier boy? How strong is your skull? You think this little hook-gun could crush it? What do you say we find out . . .'

He pressed the Maghook's cold magnetic head up against Book II's nose.

Book, held up by his neck, grabbed the Maghook with both hands, and despite his wounded arm, pushed it back toward Goliath. The Maghook went vertical, but then to Book's horror, it started to come *back* toward his face. Goliath was going to win this arm wrestle, too.

Then suddenly Book saw the way out.

'Aw, what the hell,' he said.

And so he reached forward, gripped the Maghook's launcher and pressed the button marked 'м' on it, initiating the grappling hook's powerful magnetic charge.

The response was instantaneous.

The lights on the Maghook's magnetic head burst to

436

life, and the now-charged head began searching for a metallic source nearby.

It found it in the steel plate inside Goliath's forehead.

With a powerful *thud!* the Maghook lodged itself against the big man's brow. It stuck hard, as if it were being *sucked* against the prisoner's very skin.

Goliath roared with rage, tried to extract the Maghook from his forehead, in doing so, releasing Book.

Book II dropped to the floor, gasping, clutching the ragged red hole in his bicep.

Goliath was spinning around, wrestling like an idiot with the Maghook attached to his face.

Book II kept his distance, at least until the staggering Goliath had his back to the wall. Then Book just stepped forward, grabbed the handgrip of the Maghook with his good hand and, without mercy, pulled the trigger.

The Maghook discharged with a gaseous *whump!* and Goliath's head was sent thundering backwards—his neck snapping almost ninety degrees the wrong way—his skull smashing against the wall behind him, creating a basketball-sized crater in the concrete. For his part, Book II was hurled several yards in the other direction, care of Newton's Third Law.

Still, he fared far better than Goliath. The gigantic prisoner now slid slowly to the floor, his eyes wide with shock and his head cracked open like an egg, a foul soup of blood and brains oozing out of it.

While Book II had been fighting with Goliath, the still-dazed Juliet had been trying to regather her pistol from the floor nearby.

When at last she got it and stood up, she stopped dead.

He was just standing there. Twenty yards away. On the other side of the hangar—Seth Grimshaw.

'I remember you now,' Grimshaw said, stepping forward.

Janson said nothing, just stared at him. She saw that he was still holding the Football . . . and a P-90 assault rifle, held low, one-handed, aimed right at her.

'You were at the Bonaventure when I tried to take out His Majesty,' Grimshaw said. 'You're U-triple-S. One of those chirpy little fucks who think that throwing their bodies in front of a corrupt President is in some way *honourable*.'

Janson said nothing.

She held her nickel Beretta by her side, down by her thigh.

Grimshaw had his rifle levelled at her. He smiled.

'Try and stop this.' He began to squeeze the trigger on his P-90.

Janson was ice-cool. She had one chance, and she knew it. Like all members of the Secret Service, she was an expert marksman. Grimshaw, on the other hand—like nearly all criminals—was shooting from the hip. The Secret Service had actually done probability scales on this sort of thing: in all likelihood, Grimshaw would miss with at least his first three shots.

Taking into account the time it would take for her to raise her own gun, Janson would have to hit him with her first.

Back the odds, she told herself. *Back the odds.*

And so as Grimshaw pulled his trigger, she whipped up her pistol.

She brought it up fast, superfast, and fired . . . *at exactly the same time as* Grimshaw loosed three short rounds himself.

The odds, it seemed, were wrong.

Both shooters fell—like mirror images—snapping backwards on opposite sides of the hangar, dropping to the ground in identical splashes of blood.

Janson lay on her back on the shiny polished floor of the hangar—gasping, breathing fast, looking up at the ceiling—a bloody red hole in her left shoulder.

Grimshaw, on the other hand, didn't move.

Didn't move at all.

He lay completely still, on his back.

Although Janson didn't know it yet, her single bullet had punctured the bridge of Grimshaw's nose, breaking it, creating a foul blood-splattered hole in his face. The exit wound that had blasted out the *back* of his head, however, was twice as big.

Seth Grimshaw was dead.

And the Football lay neatly at his side.

The X-rail train shot through the tunnel system.

After his talk with the President, Schofield had moved into the driver's compartment. They'd be arriving at Area 8 in a couple of minutes, and he wanted a short moment's peace.

With a soft shooshing sound, the compartment's sliding door opened and Mother entered.

'How you doing?' she said as she sat down beside him.

'To be honest,' he said, 'when I woke up this morning, I didn't think the day would turn out like this.'

'Scarecrow, why didn't you kiss her?' Mother asked suddenly.

'What? Kiss who?'

'Fox. When you took her out to dinner and dropped her home. Why didn't you kiss her?'

Schofield sighed. 'You'll never make it in the diplomatic corps, Mother.'

'Blow me. If I'm going to die today, I'm sure as hell not going to die wondering. Why didn't you kiss her? She wanted you to.'

'She did? Ah, damn it.'

'So why didn't you?'

'Because I . . .' he paused. 'I guess I got scared.'

'Scarecrow. What the *fuck* are you talking about? What were you afraid of? The girl is crazy about you.'

'And I'm crazy about her, too. I have been for a long time. Do you remember when she joined the unit, when the selection committee put on that barbecue at the base in Hawaii? I knew it then—as soon as I saw her—but back then I figured she could never be interested in me, not with these . . . things.'

He touched the twin scars running vertically down his eyelids.

He snuffed a laugh. 'I didn't talk much at that lunch. I even think she caught me staring off into space at one point. I wonder if she knows I was thinking about *her*.'

'Scarecrow,' Mother said. 'You and I both know Fox can see beyond your eyes.'

'See, that's the thing. I know that,' Schofield said. 'I know that. I just don't know what I was thinking last week. We were finally going out on a date. We'd got along so well all night. Everything was going great. And then we arrived at her front door and suddenly I didn't want to screw everything up by doing the wrong thing . . . and well, I don't know . . . I guess . . . I guess I just froze up.'

Mother started nodding sagely—then she burst out laughing.

'I'm glad you think this is funny,' Schofield said.

Mother kept laughing, clapped a hand on his shoulder. 'Scarecrow, you know, every now and then, it's nice to see that you're human. You can leap off ice cliffs and swing across giant elevator shafts, but you still freeze up when it comes to kissing the girl. You're beautiful.'

'Thanks,' Schofield said.

Mother stood up to go.

'Just promise me this,' she said kindly. 'When you see Fox next, kiss the fucking girl, will you!'

While Schofield, Mother and the President were shooting through the X-rail tunnel *under* the desert floor toward Area 8, Caesar Russell and his four remaining 7th Squadron men were zooming through the air *above* the desert in their two Penetrator attack choppers, heading in the same direction, a few minutes ahead of the X-rail train.

The small cluster of buildings that was Area 8 rose up out of the sandy landscape in front of the two helicopters.

Area 8 was essentially a smaller version of Area 7: two box-shaped hangars and a three-storey airfield control tower sat alongside the facility's black bitumen runway, complete with its sand-covered extensions that Schofield had observed earlier that day.

As the two Penetrators approached it, Caesar saw the gigantic doors to one of the complex's hangars suddenly part in the middle, and open.

It took the doors a long while to open fully, but once they had, Caesar's jaw dropped.

One of the most amazing-looking flying objects known to man rolled slowly out of the hangar.

Truth be told, what Caesar saw was actually *two* flying

objects. The first was a massive Boeing 747 jumbo jet, painted in glistening silver. The jumbo, with its imperious nose and outstretched swan-like wings, edged out from the shadows of the hangar.

It was, however, the smaller aircraft mounted on the *back* of the 747 that seized Caesar's attention.

It looked incredible.

Its paint scheme was like that of NASA's regular space shuttles: mainly white, with the American flag and 'UNITED STATES' written in bold lettering on its side, and with the distinctive black-painted nose and underbelly.

But this was no ordinary space shuttle.

It was the X-38.

One of two sleek mini-shuttles purpose-built by the United States Air Force for the tasks of satellite killing and, where necessary, the boarding, takeover or destruction of foreign space stations.

In shape, it was similar to the standard shuttles—delta planform, with flat triangular wings, a high aerodynamic tail, and three conical thrusters on its rear end—but it was smaller, much more compact. For where *Atlantis* and her sister shuttles were heavy long-haul vehicles designed for ferrying bulky satellites into space, this was the sports version, designed for blasting them out of existence.

Four specially designed zero-gravity AMRAAM missiles hung from its wings, on the outside of two enormous Pegasus II booster rockets—massive cylindrical thrusters filled to the brim with liquid oxygen—that were attached to the underbelly of the bird.

What a lot of people don't realise is that many of today's space flights are conducted with what is essentially late 1960s technology. Saturn V and Titan II boosters were used in the original US–Soviet space race in the sixties.

The X-38, however, with its 747 launch-platform and its stunning Pegasus II boosters, is the first orbiter to truly bring space flight into the 21st century.

Its specially-configured 747 launcher—fitted with new extra-powerful Pratt & Whitney turbofan engines, enhanced pressurisation systems and extra radiation protection for the pilots—can carry the X-38 to a release height of around 67,000 feet, 24,000 feet higher than a commercial jumbo can fly. Air-launch saves the shuttle one-third of its first-stage power/lift ratio.

Then the Pegasus II boosters kick in.

More powerful than Titan III by a whole order of magnitude, the boosters provide enough lift after the high-altitude launch to carry the shuttle into a low-earth orbit. Once expended, they are jettisoned from the shuttle. The X-38—now in a stationary orbit about two hundred and ten miles above the earth—can then manoeuvre freely in space, killing enemy satellites at will, and co-ordinate its landing, all under its own power.

Caesar Russell gazed at the mini-shuttle.

It was absolutely magnificent.

He turned to Kurt Logan. 'That shuttle cannot be allowed to get off the—'

He didn't get to finish the sentence, for at that moment—completely without warning—five Stinger missiles came rocketing out from the darkened hangar behind the silver 747, swooping in a wide arc around its wings before rising sharply into the air, heading straight for Caesar's two Penetrators.

Echo Unit had seen them.

*

The underground X-rail station of Area 8 was identical to the one at Area 7: two tracks on either side of an elongated central platform, with an elevator sunk into the northern track's wall.

After about seven minutes of superfast travel, Schofield's X-railcar zoomed into the station, bursting into the white fluorescent light of Area 8. The bullet-shaped engine decelerated quickly, stopped on a dime.

Its doors hissed open and Schofield, Mother and the President of the United States came charging out of it, heading straight for the elevator set into the northern wall. Trailing behind them—looking completely lost and now holding his cell phone to his ear—was Nicholas Tate III.

Schofield hit the elevator's call button.

As he waited for the lift to arrive, he noticed Tate for the first time. The White House suit was clearly rattled, freaked out by the morning's events. But it was only then that Schofield realised that Tate was *speaking* into his cell phone.

'*No*,' Tate said irritably into the phone, 'I want to know who *you* are! *You* have interrupted *my* phone call to *my* stockbroker. Identify yourself.'

'What on earth are you doing?' Schofield asked.

Tate frowned, spoke very seriously—in doing so, indicating that he had gone completely bonkers. 'Well, I *was* calling my broker. I figured by the way things are going today, I'd sell off my US dollars. So, after we got out of that train tunnel, I called him up, but no sooner do I get him on the line than this *asshole* cuts across the connection.'

Schofield snatched the phone from Tate's hand.

446

'Hey!'

Schofield spoke into it. 'This is Captain Shane M. Schofield, United States Marine Corps, Presidential Detachment, serial number 358-6279. Who is this?'

A voice came through the phone: *'This is David Fairfax of the Defense Intelligence Agency. I'm speaking from a monitoring station in DC. We have been scanning all transmissions emanating from two Air Force bases in the Utah desert. We believe that there may be a rogue Air Force unit at one of those bases and that the President's life may be in danger. I just enacted an emergency breakthrough on your friend's telephone call.'*

'Believe me, you don't know the half of it, Mister Fairfax,' Schofield said.

'Is the President safe?'

'He's right here.' Schofield held the phone out for the President.

The President spoke into it: 'This is the President of the United States. Captain Schofield is with me.'

Schofield added, 'And we are currently in pursuit of that rogue Air Force unit you just mentioned. Tell me everything you know about it—'

Just then, the elevator pinged.

'Hold on.' Schofield raised his P-90 toward the elevator.

The doors opened . . .

. . . revealing horribly blood-splattered walls and a particularly grisly sight.

The gunned-down bodies of three dead Air Force men lay strewn about the elevator—no doubt members of the skeleton crew stationed at Area 8.

'I think we got a fresh trail,' Mother said.

They hurried into the lift.

Tate stayed behind, determined not to go near any more danger. The President, however, insisted on going with Schofield and Mother.

'But, sir—' Schofield began.

'Captain. If I'm going to die today as the representative of this country, I'm not going to do it cowering in some corner, waiting to be found. It's time to stand up and be counted. And besides, it looks like you could do with some numbers.'

Schofield nodded. 'If you say so, sir. Just stay close and shoot straight.'

The elevator doors closed and Schofield hit the button for ground level.

Then he brought Tate's cell phone back to his ear.

'Okay, Mister Fairfax. Twenty-five words or less. Tell me everything you know about this rogue Air Force unit.'

In his subterranean room in Washington, Dave Fairfax sat up straighter in his chair.

Events had just got a lot more real.

First, he had picked up the cell phone call coming out of Area 8. Then he had cut across the line—interrupting some moron—and now he was speaking to this Schofield character, a Marine on the President's helicopter detail. As soon as he had heard it, Fairfax had punched Schofield's serial number into his computer. Now he had Schofield's complete military history—including his current posting on Marine One—right in front of him.

'Okay,' Fairfax said into his headset mike. 'As I said, I'm DIA, and recently I've been decoding a set of unauthorised transmissions coming out of those bases. Now, first of all, we think a team of former South African Reccondos are heading there—'

'*Don't mind them. Killed them already,*' Schofield's voice said. '*The rogue unit. Tell me about the rogue unit.*'

'Oh . . . okay,' Fairfax said. 'By our reckoning, the rogue unit is one of the five 7th Squadron units guarding the Area 7 complex: the unit designated "Echo" . . .'

At Area 8, the elevator whizzed up the shaft.

Fairfax's voice came through the cell phone. ' . . . *We believe that this unit is aiding Chinese agents in an attempt to steal a biological vaccine that was being developed at Area 7.*'

Schofield said, 'Do you have any idea how they're going to get the vaccine out of America?'

'*Uh, yeah . . . yeah I do,*' Fairfax's voice said. '*But you might not believe it . . .*'

'I'll believe just about anything, Mister Fairfax. Try me.'

'*Okay . . . I believe they're going to load the vaccine onto a satellite-killer shuttle based at Area 8 and fly it up into a low orbit where they will rendezvous with the Chinese space shuttle that launched last week. They will then transfer both themselves and the vaccine onto the Chinese shuttle and land it back inside Chinese territory where we can't get to it or them . . .*'

'Son of a bitch,' Schofield breathed.

'*I know it sounds crazy, but . . .*'

' . . . but it's the only way to get something out of the United States,' Schofield said. 'We could stop any other extraction method—car, plane, boat. But if they went up into space, we'd never be able to follow them. They'd be home by the time we got a chase shuttle onto the pad at Canaveral.'

'*Exactly.*'

'Thanks, Mister Fairfax. Call the Marines and the Army, and get them to mobilise whatever air-capable units they have—Harriers, choppers, anything—and send them directly to Areas 7 and 8. *Do not use the Air Force*. Repeat: *Do not use the Air Force*. Until further notification, treat all Air Force personnel as suspicious.'

As he spoke, Schofield saw the illuminated numbers on the elevator ticking upward: 'sl-3 . . . sl-2 . . .'

'As for us,' Schofield said, 'we have to go now.'

'What are you going to do? What about the President?'

'sl-1' became 'g' and suddenly Schofield heard muffled gunfire beyond the elevator doors.

Ping!

The elevator had reached the ground floor.

'We're going after the vaccine,' he said. 'Call you later.'

And he hung up.

A second later, the elevator's doors opened—

SIXTH CONFRONTATION

3 July, 1023 Hours

—and suddenly Schofield and the others entered a whole new ball game.

In the main hangar of Area 8, a fierce gun-battle was already underway.

Explosions boomed, gunfire roared.

Shafts of sunlight streamed in through the hangar's gigantic open doors. About fifty yards away from the elevator, filling the open doorway—partially blocking the incoming sun—was the bird-like rear-end of a silver Boeing 747.

'Son of a bitch,' Schofield breathed as he saw the streamlined space shuttle mounted on the 747's back.

Gunfire rang out from over by the hangar doors.

Five black-clad 7th Squadron commandos—the treacherous men from Echo Unit, Schofield guessed—were taking cover behind the doors, firing their P-90s at something *outside* the hangar.

'This way,' Schofield said, hurrying out of the elevator. The three of them skirted around a Humvee and a pair of cockroach towing vehicles until they could see what lay beyond the hangar doors: two black Penetrator helicopters, hovering low over the tarmac outside the hangar, *blocking the way* of the shuttle-carrying 747.

The six-barrelled Vulcan mini-guns mounted underneath the noses of the two Penetrators were raining down a storm of bullets on the Echo Unit men in the hangar—pinning them down, preventing them from dashing across the twenty yards of open ground to the wheeled stairway that led onto the 747.

Missiles lanced out from the wing-stubs of the Penetrators, zeroing in on the 747. But the jumbo must have been using the latest electromagnetic counter-measures, because the missiles never got near them—they just went berserk as soon as they got close to the big plane, rolling through the air away from it, before slamming into the ground and detonating in showers of concrete and sand.

Even the onslaught of flashing orange tracer bullets from the helicopters just veered *away* from the body of the giant jumbo, as if some invisible magnetic shield prevented them coming near it.

From his position behind the cockroach, Schofield recognised two of the men seated inside one of the helicopters: Caesar Russell and Kurt Logan.

I'll bet Caesar's not happy with Echo, he thought.

Caesar and Logan must have arrived only moments earlier—just as the men of Echo had been boarding their escape plane. Caesar's choppers, it seemed, must have opened fire before all the Echo men had been able to get on the plane, before they'd been able to get away with Kevin.

Kevin . . .

Schofield scanned the battlefield. He couldn't see the little boy anywhere.

He must already be on board the plane . . .

And then without warning the 747 powered up, its four massive jet engines blasting air everywhere, sending any loose objects tumbling across the hangar.

The plane started moving forward—away from the hangar, out onto the runway—*toward* the two black Penetrators. Its wheeled staircase clattered to the ground behind it.

It was a good tactic.

The Penetrators knew that they stood no chance against the weight of the rolling 747, so they split like a pair of frightened pigeons, moving out of the way of the massive jumbo.

It was then that Schofield saw an Echo man standing in the open side door of the 747, saw him wave to his men still in the hangar and then toss a thin rope ladder from the doorway. The rope ladder hung from the small doorway, swaying beneath the rolling plane.

At that same moment, movement near the *hangar's* entry caught his eye and he spun, and saw the five Echo men at the hangar door dash for the Humvee parked near his cockroach.

They were going to try to board the 747 . . .

. . . *while it was moving!*

As soon as the Echo men moved, a withering burst of tracer fire from the Penetrators outside flooded in through the hangar's open doorway, shredding the ground at their feet.

Two of the men fell, hit, their bodies erupting in a thousand explosions of red. The other three made it to the Humvee, clambered inside, started her up. The big car peeled off the mark, turning in a wide circle—

Shoooooom!

A missile rocketed in through the open hangar doors, heading straight for the skidding Humvee.

The Humvee's life was short.

The missile hit it square on the nose—so hard that the wide-bodied jeep was sent flailing back across the slippery hangar floor, before it slammed against a wall and filled with light and blasted outwards in a shower of metal.

'Holy exploding Humvees, Batman!' Mother said.

'Quickly!' Schofield said. 'This way!'

'What are we doing?' the President asked.

Schofield pointed at the moving jumbo outside. 'We're getting on that plane.'

As with many desert bases, Area 8's elongated runway was roughly L-shaped, with the shorter arm of the 'L' meeting the open doorway of the complex's main hangar.

Aircraft took off and landed on the longer arm of the 'L' but to get out to that runway, all planes had to taxi along the shorter strip first. While the main runway was over five thousand yards long, the shorter runway—or taxiway—was only about four hundred yards in length.

The silver 747—with the glistening white X-38 space shuttle on its back—rumbled along the taxiway, flanked by the two black Air Force Penetrators.

Windblown sand whistled all around it, the brutal desert sun glinted off its sides.

The big jumbo had reached the halfway point of the taxiway when a speeding vehicle came blasting out of the main hangar behind it.

It was a cockroach.

One of the white flat-bodied towing vehicles that had been parked inside the hangar. Looking like a brick with wheels, it thundered along the taxiway, *chasing after* the big plane.

In the cramped driver's compartment of the cockroach, Mother drove. Schofield and the President shared the passenger seat.

'Come on, Mother, pick it up!' Schofield urged. 'We've got to catch it before it gets to the main runway! Once it gets there and starts on its flight run, we're screwed.'

Mother jammed the cockroach into third, its highest gear. The towing vehicle's V8 engine roared as it leapt forward, accelerating through the shimmering desert heat.

The cockroach whipped across the taxiway, closed in on the shuttle-carrying 747.

The Penetrators opened fire on it, but Schofield kicked open the passenger-side window and unleashed a burst from *both* his and Mother's P-90 assault rifles, hitting the nose-mounted Vulcan cannon on one of the Penetrators, causing it to bank away. But the other chopper kept firing hard, kicking up sparks all around the speeding cockroach.

'Mother! Get us under the plane! We need its counter-measures!'

Mother hit the gas and the cockroach surged forward, hit its top speed. It reeled in the lumbering 747—inch by painful inch—until at last the speeding towing vehicle sped underneath the silver jumbo's high tail section.

It was like entering an air bubble.

The bullets from the second Penetrator no longer hit the ground all around them. The fireworks display of their impact sparks ended abruptly.

The cockroach kept rushing forward—now speeding along in the shadow of the shuttle-carrying 747—pushing past its rear landing gear while still remaining in the shelter of its massive body.

The cockroach weaved under the left-hand wing of the 747, the tarmac rushing by beneath it, heading for the rope ladder that dangled from the plane's still-open left-hand door.

The cockroach came to the rope ladder—

—just as the entire 747 abruptly swung right.

'God damn it!' Mother yelled as the cockroach swung out from the shelter of the jumbo into glaring sunlight.

'It's turning onto the main runway!' Schofield shouted.

Like a giant, slow-moving bird, the silver 747—with the X-38 shuttle on its back—turned onto Area 8's elongated runway.

'Get to that ladder, Mother!' Schofield called.

Mother gunned it, yanked the steering wheel hard-right, directing the cockroach—now momentarily deprived of the jumbo's electromagnetic protection—back in toward the flailing rope ladder, but not before one of the Penetrators swung quickly around in front of the turning 747 and opened fire.

A devastating line of tracer bullets impacted against the tarmac in front of the cockroach, kicking up sparks that ricocheted everywhere.

Several bullets smacked against the cockroach's windscreen, cracking it. Many more, however, bounced up *underneath* the towing vehicle's speeding front bumper and impacted against the underside of the cockroach—three of them hitting the vehicle's steering column.

The response was instantaneous.

The steering wheel in Mother's hands went haywire.

The cockroach fishtailed wildly, lurching sideways as it sped along the runway under the wing of the 747, swinging left and right.

Mother had to use all her strength just to keep a grip on the steering wheel, to keep the cockroach under control.

The 747 finished its turn, began to straighten up.

The runway in front of it stretched away into the distance—a long, straight ribbon of black that disappeared into the shimmering desert horizon.

'Mother . . . !' Schofield yelled.

'I know!' Mother shouted. 'You go! Get up on the roof! I'll bring us under the ladder! And take the Prez here with you!'

'But what about you—?'

'Scarecrow! In about twelve seconds, that jumbo is going to take off and if *you* aren't on it, we lose that kid! I have to stay at the wheel of this thing, otherwise it'll spin out!'

'But those Penetrators will kill you once we're gone . . . !'

'That's why you have to take *him* with you!' Mother said nodding at the President. 'Don't mind me, Scarecrow. You know it'll take more than a bunch of Air Force cocksuckers to get rid of *me*.'

Schofield wasn't so sure.

But he saw the look in her eye, and he knew that she was prepared to keep driving the cockroach—to her almost certain death—so long as he and the President got on board that plane.

He turned to the President. 'Come on. You're coming with me.'

*

The cockroach raced alongside the 747, once again shielded by its electronic countermeasures, swung in underneath its forward left-hand entry door—the door from which the rope ladder dangled.

The two tiny figures of Schofield and the President—still dressed in their black combat uniforms—climbed up onto the roof of the speeding towing vehicle. Conveniently, their 7th Squadron uniforms came with protective goggles, so they put them on to protect their eyes against the storm of sand blowing all around them.

Down in the driver's compartment, Mother continued to grapple with the steering wheel of the cockroach, trying with all her might to keep the rampaging vehicle on a straight course.

On the roof of the cockroach—in the face of the battering wind—Schofield reached for the flailing rope ladder. It fluttered and swayed just out of his reach—

Then suddenly a deafening *roar* filled his ears.

The 747's four wing-mounted jet engines were coming to life.

Schofield's blood ran cold.

The plane was powering up for take-off, starting its run down the airstrip. Any second now, it would accelerate considerably and pull away from the cockroach.

The rope ladder continued to flutter in the raging wind, a few feet in front of the speeding cockroach. Billowing clouds of sand flew everywhere.

Schofield turned to the President and yelled: 'Okay! I grab the ladder! You grab me!'

'What!'

'You'll understand!'

And with that, Schofield charged across the flat roof of

the cockroach and leapt off its forward edge . . .

. . . and flew through the air, reaching up with his outstretched arms . . .

. . . *and caught the bottom rung of the dangling rope ladder.*

He waved for the President to follow. *'Now you grab me!'*

With a doubtful shake of his head, the President said, 'Okay . . .'

And he ran forward and jumped—

—just as the silver 747 shot forward, its engines engaging.

The President flew through the short space of air in front of the speeding cockroach before his body *slammed* into Schofield's, and he threw his arms around the young captain's waist, clasping his hips tightly while Schofield himself held on grimly to the bottom rung of the rope ladder with both of his hands!

Mother's cockroach instantly peeled away behind them, unable to keep up. The two Penetrators also gave up the chase, wheeling to a halt in mid-air above the runway.

Hanging from the rope ladder—and travelling at close to a hundred miles an hour, with the wind whipping all around him and the President of the United States hanging from his waist—Schofield watched in horror as one of the Penetrators loosed a missile at Mother's now-unprotected cockroach.

The missile hit the cockroach's tail and detonated hard, lifting the rear end of the still-speeding towing vehicle a clear five feet off the ground.

With the missile impact, the cockroach fishtailed wildly—and shot off the runway, onto the sand, kicking up an enormous billowing dustcloud—and then it flipped—and tumbled—and rolled—once, twice, three times—before it came to a thumping crashing crushing halt, right on its cockpit, surrounded by falling sand.

And as he hung from the doorway of the accelerating 747, Schofield could only stare at the dust-covered wreck and pray that Mother had died quickly.

But right now he had other things to do.

The 747 continued to rush down the runway.

As it did so, the two tiny figures of Schofield and the President could be seen dangling from its forward left-hand doorway.

The 747 picked up speed. With the extra weight of the X-38 on its back, it required an unusually long take-off run.

Wind whipped all around Schofield and the President as they hung from the rope ladder.

'You go first!' Schofield yelled. 'Climb up my body and then go up the ladder!'

The President did as he was told.

With the runway rushing by beneath them, he first climbed up Schofield's body, using his combat webbing for hand and footholds. Then he stepped off Schofield's shoulders onto the rope ladder itself and began to climb it.

As soon as the President was on the ladder, Schofield began to haul himself up, using only his arms.

The ground continued to whip by beneath them as they ascended the rope ladder, the wind slamming into their bodies.

And then, all of a sudden, as they reached the doorway at the top of the ladder, the speeding runway beneath them just dropped away—dropped dramatically away—and receded rapidly into obscurity.

Schofield swallowed.

They were now in the air.

Caesar Russell's helicopter landed softly on the runway far beneath the rising 747, twenty yards away from Mother's crashed cockroach.

Caesar stepped out of the chopper and just gazed up after the plane.

Kurt Logan walked over to the torpedoed cockroach. It was a battered, tangled wreck. Mangled steel lay everywhere.

Its driver's compartment was completely flattened, its windshield and roof struts bent shockingly inward. It looked like an aluminium can that had been crumpled flat.

And then he saw the body. It lay face-down in the sand in front of the smashed towing vehicle—twisted and broken. Only the torso and limbs were visible, the head was not. Mother's head lay somewhere underneath the cockroach's lowered front bumper, crushed flat against the ground. Her left pants leg ended abruptly at the knee—her lower leg wrenched off by the force of the impact.

Logan returned to Russell's side. Caesar hadn't taken his eyes off the rising silver plane.

'Echo has the boy,' Logan said. 'And the Marines have the President.'

'Yes,' Caesar said, staring up at the fleeing jumbo. 'Yes. So now, regrettably, we move to the alternate plan. Which means we head back to Area 7.'

The President landed with a heavy thump inside the open doorway of the 747, absolutely breathless.

Schofield followed a few seconds later, also breathing hard. He managed to stagger to his knees and pull the door shut behind him. It sealed with a loud *whump!*

Both men were lying on the floor, still wearing their protective goggles, when one of the pilots of the 747—a commando from Echo Unit—came down the stairwell from the upper deck.

The pilot was wearing a baggy bright-orange flight-suit which Schofield immediately recognised as a pressure suit.

Pressure suits were mandatory on all high-altitude or low-orbital flights. Although baggy on the outside, they were actually quite figure-hugging on the inside, with elasticised cuffs that ran down the wearer's arms and legs. The cuffs squeezed its wearer's limbs to regulate blood-flow through the body and to stop blood draining from the head.

This man's suit had a metal ring around its neck, to which could be attached a space-flight helmet, and a plug-in hose socket on its waist, to which one connected a life-support unit.

'Ah, you made it,' the Echo pilot said as he approached them, obviously not seeing beyond their 7th Squadron outfits and filthy sand-covered goggles. 'Sorry, but we couldn't wait for you any longer. Cobra made the call.

Come on, it's only Coleman and me left. Everyone else is already up in the shutt—'

Smack!

Schofield stood quickly and punched him hard in the face, dropping him with one hit.

'Apology not accepted,' Schofield said. Then he turned to the President. 'Wait here.'

'Okay,' the Chief Executive replied quickly.

The 747 soared into the sky. Inside it, the world was tilted crazily, at an almost 45-degree angle.

Schofield hurried up the stairs that led to the 747's upper deck and cockpit. He held his P-90 poised in front of him, searching for the second pilot, the man named Coleman.

He found him as he was emerging from the cockpit. Another sharp blow later—this time with the butt of his P-90—and Coleman was also out cold.

Schofield rushed into the empty cockpit, scanned it quickly.

He'd been hoping to seize the controls and bring the plane down . . .

No dice.

A screen on the cockpit's display revealed that the plane was flying on autopilot, and heading for an altitude of 67,000 feet—the height at which the 747 would release the space shuttle on its back.

At the bottom of the screen, however, were the words:

AUTOPILOT ENGAGED.
TO DISABLE AUTOPILOT OR ALTER SET COURSE
ENTER AUTHORIZATION CODE.

Authorization code? Schofield thought.

Shit.

He couldn't switch off the autopilot. Which meant he couldn't bring the plane down . . .

So what *could* he do?

He looked about himself, saw the clouds outside, saw the unconscious body of the pilot named Coleman lying on the floor just outside the cockpit.

And as his eyes fell on the pilot's body, he got an idea.

Schofield came back down to the President, hauling the unconscious Coleman on his shoulder.

He nodded toward the other knocked-out pilot at the President's feet. 'Put on his flight-suit,' Schofield said as he dropped Coleman's body to the floor and started undressing it.

Within minutes, Schofield and the President were wearing the two pilots' bright-orange pressure suits—with SIG-Sauer pistols concealed in their thigh pockets.

'Where to now?' the President asked.

Schofield gave him a serious look. 'Where no man has gone before.'

The X-38 space shuttle was connected to the launch jumbo by a cylindrical umbilical. Half a dozen titanium struts actually mounted the shuttle onto the back of the 747, but it was the umbilical that allowed human access to and from the spacecraft.

Basically, the umbilical looked like a long vertical tube that stretched upward from the back of the jumbo into the underside of the shuttle. Its entrance was at the mid-point of the jumbo, halfway along its lower deck.

Schofield and the President hurried toward it.

On the way, they found gear that had been waiting for the two Echo Unit pilots: two white briefcase-like life-support systems—small self-contained air-conditioners just like those carried by the shuttle astronauts—and a pair of spherical gold-tinted space helmets that clicked onto the neck-rings of their pressure suits.

The reflective gold tint of the helmets' dome-shaped visors—a feature designed to protect the wearer from the brutal quantities of ultra-violet radiation one experiences at extremely high altitudes—completely hid their faces.

They came to the umbilical's entrance: a tubular vertical tunnel that disappeared into the ceiling. A thin steel ladder rose up through its core.

Now dressed completely in his space suit, his face hidden by his reflective gold visor, Schofield peered up into it.

At the top end of the tube, about thirty yards straight up, he could see the illuminated interior of the X-38 shuttle.

He turned to the President and signalled with his finger: *up*.

They climbed the ladder slowly, weighed down by their cumbersome space suits and life-support briefcases.

After about a minute of climbing, Schofield's helmeted head rose up through a circular hatch in the floor of the shuttle.

Schofield froze.

The rear cargo compartment of the space shuttle looked like the interior of a high-tech bus.

It was only a small space, compact, designed to hold anything from men to weapons to small satellites. It had pristine white walls that were lined with life-support sockets, keypads and tie-down equipment studs. At the moment, however, the cabin was in personnel-carrying mode: about a dozen heavy-looking flight seats faced forward, grouped in pairs.

And strapped into those seats, Schofield saw, were the men of Echo Unit and their Chinese conspirators.

There were five of them inside the cargo cabin, and they all wore identical space suits—gold-tinted helmets and baggy orange pressure suits with small US flags sewn onto the shoulders.

How ironic, Schofield thought.

They were also strapped tightly into their flight seats, in readiness for the high-G transit into orbit.

Through the cockpit door at the front of the cargo compartment, he saw three more space-suited individuals— the shuttle's flight team. Beyond them he could see the clear open sky.

As he stood there, sticking half out of the shuttle's floor hatch, Schofield felt his adrenalin surge.

He knew that their reflective gold helmets prevented him and the President from being recognised. But still he felt self-conscious, certain that he looked like an impostor stepping into the heart of enemy territory.

Near the front end of the compartment, there were several empty seats—waiting, presumably, for the two 747 pilots, and the five Echo commandos who had been cut off down in the hangar.

Slowly, Schofield raised himself up and out of the umbilical tunnel.

No-one paid him any special attention.

He searched the cabin for Kevin, and at first, to his horror, *didn't* see him.

No . . .

But then he noticed that one of the five space-suited figures seated inside the cabin didn't quite seem to fill out his oversized suit.

In fact, it looked almost comical. The suit's gloved arms hung limply on this figure, its booted leggings dangled clumsily to the floor. It appeared that the wearer of this suit was *way too small* for it . . .

It had to be.

Rather than bunching up the space suit to allow Kevin's hands to reach into its gloves, the Echo men had made sure that the little boy was receiving the full benefit of the pressure suit's blood-regulating cuffs, even if that meant he looked like Charlie Chaplin wearing an oversized outfit.

All right, Schofield thought as he stepped out of the umbilical's hatch. *How am I going to do this?*

Why not just grab Kevin before anyone has a chance to unbuckle themselves, then dive down into the umbilical and get back into the 747 and—

Just then a hand seized Schofield's arm, and a voice exploded in his ear.

'Yo, Coleman.'

It was one of the shuttle's pilots, faceless behind his gold visor. He had stepped back into the personnel cabin and grabbed Schofield's arm. His tinny voice came in over Schofield's helmet intercom.

'*Just you two? What happened to the others?*'

Schofield just shook his head sadly.

'*Aw, well,*' the faceless astronaut said. He pointed with two fingers to a pair of flight seats close to the cockpit door. '*Take a seat and strap in.*'

Then, with casual efficiency, the astronaut crouched down, helped the President out of the umbilical, and shut the entry hatch behind him!

Then he just strode forward to the cockpit, speaking into his intercom as he did so: '*All personnel, prepare for separation from the launch vehicle in thirty seconds.*'

The cockpit door slid firmly shut behind the pilot, sealing it off, and Schofield was left standing in the middle of the cabin, staring at the closed pressure hatch in the floor beneath him.

Holy shit . . .

They were about to go into orbit.

With the President behind him, Schofield made his way forward, to two empty seats near the cockpit door.

As he did so, he observed how the Echo men had attached themselves to the shuttle's centralised life-support system and strapped themselves into their seats.

He arrived at his seat, and plugged a secondary hose from his life-support briefcase into a socket in the seat's arm. Then he sat down and started securing his seat-harness.

The President, watching him, did the same, strapping himself into a seat on the other side of the central aisle.

Once he was safely secured, Schofield turned to look about himself.

Across the aisle from him, in the seat directly behind the President, he saw the lopsided figure of Kevin, looking very awkward in his oversized space suit.

It was then that a strange thing happened.

Kevin waved at him.

Waved at him.

It was a rapid side-to-side wave which made the little boy's over-long sleeve flap stupidly in the air.

Schofield frowned, did a double take.

He was wearing his opaque gold-tinted space helmet. There was no way Kevin could see his face.

Did Kevin know who he was?

How *could* Kevin know who he was?

Schofield dismissed the thought as stupid. Kevin must have just been waving at all of the astronauts.

He turned to check on the President—saw him draw his seatbelts tightly across his chest. The President seemed to take a long, deep breath. Schofield knew how he felt.

Suddenly, voices came in over their helmet intercoms.

'Booster ignition standing by . . .'

'Approaching launch height . . .'

'Umbilical release in three . . . two . . . one . . . mark.'

There came a loud clunking noise from beneath the shuttle, and abruptly, the whole spacecraft rose slightly in the air, felt lighter.

'Umbilical has separated . . . we are clear of the launch vehicle . . .'

There came a soft chuckle. Then Cobra Carney's voice: *'Burn it.'*

'Certainly, sir. Prepare to engage Pegasus boosters . . . Ignition in three . . .'

The shuttle beneath Schofield began to rumble ominously.

' . . . two . . .'

He waited in tense anticipation.

' . . . one . . . mark.'

It looked like someone had ignited a flamethrower.

When the X-38's Pegasus boosters fired, the space shuttle was positioned slightly above its abandoned 747 launch vehicle—its gigantic boosters pointed *directly at* the silver jumbo beneath it.

The boosters ignited, bright as magnesium flares. Two incredibly long tongues of white-hot fire blasted out from the twin cylindrical boosters on the underside of the X-38.

The two lances of fire shot like lightning bolts straight into the 747, severing it in the middle, cutting through it like a pair of blowtorches.

The 747 just snapped in half under the weight of the fiery blast, its back broken in an instant. The fuel inside its wings ignited immediately, and a split-second later, the whole gigantic plane just exploded, showering the sky with a thousand pieces of smoke-trailing debris.

Schofield never saw the 747 get destroyed. He was in a whole new world now.

The blast of the boosters igniting was like nothing he had ever heard.

It was *loud*. Booming. All-consuming.

It had been like the sound of a jet engine thundering to life—only multiplied by a thousand.

Now the shuttle tilted sharply upwards and *rocketed* forward.

Schofield was thrust back into his seat by the G-force. The whole cabin began to shake and shudder. He felt his cheeks flatten, press back against his face. He clenched his teeth.

Apart from the closed cockpit door, the only visible link between the flight deck and the rear cargo compartment was a five-inch-thick window set into the cockpit's back wall.

476

Through this window, Schofield could see right through to the forward windshield of the shuttle—through which he could actually see the sky turning purple as they rose higher.

For a few minutes the shuttle soared upward, its massive boosters lifting it high into the sky. Then, abruptly, over the roar of the rockets, the flight team's voices returned:

'*Prepare to jettison boosters and switch over to self-contained power . . .*'

'*Copy that.*'

'*Stand by for booster release. In three . . . two . . . one . . . mark.*'

Kerchunk!

Schofield felt the weight of the enormous booster rockets drop away from the rising shuttle.

He looked over at the President—the Chief Executive was gripping his armrests tightly. As far as Schofield was concerned, that was actually a good sign. It meant that the President hadn't passed out.

The X-38 rose into the sky. The shuddering and shaking had stopped now and the ride became smoother, quieter, almost as if the X-38 was floating on air.

The respite gave Schofield a chance to take in his surroundings more closely.

The first thing he saw was a keypad next to the cockpit door—a locking mechanism, presumably for use in emergencies, like when cabin pressure was lost.

Schofield also examined his space suit. There was a small unit sewn into the sleeve of his left forearm which appeared to control his helmet intercom. At the moment, the unit's display screen indicated that he was currently on channel '05'.

He looked over at the President, surreptitiously tapped his wrist unit, then held up three fingers: *Switch to channel three.*

The President nodded. A few seconds later, Schofield said, 'Can you hear me?'

'*Yes. What's the plan?*'

'We sit tight. And we wait for a chance to take over this bird.'

The shuttle flew higher.

As it did so, the view outside its forward windshield gradually changed. The sky transformed from cloudy purple to ominous black.

And then abruptly, as though a veil had been lifted, Schofield found himself looking at a glorious galaxy of stars, and beneath the starfield—glowing like an opal against the jet-black sky—the wide elliptical expanse of the Earth, curving downward at both extremities, stretching away into the distance like some unbelievably gigantic luminescent orb, so absolutely *immense* in its size that it was almost too large to comprehend.

It was breathtaking.

They weren't far up, almost exactly at the dividing line between space and the outer atmosphere, about two hundred miles.

The Earth itself—curved and massive and dazzling—filled almost three-quarters of Schofield's field of vision.

He stared at the sight, at the glowing turquoise planet hovering in front of the universe. Then he turned his gaze to the starfield above the planet. It was so clear up here, the starry sky so endless.

And then, one of the stars began to move.

Schofield blinked, looked again.

One of the stars was definitely moving.

'Holy *Christ* . . .' he breathed.

It wasn't a star at all.

It was a shuttle, a space shuttle, all but identical in shape and size to the regular American models.

It soared effortlessly in the weightlessness of space, cutting a dead-straight line toward them. The red and yellow flag on its tail was unmistakable.

It was the Chinese space shuttle.

Schofield flicked back to channel 05 in time to hear Cobra's voice say: '*Yellow Star, this is Fleeing Eagle, I have visual on you now. We are reducing thrust to begin parking orbit. You may commence your approach in thirty seconds.*'

Just then, the cockpit door slid open and two of the X-38's pilots emerged.

Schofield snapped to look up.

Now that they were in low orbit, they could move around the cabin. It was zero gravity, so they stepped lightly, using hand-grips attached to the ceiling to move around.

Both pilots still wore their gold-tinted helmets, still carried their briefcase-like life-support units at their sides. They strode past Schofield and the President, heading aft to prepare for the docking with the Chinese shuttle.

A couple of the other space-suited men in the cargo hold also began unbuckling their seatbelts, getting up to help with the transfer.

Schofield saw the chance, tuned to channel 03.

'Okay,' he turned to the President. 'This is it. Follow me.'

As casually as he could make it look, Schofield reconnected his air-hose to his life-support briefcase and began unbuckling his seatbelts.

The President did the same.

As his belts came free, Schofield felt the weightlessness take hold of him. He gripped a ceiling handhold and before anyone could stop him—or even ask him what he was doing—he casually stepped over to Kevin and began re-attaching the boy's life-support briefcase and disengaging him from his seat.

A couple of the faceless Echo astronauts looked over, curious.

Schofield gestured to the cockpit—*Wanna have a look?*

Kevin nodded.

The Echo men went back to their work.

With the President in tow behind him—holding onto the ceiling handholds—Schofield led Kevin forward, into the shuttle's cockpit.

The view from the cockpit was even more incredible.

Through the panoramic forward windshield, the Earth looked amazing, stretching away from them like an enormous aqua-blue convex lens.

The last remaining pilot in the cockpit turned in his seat as they entered.

Over to channel 05: 'Just thought we'd come up and see the view,' Schofield said, coughing through his voice to mask it.

'Not bad, huh? Just be sure to keep your visors on. Radiation's a killer, and the sun is almost blinding.'

Schofield put Kevin in the empty co-pilot's seat. Then

he turned to the President, clicked back to channel 03.

'You unbuckle his seatbelts, then use them to secure his arms. I'll take care of his life-support hose.'

'Huh—how? When?'

'After I do this . . .' Schofield said.

And with that he leaned forward, grabbed the pilot's gold-tinted visor, and wrenched it open.

'*Argh!*' the pilot roared, as raw white sunlight assaulted his eyes. Underneath his gold-tinted visor was a clear glass bubble that afforded no protection against the pure sunlight.

Schofield then ripped the man's life-support system out of its wall socket, while at the same time, the President unclasped his seatbelts and quickly looped them *behind* the man's flight seat, pinning his arms firmly to his sides.

Deprived of his life-support—and now tied to his own seat—the pilot started to gasp desperately for air.

Schofield dived for the cockpit door, slammed his fist down on a switch next to the entryway. The door slid quickly shut, enclosing the three of them inside the cockpit.

The President spun, 'So what—?'

But Schofield was still moving.

He knew he had about three seconds before someone re-opened the cockpit door from the rear cargo compartment.

There was a keypad next to the door, identical to the one on the other side.

Schofield rushed over to it.

Apart from the usual numbered keys and open/close switches, there was one long red rectangular button on the panel, concealed behind a clear-plastic safety casing. It read:

EMERGENCY USE ONLY:

COCKPIT SECURITY LOCK

Schofield flipped open the safety casing and hit the big red button.

Immediately—*thunk-thunk-thunk-thunk-thunk!*—the door's five emergency dead-bolts locked into place, sealing off the cockpit like a bank vault.

A second later, Schofield heard a weak thumping noise coming from the other side: the sound of the Echo men hammering angrily on the door.

Reflective gold helmets peered in through the five-inch-thick window in the dividing wall, waving furious fists.

Schofield didn't care.

This shuttle was now his.

He leaned over Kevin in the co-pilot's seat, the Earth and the stars laid out before him.

In addition to the view, he was confronted by another intimidating sight: the X-38's flight console—a collection of about a million tiny switches, lights, buttons and monitors. It looked like the cockpit of a jumbo jet . . . only *more* complex.

The President took the rear navigator's seat, lifting Kevin onto his lap.

'So, what now?' he asked. 'Don't tell me you know how to fly a space shuttle, too, Captain.'

'Unfortunately not,' Schofield said. He turned to face the bound and still-gagging shuttle pilot. 'But he does.'

Schofield pulled his SIG-Sauer from his thigh pocket

and held it to the choking pilot's visor. The President re-attached the man's life-support hose. The pilot stopped gasping as Schofield flicked his intercom to channel 03.

'I need you to help me bring this thing back down to earth,' Schofield said.

'*Fuck you . . .*' the pilot said.

'Hmm,' Schofield said. He then nodded to the President, who yanked the pilot's life-support hose out of its socket again. The Echo Unit pilot immediately resumed his gagging.

Schofield tried again. 'How about I put this another way: either you tell me how to pilot this thing safely back to Utah, or I do it without your help. Now, given the way I fly, either we'll burn up on re-entry or crash into a friggin' mountain. Either way, we die. So, the way I see it, you either tell me how to do it, or you get killed watching me try.'

The President re-attached the pilot's life-support hose. The bound man's face was almost blue.

'*Okay,*' he breathed. '*Okay . . .*'

'Great,' Schofield said, 'Now, the first thing I need is—'

He cut himself off as illuminated green words scrolled out rapidly across the cockpit's transparent Heads-Up Display, or HUD, in the windshield:

FLEEING EAGLE, THIS IS *YELLOW STAR*.
YOU HAVE ALTERED COURSE.
PLEASE REALIGN TO VECTOR THREE-ZERO-ZERO.

Schofield stared at the words on the HUD. They seemed to hover in the air in front of the starfield.

Then, beyond the transparent display, he saw the Chinese space shuttle, much closer now.

It glided slowly and effortlessly through the void toward his ship, about three hundred yards away and closing quickly.

FLEEING EAGLE, PLEASE CONFIRM.

'Please confirm . . .' Schofield muttered as he scanned the cockpit's enormous array of switches and found the weapons section. 'Confirm *this*.'

He flipped open a safety casing to reveal two red buttons marked 'MSSLE LNCH'.

'This is for Mother,' he said as he jammed his fingers down on both buttons.

The two shuttles faced each other in space—hovering above the outer atmosphere, lit from below by the brilliant reflected light of the world—the compact X-38 and the much larger Chinese shuttle.

And then suddenly, twin bolts of white shot out from the wings of the X-38—two missiles, sleek zero-gravity AMRAAMs. They blasted off their wing-mounts and rocketed through the vacuum between the two shuttles.

The missiles moved unbelievably fast, converging on the Chinese shuttle like a pair of giant winged needles.

They left no smoketrails in their wakes. No puffs of flame or fire, for nothing survives in a vacuum. Their tail thrusters simply glowed orange against the black star-filled sky.

There was nothing the Chinese space shuttle could do. There were, quite simply, no defensive measures it could employ up here.

The two AMRAAMs slammed into the Chinese ship at exactly the same time—one hitting it in the middle, the other in the nose.

The shuttle just *cracked*.

There was an instantaneous flash of blinding white light and the Chinese shuttle spontaneously blew out into pieces which, after the initial blast, just radiated outwards in a kind of accentuated slow motion.

The *Yellow Star* would not be returning to Earth.

The Echo men were still hammering on the cockpit door as, under the instructions of the tied-up pilot, Schofield enabled the X-38's automated re-entry procedures.

There was nothing the men from Echo Unit could do.

The cockpit door was three-inch-thick titanium. And firing a gun through the five-inch-thick glass window didn't look like a clever option.

Indeed, as the X-38 began its controlled descent out of its orbit, hit the atmosphere and engaged its heat-shields against the 4,000°F temperatures outside, they could only strap themselves back into their seats and hang on.

The shuttle rocketed downward under the autopilot. As it did so, Schofield watched the starfield above them slowly fade away, replaced by a hazy purple aura, before suddenly, brilliantly, they burst down into dazzling blue sky.

The orbiting X-38 had travelled eastward—but because it hadn't actually been up that long, only about halfway across Colorado. Looking down, and facing *west* now, Schofield saw steel-grey mountains and lush green valleys. Beyond them, on the curved horizon, he could see the sandy-yellow Utah desert.

He looked at his watch.

10:36 a.m.

They hadn't been in orbit long at all. About twelve minutes, in fact. Now, gliding downward at supersonic speed, they'd be back in Utah in only a couple more.

Suddenly, the heads-up display came to life:

SOURCE AIRFIELD BEACON DETECTED

AIRFIELD IDENTIFIED AS UNITED STATES AIR FORCE

SPECIAL AREA (RESTRICTED) 08

PROCEEDING TO SOURCE AIRFIELD

Area 8, Schofield thought.

No.

He didn't want to go there.

So far as he could see, the only way to end this challenge once and for all was to get away from these bases with the President *and* the Football.

But to do that, they needed the Football.

And the Football—whose interminable countdown still needed to be satisfied by 11:30—was last seen at Area 7, in the hands of Seth Grimshaw.

Schofield turned to his captive shuttle pilot. 'We need to get to Area 7.'

The X-38 descended rapidly, shooting westward, blasting over the barren Utah desert.

It flew down toward Area 8, roaring through the air, but as it came close, Schofield disengaged the autopilot and, now flying the shuttle manually like a regular plane, he allowed the shuttle to overshoot the base.

They covered the twenty miles to Area 7 in less than a minute, and very soon, he saw the low mountain and the cluster of hangars and buildings, and the elongated runway in the sand. In the far distance, on the horizon, he saw the wide expanse of Lake Powell, with its twisting network of water-filled canyons.

He aimed for the runway, sweeping in low over the buildings of Area 7. It ran from east to west, so he was coming straight for it.

The X-38 boomed over the Area 7 complex, shaking its walls, before touching down perfectly on its black bitumen runway.

But it came in fast—very fast.

Which was why Schofield didn't see the two black Penetrator helicopters sitting silently next to Area 7's hangars.

Didn't see one of them immediately power up and rise into the air as soon as his tyres had hit the tarmac.

The X-38 rocketed down the desert runway, its tyres smoking.

Schofield tried to rein in the speeding spacecraft, releasing a brake-parachute which fluttered to life behind it. The shuttle began to slow.

When at last it had lost all its momentum, Schofield flicked some switches, prepared to take her back to the main hangar.

He never even got to turn the shuttle around.

For at the very moment that he brought it to a halt, he saw the Penetrator helicopter swing menacingly into place in front of him, hovering above the runway like an evil bird of prey.

The space shuttle and the winged attack helicopter squared off like a pair of gunslingers on a Wild West street—the shuttle on the runway, the Penetrator floating in the air in front of it.

Inside the shuttle's cockpit, Schofield yanked off his helmet. The President did the same.

'Shit. What do we—?' the President asked.

Bang!

The cockpit door shuddered.

The men of Echo Unit were out of their seats and were once again pounding on it.

Then suddenly the voice of the Penetrator's pilot came in over the radio. It was one of Caesar Russell's 7th Squadron men.

'X-38, this is Air Force Penetrator. Be advised, we have missile lock on you. Release the boy now.'

Schofield spun to look at Kevin, thinking fast.

The world was closing in on them—the Penetrator outside, the Echo men inside, missile lock . . .

And then he saw the compartment sunk into the wall beyond Kevin's seat.

He turned to the President. 'Sir, could you help Kevin get his suit off, please.'

The President did so while Schofield hit the 'TALK' button. 'Air Force Penetrator, what are your intentions?'

As he spoke, Schofield climbed over to the wall compartment and yanked it open.

A sign on its door panel read: SURVIVAL KIT.

The Echo men continued to pound on the cockpit door.

'If you release the boy,' the Penetrator pilot said, *'we leave you in peace.'*

'Yeah, right,' Schofield muttered.

He was foraging frantically through the shuttle's survival compartment. 'Come on,' he breathed, 'there *has* to be one in here. There always is . . .'

Into his mike, however, he said, 'And if we don't release the boy?'

'Then we might just have to cut our losses and kill you all.'

It was then that Schofield found what he was looking for inside the compartment: a two-foot-long cylindrical metal tube that looked like a—

He grabbed it, snapped to look up—and found himself looking out through the five-inch-thick glass window that opened onto the rear section of the shuttle. On the other side of the glass, aimed right at his face, was a *pistol*, held by one of the Echo men!

With a flash of white light—and a silent *bang*—the pistol fired.

Schofield shut his eyes, waited for the bullet to crash through the glass and enter his head.

But the glass was too thick. The bullet just scratched the surface and pinged away.

Schofield breathed again, raced back to his seat.

'Air Force Penetrator,' he said as he climbed back into his flight seat and started doing up his seatbelts. 'All right. All right. Listen. I also have the President here.' As he spoke, he indicated for the President to undo his belts.

'*The President . . .*'

'That's right. I'm going to send him out with the boy. I'm sure you won't mind that. Now, I have your word, you won't fire on us if we send them out?'

'*That's right.*'

'Okay,' Schofield said to Kevin and the President. 'When I release the hatch, I want you two to get as far away from this shuttle as you can. All right?'

'Right,' Kevin said.

'Right,' the President nodded. 'But what about you?'

Schofield pulled the hatch release lever.

With a sharp *snap-whoosh!* a small section of the shuttle's ceiling—the part directly above the tied-up

491

shuttle pilot—went catapulting high into the air, flying end over end.

A wide square of blue sky opened over the pilot.

'Just get as far away from this shuttle as you can,' Schofield said. 'I'll be joining you in a minute. I just have a helicopter to kill.'

In the shimmering desert heat, two tiny figures emerged from the shuttle's cockpit hatch.

The President and Kevin.

The President still wore his orange flight suit, only now he was helmetless. Kevin just wore the regular clothes he'd been wearing underneath his oversized space suit.

The Penetrator loomed above them, its rotor wash shaking the air.

A plastic rope-ladder hung down from the shuttle's roof. It had unrolled automatically when the escape hatch had been jettisoned.

The President and Kevin descended the ladder quickly, under the watchful eye of the Penetrator's three crew members.

Then their feet touched the burning-hot tarmac and they hurried away from the shuttle.

Meanwhile, inside the shuttle's cockpit, Schofield was positioning the metal tube on his lap, waiting tensely for Kevin and the President to get clear.

He exchanged a glance with the still-bound shuttle pilot. 'What're you looking at?' he said—

Zzzzzzzzz!

Without warning, a spray of brilliant orange sparks exploded out from the door behind him.

Holy . . .

The Echo men were using *a blowtorch* to cut through the door!

Must wait for the President and the boy to get clear . . .

And then the Penetrator pilot's voice came through. *'Thank you, X-38. I'm sorry for misleading you, but unfortunately you must now be destroyed. Goodnight.'*

Instantly, a Sidewinder missile shot out from the right-hand wing-stub of the Penetrator, a smoketrail looping through the air behind it. It zoomed downwards, heading straight for the space shuttle's windshield.

The blowtorch's sparks sprayed into the cockpit from behind.

Screw it, Schofield thought. *Time to blow this joint.*

And with that, he yanked on the ejection lever beside his seat.

Like a New Year's Eve firecracker shooting up into the sky, Shane Schofield rocketed up into the air above the grounded space shuttle, sitting on his flight seat.

He carved a perfectly straight vertical path into the air, in the process creating a bizarre triangle between himself, the space shuttle and the Penetrator helicopter.

And then everything happened at once.

First, the Penetrator's missile *slammed* into the X-38 beneath Schofield, causing it and the Echo men inside it to explode in a billowing blasting fireball.

For his part, Schofield shot high into the air above the flaming explosion, reaching the zenith of his flight path just as he drew level with the Penetrator's shocked crew.

It was only then that the chopper's three crew members saw Schofield heft the cylindrical tube from the shuttle's survival kit onto his shoulder—*as he flew upwards on the ejection seat.*

Only it wasn't just any old tube.

It was a rocket launcher.

A compact M-72 single-shot disposable rocket launcher, supplied in the survival kit for astronauts who crash-landed in enemy territory and needed some lightweight but heavy-hitting firepower.

Hovering in the air in his ejection seat, high above the billowing fireball that had been the X-38, Schofield jammed his finger down on the rocket launcher's trigger.

Instantly, a streamlined warhead *shoomed* out from the M-72 on his shoulder, streaking through the air at pheno-menal speed, heading straight for the Penetrator's cockpit.

The warhead smashed through the helicopter's glass windshield and detonated violently. The walls of the attack helicopter blasted outwards, the chopper just disinte-grating in mid-air.

It dropped out of the sky—a blazing, flaming wreck, trailing a plume of thick black smoke—and crashed down against the tarmac, shattering into pieces.

The final episode of the sequence was the inflating of Schofield's parachute.

It blossomed to life above his ejection seat, lifting him out of it. Then the parachute carried him safely back down to earth, landing him gently on the runway a short way from the twin flaming ruins of the space shuttle and the Penetrator.

The President and Kevin rushed up to him.

'That was *so* cool!' Kevin gasped.

'Yes. Remind me never to point a loaded weapon at you,' the President said.

Schofield discarded his parachute, gazed back down the runway toward the buildings of Area 7.

Area 7 . . .

Strangely, the first thing he thought about was not the Football nor the fate of the country.

It was Libby Gant.

He'd last seen her during their battle in the pit, when Colonel Harper's Sinovirus grenade had gone off and they'd been separated.

But then he saw the helicopter.

Saw the *second* Penetrator—Caesar and Logan's Penetrator—sitting empty and abandoned outside the main hangar complex.

'Caesar came back to Area 7 . . .' Schofield said aloud. 'Why would he do that?'

It was then that he saw a figure emerge from the base of the airfield's control tower, waving one arm weakly.

It was Book II.

Schofield, Kevin and the President met Book at the base of the tower.

Book II looked pale, weary. He wore a thick bandage over a wound on his left bicep; the rest of the arm was held in a makeshift sling.

'Scarecrow. Quick,' he said, obviously still in pain. 'You better come and see this. *Now.*'

As they climbed the stairs of the control tower, Schofield said, 'When did Caesar come back to Area 7?'

'They landed only a few minutes before you did. They *were* all heading for that top door entrance when you guys arrived. I was looking after Janson up in the tower, and we saw the whole ejection-seat thing. Caesar and Logan watched it from the hangar entrance, but when you blasted their boys to kingdom come, they headed straight inside the complex again.'

'Caesar went back inside the complex ... Why?' Schofield said, thinking hard. Then he looked up. 'Any word from Gant?'

'No,' Book II said. 'I figured she was with you.'

'We got separated when that Sinovirus grenade went off before. She must still be inside the complex.'

They arrived at the top level of the tower. Juliet Janson lay slumped on a chair, a bandage over her bullet-wounded shoulder, alive but very pale.

Beside her, lay the Football.

'So what did you want me to see?' Schofield asked Book.

'This,' Book II said, indicating one particular computer screen. It was flashing:

LOCKDOWN PROTOCOL S.A.(R) 7-A
FAILSAFE SYSTEM ENACTED
AUTH CODE: 7-3-468201103

*******************************WARNING!*******************************
EMERGENCY PROTOCOL ACTIVATED.
IF YOU DO NOT ENTER AN AUTHORIZED LOCKDOWN
EXTENSION OR TERMINATION CODE BY 1105 HOURS,
FACILITY SELF-DESTRUCT SEQUENCE WILL BE ACTIVATED.
SELF-DESTRUCT SEQUENCE DURATION: 10:00 MINUTES.
*******************************WARNING!*******************************

Schofield looked at his watch.

It was 10:43.

Twenty-two minutes till the complex's thermonuclear self-destruct mechanism was set in motion.

And they'd had no word from Gant . . .

Shit.

'There's another thing,' Book II said. 'We've managed to get the generators back on line, but the power's still very low. We've been able to get a couple of systems back on, some light systems, a few communication lines and the internal broadcast system.'

'And . . . ?'

'Have a look at this.'

Book II hit a switch, and one of the console monitors blinked to life.

On it, Schofield saw the image of the control room overlooking the main hangar.

497

And standing inside the heavily battered room, looking directly into the camera as he had done on several occasions earlier that morning, was Caesar Russell.

Russell grinned at the camera.

When he spoke, his voice boomed out from the tower's speakers.

'Greetings, Mister President, people of America. I know it's a little early for my hourly update, but since, alas, it appears that my race has been run, I'm sure you won't mind an early commentary.

'My men are vanquished, my cause lost. I would commend the President and his brave bodyguards for their efforts, but such is not my way. I merely leave you all with a parting comment: this country can never be the same, not after today . . .'

Then Caesar did something that made Schofield's blood completely freeze.

He pulled open the front of his combat fatigues, revealing his chest.

Schofield's jaw dropped. 'Oh no . . .'

There, on Russell's chest, was a long vertical scar, right over his heart—the scar of a man who had had heart surgery sometime in the past.

Caesar grinned, an evil, maniacal, completely *insane* grin.

'Cross my heart,' he said, *'and hope to die.'*

'What?' the President said. 'I don't get it.'

Schofield was silent.

He got it.

He snatched a piece of paper from his pocket. It was the printout he'd got Brainiac to produce inside the

AWACS plane right at the very start of all this—when he'd needed to know if there really was a radio transmitter planted on the President's heart.

Schofield scanned the printout. It still had the circles Brainiac had drawn on it before:

He recalled Brainiac's earlier explanation.

'It's a standard rebounding signature. The satellite sends down a search signal—they're the tall spikes on the positive side—and then, soon after, the receiver on the ground, the President, bounces that signal back. Those are the deep spikes on the negative side.

'Search and return. Interference aside, the rebounding signature seems to repeat itself once every twenty-five seconds.'

'Interference aside . . .' Schofield said as he stared at the printout.

'Only there is no interference. There are *two separate* signals. The satellite needs to pick up two signals . . .' He grabbed a nearby pen and joined the four circles into two pairs.

'This graph indicates *two* distinct signal patterns,' Schofield said. 'The first and the third. And then the second and fourth.'

'What are you saying?' the President asked.

'What I'm saying, Mister President, is that you're not the only man at this complex with a radio transmitter attached to his heart. It's Caesar's trump card, his last resort, so that even if he loses, he still wins. Caesar Russell has a transmitter attached to *his* heart. So now, if he dies, the devices at the airports go off.'

'But he's inside the complex,' Book II said, wincing with pain, 'and in exactly twenty minutes, the self-destruct sequence will be initiated.'

'I know,' Schofield said, 'and so does he. Which means I now have to do something that I never thought I'd *ever* want to do. I have to go back into Area 7 and stop Caesar Russell from getting killed.'

SEVENTH CONFRONTATION

3 July, 1045 Hours

UNITED STATES AIR FORCE
SPECIAL AREA (RESTRICTED) NO. 7
1045 HOURS

GROUND LEVEL: Main Hangar

LEVEL 1: Hangar Bay

LEVEL 2: Hangar Bay

LEVEL 3: Living Quarters

LEVEL 4: Laboratories

LEVEL 5: Confinement

Flooded floor

LEVEL 6: X-rail platform

Schofield re-armed himself.

With Book II and Juliet both wounded, he was going back inside alone.

He got his Maghook back from Book, slid it into the shotgun holster on his back. He also grabbed the P-90 that Seth Grimshaw had brought out of the complex. It only had about forty rounds left in it, but that was better than nothing. He jammed Book's M9 and his own Desert Eagle pistol into his thigh holsters. And last of all, he swapped his water-damaged wrist mike and earpiece for Juliet's working unit.

Book and Juliet would remain up in the tower armed with a P-90, guarding the President, the Football and Kevin until the Army and Marine forces arrived at the base.

Schofield pulled out Nicholas Tate's cell phone, dialled the operator. He got Dave Fairfax's voice straight away, cutting into the call.

'Mister Fairfax, I need a favour.'

'*What?*'

'I need the lockdown release codes for Special Area 7,

the codes that turn off the self-destruct mechanism. Now, I can't imagine they're kept in a book somewhere. You're going to have to get onto the local network itself and somehow pull them out.'

'*How long have I got?*' Fairfax asked.

'You've got exactly nineteen minutes.'

'*I'm on it.*'

Fairfax hung up.

Schofield jammed a fresh clip into his M9. As he did so, a figure appeared at his side.

'I think she's still alive, too,' Kevin said suddenly.

Schofield looked up, appraised the little boy for a moment. 'How did you know I was thinking that?'

'I just know. I always know. I knew that Doctor Botha was lying to the Air Force men. And I could tell that you were a good man. I can't see exactly what someone's thinking, just what they're feeling. Right now, you're worried about someone, someone you care about. Someone who's still inside.'

'Is this how you knew it was me on the space shuttle?'

'Yes.'

Schofield finished loading his guns. 'Any final tips, then?' he asked Kevin.

The little boy said, 'I only saw her once, when you were both standing outside my cube. I only sensed one thing about her: she really likes you. So you'd better save her.'

Schofield gave him a wry smile. 'Thanks.'

And then he was away.

He tried the top door entrance first.

No luck.

Caesar had changed the code, manually it seemed. No time for Fairfax to crack that one.

That left only one other option: the Emergency Exit Vent.

Schofield ran for Caesar's abandoned Penetrator helicopter.

It was 10:48 a.m.

Two minutes later, Caesar's Penetrator—now flown by Schofield—landed next to the EEV in a swirling cloud of dust and sand.

The EEV hadn't been hard to find. Mr Hoeg's lime-green biplane—still sitting there on the desert floor—betrayed the exit's location quite unambiguously.

No sooner had the black helicopter touched the ground than Schofield was out of it and running toward the EEV.

He leaped down into the earthen trench and disappeared inside the exit's open steel doorway at a run.

It was 10:51 when Schofield stepped out onto the darkened X-rail tracks on Level 6, his gun raised.

The world down here was pitch black, save for the thin beam of his P-90's barrel-mounted flashlight.

He saw bodies laid out before him, shadows in the dim light—the remnants of the previous battles that day.

Air Force vs Secret Service.

South Africans vs Air Force.

Schofield and his Marines vs Air Force.

Christ . . .

But another thing weighed on his mind. Kevin, of course, had been right. Apart from saving Caesar Russell, Schofield had a far more personal reason for entering Area 7 again.

He wanted to find Libby Gant.

He didn't know what had happened to her after the Sinovirus grenade had gone off up in the main hangar, but he refused to believe that she was dead.

Schofield brought his wrist mike to his lips. 'Fox. Fox. Are you out there? This is Scarecrow. I'm back inside. Can you hear me?'

In a dark place somewhere inside Area 7, Libby Gant stirred, a voice invading her dreams.

'—*you hear me?*'

She'd been unconscious for nearly an hour now, and she didn't have a clue where she was or what had happened to her.

Her last memory was of being inside the control room upstairs and seeing something important and then suddenly . . . *nothing*.

As she blinked awake, she saw that she was still wearing her bright yellow biohazard suit, except for the helmet. It had been removed.

It was only then that she became aware of a pain in her shoulders. Gant opened her eyes fully—

—and an ice-cold chill rippled down her spine.

Her entire upper body was bound to a pair of steel girders that had been arranged in the shape of an X. Her wrists were held high above her head—crucifix-style—affixed to the arms of the cross with duct tape, while more thick tape held her throat tightly up against the junction of the X. Her legs— duct-taped at the ankles—were laid out flat in front of her.

Gant began to breathe very very fast.

What the hell was this?

She was someone's *prisoner*.

As she hung helplessly from the cross, eyes wide and terrified, she slowly began to regain her senses. She took in the area around her.

The first thing she noticed about this place was that there was no electric lighting. Three small fires illuminated the immediate area.

It was in this grim firelight that she saw Hagerty.

Colonel Hot Rod Hagerty sat immediately to her right, similarly 'crucified'—his legs stretched out on the floor in front of him, his arms outstretched on his own cross. His eyes were shut, his head bent. Every few seconds he groaned.

Gant looked at the room around them.

She was sitting underneath an overhang of some sort, in dark shadow; a stage-like structure stood out in the open space in front of her. Some children's toys lay scattered about the stage, amid shards of glass.

It looked as if—once—a glass cube of some sort had encased the stage, but now only half of that cube remained standing.

Gant realised where she was.

She was in the area that had contained Kevin's sterilised living area. Right now, she must be sitting directly underneath the observation lab that had overlooked the cube, beneath the overhang it created.

And then Gant saw the third crucified figure in the room, and she gasped in revulsion.

It was the Air Force colonel, Jerome Harper.

Or what was left of him.

He lay to Gant's left, also under the overhang, his arms taped to a cross high above his head, his head leaning as

507

far forward as the duct tape around his throat would allow.

But it was his lower body that seized Gant's shocked attention.

Harper's legs were missing.

No, not just missing.

Hacked off.

Everything from the Air Force colonel's waist down had been brutally carved away—like a carcass in an abattoir—leaving a gigantic slab of raw hacked flesh around his hips. Indeed, Harper's whole waist region was just a foul bloody mess that ended at the curved bony hook of his spinal column.

It was the most disgusting thing Gant had ever seen in her life.

Her eyes swept the room, as the full extent of her predicament became clear.

She was the prisoner of a monster. An individual who, until today, had been a guest here at Area 7.

Lucifer Leary.

The Surgeon of Phoenix.

The serial killer who had terrorised hitch-hikers on the Vegas-to-Phoenix interstate—the former medical student who would kidnap his victims, take them home, and then *eat* their limbs in front of them.

Gant looked about herself in horror.

Leary—a big man, she recalled, at least six-eight, with a hideous facial tattoo—was nowhere to be seen.

Except for Hagerty and herself, the whole observation area was completely and utterly *empty*.

Which, in a strange way, was even more frightening.

Schofield made for the stairwell at the eastern end of Level 6.

He had to get to the control room overlooking the main hangar—to enter the termination codes before 11:05; or if he couldn't do that, to capture Caesar and get him out of Area 7 before the nuke went off at 11:15.

He threw open the stairwell doorway—

—and was instantly confronted by an enormous black bear, caught in the beam of his small flashlight, rearing up on its hind legs, baring its massive claws and bellowing loudly at him!

Schofield dived off the edge of the X-rail platform as the family of bears ambled out of the stairwell—papa bear, mama bear and three little baby bears, all in a row.

Nicholas Tate had been right.

There *were* bears on the loose.

Papa bear seemed to sniff the air for a moment. Then he headed westward, toward the other end of the underground railway station, followed by his brood.

As soon as they were a safe distance away, Schofield dashed into the open stairwell.

*

Dave Fairfax was tapping feverishly at the keyboard of his supercomputer.

After five minutes' work, the computer had found a source number that represented Area 7's self-destruct release code.

Not bad progress, really. There was only one problem.

The number had 640 million digits.

He kept typing.

10:52.

Schofield bounded up the stairwell, in near pitch darkness, his flashlight beam wobbling.

As he ran, he tried to get Gant on the airwaves. 'Fox, this is Scarecrow. Can you hear me?' he whispered. 'I repeat, Fox, this is Scarecrow . . .'

No reply.

He ran past the firedoor to Level 5—the door with the thin jets of water shooting out from its edges—then came to Level 4, the lab level, hurried past its open door, heading upward.

On the other side of Level 4, Gant heard the voice again. It sounded tinny and distant.

'—repeat, Fox, this is Scarecrow—'

Scarecrow . . .

The voice was coming from Gant's earpiece, which now hung loosely from her ear. It must have been dislodged when her captor had knocked her unconscious.

Gant looked up at her left wrist, duct-taped to the cross high above her head.

She still had her Secret Service wrist mike attached to it. But there was no way she could bring it to her mouth, and the mike only worked when you spoke into it at close range.

So she started tapping her finger on the top of the microphone.

Schofield came to the floor-door that opened onto Level 2 and suddenly stopped.

He'd heard a strange tapping in his earpiece.

Tap-tap-taap. Tap-taap-tap . . .

Long and short taps.

Morse code.

Morse code that read, 'F-O-X. F-O-X . . .'

'Fox, is that you? One tap for no, two taps for yes.'

Tap-tap.

'Are you okay?'

Tap.

'Where are you? Tap out the floor number.'

Tap-tap-tap-tap.

10:53.

Schofield burst through the Level 4 firedoor, scanning the decompression area down the barrel of his gun.

It was dark.

Very dark.

This end of the floor was completely deserted—the decompression chamber was empty, as were the test chambers opposite it, and the catwalks above. The sliding horizontal doorway in the floor—the one that led down to the Level 5 cell bay—however, was still open.

The water level down on Level 5 had risen considerably over the last few hours. It had levelled off flush against the floor of Level 4. Inky black wavelets lapped up against the edges of the horizontal opening so that it now looked like a little rectangular pool.

Level 5, it seemed, was completely underwater now.

Schofield stepped past the pool—just as something slashed quickly through its waves. He spun, whipped his gun around, but whatever it had been was long gone.

This was *not* what he needed.

Dark complex. Bears moving around the stairwells. Caesar and Logan in here somewhere. Water everywhere. Not to mention the possible presence of more prisoners.

He came to the wall that divided Level 4 in two, flung its door open and snapped his gun up . . .

. . . and immediately saw Gant on the far side, beyond the shattered remains of Kevin's cube, lying spread-eagled up against a bizarre steel cross.

Schofield ran across the observation area, slid to his knees in front of Gant.

As he arrived before her, he dropped his P-90, clasped her head gently in his hands and, without even thinking, *kissed* her on the lips.

At first, Gant was a little stunned, then she realised what was happening and she kissed him back.

When he pulled away, Schofield saw the two men on either side of her.

First he saw Hagerty, out cold, similarly crucified.

Then he saw the dead Colonel Harper—saw the raw pink flesh of his hacked-off lower body, saw his exposed tail bone.

'Holy *Christ* . . .' he breathed.

'Quickly,' Gant said. 'We don't have much time, he'll be back soon.'

'Who?' Schofield started unravelling her duct-taped throat.

'Lucifer Leary.'

'Oh, *shit* . . .' Schofield started working faster. The tape around Gant's neck came free. He started on her wrists—

There came a loud resonating *boom* from within the walls.

Schofield and Gant both looked up, eyes wide.

'The aircraft elevator . . .' Schofield said.

'He must have gone upstairs,' Gant breathed, 'and now he's back. *Hurry* . . .'

Faster now, Schofield continued untying the tape around Gant's left wrist, but it was done too tightly. His fingers fumbled with the tape. This was taking too long . . .

He spun, saw some glass shards lying over by Kevin's stage-like living area—shards that he could use to cut the duct tape. He slid over toward them and sifted through them, trying to find one that was sharp enough. He found one, just as Gant called, '*Scarecrow!*' and he stood and turned—

—and found himself confronted by an extremely tall broadshouldered figure.

Schofield froze.

The figure just stood there before him—perhaps a yard away, his face shrouded in shadow—absolutely motionless. He towered over Schofield, gazing at him silently. Schofield hadn't even heard him approach.

'Do you know why the weasel never steals from the alligator's nest?' the shadowy figure asked. Schofield couldn't even see the man's mouth move.

Schofield swallowed.

'Because,' the figure said, 'it never knows when the alligator will return.'

And then the giant man stepped into the firelight—

—and Schofield saw the most fearsome, evil-looking face he'd ever seen in his life. The face was big—like its owner—and it had a hideous black tattoo covering its entire left side, a tattoo depicting five ragged claw-marks scratched down the length of the man's face.

Lucifer Leary.

He was absolutely *enormous*, too, at least six-foot-eight, with massive muscular shoulders and gigantic tree-trunk legs; almost a full foot taller than Schofield. He wore prison-issue jeans and a sky-blue shirt with the sleeves ripped off. His black eyes revealed not a trace of humanity—they just stared at Schofield like empty black orbs.

Then Leary opened his mouth, smiling menacingly, revealing foul yellow teeth.

The effect was mesmerising, almost hypnotic.

Schofield shot a glance back over at Gant, at his P-90 lying on the floor in front of her. Then, in what he thought was a quick draw, he whipped his two pistols from his thigh holsters.

The guns barely got out of their sheaths. Leary had anticipated the move.

Quick as a rattlesnake, he lunged forward and clamped his fists around Schofield's gunhands, seizing them by the wrists.

And then the bigger man started to *squeeze*.

Schofield had never felt such intense pain in his life. He dropped to his knees, teeth clenched—his wrists held in Leary's giant paws. Bloodflow to his hands ceased. It felt as if his fingers—bulging with redness—were going to burst.

He released his pistols. They clattered to the floor. Leary kicked them away.

Then, with the guns gone, he seized Schofield by the throat, lifted him clear off the ground and hurled him across Kevin's living area.

Schofield went crashing across the stage, sliding through some toys, before he exploded through a still-upright section of glass and went tumbling off the far edge of the stage.

Lucifer stalked around the elevated platform after him, his every step crunching on broken glass.

Schofield groaned, tried to stand. He needn't have bothered. Within seconds, Leary was there.

The massive killer lifted Schofield off the floor by his combat webbing and punched him hard in the face, sending his head snapping backwards.

Gant could only watch helplessly from her cross—her hands still tightly bound, Schofield's P-90 lying on the floor only inches away from her—as Lucifer pounded Schofield.

The fight was all one-way traffic.

Lucifer hit, Schofield recoiled, collapsed in a heap to the floor.

Lucifer strode forward, Schofield struggled to stand up.

And then Lucifer hurled Schofield through the doorway that divided Level 4, sending him sliding into the decompression area.

Lucifer followed him in.

Another kick and Schofield rolled—bleeding and gasping—up against the rim of the horizontal doorway in the floor, filled as it was with lapping water.

And then from out of nowhere, a giant reptilian head came bursting up out of the water and lunged at Schofield's head.

Schofield rolled quickly, avoiding the fast-moving jaws as they snapped down an inch away from his face.

Jesus!

It was a Komodo dragon. The largest lizard in the world, a known man-eater. The President had said they kept some of them here—along with the Kodiak bears, in cages down on Level 5—for use on the Sinovirus project.

The electric locks on their cages, it seemed, hadn't survived the power shutdown either.

At the sight of the Komodo dragon in the pool, a thin smile cracked Lucifer's hideous face.

He lifted Schofield off the ground and held him out over the reptile-infested pool.

As he hung above it, legs kicking, hands grappling at Lucifer's enormous fists, Schofield saw the dark alligator-like bodies of at least two dragons in the water beneath him.

Then without so much as a pause, Lucifer dropped Schofield into the pool.

Schofield splashed down into the water in an explosion of foam, a moment before Lucifer pressed a button in the floor beside the doorway, causing the hole's sliding garage-style door to close quickly over the ripples that marked the spot where Schofield had plunged into it.

Within seconds, the leading edge of the door met the opposite rim.

Ka-chunk.

Sealed. Shut.

Lucifer grunted a laugh as he heard Schofield's fists banging on the underside of the sliding door, heard the sloshing of water underneath the closed door—the sound of the dragons mauling the foolish Marine.

Lucifer smiled.

Then he headed back toward the other side of Level 4, where the pleasure of carving up the pretty female soldier awaited him.

Libby Gant gasped in horror as Lucifer Leary returned alone to the observation area of Level 4.

No.

Lucifer couldn't have . . .

No . . .

The giant serial killer strode confidently across the wide hall-like room, his head lowered, his eyes locked on Gant's.

He dropped to his knees in front of her, pushed his face close to hers. His breath was foul—it reeked of *eaten* human flesh.

He stroked her hair.

'Such a shame, such a shame,' he trilled, 'that your knight in shining armour was not the brave warrior he thought himself to be. Which only leaves us, now, to get . . . *better* acquainted.'

'Not likely,' said a voice from behind Lucifer.

The giant spun.

And there, in the doorway that led to the decompression area, his whole body dripping with water, stood Shane Schofield.

'You'll have to get rid of me,' he said grimly, 'before you lay a finger on her.'

Lucifer roared, snatched up Schofield's P-90 and let rip with an extended burst.

Schofield just stepped behind the doorway, out of sight, as the dividing wall all around the door was shredded by the hailstorm of gunfire.

Within seconds, however, the gun ran dry and Lucifer discarded it and stormed across the observation area, into the decompression area.

The horizontal door in its floor now lay open, wavelets still lapping against its rims. The large outlines of the Komodo dragons were still visible beneath the pool's rippling surface.

But, somehow, they hadn't killed Schofield.

And then Lucifer saw him, standing over by the decompression chamber, to the right of the pool.

He charged at Schofield, lashed out with a ferocious right.

Schofield ducked, walked under the punch. He was calmer now, collected. Not so caught-by-surprise. He had Lucifer's measure.

Lucifer spun, swung again. Another miss. Schofield punished the error with a crisp hit to Lucifer's face.

Crack.

Instantly broken nose.

Lucifer seemed more stunned than injured. He touched the blood that ran down from his nose as if it were an alien substance, as if no-one had ever hurt him before.

And then Schofield hit him again, a great powerful

blow, and for the first time, the big man staggered slightly.

Again, harder this time, and Lucifer took an unsteady step backwards.

Again, another step backwards.

Again—the most violent punch Schofield had ever thrown—and Lucifer's back foot touched the rim of the pool. He turned slightly—just as Schofield nailed him in the nose, causing the big man to lose his footing completely and fall backwards . . .

. . . into the Komodo-infested pool.

There was a great splash as Lucifer entered the water, and as the foam subsided, the Komodos rushed him, swarming all over his body, turning it into a writhing mass of black reptilian skin, claws and tails, and in the middle of it all, Lucifer's kicking feet and agonised screams.

Then, abruptly, the pool turned a sickening shade of red and Lucifer's legs went still. The Komodos just continued to eat his body.

Schofield winced at the sight, but then, if anyone deserved to die such an horrific painful death, Lucifer Leary did.

Then Schofield hit the button that closed the floor-door, obliterating the foul sight, and hurried back to get Gant.

10:59.

Within a minute, Gant was unbound and standing next to Schofield as he freed the bleary-eyed Hot Rod Hagerty.

Gant said, 'You know, this birthday really has *sucked*.'

She nodded toward the decompression area. 'What happened in there? I thought Leary had . . .'

'He did,' Schofield said. 'Bastard dropped me in a pool filled with Komodo dragons.'

'So how'd you get out?'

Schofield pulled out his Maghook. 'Apparently reptiles are exceptionally sensitive to magnetic discharges. I only learned that little fact this morning, from a little boy named Kevin. So I just flicked on my Maghook and they didn't want to come near me. Then I opened the floor-door up again from below and came back for you. Sadly, Lucifer didn't have a supercharged magnetic grappling hook on him when *he* fell in.'

'Nice,' Gant said. 'Very nice. So where's the President, and Kevin?'

'They're safe. They're outside the complex.'

'So why are you back in here?'

Schofield looked at his watch.

It was exactly 11:00 a.m.

'Two reasons. One, because in exactly five minutes this facility's self-destruct mechanism will be activated. Ten minutes after that, this whole place will be vapourised, and we can't allow that to happen while Caesar Russell is inside it. So we either *stop* it from going off, or, if we can't do that, we get Caesar Russell out of here before it does.'

'Wait a second,' Gant said, 'we have to *save* Caesar?'

'It seems our host decided to put a radio chip on his own heart as well as the President's. So if he dies, so does the country.'

'Son of a bitch,' Gant said. 'So what was the second reason?'

Schofield's face reddened slightly. 'I wanted to find you.'

Gant's face lit up, but she spoke matter-of-factly: 'You know, we can talk about this later.'

'I think that would be good,' Schofield said as Hagerty came free of his bonds, blinking out of his stupor. 'What do you say we do it on another date?'

Gant broke out in a grin. 'You bet.'

11:01.

Schofield and Gant rode the detachable mini-elevator swiftly up the main shaft, now armed only with Schofield's pistols—Gant with the M9, Schofield with the Desert Eagle.

Schofield had sent Hagerty down to Level 6, to escape via the Emergency Exit Vent. When he'd seen the hacked-up half-body of Colonel Harper, Hagerty hadn't argued. He was happy to get out of Area 7 as quickly as possible.

'I don't know if we'll be able to disarm the self-destruct system,' Gant said as Schofield gave her a shot of the Sinovirus vaccine to protect her against the contaminated hangar. 'You have to enter a lockdown code by 11:05 to call it off, and we don't know any of the codes.'

'I've been working on that,' Schofield said, pulling out his cell phone. He hit redial and Fairfax's voice came on the line straight away.

'Mister Fairfax, how goes it?'

'The lockdown termination code is 10502,' Fairfax said. 'Hacked into the system from behind, from the source code. Got it that way. Turns out it's the operator number of the head dude there, an Air Force colonel named Harper.'

'I don't think he'll be needing it anymore,' Schofield said. 'Thank you, Mister Fairfax. If I get out of this alive, I'll buy you a beer sometime.'

He hung up and turned to Gant.

'Okay. Time to turn off this nuclear time-bomb. Then all we have to do is capture Caesar alive.'

They rose up the side of the darkened shaft.

Its great square-shaped opening up at ground level loomed above them, backlit by orange firelight.

It turned out that Lucifer Leary had indeed brought the main elevator platform down to Level 4. When they'd arrived at the elevator shaft from the Level 4 observation lab, Schofield and Gant had found the giant platform sitting right there in front of them, piled high with no less than *fifteen* bodies—prisoners, 7th Squadron commandos, Marines and White House staff—bodies which Leary no doubt planned to dismember in strange and unusual ways.

As such, the shaft now yawned wide above Schofield and Gant, open and airy.

As they travelled quickly up it, Gant reached underneath the moving platform. She emerged with her Maghook, which she'd left attached to the underside of the mini-elevator earlier.

'Get ready,' Schofield said.

They had arrived at the main hangar.

The hangar looked like hell.

Literally.

Fires burned all over the place, bathing the enormous

space in a haunting orange glow. Bodies lay everywhere.

Assorted debris littered the area—the remains of blown-up helicopters, crumpled towing vehicles, the pieces of Bravo Unit's failed barricade over by the internal building.

Nothing, it seemed, lay unscarred.

The slanted windows of the control room overlooking the hangar were completely shattered. Even one of the giant wooden crates hanging from the overhead crane system had a gnarled piece of Nighthawk 2's tail rotor embedded in its side.

Amazingly, however, one object remained untouched by the day's mayhem.

Marine One.

It still stood on the western side of the aircraft elevator shaft, miraculously intact.

As their elevator jolted to a halt inside the hangar, Schofield and Gant looked about themselves cautiously.

11:02.

'The self-destruct computer is in the control room,' Gant said.

'Then that's where we're going,' Schofield said, heading for the internal building.

'Wait a minute,' Gant said, stopping suddenly, her eyes scanning the debris-covered floor around them.

'We don't have a minute,' Schofield said.

'You go then,' Gant said. 'Call me if you need any help. I'm gonna try something.'

'Okay,' Schofield said, charging off toward the internal building.

Gant, meanwhile, dropped to her knees and started searching through the bodies and debris around the mini-elevator platform.

Schofield burst inside the lower floor of the internal building, leading with his Desert Eagle.

He hit the stairs on the fly, charged up them. For the first time that day, he actually felt in control. He had the lockdown code—10502—and now all he had to do was punch it into the computer and disarm the nuke.

Then he would have plenty of time to find Caesar—whose men were now history—before he killed himself, and drag him out of Area 7 to face justice.

11:03.

Schofield came to the control room door, pushed it open, his gun levelled in front of him.

What he saw took him completely by surprise.

There, sitting in a swivel chair in the middle of the destroyed command room, waiting for Schofield and smiling broadly at him, was Caesar Russell.

'I thought you might be back,' Caesar said.

He was unarmed.

'You know, Captain,' he said, 'a man like you is wasted on this country. You're clever, you've got courage, and you'll do whatever it takes to win, including the bizarre and the illogical, such as saving me. You and your efforts would be unappreciated by the ignorant fools who make up this nation. Which is why,' he sighed, 'it is such a shame that you have to die.'

It was then that the gun cocked next to Schofield's head.

Schofield turned—

—to see Major Kurt Logan standing behind him, his silver SIG-Sauer pistol pointed right at Schofield's temple.

11:04.

'Come in,' Caesar said. 'Come in.'

Logan relieved Schofield of his Desert Eagle as the two of them stepped into the destroyed control room.

'Come and watch America's death sentence,' Caesar

waved at an illuminated screen behind him. It was like the one Schofield had seen outside. It read:

LOCKDOWN PROTOCOL S.A.(R) 7-A
FAILSAFE SYSTEM ENACTED
AUTH CODE: 7-3-468201103

***********************************WARNING!***********************************
EMERGENCY PROTOCOL ACTIVATED.
IF YOU DO NOT ENTER AN AUTHORIZED LOCKDOWN
EXTENSION OR TERMINATION CODE BY 1105 HOURS,
FACILITY SELF-DESTRUCT SEQUENCE WILL BE ACTIVATED.
SELF-DESTRUCT SEQUENCE DURATION: 10:00 MINUTES.
***********************************WARNING!***********************************

Schofield saw a clock at the bottom corner of the computer screen ticking upward.

11:04:29
11:04:30
11:04:31

'Tick-tick-tick,' Caesar said deliciously. 'How frustrating this must be for you, Captain. No clever plans to save you now, no space shuttles, no secret exits. Once the ten-minute self-destruct sequence is set in motion, nothing can stop it from going off. I will die, and so will you, and so too will America.'

The clock on the screen ticked upward.

Covered by Logan, Schofield could only watch helplessly as it approached 11:05 a.m.

11:04:56
11:04:57

Schofield clenched his fists with frustration.

He knew the code! *He knew it.* But he couldn't *use* it. And where the hell was Gant? What was she doing?

11:04:58

11:04:59

11:05:00

'Lift-off,' Caesar smiled.

'Shit,' Schofield said.

The screen beeped.

LOCKDOWN PROTOCOL S.A.(R) 7-A

FACILITY SELF-DESTRUCT SEQUENCE ACTIVATED.
10:00 MINUTES TO DETONATION.

A blinking countdown commenced on the screen.

10:00

9:59

9:58

At that very same moment, an army of battery-powered revolving red lights exploded to life throughout the complex—inside the main hangar, down in the aircraft elevator shaft, even inside the control room.

An electronic voice boomed out from an emergency PA system.

'Warning. Ten minutes to facility self-destruct . . .'

And just then—as they were bathed in strobing red light—Schofield saw Kurt Logan take his eyes off him, just for a split-second, to look out at the lights.

Schofield took the chance.

He drove his body into Logan's, sending both of them crashing against a computer console.

Logan brought his gun around, but Schofield grabbed

his wrist and banged it down against the console, causing the 7th Squadron commander to release the pistol.

Caesar just sat back, grinning with satisfaction, watching the fight in front of him with mad delight.

Schofield and Logan fought hard, covered in red emergency lighting. They looked like mirror images, two elite soldiers who had studied from the same manual, exchanging identical blows, employing identical evasive moves.

But Schofield was exhausted from his previous battle with Lucifer and he unleashed a loose swing which Logan punished without mercy.

He ducked beneath Schofield's wayward blow and then tackled him around the waist, lifting Schofield clear off the ground and driving him backwards toward the shattered windows of the control room.

Schofield blasted out through the destroyed windows of the command room, back-first, flying through the air. He shut his eyes and waited for the crushing impact with the floor thirty feet below.

It never came.

Instead, his fall was unexpectedly short.

Thud!

Schofield slammed down on a rough wooden surface that rocked beneath his weight.

He opened his eyes.

He was lying on top of one of the enormous wooden cargo crates that hung from the main hangar's ceiling-mounted rail network.

It had been parked just outside the control room, a little to the left, allowing the command centre a clear view of the hangar.

A triangle of thick chains connected the massive crate to the overhead rail system six feet above it. The chains were held together by a spring-loaded ring mechanism not unlike the closable circular latch one finds on a necklace.

Attached to the ring mechanism was a square control unit made up of three big buttons which presumably moved the crate back and forth along the rails.

Then suddenly, the crate rocked wildly and Schofield looked up to see that Kurt Logan had jumped out onto it after him.

Down on the hangar floor, Libby Gant had heard the crash of breaking glass and snapped to look up.

She had just found what she was looking for amid the debris on the floor when she saw Schofield come exploding out through the control room's windows and land hard on the wooden crate suspended high above the hangar floor.

Then she saw Kurt Logan jump out through the window, and land easily on the crate next to him.

'No . . .' Gant breathed.

She drew her gun, but abruptly, a barrage of bullet impact-sparks lit up the floor all around her.

She dived for cover behind a couple of dead bodies. When she finally looked up, she saw Caesar Russell leaning out from the destroyed control room windows, brandishing a P-90 and yelling, 'No, no, no! A fair fight, please!'

'Warning. Nine minutes to facility self-destruct . . .'

Up on the wooden crate, Logan kneeled astride Schofield, hit him hard in the face.

'You've made today a lot harder than it had to be, Captain.'

His face gleamed with anger in the strobe-like red light.

Another punch. Hard.

Schofield's head slammed back against the crate, his nose gushing with blood.

Logan then grabbed the control unit above his head and hit a button.

With a jolt and a sway and the clanking of mechanical gears, the crate began to move out across the hangar, toward the open aircraft elevator shaft. It was petrol-powered, so it hadn't been affected by the complex's power loss.

As the crate began to glide out over the hangar Logan kept pounding Schofield, talking as he did so.

'You know, I remember—'

Punch.

'—taking out you Marine pussies at the annual war-games—'

Punch.

'—Too fucking easy. You're a disgrace—'

Punch.

'—to the country, to the flag, and to your fucking bitch-whore mothers.'

Punch.

Schofield could barely keep his eyes open.

Christ, he was getting his ass kicked . . .

And then the crate swung out over the four-hundred-foot-deep aircraft elevator shaft and Logan pressed a button on the control unit, stopping it.

The big crate swung to a halt directly above the wide, yawning shaft.

'Warning. Eight minutes to facility self-destruct . . .'

Schofield peered over the edge of the crate, saw the shaft's concrete walls, now lined with revolving red lights, plummeting like four matching vertical cliffs down into bottomless black.

'Goodbye, Captain Schofield,' Logan said, as he lifted Schofield by his lapels and stood him at the edge of the crate.

Schofield—battered, bloody, bruised and exhausted—couldn't resist. He stood unsteadily at the edge of the crate, the great hole of the elevator shaft yawning wide beneath him.

He thought about the Maghook on his back, but then saw the ceiling. It was made of sheer flat fibreglass. The Maghook wouldn't stick to it with its magnet, nor could it get a purchase on it with its hook.

In any case, he didn't have any energy left to fight.

No more guns.

No more Maghooks.

No more ejection seats.

He had nothing that Logan didn't have more of.

And then, just as Logan was about to push him off the edge of the crate, Schofield saw Gant—a shadow amid the redness—saw her taking cover behind some bodies next to the eastern rim of the elevator shaft.

Except friends . . .

He turned suddenly to face Logan . . .

. . . and to Logan's complete surprise, he smiled, and raised his open palm, revealing his Secret Service microphone.

Schofield then looked Logan deep in the eye and said 'Sydney Harbour Bridge, Gant. You take the negative.'

Logan frowned. 'Huh?'

And then before Logan could even think to do anything, with his last ounce of strength, Schofield reached over Logan's shoulder and *unlatched* the spring-loaded ring mechanism holding the crate to the overhead rail system.

The result was instantaneous.

In a kind of hellish slow-motion that was only accentuated by the strobing red lighting, the crate—with both Schofield and Logan on it—just *fell away* from its ceiling-mounted rails, spilling the two combatants off its back . . .

. . . and the three of them—Schofield, Logan and the crate itself—dropped together into the four-hundred-foot abyss of the elevator shaft.

Schofield fell through the air.

Fast.

At first he saw the red-lit hangar rushing past him, swinging upwards—then suddenly that image was replaced by the rim of the elevator shaft, swooshing by him as he dropped into the shaft itself. Then all he saw were rapidly-rushing concrete walls speeding by in a blur of grey and he glanced up and saw the wide square up at the top of the shaft shrinking *very, very* quickly above him.

He saw Logan falling beside him, a look of absolute terror on his face. It looked as if Logan couldn't believe what Schofield had just done.

He'd just dropped *both of them* into the shaft, crate and all!

Schofield, however, just prayed that Gant had heard him.

And as he fell through the air, surrounded by red light, he coolly unslung his Maghook, initiated its magnet, selected a positive charge, and looked up in search of his only hope.

*

Gant *had* heard his call.

Now she lay on her stomach on the rim of the shaft, aiming her own Maghook—now charged negatively—down into it.

'Scarecrow,' she said into her radio mike, 'you fire first. I'll make the shot.'

As he fell down the elevator shaft, Schofield fired his positively charged Maghook into the air.

It rocketed up the shaft—flying perfectly vertical—its tail-rope wobbling through the air behind it.

Kurt Logan, falling alongside Schofield, saw what he was doing and yelled, '*No . . . !*'

'Come on, Fox,' Schofield whispered. 'Don't let me die.'

Libby Gant's eyes narrowed as she gazed down the barrel of her Maghook.

Despite all the distractions around her—the flashing red lights, the klaxons, the droning electronic warning voice—she drew a bead on Schofield's flying Maghook: an arcing dot of glinting metal shooting up out of the blackness of the shaft, coming toward her.

'Nothing's impossible,' she whispered to herself.

Then, cool as ice, she pulled the trigger on her own Maghook.

Whump!

The bulbous magnetic head of her Maghook shot out of its launcher, rushed down into the shaft, trailing its own length of rope.

Schofield's Maghook shot *up* the shaft.

Gant's Maghook shot *down* the shaft.

Schofield fell, with Logan and the crate beside him.

Gant rode her Maghook all the way down. 'Come on, baby. Come on . . .' Since they were oppositely charged, they'd only have to pass by close to each other to—

Clang!

The two Maghooks hit—*in mid-air*—like twin missiles slamming into each other in the sky!

The Sydney Harbour Bridge.

Their powerful magnetic charges held them firmly together, and up in the hangar, Gant quickly hooked her launcher into a grate in the floor.

Two Maghooks equals three hundred feet of rope.

And a three-hundred-foot fall means one hell of a jolt.

When he saw Gant's flying magnetic hook connect with his own, Schofield—still falling fast—slung his launcher under his shoulders and around his chest. Then he tensed his arms around the rope, bracing himself for the impending jolt.

This was going to hurt.

It hurt.

With an outrageous *snap*, the ropes of the two Maghooks went taut and Schofield bounced up into the air, yanked upward like a skydiver opening his parachute—while below him, Kurt Logan and the wooden crate just kept on falling, and *slammed* into the aircraft platform below them.

The wooden crate just exploded, its walls shattering into splinters as it hit the platform.

Logan met a similar fate.

He landed hard—screaming—on the jagged remains of the AWACS plane that still littered the elevator platform. His head was separated from his shoulders as his throat hit an upwardly-pointed piece of wing. The rest of his body just *flattened* with the phenomenal impact, splatting like a tomato when it hit the platform.

As for Schofield, after he was snapped upward by the ropes of the two Maghooks, he swung in toward the side wall of the shaft. He slammed into it heavily, bounced off it, and was left hanging next to the sheer concrete wall a bare eighty feet above the elevator platform, breathing hard, his shoulders and arms aching from the jolt, but alive.

The two Maghooks reeled Schofield up the shaft quickly.

'Warning. Six minutes to facility self-destruct.'

It was 11:09 when Gant hauled him up over the rim of the great pit.

'I thought you said the Harbour Bridge was impossible,' she said drily.

'Believe me, that was a very nice way to be proved wrong,' Schofield said.

Gant smiled. 'Yeah, well I only did it because I wanted another—'

She was interrupted by a thunderous line of gunfire cutting through the air all around them, ripping across both their bodies.

A ragged bullet wound burst open near Gant's right foot—shattering her ankle—while another two appeared on Schofield's left shoulder. More bullets passed so close to his face he felt their air-trails swoosh past his nose.

Both Marines dropped, gritting their teeth, as Caesar Russell came charging out of the internal building nearby, his P-90 pressed against his shoulder, firing wildly, his eyes gleaming with madness.

Schofield—hurt for sure, but far more mobile than Gant—pushed Gant behind the remains of Bravo Unit's crate barricade.

Then he grabbed her Beretta and made a loping dash the *other* way, through the strobing red-on-black world, toward the remains of Nighthawk Two over by the personnel elevator, trying to draw Caesar's fire away from Gant.

The massive Marine Corps Super Stallion was still parked in front of the regular elevator's doors—battered and dented, its entire cockpit section blasted wide open.

Caesar's stream of bullets chewed up the ground at his heels, but it was loose fire, and in the flashing red light, Caesar missed wide.

Schofield made it to the Super Stallion, dived into its exploded-open cockpit, just as the chopper's walls erupted with bulletholes.

'Come on, hero!' Caesar yelled. 'What's the matter? *Can't shoot back?* What're you afraid of? Go on! Find a gun and shoot back!'

That, however, was the one thing Schofield couldn't do. If he killed Caesar, he killed every major city in northern America.

Goddamnit! he thought.

It was the worst possible situation.

He was being fired upon by a man he couldn't fire back at!

'Fox!' he yelled into his wrist mike. 'You okay?'

A stifled grimace over his earpiece. *'Yeah . . .'*

Schofield yelled, 'We have to grab him and get him out of here! Any ideas?'

Gant's reply was drowned out by the complex's electronic voice.

'Warning. Five minutes to facility self-destruct . . .'

Through a small door-window, Schofield saw Caesar approaching the semi-destroyed helicopter from the side, pummelling its flanks with his fire.

'You like that, hero?' the Air Force general yelled. 'You like that!'

Inside the blasted-open cockpit, everything was shuddering and shaking under the weight of Caesar's fire. Schofield clenched his teeth, gripped his gun. The two bullet holes in his shoulder hurt like hell, but adrenalin was keeping him going.

Through the cracked door-window of the Super Stallion he saw Caesar—crazed and deranged—firing like a yee-ha cowboy at the chopper, striding cockily around it, heading toward its open cockpit.

Caesar would have him in about four seconds . . .

Then suddenly Gant's voice exploded through his earpiece.

'Scarecrow! Get ready to shoot. There might be another way . . .'

'But I *can't* shoot!' Schofield yelled.

'Just give me a second here!'

Over by the elevator shaft, Gant was crouched over the object she had been searching for earlier—the black box that she had pilfered from the AWACS plane down on Level 2 ninety minutes earlier, the black box that she had surreptitiously kicked away from the mini-elevator when she and the President had arrived in the main hangar before.

In the flashing light of the complex, she pulled a small

red unit with a black stub antenna from the thigh pocket of her baggy biohazard suit.

It was Russell's initiate/terminate unit—with its two 'On–Off' switches marked '1' and '2'.

It was only now that Gant understood why there were *two* switches on the unit.

This unit not only started and stopped the radio transmitter on the President's heart, *it also started and stopped the transmitter on Caesar's heart.*

Caesar was almost at the blasted-open cockpit of the chopper, his P-90 raised.

In a few seconds, he would have a clear shot at Schofield.

'I'm *coming* . . . !' he cackled.

Schofield lay slumped on the floor inside the Super Stallion, pinned down, looking out through its exposed forward section.

Trapped.

'Fox—' he said into his mike.

'—*whatever you're going to do . . . please do it soon.*'

Gant was sweating, the world around her flashing red. Her ankle throbbed painfully, but she had to concentrate—

'*Warning. Four minutes to facility self-destruct . . .*'

She'd brought up the familiar spike pattern on the black box's small LCD screen. Now she turned to the I/T unit.

The only question was *which* switch on the unit controlled the President's transmitter and which controlled Caesar's—1 or 2?

Gant had no doubt.

Caesar would make himself Number 1.

Then—in time with the spike screen on the black box, *in between* its recurring search and return signals—she flicked the switch marked '1' on the initiate/terminate unit, *switching off* Caesar's microwave signal.

As soon as she did that, she switched *on* the black box's microwave signal—using it to impersonate Caesar's signal. If she'd done it right, the satellite in orbit above them wouldn't be able to tell that it was a new return signal coming back to it.

A tiny green strobe light on top of the black box started blinking.

Gant keyed her radio mike.

'Scarecrow! I just took care of the radio signal! Nail the bastard!'

As soon as Gant said it, Caesar came into Schofield's view.

The Air Force general smiled at the sight of Schofield, slumped in the cockpit of the destroyed Super Stallion, defiantly raising his ornamental pistol in defence.

Caesar wagged a finger at Schofield. 'Oh, no, no, no, Captain, you're not allowed to do that. Remember, no shooting Uncle Caesar.'

'No?' Schofield said.

'No.'

'Oh . . .' Schofield sighed.

Then—*blam!*—quick as a flash, he snapped his gun up and shot Caesar square in the chest.

A gout of blood erupted from Caesar's torso.

Blam! Blam! Blam!

Caesar reeled with each shot, staggering backwards, his eyes bulging in astonishment, his face completely aghast. He dropped his P-90 and fell unceremoniously to the floor, landing hard on his butt.

Schofield rose to his feet, stepped out of the chopper and strode over to the fallen Caesar, kicking the general's P-90 away from his clawing fingers.

Caesar was still alive, but only just.

A trickle of blood gurgled out the side of his mouth. He looked pathetic, helpless, a shadow of his former self.

Schofield stared down at him.

'How . . . how . . . ?' Caesar stammered through the blood. 'You . . . you can't kill me!'

'As a matter of fact, I could,' Schofield said. 'But I think I'll leave that to you.'

And then he hurried off to rejoin Gant and get the hell out of Area 7.

'Warning. Three minutes to facility self-destruct . . .'

Schofield carried Gant in his arms onto the detachable mini-elevator. Her right ankle had been completely shattered by Caesar's shot, and she couldn't walk on it at all.

But that didn't stop her contributing.

While Schofield carried her, she held the most important black box in the world in her lap.

Their goal now—more than saving their own lives— was to get that flight data recorder out of Area 7 before it was destroyed in the coming nuclear blast. If its signal died now, everything they had fought for would be for nothing.

'Okay, smart guy,' Gant said, 'how are we gonna get out of this seven-storey nuclear grenade?'

Schofield hit the floor panel of the mini-elevator and it began to whiz down the wall of the shaft. He looked at his watch.

11:12:30

11:12:31

'Well, we can't get out through the top door,' he said. 'Caesar changed the code, and it took my DIA guy ten minutes to crack the lockdown codes. And I don't like our chances of getting out through the EEV in time. It took Book and me a good minute to come *down* through that vent before. I can't imagine the two of us getting *up* it in less than ten. And by then, that Escape Vent is gonna be vapour.'

'So what are we going to do?'

'There's one way,' Schofield said, 'if we can get to it in time.'

11:12:49

11:12:50

Schofield stopped the mini-elevator at the Level 2 hangar, and still carrying Gant, hustled down its length, making for the entry to the stairwell at the other end.

'Warning. Two minutes to facility self-destruct . . .'

They reached the stairwell.

11:13:20

Schofield burst into it, leapt down it with Gant in his arms, taking the stairs three at a time.

They passed Level 3, the living quarters.

11:13:32

Level 4, the nightmare floor.

11:13:41

Level 5, the flooded floor.

11:13:50

Schofield kicked open the door to Level 6.

'Warning. One minute to facility self-destruct . . .'

He saw their escape vehicle right away.

The small X-rail maintenance vehicle still sat right next to the stairwell door, on the track that led out to Lake

Powell, in the spot where it had been sitting all day.

Schofield remembered what Herbie Franklin had said about the maintenance car before. It was smaller than the other X-rail engines, and faster, too—just a round capsule and four long struts, with room for only two people in its pod-like cabin.

'Forty-five seconds to facility self-destruct . . .'

Schofield yanked open the pod's door, heaved Gant into it, then he clambered up into the small round capsule after her.

'Thirty seconds . . .'

Schofield hit the black start button on the pod's console.

The compact X-rail engine hummed to life.

'Twenty seconds . . . nineteen . . . eighteen . . .'

He looked at the tracks in front of him. They stretched away into flashing red darkness, four parallel tracks converging to a point in the far distance.

'Hit it!' Gant said.

Schofield jammed the throttle forward.

'Fifteen . . .'

The small X-rail pod leapt off the mark, thundered forward, shooting along the length of the underground subway station, crashing through the strobing red shadows.

'Fourteen . . .'

Schofield was thrust back into his seat by the speed.

The pod hit 50 mph.

'Thirteen . . .'

The X-rail pod gained speed quickly. Schofield saw the quartet of tracks both beneath and above the windshield rushing past them.

100 mph.

'Twelve . . . eleven . . .'

Then suddenly—*shoom!*—the X-shaped pod entered the tunnel leading out to Lake Powell, leaving Area 7 behind it.

150 mph.

'Ten . . .'

250 mph. Two hundred and fifty miles per hour equalled about 110 yards per second. In ten seconds, they'd be nearly a mile away from Area 7.

'Nine . . . eight . . .'

Schofield hoped a mile would be enough.

'Seven . . . six . . .'

He urged the little pod onward.

'Five . . . four . . .'

Gant groaned with pain.

'Three . . . two . . .'

The little maintenance pod rocketed through the tunnel, shooting away from Area 7, banking with every bend, moving at phenomenal speed.

'One . . .

' . . . facility self-destruct activated.'

Boom time.

It sounded like the end of the universe.

The colossal *roar* of the nuclear explosion inside Area 7 was absolutely monstrous.

For a structure that had been designed in the Cold War to withstand a direct nuclear strike, it did quite well *containing* its own supernuclear demise.

The W-88 self-destruct warhead was situated inside the walls of Level 2, roughly in the centre of the underground facility. When it went off, the whole underground complex lit up like a light bulb, and a white-hot pulse of energy rocketed through its floors and walls—unstoppable, irresistible.

Everything inside the complex was obliterated in a nanosecond—aeroplanes, test chambers, elevator shafts. Even the bloodied and broken Caesar Russell.

From his position on the floor of the main hangar, the last thing he saw was a flash of blinding white light, followed by an instant's worth of the most intense heat he had ever felt in his life. And then nothing.

But to a large extent, the complex's two-foot-thick titanium outer wall contained the blast.

The concussion wave that the momentous explosion generated, however, shook the sandy earth well *beyond* the structure's titanium walls, making it shudder and shake for several *miles* around Area 7, the wave of expanding energy fanning outward in concentric circles, like ripples in a pond.

The first thing to go was the Emergency Exit Vent.

Its tight concrete walls were assaulted by the expanding wall of energy within a second of the blast. They were turned instantly to powder. Had Schofield and Gant been inside it, they would have been pulverised beyond recognition.

It was then, however, that the most spectacular sight of all appeared.

Since the entire complex had effectively become a hollowed-out shell, the super-heavy layer of granite above the underground section caved in on it.

From the sky above Area 7, it looked as if a *perfectly-circular* earthquake had struck the facility.

Without warning, an eight-hundred-yard-wide ring of earth around the complex just gave way, turned to rubble, and Area 7's buildings—the main hangar, the airfield tower, the other hangars—were just swallowed by the earth, dropping from sight, until all that remained in the place of Area 7 was a gigantic half-mile-wide crater in the desert floor.

From his position on board a Marine Corps Super Stallion that had arrived at the complex only ten minutes earlier, the President of the United States just watched it all go down.

Beside him, Book II, Juliet Janson and the boy named Kevin just stared in stunned awe at the spectacular end of Area 7.

Down in the X-rail tunnel, it wasn't over yet.

When the nuke had gone off, Schofield and Gant's maintenance pod had been shooting through the tunnel like a speeding bullet.

Then they'd heard the *boom* of the blast.

Felt the shudder of the earth all around them.

And then Schofield looked out through the rear window of the two-person pod.

'*Son of a . . .*' he breathed.

He saw an advancing wall of falling rock, *rampaging* through the tunnel behind them!

The roof of the tunnel was caving in, shattering into pieces as the expanding pulse of the concussion wave rippled outward from Area 7.

The problem was, it was catching up with them!

The X-rail pod shot through the tunnel at two hundred and fifty miles per hour.

The advancing wall of falling rock shot forward after it, doing at least two-sixty.

Chunks of falling rock rained down on the tunnel. It was as if the passageway was now a living creature biting down at the heels of the speeding X-rail pod.

Bang!

A chunk of concrete the size of a baseball landed on the roof of the pod. Schofield snapped to look up at the sound. And then—

Bang-bang-bang-bang-bang-bang-bang-bang-bang!

A deafening hailstorm of chunks rained down on top of the pod.

No! Schofield's mind screamed. *Not now! Not this close to the end!*

551

The advancing wall of collapsing rock had caught them.

Bang-bang-bang-bang-bang-bang-bang—

Chunks assaulted the pod's windscreen, shattering it. Glass exploded everywhere.

Bang-bang-bang-bang-bang-bang-bang—

Small chunks started entering the cockpit. The whole pod started to shudder violently, as if it were about to run off its . . .

And then all of a sudden the concrete rain slowed and the pod *blasted* clear of the falling chunks.

Schofield turned in his seat and saw the moving waterfall of concrete receding into the tunnel behind them, shrinking back behind a bend, falling back like a hungry monster that had given up on the chase. The ripple-like expansion of the concussion wave had run its course and petered out.

They'd outrun it.

Just.

And as the X-rail pod continued on its way down the tunnel, Shane Schofield fell back into his seat and breathed a long and deep sigh of relief.

By the time Schofield and Gant were airlifted from the canyonway outside the X-rail loading dock adjoining Lake Powell by a Marine CH-53E, there was a veritable armada of Army and Marine Corps helicopters in the air above Area 7.

They looked like a swarm of tiny insects, black dots hovering in the clear desert sky—all keeping at a safe distance to avoid any lingering radiation.

The President was now safely ensconced in his Marine helicopter, which itself was surrounded by no less than five other Marine Super Stallions. Until the radio transmitter attached to his heart was removed, the Marines would stay by his side.

And the moment he had been lifted off the tarmac at Area 7, he had issued a standing order that all Air Force aircraft in the continental United States be grounded pending further notice.

Schofield and Gant—and their precious microwave-transmitting black box—were reunited with the President,

Book II, Juliet and Kevin at Area 8, which had been secured twenty minutes before their arrival by two Marine Recon units.

During their sweep of the base, the Marines had found no live personnel except one Nicholas Tate III, Domestic Policy Adviser to the President of the United States, rambling incoherently, saying something about calling his stockbroker.

Gant was immediately placed on a stretcher and her ankle attended to by a corpsman. Schofield was given a temporary gauze dressing for his bullet wounds, a sling for his arm, and a dose of codeine for the pain.

'Nice to see you made it out, Captain,' the President said as he came over to where they sat. 'Not so Caesar, I take it?'

'I'm afraid he couldn't make it, sir,' Schofield said. He held up the black box, its green transmission light blinking. 'But he's with us in spirit.'

The President smiled. 'The Marines who swept this base said they found something *outside* it that you might like to see.'

Schofield didn't understand. 'Like what?'

'Like me, you *sexy* thing,' Mother roared as she stepped out from behind the President.

Schofield grinned from ear to ear. 'You made it!'

The last he had seen, Mother had been flipping end-over-end inside a speeding cockroach.

'Fucking *indestructible* is what I am,' Mother said. She was limping slightly on her real leg. 'When it got hit by that missile, I knew my cockroach was done for. And I didn't figure old Caesar and his buddies would take kindly to finding me in it. But when I ran off the runway,

I kicked up a hell of a dustcloud. So I bailed out under the cover of the cloud. The cockroach flipped and smashed and I just dug a little hole for my head in the sand under its front bumper, ripped my fake leg off for added effect, and played dead until Caesar and his choppers flew off.'

'Ripped your fake leg off for added effect . . .' Schofield said. 'Nice touch.'

'I thought so,' she smiled. Then she jutted her chin at him. 'What about you? Last I saw, you and the Prez were heading off into outer space. Did you save the fucking day again?'

'I might have,' Schofield said.

'More to the point,' Mother whispered conspiratorially, 'did you do what I told you to do with You-Know-Who?' She nodded theatrically at Gant. 'Did you kiss the friggin' girl, Scarecrow?'

Schofield snuffed a laugh, cast a sideways look at Gant.

'You know what, Mother. As a matter of fact, I think I did.'

A short while later, Schofield sat alone with the President.

'So what's the word on the rest of the country?' he asked. 'Have they been watching all this every hour on the Emergency Broadcast System?'

The President smiled. 'It's funny you should ask. While you were gone, we examined the complex's power history, and we found this.'

He pulled out a printout of Area 7's source power history, pointed to one entry.

07:37:56   WARNING: Auxiliary   System   Malfunction located at
           power malfunction   terminal 1-A2
                                                   Receiving no response
                                                   from systems: TRACS;
                                                   AUX SYS-1; RAD COM-
                                                   SPHERE; MBN; EXT FAN

The President said, 'Remember you said that you blew up a junction box on one of the underground hangar levels earlier this morning? Sometime around 7:37.'

'Yeah . . .'

'Well, it seems that that junction box was kind of important. Among other things, it housed the controls for the base's auxiliary power system and its radiosphere. It also housed a system called the MBN. You know what "MBN" stands for?'

'No . . .'

'Stands for the Military Broadcast Network, the previous name for the Emergency Broadcast System. Seems the MBN's outgoing transmission cable was destroyed in that blast. And because the LBJ Protocol was never initiated this morning, Caesar's transmissions over the Emergency Broadcast System were delayed by forty-five minutes.'

'But the system was destroyed at 7:37 . . .' Schofield said.

The President smiled.

'Correct,' he said, 'which means that every time Caesar Russell spoke into his digital camera this morning, he wasn't transmitting at all. He was speaking to no-one but the people at Area 7.'

Schofield blinked, trying to comprehend it all.

Then he said: 'So the country doesn't know this happened . . .'

556

The President nodded ruefully.

'It seems,' he said, 'that the people of America have been preoccupied all day with another drama, an accident involving Hollywood's highest paid actress and her actor fiancé.

'It appears that the unlucky couple have been trapped in the Swiss Alps all day, cut off by an avalanche while hiking illegally on Swiss military property. Sadly, their unscrupulous guide was killed, but I believe that just in the last hour our two superstars have been found safe and well.

'As I understand it, CNN has been covering the whole drama all day, updating the public every hour, recycling some amateur footage of the area, giving updates. Biggest news event since Diana's car crash, they tell me.'

Schofield almost laughed.

'So they really don't know,' he said.

'That's right,' the President said. 'And that, Captain, is the way it will stay.'

Exactly six hours later, the second X-38 space shuttle from Area 8 was launched off the back of a high-flying 747.

Its mission: the destruction of a rogue Air Force reconnaissance satellite hovering in a geosynchronous orbit above southern Utah.

So far as the shuttle's pilots could tell, it appeared that the satellite in question had been sending and receiving a peculiar microwave signal down into the Utah desert.

In the end, the pilots didn't care what it was doing. They had orders, which they followed to the letter.

And so they blasted the satellite out of the sky.

With the controlling satellite destroyed, the Type-240 plasma explosives in the airports were rendered useless, apart from their proximity sensors, which would take a little more time to disable.

Over the next few hours, all fourteen bombs would be disarmed and dismantled, and then taken away for analysis.

*

In addition to the disarming of the plasma bombs, the destruction of the satellite also allowed for the removal of the radio transmitter attached to the President's heart.

The procedure was conducted by a renowned civilian heart surgeon from Johns Hopkins University Hospital under the watchful eye of three other cardiac surgeons and armed supervision by the United States Secret Service and the United States Marine Corps.

Never was a surgeon more careful—or more nervous—during an operation.

Limited anaesthesia was used. Although the public was never notified of it, for twenty-eight minutes, the Vice-President was in charge of the United States of America.

An investigatory committee would later be formed to conduct an inquiry into the Air Force's role in the Area 7 incident.

As a result of that inquiry, no less than eighteen high-ranking Air Force officers in charge of a dozen bases across the south-western United States and *ninety-nine* junior officers and enlisted men stationed at those bases were tried for treason in closed session.

It appeared that all of the men linked to the day's events were either currently serving, or had once served, at either the Air Force Special Operations Command, based at Hurlbut Field, Florida, or with the 14th and 20th Air Forces at Warren and Falcon Air Force Bases in Wyoming and Colorado. All, at one time or another, had been under the direct command of Charles 'Caesar' Russell.

Overall, in a service of nearly 400,000 men and women, one hundred and seventeen traitors was not a very large group, barely a dozen to each tainted base. But considering the aircraft and ordnance at those bases, it was more than enough to carry out Caesar's plan.

It further emerged at the trials that five of the USAF personnel involved in the plot were Air Force surgeons who at various times had performed procedures on Congressional members, including the United States senator and one-time presidential hopeful, Jeremiah K Woolf.

Circumstantial evidence presented at all the trials also suggested that every Air Force man involved in the incident was a member of an informal racist society within the United States Air Force known as the Brotherhood.

All were sentenced to life imprisonment at an undisclosed military prison, with no hope of parole. Unfortunately, the plane delivering them to the secret prison inexplicably crashed during flight. There were no survivors.

In the investigatory committee's final report to the Joint Chiefs of Staff, the subject of 'informal anti-social interest groups' within the armed forces was raised. While it was acknowledged in the report that most such societies had been removed from the military during a purge in the 1980s, the report recommended that a new investigation be initiated into their continued presence.

The Joint Chiefs, however, did not accept that such societies existed, and therefore rejected the recommendations of the investigatory committee on this point.

Over the next six months, there would be a number of unconfirmed reports from tourists in the Lake Powell area concerning the sighting of a family of Kodiak bears around the north-eastern portion of the lake.

Officers of the US Fish and Wildlife Service investigated the reports, but no bears were ever found.

A couple of weeks later, a quiet ceremony was held in a dark underground meeting room beneath the White House.

Inside the room were nine people.

The President of the United States.

Captain Shane Schofield—with his arm in a sling.

Staff Sergeant Elizabeth Gant—with crutches on account of her broken ankle.

Gunnery Sergeant Gena 'Mother' Newman—with her small bald-headed trucker husband, Ralph.

Sergeant Buck Riley Junior—with sling.

United States Secret Service Agent Juliet Janson—with sling.

David Fairfax, of the Defense Intelligence Agency—wearing his good sneakers.

And a small boy named Kevin.

The President bestowed upon Schofield and his team of Marines the Congressional Medal of Honour (Classified), for acts of valour in the field of battle despite the endangerment of their own lives.

It was, however, an award they could tell no-one about.

But then again, they all agreed it was probably better that way.

While the others stayed to eat in the White House dining room—during which dinner the President had a particularly lively conversation with Mother and Ralph about the Teamsters—Schofield and Gant took their leave, and went out, alone, on their second date.

When they got to the venue, they found that they had the place to themselves.

A single candle-lit table stood in the centre of the wide wood-panelled room.

And so they took their places and dined.

Alone.

In the President's private dining room, on the upper floor of the White House, overlooking the Washington Monument.

'Give them whatever they want,' the President had instructed his personal chef. 'Just put it on my tab.'

By flickering candlelight, they talked and talked till late in the evening.

As dessert arrived, Schofield reached into his pocket.

'You know,' he said, 'I meant to give you this on your birthday, but the day kind of got away from me.'

He pulled a crumpled piece of cardboard from his pocket. It was only small, about the size of a Christmas card.

'What is it?' Gant asked.

'It *was* your birthday present,' Schofield said sadly. 'It was in my trouser pocket all day—I had to take it with me every time I changed uniforms—so I'm afraid it got a little, well, beat up.'

He handed it to Gant.

She looked at it, and she smiled.

It was a photograph.

A photograph of a group of people standing on a beautiful Hawaiian beach. Everyone was wearing board-shorts and loud Hawaiian shirts.

And standing next to each other at the very edge of the group, smiling for the camera, were Gant and Schofield. Gant's smile was a little uncomfortable, and Schofield's kind of sad, behind his reflective silver sunglasses.

Gant remembered the day as if it were yesterday.

It had been that barbecue held on a beach near Pearl Harbor, celebrating her promotion to Schofield's Recon Unit.

'It was the first time we met,' Schofield said.

'Yes,' Gant said. 'Yes, it was.'

'I've never forgotten it,' he said.

Gant beamed. 'You know, this is the nicest birthday present I've received this year.'

Then she lifted herself up out of her seat, leaned across the table and kissed him on the lips.

After their dinner, they arrived downstairs, where they were met by a Presidential limousine. It was flanked, however, from in front and behind, by four Marine Corps Humvees, six police cruisers and four motorcycle out-riders.

Gant raised her eyebrows at the elaborate motorcade.

'Oh, yeah,' Schofield said sheepishly, 'there was something else I had to tell you about.'

'Yes?' Gant said.

Schofield opened the limousine's rear door wide—

—to reveal the small sleeping figure of Kevin lying on the back seat.

'He needed a place to stay, at least until they find him a new home,' Schofield shrugged. 'So I said I'd take him for as long as they needed. The government, however, insisted on providing a little extra security.'

Gant just shook her head and smiled.

'Come on,' she said. 'Let's go home.'

AN INTERVIEW WITH MATTHEW REILLY

THE WRITING OF *AREA 7*

How did you come up with the idea for Area 7*?*

I actually conceived the core idea for *Area 7*—namely, that a character has a transmitter attached to his heart and if his heart stops, something terrible happens—just after I finished *Ice Station*, way back in 1997. (I still remember finishing *Ice Station* and saying to myself, 'Okay, Matt, you now have two options for your next book: you can do that transmitter-on-the-heart one or you can do that Incan two-stories-told-in-parallel novel.' Obviously, I chose the latter option, and it became *Temple*.)

The thing was, back then, I couldn't figure out a way to make the transmitter-on-the-heart idea work. My main problem was that I didn't know whose heart to put the transmitter on! I had this great idea, but didn't have a story to wrap it up in. Then, nearly three years later, when I decided to do a new Shane Schofield book, I said, 'Wait a second, what if I attached the transmitter to the US President's heart and made Schofield one of his body-guards . . .' And so *Area 7* was born.

What was it like to write a sequel?

Area 7 is the first sequel I've ever written, and it was a very different experience to creating a wholly new novel. The first thing that must be said is that I didn't make the decision to do a sequel to *Ice Station* lightly. As a keen moviegoer, I am very conscious of sequels that ruin the original story. So I decided that if I was going to write a sequel to *Ice Station*, that book would have to (a) have a rip-roaringly original story that at least matched the story in *Ice Station*; and (b) somehow add to the experience of *Ice Station*. It was also important to me that *Area 7* should stand on its own, that readers who hadn't read *Ice Station* would still be able to enjoy it just as much as those who had read the earlier book. I reckon *Area 7* stands up to all three of those stipulations, but ultimately that's for my readers to decide.

So, to you, how does **Area 7** *'add to the experience of* **Ice Station***'?*

To my mind, a sequel should reveal some kind of extra dimension to the lead characters of the original. In *Area 7*, for example, we learn a little more about Schofield and Gant's relationship, and about Mother's home life. To my mind, the biggest addition comes in the character of Book II. (For those who haven't read *Ice Station*, I suggest, at this point, that you skip to the next question as I'm about to give away a couple of plot points.)

I loved the original 'Book' Riley in *Ice Station*. I loved his loyalty to Scarecrow, his nuggety strength, and his overall 'fatherly' influence on Schofield. As such, it was a big decision to kill him in *Ice Station* (his death, I've been told, shocked a lot of people; in fact, my girlfriend, Natalie, still hasn't forgiven me for doing that). And so, in *Area 7*, I thought I'd 'resurrect' Book in the shape of his son, Book II.

567

I felt it might do two things: first, it would bring Book Snr back in the new book, at least in spirit; and second, it would add something to the *Ice Station* experience by showing that the story in *Ice Station* was not quite over at the end of the book, that the events depicted there had consequences, repercussions.

Now, I know what you're thinking: Matthew Reilly books aren't exactly known for their character development. Hey, one reviewer once said that the characters in my books don't live long enough to justify any 'development'. My response, however, is simple: I want to write about action and thrills and adventure, and if developing characters slow down the action, then developing characters get the chop! The introduction of Book II, however, was an effort to give a little more character depth than usual.

Why did you choose to set **Area 7** *in the American desert?*

Several reasons. First, because I love stories about Area 51, the top-secret base where the US government supposedly keeps aliens and crashed alien spacecraft. The second reason was far more pragmatic: a blazing hot desert was the diametric opposite to the Antarctic wasteland of *Ice Station* and I figured that, visually, a sequel to *Ice Station* should be as different as possible to the original. And once I learned about the extraordinary landscape of Lake Powell, with its incongruous mix of towering canyons and watery lakes and canals, the choice of location was settled. (And, hey, I'd been to the cold for *Ice Station*, the jungle for *Temple*, and the city for *Contest*, so why not tackle a desert environment for my fourth book?)

Have you been to Lake Powell?

Yes, I have. As part of my research for *Area 7*, I went to the Utah–Arizona border just to see the lake. I'd seen pictures of it in books (and on the Internet), but decided I had to see it for myself. It is absolutely awesome. Oddly, though, when you meet Americans and ask them, 'Have you been to Lake Powell?' they say, 'Lake what?' Granted, it is very close to the Grand Canyon, so it's probably just over-shadowed by its more famous neighbour.

Some questions about technique. How do you go about writing? For example, do you set yourself certain hours in which to work each day, or are you a 'have to be in the mood' kind of writer?

I am, without question, a 'have to be in the mood' kind of writer. The simple reason for this is that I have tried writing when I *wasn't* in the mood, and I didn't like what I wrote. I had wasted my time. Now, if I'm not in the mood, I go to the library and do some research or see a movie (often just to give my mind a rest), and when I return, I am usually ready and raring to go.

The more complex reason, however, for this method of writing is that I just can't stand routine. I love variation, in the hours I work, in the amount of writing I do, in how I spend my day. (I also, it must be said, have a pathetically short attention span!) So rather than look at writing on a day-to-day basis—and say to myself, 'Okay, Matt, you *have* to write for six hours today between the hours of 9 a.m. and 3 p.m.'—I look at my writing on a weekly basis and say: 'All right, this week, I would like to get four good days' worth of writing done. Doesn't matter when I do it, as long as it gets done.' Now, I don't care if I get that writing done during the day, the evening, or the middle of the night (which can be a very good time to write since the phone—usually—doesn't ring at two o'clock in the morning!). So long as I get it done, I am happy. Working this way, on the average day, I get about eight hours of writing done.

Sounds like this would require considerable self-motivation. How do you motivate yourself to keep writing?

Generally speaking, motivation isn't a problem for me. Like everyone else, I have my bad days (who doesn't?), but they're not very common. Quite simply, I enjoy the act of writing. I am not a stereotypical 'tortured' writer, hunched over my keyboard, tearing my hair out, gnashing my teeth at the prospect of the next sentence. I like writing. I like creating. And I *love* creating big action scenes with words on a page. Since that's pretty much what I do each day, I find motivating myself fairly easy. Now, motivating myself to exercise, that's another story . . . !

Having said that, however, I should say something a little more *general* on the subject (because I am asked about motivation a lot). Writing a book does take a lot of *self-*motivation. It takes me about a year to write each novel. That's a long time to spend on a single project, so you have to really love what you're doing—and that means *wanting* to tell the story you're telling.

If you have a story to tell, no-one will force you to write it down. *You* have to do it. If you don't know the ending, no-one else is going to give it to you. *You* have to figure it out. Writing a book—to me—is one of the most invigorating mental challenges in the world. It can be hard (when I was finishing the writing of *Temple*, my head was nearly exploding with all the subplots running between the two parallel stories); it can be thrilling (it took me nearly two weeks to write the hovercraft chase in *Ice Station*, but every one of those days was just awesome; typing fast, living the action in my head); and it can be painful (I cut a killer action scene from *Temple*—before I actually wrote it, thank God—because I felt it was one too many) but when you see that manuscript sitting on your desk at the end of it all, it is enormously—*enormously*—satisfying.

On a more detailed note, when you write, do you work on a chapter-by-chapter basis?

No. I work on a scene-by-scene basis. I like to think that with my books, chapter endings are generally not the best place to stop reading. And, indeed, this is how I write—I don't stop writing when I reach the end of a chapter. I keep going, as I hope the reader will do. I stop my day's writing when I get the *scene* done. Again, the hovercraft chase in *Ice Station* is a good example. That forty-page action sequence took me nearly two weeks to write (sounds like making a movie, doesn't it?), but in it are a whole bunch of small interwoven mini-scenes— Schofield going under the hovercraft; Book Snr saving Holly; Renshaw and Schofield running alongside the cliff-edge. I did each of these mini-scenes on a different day.

Any other tips for aspiring writers?

Yes. There is no such thing as an 'aspiring writer'. You are a writer. Period. I was told that once, and I have never forgotten it.

So what's next for Matthew Reilly?

Hmmmm. Good question. With my next book, I want to re-invent what I do, and take the action thriller to the next level. It can go faster. I'm talking lean, mean and *totally* out of control. In the downtime I've had since finishing *Area 7*, I have been working on this idea, toying with new structures, figuring out ways to make the narrative just *zoom* along. I think if you want longevity as a creative individual (think of Madonna, or U2, or of great storytellers like Steven Spielberg, Michael Crichton or Joss Whedon) you have to evolve, constantly re-invent yourself, and take your craft to a new level. Reset the benchmark for yourself. So, to answer the question: the future involves pushing myself to a new level of *speed* in my next novel. And then I'm going to make a movie.

Any final comments?

As always, I just hope you enjoyed the book. Best wishes, and hopefully, I'll see you next time!

Matthew Reilly
Sydney, Australia
August, 2001

CONTEST

For Mum and Dad

ACKNOWLEDGEMENTS

Special thanks to Stephen Reilly, my brother—marketing genius, tortured writer (aren't we all?) and loyal friend. To Natalie Freer—the first person to read my work, and the most patient and giving person on this earth. To my parents for letting me watch too much television as a kid and for their unwavering support. And to Peter Kozlina for his monumental show of faith in this book before he had even read a word.

And of course, thanks once again to everyone at Pan Macmillan—Cate Paterson, for being a brilliant publisher; Jane Novak, for being a fantastic publicist (and for being the only person I know who could read *Voss* and then pick up *Ice Station* and enjoy them both!); Julie Nekich, for being an understanding editor (you have to be to work with me); and lastly, once again, all the sales reps at Pan for the countless hours they spend on the road between bookshops. Thank you.

To anyone out there who knows a writer, never underestimate the power of your encouragement.

A note from the author about *Contest*

Hello there. Matthew Reilly here.

Now before we get on with the show, I'd like, if I may, to share with you a few secrets about *Contest*.

First of all, as some of you may already know, *Contest* was my first novel. The story of how I self-published it after every major publisher in Sydney rejected it has been pretty well documented elsewhere, so I won't go into that here. Suffice it to say that only 1000 copies of *Contest* were ever released, all paid for by yours truly.

And then came *Ice Station*.

Now, many people have taken the time to tell me what a ride they found *Ice Station* to be. Such comments please me immensely because that is what it was *supposed* to be—a non-stop rollercoaster ride on paper.

What few people know, however, is that when I wrote *Ice Station*, I had one all-consuming goal: to top *Contest*.

Contest is the book that made *Ice Station* (and later *Temple*) what it was. If it doesn't seem as large in scale as its two successors, it is because it was the first. It was the prototype upon which they were built; a prototype for a different *style* of book—a superfast-paced, absolutely *non-stop* thriller. Everybody has to start somewhere. I started with *Contest*.

That said, I think the story in *Contest* is easily the fastest of all my books. It is like a sports car stripped down to its raw components—wheels, frame, engine. No fancy paintwork. No fancy upholstery. Just raw non-stop *energy*.

As any author will tell you, you only get one first book. And that first one always occupies a special place in your heart. *Contest* is like that for me. It was the first one, and now as I look back on it, I can see without a doubt that it set the tone for everything to come.

I truly hope you have as much fun reading it as I did writing it.

Matthew Reilly
November 2000

Do I dare
Disturb the universe?

– T. S. Eliot

THE NEW YORK STATE LIBRARY

THIRD FLOOR:
Study hall

Janitor's room

Stairwell

Desks

Desks

Elevators

N
W — E
S

SECOND FLOOR:
Reading/function rooms

Reading rooms

Computer room

Stairwell

Elevators

FIRST FLOOR:
Mezzanine; Internet facility

Stairwell

Internet facility

Photocopying room

Mezzanine balcony

Elevators

INTRODUCTION

From: Hoare, Shane
        Suetonius: The Picture of Rome
        (New York, Advantage Press, 1979)

'CHAPTER VII: THE FIRST CENTURY A.D.

. . . ultimately, however, it is Suetonius' classic work, *Lives of the Emperors,* that provides us with the best picture of court life in Imperial Rome. Here Suetonius might well be writing a modern day soap opera, as he outlines the lust, the cruelty, the intrigues and the numerous *insidiae*—or plots—that dominated life in the Emperor's presence . . .' [p. 98]

'. . . not least of whom was Domitian, who, although well-known for his *ex-tempore* executions of scheming courtesans, provides perhaps the most brutal of all examples of Roman intrigue—that of Quintus Aurelius.

3

A distinguished former captain in the Roman army who rose to prominence in the Senate under Domitian, Aurelius apparently fell out of favour with the Emperor in 87 A.D. Initially recruited by Domitian to aid him in military matters, Aurelius was also a prolific writer, who not only instructed Domitian on military strategy, but who also committed those instructions to his own personal record. Much of this writing has survived to the present day, dated and intact.

However, Quintus Aurelius' writing ceased abruptly in the year 87 A.D.

All correspondence between senator and Emperor was severed. Aurelius' personal record cited no further entries. There was no mention of Aurelius in Senate documents from that year onward.

Quintus Aurelius had disappeared.

Some historians have speculated that Aurelius—who, it was said, would appear in the Senate in full military attire—simply fell out of favour with Domitian, while others have proposed that Aurelius was discovered plotting . . .' [p. 103]

From: **Freer, Donald**
From Medieval to Modern: Europe 1010–1810
(London, W. M. Lawry & Co., 1963)

'. . . by comparison, the wheat riots in Cornwall were but a trifle when compared with the confusion that overwhelmed a small farming community in West Hampshire in the spring of 1092.

Historians have long pondered over the fate of Sir Alfred Hayes, the Lord of Palmerston Estate, whose disappearance in 1092 upset the entire feudal balance of his small agrarian community in West Hampshire . . .'
[p. 45]

'. . . However, the most startling aspect of the whole affair is that if Hayes did, in fact, die suddenly (of cholera or anything else for that matter), why was his death not listed in the local church register as had always been the custom? A man so renowned for his past glory on the battlefield, and of such stature in the community, would not be overlooked by the death registrar. The sad fact is that since no body was ever found, no death was ever recorded.

Writing after his lord's disappearance, the local abbot of West Hampshire observed that, apart from necessary military excursions, Sir Alfred had never left

West Hampshire before, and that during the days immediately prior to his disappearance, he had been seen about the village carrying out his business as usual. It was odd, the abbot wrote, that here was a man who could be 'certified as born', but who had, officially, never died.

Putting aside all medieval myths of witchery and demonic intervention, the facts are quite straightforward: in the spring of 1092, Sir Alfred Hayes, Lord of Palmerston Estate, West Hampshire, simply vanished from the face of the earth.' [p. 46]

CONTEST

PROLOGUE

Mike Fraser pressed himself flat against the black wall of the tunnel. He squeezed his eyes shut as he tried to block out the roar of the subway train flashing by in front of him. The dirt and dust kicked up by the speeding train hit his face like a thousand pin-pricks. It hurt, but he didn't care. He was almost there.

And then, just as soon as it had come, the train was gone, its thunderous rumble slowly fading into the blackness of the tunnel. Fraser opened his eyes. Against the black backdrop of the wall, the whites of his eyes were all that could be seen. He peeled himself away from the wall and brushed off the dirt that had clung to his clothes. Black clothes.

It was two o'clock in the morning, and while the rest of New York slept, Mike Fraser was going about his work. Silently and swiftly, he made his way up

9

the subway tunnel until he found what he was looking for.

An old wooden door, set into the tunnel wall, held shut by a solitary padlock. Pasted across the door was a sign.

NO ENTRY—BOOSTER VALVE
HIGH VOLTAGE AREA
CONSOLIDATED EDISON PERSONNEL ONLY

Fraser examined the padlock. Stainless steel, combination lock, pretty new. He checked the hinges of the old wooden door. Yes, much easier.

His crowbar fitted snugly behind the hinges.

Crack!

> *Status Check: Initialise program systems.*
> *Officials in charge of third element*
> *please confirm delivery.*

The door fell from its frame, and dangling from the padlock, swung silently into Fraser's waiting hand.

He peered inside the doorway, slipped the crowbar back into his belt and stepped inside.

Large box-shaped electricity meters lined the walls of the booster valve room. Thick black cables snaked their way across the ceiling. There was a door on the far side. Fraser headed straight for it.

Once through the booster valve room, he made his way down a narrow, dimly lit passageway until he came to a small red door. It opened easily and as Fraser looked out from the doorway, he smiled at the view.

Endless rows of bookshelves—each one rising from floor to ceiling—stretched away from him as far as the eye could see. Old and faded fluorescent lights lined each aisle, but at night only every third one was on. The lights themselves were so old that the whiteness of their fluorescent tubes had gone a mouldy ivory colour and a powder of oxidised fluorine had settled inside them. Their sickly state gave the lowest floor of the New York State Library a haunting yellowish glow.

The New York State Library. One hundred years old, a silent sanctuary of history and knowledge—and also the owner of twelve brand-new Pentium III computers whose hard drives would soon be in the back room of Mike Fraser's apartment.

Fraser checked the lock on the door.

Safety lock.

From the booster room you didn't need a key, but from the library side you did. One of those automatically closing doors designed to keep the curious out, but not to accidentally lock the electricity workers in.

Fraser thought for a moment. If he had to make a hasty escape, he wouldn't have time to pick the lock. He searched around for an answer.

That'll work, he thought, spying the nearest book-shelf. He grabbed the first book he could reach and wedged it on the floor between the red door and its frame.

The door now safely ajar, Fraser hustled down the nearest aisle. Soon the small red door marked BOOSTER VALVE—NO STAFF ACCESS PERMITTED was but a tiny square in the distance behind him. Mike Fraser didn't even notice, he knew exactly where he was going now.

Terry Ryan looked at his watch—again.

It was 2:15 a.m. Four minutes after he'd last looked. Ryan sighed. Jesus, the time crawled on this job.

> *Status Check: Officials in charge of third element confirm delivery complete.*

Idly, Ryan peered out through the massive floor-to-ceiling windows of the atrium of the New York State Library. Nothing stirred on the streets outside.

He touched the gun by his side and grunted a laugh. Security guards in a library—a *library*, for God's sake. The pay was the same, he guessed, and so long as that kept coming, Terry Ryan didn't care what they asked him to guard.

He continued to stroll around the atrium, whistling quietly to himself—

Clink-clink.

He froze.

A noise.

There it was again: *clink-clink.*

Ryan held his breath. It had come from the left. He drew his gun.

Behind the Information Desk, Mike Fraser swore as he picked his screwdriver up from the floor. He peered out over the counter.

No one to the left. Nor to the right. He let out a deep breath. No one had—

'*Freeze!*'

Fraser snapped around. He took in the scene quickly. Security guard. Gun. Maybe fifteen metres, twenty at the most. As if there was a choice.

'I said, freeze!' Terry Ryan yelled. But the thief had already made a break for it. Ryan broke into a run.

Books on shelves became streaking blurs of colour as Fraser bolted down a narrow aisle. His heart pounded loudly inside his head. And then suddenly he saw the door. And the sign: STAIRS.

Fraser hit the stairs running, grabbing the banister, sliding down the first flight. The security guard, Ryan, flew in two seconds later, taking the stairs three at a time.

Down and down, round and round, Fraser went, clinging to the banister, hauling himself around at every turn. He saw the door at the bottom. He flew down the last flight of stairs and hit the door at full speed. It burst open easily—too easily—and Fraser went sprawling face-first onto the hard wood floor.

He could hear heavy footsteps bounding down the stairs behind him.

Fraser reached for the nearest bookshelf to hoist himself up and immediately felt a searing pain rip through his right arm. It was then that he saw his wrist. It had taken the full weight of the fall, and now, bent grotesquely backwards, it was undoubtedly broken.

Teeth clenched, Fraser hauled himself up with his good arm and had just made it to his feet when—

'You stay right where you are.'

The voice was soft and sure.

Fraser turned around slowly.

In the doorway behind him stood the security guard, with his gun levelled at Mike Fraser's head.

*

Ryan pulled out his handcuffs and threw them to the injured thief.

'Put 'em on.'

Fraser closed his eyes in disgust. 'Why don't you,' he began, 'kiss ... my ... *ass*!' Then suddenly, like a wounded animal, he lunged at the guard.

Without a blink, Ryan raised his gun and fired it into the air above the fallen thief's head.

The booming shot rang out in the silence of the library.

Fraser dropped back to the floor as small white flakes of plaster began to flutter down around his head.

Ryan stepped forward into the aisle, tightened his grip on his pistol, reasserted his aim at Fraser's head.

'I said, *put 'em on*. So put—' Ryan's eyes darted left. 'What was that?'

Fraser heard it, too.

And then—ominously—it came again.

A long, slow growl. Like the snort of a pig. Only louder. Much louder.

'What the hell was that?' Fraser said quickly.

Boom. A loud, dull thud.

The floor shook.

'There's something down here . . .' Fraser whispered.

Boom. Again.

The two men stood there frozen.

15

Ryan looked down the aisle beyond Fraser. It stretched endlessly away from them, disappearing into darkness.

Silence.

Dead silence.

The wooden floor was still again.

'Let's get the fuck outta here,' Fraser hissed.

'Shh!'

'There's somethin' down here, man!' Fraser raised his voice.

Boom.

A tremor shook the floor again.

A book teetering on the edge of a shelf fell to the floor.

'Let's go!' Fraser cried.

Boom. Boom. Boom.

Books began to fall off the shelves in bundles.

Ryan leaned forward, grabbed Fraser by the collar. He pulled the thief's face up to his own.

'For God's sake, shut up,' he whispered. 'Whatever it is, it's hearing your voice. And if you keep talking—'

Ryan stopped abruptly, and frowned at Fraser. The young thief's eyes were wide with fear, his lower lip quivering madly, his whole expression one of total and utter disbelief.

Ryan felt his blood run cold.

Fraser was looking over his shoulder.

Whatever 'it' was, it snorted again, and as it did so Ryan felt a wave of hot air rush across the back of his neck.

It was behind him.

It was right behind him!

The gun went off as Ryan was yanked bodily off the floor. Fraser dropped to the ground, staring at the hulking mass of blackness before him.

Ryan screamed as he struggled uselessly in the powerful arms of the dark shape. And then suddenly, the creature bellowed loudly and hurled him through the nearest bookshelf. Books cascaded everywhere as Ryan's body doubled over and crashed *right through* the old wooden casing.

The massive black shape lumbered around the bookshelf, looking for the body on the other side. In the dull yellow light, Fraser could see long black bristles flowing over a high, arched back, saw demonic pointed ears and powerful muscular limbs, caught glimpses of matted black hair and gigantic scythe-like claws.

Whatever it was, it picked up Ryan's body like a rag doll and dragged it back around to the aisle where Fraser sat.

The flight through the bookshelf must have broken Ryan's back, Fraser guessed, but the security guard wasn't dead yet. Fraser could hear him moaning softly as the creature lifted him to the ceiling.

It was then that Ryan screamed.

A shrill, ear-piercing, inhuman scream.

To his absolute horror, Fraser saw what was going to happen next and he put his hand up over his face just as he heard the sickening *crack* and an instant later, he felt a torrent of warmth wash all over the front of his body.

Ryan's scream cut off abruptly and Fraser heard the beast roar a final time, followed by the thunderous crunching of wooden shelves.

And then there was nothing.

Silence.

Total and utter silence.

Slowly, Fraser removed his hand from his face.

The beast was gone. The guard's body lay there in front of him, twisted and mangled, motionless. One of the bookshelves to his right lay horribly askew, wrenched free from its ceiling mountings. Blood was everywhere.

Fraser didn't move, couldn't move.

And so he just sat there, alone, in the cold emptiness of the New York State Library, and waited for the dawn.

FIRST MOVEMENT

30 November, 1:27 p.m.

The sun shone brightly over Norwood Elementary School. It was lunchtime and groups of schoolchildren were out playing on the school's enormous grassy playing field.

Status Check: Initialise electrification systems.

Norwood was one of the leading private elementary schools in Connecticut. An impressive academic record— and one of the biggest building funds in America—had made it one of *the* sought-after schools for the well-to-do.

At the bottom corner of the grassy playing area, a cluster of children had gathered. And in the middle of this cluster stood Holly Swain, nose-to-nose with Thomas Jacobs.

'He is not, Tommy.'

'Is too. He's a *murderer*!'

The crowd of children gathered around the two combatants gasped at the word.

Holly tried to compose herself. The white lace collar of her uniform was beginning to feel very tight now and she was determined not to let it show. She shook her head sadly, raised her nose a little higher.

'You're so childish, Tommy. Such a *boy*.'

The girls behind her chirped similar comments in support.

'How can you call me childish when *you're* only in the third grade?' Tommy retorted. The group assembled behind him echoed their agreement.

'Don't be so *immature*,' Holly said. *Good word*, she thought.

Tommy hesitated. 'Yeah, well, he's still a murderer.'

'He is not.'

'He killed a man, didn't he?'

'Well, yes, but . . .'

'Then he's a murderer.' Tommy looked around himself for support. 'Murderer! Murderer! Murderer!' The group behind him joined in.

'*Murderer! Murderer! Murderer!*'

Holly felt her fists clench by her side, felt her collar tighten around her neck. She remembered her father. *Be a lady. Got to be a lady.*

She spun around, her blonde ponytail flinging around her shoulders. The girls around her were shaking their heads at the taunts of the boys. Holly took a deep breath. She smiled to her friends. *Got to be a lady.*

Behind her, the boys' chant continued.

'*Murderer! Murderer! Murderer!*'

Finally, Tommy called out above the chant, 'If her father's a murderer, then Holly Swain will probably grow up to be a murderer, too!'

'Yeah! Yeah, she will!' his group urged.

Holly's smile went flat.

Slowly—ever so slowly—she turned back around to face Tommy. A hush fell over the crowd.

Holly stepped closer. Tommy chuckled, glancing around at his friends. Only now his supporters were silent.

'Now I'm upset,' Holly said flatly. 'I think you'd better take back those things you've been saying. Would you, please?'

Tommy smirked and then he leaned forward. 'Nope.'

'Okay, then,' Holly said, smiling politely. She looked down at her uniform, straightened her skirt.

Then she hit him.

Hard.

The clinic had become a battlefield.

Glass exploded everywhere as test tubes exploded against the walls. The nurses leapt clear of the melee, hurriedly moving the multi-million-dollar equipment out of the line of fire.

Dr Stephen Swain burst out of the adjoining observation room and immediately set about calming the
source of the storm—a 57-year-old, 240-pound, big-
busted woman named Rosemary Pederman, a guest of St
Luke's Hospital, New York City, on account of a small
abnormality in her brain known as a cerebral aneurism.

'Mrs Pederman! Mrs Pederman!' Swain called. 'It's
okay. It's okay. Just calm down,' he said gently. 'What
seems to be the problem?'

'The problem?' Rose Pederman spat. 'The problem,
young man, is that I will not put my head in that . . .
that *thing* . . . until someone tells me exactly what it
does!'

As she spoke, she jerked her chin at the enormous Magnetic Resonance Imaging—or MRI—machine
which occupied the centre of the room.

'Come on, Mrs Pederman,' Swain said sternly.
'We've been through this before.'

Rose Pederman pouted, child-like.

'The MRI will not harm you in any way—'

'Young man. *How does it work?*'

Swain pursed his lips tightly.

At 39, he was the youngest ever partner in Borman
& White, the radiologist collective, and for a very simple
reason—Swain was *good*. He could see things in an X-
ray or a CAT-scan that no-one else could, and on more
than one occasion, had saved lives by doing so.

This fact, however, was difficult to impress upon older patients since Swain—sandy-haired and clean-shaven, with a lean physique and sky-blue eyes—*looked* about ten years younger than his actual age. Except for the fresh red vertical scar that cut down across his lower lip, a feature which seemed to age him, he could have passed for a third-year resident.

'You want to know how it works?' Swain said seriously. He resisted the urge to look at his watch. He had somewhere to be. But then, Rose Pederman had gone through six radiologists already and this had to stop.

'Yes, I do,' she said stubbornly.

'Okay. Mrs Pederman, the process you are about to undertake is called Magnetic Resonance Imaging. It's not unlike a CAT-scan, in that it generates a cross-sectional scan of your skull. Only instead of using photovoltaic methods, we use controlled magnetic energy to re-align the ambient electrostatic conductivity in your head in order to create a three-dimensional composite cross-section of your cranium.'

'What?'

'The magnet in the MRI machine affects the natural electricity in your body, Mrs Pederman, giving us a perfect picture of the inside of your head.'

'Oh, well . . .' Mrs Pederman's lethal frown instantly transformed itself into a beaming, maternal smile.

'That's quite all right then. That was all you had to tell me, lovey.'

An hour later, Swain burst through the doors of the surgeon's locker room.

'Am I too late?' he said.

Dr James Wilson—a red-haired paediatrician who, ten years previously, had been the best man at Swain's wedding—was already moving quickly toward him. He hurled Swain's briefcase to Swain. 'It's 14–13 to the Giants. If we hurry, we can catch the last two quarters at McCafferty's. Come on, this way. We'll go through the ER.'

'Thanks for waiting,' Swain hurried to keep up with his friend's rapid strides.

'Hey, it's your game,' Wilson said as he walked.

The Giants were playing the Redskins and Wilson knew that Swain had been waiting a long time for this game. It had something to do with Swain living in New York and his father who lived back in D.C.

'Say,' Wilson said, 'how's that lip healing up?'

'It's okay.' Swain touched the vertical scar on his lower lip. 'Still a bit tender. Got the stitches out last week.'

Wilson turned as he walked, grinning. 'Makes you look even uglier than you already are.'

'Thanks.'

Wilson arrived at the door to the emergency room, opened it—

—and was immediately met by the pretty face of Emma Johnson, one of the floating nurses at St Luke's.

The two men stopped instantly.

'Hey, Steve, how are you?' Emma looked only at Swain.

'Gettin' there,' he replied. 'How about you?'

A coy cock of the head. 'I'm good.'

'I'm fine, too,' Jim Wilson chimed in. 'Not that anyone seems to care . . .'

Emma said to Swain: 'You wanted me to remind you about your meeting with Detective Dickson, about the . . . *incident*. Don't forget you have to see him at five.'

'Right,' Swain nodded, absently stroking the cut on his lower lip. 'No problem. I can do that after the game.'

'Oh, I almost forgot,' Emma added. 'You got another message. Norwood Elementary called about ten minutes ago. They want to know if you can come down there right away. Holly's been fighting again.'

Swain sighed. 'Not again. Right away?'

'Right away.'

Swain turned to Wilson. 'Why today?'

'Why not?' Wilson said wryly.

'Is there a delayed telecast of the game later tonight?'

'I think so, yeah,' Wilson said.

Swain sighed again. 'I'll call you.'

Stephen Swain leaned on the steering wheel of his Range Rover as he pulled it to a stop at the traffic lights. He glanced across at the passenger seat beside him. Holly was sitting with her hands in her lap and her head bowed, her feet jutting out horizontally from the seat, unable to reach the floor. They weren't swinging wildly about as they usually did.

The car was quiet.

'You okay?' Swain asked softly.

'Hmmm.'

Swain leaned over to look at her.

'Oh, don't do that,' he said gently, reaching for a tissue. 'Here.' He dabbed at the tears that had run down her cheeks.

Swain had arrived at the school just as Holly was leaving the vice-principal's office. Her ears were red and she'd been crying. It was harsh, he thought, that an eight-year-old should get such a dressing down.

'Hey,' he said. 'It's all right.'

Holly lifted her head. Her eyes were watery and red. She swallowed. 'I'm sorry, Daddy. I tried.'

'You tried?'

'To be a lady. I really did. I really tried hard.'

Swain smiled. 'You did, huh?' He grabbed another tissue. 'Mrs Tickner didn't tell me what made you do it. All she said was that the lunchtime teacher found you straddled on top of some boy, beating the hell out of him.'

'Mrs Tickner wouldn't listen to me. She just kept saying that it didn't matter what made me do it, only that it was wrong for a lady to fight.'

The lights went green. Swain put the Range Rover into gear and moved off.

'So what did happen, then?'

Holly hesitated, then said, 'Tommy Jacobs was calling you a murderer.'

Swain closed his eyes momentarily. 'He was, was he?'

'Yes.'

'And you tackled him and punched him for that?'

'No, I punched him first.'

'But for that. For calling me a murderer?'

'Uh-huh.'

Swain turned to face Holly and nodded. 'Thanks,' he said seriously.

Holly smiled weakly. Swain turned his eyes back to the road. 'How many lines did you get?'

'One hundred times: "I must not fight because it is not ladylike".'

'Well, since this was partly my fault, what do you say you do fifty, and I'll do the other fifty in your handwriting.'

Holly smiled. 'That would be good, Daddy.' Her eyes began to brighten.

'Good,' Swain nodded. 'Just next time, try not to fight. If you can, try to *think* your way out of it. You'd be surprised, you can do a lot more damage with your brains than with your fists. And you can still be a lady at the same time.' Swain slowed the car and looked at his daughter. 'Fighting is never the answer. Only fight when it's the last option you've got.'

'Like you did, Daddy?'

'Yeah,' Swain said. 'Like I did.'

Holly lifted her head and began to peer out the window. She didn't recognise this area.

'Where are we going?' she said.

'I've got to go to the police station.'

'Daddy, are you in trouble again?'

'No, honey, I'm not in trouble.'

'Can I help you!' the harried-looking receptionist yelled above the din.

Swain and Holly were standing in the lobby of the

14th Precinct of the New York Police Department. There was activity everywhere. Beat cops hauling drug dealers away; phones ringing; people shouting. A prostitute in the corner winked sexily at Swain as he stood at the check-in desk.

'Uh, yes, my name is Stephen Swain. I'm here to see Detective Dickson. I was supposed to see him at five, but I had some time, so I—'

'That's fine, you're on the list. He's up in his office now. You can go right up. Office 209.'

Status Check: Electrification systems ready.

Swain headed for the stairwell at the rear of the bullpen. As he did so, Holly bounded to his side and grabbed his hand. Swain looked down at the blonde ponytail bobbing madly up and down beside him. Wide-eyed and interested, Holly was taking in the pandemonium of the police station with the curiosity of a scientist. She certainly was resilient, that was for sure, and with her natural blonde hair, blue eyes, button nose and sharp-eyed gaze, she was looking more and more like her mother every day . . .

Stop it, Swain thought. *Don't go there. Not now . . .*

He shook his thoughts away as they ascended the stairs.

On the second floor, they came to a door marked:

31

209: HOMICIDE. Swain heard a familiar voice shouting from within.

'I don't care what your problem is! I want that building shut down, okay!'

'But sir—'

'Don't give me that, John. Just listen for a moment, will you. Good. Now look at what we have here. A security guard found lying on the floor—*in two pieces*— and a two-bit thief who's found sitting there next to him. Yeah, that's right, he's just sitting there when we arrive.

'And this thief, he's got blood all over his face and all down the front of his body. But it's not his blood, it's the guard's. Now I don't know what's going on. You tell me. Do you think this thief is from one of those crazy sects, who goes out, chops up a security guard, rubs the blood all over himself, and then manages to overturn a couple of ten-foot-tall bookcases?'

The voice paused for a moment, listening while the other man mumbled something.

'John, we don't know shit. And until we find out more, I'm shutting down that library. Okay?'

'Okay, Sarge,' the other voice relented.

'Good,' the first voice was calm again. 'Now get down there, set up the tape around all entrances and exits, and put a couple of our guys inside for the night.'

The door opened. Swain stepped aside as a short officer came out of the office, smiled quickly at him, and then headed down the corridor and into the stairwell.

Status Check: Electrification to commence in two hours.
Earth time: sixth hour post meridian.

Swain knocked softly on the door and peered inside the office.

The wide room was empty, save for one desk over by the window. There Swain saw a large barrel-chested man seated in a swivel chair, his back to the door. He was gazing out the window, sipping from a coffee mug, savouring, it seemed, a rare moment's silence.

Swain knocked again.

'Yeah, come in,' the man didn't look up.

Swain hesitated, 'Ah, Detective—'

Captain Henry Dickson swung around in the swivel chair. 'Oh, I'm sorry, I was expecting someone else.' He got up quickly, crossed the room and shook Swain's hand. 'How are you today, Dr Swain?'

'Gettin' there,' Swain nodded. 'I had some time so I thought I'd come in and get this thing out of the way, if that's all right.'

Dickson led them to his desk where he reached into an open drawer and pulled out a file.

'Sure, no problem,' Dickson fished through the file. 'It shouldn't take more than a few minutes anyway. Just give me a minute here.'

Swain and Holly waited.

'All right,' Dickson said at last, holding up a sheet. 'This is the statement you gave on the night of the incident. What we'd like to do is include it in the departmental report, but by law we can't do it without your written consent. Is that okay with you?'

'That's fine.'

'Good, then I'll just read it to you to make sure it's okay, and then you can sign the report and we can all be out of here.'

Status Check: Officials from each system report that teleports are ready. Awaiting transmission of grid co-ordinates of labyrinth.

Dickson straightened himself in his chair.

'All right, then,' he began to read from the statement, 'at approximately 8.30 p.m. on the night of October 2, 2000, I was working in the emergency room of St Luke's Hospital, New York City. I had been called in to do a radiology consult on a gunshot wound to a police officer. X-rays, C-spines and a CAT-scan had been taken and I had just returned to the emergency ward with the films when five young Latin American men

34

wearing gang colours burst in through the main doors of the emergency ward with automatic weapons firing.

'Everyone in the ward dived for the floor as the wave of bullets smashed into everything in sight—computer screens, whiteboards, everything.

'The gang members fanned out immediately, shouting to each other, "*Find him and kill him!*" Two of them brandished automatic rifles while the other three held semi-automatic pistols.'

Swain listened in silence as Dickson recounted the events of that night. He remembered being told later that the wounded cop had been with the Vice Squad. Apparently, he'd been working undercover in Queens with a crack-dealing gang when his cover had been blown during a botched raid. He'd been winged during the shoot-out, and now the gang-bangers—incensed at his role in the bust—were here to finish him off.

Dickson kept reading: 'I was standing just outside the wounded policeman's room when the five men stormed the hospital. There was noise everywhere— people were screaming, the men's guns were booming— and I ducked behind the nearest corner.

'Then suddenly I saw one of the pistol-bearing gang-bangers rush toward the wounded cop's room. I don't know what made me do it, but when I saw him reach the doorway to the room and see the cop inside—and smile—I leapt at him from behind, tackled him hard.

'We slammed into the doorframe together, but he elbowed me sharply in the mouth—cutting my lip—and we fell apart and then suddenly before I knew what was happening, he was swinging his pistol around toward me.

'I caught his wrist in mid-flight—held the gun clear of my body—just as one of the *other* gang members arrived right in front of us.

'This second youth saw our struggle and instantly raised his own pistol at me but—still holding onto the first gang member's wrist—I whirled around and, with my free hand, punched the second youth square on the wrist of his gun-hand, causing his fingers to reflexively spring open and drop the gun. On the return journey, I used that same fist to backhand the youth across the jaw, knocking him out cold.

'It was at that moment that the first gang member started pulling indiscriminately on the trigger on his gun—even though I was still gripping his wrist. Gunshots boomed, bullets shredded the walls.

'I had to do something, so, pushing my feet off the doorframe, I hurled us both to the floor. We tumbled to the ground together—a clumsy rolling heap, so clumsy in fact that the youth's gun was pushed awkwardly up against his own head and then—'

And then abruptly—*shockingly*—the gun had gone off and the youth's head had simply exploded.

Swain didn't need to listen to Dickson any more. He could see it all in his mind's eye as if he was still there. He could remember the star of blood that had sprayed all over the door. He could still *feel* the youth's body go limp against his own.

Dickson was still reading the statement.

'—as soon as the other gang members saw their dead comrade, they fled. I believe it was about then that I passed out. This statement is dated 3/10/00, 1:55 a.m., signed Stephen Swain, M.D.'

Dickson looked up from the sheet of paper.

Swain sighed. 'That's it. That's my statement.'

'Good,' Dickson handed the typewritten statement to Swain. 'If you just sign there where it says "Consent granted", that'll just about do it, Dr Swain. Oh, and may I say once again, on behalf of the New York Police Department, thank you.'

Status Check: Grid co-ordinates of labyrinth to be transmitted to all systems upon electrification.

'We'll see you in the morning then,' Officer Paul Hawkins said as he stood inside the enormous translucent glass doors of the New York State Library.

'See you then,' the lieutenant said, closing the doors on Hawkins' face.

Hawkins stepped away from the doors and nodded to his partner, Parker, who stepped forward with a large ring of keys. As Parker began to bolt the first of four locks on the huge translucent doors, Hawkins could see the blurred outline of the lieutenant affixing bright yellow police tape across the entrance. The tape pressed up against the other side of the glass and Hawkins could make out the familiar words: POLICE LINE—DO NOT CROSS.

He checked his watch.

5:15 p.m.

Not bad, he thought. It had only taken them twenty minutes to skirt the building and seal off all the entrances and exits.

Parker finished off the last lock and turned around.

'All done,' she said.

Hawkins thought about what the other cops had said about Christine Parker. Three years his senior, she was hardly pretty—for that matter, hardly petite. Big hands, dark heavy-set features, good with a gun. Unfortunately, her image hadn't been helped along by reports of insensitivity—she was known in the department for her rather icy demeanour. Hawkins shrugged it off. If she could hold her own, that was all that mattered to him.

'Good,' he turned to face the enormous atrium of the library. 'Do you know what happened? I was only called in this afternoon.'

'Somebody broke in and slashed up a security guard. Pretty messy,' Parker replied casually.

'Broke in?' Hawkins frowned. 'I didn't see any forced entry on any of the doors we sealed.'

Status Check: 0:44:16 *to Electrification.*

Parker put her keys in her pocket and shrugged. 'Don't ask me. All I know is that they haven't determined point of entry yet. SID's coming in tomorrow morning to do that. Guy probably picked the lock on one of the storage doors. Those things have got to be at least forty years old.'

She cocked her head indifferently. 'Larry at Dispatch told me they spent most of the day just trying to clean it all up.'

Parker walked over to the Information Desk and sat down. 'Anyhow,' she put her feet up on the counter, 'this isn't so bad. Doesn't bother me if I get double time for sitting in a library all night.'

'Come *on*, Daddy!' Holly said impatiently. 'I'm missing Pokémon!'

'Okay, okay,' Swain pushed open the front door. Holly burst past him, dashed into the house.

Swain pulled his key from the door and called after her, 'Don't slide on the carpet!'

He stepped inside as Holly charged out of the kitchen, biscuit tin in one hand, a can of Coke in the other. Swain stopped in his tracks as Holly cut across his path, making a beeline for the TV.

Watching her, Swain put his suitcase down, folded his arms and leaned against the bench that separated the kitchen from the living room. He watched as, unsurprisingly, in mid-stride Holly dropped to the floor and slid gracefully across the carpet, coming to a halt inches away from the television set.

'Hey!'

Holly gave him a throwaway smile. 'Sorr*eee*.' She flicked on the TV.

Swain shook his head as he went into the kitchen. He always said not to slide on the carpet and Holly always did it anyway. It was kind of a ritual. Besides, he thought, Helen had always said it, and Holly had always ignored her, too. It was a good way for both of them to remember her.

It had been two years now since Swain's wife had been killed by a drunk driver who had tried to run a red light at fifty miles an hour. It had happened late one August evening, around eleven-thirty. They had run out of milk, so Helen had decided to walk to the 7-Eleven a few blocks away.

She never came back.

Later that night, Swain would see her body at the morgue. The mere sight of it, bloodied and broken, had knocked the wind out of him. All the life, the essence, the personality—everything that had made her *Helen*— had been sucked from it. Her eyes had been wide open, staring blankly into space, lifeless.

Death had struck—brutally, swiftly, unexpectedly. She had gone out for milk and then all of a sudden she was gone. Just gone.

And now it was just him and Holly, somehow continuing life without her. Even now, two years on, Swain occasionally found himself staring out the window, thinking about her, tears forming in his eyes.

Swain opened the fridge, pulled out a Coke for himself. As he did so, the phone rang. It was Jim Wilson.

'You missed a *great* game.'

Swain sighed. 'Oh, yes . . .'

'Man, you should've seen it. It went into—'

'No! Stop! Don't tell me!'

Wilson laughed loudly on the other end of the line. 'Now would I do that?'

'Not if you wanted to live. Want to come over and watch it all over again?'

'Sure, why not? I'll be there in ten,' Wilson said and hung up.

Status Check: 0:14:38 *to Electrification.*

Swain glanced at the microwave. The green LED clock read 5:45 p.m.

He looked over at Holly, camped less than a foot away from the television screen. On the screen, multi-coloured creatures danced about.

Swain grabbed his drink and went into the living room. 'What are you watching?'

Holly didn't move her eyes from the screen. 'Poké-mon,' she said, feeling for the biscuit tin beside her and grabbing a biscuit from it.

'Any good?'

She turned quickly, scrunched up her nose. 'Nah. Mew isn't there today. I'll see what's on the other channels.'

'No, wait!' Swain leaned forward, grabbing for the remote. 'The sport will be—'

The station changed, and a newsreader appeared on the screen.

'—while in football, fans in the national capital were not to be disappointed as the Redskins scalped the Giants twenty-four to twenty-one in an overtime thriller. At the same time, in Dallas . . .'

Swain closed his eyes as he sank back into his chair. 'Aw, man.'

'Did you hear that Daddy? Washington won. Grandpa will like that. He lives in Washington.'

Swain laughed softly. 'Yes, honey, I heard. I heard.'

Status Check: Officials attending to Earth Contestant await special instructions regarding teleportation.

Paul Hawkins strolled idly around the foyer of the library.

His every footfall echoed hauntingly in the open space of the atrium.

He stopped to survey the atrium around him. It was,

43

quite simply, a massive interior space. When one took into account the rail-lined balcony that ran in a horse-shoe above the lower floor, its ceiling was actually two storeys high. In the early evening darkness, the atrium looked almost cavernous.

Ten-foot-high bookcases loomed in the brooding semi-darkness. Indeed, with the onset of night, apart from the harsh white glow coming from the Information Desk where Parker sat reading, the only light that penetrated the gigantic room was the slanting blue light from the streetlights outside.

Status Check: 0:03:04 to Electrification.
Teleport Officials standby.

Hawkins looked over at Parker. She was still sitting behind the Information Desk, her feet up, reading some Latin book she said she'd read back in school.

Jesus, it's quiet here, he thought.

Status Check: 0:01:41 *to Electrification.*

Status Check: Officials on Earth confirm
receipt of special instructions.
Standby.

The phone rang again. Holly leapt up from the floor and grabbed the receiver.

'Hello, Holly Swain speaking,' she said. 'Yes, he's here.' She put the receiver to her chest and yelled at the top of her lungs, 'Dad*deee*! Phone!'

Swain emerged from his bedroom down the hall, doing up the buttons on a clean shirt. The belt around his jeans dangled from his waist and his hair was still dripping from the shower.

He gave Holly a crooked smile as he took the phone from her. 'Do you think the whole neighbourhood now knows I've got a phone call?'

Holly shrugged as she danced away toward the refrigerator.

'Hello,' Swain said into the phone.

'It's me again.' It was Wilson.

Swain glanced at the microwave clock. 'Hey, what are you doing? It's almost six. Where are you?'

'I'm still at home.'

Status Check: 0:00:46 to Electrification.

'Home?'

'The car won't start. Again.' Wilson said, deadpan.

Swain just laughed.

Hawkins was bored.

Idly, he poked his head inside the library's central stairwell, flicked on his heavy police flashlight. White marble stairs flanked by solid oak banisters rose in a wide spiral up into the darkness.

Hawkins nodded. Had to hand it to these old buildings, they were built to last.

Status Check: 0:00:15 to Electrification.

Parker stood up from her seat behind the Information Desk. She gazed lazily around the atrium, squinting in the darkness.

'What're you doing?' she called.
'Just looking around.'

Status Check: 0:00:09 *to Electrification.*
Standby.

Parker walked over to Hawkins. He was standing at the doorway to the stairwell, his flashlight on, peering up into the darkness.

:06

She stopped next to him.
'Nice old place,' Hawkins said.
'Yeah,' Parker nodded. 'Nice.'

:04
:03
:02
:01

Standby . . .

—Electrification initialised.

At that moment, while Hawkins and Parker stood in the stairwell, bright blue sparks flashed out from the main entrance to the library. An electric blue current shot up between the large glass doors while sizzling claws of electricity lashed out around the edges of the door frame.

Every single window of the library shook as tiny forks of blue lightning shot out from their panes. At the small side entrances to the library, yellow police tape bubbled slowly, boiling under the intense heat of the electricity now flowing through the doors.

And then, in an instant, it stopped.

All the windows and doors giving access to the library were suddenly still.

Suddenly silent again.

The State Library, old and dark, stood sombrely in the darkness of New York City, its magnificent glass doors grey in the moonlight. To the casual observer a few feet away they looked regal and austere, just as they had looked the day before.

It was only when one came close that one would see the intermittent flash of tiny blue lightning that licked out from between the two huge doors every few seconds.

Just as it did at every other entrance to the library.

Status Check: Electrification complete.
Dispatch grid co-ordinates
of the labyrinth.

Commence teleportation.

Holly grabbed onto Swain's leg. Swain shook it playfully as he spoke into the phone.

'It won't be much of a surprise anyway. I already heard who won.'

'You did?'

Swain frowned down at Holly as she reached into his jeans pocket. 'Yes. Unfortunately I did.'

Holly pulled her hand out of his pocket and frowned at the object in her hand.

'Daddy, what's this?'

Swain glanced down at her and cocked his head in surprise. 'May I?' he said.

Holly gave him the small silver object.

'What's going on?' Wilson asked.

Swain turned it over in his hand. 'Well . . . *Doctor* Wilson, maybe you can tell me. Maybe you can tell me why my daughter has just pulled a Zippo out of my jeans. *My* jeans that *you* borrowed for your little cowboy thing on the weekend.'

Wilson hesitated. 'I have absolutely no idea how that got there.'

'Why don't I believe you?'

'All right, all right, don't start.' Wilson said. 'What are my chances of getting my lighter back?'

Swain put the cigarette lighter back into his pocket. 'I don't know. Sixty–forty.'

Status Check: Teleportation sequence initialised.

'Sixty–forty!'

Holly grabbed another drink from the refrigerator. Swain shifted the telephone to his shoulder and bent down to pick her up. He grunted under the weight.

'God, you're heavy.'

Initialise teleport: Earth.

'*Dad* . . . Come on, I'm eight now . . .'

'Too old to be picked up, huh? All ri—'

At that moment the room around Swain began to brighten. A mysterious white glow filled the kitchen.

'Daddy . . .' Holly gripped his shoulders tightly.

Swain turned around slowly, staring, mesmerised, at the soft white light glowing around him—glowing around him—*growing* around him.

Growing.

The kitchen was getting brighter. The light was gathering intensity.

Swain spun. All around him, the soft white glow had become a dazzling white light. Wherever he turned, his eyes reeled at the brilliant light. It seemed to come from every direction.

He lifted his forearm to shield his eyes.

'Daddy! What's happening?'

Swain held her closer, pushed her head into his chest, guarding her from the light. He squinted as his eyes tried to penetrate the blinding wall of white light surrounding them, searching for a source.

Recoiling from the light, he abruptly looked down at his feet—and saw a perfect circle of white light ringing his sneakers.

And then Swain realised.

He was at the centre of the light.

He was the source!

Gusts of wind shot through the kitchen. Dust and paper swirled around Swain's head as he held Holly close to his chest. He shut his eyes, bracing himself against the screaming wind.

Then, strangely, above the howling of the wind, he heard a voice. A soft, faint, insistent voice saying, 'Steve? Stephen Swain, are you still with us?'

It took him a second to realise that it was the phone. Wilson was still on the line. Swain had forgotten that he was still holding onto the phone.

'Stephen, what's going on? Ste—'

The phone went dead.

A deafening thunderclap boomed and Swain was instantly plunged into complete darkness.

SECOND MOVEMENT

30 November, 6:04 p.m.

A lot of people would say that fear of the dark is nothing but a phenomenon of childhood.

A child fears the dark simply because he or she does not have the experience to know that in fact nothing is there. But as Stephen Swain knew, fear of the dark was common in many adults. Indeed, for some, the human need for sight was often as basic as the need for food.

Standing in pitch darkness, without a clue where he was, Swain felt it strange that he should be thinking of his college studies in human behaviour. He remembered his lecturer saying, 'Human fears are very often irrational constructs of the mind. How else would you explain a six-foot-tall woman being petrified by the mere sight of a single white mouse—a creature barely four inches long?'

But no fear was seen as more irrational—or more innate in man—than a fear of the dark. Academic theorists and weary parents had been saying for centuries that there was nothing in the dark that was not already there in the light . . .

But I'll bet something like this never happened to them, Swain thought as he stared into the sea of blackness around him.

Where the hell are we . . . ?

His heart pumped loudly inside his head. He could feel a wave of panic spreading slowly through his body. No. He had to stay calm—rational—had to look after Holly.

He felt for her at his shoulder. She held him tightly, frightened.

'Daddy . . .'

If he could just see *something*, he thought, trying to contain his own ever-increasing fear. A break in the darkness. A splinter of light. Anything.

He looked left, then right. Nothing.

Only black. Endless, seamless black.

A fear of the dark didn't seem quite so irrational now.

'Daddy. What's *happening*?'

He could feel Holly's head pushed close against his shoulder.

'I don't know, honey,' Swain pursed his lips in thought. And then he remembered.

'Wait a minute,' he said, stretching his hand awkwardly underneath Holly to reach into his jeans pocket. He breathed a sigh of relief as he felt the cold slippery metal of the lighter.

The Zippo flipped open with a metallic *calink!* and Swain flipped down on the cartwheel. The flint sparked for an instant, but the lighter didn't catch. Swain tried again. Another spark but no flame.

'Christ,' he said aloud. 'Some smoker.'

'Daddy . . .'

'Just hold on, honey,' Swain put the lighter back in his pocket and turned to face the darkness again. 'Let's see if we can find a door or something.'

He lifted his foot and took a hesitant step forward. As he lowered it, however, he began to understand why some people feared the dark so much. The sheer helplessness of not knowing what was right in front of you was terrifying.

His shoe hit the floor. It was hard. Cold. Like slate, or marble.

He took another step forward. Only this time, as his foot came down, it didn't find any floor. Just empty space.

'Uh-oh.'

His sense of panic began to rise again. Where the hell was he? Was he standing on the rim of a ledge? If he was, how far down did it go? Was it on every side of him?

Shit.

Swain slowly lowered his foot further over the edge.

Nothing.

Slowly. Further. Still nothing.

57

Then his foot hit something. More floor, not far below where he was standing.

Swain pushed down and forward again. Another piece of floor. He smiled in the darkness, relieved.

Steps.

Holding Holly close to his chest, Swain cautiously descended the stairs.

'Where are we, Daddy?'

In the darkness, Swain stopped. He glanced at Holly. Although everything was still dark, he could just make out the outline of her face. The hollows of her eye sockets, the shadow of her nose across her cheek.

'I don't know,' he said.

He was about to take another step forward when he snapped up to look at Holly again. The hollows of her eye sockets, the shadow across her cheek—

A shadow.

There must be a light.

Somewhere.

Swain looked closely at her face and, scanning the shadow of her nose, he suddenly saw it—a soft green glow, so dim that it barely revealed her other features. Swain leaned closer and—abruptly—the gentle glow vanished.

'Damn it.'

He slowly moved his head back and, equally slowly, the glow returned, half covering Holly's face.

Swain's eyes widened. It was his *own* shadow covering his daughter's face.

The light source was somewhere behind him.

Swain spun around.

And there, in the sheet of blackness in front of him, he saw it. It was hovering in the darkness, level with his eyes and yet completely still—a tiny green light.

It couldn't have been more than six feet away, and it shone like a small pilot light on a VCR. Swain stared intently at the tiny green light.

And then he heard a voice.

'Hello, Contestant.'

It came from the green light.

It sounded prim, proper, refined. And yet at the same time high-pitched, as if spoken by a midget.

It came again.

'Hello, Contestant. Welcome to the labyrinth.'

Swain squeezed Holly close. 'Who is that? Where are you?'

'I am here. Can you not see me?' The voice was not threatening. It was almost, Swain thought, helpful.

'No. It's too dark.'

'Oh, yes. Hmm,' the voice sounded disheartened. 'Just a moment.'

The tiny green light bounced away to Swain's left, bobbing up and down. Then it stopped.

'Ah. Here we are.'

Something clicked and some overhead fluorescent lights immediately came to life.

In this new-found light, Swain saw that he was standing halfway down a flight of wide marble stairs with banisters made of dark polished wood. The stairs seemed to spiral down several floors before disappearing into darkness.

Swain guessed he was at the top of the stairwell, since no stairs ascended from the landing above him. Only a heavy-looking wooden door led out from the landing.

His gaze moved left from the door, and suddenly he saw the owner of the voice.

There, standing next to a light switch, stood a man no more than four feet tall, dressed completely in white.

White shoes, white coveralls, white gloves.

The little man was holding something in one white-gloved hand. It looked like a grey wristwatch. Swain noticed that the small green light he had seen before was attached to the face of the wristwatch.

In addition to his completely white outfit, Swain saw that the little man wore an odd white skull cap that covered every part of his head, except for his face.

'Daddy, it looks like an eggshell,' Holly whispered.

'Shh.'

The little man in white stepped forward, so that he stood on the edge of the landing, his head a little higher than Swain's. He spoke perfect English, without trace of an accent.

'Hello. Welcome to the labyrinth. My name is Selexin and I am your guide.' He extended his little white hand. 'How do you do?'

Swain was still staring in disbelief at the little white man. He absently offered his own hand in return. The little man cocked his head.

'You have an interesting weapon,' he said, looking down at the telephone receiver in Swain's hand.

Swain glanced at the receiver. The spiral cord leading out from the phone had been cut several inches from where it met the hand-piece. He hadn't realised that he was still holding it. He quickly handed it to Holly, and shook hands awkwardly with the man in white.

'How do you do?' Selexin bowed solemnly.

'I'm gettin' there,' Swain said, warily. 'How about you?'

The man in white smiled earnestly and nodded politely. 'Oh, yes. Thank you. I am getting there, too.'

Swain hesitated. 'Listen, I don't know who or what you are, but . . .'

Holly wasn't listening. She was staring at the hand-piece of the telephone. Without a spiral cord snaking back to a base unit, it looked like a cellular.

She examined the shortened phone cord. The cut at the end of it looked as if someone had snipped it with a pair of extremely sharp scissors. It was a clean cut. A *perfectly* clean cut. The wires inside the cord were not even frayed.

Holly shrugged and put the phone in her uniform pocket. Her own cellular phone, even if it didn't work.

She looked back at the little man in white. He was talking to her father.

'*I* have no intention of harming you,' he was saying.

'You don't?'

'No,' Selexin paused. 'Well, not *me*.'

'Then if you don't mind, do you think you could tell us where we are and how the hell we can get out of here?' Swain said, taking a step up the stairs towards the landing.

The little man seemed shocked.

'*Get out?*' he said blankly. 'No one gets out. Not yet.'

'What do you mean no one gets out? Where are we?'

'You are in the labyrinth.'

Swain looked at the stairs around him. 'And where is this labyrinth?'

'Why, Contestant, this is Earth, of course.'

Swain sighed. 'Listen, ah . . .'

'Selexin.'

'Yes. Selexin,' Swain offered a weak smile. 'Selexin, if it's okay with you, I think my daughter and I would like to leave your labyrinth. I don't know what it is you're doing here, but I don't think we're going to be a part of it.'

Swain climbed the stairs and walked over to the door leading out from the landing. He was reaching for the door handle when Selexin snatched his hand away.

'*Don't!*'

63

He held Swain's hand away from the heavy wooden door. 'Like I said, no one gets out, *yet*. The labyrinth has been sealed. Look.'

He pointed to the gap between the door and its solid wooden frame. 'You see?'

Swain looked at the gap and saw nothing. '*No*,' he said, unimpressed.

'Look *closely*.'

Swain leaned closer and peered at the inside of the door frame.

And then he saw it.

A tiny blue fork of electricity licked out from the gap between the door and the frame.

He only just saw it, but the sudden electric blue flash of light was unmistakable. Swain's eyes followed the door frame up its vertical edge. Every few inches there was a distinct flicker of the bright blue charge between the frame and the door.

It was the same on all four sides of the door.

Slowly, Swain stepped back onto the landing. He spoke as he turned, his voice soft and flat.

'What the hell are you doing here?'

In the atrium of the library, Officer Paul Hawkins was pacing back and forth in front of the Information Desk.

'I'm telling you, I saw it,' he said.

Parker was sitting with her feet up on the desk, chewing on a candy bar, now happily reading a back issue of *Cosmopolitan*.

'Sure you did.' She didn't even look up as she spoke.

Hawkins was angry. 'I said, *I saw it.*'

'Then go and check it out for yourself,' Parker offered him a dismissive wave. As far as she was concerned, Hawkins was green. Too young, too fresh and far too eager. And like every other rookie, always suspicious that the crime of the century was happening right under his nose.

Hawkins walked off toward the bookcases near the stairwell, mumbling to himself.

'What'd you say?' Parker called lazily from behind her magazine.

'Nothing,' Hawkins muttered as he stalked off. 'I'm going to see if it happens again.'

Parker looked up from her magazine to see Hawkins disappear through the stairwell doors. She shook her head.

'Rookie.'

Slowly, Hawkins climbed the wide marble stairs, peering around every turn, hoping to see it happen again. He leaned out over the banister and looked up into the shaft.

With the stairwell lights out, he knew he would barely be able to see beyond the first landing—

There was a light!

Up at the top.

One of the fluorescent lights up at the very top of the stairwell was on—and it hadn't been on before.

Hawkins felt his adrenalin surge.

Someone was in here.

What should he do now? Get Parker? Yes, backup— backup was good. No, wait. She wouldn't believe him. She hadn't before.

Hawkins peered back up into the shaft and saw the light. He took a hesitant step up the stairs.

And then it happened.

Hawkins immediately leapt back from the banister as

a blinding stream of white light burst up through the central shaft of the stairwell, instantly illuminating everything around it.

Flecks of dust swirling around the hollow core of the stairwell suddenly came to life as the rising light struck them, creating a dazzling column of vertical white light.

Hawkins stared at it in awe. It was exactly what he had seen before—a brilliant stream of white light pouring through the shaft of the stairwell.

And yet, somehow, this time it was different.

The *source* was different. This time, it wasn't coming from somewhere high up in the stairwell.

No, this time it was coming from below.

Slowly, Hawkins peered out over the edge of the banister, looking down into the shaft.

The light seemed to be coming from underneath one of the landings below him. All he could make out was the edge of what looked like a large glowing sphere of pure white—

It went out.

It didn't fade. It didn't flicker. It just disappeared to black. Just as it had done before.

Hawkins suddenly found himself standing in the empty stairwell again, the hollow shaft in the centre now no more than a silent, gaping hole of blackness.

He looked back over his shoulder toward the atrium. Beyond the bookcases, he could see Parker's feet resting lazily on the counter of the Information Desk. He thought about calling to her, but decided against it.

He turned back to face the darkened stairwell.

He swallowed, and suddenly forgot all about the fluorescent light that had been turned on upstairs.

Hawkins pulled his heavy police-issue flashlight from his belt and switched it on.

Then he began his descent into the darkness.

Selexin was still holding the grey wristband. It was heavy in his hand, mainly because of the thick metal straps used to clasp it to its wearer's wrist.

He glanced at the face. It was rectangular—like an elongated digital watch—broad in width, short in height. At the top of the face, the little green pilot light burned brightly. Next to it was another light, slightly larger than the green one, dull red in colour. At the moment it was lifeless.

Good, Selexin thought.

Beneath the two lights there was a narrow oblong display that read:

INCOMPLETE—1

Selexin looked up from the watchface. He saw Swain and Holly standing at a window, gazing out, both careful to stay a safe distance from the electrified window panes.

Selexin grunted, shook his head sadly, and looked back down at the wristband. The display flickered:

INCOMPLETE—1

The words disappeared for an instant. When they returned, they had changed. The display now read:

INCOMPLETE—2

And it was stable again.

Selexin walked over to Swain at the window and stopped beside him.

'Now do you understand?'

Swain continued to stare out the window.

After he had seen the electrified door at the top of the stairwell, he had immediately come down the first flight of stairs and opened the nearest door. It was a large fireproof door marked with a red '3'.

It had opened onto an extremely broad, low-ceilinged room, perhaps fifty yards wide. Swain had gone straight across it—winding his way through a forest of odd-looking steel-framed desks—heading directly for the nearest window.

The room was completely filled with the peculiarly

shaped desks. Each had a vertical partition attached to the rear edge, so that it formed an L-shape with the horizontal writing surface. Hundreds of these desks, bunched together in tight clusters of four, covered the vast floorspace of the room.

Now, as he looked out the window and saw the familiar inner city park, surrounded by the darkened streets of New York City, Swain began to understand.

'Where are we, Daddy?'

Swain's eyes took in the multitude of partitioned desks in the room around them. In the near corner of the room was a heavy-looking maintenance door, next to which was a sign:

QUIET PLEASE.
THIS ROOM IS FOR PRIVATE STUDY ONLY.
NO CARRY BAGS PERMITTED.

A study hall.

Swain turned to face Selexin. 'We're in the library, honey. The State Library.'

Selexin nodded. Correct.

'This,' he said, 'is the labyrinth.'

'This, is a *library*.'

'That it may well be,' Selexin shrugged, 'but that is of little concern for you now.'

Swain said, 'I think it's of a lot of concern for me

now. What are you doing here and what do you want with us?'

'Well, first of all,' the smaller man began, 'we do not exactly want both of you.' He looked at Swain. 'We actually only want *you*.'

'So why did you bring my daughter too?'

'It was unintentional, I can assure you. Contestants are strictly forbidden to have assistance of any kind. She must have entered the field just before you were teleported.'

'Teleported?'

'Yes, Contestant,' Selexin sighed sadly. 'Teleported. And you can count yourself extremely fortunate that she was fully inside the field at the time. If she had been only partially inside the field, she might have been—'

There was a loud rumble of thunder outside the window. Swain looked out through the glass and saw dark storm clouds rolling across the face of the moon. It was well and truly dark outside now. Streaks of rain began to appear on the window.

He turned back. 'The white light.'

'Yes,' Selexin said, 'the field. Everything inside the field at the time the systems are initialised is teleported.'

'Like the phone,' Swain said.

'Yes.'

'But only half the phone came with us.'

'Because only half the phone was inside the field.'

71

Selexin said. 'In its simplest form, the field is merely a spherical hole in the air. Anything inside that sphere is, at the time of teleportation, lifted up and placed else-where, whether it is attached to something else or not.'

'And you determine where we go. Is that right?' Swain said.

'Yes. Now, Contestant—'

Swain held up his hand. 'Wait a minute. Why do you keep calling me that?'

'Calling you what?'

'"Contestant". Why do you keep calling me "Contestant"?'

'Because that is what you are, that is why you have been brought here,' Selexin said, as if it was the most obvious thing in the world. 'To compete. To compete in the Seventh Presidian.'

'Presidian?'

Now it was Selexin who frowned.

'Yes,' his voice tightened. 'Hmmm, I suspected this might happen.' He gave a long sigh and looked impatiently at the metal wristband in his hand. Its green light was still burning and its display still read:

INCOMPLETE—2

Selexin looked up and spoke to no-one in particular: 'Well, since there is still time, I will tell you.'

Holly stepped forward, pointed to the grey wrist-watch. 'What is that?'

Selexin gave her a sharp look. '*Please*, I will come to that. Just listen for a moment.'

Holly backed away immediately, reaching for Swain's hand.

Selexin was taking short, quick breaths, showing his irritation. As Swain watched him, it seemed increasingly obvious that the little man in white simply did not want to be here.

'The Presidian,' Selexin began, 'has been held on six previous occasions. And this,' he said, looking at the study hall around him, 'is the seventh. It is held approximately once every thousand Earth years, each time on a different world, and in every system, except Earth, it is held in only the highest esteem.'

'Systems?' Swain asked.

'Yes, Contestant, *systems*.' Selexin's tone was now that of a weary adult addressing a five-year-old. '*Other* worlds. *Other* intelligent life. There are seven in total.'

Selexin paused for a moment, lifted a hand to massage his brow. He looked as if he was trying very hard to keep himself calm.

Finally, he looked up at Swain. 'You didn't know that, did you?'

'The part about other worlds and other intelligent life? Ah, no.'

'I am dead,' Selexin whispered, presumably to himself. Swain heard him clearly.

'Why?' he asked innocently. 'Why are you dead? What is this Presidian?'

Selexin sighed in exasperation. He held his hands out, palms up.

'What do you *think* it is?' he said sharply, barely concealing the condescension in his voice. 'It is a *competition*. A *battle*. A *contest*. Seven contestants enter the labyrinth and only one leaves. It is a fight to the death.'

He could see the disbelief spread across Swain's face. Selexin threw up his hands. 'By the Gods, you do not even understand what you are here for! Do you not see?'

Selexin slowed down for a moment, lowering his voice, trying desperately to control himself.

'Let me begin again. You have been chosen to represent your species in the ultimate contest in the universe. A contest that dates back over six millennia, that bases itself on a principle that goes light years beyond any notion of "sport" that you could possibly imagine. *That* is the Presidian.

'It is a battle. A battle between hunters, athletes, warriors; creatures coming from every corner of the universe, possessed of skill, courage and intelligence, prepared to stake their very lives on their extraordinary talents—talents at hunting, stalking and killing.'

Selexin shook his head.

'There is no coming back from defeat in the Presidian. There is no return match. Defeat in the Presidian is no loss of pride, it is *loss of life*. Every contestant who enters the labyrinth accepts that in this contest the only alternative to ultimate victory is certain death.

'It is quite simple. Seven will enter. The best will win, the lesser will die. Until only one remains.' The little man paused. 'If, of course, one *does* remain.

'There is no place for the ordinary man in the Presidian. It is a contest for the extraordinary—for those prepared to risk the ultimate to attain the ultimate. On Earth you play games where you lose nothing in defeat. "Winning isn't everything," you say. "It doesn't matter if you win or lose, but how you played the game."' Selexin grunted disdainfully. 'If that is the case, why should anyone even *try* to win?

'Winning is devalued where defeat involves no loss, and humans are quite simply unable to comprehend that idea. Just as they are unable to comprehend a contest like the Presidian, where defeat means exactly that— losing *everything*.'

The little man looked Swain squarely in the eye. 'Winning *is* everything when you have everything to lose.'

The little man laughed weakly. 'But your kind will never understand that . . .'

Selexin paused, dropping his head, withdrawing into

himself. Swain just stood there, entranced, staring in amazement at the little man before him.

'And that is why I am dead,' Selexin looked up. 'Because *my* survival depends on *your* survival. It is a highly prized honour to guide a contestant through the Presidian—an honour bestowed upon my people since we are prevented by our size from competing in the contest—but when one accepts that honour, one also accepts the fate of his contestant.

'So when you die, I die. And as I see it now,' he raised his voice, 'since you appear to know *absolutely nothing* about the Presidian or anything it entails, I would say quite confidently that at the moment our collective chances of survival are approximately zero!'

Selexin looked Swain up and down. Sneakers, jeans, a loose-fitting shirt with the sleeves rolled up, hair still slightly wet. He shook his head.

'Look at you, you haven't even come *prepared* to fight!'

He began to pace, gesturing with his arms, despairing for his situation, until finally he was totally indifferent to Swain and Holly's presence: 'Why me? Why this? Why the *human*? Keeping in mind the distinguished history human participation has had in the Presidian . . .'

Swain watched the little man pace back and forth in front of him. Holly just stared at him.

'Hey,' Swain said, stepping forward. Selexin continued to mutter to himself.

'*Hey!*'

Selexin stopped. He turned and stared at Swain.

'What?' he said angrily. In his anger, the little man possessed a ferocity that belied his size.

Swain cocked his head. 'Are you saying that humans have been in this thing before? In this contest?'

Selexin sighed. 'Yes. Twice. In the last two Presidia, humans have participated.'

'And what happened to them?'

Selexin laughed sadly. 'Both were the first to be eliminated. Neither one ever stood a chance.' He cocked an eyebrow. 'Now I know why.'

He looked down at the wristwatch. It now read:

INCOMPLETE—3

Swain said, 'And how exactly were they selected for this thing?'

As Selexin explained, but for one crucial modification, the process for human selection for the Seventh Presidian was largely unchanged from that which had operated for the two Presidia before it. Beings unable to accept the fact that other lifeforms existed in the universe could hardly be expected to choose a contestant of their own accord, let alone appreciate the concept of the Presidian.

After all, humans had not even been considered for inclusion in any Presidian until two thousand years ago—human development having been disappointingly slow.

All six of the other systems chose their own representatives for the millennial Presidian either by holding a competition of their own or by choosing their greatest sportsman, huntsman or warrior. Earth, on the other hand, would be surveyed for some time, and from that surveillance, a worthy contestant would be chosen.

'Well, they didn't look too hard this time,' Swain said. 'I've never picked a fight in my life.'

'Oh, but—'

'I'm a *doctor*,' Swain said. 'Do you know what a doctor is? I don't kill people. I—'

'I know what a doctor is, and I know precisely what they do,' Selexin shot back. 'But you have forgotten what I said earlier—*one crucial modification* was made to the selection criteria this time.

'You see, for the last two Presidia the choice of the human contestant was based largely on combat skills, and combat skills alone. This was obviously a mistake. After the dismal performance of those two human contestants, it was decided that other, less obvious skills should be taken into account in the selection process for this Presidian.

'Of course, fighting skills would be necessary, but this time they would *not* be conclusive. Now, from our observations of your planet, we could see that human warriors were adept at using artificially propelled weapons—firearms, missiles and the like. But such weapons are forbidden in the Presidian. Only *self*-propelled weapons are allowed—throwing knives, bladed weapons. So, first of all, we needed a human proven in hand-to-hand combat. Naturally, several warriors of your race fulfilled this requirement.

'But other skills were also deemed necessary, skills which are not often found in your warrior types. High mental aptitude levels were a primary consideration—in particular, the ability to respond to a crisis, objective rational thinking in the face of the potentially bizarre, and most importantly, adaptive intelligence.'

'Adaptive intelligence?'

'Yes. The ability to evaluate a scenario in an instant, take in all the immediately available solutions, and then *act*. We often call this reactive thinking—the ability to think clearly under pressure and use *any* available means to solve one's problem. Based on our prior experience with humans, it was anticipated that the human contestant would probably not be an *offensive*, proactive contestant. Rather, he or she would be more defensive, *reactive* to a situation of someone else's making. So a quick-thinking, adaptive personality was required. You.'

Swain shook his head. He hardly thought of himself as a quick-thinking, adaptive personality. He saw himself as a good doctor, but not brilliant. He knew of countless other surgeons and physicians who were miles ahead of him in both knowledge *and* ability. He was just good at what he did, but quick-thinking or adaptive?

'Make no mistake, Contestant, your skills as a physician have been under scrutiny for some time now. Clear, *reactive* thought, under intense pressure—have you ever experienced that before?'

'Well, yes, lots of times, but still . . . I mean, God, I've never been in combat—'

'Oh, but you have,' Selexin said. 'Your selection was based on your response to a life-threatening combat situation not so long ago, a situation that involved multiple enemies.'

Swain thought about it. A life-threatening combat situation involving multiple enemies. He wondered if college football counted as life-threatening. Christ, it sounded like something that would be better suited to somebody in the army or the police force.

The police force . . .

That night . . .

Swain thought about that night one month ago in

October, when the five heavily-armed gang members had stormed the ER at St Luke's. He remembered his fight with the two pistol-toting youths—remembered tackling the first one, then punching the second one in his wrist, dislodging his gun—and then struggling with the first one again—and falling to the floor in a heap—and then hearing the gun discharge that final fatal shot.

Life-threatening? Definitely.

Swain suddenly realised that he was rubbing the cut on his lower lip.

'There is another thing,' Selexin said, interrupting his thoughts. The little man lifted his small white hand, offering the grey wristband to Swain.

'Take it, put it on. You will need it. Especially if we are separated.'

Swain took the wristband but did not put it on. 'Now, wait just a minute. I haven't agreed to be a part of this little show of yours yet—'

Selexin shook his head. 'You have not understood what I have been telling you. Your selection for the Presidian has been finalised. You no longer have any choice in the matter.'

'It doesn't seem like I ever did.'

'Please, just look at your wristband.'

Swain looked at the watch, at the display beneath the glowing green light. It read:

INCOMPLETE—3

Selexin said, 'See that number—three. Soon that number will reach seven. When it does, we will know that all seven contestants have been teleported into the labyrinth. Then the Presidian will begin.' He looked seriously at Swain. 'You are here now, and whether you like it or not, you have become an integral part of this contest.'

Selexin pointed at the wristband. 'And when that number hits "7" you will become fair game for six other contestants who all have the same goal that you have. To get out.'

'What's that supposed to mean?'

'Remember what I told you,' Selexin said. 'Seven enter, but only one leaves. The labyrinth is completely electrified. There is absolutely no way out. Except by teleport. And that is initialised *only* when one contestant remains in the labyrinth. *That* is the exit from the labyrinth—and only the winner leaves. If, of course, there is a winner.'

Selexin slowed down. 'Mr Swain, the other contestants, they don't care whether or not you decide to accept your status as a contestant. They will kill you anyway. Because they are all well aware that unless every contestant bar one is dead, *no-one* leaves the labyrinth. The ultimate contest, Mr Swain.'

Swain looked at the little man in disbelief. He let out a slow breath through his nose. 'So you're telling me that not only are we stuck in here, but that soon there will be six other guys in here too, whose only way out is to make sure that I'm dead.'

'Yes. That is right.'

'Holy shit.'

Swain stood in the stairwell, by the fire door leading to the study hall. Holly stood behind him, holding onto his shirt tail.

He looked at the thick grey wristband now clasped firmly around his left wrist. It looked like a manacle from the arm of an electric chair—thick and solid, and heavy too. The little green light glowed while the display still read:

INCOMPLETE—3

Swain turned to Selexin, 'So there are only three of us in here now. Is that right?'

'Yes. That is right.'

'Does that mean that we can walk around safely now?'

'I do not understand.'

'Well, not everyone is in the labyrinth yet,' Swain said. 'So say I want to wander around and have a look at this place—what happens if I bump into another contestant? He can't kill me, can he? Not yet.'

Selexin said, 'No, he cannot. Combat of any kind between contestants is strictly prohibited until *all seven* have entered the labyrinth. In any case, I would advise you against "wandering about".'

'Why not, if they can't hurt us, we can safely have a look around the library.'

'That is true, but if you decide to wander, you do hazard the risk of being sequenced.'

'Sequenced?'

'Yes. If you do happen to meet another contestant before all seven have been teleported into the labyrinth, you can be assured that he—or she—cannot hurt you in any way. You may converse with other contestants if you want to, or you may ignore them completely.' Selexin spread his palms. 'Very simple.'

Then he held up a finger.

'However. If you do meet another contestant, there is nothing to stop that contestant *following* you until the remaining contestants *have* been teleported into the labyrinth, and the Presidian has commenced. That is sequencing, and it has proved to be a common tactic in previous Presidia.

'Another contestant can quite rightfully walk two feet behind you for the whole time until the Presidian commences and you cannot touch him—for just as he cannot hurt you, you cannot hurt him either. And once the last contestant has been teleported into the labyrinth and your wristband reads "7", well . . .' Selexin shrugged. 'You had better be ready to fight.'

'Great,' Swain said, frowning at the thick grey wristband clamped to his wrist.

At that moment, the display flickered.

Swain was momentarily startled. 'What's this?'

Selexin looked at the wristband. The display read:

INCOMPLETE—3

Then it vanished and the screen came up again, reading:

INCOMPLETE—4

'What's that mean?' Swain asked.

'It means,' Selexin said, 'that another contestant has arrived in the labyrinth.'

In the atrium of the library, Officer Christine Parker sat behind the Information Desk with her mouth agape and her eyes wide.

She was staring at the hulking seven-foot figure

standing before her, in front of the massive glass doors of the library.

Parker remembered how Hawkins had wandered off twenty minutes ago, looking for some damned white light that he thought he had seen. She also remembered laughing loudly when he'd told her about it.

Now she didn't feel like laughing.

Moments ago, she had seen a perfect sphere of brilliant white light appear in front of her. It was fully ten feet in diameter and it lit up the whole cavernous space of the atrium like an enormous light bulb.

And then it had vanished.

Extinguished in an instant.

Gone.

And now in its place stood a figure that looked something like a man. A seven-foot-tall, perfectly proportioned man—with broad muscular shoulders narrowing to an equally muscular waist.

A man clad entirely in black.

Parker stared at him in awe.

The streams of soft blue light that filtered in through the great glass doors of the library surrounded the tall black figure before her, creating a spectacular silhouette, while at the same time highlighting one particularly distinguishing feature of the man.

The 'man' had horns.

Two long beautifully tapered horns that protruded from both sides of his head, and then stretched upwards so that they almost touched two feet above his head.

He stood absolutely still.

Parker thought he might have been a statue, but for the slow, rhythmic rise and fall of his powerfully built chest. Parker's eyes searched the head for a face, but with the light source behind him, all she could see beneath the two sharp rising horns was an empty space of ominous black.

But there was something wrong with the silhouette.

Something on the man's shoulder that was not black, something that broke the perfect symmetry of his body. It was a lump. A small white lump that seemed to slump over his left shoulder.

Parker squinted in the darkness, tried to determine what the small lump was.

She leaned back in her seat, her eyes wide.

It looked like another man . . .

A very small man. Dressed completely in white—

And then, suddenly, there was light again.

Sharp, sudden, *brilliant* white light filled the atrium of the State Library. Blinding spheres of light, four feet in diameter—half the size of the one she had seen before—illuminated everything around Parker.

Parker saw two small spheres of light before her . . .

then three . . . then four. Loose sheets of paper began to blow about all around her, just as they had done before.

She looked beyond the swirling sheets of paper, trying to catch a glimpse of the tall man in black. But amid the billowing pages and the blinding light, the horned man remained completely still, impervious to distraction.

And then, in a flare of white, Parker saw the man's face.

He was staring at her.

Straight at her.

It was terrifying. Their eyes locked and a flood of adrenalin instantly rushed through Parker's body. All she could see were deep blue eyes set against a harsh black face. Eyes devoid of emotion. Eyes that simply stared.

Stared right at her.

Sheets of paper fluttered wildly around his unmoving frame and then—

And then abruptly, darkness again.

The four white spheres of light had vanished instantly. The wind stopped abruptly, and all over the atrium, sheets of paper glided softly to the floor.

Parker spun to face the spot where one of the spheres had been—

—only to see something small scuttle away behind a nearby bookcase, its long black tail lashing against the bottom shelf of the bookcase as it disappeared from view.

An eerie silence filled the atrium.

The enormous room was once again bathed in the soft blue light of the street lamps outside.

Parker looked back from the bookshelf, saw the carpet of loose paper spread out on the floor before her. In the silence, she could hear herself breathing heavily.

'*Salve, moriturum es!*'

A voice—a deep, baritone voice.

Echoing loudly in the atrium.

Parker's head snapped up. It had come from the silhouetted man.

'*Salve, moriturum es!*' he repeated, loudly. His face was again masked by blackness, shadowed by the blue light behind him. Parker couldn't even see his lips move.

She heard the words. *Salve moriturum es.* They sounded vaguely familiar, like something she had learned at school, something that she had long since forgotten . . .

The big man took a step toward her. A glint of gold flashed off his dark shadowed chest.

Now she could see the small white lump on his shoulder quite clearly. It was a man all right, a small man, held in a fireman's carry over the horned man's shoulder. The little man groaned as the tall horned man moved toward the Information Desk.

Behind the counter of the desk, Parker leaned back, and slowly—silently—eased her Glock 20 semi-automatic pistol from its holster.

The tall man spoke.

'Greetings, fellow competitor. Before you stands Bellos. Great-grandson of Trome, the winner of the Fifth Presidian. And like his great-grandfather and two Malonians before him, Bellos shall emerge from this battle alone, conquered by none and not undone by the Karanadon. Who be'st thou, my worthy and yet unfortunate opponent?'

There was silence as the man waited for an answer.

Parker heard a soft, insistent scraping sound from the bookshelves to her left. It sounded like long fingernails moving quickly back and forth on a blackboard. She turned back to face him.

The man—Bellos—was looking at her, examining her, up and down, right and left.

Parker swallowed. 'I don't—'

'Where is your guide?' the deep baritone voice suddenly interjected. A demand, not a question.

'My guide?' Parker's face displayed her incomprehension.

'Yes,' Bellos said. 'Your guide. How will you confirm any conquest without a guide?'

Beneath the counter, Parker's hand gripped her gun tightly. 'I have no guide,' she said coolly.

The big man cocked his head, his sharp horns tilting to the side. Parker watched him carefully as he pondered over her comment for a moment. He glanced down at the large metal band attached to his wrist. It had a green light on it . . .

The scraping sound behind the bookshelf got faster, more intense.

Impatient.

Bellos looked up from his wristband and levelled his eyes at Parker.

'You are not a contestant in the Presidian, are you?'

He looked at the wide atrium around him, at the bookshelves to his left and right. Then he looked back at Parker, a glint of menace in his eyes.

'Good,' Bellos said, smiling. '*Kataya!*'

The attack came from Parker's left. From the bookshelves.

The creature sprang forward, leaping at the counter of the Information Desk with frightening speed. It hit the counter hard, grabbing the edge with two vicious-looking foreclaws, baring twin rows of long, razor-sharp teeth, squealing a loud reptilian squeal.

Parker reeled back in horror, staring in shocked disbelief at the creature before her.

It was the size of a large dog, about four feet tall, with hard scaly skin that was gunmetal black in colour.

It had four bony-but-muscular limbs and a long, black scaled tail that slithered madly behind its body.

Stunned, Parker just stared at the creature as it struggled to climb over the counter.

Supported by a thin black neck, its head was totally bizarre. Two lifeless black eyes sat on either side of a round black skull, whose sole purpose it seemed was to accommodate the creature's enormous jaws.

The creature lashed out at Parker, clamping its pointed teeth down in front of her.

Parker pulled back from the counter, away from the creature, raised her gun—

—and then in a strange, flashing instant she saw the creature's limbs on the counter.

It was not struggling to climb over the counter anymore—*it was already there*.

It lashed out at her again. Missed again.

Parker was momentarily startled.

It wasn't even *trying* to get her. It was as if this creature were merely trying to keep her attention . . .

It was then that a second creature hit her from the side. Knocking the wind out of her, jolting the pistol from her hand.

Parker stumbled from the impact, catching a split-second glimpse of what had hit her—another creature, identical to the first.

A third creature charged her from behind, pitching her forward, face-first onto the ground. Parker rolled quickly onto her back and suddenly felt a heavy weight slam down onto her chest.

A loud reptilian squeal pierced her ears as two rows of long jagged teeth opened wide in front of her eyes.

It was standing on top of her!

Parker screamed as the creature slashed its long fore-claw across her stomach and ducked its head.

And as she lay on the floor, helpless to resist the slicing of the creatures' sharp teeth as all four of them began to feed on her belly, Officer Christine Parker suddenly remembered—quite irrationally—what the words '*Salve moriturum es*' meant.

They were Latin words—words similar to those spoken by Roman gladiators when they were presented to the cheering crowd before combat—'We who are about to die, salute you'.

However, as Parker sank to the floor, her strength fading, and the weight of the four creatures now pressing down heavily on her body, she realised that Bellos had changed the words slightly, changing the meaning.

'*Salve moriturum es*' meant: 'I salute you, *you* who are about to die.'

'I am not sure this is such a good idea,' Selexin said as he followed Swain and Holly through the fire door into the stairwell.

Swain peered down into the shaft, ignoring Selexin. Holly, however, turned to face the little man.

'If you're from another planet,' she said, 'how come you speak English so well?'

Selexin said, 'My native tongue is based on an alphabet comprised of seven hundred and sixty-two distinct symbols. With only twenty-six base letters to choose from, your language is exceedingly simple to learn apart from the dreadful idioms.'

'Oh.'

Swain continued to stare down the shaft.

'I was saying,' Selexin repeated for him, 'that I am not sure this is a very good idea. The chances of sequencing increase as more contestants enter the labyrinth.'

Swain was silent for a long moment.

'You're probably right,' he said, looking down into

the dark shaft. Then he turned to face Selexin. 'But then again, if I'm going to be running for my life in this place, I don't want to be doing it in rooms and corridors that I don't know. At least if we look around, we might get to know where we can and can't run if we are followed. I sure as hell don't want to run into a dead end with some half-cocked killer behind me. And besides,' he shrugged, 'we might even find somewhere to hole up if we have to.'

'Hole up?'

'Yes, hole up. Hide,' Swain said. 'You know, escape. Maybe even just stay in the one place until everybody else has killed each other.'

'That is improbable,' Selexin said.

'Why is it improbable? Surely it must be the best way to survive this whole damn thing. We just hide away somewhere, let the others do the fighting and maybe they'll . . .'

Selexin wasn't listening. He was just standing there, staring at Swain, waiting for him to stop talking.

Swain said, 'What? What is it?'

Selexin cocked his head to one side. 'If you remember what I told you before, you will understand.'

'What? What did you tell me before?'

'As I have said from the beginning, only one contestant leaves the labyrinth. And if not one, none.'

Swain nodded. 'I remember. But how can that happen? If only one contestant is left in the maze, he's safe to find the exit and leave, because there's nothing left to kill him . . .'

Selexin did not answer.

Swain sighed, '. . . unless there's something else in here.'

Selexin nodded. 'That is right,' he said. 'The third element of the Presidian.'

'The *third* element?'

Selexin stepped back into the study hall and sat down at one of the L-shaped desks. Swain and Holly followed.

'Yes, an outside agent. A variable. Something that is capable of altering the conditions of combat instantly. Something that can turn victory into defeat, life into death. In the Presidian, the third element is a beast, a beast known throughout the galaxy as the Karanadon.'

Swain was silent.

'It is a most powerful beast, like no other,' Selexin said. 'As tall as the ceiling, as broad as three men, and as strong as twenty—and its considerable strength is only matched by its unbridled aggression—'

'Okay, okay,' Swain said, 'I think I get the picture. This thing, it's in here too, right? Trapped inside, like the rest of us?'

'Yes.'

'So what does it do? Does it just wander around killing whoever it pleases?'

Selexin said, 'Well, for one thing, it does not just wander around . . .'

Swain let out a breath in relief.

'. . . all of the time.'

Swain groaned.

'But if you will just look at your wristband for a moment,' Selexin said, 'I will explain everything.'

Swain looked down at the heavy grey band on his wrist. The display still read:

INCOMPLETE—4

'You will remember,' Selexin said, 'that when I gave you your wristband, I told you it would be of vital importance to you, yes? Well, it is more than that. Without it, you will not survive the Presidian.

'Your wristband serves many purposes, one of which is to identify you as a contestant in the Presidian. For example, you cannot win the Presidian unless you are wearing your wristband—you will simply be denied entry into the exit-teleport when it is opened. In the same way, other contestants will know that you are competing in the Presidian because they will see your wristband. This will protect you in the time before the Presidian commences—but it will also tell others that you are still a competitor who must be eliminated.

'However, in addition to this, your wristband provides several other, more important functions. First of all, as you have no doubt already noticed, there is a glowing green light on it. That light answers your previous question: no—the Karanadon does not just "wander" around. The green light you see indicates that the beast is at present dormant, nesting somewhere within the labyrinth. Or more simply, asleep. Wherefore, movement throughout the labyrinth is, at least for the moment, uninhibited by the Karanadon. Hence the green light.'

'The band can tell when it's asleep?' Swain said doubtfully.

'It is done through a device, surgically implanted in the beast's larynx, that electronically measures its rate of respiration. Respiration below a certain rate indicates sleep, respiration above—animation. That device, however, also provides some degree of control over the beast. It can, at official command, either secrete a sedative that will put the beast to sleep or inject a hormone that will rouse it immediately.'

'When would that happen?' Swain asked. 'When would you *want* it to wake up?'

'Why, when there is only one contestant left, of course,' Selexin said. 'Perhaps I can explain this another way. There have been six previous Presidia. Three have been won by Malonians, one by a Konda, and one by a Crisean.'

'Okay.'

Selexin stared at Swain. 'Well, that's it. That's the point.'

'What's the point?'

'There have been six Presidia, while there have been only five winners,' Selexin said.

The little man sighed. 'That is what I am trying to tell you. There may be *no* winner in the Presidian—unless one is worthy, none are worthy. There was no winner in the last Presidian, because the Karanadon killed all of the final three contestants when they happened upon its nest during combat. In the space of two minutes, the Presidian was over, due solely to the beast.'

'Oh.'

Selexin went on: 'And, as has always been the case, when only one contestant remains, and the exit-teleport to the labyrinth has been opened, the Karanadon is roused. One may choose to avoid it and search the labyrinth for the exit. Or one might attempt to kill it if he dares.'

Swain said, 'And has anybody ever done that before? Killed one?'

Selexin looked at Swain as though he had asked the most stupid question in the world.

'In a Presidian? No. Never. Not ever.' There was a short pause. Selexin moved on. 'But, anyway, as you will hopefully live to see later, when the beast is awake, the red light on your wristband will ignite.'

'Uh-huh. And this beast, this Karanadon, it was teleported into the library at the same time I was?'

'No,' Selexin said, 'the Karanadon is traditionally teleported into the labyrinth at least a day before the Presidian is to commence. But that does not really matter, because it would have been asleep all that time. Unless, of course, it was aroused. But that is unlikely.'

'I have one more question,' Swain said.

'Yes?'

'What if someone got out of this maze of yours? Now I know you think it can't happen, but what if it did? What happens then?'

'You credit me with a faith I do not possess. No, I accept your question quite easily, because it can happen. In fact, it *has* happened. Contestants have been known to be ejected from the labyrinth, either by design or by simple accident.'

'So what happens?'

'Again, it is your wristband that governs this situation,' Selexin said. 'As you know, an electric field covers this labyrinth. Your wristband operates in accordance with that field. If for some reason your wristband detects that it is no longer surrounded by the electric field, it automatically sets a timer for self-detonation.'

'A timer for self-detonation,' Swain said. 'You mean it explodes?'

'Not instantly. There is a time limit. You are allowed fifteen min—'

'Jesus Christ! You put a goddamn bomb on my wrist! Why didn't you tell me that before!' Swain couldn't believe it. It was incredible. He began to fiddle hurriedly with the wristband, trying to get it off.

'It won't come off,' Selexin said calmly. 'It *can't* come off, you waste your time even trying.'

'Shit,' Swain muttered, still grabbing at the solid metal band.

'Language,' Holly said, waving an admonishing finger at Swain.

'As I was saying,' Selexin said, 'if by some chance you are expelled from the labyrinth, you will have fifteen minutes to re-enter it. Otherwise, detonation will occur.'

He looked sadly at Swain, still fiddling with the wristband. Finally Swain gave up.

'You needn't worry,' Selexin said. 'Detonation will only occur upon expulsion from the labyrinth, and as I admit that it has happened before, I also add that it has not happened often. No-one gets out. Mr Swain, you must see now that whichever way you go there remains but one answer. Unless you leave this contest as the victor, you do not leave at all.'

Hawkins stood at the base of the stairwell, the beam of his flashlight the only light. There were no more stairs going down from here. Nothing but concrete walls and a large fire door that read: SUB-LEVEL 2.

Must be the bottom.

Hawkins moved cautiously over to the fire door. The handle turned easily and he slid the door open. He peered around the doorframe and instantly felt a rush of bile rise up the back of his throat. He turned back into the stairwell and vomited.

Several moments later, wiping his mouth and coughing to clear his throat, Hawkins looked back out through the doorway.

Aisles of bookcases stretched endlessly away from him, disappearing into darkness, beyond the reach of the mouldy overhead lights. But it was the aisle directly in front of him that seized his immediate attention.

The bookshelf to his left—twelve feet high and twenty feet long—had been wrenched free from its ceiling mounts and was now leaning backwards against the bookcase in the aisle behind it. Like two enormous dominoes: one upright, holding up its fallen neighbour.

The opposite bookshelf—to Hawkins' right—remained upright. It simply had a gaping hole of splintered wood bored through its core. For some reason, books littered the aisle behind it, as though, Hawkins thought, something had—well—something had been hurled right *through* this bookshelf . . .

And then there was the aisle in between.

The flat pool of blood that filled the aisle had dried somewhat in the past twenty-four hours, but the stench still remained.

Of course, the body had been removed, but as Hawkins noticed, the sheer amount of blood was staggering. It lay everywhere—on the floor, on the ceiling, spattered all over the stairwell door. Those books that had remained on the shelves had been sprayed with flying blood. Those that had fallen to the floor had simply changed colour. They were maroon.

Hawkins swallowed as he saw the trail of smeared blood that stained the floor around the shelf with the hole in it. It looked as if someone had been dragged *around* the shelf, back into the original aisle.

By New York Police Department standards, Paul Hawkins was young. Twenty-four. And his youth, combined with his relative inexperience, had made him the obvious choice for baby-sit assignments like this one. Domestic violence protection, post-trauma custody, that sort of thing. He'd seen battered wives and beaten-up teenagers, but in sixteen months of duty, Paul Hawkins had never seen a murder scene.

He felt it odd that the first thing that struck him about the scene was how the movies got it all wrong. Even the most violent film could never successfully achieve the sheer *ugliness* of a murder scene. This was it, he thought, as he stared at the wide pool of dried blood before him.

It was ugly. Dirty and crude and brutal. Hawkins wanted to be sick again.

He looked up at the endless rows of bookshelves that lined Sub-Level Two.

Someone—something—is down here.

He lifted his flashlight. And then slowly, cautiously, he ventured out into the aisles.

'Daddy,' Holly said, following her father into the stairwell.

'In a second, honey,' Swain turned to Selexin. 'Are you sure there isn't anything else you should tell me about before we go any further? No more exploding devices?'

'Daddy.'

Selexin said, 'Well, there is one thing—'

'Dadd*ee*!'

Swain stopped. 'What is it, honey?'

Holly held up the telephone receiver, giving her most winning smile. 'It's for you.'

Swain bent down and took the dead phone. He spoke into it while looking at Holly. 'Hello? Oh hi, how are you?—Yeah?—Is that so?—Well, I'm kinda busy at the moment. Can I call you back? Great. Bye.' He gave the phone back to Holly. Satisfied, she grabbed Swain's hand and fell back into step with him and the egg man.

Selexin spoke quietly, 'Your daughter is really quite charming.'

'Thanks,' Swain said.

'But she provides far more risks to your safety than you should be willing to accommodate.'

'What?'

'I am merely suggesting that you might be better off without her,' Selexin said. 'It might be wise for her to "hole up", as you say. Hide for the duration of the Presidian. If you survive, you will be able to come back for her. If, of course, you care for her that much.'

'Which I do.'

'And likewise,' Selexin went on, 'if you are defeated, she will not also be killed. In any case, to what efficiency can you aspire if you are defending her life as well as your own? An act to prevent her from injury might—'

'Might jeopardise my own life,' Swain said, 'and therefore jeopardise yours. This is my daughter. Where I go, she goes. *Not* negotiable.'

Selexin took a gentle step back.

'And another thing,' Swain said, 'if something does happen and we are separated, I expect *you* to look after her. Not to hole her up and hope nobody stumbles onto her, but to make sure that nothing—*nothing*—happens to her. Do you understand?'

Selexin bowed. 'I have been at error and I apologise with all my heart. I was unaware of your attachment to your child. In as much as I can, I will do my utmost to serve your wishes should such an eventuality occur.'

'Thank you. I appreciate that,' Swain said, nodding. 'Now, you were saying there was something else. Something I should know about.'

'Yes,' Selexin regathered himself. 'It pertains to combat, or rather, the end of any fighting. Whenever any contestant defeats another—either in combat or ambush or otherwise—the conquest must be confirmed.'

'Okay.'

'And that is my purpose,' Selexin said.

'You confirm a kill? Like a witness?' Swain asked.

'Not exactly. I am not the witness. But I do provide the window *for* the witness.'

'Window?'

Selexin stopped on the steps. He turned to Swain.

'Yes. And only at your command can the window be initialised. If you would be so kind, would you please say the word "Initialise".'

Swain cocked his head. 'Initialise? Why—'

And then it happened. A small sphere of brilliant white light—perhaps a foot in diameter—burst to life above Selexin's white skull cap, illuminating the entire stairwell around them.

'What is it?' Swain asked.

'It's coming from the egg—' Holly marvelled.

Selexin looked at Holly, somewhat surprised. 'Yes. You are correct. My rather odd-looking hat is the source of this teleport, small as it is. If you will, Mr Swain, please say "Cancel" lest my superiors believe you actually have killed somebody.'

'Oh, okay. Ah . . . cancel.'

The light disappeared instantly.

'You say it's a teleport. Like before?' Swain asked.

'Yes,' Selexin said, 'exactly the same as before— simply a hole in the air. Only much, much smaller, of course. There is merely another official like myself who is watching at the other end of this teleport. He is your witness.'

Swain looked at the white skull cap on Selexin's head. 'And it comes from that?'

'Yes.'

'Uh-huh,' Swain said, continuing down the stairs.

Selexin followed in silence. Finally he said, 'If I may be so bold as to inquire, where are we going?'

'Down,' Holly said, shaking her head. '*Derrr.*'

Selexin frowned, puzzled.

Swain shrugged. 'Like the lady said, down.'

He gave Holly a quick wink—masking his own very real fear—and she grinned back at him, reassured by the almost conspiratorial nature of the gesture.

They continued down the stairs.

The switchboard operator stared at the panel before her in stunned disbelief.

When is this going to stop? she thought.

On the switch in front of her, two rows of incessant flashing lights indicated that there were a hell of a lot of phone calls waiting to be answered.

She took a deep breath and pressed the flashing square that read '9', and began:

'Good evening, Con Edison Customer Service Line, my name is Sandy. How may I help you?'

Her headset rattled with the tinny voice of yet another disgruntled New Yorker. When finally it stopped, she punched the code—401—into her computer console.

That made fourteen in the last hour, on her panel alone. All coming from inside grid two-twelve—central Manhattan.

A 401—power out due to a probable short in the electrical main. The switchboard operator looked at the words on her computer screen: 'Probable short in the electrical main'. Electronically, she didn't know what a short in the main meant nor how it was caused. She simply knew all the symptoms of power cuts and failures and, in much the same way as a doctor identifies an illness, all she did was add up the symptoms and identify the problem. To know how it was caused was someone else's job.

She shrugged, leaned forward and pressed the next flashing square, ready to face the next complaint.

The lowest floor of the New York State Library is called the 'Stack'. It contains no toilets, no offices, no desks, and no computers. In fact, the Stack holds nothing but books, lots and lots of books.

Like other large libraries, the State Library of New York is less a borrowing library than it is an information library—chiefly computers, Internet, microfilm and CD-ROMs.

As far as actual books are concerned, only the more recent and popular are on display on the Ground Floor. If patrons seek other books, then they are to be found—by staff only—in the Stack, Sub-Level Two.

Wherefore, the Stack acts as little more than a holding pen for several million books.

Lots of books. In *lots* of bookshelves. And these

bookshelves are arranged in a vast rectangular grid formation.

Twenty-two long rows of bookshelves stretch the length of the floor, while horizontal passageways cut across these longer rows at intervals of twenty feet—creating an enormous maze of right-angled twists and turns, blind corners, and long straight aisles that stretch away into infinity.

An enormous maze, thought NYPD Officer Paul Hawkins as he wandered through the Stack. *Wonderful.*

Hawkins had been wandering through the dusty aisles for several minutes now and had so far found nothing.

Damn it, he thought, as he turned back for the stairwe—

A soft noise.

From off to the right.

Hawkins' hand whipped to the automatic by his side. He listened intently.

There it was again.

A low, rasping sound.

Not breathing, he thought. No. More like . . . *sliding*. Like a broom sweeping slowly over a rough wooden floor. Like something *sliding* along the dusty floor of Sub-Level Two.

Hawkins drew his gun and listened again. It was

definitely coming from the right, from somewhere within the maze of bookshelves around him. He swallowed.

There's someone in here.

He grabbed the radio on his belt.

'Parker!' he hissed. 'Parker! Do you copy?'

No answer.

Jesus.

'Parker, where are you?'

Hawkins switched off the radio and turned to look back at the receding rows of bookshelves before him. He pursed his lips for a moment.

Then he lifted his gun and ventured out into the maze.

Gun in hand, Hawkins quietly zig-zagged his way between the bookshelves, moving quickly and easily, searching for the source of the sound.

He came to a halt at the base of a bookcase full of dusty hardcovers. Held his breath for a moment. Waited . . .

There.

His eyes snapped left.

There it was again. The sweeping sound.

It was getting louder—he must be getting closer.

Hawkins darted left, then right, then left again—

moving smoothly in and out of the aisles, stopping every few metres at the flat end of a bookcase. It was disorienting, he thought. Every aisle looked the same as the one before it.

He stopped again.

Listened.

Again, he heard the soft brushing sound. Like a broom on a dusty wooden floor.

Only louder now.

Close.

Very, very close.

Hawkins hurried on along a passageway that cut across the long vertical aisles of the Stack until suddenly he was confronted by a wall of bookshelves—a solid wall of bookshelves that seemed to stretch away into darkness in both directions.

A wall? Hawkins thought. He must be at the edge of the floor—at one of the long sides of the enormous rectangle.

The sound came again.

Only this time, it came from . . . behind him.

Hawkins spun, raised his gun.

What the hell—? Had it turned?

Cautiously, he edged his way down the alleyway of books.

The aisle closed in around him. The nearest cross-passageway branched away to his right—there was nothing but the unbroken wall of bookshelves to his left—about twenty feet away. It was cloaked in shadow.

Hawkins stepped forward slowly. The passageway came fully into view.

It was different.

It wasn't a T-junction, like the last one. More like an L-shape.

Hawkins frowned, and then he realised. It was a corner—the very corner of the floor. He hadn't realised that he'd come this far from the stairwell at the centre.

Listening.

Nothing.

He came to the L-junction and listened again. There was no sound.

Whatever it was, it was gone now.

And then Hawkins began to think. He'd followed the sound, the source of which had presumably been unaware of his presence. But its last few movements had been odd.

It was as though whoever it was had lost direction and had started circling . . .

Circling, Hawkins thought.

No-one would consciously go in a circle, would they, unless they were lost or . . . *or unless they knew someone was following them*.

Hawkins' blood went completely cold. Whoever it was, it wasn't just circling.

It was doubling back.

It knew he was here.

Hawkins spun to face the long aisle behind him, jamming his back into the corner shelving.

Nothing.

'Damn it!' he could feel the beads of cold sweat forming on his forehead. 'Damn it, shit!'

He couldn't believe it. He'd walked right into a corner. A goddamn corner! Two options—straight or left. Shit, he thought, at least among the bookshelves he'd have had four. Now he was trapped.

And then suddenly he saw it.

Off to the left, moving slowly and carefully, out into the passageway.

Hawkins' eyes widened.

'*Holy* shit.'

It looked like nothing he had ever seen before.

Big and long, but low to the ground like an alligator, the creature looked almost dinosaurian—with black-green pebbled skin, four powerful stubby limbs and a long, thick counterbalancing tail.

Its head was truly odd. No eyes, and—seemingly—no mouth. The only distinguishing feature: a pair of long spindly antennae that jutted up from its forehead and clocked rhythmically from side to side.

It was twenty feet away from Hawkins when the tip of its tail finally came into view. The tail itself must have been eight feet long, and it slid across the floor in long, slow arcs, creating the soft sweeping sound. Hawkins saw that the tail tapered sharply to a point at its tip. The whole animal must have been at least fourteen feet long.

Hawkins blinked. For an instant there, behind the tail, he thought he caught a glimpse of a man, a small man, dressed completely in white—

And then the creature's head eased slowly upward— the folds of its skin peeling back to reveal a hideous four-sided jaw that opened with a soft, lethal hiss. Four rows of hideously jagged, saliva-covered teeth appeared.

'Jesus *Christ*,' Hawkins stared at the creature.

It moved forward.

Toward him.

One of the animal's forelegs caught his attention. A green light glowed from a thick grey band strapped to the creature's left forelimb.

It was close now—its jaws wide, salivating wildly, dripping goo all over the floor. Hawkins' eyes were locked on the swaying antennae on its head, clocking from side to side like a pair of metronomes.

It was three feet away . . .

Two feet . . .

Hawkins tensed to run, but for some terrifying reason, his legs wouldn't move. He tried to raise his gun, but couldn't—it was as if every muscle in his body had gone completely, instantly limp. He watched helplessly as, to his horror, his gun slipped from his unresponsive hand and dropped loudly to the floor.

The antennae kept swaying.

One foot . . .

Hawkins was sweating profusely, breathing in short, rapid breaths. He just couldn't take his eyes off them. The antennae. They seemed to move in perfect rhythm, swaying in smooth hypnotic circles . . .

He watched—completely defenceless—as the creature's sinister-looking head came slowly up to his knee.

Ohshit. Ohshit. Ohshit.

And then, suddenly, unexpectedly, like a cobra coiling up off the ground, the creature's long, pointed, eight-foot tail lifted off the floor and swung forward— over its low reptilian body—so that now it was pointing *forward*, arcing over its frame like a scorpion's stinger, the tip of the tail *pointing right at the bridge of Paul Hawkins' nose.*

Hawkins saw it happen and his terror hit fever pitch. He desperately wanted to shut his eyes, so he wouldn't see it happen, but he couldn't even do that—

'*Hey!*'

The creature's head snapped left.

And in an instant, the trance was broken and Hawkins could move again. He looked up and saw . . .

. . . *a man*.

A man, standing a short way down the aisle. Hawkins

hadn't even seen him approach. Hadn't even heard him. Hawkins took in the man's appearance. He had wet hair, and was wearing jeans and sneakers and a white shirt that hung out at the waist.

The man spoke to Hawkins.

'Come over here. Now.'

Hawkins looked down warily at the big alligator-like creature at his feet. It ignored him completely, simply faced the man in jeans, its body dead still.

If it had eyes, Hawkins thought, it was definitely *glaring* at him. A low rumbling noise rose threateningly from the back of its throat.

Hawkins glanced back questioningly at the man. The man just kept his eyes levelled at him.

'Come on,' the man said calmly, eyes unmoving. 'Just leave the gun there and walk very slowly over to me.'

Tentatively, Hawkins took a step forward.

The creature at his knee didn't move. It remained steadfastly focused on the man in jeans.

The man pushed Hawkins behind him and slowly stepped backwards, away from the creature.

Hawkins looked down the aisle behind them and saw two figures standing maybe forty feet away—a small one in white, and another, equally small, who looked like . . . he squinted . . . like a little girl.

'Move,' Swain said, pushing Hawkins down the aisle, his back to him.

Swain kept his eyes up, focused on the bookshelves, *away* from the creature's swaying antennae, watching it only out of his peripheral vision.

The two men stepped slowly down the aisle, away from the frozen creature.

And then suddenly it began to follow them, moving around the corner in a darting crab-like manner that belied its size. Then it stopped.

Swain pushed Hawkins further down the aisle. 'Keep moving. Just keep moving.'

'What the—'

'Just *move*.'

Swain was walking backwards, still facing the creature. Again it made a darting, scuttling movement ten feet forward, and then stopped again, well short of Hawkins and himself

It's being cautious, he thought.

And then it charged.

'Oh, *shit!*'

The large animal bounded down the narrow confines of the aisle.

Swain looked frantically for somewhere to run. But he was still ten feet away from the nearest passageway into the maze of bookshelves.

There was nowhere to go!

Swain braced himself, the ground beneath him vibrating under the thumping weight of the fast-approaching creature. *Christ, it must weigh nearly four hundred pounds.*

Hawkins turned. He saw it over Swain's shoulder. '*Holy* Christ . . .'

Swain just stood there, feet spread wide, taking up the whole aisle.

The creature kept coming. It wasn't stopping.

'It's not stopping!' Hawkins yelled.

'*It has to!*' Swain called. '*It has to stop!*'

The creature bounded forward, bearing down on Swain like a runaway freight train, until abruptly, three feet short of him, it reared on its hind legs and clasped the bookcases on either side of it with its clawed forelimbs, bringing it to a sudden, lunging stop.

The four-sided jaw stopped just inches away from Swain's unmoving face.

The creature hissed fiercely, challenging him. Its saliva dripped down onto the floor in front of his shoes.

Swain averted his gaze, stared at a nearby bookshelf, keeping his eyes off the animal's oscillating antennae. The horrifying alligator-like creature, now standing up on its hind legs, towered over him, *looming* above him like an evil apparition.

Swain wagged an admonishing finger at the infuriated animal: 'Ah-ah-ah. No touching.'

And he began to walk backwards again, pushing Hawkins.

Hawkins stumbled down the aisle, looking back over his shoulder every few seconds. This time the creature didn't follow them, at least not immediately.

They reached the little white man and the girl, and were a good thirty feet from the creature when it began moving toward them again.

The little man spoke: 'Sequencing! She's sequencing!'

The man in the loose-fitting shirt and jeans looked at Hawkins, standing there in his well-pressed police uniform.

'We don't have time to talk right now, but my name is Stephen Swain, and at the moment we're all in big trouble. You ready to run?'

Hawkins answered without thinking. 'Yuh-huh.'

Swain looked back down the aisle at the large dinosaur-like creature. Twenty feet. He picked up Holly.

'You know the way back to the stairwell?' he asked Hawkins.

The young cop nodded.

'Then you lead the way. Just keep zig-zagging. We'll be right behind you.' He turned to the others. 'You two ready?' They nodded. 'Okay then, let's move.'

Hawkins broke into a run, the others close behind him.

With a great lunge, the creature leapt forward in pursuit.

Swain brought up the rear, carrying Holly on his hip. He could hear the pounding of the great weight on the floor behind him.

The stairs. The stairs. Got to reach the stairs.

Left, right, left, right.

He could see the cop weaving up ahead, and then finally, beyond the policeman, he saw the central stairwell block. But he couldn't see the doorway.

They were coming from the wrong side.

'Daddy! It's *catching up*!' Holly yelled from his shoulder.

He looked behind him.

The creature was indeed closing in on them—a giant black-green monster galloping down the narrow aisle with its salivating jaws bared wide.

Swain wasn't worried for himself. Selexin had been right about that. Whatever it was, it was another contestant, and it couldn't touch him. Not yet. Not until that number on his watch read '7'.

But if it got Holly . . .

He saw the cop round the central stairwell block up ahead, then Selexin. Swain rounded the concrete block last of all, panting hard.

The door!

He saw Selexin duck inside it, and then the policeman appeared in the doorway, his hand outstretched.

'Come on!' he was yelling.

Swain heard the creature slide around the corner behind him.

He kept running, kept holding Holly to his chest. He was breathing very heavily now. He was sure he was running too slowly. He could hear the creature's snorting grunts close behind him. Any second now it would be all over him, ready to pluck his daughter—the only family he had left—right from his very arms . . .

'*Come on!*' Hawkins called again.

Behind him, Swain heard the creature's tail slam against a bookcase, heard the sound of books crashing to the floor. Then suddenly, he was at the door and he reached for Hawkins' outstretched arms and Hawkins grabbed his hand and hurled him and Holly inside the stairwell just as Selexin slammed the door shut behind them.

Selexin turned, breathless, exhilarated. 'We made it—'

Bang!

The door behind him shuddered violently.

Swain lifted himself up from the floor, gasping for air. 'Come on.'

They were a whole floor up the stairwell when they heard the door to Sub-Level Two bang open with a loud bone-jarring *crack!*

INCOMPLETE—6

Swain frowned at the wristband. He'd missed the arrival of the last two contestants. Now there was no knowing when the next—and last—contestant would enter the library.

No knowing when the Presidian would begin.

The group had left the stairwell and were now hiding in an office on Sub-Level One. Like all the others around it, this office was partitioned by waist-high wood panelling with glass reaching the rest of the way up to the ceiling. Everyone was careful to stay low, out of sight, below the glass.

Swain had found a directory of the library attached to the wall of the stairwell and wrenched it free. He was looking at it now while Selexin sat behind the desk, quietly explaining their situation to Hawkins. Holly was sitting on the floor nestled up to Swain, holding him tightly, sucking her thumb. She was still a little shell-shocked by their close encounter with the big creature downstairs.

The directory showed a cross-section of the library.

Six floors—four above ground, two below—each a different colour. The two sub-levels below the Ground Floor were both shaded grey and stamped with the label NO PUBLIC ACCESS. The others were brightly coloured:

THIRD FLOOR—STUDY HALL
SECOND FLOOR—READING ROOMS,
FUNCTION ROOMS,
COMPUTER SERVICES
FIRST FLOOR—ON-LINE SERVICES,
CD-ROMS, COPIERS,
MICROFILM
GROUND FLOOR—CATALOGUES,
CD-ROMS, REFERENCE

Swain remembered the study hall on the top floor with its odd-looking desks. He tried to memorise the rest. Small blue squares picturing a stick-man and woman indicated toilets on every other floor. Another blue square, with a car pictured in it, was tacked to the edge of Sub-Level One. The parking lot.

He checked his wristband again.

INCOMPLETE—6

Still '6'. Good.

He looked over at Selexin and the policeman, and shook his head in wonder.

That young cop was lucky to be alive. It had been only blind luck that had led Swain to his rescue—the instant when he, Holly and Selexin had been descending the stairs and seen a long shadow stretch out onto the landing below them.

They had watched from the shadows above as the creature—Selexin said its name was Reese—stepped slowly into view, accompanied by its guide. It stopped on the landing, seemed to examine the floor with its snub dinosaur-like snout, and then peered down the stairwell.

Then it had slithered quickly down the stairs.

Something had caught its attention.

Curious, they had then followed it down into the Stack and seen it weave purposefully in and out of the bookshelves for several minutes—stalking something, leading it on. It was only at the last moment that Swain had ventured out into the furthermost aisle to actually see Reese's quarry—a lone policeman, trapped in the corner.

He'd moved instantly—stopping only for a piece of

last-minute advice from Selexin: avoid all eye contact with Reese's antennae.

And so they had met Hawkins.

Swain turned to Selexin. 'Tell me more about Reese.'

'Reese?' Selexin said. 'Well, for one thing, Reese is, in human terms, female. Her tail tapers sharply to a point, like a spear. Males of her species possess only blunted tails. This is because in their clans, the female is the hunter, and her chief weapon is her sharp pointed tail.

'Didn't you see, when Reese was moving in on your new friend here,' Selexin nodded to Hawkins, 'that her tail was poised high over her body, in a large arc, pointing *forward*? And *he* couldn't move an inch.

'That is why I told you not to make prolonged eye contact with her antennae. Any extended visual contact with them will cause instant paralysis. Just like it did with him.' Selexin gave Hawkins a look. 'That is how Reese hunts. You look at her antennae for too long and you suffer hypnotic paralysis, and—*bang!*—before you know it, she's got you with that tail. Right between the eyes.'

The little man smiled. 'I would say she bears a rather strong resemblance to the female of your own species, aggressive *and* instinctive. Wouldn't you say?'

'*Hey*,' Holly said.

Swain ignored the remark. 'Tell me more about her hunting methods. Her stalking methods.'

Selexin took a breath. 'Well, as you no doubt noticed, Reese has no eyes. For the simple reason that she does not need them. She comes from a planet surrounded by opaque, inert gases. Light cannot enter their atmosphere, and the inert gases are impervious to any chemical change. Her race has simply adapted over time to utilise and enhance their other senses: increased auditory acuity, sensitive ampullae for detecting the distressed heartbeat of frightened or wounded prey, and, most of all, a highly evolved scent detection mechanism. In fact, I would say that her sense of smell is her most well-developed hunting tool.'

'Wait a second,' Swain said, alarmed, 'she can *smell* us?'

'Not now. Reese's sense of smell has a very limited range. No farther than, say, a couple of feet.'

Swain breathed in relief. Hawkins did, too.

'But *within* that range,' Selexin went on, 'her sense of smell is incredibly astute.'

'What do you mean?'

'I mean,' Selexin said, 'that the manner by which she detected *him*,'—Selexin pointed roughly to Hawkins—'was by his scent.'

'But I thought you said her range wasn't that good. How could—'

Swain cut himself off. Selexin was waiting for him again, giving him an expectant 'are-you-finished?' look.

'That is correct,' Selexin said, 'in a way. You see, Reese didn't smell *him*. What she smelled was the *scent* he left behind. Do you remember when Reese first came into our view in the stairwell? She bent low and sniffed the floor?'

Swain frowned. 'Yeah . . .'

'Footprints,' Selexin said. 'A trail not long cold. With any fresh trail like that, Reese doesn't *need* to smell anything beyond two feet, because she just follows the scent of the trail itself.'

'Oh,' Swain said.

And then it hit him.

'Oh, *shit!*'

He shot up to look out through the glass partition above him—

And found himself staring at Reese's menacing four-pronged jaws—wide open, foully salivating—pressed up against the other side of the glass, only inches away.

Swain fell backwards, stumbled away from the glass.

Hawkins leapt to his feet, mouth agape.

Reese slammed against the partition, smearing saliva everywhere.

'Eyes down!' Swain yelled, snatching Holly up in his

arms. Reese rammed the partition again—hard—and the whole office shook. 'Keep your eyes away from the antennae! Go for the door!'

There were three glass doors to this square-shaped office—one west, one south and one east. Reese was banging on the western wall of the room.

Swain ran for the eastern door, threw it open and charged into the next office, Selexin and Hawkins close behind him.

With Holly in the crook of his arm, he slid smoothly over a desk in the centre of the office, opened the next door.

'Close the doors behind you!' he yelled back.

'Already doing it!' Hawkins called forward.

And then, from behind them, there came a loud crashing sound—the sound of breaking glass.

Up ahead, Swain continued to run. Over desks, through doorways, dodging filing cabinets, sending paper flying everywhere. Then he came out of the last office and was suddenly faced with something different.

A heavy blue door set into a solid concrete wall.

Hawkins was yelling, 'She's *coming*! And she seems really *pissed off*!'

Swain looked at the heavy blue door. It looked strong, with a hydraulic opening mechanism. At the end of the short corridor to his right, he saw another option—a glassed-in elevator bay. He glanced back at Hawkins racing through the offices behind him.

Better do something . . .

With Holly still in his arms, Swain turned the knob on the hydraulic door. It opened.

Three concrete stairs. Going down.

He stepped through the doorway, pulled Selexin with him and waited for Hawkins. Hawkins was running hard, through the last glass-walled office.

Beyond Hawkins, Swain could see nothing but offices divided by glass partitions.

And then he saw it. Saw the long pointed tail flashing up above the waist-high wood panelling. It was barging through anything that lay in its path—like a great white shark's fin slicing through water—launching desks and filing cabinets and swivel chairs high into the air.

Two offices away and heading directly toward them.

Moving fast.

Closing in.

Hawkins ran past Swain, through the doorway, and Swain shut the big hydraulic door behind him. It closed with a dull thud.

Strong door. Good. It would give them some time.

Holding Holly, Swain took the lead again, heading down the three concrete stairs. White fluorescent lights lit a modern grey-painted corridor. Black piping snaked its way along the ceiling.

The four of them followed the winding corridor for about twenty yards before, suddenly, they burst into open space.

Swain stopped and took in the scene before him.

An underground parking lot.

It looked new—almost brand new, in fact. Glistening newly paved concrete, white-painted floor markings, shiny yellow wheel clamps on the ground, pristine white fluorescent lights. It was quite a contrast to the old dusty library they had seen so far.

Swain scanned the parking lot.

No cars.

Damn.

There was a Down ramp in the centre of the lot, about twenty yards in front of them. Swain figured that the Exit ramp going up to the street must be on the other side of the Down ramp.

There came a sudden, loud bang from somewhere behind them.

Swain spun.

Reese was through the door.

He quickly led the others to the Down ramp. It was wide—wide enough for two cars to pass each other side-by-side. They had just reached the top of the ramp when he heard a hissing sound from behind them.

Swain turned around slowly.

Reese was standing at the entrance to the parking lot, her guide positioned silently behind her.

Swain swallowed—

—and then, suddenly, he heard another sound.

Clop . . .

Clop . . .

Clop . . .

Footsteps. Slow footsteps. Echoing loudly in the deserted parking lot.

Swain, Holly, Selexin and Hawkins all spun at the same time and they saw him instantly.

Coming up the Down ramp.

Walking slowly, purposefully.

A six-foot bearded man, dressed in a broad-shouldered animal-skin jacket, dark pants and knee-high black boots that clip-clopped loudly on the concrete ramp.

And behind him, yet another guide, dressed completely in white.

As the big bearded man stepped onto level ground and stopped, Swain instinctively pushed Holly behind him.

At the sight of the new contestant, Reese became visibly agitated. She hissed even louder.

They all stood in silence—the three groups forming a precarious, unspeaking triangle.

It was then that Swain looked down at his wristband. It now read:

INITIALISED—7

Seven.
Swain looked up slowly.

The Presidian had begun.

THIRD MOVEMENT

30 November, 6:39 p.m.

The parking lot was silent.

Somewhere off to his left Swain could hear the drone of New York traffic, the honking of car horns. The sounds of the outside world—the ordinary world.

Selexin drew up beside him.

'Just keep looking forward,' Selexin was staring intently at the tall bearded man before them.

'He is Balthazar. The Crisean. Small-blade handler: knives, stilettos, that sort of thing. Technologically, the Criseans are not well-developed, but with their hunting skills, they don't need tech—'

Selexin cut himself off.

The bearded man was staring right at them. Looking directly at Swain.

Swain kept his eyes locked on Balthazar.

Just then the big man turned slightly, revealing something hanging from his waist. Something that glinted under the harsh electric light of the parking lot.

A blade.

A sweeping, curving, vicious-looking blade. An extra-terrestrial cutlass.

Swain lifted his gaze. A thick leather-like baldric hung over Balthazar's shoulder, attaching itself to the belt at his waist. Fastened to the leather strap were various sheaths and scabbards—and in them, a whole assortment of lethal throwing knives.

'You see them?' Selexin whispered.

'I see them.'

'Criseans,' Selexin said respectfully. 'Very impressive bladesmen. Very quick, too. Fast. Take your eyes off him for a second and before you know it, you'll have a knife lodged in your heart.'

Swain didn't answer. Selexin turned to him.

'Sorry,' he whispered. 'I shouldn't have said that.'

'Daddy . . .' Holly said. 'What's happening?'

'We're just waiting, honey.'

With one eye on Balthazar, Swain scanned the parking lot. Looking for something . . . looking for a way out . . .

There.

In the south-west corner of the lot, maybe twenty yards away from them—a pair of elevators, encased inside a brightly lit glass-walled foyer. It was the same elevator bay he had seen earlier, only here it opened out onto the parking lot.

Swain handed Holly to Hawkins, at the same time as he pulled Hawkins' heavy police flashlight from his gunbelt.

'Whatever happens here,' Swain said, 'I want you to run as fast as you can to those elevators over there, okay?'

'Okay.'

'Once you're inside and the doors are shut, let it go halfway up a floor and press the Emergency Stop button. Okay?'

Hawkins nodded.

'You should be safe there,' Swain said, rolling the big flashlight over in his hand. 'I don't think they'll have figured out how to use elevators yet.'

Beside them, Selexin was watching the other two contestants warily. 'What happens now?' Swain asked him.

At first there was no reply. The little man just stared intently at the empty car park. And then, without turning his head, Selexin said, 'Anything.'

Reese moved first. Darting towards Swain. Heavy, bounding steps.

Swain felt adrenalin surge through his body. He swallowed, gripped the flashlight tightly.

Reese kept coming.

Christ, Swain thought, *how the hell do you fight a thing like that?*

He tensed to run, but suddenly Selexin grabbed his arm. '*Don't*,' he whispered. 'Not yet.'

'Wha—?' Swain watched Reese charge toward them.

'Trust me,' Selexin's voice was like ice.

Reese was *bounding* toward them now. Swain wanted desperately to run. Out of the corner of his eye he saw Balthazar slowly unsheath a pair of throwing knives—

And then Reese turned.

Sharply and unexpectedly. *Away* from Swain and the group.

Toward Balthazar.

'Ha! She had to,' Selexin whispered proudly. 'Had to. Classic huntsman behaviour . . .'

Then suddenly, in a blur of motion, Swain saw Balthazar's right arm move in a rapid throwing action— and abruptly two flashes of silver fanned out from his hand, whistling through the air.

Thud!

A glinting steel throwing knife embedded itself in the *concrete* pillar between Swain and Hawkins, missing them both by inches!

The second futuristic-looking knife was intended for Reese, but unlike Swain, she was ready for it. Running low and fast, she rolled right when she detected the flying blade coming toward her and—*crack!*—the throwing knife, flying downward, lodged in the floor of the parking lot underneath her, cracking the shiny new concrete, standing almost upright.

Selexin was still praising his tactical decision. 'I tell you, classic huntsman behaviour. You take out the more dangerous prey first, catch it off-guard—'

'Tell me about it later,' Swain said as he glanced over his shoulder to see Reese—shrieking wildly—slam into Balthazar, toppling him over backwards.

Swain pushed Hawkins toward the elevator bay. 'Go!'

Hawkins took off, holding Holly close to his chest, running straight for the elevators.

Swain was about to follow them when he turned for a final look at the battle behind him.

Reese had Balthazar pinned to the ground beneath her, jamming his hands down beneath her powerful stubby forelimbs. Balthazar was struggling desperately, reaching for his cutlass on the floor, inches out of his reach.

But the weight was too much.

Reese's jaws were salivating wildly above his head, the saliva gushing in heavy torrents all over Balthazar's face. And then Reese began to slash at him with her foreclaws—vicious sweeping slashes that drew whole chunks of flesh from Balthazar's chest.

It was disgusting, Swain thought. Disgusting, violent and brutal.

He watched in horror as Balthazar shook his head rapidly from side to side, screaming in pain trying to avoid eye contact with Reese's swaying antennae, trying to get his head clear of the blinding saliva, while at the same time feebly attempting to fend off her savage blows. It was *desperation*. The total and utter desperation of a man fighting for his very life.

And Stephen Swain felt angry. Indignant and furious at the whole scene in front of him.

He spun quickly to see Hawkins and Holly reach the glassed-in elevator bay and enter it. Hawkins quickly pressed the UP button on the wall. Neither of the two elevators opened immediately. The lifts were on the way.

They'd be safe.

Swain turned back to face the battle, the anger welling up inside him. Balthazar was still struggling, swishing his head from side to side, his cries of pain drowned out by the saliva gushing down into his screaming mouth. Reese was still firmly on top of him, violently slashing, squealing maniacally.

And then Swain saw Reese's tail rise. Slowly and silently behind her, like an enormous scorpion, out of Balthazar's view.

And with that, Swain knew what he had to do.

He ran.

Straight at them.

Reese's tail was poised now, arcing high over her head . . . ready to strike . . . and then Balthazar saw it too and he began to scream . . .

With Hawkins' heavy police flashlight in front of him, Swain slammed into Reese, knocking her off Balthazar, sending all three of them sprawling onto the concrete floor.

Reese fell onto her back and Swain tumbled on top of her. She let out an ear-piercing shriek as her body writhed about on the concrete, bucking and kicking, trying desperately to throw Swain clear.

Swain's grip on her slipped and suddenly he was in mid-air and all he could see was a kaleidoscope of grey walls, white fluorescent light and concrete pavement. He hit the floor hard, chest-first, and rolled onto his back—

—only to see Reese's sharp tail rushing toward his face!

Swain swerved his head left and the tail hit the concrete with a loud thud.

Swain glanced quickly at the spot where his head had been. Broken chunks of cement surrounded a small crater the size of a tennis ball in the concrete floor.

Jesus Christ.

Swain was still on the floor, rolling fast. Reese was crab-walking next to him, moving equally fast, banging her tail down like a piledriver.

The tail came crashing down again, *right next to Swain's head*.

In the nanoseconds of time in which the mind operates, Swain tried to weigh up his options. He couldn't run. There was no way he could get up and clear in time. And he couldn't *fight* Reese. Christ, if a warrior like Balthazar couldn't beat her, how the hell could he?

No, somehow he had to get out of here. But to do that, he had to do something that would buy him enough time to get clear.

And so Swain did the only thing he could think to do.

With all his strength he swung Hawkins' heavy police flashlight—baseball-style—at Reese's tail, planted in the concrete.

He aimed for the tip of the tail, the thinnest part, from the side.

The flashlight hit its mark—hard—impacting against the tapered tip of the tail. There was a loud, blood-curdling *snap!* of breaking bone as the tail bent instantly and Reese roared in agony, instantly pulling away from Swain.

Swain seized the chance.

He leapt to his feet and looked over at the two elevators inside the glass-walled foyer. The doors to the left-hand elevator were opening and Hawkins, carrying

Holly, was getting inside, looking back questioningly at Swain with every step.

'Go! *Go!*' Swain yelled. 'I'll catch up!'

Hawkins ducked inside the elevator and hit a button and the elevator doors closed. Swain swung back to the fight.

Reese had backed off several steps, consumed with her broken tail. Balthazar was now rising unsteadily to his feet, his head bent as he tried to clear the saliva from his eyes.

Swain stumbled over to Balthazar. The big man's eyes were still covered in gooey saliva, the exposed skin on his chest horribly shredded and caked in thick blood, his face locked in a grimace of extreme pain.

Swain grabbed his arm and simply said, 'Come with me.'

Balthazar said nothing, merely allowed Swain to take his arm and pull him away. Swain looped the big man's arm over his shoulder and helped him towards the elevators.

Selexin just stood there, gaping at Swain in utter amazement.

'You coming?' Swain said as he dragged Balthazar past the little man.

Stunned, Selexin looked from Swain to Balthazar's guide—who just shrugged uncomprehendingly—then to

Reese, and then finally to the elevators. Then he hurried after Swain.

Swain burst into the glass-walled elevator bay, hit the UP button. Balthazar was still draped over his shoulder, his guide right behind him. Swain spun to see Reese banging her tail on the concrete floor. Two loud bangs were followed by a third that emitted a sickening cracking sound.

Reese roared savagely and Swain knew at once what that meant. She had straightened the fracture. Once she was over the instant pain she would be moving again—

Reese was moving again. Toward the elevator.

Swain jammed his finger down on the UP button. 'Come on! Come on!'

Reese was darting left and right, scuttling in a crab-like manner across the wide parking lot floor, coming closer . . .

She stopped. Fifteen yards away from the elevator bay.

Swain noticed that this time her tail didn't swish menacingly back and forth behind her. It just sat there, limp on the floor, motionless.

Reese hissed softly in the silence of the parking lot, her antennae swaying hypnotically above her head. Swain watched her through the glass walls of the elevator bay, entranced.

Selexin shoved him hard, jolting him sideways. '*Don't* look at the antennae!'

Swain blinked back to his senses. He couldn't even *remember* looking at the antennae . . .

There was a loud *bing* from behind him and he spun to see the second elevator's doors grinding open.

'Everybody inside,' he said, suddenly back to life, hurling Balthazar into the lift. Once inside, he hurriedly pressed '1' and then **DOOR CLOSE**.

Nothing happened.

Swain looked out and saw Reese bounding toward the glass elevator bay.

He pressed **DOOR CLOSE** repeatedly.

The doors remained open.

Reese was getting closer, charging.

Suddenly there was a click and the elevator doors slowly began to close.

Smash!

Glass exploded everywhere as Reese burst through the clear glass door of the elevator bay. She landed clumsily inside the small foyer, sliding across the floor on a carpet of tiny glass fragments, sprawled out on all four legs.

The doors were inching closer.

And then, to Swain's horror, Reese slid to a halt *right in front of the elevator* and started getting to her feet.

The doors kept closing. Reese was on her feet again. The doors were almost joined. Reese tensed herself to leap—

And the doors joined.

And the lift began to move upward.

Swain exhaled with relief.

And then with all her weight Reese hit the exterior doors.

Hard and loud. Denting the doors inward, tearing them apart at the centre, shaking the whole elevator and *stopping* it with a loud scraping lurch.

Two feet above the ground.

The lift rocked. Selexin clutched at Swain's leg for balance. Balthazar sat in the rear corner, head bent, body limp, swaying with the elevator's movement.

Swain regained his balance and saw the doors, pushed inward, creating a gap one foot wide at the centre.

Too narrow, he thought. *She can't get in.*

Reese rammed the doors again.

The elevator shook. The gap widened.

Swain pressed the UP button on the panel, but the elevator still didn't move. The large inward dent in the doors was keeping them from closing, and the lift wouldn't move again until they were shut.

Reese now had her snout and antennae inside the elevator doors. She was snapping her jaws ferociously from side to side, flinging saliva everywhere, desperately trying to force the doors open—her antennae slicing through the air like twin whips.

Swain tightened his grip on Hawkins' flashlight and stepped toward her.

Suddenly Reese surged forward, rocking the elevator. Swain fell, slipping on the wet floor, falling backwards, the flashlight flying from his hand into the corner of the lift. He looked up to see Reese lunging ferociously at his feet, snapping wildly, held back by the doors—saw the frenzied, salivating jaws, the four sets of bared, jagged teeth only inches away from his feet. About to—

Swain turned his eyes clear, took a deep breath and in a flashing instant thought, *I can't believe I am going to do this*. Then he kicked hard, landing the sole of his shoe squarely on Reese's front teeth, breaking three instantly.

Reese recoiled, shrieking fiercely as she fell backwards onto the floor below.

Swain kicked again, this time at the doors, in a vain attempt to straighten the large inward dents. He gave them three hammering blows, but barely made an impression. The doors were double-strength, too strong.

And then suddenly—*whack!*—a giant leather boot came crashing down on the battered doors, and the dents straightened markedly.

It was Balthazar!

He had slid over to where Swain was lying and,

despite his injuries, had unleashed a powerful kick of his own at the doors.

Whack! Whack!

Two more thunderous blows and the dents straightened fully and the doors eased shut and Balthazar fell to the floor in exhaustion and the elevator lifted and at last, there was silence.

'Grid two-twelve,' the assistant said, reading from his clipboard. 'The area bounded by 14th Street and Delancey on the north–south axis. Medium rise zone: standard commercial–residential area, couple of buildings on the National Register, a few parks. Nothing special.'

Robert K. Charlton sat back in his chair.

'Nothing special,' he said. 'Nothing special, except that in the last couple of hours, we've had over *a hundred and eighty* complaints from an area that hardly ever says boo.'

He handed a sheet of paper over his desk to his assistant.

'Take a look at that. It's from the switch. One girl down there has had—what is it now?—fifty-one, no, fifty-two probable 401s on her own. All from two-twelve.'

Slightly overweight, 54 years old, and a man who had spent *way* too much time in the same job, Bob Charlton was the evening watch supervisor for Consolidated

Edison, the city's main electricity supplier. His office was situated one floor above Con Ed's switchboard and it was hardly ostentatious. It comprised a wraparound Ikea desk—with a computer on it—surrounded by that beige-coloured shelving common to middle-management offices the world over.

'And do you know what that means?' Charlton asked.

'What?' his assistant said. His name was Rudy.

'It means that somebody has got to the main,' Charlton said. 'Cut it off. Shut it down. Or maybe even overloaded it. Shit. Run down to Dispatch and see if any of our guys were down in that grid today. I'll give the cops a call, see if they've found any punks cutting cables.'

'Yes, sir.'

Rudy left the room.

Charlton swung around in his swivel chair to face a map of Manhattan Island he had pinned to the wall behind his desk.

To Charlton, Manhattan looked like a warped diamond—three perfectly straight sides, with one side, the north-eastern, jagged and twisted. Electrical grids stretched across the island's breadth like lines on a football field.

He found the horizontal rectangle that displayed grid two-twelve. It was down near the southern end of the island, a few miles north of the World Trade Centre.

He thought about the report.

Medium rise zone. Standard commercial–residential area, couple of buildings on the National Register. A few parks.

The National Register.

The National Register of Historic Places.

He thought about that. Lately Con Ed had been bullied by the Mayor's Office into linking up some of the older buildings of the city to the new mains. Not surprisingly, there had been a truckload of problems. Some of the older buildings had circuitry dating back before the First World War, others didn't even have circuitry. Linking them up had been unusually difficult and it wasn't uncommon for one building's overload to screw up the networking for an entire city grid.

Charlton flicked on his computer and called up the file on the National Register. It wouldn't have *all* the historically protected buildings in the city, only the ones that Con Ed had worked on. That would be good enough.

He called up grid two-twelve. There were five hits. He pressed DISPLAY.

The screen scrolled out a more detailed list of names and Charlton was leaning forward to read them when the phone rang.

'Charlton.'

'Sir, it's me.' It was Rudy.

'Yes?'

155

'I'm down in Dispatch, and they say that none of their guys has been in two-twelve for nearly three weeks.'

Charlton frowned. 'You sure?'

'They've got records on disk if you want them.'

'No, that will be fine. Well done, Rudy.'

'Thank you, si—'

Charlton hung up.

'Damn.'

He was hoping it had been someone from Dispatch. At least then it would have been traceable. There would be a record of where the break—or shutdown, or overload—in the main was. A record of where the work had been done.

Now there was no knowing where the break was. Other shorts could be detected with Con Ed's computers, tracing every line. But for that you needed the main to be on-line.

But with the main down in a particular grid, that grid became a black hole as far as computer tracing was concerned. And the break lay somewhere within that black hole.

Now it was guesswork.

Charlton swore. The first thing to do was call the police. See if they had pulled in someone in the last twenty-four hours hacking at the cables somewhere. Anything like that.

He sighed. It was going to be a long night. He picked up the phone and dialled.

'Good evening, this is Bob Charlton, I'm the evening watch supervisor down here at Consolidated Edison. I'd like to speak with Lieutenant Peters, please. Yes, I'll hold.'

As he waited on hold, Charlton looked idly back at the map of Manhattan Island. Soon his call was put through and he turned away from the map altogether.

All the while the computer screen on his desk remained on.

And for the whole time he was on the phone, Bob Charlton never noticed the last line of the list of historic buildings on the screen. The line read:

GRID 212: LISTING No. 5
NEW YORK STATE LIBRARY (1897)
CONNECTED TO NETWORK: 17 FEBRUARY
1995

After a few moments, Charlton said excitedly, 'You *did*—when? I'll be down there in twenty minutes.' Then he hung up, grabbed his coat and quickly left his office.

A few seconds later, he returned and leaned across his desk.

And switched off his computer.

Swain pressed the red EMERGENCY STOP button and the elevator creaked loudly to a halt. He reached up for the hatch in the ceiling.

Balthazar, his energy now completely spent after repairing the elevator doors, sat propped up against the corner of the lift, his head bowed, groaning. His guide stood unsympathetically beside him, glaring at Selexin.

Swain was opening the hatch in the ceiling of the elevator when the other guide spoke. 'Come on, Selexin, get on with it.' He nodded at Balthazar. 'Finish it.'

Swain stopped what he was doing and turned to face the others.

Selexin said, 'That is not for me to decide. You of all people know that.'

The other guide spun to face Swain. '*Well?* Look at him'—a jerk toward Balthazar in the corner—'he cannot fight anymore. He cannot even defend himself. Finish it. Finish it now. Our fight is over.'

Swain swallowed. The little guide possessed an

unusual strength in his defiance—the strength of a man who knows he is about to die.

'Yes,' Swain said slowly to himself. 'Yes.'

He looked again at Balthazar. It was only then that he noticed just how big the bearded man was. Not six foot. More like six-eight. But that didn't seem to matter now.

Balthazar lifted his head and stared up at Swain. His eyes were severely bloodshot, red-rimmed; his chest ripped to shreds.

Swain took a slow step forward and stood over him.

Selexin must have noticed his hesitation. 'You must,' he said, softly. 'You have to.'

Balthazar never took his eyes off Swain. The big bearded man took a deep breath as Swain reached down and slowly—very slowly—unsheathed one of the long daggers from the baldric draped across his chest. The dagger hissed against the sheath as Swain pulled it out.

Balthazar shut his eyes, resigned to his fate, unable to offer any defence.

Knife in hand, Swain shot a final questioning glance at Selexin. The little man nodded solemnly.

Swain turned back to Balthazar, lowered the knife, pointed it at the big man's heart. And then he did it.

He slid the blade gently back into its sheath.

And then he stepped away, back toward the hatch in the ceiling of the elevator, back to what he'd been doing.

Balthazar's eyes opened, puzzled.

Selexin rolled his eyes.

The other guide was simply thunderstruck. He said to Selexin, 'He can't do that.' Then to Swain, who was back at the ceiling, tossing open the hatch, 'You can't do that.'

'I just did,' Swain said. The hatch banged open.

He turned, not looking at the other guide, but rather, straight at Selexin. 'Because that's not what I do.'

With that, Swain grabbed Hawkins' police flashlight and poked his head up through the open hatch. He had something else on his mind.

He peered up into the dark elevator shaft, flicking on the flashlight. He was hoping that Hawkins had done what he had told him to do.

He had.

The other elevator lay right there, only a few feet away, right alongside Swain's elevator, halted halfway between this floor and the one above. Swain aimed the beam of the flashlight up into the shaft. Greasy cables stretched up into the darkness. The doors to the next floor were about eight feet above him. On them were written the black-painted words: **GROUND FLOOR**.

The shaft was silent.

The other elevator sat still, perhaps a foot above Swain's, a small slit of yellow light betraying a crack in its side panelling.

'Holly? Hawkins?' Swain whispered.

He heard Holly's voice—'Daddy!'—and he felt a wave of relief wash over him.

'We're here, sir,' Hawkins' voice said. 'Are you all right?'

'We're fine here. How about you two?'

'We're okay. Want us to come over?'

'No. You stay where you are,' Swain said. 'Our elevator has taken a beating, the doors are busted. They probably won't open again, so we'll come over there. See if you can open the hatch in the roof.'

'Okay.'

Swain dropped back into his elevator and surveyed the group around him—Balthazar and the two guides. Hmmm.

'All right, everyone, listen up. We're all going over to the other elevator. I want you two little guys to go first. I'll handle the big fella. Got it?'

Selexin nodded. The other guide just stood there, his arms folded defiantly.

Swain scooped up Selexin and held him up to the hatch. The little man disappeared into the darkness.

Swain poked his head up through the hatch after him and saw Selexin step up onto the roof of the other elevator. A weak haze of yellow light appeared above the other lift. Hawkins must have opened the hatch.

Swain motioned to the other guide. 'Your turn.'

The guide looked cautiously at Balthazar, then said something in a grunting guttural language.

Balthazar responded with a dismissive wave and grunt.

As a result, the guide reluctantly offered his arms to Swain, who duly lifted him up through the hatch. The guide disappeared into the shaft.

Swain turned back to face Balthazar.

The big man was still sitting slumped in the corner. Slowly, he looked up at Swain.

Whatever he was, Swain thought, he was badly injured. His eyes were red, his hands bloodied and scratched. Some of Reese's saliva still bubbled on his beard.

Swain spoke gently, 'I don't want to kill you. I want to help you.'

Balthazar cocked his head, not understanding.

'Help,' Swain held out his hands, palms up—a gesture of aid, not attack.

Balthazar spoke—softly—in his strange guttural tongue.

Swain didn't understand. He offered his hands again.

'Help,' he repeated.

Balthazar frowned at the communication breakdown. He reached down for the long dagger Swain had held before, now back in its sheath across his chest.

He pulled it out.

Swain stood dead still—unflinching—staring Baltha-zar squarely in the eye.

He can't do that. He can't.

The bearded man reversed the knife in his hand, and placed the handle in Swain's palm. Swain felt the warmth of Balthazar's hand as they both gripped the knife—pointed at Balthazar's chest.

Balthazar then pulled their hands toward his chest. Swain didn't know what to do, except allow Balthazar to pull the glistening blade closer, and closer, and closer to his body . . .

And then Balthazar guided their hands sideways, sliding the knife back into its sheath.

As Swain had done before.

He looked up at Swain, his eyes bulging red, and nodded.

And then Balthazar spoke again—slowly, deep-throated—trying to get his mouth around the word Swain had just used.

'Help.'

The elevator doors rumbled open and Stephen Swain peered out to see the First Floor of the State Library.

Dark and quiet.

Empty.

The first thing Swain noticed about the First Floor was the peculiar way it had been arranged: it was an enormous U-shape, with a wide gaping hole in the centre, so that one could look down onto the Ground Floor atrium.

Clearly, the floorspace of this floor had been sacrificed to provide for a grander, higher-ceilinged Ground Floor—in the process, making the First Floor of the State Library little more than a glorified balcony. A mezzanine.

The elevators themselves stood at the south-east corner of the floor, to the right of the curved base of the U-shape. Opposite them—at the open-end of the U—stood the enormous glass doors of the library's main entrance.

Off to his left, Swain saw a room filled with photo-copiers. A door at the far end of the room had **INTERNET FACILITY** stamped on it. The rest of the floor was deserted and dark, save for the blue streams of reflected city light that penetrated the enormous glass doors and windows way over at the other end.

Swain pulled Balthazar out of the lift and dragged him over to the hand-railing overlooking the Ground Floor. He was propping the big man up against the railing when the others joined them.

'What do we do about that?' Hawkins said, indicating the open elevator behind them. He spoke softly in the darkness.

'Turn the light off,' Swain whispered. 'If you can't find the switch, just unscrew the fluorescent tube. Apart from that,' he shrugged, 'I don't know, leave it there. As long as it's here, nobody else can use it.'

As Hawkins headed back toward the elevator, Swain saw Selexin draw up alongside him. The little man was peering cautiously up at the ceiling all around them.

'What are you doing?' Swain asked.

Selexin sighed dramatically: 'Not all the creatures in this universe walk on *floors*, Mister Swain.'

'Oh.'

'I am looking for a contestant known as the Rachnid. It is a trap-laying species—large and spindly, but not particularly athletic—known for lying in wait in elevated caves and hollows for long periods of time, waiting for its prey to step underneath it. It then lowers itself silently to the floor behind its victim, clutches it within its eight limbs, and constricts it to death.'

'Constricts it to death,' Swain said, glancing nervously up at the uneven shadow-covered ceiling above him. 'Nice. Very nice.'

'Daddy?' Holly whispered.

'Yes, honey.'

'I'm scared.'

'Me too,' Swain said softly.

Holly touched his left cheek. 'Are you all right, Daddy?'

Swain looked at her finger. It had blood on it.

He dabbed at his cheek. It felt like a cut, a big one, running down the length of his cheekbone. He looked down at his collar and saw a large red stain on it—a lot of blood had been running down his face.

When had that happened? He hadn't felt it. And he certainly didn't remember feeling the sting of being cut. Maybe it was when he was thrown on top of Reese, after bowling her over. Or when Reese was bucking and kicking like a mad horse. Swain frowned. It was a blur. He couldn't remember.

'Yeah, I'm okay,' he said.

Holly nodded at Balthazar, up against the steel railing. 'What about him?'

'Actually, I was just about to check,' Swain said, getting up onto his knees, hovering over Balthazar. 'Could you hold this for me?' he offered Holly the heavy police flashlight.

Holly flicked on the torch and held it over Swain's shoulder, pointed at Balthazar's face.

The big man winced at the light. Swain leaned forward, 'No, no, don't shut your eyes,' he said gently. He held Balthazar's left eye open. It was heavily blood-shot, reacting badly to Reese's saliva.

'Could you bring the light in a bit closer . . .'

Holly stepped forward and as the light came nearer, Swain saw Balthazar's pupil dilate.

Swain leaned back. That wasn't right . . .

His eyes swept over Balthazar's body. Everything about him suggested that he was human—limbs, fingers, facial features. He even had brown eyes.

The eyes, Swain thought.

It was the eyes that were wrong. Their reaction to the light.

Human pupils *contract* when hit by direct light. They dilate—or widen—in darkness or poor light, so as to allow as much light as possible onto the retina. These eyes, however, dilated in the face of brighter light.

They were not human eyes.

Swain turned to Selexin. 'He looks human, and he acts human. But he's not human at all, is he?'

Selexin nodded, impressed. 'No, he is not. Almost, though—in fact, as close as he can be. But no, Balthazar is definitely not human.'

'Then what is he?'

'I told you before, Balthazar is a Crisean. An excellent blade-handler.'

'But why does he look human?' Swain asked. 'The chances of some alien from another world evolving to look exactly like man would have to be a million to one.'

'A billion to one,' Selexin corrected him. 'And please, try not to use the term "alien" *too* liberally. Such a harsh word. And besides, in your current situation, aliens do form the standing majority.'

'Sorry.'

'Nevertheless,' Selexin went on, 'you are correct. Balthazar is not human, nor is his form. Balthazar, and for that matter one other contestant named Bellos, is amorphic. Able to alter his form.'

'Alter his form?'

'Yes. Alter his exterior shape. Just as your chameleon can change its skin colour to blend in with its surroundings, so too can Balthazar and Bellos do the same, only they do not alter their colour: they alter their entire external shape. And it makes sense. One makes one's self human when competing in a human labyrinth, because any doors or handles or potential weapons will all be made for the human form.'

'Uh-huh,' Swain said, turning back to attend to Balthazar.

Hawkins came back from the elevator.

'It took a bit of doing,' he said, 'but I finally got the tube out of its—'

Swain held Balthazar's other eye open, peering at it under the light of the flashlight.

'Out of its . . . what?' he said, not turning around.

Hawkins didn't reply.

Swain looked up. 'What is it—' he cut himself off.

Hawkins was staring out over the railing, at the Ground Floor atrium down below. Swain swivelled around, following Hawkins' gaze down into the atrium.

'*Oh my God*,' he said slowly. And then quickly he turned to Holly, reaching for the flashlight. 'Quick, turn it off.'

The flashlight went out. Blue moonlight covered them again and Stephen Swain peered out over the railing.

The man was just standing there. Tall and black. Two tapering horns rising high above his head. The soft moonlight glinted off the lustrous gold metal attached to his chest.

He was standing next to a glass display case down in the atrium. Just standing there, staring intently into one of the aisles in front of him, at something out of Swain's view.

Swain felt a chill.

He's not staring, he thought. *He's stalking.*

Selexin came up beside him.

'Bellos,' he whispered, not taking his eyes off the horned man in the atrium below. There was a sense of awe in his voice, a reverence that was unmistakable. 'The Malonian contestant. Malonians are the most lethal huntsmen in the galaxy. Trophy collectors. They have won more Presidia than any other species. Why, they even conduct a six-way internal hunt to determine who amongst them will compete in the Presidian.'

Swain watched as he listened. The horned man—Bellos—was a magnificent specimen of a man. Tall and broad-shouldered, built like a house, and, except for his golden chest, completely dressed in black. An imposing figure.

'Remember. Amorphic,' Selexin said. 'It makes sense to adopt the human form. Makes better sense to adopt a *highly developed* human form.'

Swain was about to reply when he heard Hawkins whisper behind him, '*Oh Christ*, where's Parker?'

Swain frowned. Hawkins had said something about that before. Parker was his partner. Stationed in here for the night with him. Maybe she was still here, somewhere inside . . .

'*Salve, moriturum es!*'

The voice boomed throughout the atrium. Swain jumped, a wave of ice-cold blood shooting through his veins.

He's seen us!

'Greetings, fellow competitor. Before you stands Bellos . . .'

Swain's mind was racing. Where could they go? They'd have a good head start. They were still one whole floor above him.

'. . . Great-grandson of Trome, the winner of the Fifth Presidian. And like his great-grandfather and two Malonians before him, Bellos shall emerge from this battle alone, conquered by none and not undone by the Karanadon. Who be'st thou, my worthy and yet unfortunate opponent?'

Swain swallowed. He took a deep breath and was about to stand up and reply when he heard another noise—a strange clicking–hissing noise.

Coming from below.

From somewhere else in the atrium.

Swain dropped like a stone, out of sight. Bellos hadn't seen them.

He was challenging someone else.

And then, slowly, another contestant came into view. From the left. A dark, skeletal shadow creeping slowly amongst the bookcases.

It moved stealthily toward Bellos.

Whatever it was, it was large—at least six feet long—but thin, insect-like, with long angular limbs not unlike those of a grasshopper, that clung to the vertical side of one of the bookcases. Although Swain couldn't see its face very well, he could see that its sinister-looking head was partially covered by a steel, mask-like object. Its movements were accompanied by a strange mechanical breathing noise.

'What is it?' he whispered.

'It is the Konda,' Selexin said. '*Very* vicious warrior species from the outer regions; remarkably evolved insectoid physique; and, according to those who gamble on the Presidian, highly fancied to take it out. Keep your eyes on its two foreclaws—the tips of each thumbnail secrete a highly poisonous venom. If the Konda punctures your skin and then inserts its thumbnail into the wound, believe me, you will die screaming. Its only weakness: its lungs cannot handle the toxicity of your atmosphere, hence the breathing apparatus.'

The Konda was getting closer to Bellos, an ominous shadow moving steadily along the vertical sides of the bookcases.

Bellos didn't move. He just stood beside the display case, rooted to the spot.

Swain felt a strange sensation as he looked down on the atrium. A kind of voyeuristic thrill to be watching something that no-one else would ever see. That no-one would ever want to see.

The Konda crept cautiously toward Bellos, picking up speed as it closed in—

Suddenly, Bellos held up his hand.

The grasshopper-like Konda stopped instantly.

Swain frowned.

Why had it—?

And then something else caught his eye.

Something in the foreground, something *in between* Swain and the Konda.

It was small and black—a shadow superimposed on the darkness—slinking swiftly and silently across the bare wooden tops of the bookshelves, heading towards the Konda from behind.

From behind.

Swain watched in amazement as another identical creature made its way across the tops of the bookshelves from the other direction. Its movements resembled that of a cat. Menacing in its supreme stealth.

Selexin saw them, too.

'Oh, sweet Lords,' he breathed, '*hoodaya.*'

Swain turned to face the little man. Selexin was staring off into space, wide-eyed and white with fear.

Swain spun back around.

Two more of the small creatures—each about the size of a dog—were creeping on all fours across the tops of the bookshelves, jumping easily from top to top, across the aisles below. Swain saw their jet-black heads— saw their long needle-like teeth and their bony but muscular limbs—saw their thin snaking tails swishing menacingly behind them.

Selexin was whispering to himself: 'He can't do that. He *can't*. Good lord, *hoodaya*.'

The four smaller creatures—hoodaya, Swain guessed—had now formed a wide circle above the aisle containing the insect-like Konda.

The Konda hadn't moved an inch. It hadn't noticed them.

Not yet.

Bellos lowered his hand. And then he turned away.

Swain saw the Konda immediately shift its weight.

It hasn't got a clue, he thought as he gripped the railing. *Hasn't got a prayer . . .*

It was then that the four hoodaya leapt down from their perches.

Into the aisle below.

Hideous, high-pitched, *alien* shrieks filled the atrium. The bookshelves on either side of the aisle shook as the Konda flung itself violently from side to side in the face of the sudden onslaught.

Swain saw Hawkins' face go blank with horror. Selexin was just stunned. Swain pulled Holly close to him, turned her face away from the scene, 'Don't watch, honey.'

The godawful shrieking continued.

And then, without warning, the near bookcase fell over and suddenly Swain saw the whole grisly scene—saw the Konda, screaming madly, completely covered by the four hoodaya, its two venom-tipped forelimbs splayed wide, pinned to the ground by two of the hoods, while the other two attack creatures tore ferociously at its face and stomach. In seconds the Konda's steel breathing mask was ripped from its head and the hapless creature's shrieks became desperate, hoarse gasps.

And then, abruptly, the pained gasping stopped and the Konda's body slumped to the ground, limp.

But the hoodaya didn't stop. Swain saw their long needle-like teeth open wide and plunge into its hide. Blood spurted out in all directions as one hoodaya ripped a large chunk of flesh from the Konda's carcass and held it aloft in triumph.

Swain's head snapped left as he heard another noise.

Footsteps.

Rapid footsteps. Soft, barely audible, getting softer. Running away.

One of the hoods heard it, too—lifted its head from its feeding. It leapt from its mount on the Konda's body and raced off into the nearest aisle, heading for the stairwell.

Swain didn't know what was going on until he heard a stumbling noise, like someone being crash-tackled to the floor.

And then he heard another scream—a desperate, pathetic yelp—that stopped no sooner than it had begun.

Swain heard Selexin gulp next to him and he realised.

It had been the guide. The Konda's guide. Swain saw the look on Selexin's face. The other guide had never stood a chance.

Swain looked back at the dead Konda and the hoods on top of it.

'Selexin.'

No reply.

Selexin was simply staring into space, in shock.

'*Selexin*,' he whispered, nudging the little man back to his senses.

'W . . . what?'

'Quickly,' Swain said harshly, trying to get Selexin out of his daze. 'Tell me about them. These hoodaya, or whatever the hell it is you call them.'

Selexin swallowed. 'Hoods are hunting animals. Bellos is a hunter. Bellos uses hoods to hunt. Simple.'

'Hey,' Swain said. 'Just tell me, okay.'

'Why? It won't matter. Not anymore.'

'Why not?'

'Mister Swain, I commend you. Your previous efforts had until now given me some hope of survival. Already you have exceeded any previous human effort in the Presidian. But now,' Selexin was talking quickly, desperately, 'now I have the misfortune to tell you that you have just witnessed the signing of your own death warrant.'

'What?'

'You cannot win. The Presidian is over. Bellos has defiled the rules. If he is discovered, which he won't be because he is too clever, he will be disqualified—killed. But if he isn't, *he will win*. No-one can escape Bellos if he has hoods. They are the ultimate hunter's tool. Remorseless and vicious. With them by his side, Bellos is unstoppable.'

Selexin shook his head.

'Do you remember the Karanadon?' he said, pointing to the green light on Swain's wristband.

'Yes.' Swain had actually forgotten about it, but he didn't tell Selexin that.

'Only one hunter being has ever successfully killed a Karanadon in the wild. And do you know who that was?'

'Tell me.'

'Bellos. *With his hoods.*'

'Great.'

There was an awkward silence.

Then Swain said, 'Okay then, how did he get them here? If he was brought here just like I was, wouldn't you guys have made sure that he didn't bring anything with him?'

'That's exactly right, but there must have been a way . . . something he found that no-one thought of . . . some way to teleport them in—'

'Hey,' Hawkins touched Swain's shoulder. 'He's doing something.'

Bellos was bent over the Konda's body, doing something that Swain couldn't see. When at last he stood, Bellos had the Konda's breathing mask in his hands. A trophy.

He fastened the mask to a loop on his belt, and then he barked a sharp order to the three hoods that were still feasting on the Konda's torso. They immediately jumped off the dead contestant's body and stood behind Bellos, at the same time as the fourth hood returned from the stairwell, large shreds of blood-stained white cloth dangling from its teeth and claws.

Then Bellos walked over to a semi-circular desk in the middle of the atrium. Swain could just make out the words on the sign hanging above it: INFORMATION.

Behind him, he heard Hawkins take a quick breath.

Bellos bent down behind the Information Desk, picked up something in one of his large black hands and carried it back over to the Konda's body.

As soon as he saw it, Swain knew what it was. It was small, white and limp. Bellos' own guide.

Bellos said something quickly, and the hoods darted behind the Information Desk. Then he draped his guide's lifeless body over his shoulder and pointed it toward the dead contestant.

'*Initialise!*' Bellos said, loudly.

Instantly, a small sphere of brilliant white light appeared above the dead guide's head, illuminating the wide open space of the atrium. Instinctively, Swain bent lower behind the railing, away from the light. The white sphere glowed for about five seconds until it vanished abruptly and the atrium was dark once more.

Selexin turned solemnly to Swain. 'That, Mister Swain, was Bellos confirming his first kill.'

Swain turned to the group gathered around him. 'I think it's time to get out of here.'

'I think you're right,' Hawkins was already moving away from the railing.

Swain grabbed Balthazar and heaved him onto his shoulder. 'Holly,' he whispered, 'quick honey, the elevator.'

'Okay.'

He turned to Hawkins, 'We'll go back to the elevator. Stop it between floors again. That's been the safest place to hide so far.'

'Fine by me,' Hawkins said.

Swain began dragging Balthazar away from the railing, with Holly by his side and Hawkins, Selexin and Balthazar's guide in front. They all headed for the open, darkened elevator.

And then it happened.

The elevator's doors began to close.

Swain shot a look at Hawkins, who immediately

dashed forward, trying to get to the doors in time. But the doors joined just as he got there.

'Damn it!' he cursed.

Swain came up beside him, looked up at the numbered display above the elevator doors. The illuminated number was moving down the line from 1 to G and then to SL-1.

'The elevator . . .' he whispered.

'Jesus Christ,' Hawkins said, realising, '*they figured out how to use the goddamn elevator.*'

'They're intelligent—' Selexin said.

'They're *animals*, for God's sake,' Hawkins said, perhaps a little too loudly.

'Alien, yes. Animal, no,' Selexin whispered. 'I would say understanding a contraption like your elevator would be regarded as remarkably intelligent.'

Hawkins was about to say something in retort when Swain cut in, 'All right. It doesn't matter. We'll find somewhere else to . . .'

'Hey Daddy, don't be silly,' Holly said, standing next to the elevator call button. 'I can get the elevator back for you.'

Swain's eyes went wide with horror.

'Holly, no!' He lunged to stop her, but it was too late.

Holly pressed the UP button.

Swain closed his eyes and bowed his head. The round

181

UP button glowed brightly in the darkness of the First Floor.

He couldn't believe it. Now, whoever was using the lift wouldn't even have to *guess* which floor they were on. Nor would they even have to figure out how to use the elevator. Because now that Holly had pressed the call button, once the elevator picked up its new passenger, it would *automatically* stop here, on the First Floor.

Holly said, 'What did I do? Didn't I do the right thing, Daddy?'

Swain sighed, 'Yes. Thank you, honey. You did the right thing.' He handed Balthazar over to Hawkins, and walked quietly back to the balcony overlooking the atrium.

Bellos was still standing behind the Information Desk, putting down his guide, oblivious to their presence.

At least that's good, Swain turned back toward the elevator, head down in thought. They still had to go. Something would be coming up in that elevator very soon and he didn't want to be here when it did.

Finally he looked up toward the elevator.

Holly was staring straight at him.

Selexin and the other guide both stood there with their mouths wide open.

Hawkins was just standing there, too, propping up Balthazar, staring fixedly at Swain.

But it was Balthazar who seized Swain's attention.

The tall bearded man had his left arm draped over Hawkins' shoulder for support. His right was held high, a glistening, evil-looking silver blade in his hand.

Poised.

Ready.

Swain didn't know what to do. What had happened? Balthazar was ready to throw a knife at him and the others weren't doing anything . . .

Balthazar threw the knife.

Swain waited for the impact. Waited to grab his chest and feel the burning pain as the blade lodged deep into his heart . . .

The knife whistled through the air at astonishing speed.

Right past him.

Swain heard a thud as the nasty-looking knife lodged into the railing behind him. The *steel* railing.

Then Swain heard the scream.

A piercing, wailing scream of pure agony.

Swain spun to see that Balthazar's knife had pinned the hood's left foreclaw to the steel railing. The force of the throw was so strong that it had lodged the knife several inches into the steel. It had caught the hood as it had been attempting to climb over the railing from the Ground Floor below—*right behind Swain.*

The hood screamed, and for an instant Swain saw its

features up close. Four muscular black limbs, all with long dagger-like claws; a long slashing tail; and strangest of all, the head. It seemed as if the head of this dog-sized animal was nothing more than two gigantic jaws. There were eyes on it somewhere, but all Swain could see were its needle-like teeth, bared wide with the help of its massive lower jaw.

And beyond the hood, Swain caught a glimpse—a split-second glimpse—of Bellos, standing by the Information Desk.

Gazing up at him.

Smiling.

He had known all along . . .

Swain turned away, stumbling away from the railing as the hood wrenched at its pinned foreclaw. It seemed to Swain that the knife fixing the claw to the railing was the only thing holding the hood up.

At that moment there was another whistling through the air and suddenly a *second* knife thudded into the forearm of the hood, slicing right through the narrow bone just above its pinned foreclaw, *cutting the claw clean off!*

With a shriek, the hood dropped instantly out of sight, falling to the atrium way below—leaving in its place a bony five-fingered claw, impaled on the railing by the first throwing knife.

Hawkins yelled to Swain, 'Here! Over here!'

Swain saw the ramshackle group hurrying toward the photocopying room to his right. He ran after them and when he reached the door to the photocopying room, he looked back over his shoulder to see the first of the remaining hoods slink slowly and menacingly over the railing.

Swain shut the door behind him and looked around the photocopying room.

Hawkins was leading the way with Balthazar over his shoulder, throwing open the other door at the far end of the room, the one that read: INTERNET FACILITY. Apart from that door, a solid concrete wall separated the two rooms. Swain followed as Holly and the others hurried through the doorway behind Hawkins.

Swain paused at the threshold. He was standing on a dusty handwritten sign that must have fallen from the door some time ago. It read:

STATE LIBRARY OF NEW YORK
INTERNET/ON-LINE SERVICES FACILITY
CLOSED FOR REPAIRS.
WE REGRET ANY INCONVENIENCE.

'I don't know if this is such a good idea,' he stepped inside, shutting and locking the door after him.

Suddenly, there was a loud *bang* from somewhere behind him and Swain spun around. He peered out through a small rectangular window set into the door— and saw that the hoods were pounding on the *outer* door of the photocopying room.

He turned to face the Internet room.

'Sorry,' Hawkins said, lowering the weary-looking Balthazar to the floor.

The Internet facility of the State Library of New York—a relatively new addition to a relatively old building—was little more than a wide empty room, with open-ended wires hanging down from an unpainted ceiling and bared electrical outlets on the walls. No computers. No modems. Even the light switch next to the doorway was merely a stumpy metal housing with lots of frayed wires. A corner room, there were windows along two of its sides, but no other doors.

There was only the one entrance.

It was a dead end.

Wonderful, Swain thought.

The banging outside continued. He looked back out through the small rectangular window in the door. The photocopying room's outer door was still, except that every few seconds it would vibrate suddenly as the hoods rammed it from the other side.

Hawkins and Holly were standing at the windows, gazing out helplessly over the park outside.

Swain pulled Holly back protectively. 'Don't get too close,' he said, pointing at the window frame, at the tiny blue talons of electricity that lashed out around its edges.

'Uh, excuse me, but I think we have more pressing problems than the *windows*,' Selexin said impatiently.

The pounding of the hoods on the outer door continued.

'Right.' Swain's eyes swept the room, looking for something he could use. Anything he could use. But there was nothing here. Absolutely nothing. The room was completely bare.

And then, with a sudden, loud crash, the outer door to the photocopying room burst inwards.

'They're inside,' Hawkins said, racing to the door, peering out through its small window.

'Christ,' Swain said.

In an instant, the first hood hit the door. Hawkins stepped back as the whole door shook.

'Get back!' Swain said. 'They'll go for the window!'

The second hood went for the window set into the door.

Shards of glass sprayed everywhere as the window exploded inwards. The hood clung to the broken window, reaching into the room, lashing out indiscriminately with a single claw.

The other hoods were ramming the door, pounding it repeatedly.

'What do we do?' Hawkins yelled. 'It won't hold for long. The other door didn't!'

'I know! I know!' Swain was trying to think.

The hoods continued to pound loudly on the door. The door's hinges creaked ominously. The hood with its arm inside the broken rectangular window was now trying to stick its head through, but the gap was too small. It hissed and snarled maniacally.

Swain spun. 'Everyone to that corner,' he pointed to the far corner. 'I want—'

He stopped—listened to the sound of the soft rain pattering against the windows. Something had changed. Something he almost hadn't noticed. He listened in the silence.

The silence.

That was it.

The pounding had stopped.

What were they doing?

And then Swain looked at the door.

Slowly, almost imperceptibly, the doorknob began to rotate.

Hawkins saw it, too. '*Holy* shit . . .' he gasped.

Swain dived for the door.

Too late.

The knob continued to rotate and then . . .

. . . *click!*

It was locked. Swain breathed again.

The knob turned again. Clicked again.

Turned. Clicked.

They're testing it, over and over, he thought in horror.

It was at that moment, as Swain was staring up at the door from the floor, that a long black claw slid slowly and silently through the broken window.

The bony black arm reached downward, slowly flexing its jagged razor-sharp fingernails. The lethal black claw was moving across and down to the right when suddenly Swain realised what it was doing.

Swain snapped round to look at Balthazar—to see if the big man could throw another knife at the claw. But, having thrown the two knives earlier, Balthazar was now spent. He just sat on the floor with his head bowed. Swain saw the knives on his baldric, thought about using one, but then decided he didn't want to get too close to the hood's vicious-looking claw.

'Quickly,' he said to Hawkins. 'Handcuffs.'

Puzzled, Hawkins reached for his gunbelt and pulled out a pair of handcuffs. Swain grabbed them.

The clawed hand edged slowly downwards, coming closer to the doorknob.

'*It's trying to unlock the door* . . .' Hawkins breathed in awe. As soon as it turned the knob from the inside, the door would unlock straight away. Unlock. And open . . .

Swain reached up to the door, trying to prise open the cuffs. But the cuffs wouldn't open.

The doorknob rattled again and Swain jumped, ready for it to burst open.

The door remained shut.

It had come from the outside. One of the hoods outside was trying to turn the knob again. The door was still locked. But the clawed hand on the *inside* was still getting closer to the knob on this side.

'They're locked! The cuffs are locked!' Swain shouted in disbelief, fumbling with the cuffs.

'Shit, of course.' Hawkins pulled some keys from his pocket. 'Here. The smallest one.'

Swain took the keys, hands shaking, and tried to insert the smallest key into the cuffs.

'*Hurry up!*' Selexin said.

The claw was at the knob now. Feeling.

Swain's hands were shaking so much that the key slipped out of the cuffs' keyhole.

'*Quickly!*' Selexin yelled.

Swain inserted the key again, turned it. The cuffs popped opened.

'There!' he said, moving across the floor, sliding underneath the doorknob.

The clawed hand was moving over the knob now, trying to get a grip on it.

Swain reached for the light switch next to the door. Its wired remains flowed out from a solid, stumpy metal housing. Swain clamped one ring of the cuffs through a gap in the metal housing.

The clawed hand slowly began to turn the doorknob.

Swain reached up to the knob, sliding the second ring of the cuffs in behind the clawed hand and around the narrowest part of the doorknob—the part closest to the door itself.

Then he clamped the cuff tightly around the doorknob *just as* the clawed hand turned it fully. There was a loud *click!* as the door unlocked. The door swung slightly inward, opening an inch.

And then suddenly, shockingly, the door was rammed from the outside.

The handcuffs went instantly taut, securing the door to the metal housing on the wall.

The door was open six inches now and Swain fell backwards as one of the hoods swiped viciously at him through the narrow gap between the door and its frame.

The hoods were snarling loudly now, scratching at the doorframe, hurling themselves bodily at the door.

But the cuffs held.

The gap between door and frame was too narrow.

The dog-sized hoods couldn't get in.

'Well done,' Hawkins said.

Swain wasn't impressed. 'If they can't open it, they'll soon break it down. We have to get out of this room.'

The hoods kept pounding on the door.

Swain turned around—searching for another way out—when suddenly he saw Holly standing over by one of the windows. She was bent over the window sill as if she were injured.

'Holly? You all right?' He hurried over to her.

'Yes . . .' Distracted.

The pounding continued. The hoods' snarling and hissing filled the room.

'What are you doing?' he said quickly.

'Playing with the electricity.'

Swain stole a glance back at the door as he came up beside her and looked over her shoulder. Holly was holding the broken telephone receiver two inches away from the window sill. As she moved it closer, the small forks of blue lightning seemed to pull *away* from it in a wide circle—away from the phone.

Swain had forgotten Holly still had the phone receiver at all. He frowned at what he saw, though. He didn't know why the electricity should move away from the phone receiver. After all, the phone was dead . . .

The pounding and the grunting of the hoods continued.

The door still held.

'Can I have that?' Swain said quickly. Holly gave him the phone as he looked back at the door.

Then, abruptly, the pounding and the snarling stopped.

Silence.

And then Swain heard the hoods scamper out of the photocopying room.

'What's going on?' Hawkins said.

'I don't know.' Swain moved to look out through the gap in the door.

'Are they coming back?' Selexin said.

'I can't see them,' Swain said. 'Why did they leave?'

Peering out through the gap in the door, Swain saw the outer door to the photocopying room swinging wide open, left ajar by the hoods. Beyond that, quite a way away and shrouded in darkness, the doors to the elevators.

And then he saw the reason why the hoods had left so abruptly.

With a soft *ping* the doors to the far elevator slowly began to open.

Slow night, Bob Charlton thought wryly as he stepped into the bustling offices of the New York Police Department's 14th Precinct.

He had been here a few times before, but this time the main foyer was much less crowded—there were only about eighty people here tonight. He stepped up to the reception desk and shouted above the din: 'Bob Charlton to see Captain Dickson, please!'

'Mr Charlton? Henry Dickson,' Dickson said, extending his hand as Charlton entered the relative silence of his office. 'Neil Peters said you'd be coming down. What can I do for you?'

'I've got a problem downtown that I was told you could help me with.'

'Yeah . . .'

Charlton said, 'Sometime in the last twenty-four hours we lost a main in one of the south–central grids.

194

Lieutenant Peters said that you picked up a guy in that area earlier today.'

'Where's your grid?' Dickson asked.

'It's bounded by 14th and Delancey on the north–south axis.'

Dickson looked at a map on the wall next to him.

'Yeah, that's right. We did pick up a fella in that area. Just this morning,' Dickson said. 'But I don't think he'll be much use to you. We picked him up in the old State Library.'

'What was he doing there?'

'Small-time computer thief. Apparently they've just put in a new set of Pentiums down there. But this poor bastard must have stumbled onto something bigger.'

'Something bigger?' Charlton asked.

'We found him covered in blood.'

Charlton blinked.

'Only it wasn't his blood. It was a security guard's.'

'Oh my God.'

'Damn right.'

Charlton leaned forward, serious. 'How did he get inside? Inside the library, I mean.'

'Don't know yet. I've got a couple of babysitters down there now. As you can see, we're pretty busy round here. Site squad'll be going in there tomorrow to determine point of entry.'

Charlton asked, 'This thief, is he still here?'

'Yeah. Got him locked up downstairs.'

'Can I talk to him?'

Dickson shrugged. 'Sure. But I wouldn't get your hopes up. He's been talking gibberish ever since we brought him in.'

'That's okay, I'd like to try anyway. Some of those old buildings have booster valves in funny places. I'm thinking he might have busted something on his way in. That okay with you?'

'Sure.'

Both men stood up and walked toward the door. Dickson stopped.

'Oh, a word of warning, Mr Charlton,' he said. 'Try to hold your stomach, this ain't gonna be pretty.'

Charlton winced as he looked again at the black man in the small cell in front of him.

Quite obviously, they hadn't been able to get all the blood off his face. Perhaps those designated to wash him had retched, too, Charlton thought. Whatever the case, they hadn't finished the job. Mike Fraser still had large vertical streaks of dried blood running down the length of his face, like some bizarre kind of warpaint.

Fraser just sat there on the far side of the cell, staring

at the concrete wall, talking rapidly to himself, making darting gestures at some invisible friend.

'That's him,' Dickson said.

'Jesus,' Charlton breathed.

'Hasn't stopped talking to that wall since we put him in here. Blood on his face has dried, too. He'll have to get it off himself later, when he's got sense enough to use a shower.'

'You said his name was Fraser . . .' Charlton said.

'Yep. Michael Thomas Fraser.'

Charlton stepped forward.

'Michael?' he said gently.

No response. Fraser kept talking to the wall.

'Michael? Can you hear me?'

No response.

Charlton turned his back on the cell to face Dickson. 'You never found out how he got into the library, is that right?'

'Like I said, site squad goes in tomorrow.'

'Right . . .'

Dickson said, 'You won't get anything out of him. He hasn't said a word to anyone all day. Probably can't even hear your voice.'

'Hmmm,' Charlton mused. 'Poor bastard . . .'

'*It's hearing your voice,*' Mike Fraser whispered into Bob Charlton's ear.

Charlton jumped away from the cell.

Fraser was right up close to the bars, only inches away from Charlton's head. Charlton hadn't even heard him come across the cell.

Fraser kept talking in an exaggerated whisper, '*Whatever it is, it's hearing your voice! And if you keep talking . . .*'

The black man was pressing his bloodstained face up against the bars, trying to get as close to Charlton as possible. The streaks of dried blood running vertically down his face gave him an aspect of pure evil.

'*Whatever it is, it's hearing your voice! And if you keep talking!*' Fraser hissed crazily. He was starting to wail.

'*And if you keep talking! Talking! Talking! Ah-ah-ah!*' Fraser was looking up at the ceiling, at some imaginary creature looming above him. He held up his hands to ward off the unseen foe. '*Oh my God! It's here! It's after me! It's here! Oh God, help me! Somebody help me!*'

Frantically, he began to shake the bars of the cell. Finally he fell limp, his arms hanging through the bars. At last Fraser looked up at Charlton.

'Don't go there,' he hissed.

Charlton leaned closer, spoke gently. 'Why? What's there?'

Fraser offered a sly, evil grin through his mask of

dried blood. 'If you go, you go. But you won't come back alive.'

'He's nuts. Lost it, that's all,' Dickson said as they walked back to the main entrance of the station.

'You think he killed the guard?' Charlton asked.

'Him? Nah. Probably stumbled on the guys who did, though.'

'And you think they messed him up? Scared him to death by painting him in the guard's blood?'

'Something like that.'

Charlton stroked his chin as he walked. 'I don't know. I think I better check out our links with that library. It's worth a shot. Might be that whoever got hold of Michael Fraser decided to hack up my junction line, too. And if they hacked the junction at the booster valve, it would definitely be possible to bring the whole main down.'

They reached the doors.

'Sergeant,' Charlton said as the two men shook hands, 'thank you for your time and help. It's been, well, interesting, to say the least.'

Stephen Swain peered out from behind the handcuffed door of the New York State Library's rather generously named Internet Facility.

The doors of the darkened elevator were fully open now but nothing was happening.

The elevator was just sitting there.

Open and silent.

For their part, the hoods were nowhere to be seen. Having hustled out of the photocopying room, they must have been out on the balcony somewhere. Hiding . . .

Swain watched intently, waiting for something to emerge from the lift.

'Could be empty,' Hawkins whispered.

'Could be,' Swain replied. 'Maybe whoever pressed the button never got in.'

'Shhh,' Selexin hissed, 'something is coming out.'

They turned back to face the elevator.

'Uh-oh,' Hawkins said.

'Oh *man*,' Swain sighed, 'doesn't this guy ever quit?'

The tail emerged first, pointing forward, hovering horizontally three feet above the ground. Swain could easily see the slight kink in the tail a few inches from the tip where he had broken the bone. The antennae came next, followed by the snout, cautiously moving out from the elevator.

'She is not a *guy*,' Selexin said. 'I *told* you that before, Reese is female.'

'How did she figure out the elevator?' Hawkins asked as they watched Reese lower her snout and sniff the floor.

'I imagine,' Selexin said, 'she smelled Mister Swain's residual scent on one of the buttons—'

Abruptly, Reese's snout snapped up and pointed directly at them. Swain and Hawkins ducked instantly behind the door. Selexin didn't move.

'What are you doing? She cannot *see* you,' he whispered. 'She can only smell you. To hide behind the door won't extinguish your scent-trail. Besides,' he added sourly, 'she probably already knows we are here.'

Swain and Hawkins resumed their positions at the door.

Hawkins said, 'So why isn't she coming after us?'

Selexin sighed. 'Honestly, it is a wonder that I bother explaining anything to you. I would think that the reason why Reese has not come directly after us is perfectly obvious.'

'And what is that?' Hawkins said.

'Because she smells something else,' Selexin said. 'Some other creature that I would safely assume is far more worrisome to her than you are.'

'The hoods,' Swain said, not taking his eyes off Reese. She was standing perfectly still at the mouth of the elevator.

'Correct. And since they were out there only very recently, their scent is probably very strong,' Selexin said. 'I would therefore assert that at the moment, Reese is feeling particularly concerned.'

For a long minute they watched Reese in silence. Her long, low, dinosaur-like body didn't move an inch. Her tail was poised high, tensed, ready to strike.

Hawkins said, 'So what do we do?'

Swain was frowning, thinking.

'We get out,' he said finally.

'*What!*' Selexin and Hawkins said at the same time.

Swain was already reaching up for the handcuffs, unlocking them.

'For one thing, we can't stay here,' he said. 'Sooner or later one of those bastards out there is going to break down this door. And when that happens, we'll be trapped. I say we get ready to run as soon as something happens.'

'As soon as *something happens*?' Selexin said. 'A rather inexact plan if you don't mind my saying so.'

Swain put the cuffs in his pocket and shrugged at the little man. 'Let's just say that I've got a feeling something is about to happen out there. And when it does, I want all of us to be ready to make a break for it.'

Several minutes later, Swain had Balthazar draped over his shoulder while Hawkins held Holly by the hand. The door was open a full two feet.

Outside, Reese stood rigidly in front of the elevator, visibly tensed, alert.

They waited.

Reese didn't move.

Another minute ticked by.

Swain turned to face the group. 'All right, when I say go, run straight for the stairwell. When you get there, don't stop, don't look back, just go straight up. When we hit the Third Floor, I'll lead the way from there. Okay?'

They nodded.

'Good.'

Another minute passed.

'It does not look like anything is going to happen,' Selexin said sourly.

'He's right,' Hawkins said. 'Maybe we better put the cuffs back on the door . . .'

'Not just yet,' Swain said, staring intently out at Reese. 'They're out there, and Reese knows it . . . *There!*'

Abruptly, Reese spun to her right, away from them. Something had caught her attention.

Swain tightened his grip on Balthazar. 'All right everybody, get ready, this is it.'

Slowly, Swain pulled the door open and ventured into the photocopying room. The others followed him to the outer door.

Reese was still facing the other direction.

Swain rested his free hand lightly on the outer door, his eyes locked on Reese, praying that she wouldn't turn around and charge.

He opened the door wider, and stepped out.

He could see the stairwell now, off to the left. Reese and the elevators were about twenty feet to the right. Beyond Reese, he could see the wide empty space that fell away to the Ground Floor atrium below. He figured if he could just ease out of the doorway and quietly make his way to the—

Suddenly, Reese whirled around.

For an instant Swain's heart stopped. He felt like a

thief discovered with his hands in the till—totally exposed. Caught in the act.

He froze.

But Reese didn't stop to face him.

She just kept turning until she came a full three hundred and sixty degrees. A full circle.

Swain breathed again. He didn't know what was happening until he realised that Reese's quick circling movement wasn't a threatening move at all.

It was a defensive move.

Reese was frightened, agitated, desperately looking— no, *smelling*—in every direction.

She's surrounded, Swain thought. *She knows we're here, but she's decided we're not worth worrying about. There's something else out there, something more dangerous* . . .

There was no time to waste.

This was the chance.

Swain turned to the others and whispered, 'Come on! We're moving now.'

Swain half-dragged, half-carried Balthazar out through the doorway, not daring to take his eyes off Reese. The others raced past him and headed for the open stairwell. Swain limped as fast as he could toward the stairwell, straining under Balthazar's dead weight. He was almost at the stairwell when the attack on Reese began.

A hood.

Squealing fiercely, it leapt over the railing from the Ground Floor, claws extended, jaws wide open.

Swain heaved Balthazar into the stairwell, trying as he did to watch what was happening behind him. And as he disappeared into the stairwell, the last thing Swain saw was a fleeting glimpse of Reese, shrieking madly, swinging her tail around to defend herself against the onslaught of incoming hoods.

Feet pounding, Swain hurried up the stairs, Balthazar's weight pressing heavily down against his shoulders.

The others were waiting for him at the fire door marked '3'. When he joined them, Swain passed Balthazar over to Hawkins.

'Why are we stopping here?' the young cop asked. 'Shouldn't we keep going up?'

'We can't go any higher,' Swain said. 'We can't get out there. The door to the roof's electrified.'

'Daddy, what are we doing?' Holly said.

Swain eased the fire door open slightly. 'Looking for a hiding place, honey.'

'Daddy, where are the monsters?'

'I don't know. Hopefully not up here.'

'Daddy . . .'

'Shh. Just wait here,' Swain said. Holly stepped back, silent.

Swain stepped through the doorway and scanned the room.

Yes. He was where he wanted to be.

The wide low-ceilinged study hall stretched away from him, its L-shaped desks creating a waist-high maze that spread right across the room. The whole room was dark, save for the soft blue city light that filtered in through the windows on the far side.

Slowly, Swain bent down to look under the desks. Through the legs he could see all the way across the room. There were no feet—or whatever the hell these creatures walked on—in sight.

The study hall was empty.

He poked his head back through the fire door. 'Okay everyone. Inside, quickly.'

The others filed into the study hall. Swain took Holly's hand and led her through the winding maze of desks.

'Daddy. I don't like it here.'

Swain was looking around the room. 'Yeah, me neither,' he said, distracted.

'Daddy?'

'What, honey?'

'Daddy, can we go now—?'

Swain pointed to a corner near the windows. 'There it is.' He quickened his pace, pulling Holly harder.

Hawkins was walking behind them. 'What is it?' he asked. All he could see was a sign on the wall reading:

QUIET PLEASE.
THIS ROOM IS FOR PRIVATE STUDY ONLY.
NO CARRY BAGS PERMITTED.

'Next to the sign,' Swain said.

Beside the sign on the wall, Hawkins saw a large, solid, grey door. It looked like some sort of maintenance door.

Swain reached for the knob. It turned easily. Unlocked.

The door opened slowly, with the distinctive hiss of a hydraulic valve. Swain didn't think much of it. All the big doors at the hospital needed hydraulics to help people open them, they were that heavy.

He reached for the light switch, but decided against it. Any light would be a certain giveaway.

He surveyed the room before him. Cold grey concrete walls, a janitor's cart filled with buckets and mops, shelves packed with bottles of detergent and floor wax, and several tarps stretched over large mounds of more janitorial equipment.

Diffused white light from the streetlights outside

streamed in through two long rectangular windows high up on the left-hand wall. Directly opposite the door, dividing the room in two, was a floor-to-ceiling cyclone fence with a rusted iron gate in its centre. Beyond the fence were more shelves of detergent and a few more piles of equipment covered in dark hessian cloth.

The group moved inside and Swain closed the door behind them. The hydraulic door shut with a soft *whump*.

Holly sat away from the door, up against the cyclone fence. Hawkins put Balthazar on the floor beneath the windows and scanned the maintenance room, nodding. 'We should be safe here.'

'For a while, yes,' Swain said.

Selexin asked, 'How long do you think we should stay here?'

'As long as we can,' Swain said.

'Hooray,' Hawkins said blandly.

'And how long is that?' Selexin again.

'I don't know. Maybe right up till the end. At the moment I'm not quite sure.'

'You cannot forget that there will always be *something* out there,' Selexin said. 'Even when all the contestants are dead, you will still have the Karanadon to face.'

'I don't have to face anything,' Swain said harshly.

'What does that mean?'

'It means, I'm not here to fight. It means I'm not

here to win your stupid contest. It means that at the
moment all I'm worried about is getting my daughter
and the rest of us out of here alive.'

'*But you can't do that unless you win*,' Selexin said
angrily.

Swain looked hard at the little man. He was silent for
a few seconds.

'I wouldn't be so sure of that,' he said softly, almost
to himself.

'What was that?' Selexin said. It was an argument now.

'I said, I wouldn't be so sure of that.'

'You believe you can get out of the labyrinth?' Selexin
challenged.

Swain was silent. He looked over at Holly by the
cyclone fence, sucking her thumb.

Selexin said again, 'Do you seriously think you can
get out of the labyrinth?'

Swain was silent.

Hawkins whispered to him, 'You think we can get
out?'

Swain looked at the windows near the ceiling, thinking to himself. At last he spoke. 'Yes.'

'Impossible.' Balthazar's guide stepped forward.
'Absolutely impossible.'

'You stay out of this,' Selexin snapped angrily.

Swain stared at Selexin. The little man had been

indignant before, distressed even, but he had never been downright angry.

Balthazar's guide stepped back immediately. Selexin spun back to face Swain.

'*How?*' he demanded.

'How?'

'Yes, how do you propose we get out?'

'You *want* to get out?' Swain couldn't believe it. After the lecture he had received before about the grandeur and honour associated with the Presidian, he found it difficult to believe that Selexin would *want* to get out.

'As a matter of fact I do.'

Balthazar's guide interrupted again, 'Oh, you do, do you? Well forgive me for reminding you of an unpleasant fact, Selexin, but you *can't!*'

Selexin didn't say anything.

Balthazar's guide went on. 'Selexin, the Presidian has begun. It *cannot* and *will not* be stopped until a winner has been found. It is the only honourable way.'

'I think any honour this thing had went flying out the window when your friend Bellos brought his blood-hounds along,' Swain said.

'I agree,' Selexin said, glaring at Balthazar's guide. 'Bellos has broken the rules. And with hoodaya, he cannot and will not be stopped. We must get out.'

'And do what?' the other guide sneered, 'use our witnessing teleports to call for help? They transmit vision only, Selexin, not sound.'

'Then *anything*,' Selexin said. 'If two contestants leave the labyrinth and initialise their witnessing teleports and wave for the cameras, the controllers of the Presidian will have to realise that something is amiss.'

The other guide stared at Selexin. 'I do not think our two contestants will last very long outside the labyrinth,' he said smugly.

'Why?'

'As a matter of fact,' the other guide smiled, 'I would say that they would not last any longer than exactly fifteen minutes.'

'Oh,' Selexin frowned, remembering. 'Yes.'

Swain was bewildered. It was as if Selexin and Balthazar's guide were speaking in another language.

'What does that mean?' he asked Selexin.

Selexin spoke sadly. 'Do you remember what I told you before about your wristband?'

Swain looked down at the heavy grey band around his wrist. He'd forgotten about it entirely.

The little green light still glowed brightly. The display now read:

INITIALISED—6

Six? Swain thought. He remembered the contestant on the Ground Floor—the Konda—that had been killed by the hoods. The wristband, it appeared, was counting *down* now. Striking out a number as each contestant was eliminated. Until only one remained.

And when only one was left, then came the Karana-don that Selexin kept talking about. Whatever *that* was.

'Do you remember?' Selexin said again.

'Yes, I think I remember.'

'Do you recall that if your wristband detects that it is outside the electronic field surrounding the labyrinth, it will automatically set itself to detonate?'

Swain frowned. It all suddenly made sense. 'And I get fifteen minutes to get back inside.'

'*Exactly.*' Balthazar's guide spat.

Nobody spoke. There was silence for a full minute. Someone took a long, deep breath.

Balthazar's guide spoke: 'So even if you get out, you are still a dead man.'

Swain looked at him and snorted. 'Thanks.'

'You know, you're a real great help,' Hawkins said to the little man.

'At least I am realistic about my situation.'

'At least I give a shit about somebody else's life,' Hawkins said.

213

'I would be more concerned about taking care of my own if I were you.'

'Yeah, well you're not me—'

'All right. All right,' Swain said. 'Settle down. We've got to find a way out of this, not fight among ourselves.' He turned to Selexin. 'Is there *any* way we can get this thing off my wrist?'

Selexin shook his head. 'No. It doesn't come off . . . unless you . . .' he shrugged.

'I know, I know. Unless I win the Presidian, right?'

Selexin nodded. 'Only the officials at the other end have the proper equipment to remove it.'

'Can we break it open?' Hawkins suggested.

'Can anyone here break down that door?' Balthazar's guide asked, pointing to the maintenance room's heavy hydraulic door, knowing the answer. 'If not, then no-one here can break open that wristband. It's too strong.'

The group went silent.

Swain looked down at the wristband again. In the last minute it had suddenly begun to feel a lot heavier. He crossed the room and sat next to Holly, resting his back up against the cyclone fence.

'How are *you* doing?' he asked softly.

She didn't answer.

'Holly? What's up?'

Still no answer. Holly was staring vacantly straight ahead.

'Come on, Hol, what is it? Did I do something?' he waited for a response.

This was not unusual. Holly would often refuse to talk to him when she felt rejected or left out or just plain stubborn.

'Holly, please, we don't have time for this now,' Swain shook his head in exasperation.

Holly spoke, 'Daddy.'

'Yes.'

'Be very quiet, Daddy. Be very, *very* quiet.'

'Why—?'

'*Shh.*'

Swain went mute. The others had sat down over near Balthazar, beneath the high windows. Everyone sat in complete silence for ten seconds. Holly leaned over to Swain's ear.

'Do you hear it?' she whispered.

'No.'

'*Listen.*'

Swain looked at Holly. She was sitting dead still, her eyes wide open, her head set rigidly upright, backed up against the cyclone fence. She looked frightened. Frightened out of her mind. She spoke again.

'Okay Daddy, get ready. Listen . . . *now.*'

And then he heard it.

The sound was barely audible, but it was unmistakable. A long, slow inhalation.

Something breathing.

Something not very far away.

Suddenly, there was a snorting sound, like the soft grunting of a pig. It was followed by a shuffling sound.

Then the inhalation came again.

It was slow and rhythmic, like the breathing of someone sleeping.

Selexin heard it, too.

At the grunting sound, his head snapped up immediately. He scrambled silently on all fours across the concrete floor to Swain.

'We have to get out,' he hissed in Swain's ear. 'We have to get out *now*.'

The inhalation came again.

'It's in here,' Selexin said. 'Quickly, give me your wrist.'

Swain offered his wristband for Selexin to see.

The green light was still on.

'Phew,' Selexin breathed.

'It?' Swain asked. 'What is *it*?'

'It's behind us, Daddy,' Holly hissed, her body frozen.

'Oh, Jesus Christ . . .' Hawkins gasped, getting to his feet on the other side of the room. He was looking through the cyclone fence. 'I think it's time to get the hell out of here.'

The inhalation came again, louder this time.

And then slowly, ever so slowly, Stephen Swain turned around.

It was over by the far corner of the cage, under some shelves mounted high up on the wall. In the dark it looked like just another large mound of equipment covered in a tarp.

Only it was moving.

Slowly and steadily.

Rhythmically rising and falling, in time with the deep inhalations.

Swain's eyes followed the outline of the 'mound'. It was big. In the dim light of the storage room he could just make out long spiky bristles on top of an arched back—

There was a loud grunt.

Then *the whole mound* rolled over onto its side and the deep inhalations resumed.

Selexin was tugging on Swain's shirt. 'Let's go! Let's *go*!'

Swain rose to his feet, plucked Holly from the floor, headed for the door. He was reaching for the door's handle when he heard a soft, insistent beeping.

It was coming from his wristband. The little green light was flashing.

Selexin's eyes went wide with horror.

'It's waking up! Get out!' he screamed. '*Get out now!*'

He barged past Hawkins, hauled open the door, pushed Swain through it, screaming, 'Out! Out! Out!'

Swain and Holly were out in the empty study hall again. Hawkins emerged from the janitor's room with Balthazar over his shoulder, the other guide close behind.

Selexin was already charging in amongst the L-shaped desks of the study hall. 'Don't stop! Don't stop! Keep moving, we have to get as far away from here as possible!'

Swain followed with Holly in his arms—weaving quickly between the desks, away from the janitor's room—the others close in tow.

Up ahead, Selexin was darting between the desks, constantly looking back to see if Swain was still with him.

'The band! The band! Look at your wristband!' he called.

Swain looked down at the wristband. It was beeping horribly loudly now, and quicker, too.

And then he stopped.

The green light on the wristband had gone out.

Now the red one was on.

And it was flashing rapidly.

'Uh-oh.'

Hawkins caught up with them. He was panting desperately. 'What is it?'

'We're about to be in for some serious trouble,' Swain said.

At that moment the heavy hydraulic door to the janitor's room exploded from its hinges and flew out into the study hall, landing with a deafening *bang!*, crushing several desks.

It was followed by a blood-curdling roar that boomed out from within the janitor's room.

'Oh, man,' Hawkins breathed.

'Let's move!' Swain took off, winding through the maze of desks, heading for the stairwell in the opposite corner of the room.

He was glancing over his shoulder when it emerged from the janitor's room.

It was *huge*.

Absolutely huge. It had to double over just to fit through the wide doorway that no longer had a door.

Selexin saw it, too. 'It's the Karanadon!'

They were halfway across the wide study hall, crossing it diagonally, when the Karanadon cleared the doorway and rose to its full height, almost touching the ceiling.

Swain pressed on, carrying Holly toward the stairwell. Hawkins was losing ground behind him, weighed down by Balthazar. Last of all was Balthazar's guide—pushing and shoving—trying desperately to get Hawkins and Balthazar to move faster, constantly looking behind him, to see if the Karanadon was coming after them.

Swain glanced over his shoulder again to get another look at the fearsome beast.

It continued to stand by the door to the janitor's room, watching them.

It hadn't moved yet.

It just stood there.

Despite the noise they were making as they scrambled in a panic through the desks for the stairwell, it just stood in front of the doorway in silence.

Swain rounded another desk. Twenty yards to the stairwell. He looked back again.

Christ, it was big all right—at least fourteen feet tall.

It had the body of an enormous, hairy, broad-shouldered gorilla—all black, hunched forward, with a series of long spiky bristles that flowed over its high arched back. Long muscular arms hung down from its massive shoulders so that the knuckles dragged on the ground.

The head was two-and-a-half feet long, and it reminded Swain of a jackal. High pointed ears. Black, lifeless eyes. And menacing canine fangs that protruded from a dark wrinkled snout, frozen in an eternal snarl.

It moved.

The Karanadon leapt forward and bounded after them at frightening speed. It stomped on the fallen hydraulic door, cracking it in the middle, breaking it in two.

Swain tightened his grip on Holly and bolted for the

stairwell. Hawkins struggled to pull Balthazar forward. Balthazar's guide was looking frantically behind them, pounding on Hawkins' back, screaming for him to move faster.

The Karanadon ploughed through the L-shaped desks like an icebreaker through a frozen sea, hurling them in all directions, crushing them under its feet. When they happened to hit the ground, the big beast's footsteps sounded like cannon fire.

Boom. Boom. Boom.

Swain and the others continued to weave in and out between the desks. The Karanadon kept coming in a straight line.

Selexin was at the stairwell, Swain ten yards away. He checked behind him.

Hawkins, Balthazar and the other guide were not going to make it. The Karanadon was closing in on them too quickly.

Better think fast, Steve.

Boom. Boom. Boom.

He let Holly drop to the floor and quickly scanned the wide study hall.

It was roughly square in shape. He and Holly were almost at the stairwell, on the western side of the floor. The janitor's room was roughly opposite them, on the north-eastern corner of the floor. On the south-eastern corner were the elevators.

Boom. Boom. Boom.

'Move faster!' Balthazar's guide was screaming at Hawkins. 'For God's sake, it's getting closer!'

The Karanadon crunched through another desk.

And then Swain pushed Holly *away* from the stairwell, toward the elevators. 'Let's go, honey. We're gonna make a run for the elevators.' He called to Selexin at the stairwell door. 'This way! We're going this way!'

Boom. Boom. Boom.

'*That* way!' Selexin screamed back. 'What about the stairs!'

'Will you just do it, okay!'

The Karanadon was right on top of the others now.

It lunged at Balthazar's guide, swiping at him with one of its long arms. The guide ducked and the massive claw swished over his head and smashed into a nearby desk. The desk shattered and Balthazar's guide stumbled forward, tripping over Hawkins' legs, sending all three of them—the guide, Hawkins and Balthazar—sprawling forward.

Hawkins hit the ground hard, landing heavily on his shoulder. Balthazar fell on top of him. His guide landed helplessly at their feet.

Boom.

There was a sudden, terrifying silence.

The Karanadon had stopped.

Hawkins was sweating profusely. He wriggled desperately, tried to pull himself to his feet, but his right arm was jammed beneath Balthazar. His left wasn't even responding, the shoulder dislocated by the fall.

Down near his feet he saw the little guide frantically clutching at his trouser leg, trying desperately to stand up.

'Help me! *Help me!*' the guide pleaded, petrified.

And then suddenly—violently—the guide was sucked from Hawkins' view.

Over by the wall, Swain watched in horror as his three companions fell below the deskline.

The Karanadon had stopped a few feet short of them. Then it had bent down behind the desks, out of view. When it reappeared, it had the distinctive white shape of Balthazar's guide in one of its massive black claws.

The guide was waving his arms wildly, screaming at the monster. The Karanadon pulled him up to its snout and curiously examined the noisy little creature it had found.

And then, one-handed, the Karanadon held the guide out at arm's length and viciously slashed across the front of his body with its free claw.

Swain's jaw dropped.

223

Hawkins' eyes went wide with terror.

Three deep slits of red exploded across the guide's chest. One slashing tear sliced across his mouth. The guide's body went instantly limp.

The room was suddenly silent.

The Karanadon shook the body once. It didn't respond. The big beast shook the lifeless body again—like a toy that didn't work anymore—and then flung it away.

Swain still couldn't see Hawkins.

He ducked down to look through the legs of the desks—and he saw him. Hawkins was lying flat on the floor, wedged underneath Balthazar, unable to move, but trying anyway.

Christ, he had to do something for him . . .

Boom.

Hawkins was struggling to free himself when he felt the floor shake beneath him. He froze, and then slowly turned to look upward.

And saw the massive jaws of the Karanadon, wide open, rushing down at him.

He shut his eyes. It was too—

'*Hey!*'

The Karanadon's head snapped up instantly.

'Yeah, that's right, I'm talking to you!'

Hawkins opened his eyes.

What the hell—?

The Karanadon slowly turned to face Swain. It cocked its head curiously, staring at this bold creature that had dared to interrupt its kill.

Swain was waving his arms, yelling angrily at the fourteen-foot-tall beast that stood barely fifteen yards away from him.

'Yeah, get up! It's okay!' Swain barked, his face twisted in a fierce growl, never taking his eyes off the monster before him.

He raised his voice. It was angry, challenging. '*Move!* I've got it covered! It's looking at me now! Get up and go for the stairwell!' It was like talking to a dog—the beast heard the intonations, but made no sense of the words.

Hawkins suddenly realised what was happening— Swain was talking to him. Immediately, he began struggling again to shift Balthazar off him. In a few seconds, he got him off, and began to drag him across the floor, away from the Karanadon while Swain kept it occupied.

The Karanadon seemed dumbstruck by this challenging display. It roared fiercely at Swain.

'Oh, yeah! Well . . . well, fuck you, too!' Swain yelled back.

Out of the corner of his eye he saw Holly and Selexin

reach the elevators over by the southern wall. In the other direction, he saw Hawkins and Balthazar reach the stairwell.

Unfortunately, the Karanadon was still staring straight at him, totally exposed, halfway between the elevators and the stairs.

Shit. What could he do now? *Nice going, Steve.*

Boom.

The Karanadon took a slow step toward him.

Boom. Boom.

Two more and suddenly the gap was seven feet. Almost within striking distance.

'Hey!'

The Karanadon's head snapped left, toward Selexin and Holly by the elevator.

'Yes! That is right! I am talking to you!' Selexin yelled.

The big creature took a step toward the elevators, growling. It roared.

Selexin braced himself, pointed a finger, and yelled, 'Oh, yeah, well *fuck you, too*!'

Swain coughed back a laugh.

The Karanadon roared in outrage and stepped away from Swain, heading for the elevators. It was gaining speed when a third voice called loudly.

'Hey!'

The Karanadon stopped in its tracks a third time.

'Yeah, you!' It was Hawkins.

Swain swung his head back and forth between the elevators and the stairwell, amazed.

Now totally confused, the Karanadon swung to face Hawkins at the stairwell. Swain took the chance and ran for the elevator. When he got there, he pressed the call button.

Hawkins was waving wildly at the Karanadon as it approached. When it got to within fifteen feet of him, Swain took over and called again from the elevators.

'Hello there! Hey, buddy! What about me!'

The Karanadon swung around slowly.

It snorted.

Boom.

Swain looked up at the numbered display above the left-hand elevator. The elevator was moving from '1' to 'G'. It was going *down*. What the hell? The right-hand elevator—with its inwardly dented doors and last seen by Swain stopped halfway between the First and Ground Floors—didn't seem to be operating at all.

Boom. Boom. Boom.

'Hey!' Hawkins called again. But this time, the beast didn't respond. It kept moving toward Swain and the elevators.

Boom. Boom. Boom.

'Hey!' Hawkins yelled. The Karanadon didn't stop. It just kept ploughing forward, toward the elevators.

'We have got trouble,' Selexin said flatly.

'We've got deep trouble,' Swain agreed.

Boom. Boom. Boom.

Swain spun around. Options, options. There were none. He checked the numbers above the elevators. Left—still on the Ground Floor. Right—still no movement at all.

He stared at the elevators for a second and suddenly had an idea.

'Quickly,' he said, moving over to the *right*-hand elevator. 'Selexin, Holly, you two grab the other side of this door and pull. We've got to get it open.'

Boom. Boom. Boom.

The Karanadon was closing in—getting faster and faster as it got closer and closer.

The elevator doors slowly came apart. 'Keep pulling,' Swain said. The black elevator shaft opened wide before him.

Boom.

'That's it,' Swain said, easing in between the doors—spreading his legs, holding them apart—while still facing the study hall. The dark elevator shaft yawned wide behind him.

It was then that Swain noticed the silence. No more booming footfalls.

The Karanadon had stopped.

Slowly, ever so slightly, Swain lifted his head.

It was *right there*!

Five feet away.

And it just stood there, looming over the three of them, its enormous black frame dwarfing them all. It tilted its head and glared down at Swain. One of its long pointed ears twitched.

'Holly, Selexin,' Swain whispered, without moving his mouth, 'I want both of you to grab hold of my legs. One each. *Right* now.'

'Daddy . . .' Holly whimpered.

'Just grab my leg, honey.'

There was a scratching sound, and Swain saw that it was the big beast's claws scraping against the marble floor as it flexed its huge black fists.

Getting ready to attack.

Holly clasped onto Swain's left leg. Selexin took the right.

'Hold tight,' Swain said, taking a deep breath as the Karanadon lifted its arm high.

The arm came down fast—but not fast enough. It hit nothing but air as Swain shifted his weight backwards and jumped into the darkness of the elevator shaft.

The elevator cable was greasy, but his grip held.

There were three vertical cables, so Swain held the middle one. Behind him, the elevator doors had shut automatically as soon as he had stopped holding them apart.

The elevator shaft was pitch black and deathly silent. If the Karanadon was roaring, they couldn't hear it in here.

'Selexin,' Swain said, his voice echoing loudly in the empty shaft. 'Grab hold of the cable.'

Selexin reached out from Swain's leg and caught hold of the elevator cable.

'All right now, slide down. Down to the elevator.'

Selexin slid down the cable, disappearing into the murky darkness of the shaft.

'Holly, you okay?'

'Yeah.' A whimper.

'All right, then, it's your turn now. Just reach out and grab the cable.'

'O-*kay*.'

Her hand shaking, Holly reached for the cable. Her fingers hesitated for an eternity just short of the greasy metal rope. She grabbed it.

And then suddenly the elevator doors burst open.

Soft blue light streamed into the elevator shaft, silhouetting the monstrous shape of the Karanadon as it held the doors apart.

It was only a few feet away and Swain was completely exposed, holding onto the elevator cable for dear life, with Holly dangling from his leg.

It roared loudly, leaning out into the shaft, swiping viciously at Swain, only to see him loosen his grip on the cable and drop out of the way a second ahead of the impact.

Swain fell like a stone, whizzing down the greasy cable into the darkness, with Holly hanging from his left leg.

They slid down the cable fast, the grease on the cable preventing Swain's hands from burning, and arrived at the roof of the right-hand elevator. Selexin was there waiting.

The elevator's hatch was still open and the light inside it still on. The lift was exactly where they had left it before, when Swain, Balthazar and the two guides had climbed across to meet Hawkins and Holly in the other one.

'Let's get inside, and see if we can get to another

floor,' Swain said, grabbing Holly's hand and lowering her into the elevator. Selexin climbed in next. Swain jumped down last of all.

In the light of the elevator Swain could see how filthy they had become. The black grease from the cable covered their clothes. He felt his cheek. The bleeding had stopped.

'Where do we go now?' Selexin asked.

'I think we should go home, Daddy,' Holly suggested.

'Good idea,' Swain said.

Selexin said, 'Well, we had better figure out some-thi—'

Suddenly, the elevator jolted and they were all thrown sideways.

'Oh my God,' Swain said, 'the cable!'

The elevator rocked violently, hurling them all to the ground. A loud *creaking* sound echoed throughout the shaft.

'It's got the cable!'

The elevator swayed dramatically and Selexin was thrown bodily into the side wall, hitting his head, falling to the floor in a heap. Swain tried to fight his way across the swaying lift to reach the button panel, but was jolted backwards. The back of his head banged into one of the elevator's doors, and for a second, he saw spots. The whole elevator groaned again at the tremendous strain being put on the cable.

And then, as quickly as it had begun, the rocking stopped and the elevator was still once more.

Holly was curled up in the corner, vigorously sucking her thumb. Selexin was out cold, face down on the floor. Swain staggered across the lift, rubbing the back of his head, looked up through the hatch.

He had just walked under the open hatch when he felt the elevator move again. Another jolt. But not like the previous ones. It was not as sharp, somehow different.

The elevator swayed again and Swain felt his knees buckle.

And then he realised.

They were going up.

It was *lifting* them up the shaft!

'Okay,' he said to himself, 'how the *hell* are we going to get out of this one?'

The lift continued upward, scraping loudly against the metal lining of the shaft.

Swain looked up through the hatch and could just make out the big arms of the Karanadon heaving on the elevator cable, hauling on it hand over hand, claw over claw.

The lift kept rising, moving higher into the shaft.

There's got to be a way out, he thought, *got to be.*

The Karanadon roared. They were close now, maybe a floor away. The hatch was still open. The Karanadon was glaring down at the elevator with animal fury as it heaved and pulled on the cables.

The cables, Swain thought.

He pondered the idea for a second. It was dangerous, yes. But it *could* work. At the moment it didn't look like he had much choice. He shrugged. Hell, anything was better than nothing.

He looked back at Holly. She was slumped in the corner of the lift, still sucking her thumb.

Yes. It could work.

It had to.

And with that, Stephen Swain reached up and climbed out through the hatch, up onto the roof of the elevator.

The study hall was closer than he thought.

They were about seven feet below the Third Floor doors where the Karanadon stood—and the lift was still moving upward.

The Karanadon saw him. And stopped.

Swain just stood there, on top of the elevator, staring at the beast.

Suddenly the Karanadon lashed out, swiping at him with its spare claw. Swain·stepped back, out of reach. The beast swung again, missed again.

'Come on!' Swain yelled. 'You can do better than that!'

The big beast roared in frustration and lashed out at

him again, harder this time, missing Swain, but hitting one of the cables.

The cable snapped like a thread and the elevator lurched. But the Karanadon was still holding it up.

With one hand!

The big beast swung again, and Swain dived to his left. It missed, and cable number two snapped.

One more, Swain told himself. *One more, and we're out of here.*

This was getting to be too much for the Karanadon. It roared again in animal anger, like a dog barking at a cat that it will never catch.

'Come on, big boy,' Swain teased. 'One last swipe, and then you can get me the hell out of here.'

It was then that the Karanadon raised its arm one final time.

But it didn't swing.

It jumped.

Onto the roof of the elevator!

Swain didn't have time for disbelief. The elevator just plummeted straight down!

A piercing metal-on-metal screech attacked Swain's ears as the elevator descended in a freefall down the shaft. Wind whipped all around him as sparks flew out from every corner of the falling elevator.

The big beast stood on the other side of the roof oblivious to what it had done. It glared at Swain.

What sort of stupid creature jumps onto an elevator that it's holding up? Swain's mind screamed.

But Swain didn't have time to think about that now. He dived for the hatch, fell through it, landed heavily on the floor of the elevator.

'Get down!' he called to Holly, above the wail of the falling elevator. 'Get down on the floor! *Flat* on the floor! Rest your *head* on your *arms*!'

The elevator screamed down the shaft.

Holly did exactly as she was told, lay flat on the floor. Swain scrambled alongside her, covering her with one arm, and did the same—lay flat on his belly, spreading his legs wide, burying his head in his other forearm, using it as a cushion.

The last of the cables must have broken by now, he thought as he lay on the floor, waiting for the bone-jarring crash that would come any second now.

The Karanadon poked its huge head through the small hatch—upside-down. It wanted to get inside, but it would never fit.

The elevator roared down the shaft, sparks flying from all sides, its high-pitched wail getting higher and higher and higher.

And then it hit the bottom.

The impact was stunning.

Swain felt his whole body shudder violently as the elevator went from thirty-five miles an hour to zero in a split second.

The muscles on his forearms cushioned his head. And his body, since it was already flush against the floor, stifled most of the force of the impact.

The same happened with Holly. Swain hoped Selexin was all right, since he had already been on the floor, knocked out.

As the elevator hit the bottom of the shaft with a horrendous *bang!*, the roof beneath the Karanadon gave way and the big beast burst right through it, crashing to the floor of the elevator, landing heavily on its back— *right next to* Swain—in a cloud of dust and shattered plastic.

A minute passed.

Slowly, Swain lifted his head.

The first thing he saw was the dark wrinkled snout

237

and the enormous white fangs of the Karanadon, right in front of his eyes.

He started. But the beast did not move.

Swain quickly looked at his wristband and sighed. The green light was back on. The Karanadon was out cold.

He lifted his body and all sorts of debris fell from his back onto the floor. Half the roof of the old, wide elevator had fallen in under the weight of the big beast, and pieces of the ceiling and shards of fluorescent light bulbs lay strewn all over the elevator.

Christ, he thought, it looked as if a bomb had gone off here: white dust floating through the air, the roof caved in, half the lights flickering, the other half destroyed beyond recognition.

Swain stood up. He touched the large bruise that was forming on the back of his head. His lower back ached from the thunderous impact. He lifted his arm off Holly.

'Holly?' he said, quietly. 'Are you okay?'

She stirred gently, as if coming out of a deep, painful sleep.

'Wha . . . what?'

Swain shut his eyes in relief and gave her a kiss on the forehead.

'Are we there yet, Daddy?' she whimpered, her head still buried in her forearms.

'Yes, honey, we're here,' he smiled.

Across the lift, Selexin groaned. He slowly raised his head and stared, unfocused, at Swain. Then he looked across the lift at the limp—but live—body of the Karanadon.

'Oh my goodness . . .'

'Tell me about it,' Swain said dryly.

'Where are we?'

'We're at the bottom of the shaft, I guess. We took the quick trip down.'

'Oh,' Selexin said absently.

He didn't seem too worried about anything right now, and for that matter, neither did Swain. He figured they could stay here for a while. The Karanadon wouldn't be waking up in the very near future, and no-one would be able to find them here.

He sat up, gently placing his daughter's head in his lap, and leaned up against the wall of the semi-destroyed elevator and smiled sadly at the destruction all around him.

Bob Charlton stopped his Chevy at a red light and dialled his office. It had barely rung once when Rudy answered. '*Robert Charlton's phone.*'

'Rudy?' Charlton said.

'*Yes, sir. Where are you?*'

'At the moment, stuck in downtown traffic. I'm on my way. I'll be back in about five minutes.'

At the other end of the line, Rudy Baker paused, and glanced nervously around Charlton's office.

'Okay, sir,' he said. 'Is there anything you want me to do in the meantime? Look up something for you?'

Charlton's voice said, '*Good idea, yes. While you're waiting, check the computer. See if the New York State Library was linked up with the main when we did that National Register of Historic Places thing a few months back. If it was, run down to Records and pull the plans.*'

Get the blueprints and see if you can find out where the damn booster valve is.'

'Uh . . . okay, sure,' he hesitated again.

'*What is it, son?*' Charlton said. '*Something wrong down there?*'

'No, sir. Not here,' Rudy lied. 'I'll see you when you get back.'

'*All right then.*' Charlton hung up.

In the office, Rudy leaned forward and switched off the speakerphone.

'Well done, son,' a voice behind him said. 'Now, why don't you just take a seat with the rest of us, and we can all wait here together until your boss comes back.'

Charlton hurried out of the elevator and walked quickly down the hallway to his office.

He looked at his watch.

It was 7:55 p.m.

He hoped that Rudy had got those files on the State Library. If he had, with a bit of luck they might be able to have the main up and running again by midnight.

Charlton charged into his office and stopped instantly.

Rudy was sitting in the chair behind Charlton's desk. He looked up helplessly.

Five other men, all dressed in dark suits, sat in a neat row in front of the desk.

As Charlton walked in, one of the men stood up and walked over to him. He was short and stocky, with red hair and a big orange walrus-style moustache.

'Mr Charlton, Special Agent John Levine,' he flashed his wallet, revealing a photo ID. 'I'm from the National Security Agency.'

Charlton examined the ID card. He wondered what the NSA would want with Con Ed.

'What seems to be the problem, Mr Levine?'

'Oh, there's no problem,' Levine said quickly.

'Then what can I do for you?' Charlton's eyes wandered warily around his office, scanning the four other men seated there.

They were all big men, broad-shouldered. Two wore sunglasses even though it was nearly eight in the evening. They were very intimidating.

'Please, Mr Charlton, take a seat. We just came by to ask you a few questions about your inquiry into the New York State Library.'

'I'm not looking at the Library itself,' Charlton said, sitting down in a spare chair. Levine sat opposite him. 'I'm just looking for a break in our main electrical line. We've had quite a few calls from that area, complaints about the power cutting out on people.'

Levine nodded. 'Uh-huh. So. Apart from being in the same area, what is the connection between these complaints and the State Library?'

'Well,' Charlton said, 'the Library is on the National Register of Historic Places, you know, one of those lists of old buildings that aren't allowed to be demolished.'

'I know it.'

'Anyway, we linked a few of them up to the main a few months back, and we've found that when they go down, sometimes they take the whole damn system with them.'

Levine nodded again. 'So why have you begun to focus on *this* building? Surely there are others in the area that deserve similar attention?'

'Mr Levine, I've been doing this sort of thing for ten years now and when you get a break in the main it can mean a shitload of problems. And that means you have to check *everything*. Every possibility. Sometimes it's kids hacking at the cables with daddy's chainsaw, sometimes it's just an overload. I've always found it prudent to go down and check with the police and see if they've pulled in someone from that area lately.'

'You went to the police?' Levine raised an eyebrow.

'Yes.'

'And did you find anything?'

'Yes, I did. In fact, it was the police who put me on to the Library in the first place.'

'If you don't mind me asking,' Levine said, 'which police station was this?'

'14th Precinct,' Charlton said.

'And what did they tell you?'

'They told me they picked up a small-time computer thief in the State Library last night, in relation to the murder of a security guard. I saw the fellow, too—'

'A murdered security guard?' Levine leaned forward.

'Yes.'

'A guard from the State Library?'

'Yes.'

'And the police said he was killed last night?'

'That's right. Last night,' Charlton said. 'They found the thief right next to him, covered from head to toe in the guard's blood.'

Levine looked around at his fellow agents. Then he said, 'Do they think the thief did it?'

'No. He was just a scrawny little guy. But they think he must have stumbled upon the guys who did. Then they roughed him up. Something like that.'

Levine stopped for a moment, deep in thought.

Then he asked very seriously, 'Have the police put any men inside the building? Inside the library?'

'The detective I spoke to said they have two officers down there right now,' Charlton said. 'You know, baby-sitting the building overnight, until some site team can go in tomorrow.'

'So there are police officers inside that building right now?'

'That's what they told me.'

At that, Levine turned to his men and nodded at the nearest one, who stood immediately.

'14th Precinct,' Levine said to him. He glanced back at Bob Charlton. 'Mr Charlton, can you remember the name of the detective to whom you spoke?'

'Yes. Captain Henry Dickson.'

Levine just turned to the standing agent and nodded curtly. The agent didn't reply. He just ran straight from the room.

Levine faced Charlton again. 'Mr Charlton, you have been very helpful. I thank you for your co-operation.'

'Not at all,' Charlton said, rising from his chair. 'If that's everything, gentlemen, I have a main to fix, so if you'll excuse me, I've got to go and check out that library—'

Levine stood, placed his hand on Charlton's chest, stopping him.

'I'm sorry, Mr Charlton, but I'm afraid your inquiry into the New York State Library stops here.'

'*What?*'

Levine spoke calmly. 'This is no longer a matter for

you or your company, Mr Charlton. The National Security Agency will take care of it from here.'

'But what about the main?' Charlton objected. 'Or the electricity? I have to get it back on.'

'It can wait.'

'Bullshit, it can wait.' Charlton stepped forward angrily.

'Sit down, Mr Charlton.'

'No, I will not sit down. This is a serious problem, Mr Levine,' Charlton paused. 'I'd like to speak with your superior.'

'*Sit down*, Mr Charlton.' Levine said, a new authority in his voice. Immediately, two agents appeared at Charlton's sides. They didn't touch him, just stood by his shoulders.

Charlton sat, frowning.

Levine said, 'All I will tell you is this, Mr Charlton. In the last two hours, that library has become the focus of a major NSA investigation. An investigation that will not be stopped because one hundred and eighty-seven New Yorkers won't be able to watch *Friends* for one night.'

Charlton just sat there, silent. Levine walked over to the doorway.

'Your inquiry is concluded, Mr Charlton. You will be advised as to when you may proceed.' Levine stepped through the doorway, taking one agent with him, leaving Charlton in the office with Rudy and the other two agents.

Charlton couldn't believe it. 'What? You're *keeping* me here? You can't do that!'

Levine stopped in the doorway. 'Oh yes I can, Mr Charlton, and I will. Under Federal law, it is within the power of an investigating officer to detain anyone concerned in a matter of national security for the duration of that investigation. You *will* remain here, Mr Charlton, with your assistant, under supervision, until this investigation is substantially concluded. Thank you for your co-operation.'

Down the hall, Levine stepped into the elevator and pulled out his cellular phone.

'*Marshall, here,*' a crackled voice said at the other end. There was a lot of static on the line.

'Sir, it's me, Levine.'

'*Yes, John, what is it? How did it go?*'

'Good and bad, sir.'

'*Tell me the good news first.*'

Levine said, 'It's definitely the State Library.'

A pause, then, '*Yes.*'

'And we got to Charlton just in time. He was just about to go there.'

'*Good.*'

Levine paused, nervously fingering his red walrus moustache.

Marshall's voice said, '*And the bad news?*'

Levine bit his lip. 'We had to detain him.'

There was silence on the other end of the line.

'There was no choice, Mr Marshall. We had to keep him away from the library.'

The man named Marshall seemed to be thinking it over. Finally he spoke, as if to himself. '*No. No. That's okay. Charlton will be all right. Besides, if this thing comes off, any flak the Agency gets from him will be water off a duck's back. What else?*'

Levine held his breath. 'There are two cops inside the building.'

'*Inside?*'

'Yes.'

'*Oh, fuck,*' Marshall's voice said. '*That is a problem.*'

Levine waited in silence. The phone hissed with static. Marshall lapsed into thought again. When he spoke, his voice was soft, deliberate.

'*We'll have to take them with us.*'

'The cops? Can we do that?'

Marshall said, '*They're contaminated. It doesn't look like we have much choice.*'

Levine said, 'What do you want me to do now?'

'*Get over to the library and, for the moment, stay out of sight. The boys from Sigma will be there shortly,*' Marshall said. '*I'll be landing in a couple of minutes. There's a car waiting on the runway, so I'll be there in about thirty minutes.*'

'Yes, sir.'

Levine hung up.

James A. Marshall sat in the executive compartment of the National Security Agency's Director's Lear as it began its descent into Newark.

As the Divisional Agent in Charge of the NSA's ultra-secret Sigma Division, Marshall was officially based in Maryland, but lately he found that he was spending most of his time out in the western states, New Mexico and Nevada.

Marshall was a tall man of fifty-two, mostly bald, with a white-grey beard and hawk-like black eyebrows that narrowed at his nose, giving him a perpetual look of deadly seriousness. He had been in charge of Sigma Division—the NSA's elite high technology discovery division—for six years now.

Back in the seventies and eighties, the NSA had been the US intelligence community's pride and joy, electronically compressing billions of encryption algorithms that were to become the foundation of its world-renowned code-breaking computers. Then, in the early nineties,

Sigma added to this lustre when it utilised semiconductor technology to make the greatest breakthrough in the history of code making and breaking—it successfully created the world's first quantum computer.

But with the subsequent thawing of the Cold War, code-cracking began to assume a lesser priority in the eyes of the government. Budgets were cut. Money was diverted to other sectors of the intelligence community and the military. The NSA had to find something *new* to excel in—something that would justify its continued existence. Otherwise it would almost certainly get folded into the Army.

James Marshall and Sigma Division were tasked with finding this new expertise.

Within weeks, Sigma's resources were focused upon a new and remarkably different goal. Only this was a goal that did not require the *creation* of new technology, but which rather was centred on the search for, discovery of, and *deciphering* of, a very special kind of technology.

Highly advanced technology.

Technology that man himself could not create.

But technology which the NSA—and the NSA alone, with its new quantum supercomputers—would be in a unique position to decipher and exploit.

Extra-terrestrial technology.

Marshall took it all with a grain of salt. Sure, the Air Force had built underground warehouses in New

Mexico and Nevada. But despite the reports of television specials asserting that they had in fact found, captured and studied alien spacecraft and lifeforms—one such special even suggested that the technology behind the Stealth Bomber came from such studies—those warehouses had remained irrefutably and unequivocally empty.

In short, the Air Force had found nothing. And in the ever-competitive quest for budget dollars, that provided the NSA with an opportunity . . .

Like tonight, Marshall thought.

And as his plane made its descent, he looked at the printout in his lap for the hundredth time.

Two hours ago, at 6:01 p.m. Eastern Standard Time, an NSA satellite, *LandSat 5*, during a random sweep over the north-eastern tip of America, detected and quantified an unusually large electronic displacement that seemed to be emanating from Manhattan Island.

The displacement had not been present during any previous sweeps, and its amperage was dangerously similar to that of previously recorded electronic scrambling—or jamming—frequencies used by North African guerilla forces, in particular those used by Libya.

And after the bombing of the World Trade Centre in 1993 by North African extremists and the destruction of two American embassies in Africa in 1998, no-one in the NSA was willing to take any chances.

The response was immediate.

The *LandSat 5* results were bounced immediately to NSA headquarters at Fort Meade, Maryland. A KH-11E counter-intelligence electronic surveillance satellite—more commonly known by its call-sign 'Eavesdropper'—was sequestered from the National Reconnaissance Office, and retasked so that it would pass over New York.

By chance, the Eavesdropper happened to be in the right place at the right time and was on the scene in minutes, and the first set of results were soon in the hands of the NSA's crisis management team in Maryland—a team that had included Marshall.

Once those results had been reviewed, in the space of nine minutes all records of correspondence between satellite control in Maryland, *LandSat 5* and the Eavesdropper had been destroyed.

LandSat 5 was retasked for immediate splashdown somewhere in the Pacific Ocean, while the Eavesdropper continued to monitor the Manhattan area with every pass.

It was then that the mission had been handed to James Marshall and his boys at Sigma Division.

Time was short, and Marshall had wasted no time.

He had raced to the airport immediately and as he

stepped onto the Director's Lear, someone at Sigma was already preparing a press release that would explain the unfortunate and regrettable loss of the two satellites.

And so here he was. On the NSA Director's Lear ready for touchdown in New York.

Marshall reached into his suitcase for a final look at the report from the Eavesdropper.

Judging by the long stretch of time covered in the report, Marshall noted, the Eavesdropper could hold its field of view on a single target for a full fifty minutes. Its orbital velocity must have been much slower than that of the smaller *LandSat 5*.

Marshall read the transcript.

LSAT-560467-S
DATA TRANSCRIPT 463/511–001
SUBJECT SITE: 231.957 (North-eastern seaboard: CT, NY, NJ)

NO.	TIME/EST	LOCATION	READING
1.	18:03:48	CT.	Isolated energy surge/Source: UNKNOWN
			Type: UNKNOWN / Dur: 0.00:09
2.	18:03:58	N.Y.	Isolated energy surge/Source: UNKNOWN
			Type: UNKNOWN / Dur: 0.00:06

3. 18:07:31   N.Y.   Isolated energy surge/Source: UNKNOWN
                           Type: UNKNOWN / Dur: 0.00:05

4. 18:10:09   N.Y.   Isolated energy surge/Source: UNKNOWN
                           Type: UNKNOWN / Dur: 0.00:07

5. 18:14:12   N.Y.   Isolated energy surge/Source: UNKNOWN
                           Type: UNKNOWN / Dur: 0.00:06

6. 18:14:37   N.Y.   Isolated energy surge/Source: UNKNOWN
                           Type: UNKNOWN / Dur: 0.00:02

7. 18:14:38   N.Y.   Isolated energy surge/Source: UNKNOWN
                           Type: UNKNOWN / Dur: 0.00:02

8. 18:14:39   N.Y.   Isolated energy surge/Source: UNKNOWN
                           Type: UNKNOWN / Dur: 0.00:02

9. 18:14:40   N.Y.   Isolated energy surge/Source: UNKNOWN
                           Type: UNKNOWN / Dur: 0.00:02

10. 18:16:23   N.Y.   Isolated energy surge/Source: UNKNOWN
                           Type: UNKNOWN / Dur: 0.00:07

11. 18:20:21   N.Y.   Isolated energy surge/Source: UNKNOWN
                           Type: UNKNOWN / Dur: 0.00:08

12. 18:23:57   N.Y.   Isolated energy surge/Source: UNKNOWN
                           Type: UNKNOWN / Dur: 0.00:06

13. 18:46:00   N.Y.   Isolated energy surge/Source: UNKNOWN

Type: UNKNOWN / Dur: 0.00:34

Marshall frowned at the transcript.

At the moment it meant nothing to him.

Twelve strong surges of some unknown kind of energy—the sources of which were also unknown—had all occurred in New York City between 6:03 and 6:46 p.m.

Added to that, the first surge, which had come from somewhere inside Connecticut. Curious also was the last surge—distinctive because it had lasted thirty-four seconds, more than three times longer than any of the others. Not to mention the four consecutive two-second surges that Marshall had underlined.

What it amounted to was a puzzle, a puzzle Marshall wanted to solve.

And Levine's news was good. The taps on Con Edison's phones had been worthwhile, if not altogether legal. The theory that large energy surges would affect local electricity systems had turned out to be correct.

Robert Charlton had led them right to the source of the energy surges.

The New York State Library.

Now they had the location. And they were going to get whatever was there.

James Marshall grinned at the thought as his Lear hit the tarmac at Newark.

Hawkins lowered Balthazar to the floor, resting him up against the concrete wall of the janitor's room. Then he himself collapsed, breathless, alongside the big bearded man.

'You're one heavy bastard, you know that?'

The janitor's room was a complete mess. The cyclone fence cutting across the middle of the room had been crumpled by the Karanadon. The splintered remains of smashed wooden boxes lay strewn everywhere. And without the big hydraulic door, the doorway was nothing more than a gaping hole in the wall.

Hawkins glanced at Balthazar by his side. He wasn't looking good. Eyes still badly bloodshot. A red rash forming on the surrounding skin. Bubbles of saliva still running through his bushy beard.

Balthazar groaned, and then as if testing himself, he put a hand to the floor to get up, but immediately fell awkwardly back against the wall.

They would have to hole up here for a while. But

first, Hawkins thought, he had to do something about that doorway.

At last, Selexin got up and walked across the elevator and stared at the massive body of the unconscious Karanadon. He bent down and peered at the long white fangs that protruded from the jet-black snout.

He made a face of pure disgust. 'Hideous,' he said. 'Truly hideous.'

Swain was holding Holly in his lap. She had gone to sleep quickly, complaining of a terrible headache. 'Yeah, not too bright, either,' he said. 'Have you ever seen one before? Up close?'

'No. Never.'

Swain nodded and they both just stared at the gigantic black beast in silence. Then he said, 'So what do we do? Do we kill it? *Can* we kill it?'

'I do not know,' Selexin shrugged. 'No-one has ever done this before.'

Swain offered a crooked smile and spread his hands. 'What can I say?'

Selexin frowned, not comprehending. 'I am sorry, but I am afraid I do not understand. What exactly *can* you say?'

'Don't worry. It's just a saying.'

'Oh.'

'Yeah,' Swain said, 'like "Fuck you".'

Selexin blushed. 'Oh, yes. That. Well, I had to say *something*. My life was in the balance too, you know.'

'Hell of a thing to say to something like *that*,' Swain nodded at the Karanadon.

'Oh, well . . .'

'But it was pretty bold. And I needed it. Thanks.'

'Think nothing of it.'

'Well, thanks anyway,' Swain said. 'By the way, are you allowed to do that? Allowed to help me?'

'Well,' Selexin said, 'technically, no. I am not supposed to help you physically in any battle—whether against another contestant or the Karanadon. But considering what Bellos has done by bringing hoods into the Presidian, then, to use another of your sayings, I think that all gambling has been cancelled.'

'Huh?'

'Is that not how you say it? "All gambling has been cancelled." It means that the rules no longer apply.'

'I think what you're trying to say is, *All bets are off*,' Swain said gently. 'But you were close. Very close.'

Selexin preened at that, pleased with himself.

Swain turned back to the Karanadon. The long spiked bristles on the beast's back were rising and falling in time with its loud, strained breathing. It was absolutely enormous.

'So can we kill it?'

'I thought you did not kill defenceless victims,' Selexin said.

'That only counts for people.'

'Balthazar was not a person, and you did not kill him. He is amorphous, remember. As a matter of fact, I am sure that you would be rather surprised at Balthazar's true form—'

Swain said, 'All right. Only for things that *look like* people, then. And besides,' he looked at the Karanadon, 'Balthazar wasn't going to rip my head off if he decided to fight back.'

Selexin looked as if he was about to object but stopped himself. He merely said, 'Okay.'

'So. What do you think? Can we kill it?' Swain asked.

'I don't see why not. But what will you kill it with?'

They surveyed the elevator. There wasn't much to be found by way of weapons. The roof of the lift had been made of thin plasterboard and one whole half of it had simply disappeared, destroyed by the Karanadon's fall. Large jagged shards of frosted plastic from the fluorescent lights lay strewn across the floor. Swain picked one up. In his hand, it looked like a pretty pathetic weapon.

Selexin shrugged. 'It *could* work. Then again, it might not do anything except wake it up.'

'Hmm,' Swain didn't like the thought of that.

He didn't want to rouse the Karanadon. It was fine now. Out cold. But for how long? And killing something that was bigger and stronger than a grizzly bear, by hand, with a shard of plastic, somehow didn't seem very likely.

At that moment, the Karanadon's right claw reached up lazily and swatted at something buzzing around its snout. Then the claw resumed its position by the creature's side and the big beast continued its slumber as if nothing had happened.

Swain watched it intently. Frozen.

The Karanadon snorted loudly, shuffled onto its side, rolled over.

'You know, upon further reflection, I am not so sure that killing it is a very good idea,' Selexin whispered.

'I was just thinking the same thing myself,' Swain said. 'Come on, let's go.' He stood up and lifted Holly.

'Come on, honey. Time to go.'

She stirred groggily, '—my head hurts.'

'Where to?' Selexin asked.

'Up,' Swain said, pointing to the big hole in the roof of the elevator.

After heaving the outer elevator doors open, Swain looked out into the musty yellow gloom to see row upon row of bookshelves stretching away to his left and right.

It was Sub-Level Two.

The Stack.

They were standing on what was left of the roof of the destroyed elevator, five feet below the floor level of Sub-Level Two. The concrete bottom of the elevator shaft, it seemed, was still a fair way below Sub-Level Two.

Swain climbed out first and saw that on this floor, the elevators were embedded in the wall of bookshelves.

He looked out from the doors and immediately realised that they were on one of the long ends of the rectangular floor. The southern wall.

Swain remembered finding Hawkins on this floor, and seeing Reese for the first time, and running blindly through the maze of shelves to the safety of the stairwell. But that, he remembered, had happened on the other side of the floor.

He turned back to the elevator shaft and pulled Holly and Selexin out.

'I remember this part of the labyrinth,' Selexin said, seeing the bookshelves around him. 'Reese.'

'That's right.'

'Daddy, I have a headache,' Holly said wearily.

'I know, honey.'

'I want to go home.'

'So do I,' Swain said, reaching down, touching her head. 'We'll see if we can find something for your headache, and at the same time, somewhere to hole up. Come on, let's go.'

They began walking left, down the southern wall of the Stack. After walking some distance, their aisle turned sharply to the right, and they headed up the shorter western wall of the floor. They had gone about twenty yards along the wall when Swain noticed something odd.

Just ahead of them, flush against the outer wall of shelves, something was ajar, sticking slightly out into the aisle. Something red.

As they came closer, Swain realised what it was.

It was a door.

A small red door, slightly opened. It was tucked into the outer wall of shelves, very unobtrusively. Indeed, Swain had seen it only because he had almost walked right past it. Anyone conducting a cursory examination of the Stack would almost certainly miss it.

The small red door had writing on it.

'"No Staff Access Permitted",' Selexin read aloud. 'What is that supposed to mean?'

But Swain wasn't paying any attention to Selexin. He was already kneeling in front of the door, peering down at its base.

Selexin said, 'I thought the staff were allowed to go everywhere in a place like this—'

'Shh,' Swain said. 'Look at this.'

Selexin and Holly crouched beside him and stared down at the book lying on the floor, wedged in between the door and its frame.

'It looks like it is holding the door open . . .' Selexin said.

'It *is* holding the door open,' Swain said, 'or at least stopping it from closing.'

'Why?' Holly asked.

Swain frowned. 'I don't know.' He looked at the door handle. On the library side, it had a keyhole in the middle of a plain silver knob. On the other side, though, he could not see any lock or keyhole. High up near the hinges he saw the closing mechanism.

'It's spring-loaded,' he said. 'To make sure it shuts every time. That's why someone used the book.'

'Why is no staff access permitted?' Selexin asked.

'Probably because this door has nothing to do with the library. And only staff are allowed in the Stack. I'd say it's probably a gas or electricity meter. Something like that,' Swain said. 'Something the staff are not supposed to touch.'

'Oh.'

Holly said, 'Can we get out through there?'

Swain looked to Selexin. 'I don't know. Can we?'

'The labyrinth was *supposed* to be sealed at the time of electrification. I cannot know what would happen if one entrance was not fully closed at that time. But I can guess.'

'So guess.'

'Well,' Selexin peered around the rim of the small red door marked NO STAFF ACCESS PERMITTED. 'I see no visible sign of electrification here. And unless there is another door *beyond* this one that was closed at the time of electrification, my guess is that we may have just found a way out of the labyrinth.'

'A way out?' Holly said hopefully.

'Yes.'

'Are you sure?' Swain whispered.

'There is only one way to find out,' Selexin said. 'We have to see if there is another door beyond this one.'

'Do we?' Swain said, thinking.

'Why, yes,' Selexin said. 'Unless you can think of another way.'

Crouching on the floor, Swain looked up at the little man, and said, 'As a matter of fact, I think I can.'

And with that, Stephen Swain thrust his left arm— with the thick grey wristband attached to it—*through* the gap between the small red door and its frame.

Immediately they heard a loud, insistent beeping coming from outside the door, and after a couple of seconds, Swain pulled his wrist back inside.

The beeping stopped instantly.

265

They all looked at the thick grey wristband. Its display now read:

INITIALISED—6
DETONATION SEQUENCE INITIALISED.
AT * 14:57 * DETONATION SEQUENCE
CANCELLED
RESET.

14:57 was flashing.

Swain smiled at Selexin. 'There's no outer door. This is the last one.'

'How do you know, Daddy?' Holly asked.

'Because,' Selexin said, 'your father's wristband is set to initialise an automatic detonation sequence of fifteen minutes as soon as it senses that it is outside the energy field of this labyrinth.'

'What?' Holly said.

Swain said, 'He means that if I move outside the electric field that's all around this building, this wristband will explode unless I get back inside in fifteen minutes.'

'And do you see that?' Selexin pointed to the read-out, the flashing 14:57. 'The countdown started when he put his wrist outside the door.'

'Which means,' Swain continued, 'that once we're

outside this door, we're outside the electrical field, and outside the labyrinth.'

'Right,' Selexin said.

'So let's go,' Holly said. 'Let's get out of this place.'

'We can't,' Swain said sadly, 'or, at least, *I* can't. Not yet.'

'Why not?' Holly said.

'Because of the wristband,' Selexin sighed.

Swain nodded. 'I can't get it off. And if I don't, I'll only last fifteen minutes before this thing explodes.'

'Then we had better find a way to get it off,' Selexin said.

'How?' Swain said, shaking his wrist. The wristband was hard and strong, a thick steel clamp. 'Look at it. It's as solid as a rock. We'd need an axe or a hammer to break it open, *and* someone strong enough to crack it.'

'I bet Balthazar could do it,' Holly said. 'He's really big. And I bet he's really strong, too.'

'And when we last saw him, he was not strong enough to stand up by himself,' Selexin said sourly.

'We don't even know if he and Hawkins are still alive,' Swain said. 'There has to be another way.'

Selexin said, 'Maybe they have a vice around here that we could squeeze it in. Snap it open with the pressure.'

'In a library? Not likely.'

Frustrated, Selexin sat down next to the semi-opened door, staring at the escape he couldn't use. Swain was also gazing at the door, deep in thought. Holly held him tightly by the arm.

'Well, first of all,' Swain said, 'we have to get you guys out. After that, I'll just have to find a way to get this thing off and then meet you outside.' He snorted. 'Hmph. Maybe I should go and ask Bellos if he'd like to have a try. I'm sure he'd like that.'

'He'd definitely be strong enough,' Selexin said.

'But would he do it?' Swain scoffed.

'Gladly,' a deep baritone voice said from somewhere behind him.

Swain spun.

There, right in front of him, standing in one of the aisles perpendicular to the western wall, stood Bellos.

Swain felt a chill at the sight of the man. His body, his face, his long tapering horns, everything about him was black. Except for his breastplate, which Swain now clearly saw to be beautifully crafted in gold.

And he was tall, taller than he had seemed before. At least seven feet.

'Greetings, fellow competitor. Before you stands Bellos—'

'I know who you are,' Swain said softly.

Bellos cocked his head in astonishment.

'Where are your hoods?' Swain asked calmly, as Selexin and Holly slowly got to their feet beside him. 'You don't fight without them, do you?'

Bellos chuckled evilly. As he did so, Swain saw something jingle at his side—something attached to his belt.

It was the Konda's breathing mask.

With a tinge of horror, Swain recalled Selexin's earlier description of Bellos: *the trophy collector.*

And then suddenly he caught sight of a second object clipped to Bellos' belt, something that glinted dull gold in the mouldy yellow light of the Stack. Swain's eyes widened when he saw what it was.

It was a New York Police Department badge.

Hawkins' partner . . .

Bellos spoke, releasing Swain from his thoughts. 'You attempt to show courage you do not possess, little man. There are no hoods here. Just you. And me.'

'Really,' Swain said. 'I don't believe you.'

Bellos stepped forward. 'You use strong words for a man who is *moriturum esse.*'

'*Moriturum esse,*' Swain repeated. Out of the corner of his eye, he watched for the hoods, expecting one of them to spring from one of the nearby aisles at any moment now. 'About to die, huh. If that's the case, why don't you just *osci assinum meum* then,' he said.

Bellos frowned, not understanding.

'*Osci assinum meum?*' he repeated, perplexed. 'You want me to kiss your mule, your ass?'

Swain surreptitiously kicked the book wedged in the doorway clear from the small red door. The spring-loaded door immediately began to close and he caught it in his hand—behind his back.

'When they attack,' he whispered to Selexin and

Holly, 'I want you two to run straight through the door. Don't worry about me.'

'But—'

'*Just do it*,' Swain said, never taking his eyes off Bellos.

Bellos sneered, 'Do you just stand there, little man, *or do you fight?*'

Swain said nothing, just looked left. Then right. Waiting for the hoods.

They attacked.

Suddenly. Without warning. From the front. Not the sides. From *behind* Bellos' shoulder.

It was a single hood, springing forward, claws bared. Straight at Swain.

With his free hand Swain swiped at the creature backhanded, hitting it squarely in the head, sending it crashing to the floor with a squeal.

Swain immediately opened the door behind him. 'Go!' he yelled to Selexin and Holly. 'Go! Go!'

And then the second hood attacked.

This one came from the left, slamming into Swain's back, knocking him to the floor, making him let go of the door.

The spring-loaded door began to close.

The second hood leapt at Swain again as he rolled onto his back. Swain threw a desperate arm up at the approaching hood and caught its narrow throat in his hand. Its massive jaws clamped viciously open and shut, trying madly to reach his face, as Swain held it out at arm's length.

Its claws swatted wildly, lashing out at his chest— but they weren't long enough. So it went for his arm instead—slashing ferociously. Five bloody gashes appeared instantly across Swain's forearm.

It was then that Swain saw the door closing.

'The door! *Get the door!*' he yelled to Holly and Selexin.

But Holly and Selexin just stood there. Dead still. Staring off to the right, down the western wall.

Swain was looking desperately at the rapidly closing door. It was almost shut when, as a last resort, he thrust his leg out and wedged his foot between the door and its frame.

'Go!' he yelled, kicking the door open again as he wrestled with the hood.

But Selexin and Holly weren't moving.

They were watching the third and fourth hoods as they stalked ominously out into the aisle.

Swain got up on one knee, still holding the second hood at arm's length. The animal decided on a new tactic. Instead of writhing about maniacally in his grip, lashing out with its claws, it grabbed hold of Swain's forearm with both its claws, clinging to him, and started *squeezing*, hoping to break his grip on its neck.

'Jesus! Go! Get out!' Swain yelled, his foot holding the door wide open. 'I can't hold it open much longer!'

But Holly and Selexin didn't move, and when at last he saw what they were looking at, Swain had a fleeting thought that came a second too late.

Where did that first hood go?

The first hood slammed into Swain at a crunching speed—hurling itself, Swain and the second hood into the open door. Swain bounced off the door and into the dark corridor beyond it, the two hoods with him.

'*No!*' he cried, as he saw the door behind him start closing again.

He still had the second hood's throat gripped tightly in his hand—just as it still held his forearm. Ruthlessly, he banged its head twice against the hard concrete floor and the hood immediately released its grip and its body went limp and Swain threw it aside and dived for the closing door.

There was noise everywhere. The hoods squealing, a loud electronic beeping coming from his wristband, and then—worst of all—the sound of Holly screaming inside the library.

Still diving, Swain landed a few feet short of the door and slid the rest of the way on his chest, arms out-stretched . . .

Too late.

The door shut.

The lock clicked.

And a blinding burst of sizzling blue electricity exploded out from the hinges and the handle.

Electrified.

There was a sudden, terrifying silence, broken only by the loud insistent beeping noise that came from Swain's wristband. Swain looked down at it. It read:

INITIALISED—6
DETONATION SEQUENCE INITIALISED.
* 14:55 *
AND COUNTING

Stephen Swain looked up at the electrified door in horror.

He was now outside the labyrinth.

FOURTH MOVEMENT

30 November, 8:41 p.m.

Holly and Selexin ran flat out down one of the aisles of Sub-Level Two.

Holly could hear nothing but her own rapid breathing as they raced down the narrow canyons of bookshelves. Beside her, Selexin was holding her hand, pulling her along, constantly looking behind them.

They came to a junction of aisles and made a quick right-left, zig-zagging their way toward the stairs at the centre of the massive subterranean floor.

Holly had started screaming as soon as she'd seen Swain tumble backwards through the doorway under the weight of the two hoods, but Selexin had suddenly come to life, seizing her hand, pulling her down the nearest aisle.

Behind them, they could hear the snarls and grunts of the hoods in hot pursuit.

Not far behind.

And gaining. Fast.

Selexin pulled Holly harder. They had to keep running.

Swain surveyed the dark passageway around him. Mouldy yellow fluorescent lights illuminated the tiny corridor.

The hood by his feet groaned softly. It lay on the floor, dazed by the two pounding blows Swain had given it against the hard concrete floor.

The other hood was nowhere in sight.

Swain crouched beside the hood on the floor. It hissed defiantly at him, but it was too badly injured to move.

Swain looked at his wristband, at the countdown in progress.

14:30

14:29

14:28

There was no time to waste. He had fourteen minutes to get back inside before his wristband exploded.

No. More important than that. He had fourteen minutes to get back to Holly.

Swain grimaced and picked up the injured hood by its narrow throat. It wriggled weakly in his grip—a futile gesture. Then Swain closed his eyes and banged the creature's head a final time against the concrete floor. The body went limp immediately. Dead.

Swain discarded the carcass and headed cautiously down the narrow corridor.

The other hood was still nowhere to be seen.

At the end of the passageway, he came to a small room filled with large box-like electricity meters attached to the walls. A big sign above one of the meters read: **BOOSTER VALVE**.

Swain noticed a small talon of jagged blue electricity licking intermittently out of a gap in the ceiling, touching the booster valve meter, causing it to short. Con Ed would love that, he thought.

There was a small doorway on the other side of the room.

With no door.

With his wristband still beeping insistently, Swain eased his way through the doorway and found himself standing beside the train tracks of the New York Subway.

It was quiet in the train tunnel. The walls were all painted black, with long white fluorescent tubes spaced every fifteen yards or so. An old wooden door swayed from a sturdy padlock by the side of the doorway. Swain wondered how the door had come to be pulled from its hinges.

There was a rustling sound from his right.

Swain turned.

The second hood was *right there*!

Three yards away, its back turned, its head shaking violently from side to side. In its mouth, the remains of what was once a rat.

Swain was about to move away from the hood when there came a soft rumble from deep within the tunnel. The tracks beside him began to hum.

Vibrating.

A soft white glow appeared around of the corner of the tunnel.

Suddenly a subway train burst through the silence, its wheels screaming a deafening, high-pitched wail, its brightly lit windows flashing rapidly by.

Immediately, Swain dropped to the black sooty ground of the tunnel, and in the flashing light of the train saw the hood's head snap up and see him.

The train roared by, kicking up specks of dust and dirt, throwing them at Swain's face. He squeezed his eyes shut.

And then, in an instant, the train was gone, and the tunnel was silent once more. The wristband continued beeping.

Slowly, Swain raised his head.

The tunnel was empty. He glanced over to where the hood had been—

It was gone.

Swain spun around.

Nothing.

He could feel his heart thumping loudly inside his head now. His right forearm stung like crazy where dust from the passing train had fallen inside the five deep claw-marks. He began to sweat.

13:40

13:39

13:38

He didn't have time for this. He rolled onto his side, and—strangely—felt something in his left jeans pocket.

It was the broken phone receiver. He had forgotten all about that. Holly had given it to him back on the First Floor. He checked his other pocket.

The handcuffs.

And Jim Wilson's useless Zippo lighter.

He checked the time again.

13:28
AND COUNTING

The words were flashing.

Christ, he thought, *and counting. I know that. I know that!*

Shit.

281

Fearfully, Swain scanned the tunnel around him, searching for the hood. Time was running out. He had to get back inside.

And then, without a sound, the hood attacked him from behind, slamming into his back, sending them both sprawling onto the train tracks. The handcuffs fell to the ground; the lighter, too.

The hood leapt onto his back, but Swain rolled quickly, hurling it clear.

Like a cat, the hood landed smoothly on its feet and immediately spun around and launched itself again at Swain. Swain caught it by its narrow throat, and fell onto his back in between the train tracks.

The hood hissed and squealed and writhed madly about, desperately trying to break Swain's grip. It flailed its razor-sharp claws in every direction—one claw slashing down Swain's chest, ripping the buttons off his shirt, drawing blood, the other swiping viciously at his arm.

Swain lay on his back, on the concrete sleepers *in between* the train tracks, holding his hand outstretched, keeping the frenzied hood at arm's length. Better to let it cut his forearm a few times than let it get at his body—

And then he froze.

He heard it.

A soft, distant rumble.

The hood paid no attention, it just kept jerking its body about fitfully.

And then, on either side of Swain, the train tracks began to hum.

Vibrating.

Oh, no . . .

Oh, no!

Swain's face was right next to the railway track, his eyes level with one of the large circular hooks—on the inside of the tracks—that held the rails to the sleepers.

The hooks, he thought.

The hood was still twisting and turning as Swain rolled suddenly.

Searching.

The hum of the tracks grew louder.

Swain looked desperately about himself. *Where were they?*

Louder still.

Where . . .

This side. That side. Searching. Searching . . .

He could hear the metallic rattling of the approaching train. It would be on them any second now—

There!

The handcuffs lay on the ground, beside another of the big round hooks on the inside of the tracks.

Swain reached over with his free hand and grabbed the cuffs and in one swift movement brought them up to the hood's throat and snapped them around its narrow neck.

283

Calick!

The hood was momentarily startled by the single handcuff locked around its throat.

Swain looked up and saw a hazy white light growing around the corner of the tunnel. The rumbling was very loud now.

Then he quickly dropped the hood and latched the other cuff around the nearest hook on the inside of the track.

Calick!

The scream of steel wheels filled the air. The train rounded the corner.

Swain grabbed the hood by its tail, and dived clear of the tracks, yanking the animal with him.

The handcuffs went instantly taut.

And the hood was left with its head cuffed to the hook on the *inside* of the track, and its body held to the *outside* by Swain.

The train shot past Swain, and there was a loud, sickening *crunch!* as its steel wheels carved through the bone of the hood's neck, decapitating it.

The train roared by, windows flashing, and then disappeared into the tunnel.

There was silence again, except for the wristband's incessant beeping.

Slimy black ooze dripped slowly from the hood's headless body. Swain touched the large droplets of blood that had splattered all over him as the train had sliced the hood's head off.

He dropped the body and looked at his wristband.

11:01
11:00
10:59
AND COUNTING

Only eleven minutes to get back inside.

There wasn't much time.

Swain hurriedly picked up the lighter and leapt from the black floor of the subway tunnel and began to run down the tracks into the darkness.

John Levine sat in the passenger seat of a black Lincoln sedan parked across the street from the main entrance to the State Library of New York.

The building looked peaceful. Quiet. Dead.

Levine looked at his watch. 8:30 p.m. Marshall should have been here by now.

His cellular rang.

'*Levine,*' the voice said. '*It's Marshall. Are you at the library?*'

'Yes, sir.'

'*Is it secure?*'

'Affirmative, sir,' Levine said, 'as quiet as a mouse.'

'*All right, then,*' Marshall said, '*the insertion team is en route. They'll be there in five minutes. I'll be there in two. Break out the tape. I want a thirty-yard perimeter set all the way around that building, okay. And Levine . . .*'

'Yes, sir?'

'*Whatever you do, don't touch the building itself.*'

*

Selexin and Holly could see the stairwell now.

Up ahead. Thirty yards away.

Panting madly, they kept running down the narrow aisle.

They were approaching the intersection of two aisles when suddenly a hood leapt across their path, its claws raised, its jagged teeth bared wide.

Holly and Selexin skidded to a stop and the hood crashed down onto the hard wood floor in front of them.

It got to its feet again, quickly blocking their path down the aisle. Not far beyond the animal, they could see the open door to the stairwell.

Selexin spun to go back the other way but stopped instantly.

There behind them, stepping slowly into the narrow aisle, was the second hood.

Swain ran down the tunnel, toward a light around the bend.

It was a subway station. Which one, he didn't care.

10:01

10:00

9:59

Swain burst into the white light of the subway station and heaved himself up from the tracks onto the platform.

287

A murmur arose among the commuters standing on the platform. They all stepped back in horror as Swain pushed past them, oblivious to how he must have looked.

His jeans were covered with black streaks of grease, and his shirt—filthy black with subway soot, elevator grease and hoodaya blood—was ripped from neck to navel. A single vertical line of blood stretched down his chest, while his right forearm was soaked red from the deep gashes inflicted by the hood. The bloody red scar across his left cheek was indistinguishable on his black sooty face.

Swain barged through the crowd and raced up the stairs toward the surface.

'What do we do now?' Holly whispered fearfully.

'I don't know, I don't know,' Selexin said.

The two hoods stood at both ends of the aisle, trapping Holly and Selexin in the middle.

Selexin, four feet tall, and Holly, about the same, were scarcely bigger than the two hoods.

Selexin looked anxiously around himself, at the bookshelves that stretched up to the ceiling. They seemed to form an impenetrable wall on either side of the aisle.

The hood in front of them edged closer. The other didn't move.

Holly noticed why.

The second hood, the one preventing their retreat, had no left foreclaw. Just a bloody stump at the end of its bony black arm. It must have been the one that Balthazar had pinned to the railing with his knife up on the First Floor.

Holly jabbed Selexin with her elbow and pointed at the hood and he saw it, too.

Selexin edged away from the first hood, toward the injured one, still eyeing the impenetrable walls of shelves on either side of them.

Wait a minute, he thought.

He scanned the bookshelves again.

They weren't *impenetrable* at all.

'Quickly,' he said. 'Grab the books. The ones here,' he pointed to a low shelf. 'Grab them and start throwing.'

He reached down to the bottom shelf and grabbed a large hardback and hurled it at the able-bodied hood, striking it in the face. The hood snarled angrily back at him.

A second book hit it again. Then a third. The fourth book hit the injured hood.

'Keep throwing them,' Selexin said.

They kept hurling books at the hoods, who backed off slightly. Holly threw another and was reaching down for more when suddenly she understood what Selexin was doing.

He wasn't just using the books to keep the hoods at bay. He was using them to create a hole in the bookshelf. The more books they threw from the shelf, the bigger the gap in the shelf became. Soon Holly could see through to the next, parallel aisle.

'Are you ready?' Selexin said, throwing a book, hitting the injured hood on its wounded forelimb. The black creature howled in agony.

'I think so,' Holly said.

The able-bodied hood began to move in.

'All right,' Selexin said. 'Go!'

Without a second thought, Holly dived cleanly through the gap in the bookshelf and landed with a thud in the next aisle.

But Selexin continued to stand in the original aisle.

The injured hood stepped cautiously forward.

The two hoods closed in on either side of the little man.

'Come on!' Holly said from the next aisle. 'Jump through!'

'Not yet,' Selexin didn't take his eyes off the approaching hoods. 'Not *yet*.' He threw another book at the injured hood. It hit. The hood hissed angrily.

'Come *on*!' Holly said.

'Just get ready to run, okay,' Selexin said.

Holly looked frantically down her aisle. On one side she could see the stairwell. On the other . . .

She froze.

It was Bellos.

Striding down the aisle toward her with long strong powerful steps.

'Selexin, jump! Jump *right now*!' she screamed.

'They're not close enough yet . . .'

'Just *jump*! He's almost here!'

'He . . . ?' Selexin was momentarily startled. The hoods were very close now.

'Oh! *Him!*' Realising, Selexin immediately dived through the gap in the shelf, landing in a heap at Holly's feet. She pulled him up and they ran for the stairwell.

Behind them, Bellos began to run.

They bolted down the aisle. Holly could hear the able-bodied hood grunting and snorting as it ran down the parallel aisle.

They hit the stairs running and climbed them two at a time.

Behind them they heard the distinctive scratching sound of claws on marble as the hood charged into the stairwell. That sound was quickly followed by a sudden thudding, crashing sound as the hood lost its footing on the slippery marble floor and slammed into the concrete wall.

Breathlessly, Holly and Selexin kept climbing and climbing until they could hear nothing behind them.

The stairwell was silent.

They kept hurrying upward.

And then there came a voice, from way down at the bottom of the shaft, echoing loudly through the stairwell.

'Keep running!' Bellos' voice boomed. 'Keep running, tiny man! We will find you! We will *always* find you! The hunt has begun, and you are the game. I will hunt you, and I will find you, and when I do, tiny man, you will wish to God that somebody else *had found you first*!'

The voice stopped. And as Holly and Selexin climbed higher, an evil laugh resounded throughout the stairwell.

'Here they come,' Levine said to Marshall as they stood beside his car.

A massive blue van rounded the corner and stopped behind Levine's Lincoln. It looked like a big TV van, with a revolving satellite dish on the roof and flashing blue police lights.

Levine shielded his eyes from the glare of the van's headlights as a barrel-chested man dressed completely in blue stepped down from the passenger-side door and stood to attention before Marshall.

It was Harold Quaid.

Commander Harold Quaid.

Levine hadn't actually worked with Quaid before, but his reputation was legendary. Apparently Quaid had given himself the title of 'Commander'—there was no such rank in the NSA—when he had assumed command of Sigma Division's field team. Rumour had it that he had once killed a civilian by mistake while following up a bogus alien sighting. No investigation into the incident was ever held.

Tonight he was dressed exactly like a SWAT team member: blue fatigues, bulletproof vest, boots, cap and gunbelt.

'Sir,' Quaid said to Marshall.

'Harry,' Marshall nodded. 'You made good time.'

'As always, sir.'

Marshall turned to Levine. 'You've cordoned off the site?'

'They're finishing now,' Levine said. 'Tape's set up all around the building. Thirty yards. Even in the park.'

'Nobody's touched the building?'

'They were given strict instructions.'

'Good,' Marshall said. On the Eavesdropper satellite's last pass—now targeted directly at the New York State Library—an unusually large amount of electromagnetic energy had been detected surging through the outer surface of the building. Marshall didn't want to take any chances.

He turned to Quaid. 'I hope your boys are ready. This is the big one.'

Quaid smiled. It was a cold, thin smile. 'We're ready.'

'You'd better be,' Marshall said, 'because as soon as we figure out how to bring down the electric field around that building, you're going in.'

For the first time that night, Stephen Swain beheld the exterior of the New York State Library.

It was a beautiful building. Four storeys high, square-shaped, flat-roofed, with six majestic Corinthian columns stretching all the way up from the front steps to the roof.

In fact, it looked like an old Southern courthouse, grandly situated in the middle of a beautiful inner-city park, as if part of a town square. Only this was a dated town square, dwarfed by the skyscrapers that had grown up around it.

Swain watched the library from across the street, from the entrance to the subway station. He was breathing hard, and the wounds to his chest and forearms burned.

His wristband was still beeping.

8:00

7:59

7:58

Time was running out and the situation didn't look good.

The library had been sealed off.

A single ribbon of bright yellow police tape stretched from tree to tree in the park surrounding the big dark building, leaving at least thirty-odd yards of open ground between the tape and the walls of the library.

Half a dozen unmarked cars—their headlights still on—formed a tight circle in front of the main entrance to the library. And in the centre of the circle, towering above the cars, stood a big blue police van with a revolving dish on its roof. Next to the dish, flashing blue police lights spun crazily, splashing the park around the library in a strobe-like blue haze.

Damn it, Swain thought, as he watched the big blue van.

For the last two hours all he had wanted to do was get *out* of the library—to get himself and Holly away from Reese and Bellos and the Karanadon—to get out of the electrified cage the library had become.

And now?

Swain smiled sadly.

Now he had to get back *in*.

To get back in and stop this bomb on his wrist from going off. To get back inside the cage, where Reese and Bellos and the Karanadon were waiting for him, waiting to kill him.

But most importantly of all, to get back inside and save Holly. The mere thought of his only daughter trapped inside the library with those monsters made him feel ill. The thought of her being trapped in there *after he was dead*, made him feel terrible. She'd already lost one parent. She wasn't going to lose another one.

But he still had to penetrate the electrified walls.

And who were these new people?

7:44

Swain's gaze came to rest on some shadows at the rear of the library building. Darkness there. Good. It was a chance.

Swain ran across the street.

The park surrounding the State Library was a pretty one, flat and grassy, with evenly spaced oaks spread around three sides of the central building—only now, the oak trees were joined by the bright yellow tape.

Outside the perimeter of oaks, on the eastern side of the building, stood a splendid white rotunda. It was essentially an elevated circular stage, free-standing, with six thin pillars supporting a beautiful domed roof twenty feet above the stage itself. A lattice handrail circled the stage.

It was a beautiful structure, popular for outdoor weddings and the like. Swain even remembered taking Holly to the pantomimes they held here in the summer—*Wizard of Oz*-type shows that involved clouds of coloured smoke and the deft use of a trapdoor in the centre of the stage.

Swain scampered across the open grass and ducked behind the rotunda's stage, out of sight.

Twenty yards to the nearest oak.

Thirty yards from the oak to the library.

He was about to run for the treeline when he saw a garbage bin next to him.

He stopped. Thinking.

If they had set up police tape around the library, it was likely they would have someone patrolling the building, warding off any would-be intruders. He had to find a way . . .

Swain rummaged through the bin and found some crumpled old newspapers. He was grabbing a handful of them when he caught sight of something else.

A wine bottle.

He picked it up and heard the sloshing of liquid still inside it. Excellent. Swain upended the bottle and poured the excess wine onto his hands. The alcohol stung the scratches on his hands.

Then, with bottle and newspapers in hand, he bolted for the treeline.

7:14

7:13

7:12

Swain thrust himself up against the thick trunk of the tree and felt his pockets.

The broken phone receiver and the equally broken lighter were still there. He cursed himself for leaving the handcuffs back at the train tracks.

In the flashing blue light of the van, he saw the nearest corner of the building.

Thirty yards.

He took a deep breath.

And ran out into the open.

Levine yawned as he leaned on the bonnet of the Lincoln. Marshall and Quaid had gone off to check out the parking lot while he had been left to watch the front of the building.

His radio crackled. It would be Higgs, the agent in charge of the surveillance team he had just sent out.

'Yeah,' Levine said.

'*We're on the western side of the building and there's nothing here, sir,*' Higgs' tinny voice said.

'Okay,' Levine said. 'Just keep circling the building, and let me know if you find anything.'

'Roger that, sir.'

Levine clicked off the radio.

*

Swain reached the south-eastern corner of the building and ducked into the shadows of the southern wall.

He was breathing hard now, his heart pounding loudly inside his head.

He scanned the wall.

7:01

7:00

6:59

There. Near the far corner.

Swain ran forward and dived to the ground.

The radio crackled again. Higgs' voice.

'*We are approaching the south-west corner, sir. Still nothing to report.*'

Levine said, 'Thank you, Higgs.'

Swain lay on the grass next to the southern wall of the State Library, still holding the newspapers and the wine bottle.

He was peering at a small wooden window set into the wall at ground level, not far from the south-western corner of the building. The window was old and dusty, and it looked like it hadn't been opened in years. His wristband still beeped softly.

6:39

Swain leaned close and saw a jagged fork of tiny blue lightning lick out from the old window's frame—

A twig snapped.

Somewhere close.

Swain pulled the newspapers to his body and immediately rolled up against the library wall, his eyes inches away from the tiny sparks of electricity that licked out from the window.

Silence.

And then a soft *beep . . . beep . . . beep.*

The wristband!

Swain thrust his left wrist under his body to muffle the sound of the beeping just as he saw three sets of black combat boots step slowly around the corner.

NSA Special Agent Alan Higgs lowered his M-16 and winced at the figure lying huddled up against the wall before him.

A filthy body, curled up in the foetal position, wrapped in crumpled newspapers in a vain attempt to counter the cold. His clothes were filthy rags and the man's face was covered in black grime.

A bum.

Higgs put his radio to his mouth. 'Higgs here.'

'*What is it?*'

'Just a bum, that's all,' Higgs said, nudging the body

with his boot. 'Rolled up tight next to the building. No wonder nobody saw him when they set up the perimeter.'

'*Any problem?*'

'Nah,' Higgs said. 'This guy probably never even noticed the perimeter going up himself. Don't worry about it sir, we'll have him out of here in no time. Higgs out.'

Higgs bent down and shook Swain's shoulder.

'Hey, buddy?' he said.

Swain groaned.

Higgs nodded to the other two agents—like himself, they were dressed in full SWAT gear—who slung their M-16s and bent down to pick up the man.

As they did so, the bum grunted loudly and rolled sleepily toward them, feebly stretching out with one hand, pressing it against the face of one of the agents, as if to say, 'Go away, I'm sleeping here.'

The agent made a face and pulled back. 'Oh, man, does this guy *stink*.'

Higgs could smell the wine from where he stood. 'Just pick him up and get him the hell out of here.'

Swain kept the beeping wristband pressed tightly against his stomach and covered in newspapers as he was carried away from the library building, back into the park.

To his ears it was beeping louder than ever, almost certain to be heard.

But the two men carrying him didn't seem to notice. In fact, they seemed to be trying to keep their bodies as far away from his as possible.

Swain began to sweat.

This was taking too much time.

He desperately wanted to look at the wristband. To see how much time was left.

They couldn't take him away.

He had to get back inside.

'Ambulance?' one of the two carriers asked the third—and presumably superior—man walking in the lead.

Swain's body tensed as he waited for the response.

'Nah,' the third man said. 'Just get him outside the perimeter. Let the police pick him up later.'

'Roger that.'

Swain breathed a sigh of relief.

But if they weren't taking him to a hospital to clean him up, and if they weren't police officers, then there were still two questions to answer: where *would* they take him, and *who the hell were they?*

The heavily armed men carried Swain through the treeline and across the park, toward the rotunda.

Okay. You can put me down now, Swain willed them. *You're taking too long . . .*

They carried him up the steps of the rotunda and laid him down on the circular wooden stage.

'Here will do,' the senior one said.

'Good,' the one whom Swain had rubbed in the face said as he released Swain's arm.

'Come on, Farrell, he doesn't smell that bad,' the senior one said.

Swain breathed again, and his body relaxed.

There would still be time.

Now go, boys. That's good. Keep going . . .

'Wait a minute . . .' the one named Farrell said.

Swain froze.

Farrell was looking down at his gloves. 'Sir, this guy is bleeding.'

Oh shit.

'He's what?'

'He's bleeding, sir. Look.'

Stay calm. Stay calm.

They are not going to come over.

They are not going to look at your arm . . .

Swain's whole body tensed as Farrell held out his gloved hands and the senior man came over.

Higgs examined the blood on Farrell's gloves. Then he looked down at Swain, at the newspapers covering his arms, at the tiny splotches of red that had seeped through the newsprint on his right arm. The strong odour of wine pervaded it all.

Finally, he said, 'Probably just a cut he got falling into a gutter. Leave him be, I'll radio it in. If they think it's necessary, the others can come by later and check him out. I don't think this guy will be going anywhere fast. Come on, let's get back to work.'

They headed back towards the main entrance.

Swain didn't dare move until the sounds of the footsteps had faded off into the night.

Slowly, he lifted his head.

He was in the rotunda, on the stage. He looked at his wristband:

2:21

2:20

2:19

'Why don't you take your time next time, boys?' he said aloud. He couldn't believe it had taken only four minutes. It had felt like an eternity.

But now he only had two minutes left. He had to move.

Fast.

With a final look through the white lattice handrail of the rotunda stage, Swain leapt to his feet, and ran down the stairs.

2:05

Into the treeline, and he stopped beneath one of the heavy oaks.

He reached up and grabbed a thick low-hanging branch and snapped it from the tree. Then he ran out onto open ground again, toward the library building.

1:51

1:50

1:49

In the shadows of the southern wall, Swain came to the ground-level window he had seen before and dropped to his knees. He tightened his grip on the long thick branch and prayed to God that this would work.

He swung the branch down hard at the window. The small window shattered instantly. Glass exploded everywhere.

Instantly, however, a crackling grid of silver-blue electricity burst to life across the width of the window.

Swain's eyes went wide with dismay.

Oh, no. Oh . . . *no*.

1:36

Swain swallowed.

He hadn't thought that *that* would happen. He had hoped that the gap would be too wide, that the electricity would not be able to jump the width of the small window.

But the window was too small.

And now he was left with a wall of jagged, criss-crossing lines of pure electricity in front of him.

1:20

1:19

1:18

Only a minute left.

Think, Swain! Think! There has to be a way! There *has* to be!

But his mind was now a blur of panic and incredulity. To have got so far, and to end it all like this . . .

Images of the night flashed across his mind.

Reese in the Stack. Meeting Hawkins. The parking lot. Balthazar. Up to the First Floor. Bellos and the hoods and the Konda in the atrium . . .

1:01

1:00

0:59

. . . the Internet Facility and the handcuffs on the door. Up to the Third Floor. The janitor's room. The Karana-don. The elevator shaft. Back down to the Stack. The small red door. Falling through the door with the hoods.

Outside. In the tunnel. The subway train.

0:48

0:47

0:46

Wait.

There was something there.

Something he had missed. Something that said there was a way in.

0:37

0:36

0:35

What was it? *Shit!* Why couldn't he remember? Okay, slow down. Think. Where did it happen?

Downstairs? No. Upstairs? No. Somewhere in between. The First Floor.

What had happened on the First Floor?

They had seen Bellos, seen the hoods attack the Konda. Then Balthazar had thrown a knife and pinned one of them to the railing . . .

0:29

0:28

0:27

Then Holly had pressed the elevator button and they had run into the Internet room.

Holly . . .

Then the door. And the handcuffs.

0:20

0:19

0:18

What was it?

Holly . . .

It was there! Somewhere in the back of his mind. A way in! Why couldn't he remember it?

0:14

0:13

0:12

Think, Goddamn it, think!

0:11

0:10

Swain pursed his lips, frowning.

0:09

He swung his head from right to left. No other windows. Nowhere else to go.

0:08

Think back. First Floor. Bellos. Hoods.

0:07

Balthazar. Knife.

0:06

Elevator. Holly pressing the button. *Holly* . . .

0:05

Holly? Something about Holly.

0:04

Something Holly *said?*

0:03

Something Holly *did?*

0:02

And with the expiration of the countdown came the horror of the realisation.

Stephen Swain was dead.

FIFTH MOVEMENT

30 November, 8:56 p.m.

In the janitor's room on the Third Floor, Paul Hawkins sat down against the wall beside Balthazar, and nodded, satisfied.

Across the floor from him, in front of the open doorway of the room, lay a large puddle of highly flammable methylated spirits—and next to him, a box of old-fashioned phosphorus-tipped matches. He had been pleasantly surprised at what he had been able to find on the shelves of the old janitor's room.

He felt a little safer now. Any unwanted guests passing through that doorway would be in for a big—

And then, abruptly, he heard it.

The windows above him rattled slightly, while the floor shook gently.

Hawkins couldn't quite guess what it was.

But it sounded like a muffled explosion.

Selexin and Holly stopped at the top of the stairwell as the wooden banister beside them began to shudder.

'Did you hear that?' Selexin asked nervously.

'I felt it,' Holly said. 'What do you think it was?'

'It sounded like a blast of some sort. An explosion. From somewhere outside—'

He cut himself off.

'*Oh no . . .*'

'*Clear!*' 'Commander' Harry Quaid called again.

Marshall ducked behind the wall at the top of the ramp as Quaid rounded the corner and joined him.

The second blast rushed outward from the bottom of the concrete entry ramp. A billowing cloud of grey smoke raced up the ramp and shot out onto the street, thundering past Marshall and Quaid.

Fragments of metal—the remnants of what had been the steel grating that closed off the library's parking lot—clattered loudly to the ground.

The smoke cleared and Marshall, Quaid and a small cohort of NSA agents made their way down the charred ramp, stepping over the gnarled pieces of steel that now littered the slope.

Marshall stopped at the bottom of the ramp and stared in awe at the sight before him.

Across the wide rectangular opening of the parking lot—filling the exploded round hole in the middle of the steel grating—was an enormous grid of bright blue electricity, crackling and sizzling, lashing out every few seconds with long fingers of high-voltage lightning.

Marshall folded his arms as Quaid stood beside him, gazing at the criss-crossing grid of light before them.

'We knew it,' Quaid said, not taking his eyes off the wall of blue light.

'We did indeed,' Marshall said. 'So. They electrify the whole building, cutting it off, sealing it so that nothing can get in or out . . .'

'Right.'

'So, why have they done it?' Marshall asked. 'What the hell is going on inside this building that we're not supposed to see?'

Holly tapped her foot impatiently as she waited on the Third Floor landing of the stairwell. Selexin was peering around the open fire door into the study hall.

The room was a mess.

An absolute mess.

A diagonal line of pure destruction ran all the way across the study hall—from the doorway to the janitor's room in the far corner, right up to the stairwell door. Desks crushed beneath the weight of the Karanadon lay in splinters, strewn all over the floor.

In the dim blue city light, Selexin could just make out the doorway to the janitor's room on the far side of the room. There didn't seem to be anybody there at the moment. In a dark corner of his mind, Selexin wondered what had happened to Hawkins and Balth—

Suddenly a shadow cut across his view of the janitor's room.

A dark shape, barely distinguishable in the hazy blue darkness, about the size of a man, but much, much thinner, moving stealthily between the desks of the study hall, heading toward the janitor's room.

Selexin ducked back behind the stairwell door, hoping that it hadn't seen him.

Then he grabbed Holly's hand and they began to descend the stairs.

In the janitor's room, Hawkins leaned back wearily against the concrete wall. He was watching Balthazar walk gingerly around the room.

Now that his eyes were clear of Reese's saliva and his vision seemingly restored, Balthazar seemed to be getting his strength back. A few minutes before, he had managed to stand up on his own. Now he was walking.

Hawkins looked out through the doorway—over the wide puddle of methylated spirits he had poured—into the study hall.

Everything was silent.

Nobody was out there.

He turned back to watch Balthazar pace awkwardly around the room, and as he did so, he failed to notice a sharp triangular head loop itself smoothly and silently around the doorway.

It looked inside, slowly tilting its head from side to side, alternating between Balthazar and Hawkins.

It never made a sound.

Hawkins turned idly and saw it. He stopped cold.

The head was a long, sharp, flat isosceles triangle, pointing downwards. No eyes. No ears. No mouth. Just a flat, black triangle, slightly larger than a man's head.

And it just hovered there, in the doorway.

The body was still out of view, but Hawkins could clearly see its long thin 'neck'.

Now, inasmuch as everything he had seen so far was basically 'animal'—with eyes, limbs and skin—this thing, whatever it was, was *totally* alien.

Its 'neck' was like a string of white pearls flowing down from the flat, two-dimensional triangular head. Presumably it flowed into a body that was still out of his sight.

Hawkins continued to stare at the creature—just as it seemed to stare curiously back at him.

And then Balthazar spoke. A deep, husky voice.

'Codex.'

'What?' Hawkins said. 'What did you say?'

Balthazar pointed at the alien. 'Codex.'

The Codex moved forward—effortlessly, smoothly—floating through the air.

It crossed the threshold of the room and Hawkins saw that it had no body at all. The string of pearls that formed its neck was, in fact, about five feet long. And it dangled down from the head, curling upward at the tip, never touching the ground.

And at the tip of the tail, burning brightly, was a green light that glowed from a tight grey metal band. The Codex was another contestant.

The tail slithered back and forth like a snake's, hovering upright, one foot above the ground.

'Oh man,' Hawkins grabbed the matchbox and pulled out a phosphorus-tipped match. He struck it on the floor.

The flare of white light made the Codex hesitate. It stopped above the pool of methylated spirits.

Hawkins held the match aloft, the flame slowly burning its way down the white wood of the matchstick, blackening it.

He swallowed.

'Aw, what the hell,' he said. And he dropped the match into the pool.

Levine was standing out in front of the library when his radio sputtered to life.

'*Sir! Sir! We have a light! I repeat: we have a light! Looks like a fire. Third floor. North-east corner.*'

'I'm on my way,' Levine said. He switched channels on his radio. 'Sir?'

'*What is it, Levine?*' James Marshall sounded irritated by the interruption.

'Sir,' Levine said, 'we have confirmation of activity

inside the library. I repeat, confirmation of activity *inside* the library.'

'*Where?*'

'North-east corner. Third Floor.'

Marshall said, '*Get over there. We're on our way.*'

The walls of the janitor's room flared bright yellow as a curtain of fire burst upward from the pool of methylated spirits, engulfing the Codex.

Hawkins and Balthazar stepped back from the flames, shielding their eyes. The Codex could not be seen through the blazing wall of fire.

And then it emerged.

Floating forward. Through the flames. Oblivious to the heat.

It moved inside the janitor's room, clear of the fire.

'Oh, *man*,' Hawkins said, edging backwards.

Balthazar spoke—again, just one word in a flat monotone.

'Go.'

Hawkins said, 'What?'

Balthazar was staring intently at the Codex. 'Go,' he repeated solemnly.

Hawkins didn't know what to do. The Codex was hovering right in front of them. And even if he got past it, he still had to get through the fire—the fire that he had set up to keep intruders *out*. It had never occurred to him that that same fire might serve to keep him *in*.

There was no way out. There was nowhere *to* go.

Balthazar turned to Hawkins and looked him squarely in the eye. 'Go . . . *now*!'

And with that Balthazar launched himself at the Codex.

Hawkins watched in astonishment as the Codex leapt forward at the same moment and coiled its thin body three times around Balthazar's throat.

With both hands, the big man pulled desperately at the Codex's stranglehold around his neck. He stumbled backwards into the remains of the cyclone fence that divided the room, tripped, and fell to the floor beneath the shelves packed with detergents and cleaning agents.

Hawkins was still just standing there, stunned, watching the battle in awe, when Balthazar cried, 'Go!'

Hawkins blinked and turned immediately. He saw the fire, spreading across the room, creeping across the floor toward him. He saw the dusty methylated spirits bottle he had used, lying on the floor, inches away from the approaching flames.

Too late.

The flames devoured the bottle as Hawkins dived over the nearest pile of wooden boxes.

Under the intense heat, the glass bottle—still half full—exploded like a Molotov cocktail, shooting out missiles of glass and fire in every direction.

Beyond the cyclone fence, Balthazar was back on his feet again, struggling with the Codex.

He fell back heavily against the wooden shelves and they collapsed under him. Glass spirit bottles, plastic detergent bottles and a dozen aerosol spray cans crashed to the floor.

Hawkins saw the shelves collapse, saw all the bottles hit the floor—cleaning agents and detergents that carried conspicuous red warning signs: **DO NOT MIX WITH DETERGENTS OR OTHER CHEMICALS**, and highly flammable aerosols with their own glaring warning labels.

The fire moved inexorably forward, across the room.

'*Oh my God,*' Hawkins' eyes darted from the fire on the floor to the chemicals lying in its path.

Behind the cyclone fence, the Codex's body was still coiled tightly around Balthazar's throat. Balthazar's face was twisted in a tight grimace, his cheeks beetroot red.

Hawkins spun to warn him about the fire and in that instant their eyes met, and Balthazar, staring intently at Hawkins, tightened his grip on the Codex's snake-like body.

Hawkins saw it in the big man's eyes. Balthazar knew what was going to happen. The fire. The chemicals. He was going to stay in the room. And keep the Codex with him.

'No!' Hawkins cried, realising. 'You can't!'

'Go,' Balthazar gasped.

'But you'll—' Hawkins saw the flames creeping steadily across the floor. He had to make a decision fast.

'*Go!*' Balthazar yelled.

Hawkins gave up. There was no more time. Balthazar was right. He had to go.

He turned back to face the fast-approaching wall of fire, and, with a final glance back at Balthazar—locked in battle with the Codex—Hawkins said softly, 'Thank you.'

Then he covered his face with his forearm and plunged into the fire.

Levine arrived at the north-east corner of the library building just as Quaid and Marshall came running up. The agent in charge of the perimeter, Higgs, was there waiting.

'Up there,' Higgs said, pointing at two long rectangular windows up on the third floor, just below the overhang of the library's roof.

The two windows glowed bright yellow, with the occasional flash of orange flames.

'Jesus Christ,' Marshall shook his head. 'The goddamn building is *on fire*. That's just what I need.'

'What do we do?' Levine said.

'We get inside,' Harry Quaid said flatly, gazing up at the glowing windows. 'Before there's nothing left.'

'Right,' Marshall scowled, thinking. 'Damn it. *Damn* it!' Then he said, 'Levine.'

'Yes, sir.'

'Call the fire department. But when they get here, tell them to hold off. We don't want them going in there until we've had a good look inside. I just want them here in case that fire gets out of con—'

'Hey. Hold on a minute . . .' Quaid called. He had wandered off down the side of the building and was now standing at the south-eastern corner.

'What is it?' Marshall said.

'*What the fuck . . . ?*' Quaid disappeared down the southern side of the building.

'What is it?' Marshall followed, rounding the corner after Quaid.

Quaid was thirty yards down the southern wall, almost at the south-western corner of the building. He called back to the group. 'Special Agent Higgs, you in charge of surveillance tonight?'

'Yes, sir.'

'Tell me, did you find anybody around here earlier? Anybody near this wall?'

Higgs didn't understand what was going on. Quaid

was peering at the base of the wall, at what appeared to be a small window down near the ground.

'Well—uh—yes, sir. Yes, we did,' Higgs said. 'We found a drunken bum asleep up against this wall not long ago.'

'Was he down near this corner? Near the window down here?' Quaid asked.

'Uh, yes. Yes he was, sir.'

'And where is this drunken bum now, Higgs?' Quaid asked, kneeling on the grass, still looking at the base of the building.

Marshall, Levine and Higgs came closer.

Higgs swallowed. 'We put him in the rotunda over there, sir.' He pointed back over his shoulder. 'I was going to call it in, but I didn't think there was any hurry.'

'Special Agent Higgs, I want you to go straight to that rotunda and find that bum for me, right now.'

Higgs hurried off immediately.

Quaid glanced up at the others as they saw what he had been looking at.

'What the . . . ?' Levine gasped.

'Well would you look at that,' Marshall said as he saw the spiderweb of electricity that spread across the small ground-level window. Tiny shards of glass lay strewn on the grass around the base of the window.

There was nobody in sight.

Quaid leaned close to the window. It was just big enough for a man to fit through. But why would somebody break it? That would serve no purpose whatsoever.

Unless they wanted to get in . . .

Higgs came running back. He spoke breathlessly.

'Sir, the bum is gone.'

Hawkins burst through the flames and fell out of the doorway and dropped to the floor of the study hall.

He checked his body. His police trousers and parka had survived the dash through the fire intact and unharmed. But for some reason his head stung like crazy.

He reached up to touch the crown of his head and suddenly felt the searing heat.

His hair was on fire!

Hawkins frantically took off his parka and smothered the tiny flames on his head with it. The heat died down quickly, and he began breathing again.

The janitor's room was glowing bright yellow now, lighting up the study hall outside. Flames flared out through the doorway.

It wouldn't be long now, he thought.

Hawkins crawled to the side of the doorway, pushed his back up against the wall.

He only had to wait a few seconds.

The chemicals inside the janitor's room combined

well. After the first aerosol can exploded in a ball of gaseous blue flame, a chain reaction of chemical explosions was set in motion.

The concrete wall behind Hawkins cracked under the weight of the shock wave as a golden fireball blasted out through the doorway, rocketing past Hawkins, setting the study hall aglow in a flash of brilliant yellow light.

Marshall, Levine and Quaid all looked up at the same time as the entire third floor of the building flared like a fiery flashbulb, lighting up the night.

Voices came in over their radios:

'—*fire is spreading!*—'

'—*corner room just exploded*—'

'Holy shit,' Levine breathed.

It sounded like thunder.

Close, booming thunder.

The whole building rocked under the weight of the explosions.

On the Second Floor of the library, Holly and Selexin reached desperately for handholds as they tried to stay on their feet.

The Second Floor of the New York State Library was

comprised mainly of two large computer rooms. In the centre of each room, long wooden tables were covered with PCs. A tangle of air-conditioning units and aluminium air ducts hung from the ceiling, providing much-needed humidity control for the computers. Glass-walled reading rooms lined the perimeter of the floor.

The explosions from the Third Floor were growing in intensity, and on the Second Floor they were received with all their violent force.

The glass walls of the reading rooms shattered all around Holly and Selexin. Computers fell from the edges of the tables, crashed to the floor.

Selexin pulled Holly under one of the long tables in the centre of the floor and they huddled together, covering their ears, as the building shook and the explosions boomed and monitors and keyboards fell from the tables all around them, smashing down onto the floor.

Chaos. Absolute chaos.

In the study hall, Hawkins pressed his hands tightly against his ears as waves of flames lashed out from the doorway next to him.

Several of the L-shaped desks around him were on fire—ignited by the initial flamethrower-like finger of fire that had blasted out from the janitor's room.

The explosions were bigger now—bigger than he had expected them to be, bigger than any chemical fire he knew.

They were almost, well . . . *too* big.

Why had that—?

Hawkins froze. Something else must have happened. *But what?*

And then he saw it.

A small pipe, running horizontally, high up on the wall near the ceiling.

It ran out from the janitor's room, across the wall of the study hall—above the northern windows—and then, halfway across, it turned abruptly downwards and ran down to the floor, and then *through* the floor down to the other floors below . . .

A gas pipe.

There must have been a gas valve in the janitor's room that he hadn't seen. A gas water heater or a gas—

The small pipe ignited.

Hawkins watched in horror as a yellow-blue flame sped in a thin line across the pipe's horizontal length, and then turned as the pipe did, darting downwards, heading for the lower floors.

Hawkins watched as a droplet of fire fell from the gas pipe and landed on one of the wooden desks. With a sudden *whoosh*, the desk went up in flames.

Hawkins leapt to his feet. The explosions from the

janitor's room were finally beginning to die, but that didn't matter anymore.

A fire was spreading through the gas piping.

Soon the whole building would be alight.

He had to find a way out.

In a small toilet on Sub-Level One, somebody else was feeling the shuddering explosions that were rocking the New York State Library.

Stephen Swain MD sat with his back pressed up against the white-tiled wall of a cubicle in the ladies' room of Sub-Level One. The water in the toilet bowl next to him splashed about wildly as the building around it tilted and swayed.

Another explosion boomed and the building shook again, although not as drastically as it had before. The explosions seemed to be losing their muscle.

Swain checked his wristband. It read:

INITIALISED—6
DETONATION SEQUENCE TERMINATED AT:
* 0:01 *
RESET

The top line flickered, then changed to:

INITIALISED—5

High above Swain's head, just below the ceiling, the grid of blue electricity was still sizzling. Beyond the glowing window he could hear the faint voices of the NSA agents.

He pressed himself closer against the tiles and breathed deeply.

He was back inside.

It was the thought of Holly that had done it.

Holly on the First Floor, in the dilapidated Internet Facility. When the hoods had been pounding on the door and Swain had handcuffed it shut, he had found Holly over by the window.

She had been holding the broken telephone receiver up against the electrified window. When the phone was brought in close to the window, the electricity seemed to pull back in a wide circle.

Away from the phone.

At the time, Swain hadn't realised what was happening, but he knew now.

It wasn't the phone that the electricity had been pulling away from, but the *magnet* inside the phone. The earpiece of a telephone is like a common stereo speaker: at its centre one will find a relatively high-powered magnet.

And as a radiologist, Stephen Swain knew all about magnetism.

People commonly associate radiologists with X-rays, but in recent years radiologists have been endeavouring to discover new ways to obtain cross-sections of human bodies—views taken by looking *down* on the body from above the head.

There are a number of techniques used to obtain these cross-sections. One well-known method is the CAT-scan. Another more modern method involves the splicing and ordering of atomic particles and is called Magnetic Resonance Imaging.

Basically—as Swain had explained to the troublesome Mrs Pederman earlier that day—MRI works on the principle that electricity reacts to magnetic interference.

And that was exactly what had happened when Holly had held the receiver to the window—the *magnetic* waves disrupted the very structure of the *electronic* waves and, hence, made the wall of electricity pull away from the magnet in order to maintain their frequency.

To get inside again, Swain had grabbed the receiver from his pocket and held the ear-piece to the window. The electricity had instantly pulled back from the receiver, forming a wide two-foot hole in the grid, and Swain had simply thrust his arm in through the hole.

The wristband, once detecting itself to be inside the electric field again, stopped its countdown immediately.

Just in time.

After a minute's careful wriggling and squirming—to make sure he did not move his body beyond the two-foot magnetic circle in the electric grid—Swain was back inside.

In fact, he had just pulled his right foot inside the window when he fell from the high window sill. The electric grid sizzled immediately back into place and Swain fell clumsily onto the toilet seat below.

Inside.

Paul Hawkins was halfway across the study hall when the explosions ceased.

Only the loud crackling sounds of a fire out of control remained. The desks over by the janitor's room were now blazing wildly. The janitor's room itself was still glowing bright yellow. The whole study hall was bathed in a flickering golden haze.

Suddenly there came a crashing sound from behind him and Hawkins spun.

There, hovering in the doorway to the janitor's room, silhouetted by the flickering yellow flames behind it, was the Codex.

Hawkins froze.

Then he saw it wobble slightly.

The Codex was hovering unsteadily. It began to swirl dizzily. And then, abruptly, its flat triangular head snapped upward and the Codex fell, crashing down on top of a crumpled desk.

After that, it didn't move.

Hawkins sighed with relief.

He was about to turn back for the stairwell when he caught sight of something on the floor not far from the door to the janitor's room. Something white. Slowly, Hawkins stepped forward until he could see what it was . . .

He stopped cold.

It was a guide. Or at least what was left of him.

It had probably been the Codex's guide, stationed outside the janitor's room while the Codex had gone inside for the kill.

The guide's body lay in a wide pool of blood underneath one of the L-shaped desks and it had been mangled beyond recognition.

Small clusters of parallel red slashes ran across its face, arms and chest—one of which had broken its nose, making for an especially gruesome excess of blood. Deep scratches on the little man's palms suggested futile defensive efforts. His eyes and mouth were wide open—frozen in eternal terror—a snapshot of his horrifying final moments.

Hawkins winced at the sickening sight—it was disgusting, brutal. And then, as he looked more closely at the clusters of slashing cuts all over the guide's body, he had a sudden, terrifying realisation. Parallel cuts indicated claws . . .

Bellos' hoods had done this.

It was time to get out of here.

Hawkins immediately turned back for the stairwell—

—only to see a big black hand rush toward his face.

And then he saw nothing.

Stephen Swain stepped cautiously out from the ladies'
room and saw the familiar glass-walled offices of Sub-
Level One.

He checked his wristband and found that the screen
had changed again.

INITIALISED—4

Another contestant was dead. Only four were left
now.

Swain wondered which contestants were still alive.
He shrugged off the thought. Hell, he only really knew
of three others—Balthazar, Bellos and Reese. Including
himself, maybe they were the only four left.

Got to find Holly, he told himself. *Holly*.

He stepped out among the offices. Across the floor,
through the glass partitions, he saw the elevator bay. He
also saw the heavy blue door that led out to the parking
lot. It was open.

Swain hastened over to the door and examined it. It

had been torn from its hinges, presumably by Reese when she had been chasing them before.

He remembered the chase into the parking lot, remembered Balthazar coming up the concrete ramp from the floor below . . .

The floor below.

Sub-Level Two, the Stack.

That was where he had been separated from Holly and Selexin, so it was the obvious place to start looking for them.

He had to get down there.

Go down the stairwell?

No. There was another way. A better way.

He remembered Balthazar again, coming up the ramp in the parking lot. *That* was the way in. Balthazar had come from another, lower, parking level. And that level had to have an entrance of some sort, a door that would open onto Sub-Level Two.

With that Swain ran through the big blue door and out toward the parking lot.

From the outside it looked like a scene from *The Towering Inferno*. The State Library of New York—standing proudly in the centre of a beautiful inner city park—with long flaming tentacles spraying out from two flat rectangular windows up near its roof, while rows of windows on the third and second floors were illuminated by a glowing golden haze.

John Levine was back at the front of the library, watching as the building before him burned.

Behind him, the big blue NSA van pulled out from the kerb and headed for the western side of the library building.

Levine watched as the van jumped the kerb and drove straight onto the grass lawn surrounding the library. Then it disappeared around the corner.

He turned back to see headlights—lots of headlights —and he knew what that meant. The fire department was arriving—closely followed by the media.

Multi-coloured vans screeched to a halt just outside

the perimeter of yellow tape. Sliding doors were flung open and cameramen charged out. Behind them, pretty reporters emerged from their vans, fluffing and primping.

One bold young reporter hustled straight over from her van, ducked under the yellow police tape and walked straight up to Levine and thrust a microphone into his face.

'Sir,' she said, in her best, most serious voice, 'can you tell us *exactly* what is happening here? How did the fire start?'

Levine didn't answer. He just stared at the young woman, silent.

'Sir,' she repeated, 'I said, can you tell us—'

Levine cut her off, speaking softly and politely, facing the young reporter, but clearly addressing the three NSA agents standing nearby.

'Gentlemen, please escort this young lady outside the perimeter and inform her that if she or anyone else crosses that line again they will be arrested on the spot and charged with Federal offences relating to interference with matters of national security, sentences for which range between ten and twenty years, depending on what sort of mood I'm in.'

The three agents stepped forward and the reporter, mouth agape, was led ignominiously back to the perimeter.

Levine was watching her legs as she walked off when his radio came to life. It was Marshall.

'Yes, sir?'

'*Quaid and I are at the entrance to the parking lot,*' Marshall said. '*TV there yet?*'

'They're here all right,' Levine said.

'*Any trouble?*'

'Not yet.'

'*Good. We'll be down here from now on. This fire has raised the stakes. Now we have to get inside before the whole place burns down. Is the truck on the way?*'

'It just left,' Levine said. 'You'll be seeing it any second now.'

The ramp leading down from the street to the underground parking lot was on the western side of the library building.

Marshall was standing at the base of the ramp, not far from the metal grille that closed off the parking lot. In the centre of the grille, just touching the ground, was the large circle of criss-crossing blue electricity.

Behind him, the big NSA van reversed around the corner and backed slowly down the ramp.

'Okay,' Marshall said into his radio, seeing the van, 'it's here. I'll call you back soon. For now, you just keep those firemen and reporters behind the tape. Okay?'

'*Okay,*' Levine's voice said as Marshall hung up.

The van stopped and the back doors burst open and four men dressed in SWAT gear jumped down onto the ramp. The first of them—a young technician—came straight up to Quaid and they spoke quietly. Then the technician nodded vigorously and disappeared inside the van. He re-emerged several seconds later carrying a large silver box.

Quaid walked over to Marshall, standing in front of the electrified metal grille.

Marshall said, 'How long will it—?'

'We'll be in there soon,' Quaid said calmly. 'We just have to do the math first.'

'Who are you going to get to do it?'

'Me,' Quaid said.

The technician placed the heavy box down on the concrete next to Quaid, then bent down and flipped open its silver lid to reveal three digital counters. Each counter displayed red numbers, which at the moment read: 00000.00.

Quaid then pulled a long green cord out from the box and led it over to the metal grille. The cord had a shiny steel bulb at the tip.

Another heavily armed agent came over and handed

him some insulated black gloves and a long pole with a loop of rope attached to its end. Quaid put the gloves on and inserted the steel bulb into the loop at the end of the pole.

He took a long, slow breath. Then he pointed the pole away from his body, toward the wall of criss-crossing blue lightning.

The steel bulb at the end of the pole glistened as it edged closer and closer to the wall of blue light.

Marshall watched tensely. Quaid swallowed.

The NSA team stared in anticipation.

None of them knew what would happen.

The bulb touched the electricity.

The counters in the steel box immediately began to tick upward slowly, measuring the voltage. They sped up slightly, the numbers getting larger and larger.

And then they went into overdrive.

On the Second Floor of the library, Holly and Selexin huddled together underneath one of the large central tables. On the floor all around them lay the crumpled remains of a dozen shattered computers.

The glass walls of the Reading Rooms had once been like the glass partitions on the First Floor—glass from the waist up, wood from the waist down—only now they had been shattered beyond recognition by the explosions, reduced to little more than gaping windows with jagged edges.

Worse still, on the eastern side of the floor, in two of the reading rooms, fires had started.

Selexin sighed sadly. Next to him, Holly was sobbing.

'Are you all right?' he asked, concerned. 'Are you hurt?'

'No . . . want *Daddy*,' she whimpered. 'I want my Daddy.'

Selexin looked over at the doorway leading to the stairwell. It was shut. 'Yes. I know. I do, too.'

Holly stared at him, and Selexin could see the fear in her eyes. 'What's *happened* to him?' she sniffed.

'I do not know.'

'And those *things* that pushed him out through the door? I hope they die. I *hate* them.'

'Believe me,' Selexin said, still eyeing the door, 'I dislike them intensely, too.'

'Do you think Daddy's coming back inside?' Holly asked hopefully.

'I am *sure* he is already back inside,' Selexin lied. 'And I would wager that at this very moment he is probably somewhere in the building looking for us.'

Holly nodded, wiping her eyes, encouraged. 'Yeah. That's what I think, too.'

Selexin smiled weakly. As much as he wanted to believe that Stephen Swain was still alive, he was extremely doubtful. The labyrinth was electronically sealed for the sole purpose of keeping the contestants *in*. Only an inexplicable fluke had created an opening in the building at the time of electrification—it was highly unlikely that another existed.

And besides, he had *heard* the explosion himself. Stephen Swain was most certainly dead . . .

And then, out of the corner of his eye, Selexin saw movement.

It was the stairwell door.

It was opening.

Swain hurried down the grey corridor and stepped out into the white fluorescent light of the car park.

It was exactly as he remembered it. Clean, shiny concrete, white floor markings, the DOWN ramp in the centre.

And it was quiet. The car park was totally empty.

Swain hurried over to the DOWN ramp and had just started to descend it when he heard someone shouting.

'Hello! *Hey!*'

Swain turned around, puzzled.

'Yes, you! The guy at the top of the ramp!'

Swain searched for the source of the shouts. His gaze fell on the entry ramp. It was off to the left, down a long, narrow passageway, closed off to the outside world by a big steel grille. At the bottom of the grille was a round exploded hole that glowed blue with criss-crossing lines of electricity.

Beyond the hole in the grille, however, was a man, dressed in blue combat attire.

And he was shouting.

Holly sat frozen underneath the long wooden table. Selexin stared at the slowly opening door.

Apart from the muffled crackling of flames that came from the fire in the reading rooms, the Second Floor of the New York State Library was completely silent.

The door to the stairwell continued to open.

And then slowly—very slowly—a big black boot stepped through the doorway.

The door opened wide.

It was Bellos. He was alone. The two remaining hoods were nowhere to be seen.

Selexin raised a finger to his lips and Holly, her eyes wide with fear, nodded vigorously.

Bellos walked into the open central area of the Second Floor.

His boots crunched softly on the broken glass of the computer monitors as he passed within a foot of the table under which Holly and Selexin hid.

He stopped.

Right in front of them!

Holly held her breath as the big boots swivelled on the spot, the body above them looking around in every direction.

Then the knees began to bend and Holly almost squealed at the prospect of it: Bellos was going to look under the table!

Bellos' legs crouched and a wave of terror swept through Holly's body.

The long tapering horns appeared first.

Then the evil black face. Upside down. Peering at them.

And at that moment, a wicked grin broke out across Bellos' face.

In the parking lot, Swain edged cautiously toward the exit ramp.

'*Hellooo!*' the man behind the grille called. 'Can you hear me?'

Swain didn't reply. He moved forward, toward the grille, focusing on the man on the other side.

He was a stocky man, dressed in blue fatigues and a bulletproof vest, like a member of a tactical response team.

The man called again. 'I said, *can you hear me?*'

Swain stopped, twenty yards away from the electrified grille.

'I can hear you,' he said.

At the sound of Swain's voice, the man behind the grille turned instantly and spoke to someone else, someone Swain could not see.

The man turned back, held up his palms and spoke very slowly. 'We mean you no harm.'

'Yeah, and I come in peace,' Swain said. 'Who the hell are you?'

The man continued to speak in that kind of slow, articulate voice one uses with an infant.

Or, perhaps, an alien.

'We are *representatives* of the government of the *United States of America*. We are'—the man spread his arms wide—'*friends.*'

'All right, friend, what's your name?' Swain said.

'My *name* is *Harold Quaid*,' Quaid said earnestly.

'And what department are you from, Harold?'

'The *National* Security *Agency.*'

'Yeah, well, I've got some bad news for you, Harold Quaid of the National Security Agency. I'm not the alien you're looking for. I'm just a guy who was in the wrong place at the wrong time.'

Quaid frowned. 'Then who are you?'

Something inside Swain's head told him not answer that question.

'I'm just a guy.'

'And where are you from?'

'Around.'

'And what are you doing in a building that's got a hundred thousand volts of electricity running through its walls?'

'Like I said, Harold, wrong place, wrong time.'

Quaid changed tack. 'We can help you, you know. We can get you out of there.'

'I've already been out, thanks,' Swain said. 'It's hazardous to my health.'

Quaid turned away for a second and conversed briefly with the man behind him. He turned back to Swain. 'I'm afraid I didn't catch that last thing you said,' he called. 'What was it again? Something about your health?'

'Forget it,' Swain said, rapidly losing interest in this conversation.

The NSA was not so selfless as to come all the way out here to save innocent humans caught up in an electrified library. It was bigger than that, it had to be. The NSA was here for contact—*extra-terrestrial* contact. Somehow they must have figured out that something was going on inside the library and now they wanted the aliens.

And, presumably, anyone who had come into contact *with* the aliens.

'No, I mean it,' Quaid said reasonably, 'come a little closer and say it again.'

Swain took a step back. 'I don't think so, fellas.'

'No, no. Please! Listen. We're not going to hurt you. I promise.'

'Uh-huh.'

'But if you'll just step a little closer . . .'

The dart whizzed by Swain's head, missing it by inches.

It had come from behind Quaid—from somebody who must have crept up behind him while he had kept Swain occupied. They must have shot the tiny dart *through* a gap in the electric field.

Swain didn't wait to think about it. He turned and ran, bolting for the DOWN ramp in the centre of the parking lot.

And as he raced down the ramp toward Sub-Level Two, the last thing he heard was the echoing voice of Harold Quaid of the National Security Agency shouting fiercely at some poor unseen subordinate.

At the base of the outer ramp, Quaid swore.

'*Fuck!* We had him!'

He turned to the Lab agent holding the tranquilliser gun. 'How the *fuck* did you miss? I can't believe you could miss him from—'

'Hold on, Quaid,' Marshall said, resting a hand on his shoulder. 'We may have lost the guy, but I think we just hit the jackpot. Take a look at that.'

Quaid turned. 'Take a look at what?'

Marshall pointed at the parking lot and Quaid followed the line of his finger. His jaw dropped immediately.

'What the hell is *that*?' he breathed.

'I don't know. But I want it,' Marshall said.

Through the grid of blue electricity they could see it clearly, whatever it was.

It looked monstrous, like a large, low-bodied dinosaur—at least fifteen feet long, with a rounded, blunt snout and two long antennae that clocked rhythmically from side to side above its head.

Quaid and Marshall watched, entranced, as the creature limped slowly across the parking lot. It stopped at the top of the DOWN ramp, where it seemed to sniff the ground for an instant.

Then it slithered quickly down the ramp and out of sight.

'Well, well, well. What *do* we have here?' Bellos said, peering under the table.

Selexin was trying hard to keep his body from shaking—and obviously not succeeding. Holly sat frozen beside him.

'Why, tiny man, your memory is as short as you are. I told you I would find you. Or did you forget?'

Selexin swallowed. Holly just stared.

'Perhaps your memory needs a little . . . *refreshing*.' Bellos began to stand. 'Get out from under there.'

Holly and Selexin scrambled out to the far side of the table. Bellos stood on the other side, his wounded guide draped over his shoulder. The flickering fires in the nearby reading rooms were now looking decidedly out of control.

Bellos cocked his head mockingly, 'Where will you run to now, tiny man?'

Selexin glanced over toward the stairwell, and saw the two hoods step menacingly into the open doorway, cutting off their only escape.

'Uh-oh,' he whispered.

When he looked at Bellos again, he saw that his golden breastplate was now smeared with thick red streaks of blood. On the black background of Bellos' forearm, Selexin saw his grey wristband clearly.

And saw the glowing green light suddenly flicker off.

The red light next to it blinked to life.

'*Uh-oh*,' Selexin said again.

Bellos began to strut around the long table. He

seemed to be in no hurry. Savouring the moment. He didn't appear to notice the red light now illuminated on his wristband.

'Why have you done this?' Selexin asked.

'Done what?'

'Broken the rules of the Presidian. Cheated. Why have you done this?'

'Why not?'

'You have broken the rules of the contest in order to win it. How can you respect the prize if you cannot respect the tournament? You have cheated.'

'When one is *caught* breaking the rules, one is a cheat,' Bellos said, walking around the end of the table. 'I do not plan to be caught.'

'But you *will* be caught.'

'How?' Bellos asked, as if he already knew the answer to the question.

Selexin spoke quickly. 'A contestant can expose you. He can say 'Initialise' and show those watching at the other end that you have hoods with you.'

'It would be a brave man who would attempt such a thing *while he was running for his life*. Besides,' Bellos said, 'who here knows that I have hoods?'

'I do.'

'But *your* master was last seen falling out of the labyrinth. And he is the only one who can initialise the teleport on your helmet.'

Selexin paused for a moment. Then he said, 'Reese.'

'What?'

'Reese knows,' Selexin said, remembering the hoods attacking Reese back on the First Floor.

'But you do not know if Reese is still alive.'

'Is she still alive?'

'Amuse me,' Bellos said. 'Let us suppose for the moment that Reese is still alive.'

'Then she can report you. She can initialise the teleport on her guide's helmet and expose you.'

'And what about her guide?'

'Excuse me?' Selexin frowned.

'Her *guide*,' Bellos said smugly. 'Surely you cannot believe that if I let Reese live, I would also allow her guide to do so.'

'You killed Reese's guide *before* you attacked Reese?'

Bellos smiled. 'All's fair in love and war.'

'Clever,' Selexin said. 'But what about the hoods? How did you plan to get the hoods out of the labyrinth. Surely you were not just going to leave them here.'

'Trust me, the hoodaya will be long gone from the labyrinth by the time I step through the final teleport,' Bellos said.

Selexin frowned. 'But how? How can you remove them from the labyrinth?'

'I will simply use the same method I used to bring them here.'

'But that would require a teleporter . . .' Selexin said, '*and* the co-ordinates of the labyrinth. And no-one but the organisers of the Presidian knows the location of the labyrinth.'

'On the contrary,' Bellos looked down at Selexin, 'guides like *you* know the co-ordinates of the labyrinth. You have to, because you are teleported with each contestant into the labyrinth.'

Selexin thought about that.

The process of teleportation involved a guide being sent to the contestant's home planet. There, the guide and the contestant would enter a teleporter, *alone*. Once inside, the guide would enter the co-ordinates of the labyrinth and the two of them would be teleported.

Selexin's case had, of course, been different, since humans knew nothing of teleporters and teleportation. He and Swain had been teleported separately.

'But you would still need a teleporter to get the hoods out of here,' Selexin said. 'And there are no teleports to be found on Earth.'

Bellos offered an indifferent shrug, conceding the point. 'I suppose not.'

Selexin was angry now. 'You forget that this is all based on the assumption that you will be the last contestant remaining in the labyrinth. And *that* is yet to be determined.'

'*That* is the risk I take.'

'Your great-grandfather won the Fifth Presidian with no need for treachery,' Selexin said spitefully. 'Imagine what he would think of you now.'

Bellos waved a dismissive hand. 'You do not realise, do you? My people *expect* me to win this contest, just as they expected my great-grandfather to do so, too.'

'But you are not the huntsman your great-grandfather was, are you, Bellos?' Selexin said harshly.

Bellos' eyes narrowed. 'My, my. How boldly we speak when we are about to meet our maker, tiny man. My great-grandfather did what he had to do to win the Presidian. So will I. Different methods, for sure, but tiny man, you must realise that the end does justify the means.'

'But—'

'I think I have had enough of your talk,' Bellos cut him off. 'It is time for you to die.'

Slowly, Bellos rounded the near corner of the table, moved toward Selexin and Holly. Selexin looked desperately about himself. There was nowhere to run to now. Nowhere to hide.

He stood there rooted to the spot, in front of Holly, watching Bellos come closer.

And then—slowly, silently—something behind Bellos caught Selexin's eye.

Movement.

From above.

From behind one of the air-conditioning ducts in the ceiling.

Slowly, ever so slowly, a spindly black body began to unfold itself from the ceiling *behind* Bellos.

It made no sound.

Bellos hadn't noticed it. He just kept approaching Selexin and Holly—while behind him, the large spindly creature assumed its full, ominous, nine-foot height.

Selexin was dumbstruck.

It was the Rachnid.

The seventh and last competitor in the Presidian. It looked like a giant stick insect, small-headed, multi-limbed. He saw its eight bone-like limbs slowly expand, preparing to wrap themselves around Bellos' body and squeeze him to death.

Then suddenly the Rachnid struck—quickly, violently—closing its arms around Bellos with stunning speed, wrenching him off his feet, lifting him high into the air.

At first, Selexin and Holly were stunned by the sheer rapidity of the attack. It had happened so fast. The slow ominous descent of the Rachnid had instantaneously transformed itself into brutal violence. And now all of a sudden Bellos was in the air, in the grip of the Rachnid, struggling with this new opponent.

The hoods moved immediately.

The able-bodied one galloped from the doorway,

leapt up onto the table and flung itself at the Rachnid, jaws bared, defending its master. The second, injured hood moved more slowly, but with equal fervour, clambering up onto the table and diving into the fray.

The element of surprise now appeared completely worthless as the Rachnid—confronted by the unexpected appearance of the two hoods—dropped from the ceiling, shrieking. It landed with a loud *smack!* on the table below, its eight spindly limbs flailing wildly in a desperate attempt to ward off the three-pronged attack.

Holly and Selexin were both staring at the scene in amazement when suddenly they both had the same thought.

Get out of here.

They bolted for the stairwell door and burst into the darkened stairway.

'Up or down?' Holly asked.

'Down,' Selexin said firmly. 'I saw another contestant up on the Third Floor before.'

They had barely taken five steps down the stairs when there came a deafening—but familiar—roar from the bottom of the stairwell.

'The Karanadon,' Selexin said. 'It's awake again. I saw the red light on Bellos' wristband. Come on,' he grabbed Holly's hand. 'Upstairs.'

They started up the stairs again, and as they ran past the door to the Second Floor, Selexin glanced inside and saw a flashing glimpse of Bellos on the table, kneeling astride the Rachnid, locked in combat.

But now Bellos clearly had the upper hand.

The hapless Rachnid was pinned beneath him, flat on its back, squealing insanely as one of the hoods ripped one of its arms clean off. The Rachnid shrieked. Off to one side, the other hood—the injured one—was busy mauling the Rachnid's guide.

And then Bellos coldly broke the Rachnid's neck and in an instant the squealing stopped. Then Bellos stood and called the hoods to stand behind him, and pointed his guide's head toward the dead body on the table.

'Initialise!' he said loudly.

A small sphere of brilliant white light appeared above the guide's head and Selexin was suddenly captivated.

Holly pulled on his arm. 'Come on, let's go!'

Selexin ducked back behind the door and the two of them hurried up the stairs.

The first thing that struck Stephen Swain about the lower parking level was its size. It was smaller than the parking floor above it. And it had no exit for cars. You could park down here, but you had to go back up to the floor above to get out.

There were three doors, each set into a different wall. One, leading east, had emblazoned across it, EMERGENCY EXIT. Opposite that door was another that read TO STACK. A third door—an older one—lay on the southern side of the parking lot. A few letters were missing from its nameplate. It simply read:—LER ROOM—NO ENTRY.

And there was a car in this parking lot.

A single, solitary car.

A tiny Honda Civic turned silently into the northwest corner, waiting patiently for its owner to return.

Swain tensed at the sudden thought that perhaps there was someone else inside the library. The owner of the car, somebody they had not seen yet.

No, he told himself. *Couldn't be.*

Then he began to think of the other possibilities—like sending the little hatchback blasting through the electrified grille in a fiery blaze of glory, and maybe getting out of the library.

But as he came closer to the little Civic, all his grandiose thoughts faded to nothing.

He sighed.

The car's owner would not be here.

And the car itself would not be blasting through any electrified grille.

This car wouldn't be going anywhere.

Swain looked sadly at the two heavy yellow clamps that held the little car firmly to the concrete floor of the parking lot, and then at the painted blue stripe on the concrete beneath it.

The car had been parked in a handicapped zone, and since it didn't have a sticker on the windshield, the authorities had put the clamps on it.

Swain smiled sadly at the useless car in front of him. At the hospital he'd seen it happen a thousand times, and he always felt that the creeps who parked in the handicapped zones deserved to get clamped.

But now, in the parking lot of the New York State Library, this car offered him absolutely nothing. A gun without any bullets.

It was then that Swain noticed the low hissing noise.

He turned around.

'You never give up, do you?' he said aloud.

For there, standing at the base of the DOWN ramp—her tail slinking back and forth behind her, her antennae clocking from side to side, and her four-sided jaw salivating wildly—stood the very first contestant Stephen Swain had met that night.

Reese.

Holly and Selexin clambered up the dark stairwell and stopped once again on the Third Floor landing. From the bowels of the stairwell came another deafening roar.

The Karanadon.

Somewhere down there.

Selexin stopped in front of the closed door to the study hall, remembering the thin shadow he had seen in there before—the shadow of the Codex.

'The door's closed,' Holly whispered.

'Yes . . .' Selexin said as if it were quite obvious.

'Well—'

'Well what?'

Holly leaned close. 'Well, *we* didn't close it. When we were here before, we just left. We didn't close the door. Remember?'

Selexin didn't remember, but at the moment he

didn't care whether the door had been closed or not, they had to go somewhere.

'You are probably right,' he said, gripping the door handle. 'But right now, there is nowhere else to go.'

The little man turned the handle and opened the fire door. He pulled it wide.

And then he fell instantly backwards.

Beside him, Holly turned and vomited explosively.

'Bring it over! Bring it over!' Quaid called. It had started to drizzle softly and a light rain now fell on his head. Quaid didn't even notice it.

The four NSA agents carrying 'it' heaved and grunted as they lowered it to the ground beside the electrified grille.

As they did so, Quaid looked down at the silver box with the counters.

The middle counter read: **120485.05**.

One hundred and twenty *thousand* volts. One hundred and twenty thousand volts of pure, borderless electric current. Kind of like an electrified fence, only without the fence.

Quaid turned his attention to the object that the four agents had just put down beside him. 'It' was the thick lead casing for Sigma Division's portable Radiation Storage Unit.

A portable RSU is basically a pressurised vacuum set inside a four-foot-high lead cube. It is used to contain any radioactive object discovered in the field until it can be brought back for study at the huge electromagnetic Radiation Storage Facility in Ohio.

In other words, it was a glorified thermos flask, surrounded by a thick, waist-high lead casing.

Quaid had ordered that the portable RSU in the van be dismantled and the heavy lead casing be brought out.

'It won't work,' Marshall said, looking down at the big lead cube, which now had its top and bottom faces removed.

'We'll see,' Quaid said.

'That electric field will cut right through it.'

'Eventually, yes, but maybe not right away.'

'What does that mean?'

'That means that it might buy us enough time to get a couple of men inside.'

Marshall frowned. 'I'm not sure . . .'

'You don't have to be sure,' Quaid said roughly. 'Because you are not the one who'll be going in.'

Selexin never took his eyes off the doorway. Beside him, Holly was still retching over a puddle of vomit, tears welling in her eyes.

Slowly, clumsily, Selexin got back to his feet, all the while staring wide-eyed up into the doorway.

There, silhouetted grimly by the blazing yellow flames inside the study hall, hanging upside down from the ceiling, drenched in glistening blood, was the horribly mutilated body of New York Police Officer Paul Hawkins.

In the lower parking lot, Swain kept his eyes fixed on Reese's tail, trying to avoid eye contact with her paralysing antennae.

She moved forward.

Toward him.

Slowly.

Then abruptly her forefoot tripped and she stumbled slightly.

It was only then that Swain remembered where he had last seen Reese. It was back on the First Floor, when the hoods had attacked her, and he and the others had fled for the stairs.

There was no doubt about it. Reese was injured. Battered and bruised from a fight with the hoods that she had only just survived.

Swain looked at himself, covered in the filthy black grime of the elevator shaft and the subway tunnel. He glanced at his wristband.

INITIALISED—3

Another contestant was dead. There were only three of them left now. The Presidian was nearing completion and the remaining contestants were injured and dirty and exhausted. It was now a battle of endurance.

There was a sudden flare of yellow from the right and Swain saw a gas pipe near the ceiling catch fire.

He stole a glance back at Reese—still trudging wearily forward—then at the little Honda Civic next to him—still utterly useless.

Then back up at the gas pipe. At the soft blue-yellow flame that began to shoot along its length. Swain's eyes followed the pipe, ahead of the flame. The pipe disappeared into the wall, right above the mysterious door marked—**LER ROOM—NO ENTRY**.

Then Swain had a sickening thought.

Gas. Gas mains.

'—**LER ROOM**.'

Boiler room.

Oh my . . .

The racing blue-yellow flame scooted across the ceiling, following the path of the gas pipe. Then it disappeared into the wall above the door.

A long silence ensued.

Then . . .

The explosion was huge. It sounded like a cannon

going off as the door to the boiler room blasted outward in a thousand pieces, followed by a billowing cloud of smoke and flames. Swain was thrown backwards onto the bonnet of the Civic.

Quaid wobbled slightly as the ground shook. An explosion somewhere.

'We have to go in now,' he said to Marshall.

'How many—?'

'As many as we can.'

'How do you know you'll get through?' Marshall asked.

'How do you know we won't?' Quaid said.

Marshall pursed his lips. 'No-one has ever seen anything like this before . . .'

Quaid just stared at him, waiting for him to make the call.

Then Marshall's eyes narrowed. 'Okay, do it.'

Swain rolled off the bonnet of the little Honda to see Reese turn to face the blazing boiler room.

Overhead sprinklers came instantly to life, dousing the whole parking lot with streams of water. It was like standing in a thunderstorm—booming explosions from the boiler room amid the pouring rain of the sprinklers.

Swain brushed the torrents of water from his eyes as he tried to see what Reese was doing. To his right—halfway between Reese and himself—he caught a glimpse of the door on the western wall of the lot, the door he wanted.

The door that read: TO STACK.

'Ready? Okay, push!' Quaid yelled.

The NSA team heaved on the big lead casing, pushing it toward the electrified grille of the parking lot.

Quaid had got them to turn the big lead cube onto its side, so that the open ends—the top and bottom—were now pointed sideways, toward the crackling grid of blue electricity.

When the lead cube was a foot away from the blue lightning, Quaid, now dressed in full assault gear—helmet, bulletproof vest—called them to a halt.

Marshall handed him an M-16 assault rifle, equipped with a high-tech-looking underslung unit. It looked like an M-203 grenade launcher, except that it had two sharp silver prongs at its end instead of a wide gunbarrel. It was a Taser *Bayonet*—a modern version of an ancient weapon. Instead of attaching a long dagger to the end of your rifle, you attached a couple of thousand volts.

'Some firepower,' Marshall said.

'Don't leave home without it,' Quaid said, taking the weapon.

Marshall reached into his coat.

'One more thing,' he said, pulling a sheet of paper from his pocket. It was the list of times and energy recordings taken from the Eavesdropper satellite. 'Have you got your copy?'

Quaid patted his back pocket. 'Don't you think I know the damn thing off by heart by now? Thirteen surges of energy after we picked up the initial electricity field in the city. That's the starting point. Thirteen things for us to find.'

'If you get in,' Marshall said.

'Yeah,' Quaid said grimly, 'if I get in. You just make sure you're ready for whatever I bring out.'

'If we're not ready, it'll be because we're already inside with you.'

'Good,' Quaid turned to the agents around him. 'Okay, boys. Let's do it.'

The agents began pushing the lead cube toward the wall of criss-crossing blue electricity. Quaid walked slowly behind it, waiting at the open rear end of the cube.

The front end of the cube touched the electricity.

Sparks flew.

Quaid ducked instantly to look through the open

rear end of the lead cube. He could see right through it. The electricity wasn't able to cut through the lead.

The NSA agents kept pushing until the cube was half inside, half outside the blue wall of light.

The lead was still holding.

They now had a tunnel through which Quaid could crawl *through* the electrified wall.

Gun in hand, Quaid dived inside the cube—and for a moment, disappeared from sight—and then he emerged on the other side of the electric grid, thumbs up.

'All right,' he called back. 'Send the others through.'

The rest of the NSA entry team—all of them armed with Taser-equipped M-16s—were lined up behind the cube.

The first agent in the line, a young Latin-American named Martinez, immediately dived head-first into the cube.

There came a sudden gut-wrenching *crack!* just as Martinez's legs disappeared inside the tunnel.

'Quickly, move! Before she goes!' Marshall yelled.

And then, without warning, the thick lead cube snapped like a twig under the weight of the surging electric wall *just as* Martinez emerged from the other side, his gun hand trailing behind him. The cube collapsed instantly, cut clean across its middle—likewise Martinez's M-16, which was sheared right through its trigger guard, the lethal electricity missing the young commando's fingers by millimetres.

The wall was back in place.

Quaid and Martinez were cut off.

'You guys all right?' Marshall asked through the grille.

'One gun down, but we're okay,' Quaid said, handing Martinez his own SIG-Sauer pistol, to replace the younger man's ruined M-16. 'Guess we're on our own from here. Be back soon.'

Quaid and Martinez hustled off into the parking lot, heading toward the DOWN ramp.

Marshall watched them go. When finally they were gone, his face creased into a smile.

They were inside the library.

Yes.

Swain stood in the corner of the lower parking lot, drenched in the pouring rain. On the other side of the floor, billowing flames lashed out from the boiler room, impervious to the relentless downpour of the ceiling sprinklers.

Reese continued to limp toward him.

Somehow, she seemed determined to reach him despite the protests of her aching body; consumed by an obsession that would not rest until Stephen Swain was dead.

Swain began to think. He couldn't kill Reese, she was just too big, too strong. And even if she was injured, she would still rip him apart in a fight.

How do you do it? he thought. *How do you kill a thing like that?*

Easy. You don't.

You just keep running.

Swain took a step backwards and felt his legs touch the little Honda.

He was in the corner.

Wonderful.

He stepped out along the wall of the parking lot, away from the car, toward the door leading to the Stack.

Reese moved quickly, paralleling the move, cutting off his escape.

Swain stopped about ten feet from the Honda, his back to the wall. He could feel the thick spray of the sprinklers hammering down against his head.

He looked at his feet, at the thick pool of water that seemed to be growing around him. It wasn't even a centimetre deep, but it stretched nearly all the way across the vast concrete floor, constantly expanding as the overhead sprinklers supplied it with a constant rain of water.

He was standing in it. Reese was, too.

His eyes followed the path of the spreading pool of water.

The pool seemed to be branching out in every direction, even over toward the eastern wall, toward the door marked **EMERGENCY EXIT**.

The Emergency Exit.

Swain's mind began to race.

The Emergency Exit would have to be an exterior door, a door leading directly outside.

And if it was, then . . .

He froze in horror. Reese still stood opposite him. The expanding pool of water crept slowly toward the Emergency Exit.

If it was an exterior door, *then it would be electrified*.

And if the pool of water reached it . . .

'Oh dear,' Swain said aloud as he looked at the water in which he was standing. 'Oh *dear* . . .'

Run! his mind screamed. *Where? Any—*

'*Don't move!*' a voice shouted.

Swain's head jerked upright.

Reese snapped around.

Two men stood at the base of the ramp in the centre of the parking lot.

It was Harold Quaid of the National Security Agency and another agent, both dressed in SWAT gear. Quaid held a strange-looking M-16 assault rifle in his hands. The other agent held a silver semi-automatic pistol.

Swain froze.

He glanced over at the Emergency Exit—at the sprinklers on the ceiling that showed no sign of stopping—at the growing pool of water that continued to edge closer to the door.

It was three feet away.

He must have made to move because Quaid called again. 'I mean it! *Don't move!*'

Swain stood stock still.

The water edged closer to the door.

Reese scuttled off to Swain's left, away from Quaid.

Quaid and his partner edged out from the ramp, their respective guns up, eyeing Reese, eyeing Swain. They stepped out into the water.

The spreading pool was now two feet from the door.

Rain from the sprinklers kept falling.

Swain wanted to run—

'Just stay there!' Quaid barked, aiming his gun threateningly at Swain. 'I'm coming over!'

One foot . . .

The water was almost at the door . . .

Screw it, Swain thought. *Either way, I'm going to die.*

'*Don't move*—' Quaid yelled as Swain broke into a run, racing for the Civic in the corner, every step splashing in the water.

Gunfire erupted.

Swain sprinted along the concrete wall, inches ahead of a line of bulletholes.

I'm not going to make it, he thought as heavy drops from the sprinklers pounded against his face. *Not going to make—*

He dived for the car.

The water touched the door.

Swain landed on the bonnet of the little Honda with a loud thud and covered his head with his hands. At the same moment, Quaid's gunfire ceased.

Swain wasn't sure what he expected to hear. The sizzling of electrostatic currents shooting through the water. Maybe even a scream from Quaid, whom he had last seen standing in the middle of the pool of water, firing at him.

But nothing happened.

Nothing at all.

The parking lot remained dead silent, save for the constant *shoosh* of the sprinklers.

Swain slowly lifted his hands from his head and saw Quaid and the second NSA agent—still standing near the central concrete ramp, their feet still in the pool of water—staring curiously at him as he lay on the car bonnet.

Reese, however, was nowhere in sight.

The pool of water had reached the Emergency Exit and flowed right under it without incident.

Swain could think of only one explanation. It wasn't an exterior door. It hadn't been electrified. There must be another door beyond it.

Sprinkler rain continued to fall.

And then suddenly—*ferociously*—Reese burst for-fjward from behind the second NSA agent, and abruptly, the man's ribcage exploded, replaced in an instant by the pointed tip of her tail, protruding grotesquely from his chest.

Quaid spun but he was too slow.

Reese was already moving—extracting her tail from Martinez's body, letting the corpse drop to the floor like a rag doll—and then trampling roughly over the body and hurling herself at Quaid, bounding into him, pitching him forward, knocking him to the floor with a splash.

She must have circled the central ramp, Swain realised, and then come up *behind* the two NSA agents, who had been threatening him.

Threatening *her* kill.

But Quaid was not giving in without a fight. He rolled onto his back just as Reese leapt onto his chest, jaws salivating, antennae swaying. Quaid reached up with his M-16, holding it above the water, and vainly sprayed the ceiling with automatic gunfire. At the same time, Swain thought he saw a flicker of white light flash out from the high-tech-looking unit attached to the barrel of Quaid's assault rifle.

The struggle continued in the pouring indoor rain—but Reese was too strong, too heavy.

Her thick right forelimb came crashing down on Quaid's right arm—his gun arm—and Swain heard the nauseating crunch of breaking bone.

The gun stopped firing instantly, and as Quaid's arm broke horribly in two, the M-16 flew from his grasp, skittling across the water-covered floor of the parking lot, landing a few feet away from Swain's Civic.

His face covered with saliva, Quaid screamed madly as blood streamed out from his cracked right elbow. With his other arm he tried pathetically to hold Reese at bay.

And then Swain saw Reese's tail arch.

Smoothly and gracefully, behind her flailing antennae. Out of Quaid's sight.

Swain didn't have time to move.

The tail came down hard.

Viciously hard.

The pointed tip penetrated Quaid's head in an explosion of red, shooting straight through the skull, emerging on the other side. Quaid's body spasmed violently with the impact, his feet lifting off the ground, and then abruptly his body went completely limp.

Swain watched in horror as Reese coldly withdrew her tail from the dead man's skull. Her tail came clear and the bloodstained head dropped to the floor with a soft splash.

Then she looked up at Swain.

And hissed at him fiercely.

Your turn.

Reese stepped clear of Quaid's body, her whole body coiled, tensed, invigorated by the scent of battle.

Sprinkler rain hammered down on her pebbled dinosaurian back.

Swain stepped off the little Honda, eyeing her cautiously, wondering what the hell he was going to do now. And then, out of the corner of his eye, he saw it.

Quaid's M-16.

Lying in the water to his right, five yards away. Lifeless. Abandoned.

Swain didn't waste a second. He dived for the gun.

Reese leapt forward.

Swain's fingers slapped hard against the water as he grabbed the gun, lifted it clear of the pool and whirled it around to face the charging Reese.

He jammed down on the trigger.

Click!

No bullets! Quaid must have run it dry.

Not fair!

Reese was close now. She leapt at him in the driving rain, flying through the air, forelimbs raised, jaws bared—a giant attacking alligator.

Swain somersaulted left, just as Reese came crashing down on the spot he had just occupied, landing in the shallow water with a massive splash.

Swain got to his feet, turned to see where Reese was—

Thwack!

An immense weight crunched into his chest, driving him backwards. It was Reese's shoulder, slamming into him.

Swain was lifted fully off the ground by the impact and then suddenly—*whump*—he landed with a thud on the bonnet of the parked Honda.

The car beneath him shuddered violently on its suspension and then before he knew it his ears were filled with the most terrifying sound he had ever heard in his life and he opened his eyes to find that he was looking into Reese's wide-open jaws from a distance of six inches.

It made for a very peculiar sight: Swain—on his back, on the bonnet of the Civic, his arms splayed wide, dangling over its sides—with Reese, standing upright, her hind legs resting on the parking lot floor, her stubby forelimbs planted firmly on the bonnet of the car on either side of him.

She lowered her snout over his chest, as if sniffing him, smelling him, savouring her victory over him.

Swain kept his eyes averted—not daring to look at her antennae—while also keeping them clear of the torrent of saliva that now splattered down onto his chest.

Through the sprinkler rain, he could see their combined shadows on the wall nearby—her body bent over his—resting on the shadow of the car.

She had him.

Reese hissed fiercely.

And at that moment, on the wall, Swain saw the shadow of her tail rise behind her back.

This was it.

This was the end.

Reese knew it. Swain did, too.

And then suddenly he felt it—*somehow* it was still in his hand, hanging over the edge of the bonnet—and like the dawn of a new day, a new realisation hit him and Swain looked up into Reese's eyeless face and said, 'I'm sorry.'

And with that Swain jammed down on the *second* trigger of the M-16 he was still holding—the trigger that was attached to the gun's barrel-mounted Taser—and fired it into the pool of water beneath the car.

*

A bolt of electricity flashed out from the prongs of the *Bayonet* and slammed into the water at the base of the Honda.

Instantly, a blinding flare of light illuminated the parking lot as a thousand branches of jagged white lightning snaked out across the surface of the water at astonishing speed.

Reese shrieked in agony as the electricity from the M-16's underslung Taser shot through the water and up into her body—via her hind legs which were still planted in the shallow pool.

She shuddered violently, her whole lizard-like frame convulsing and spasming, causing the Honda beneath her to rock.

Swain just tried to keep himself clear of her body as it absorbed the stunning surge of electricity.

And then, in a final, lurching fit of electrocution, Reese vomited all over his chest—a disgusting greeny-brown slime—before she reared up on her hind legs and fell to the ground, splashing into the pool of water.

Dead.

For its part, the little Honda Civic—with Swain still on it—stood its ground as the electricity from the *Bayonet* hit its tyres but proceeded no further, its attempts to climb the car frustrated by the rubber.

*

Moments later, the sprinklers stopped.

The parking lot was silent once more.

Flat on the bonnet of the Civic, Swain breathed again. The initial flare of white light was gone and now only weak glints of electricity flickered up from the water.

The surge of power from the M-16's *Bayonet* had dissipated. The water was back to normal. The *Bayonet* itself was spent, sizzling, shorted out by the water contact. Swain let the gun splash to the ground.

He looked down at Reese. Strangely, in death her bulky dinosaurian body seemed even larger than it had in life. He also saw the bodies of the NSA agents, Quaid and Martinez, lying motionless on the watery floor.

He shook his head in astonishment, wondering how the hell he had managed to survive this confrontation.

And then his wristband beeped.

INITIALISED—2

Now there was only one other contestant left—and he still hadn't found Holly and Selexin.

Swain took a deep breath and heaved himself off the car. His feet hit the concrete with a soft splash.

It wasn't over yet.

'We have to,' Selexin said urgently.

'You can. But I'm not,' Holly said.

'I am not going to leave you here.'

'Then we can just stay here together.' Holly folded her arms resolutely.

They were still standing on the Third Floor landing of the stairwell, outside the study hall.

After seeing Hawkins' mutilated body suspended from the ceiling and throwing up, Holly had slumped down against the nearest wall and stared off into space. Now she was flatly refusing to enter the study hall, which meant walking past the body, and—worse still—through the blood.

Selexin looked about himself nervously. Down the stairs, he could see the open door to the Second Floor. Inside the study hall, upside down, he saw Hawkins' body swaying gently from the ceiling.

Whatever had done this—Selexin suspected it had been Bellos and his hoods—it had ripped his arms right out of their sockets and torn off his head, accounting for the enormous pool of blood underneath the swinging body. Clusters of parallel gashes cut across Hawkins' body—claw marks. Hood marks. When combined with the ominous yellow glow of the fire in the study hall, it made for a particularly grisly sight.

'You can shut your eyes,' Selexin suggested.

'No.'

'I can carry you.'

'No.'

'You must realise, we cannot stay here.'

Holly remained mute.

Selexin shook his head in frustration and again looked down the stairs.

He froze.

And then he turned back to Holly, picking her up roughly whether she liked it or not.

'Hey—'

'*Shh!*'

'What are you doing—?'

'We're going inside. *Right now*,' Selexin said, pulling her toward the door, looking over his shoulder.

Resisting, Holly followed his gaze down the stairwell. '*I said*, I don't want—'

Her voice trailed off as her eyes came to rest on the door to the Second Floor. She fell silent.

A faint rectangle of light stretched out onto the

Second Floor landing, and slowly—very slowly—Holly saw a dark shadow extend into it.

The source of the shadow appeared and Holly watched in terror as a hood stepped out onto the landing and looked up into her eyes.

The M-16's underslung unit had writing on it: TASER BAYONET-4500.

Jesus, Swain thought, as he stood over the body of Harold Quaid, it made it sound like a new model motorcycle.

Swain had seen Taser shock victims before. Usually you recovered with a monster of a hangover, chiefly because police Taser sticks were unchangeably set at minimum voltage.

But this rifle-mounted Taser unit was *not* standard police issue. And if Quaid really was NSA, who knew what sort of voltage it was packing.

Swain looked down at Reese, lying face down in the shallow pool of water. One thing was certain: NSA Tasers weren't set to simply stun. This one had carried enough voltage to kill Reese.

Swain held the M-16 in his hands. With its magazine empty and the Taser shorted out, it was useless. He discarded the assault rifle and bent down to examine the bodies of Quaid and Martinez. They might have something else on them.

Martinez's SIG-Sauer pistol, or what was left of it, lay half-submerged in the water. It had been completely flattened—Swain guessed Reese must have stepped on it—and now it was little more than a collection of bent metal and broken springs.

Swain rummaged through the pockets of the two NSA men's uniforms. He found a pair of small Motorola walkie-talkies, four extra batteries for the Taser unit, extra clips for the SIG-Sauer, two telescoping truncheon sticks, and each man had two CS tear-gas grenades.

Swain wondered if Karanadons were susceptible to tear gas—probably not. Hell, if he used the grenades, Swain thought, he'd probably only succeed in incapacitating himself. The radios were no help—after all, who was he going to call? And he didn't like his chances with the truncheons against someone like Bellos. No, Harold Quaid and his partner had little to offer him.

He wondered how they had got inside the library in the first place. The parking lot presumably. But something must have gone wrong—otherwise they would have had ten more guys with them, and much more artillery. Surely they wouldn't come searching for aliens with only two guns between them.

Then Swain found something.

In Quaid's back pocket. A sheet of paper. A list:

LSAT-560467-S

DATA TRANSCRIPT 463/511–001

SUBJECT SITE: 231.957 (North-eastern seaboard: CT, NY, NJ)

NO.	TIME/EST	LOCATION	READING
1.	18:03:48	CT.	Isolated energy surge/Source: UNKNOWN
			Type: UNKNOWN / Dur: 0.00:09
2.	18:03:58	N.Y.	Isolated energy surge/Source: UNKNOWN
			Type: UNKNOWN / Dur: 0.00:06
3.	18:07:31	N.Y.	Isolated energy surge/Source: UNKNOWN
			Type: UNKNOWN / Dur: 0.00:05
4.	18:10:09	N.Y.	Isolated energy surge/Source: UNKNOWN
			Type: UNKNOWN / Dur: 0.00:07
5.	18:14:12	N.Y.	Isolated energy surge/Source: UNKNOWN
			Type: UNKNOWN / Dur: 0.00:06
6.	18:14:37	N.Y.	Isolated energy surge/Source: UNKNOWN
			Type: UNKNOWN / Dur: 0.00:02
7.	18:14:38	N.Y.	Isolated energy surge/Source: UNKNOWN
			Type: UNKNOWN / Dur: 0.00:02

8.	18:14:39	N.Y.	Isolated energy surge/Source: UNKNOWN
			Type: UNKNOWN / Dur: <u>0.00:02</u>
9.	18:14:40	N.Y.	Isolated energy surge/Source: UNKNOWN
			Type: UNKNOWN / Dur: <u>0.00:02</u>
10.	18:16:23	N.Y.	Isolated energy surge/Source: UNKNOWN
			Type: UNKNOWN / Dur: 0.00:07
11.	18:20:21	N.Y.	Isolated energy surge/Source: UNKNOWN
			Type: UNKNOWN / Dur: 0.00:08
12.	18:23:57	N.Y.	Isolated energy surge/Source: UNKNOWN
			Type: UNKNOWN / Dur: 0.00:06
13.	18:46:00	N.Y.	Isolated energy surge/Source: UNKNOWN
			Type: UNKNOWN / Dur: 0.00:34

Swain stared at the list, bewildered.

Numbers and times and energy surges and the constant repetition of the word UNKNOWN. And presumably it all had something to do with the library.

Thirteen surges of energy in all. One in Connecticut and twelve in New York.

Okay.

Swain looked at the times of the first few surges.

18:03:48. A surge—source unknown, type unknown—detected in Connecticut, lasting *nine* seconds.

Exactly *ten* seconds after that initial surge began, at 6:03:58 p.m., a surge appeared in New York.

All right. That was easy. That was Swain himself and Holly being teleported from his home in Connecticut to the library in central Manhattan.

Six other surges of roughly the same duration—five to eight seconds—accounted for the other contestants and their guides being teleported into the library for the Presidian.

Swain remembered that Selexin had already been inside the library when he had arrived. His teleportation must have occurred too early to be on this list.

But that still left five other surges.

Swain scanned the list further and saw the entries numbered 6 through 9—the four two-second surges that had come in rapid succession one second after the other. They had been underlined.

Swain frowned at the fifth surge.

18:14:12. A six-second surge. Nothing special about that, just another contestant and his guide being teleported inside. But twenty-five seconds after that surge came the four rapid surges in quick succession.

The hoods! he thought, realising.

They were small, so teleportation must not have taken very long. Only two seconds each.

And that explained the variation in the times needed for the other teleportations—some contestants were bigger or smaller than others, so they required more or less time to be teleported into the labyrinth, somewhere between five and eight seconds.

Swain smiled, this was coming together nicely.

Except for one thing.

The last energy surge.

It had come more than *twenty-two minutes* after all the other surges, which themselves had all occurred *within* twenty minutes.

And it had lasted thirty-four seconds. The longest surge before that had lasted only nine seconds.

What was it? An afterthought perhaps? Was it something the organisers of the Presidian had forgotten to put inside the labyrinth?

It wasn't the Karanadon. Selexin had told Swain that the Karanadon had been placed inside the labyrinth almost a day *before* the Presidian was to commence.

Swain couldn't figure it out now, so he let it be for the moment. It was time to go.

He put the sheet of paper in his pocket and with a final glance at Reese's motionless body, he headed for the door marked **TO STACK**.

The study hall was bathed in the yellow glow of a fire out of control.

In the far corner of the wide room, beyond the flames, the janitor's room stood sombrely—dark and charred, the fire inside it having burned itself out.

Holly shut her eyes as Selexin led her around the bloody corpse swinging from the ceiling. Her feet slipped suddenly on the pool of blood, but Selexin steadied her before she fell.

They could hear the hoods climbing the stairs behind them, grunting, snorting.

Selexin pulled harder, guiding Holly in among the L-shaped desks of the study hall.

'The elevator!' Holly whispered. 'Go for the elevator!'

'Good idea,' Selexin said, pressing on through the tangle of standing and fallen desks.

There must have been hundreds of desks in the study hall, half of which still stood, undisturbed. The other half had not been so fortunate, crushed or thrown by the Karanadon, torn to pieces, smashed beyond recognition.

The elevators were close now.

The doors to the left-hand elevator were still pulled wide, revealing the black abyss of the elevator shaft. The Karanadon must have pulled them open so hard that they had stayed open.

Selexin hit the call button on the run, slammed into the wall, spun around.

In the flickering glow of the fire, he saw Hawkins' body spinning slowly from the ceiling above the entrance to the stairwell.

And beneath the body, stepping slowly and cautiously into the study hall, was a hood.

Through the tangled forest of desk legs, Selexin saw the second hood join its partner and he felt a chill.

They were scanning the study hall very slowly, peering across the room, under the desks.

Selexin watched intently. It was as though the hoods were more resolved now, more serious. It was time to kill. Play was over. The hunt had begun.

Holly snapped round to look at the open elevator shaft behind them.

The cables that had run vertically down the shaft

were all gone now, snapped by the Karanadon, probably resting at the bottom with the rest of the battered lift. They couldn't slide down this time.

The numbered display above the other elevator was still working though: one number after the other slowly ignited as the elevator crawled upwards.

LG glowed yellow. Then faded.

G glowed yellow, faded.

1 glowed—

Holly felt Selexin tug on her shoulder. 'Come on,' he said. 'We can't stay here.'

'But the lift . . .'

'It will not get here in time.' Selexin grabbed her arm and pulled her away from the elevators just as she caught a glimpse of the hoods moving in from the left.

Selexin pulled hard, dragging Holly to the right, watching the hoods through the legs of the desks.

The hoods were twenty feet away, moving with the cold stealth of seasoned hunters.

In the strobe-like light of the fires, Selexin could see them clearly. The needle-like teeth protruding from the spherical head; the bony black forelegs with their blood-ied claws scraping on the floor; the powerful, muscular hind legs; and the long scaly tail that swished menacingly behind the black torso as if it had a mind of its own.

The perfect hunter.

Remorseless. Relentless.

Selexin swallowed as he jumped over a fallen desk and found himself standing before the janitor's room. In the corner.

Dead end.

He looked back. The hoods had stopped now, still twenty feet away. They were just standing there, staring at their diminutive prey.

A moment later, they moved again.

In opposite directions.

They were splitting up.

'Not good,' Selexin said, 'this is not good.' It was better when they were together, because at least then he could see them both at the same time. But now . . .

'Quickly,' he said to Holly, 'get on the desks.'

'What?'

'*Get on them*,' Selexin insisted. 'They are seeing us through the legs. If we get onto the desks, they will not know where we are.'

Holly climbed like a monkey onto the nearest L-shaped desk. Selexin jumped up quickly behind her.

'Let's go,' she whispered, obviously in her element now, jumping easily across to the next desk.

'Just be careful,' Selexin said, stumbling after her. 'Do not fall off.'

Holly danced nimbly from desk to desk, skipping over the gaps with ease. Behind her, Selexin did the same.

Beneath them, they could hear the snorting and grunting of the hoods.

There was a sudden *bing!* and Selexin looked over his shoulder and saw—across the sea of desks—the upper half of the elevator doors.

They were opening.

'Oh no,' he said, running across the desk tops.

Holly saw them, too. 'Can we get there?'

'We have to try,' Selexin said.

Holly changed her course, turning in a wide semi-circle, jumping across the desks. She was about to leap across a wide gap between two desks when the able-bodied hood, claws raised to attack, sprang up from the floor into her path.

Holly fell backwards onto the desk and the hood dropped from sight.

Selexin caught up with her. 'Are you—?'

With a loud squeal, the hood leapt up again, onto an adjacent desk, and lashed out at Holly with a scythe-like foreclaw.

Holly screamed as she rolled clear, *off the desk*, falling to the floor. Selexin watched her fall out of sight.

'No!'

The hood swung viciously at Selexin—backhanded—hitting him squarely in the face. He recoiled sharply, losing his balance, falling backwards onto his desk.

With frightening speed, the hood leapt at him as he

landed, but Selexin rolled and the hood smashed into the upright partition of the L-shaped table.

The weight of the impact rocked the desk, and in an instant Selexin's horror became complete as he saw the world tilt crazily and felt the desk he was sitting on keel over backwards.

From the floor, Holly watched fearfully as the desk on which Selexin and the hood fought lurched backwards and tipped over. It seemed to fall in slow motion.

Selexin fell first, hitting the floor hard, his white eggshell hat flying from his head. He rolled clear of the falling desk.

The hood slid off the tilting desk, landing on its feet like a cat, right in front of Selexin.

Selexin was totally exposed, and the hood was tensing itself to attack when abruptly the desk came crashing down on its back.

Pinned to the floor, shrieking like a mad animal, the hood writhed about in a frenzy, attempting to free itself. Its jaws snapped and snarled as it still tried—despite its own predicament—to get to Selexin.

Selexin was scrambling backwards on his butt, away from the wailing creature when, from behind him, Holly tipped over a second desk.

This time the L-shaped table fell forward, and the

hood looked up in horror at the desk rushing down toward it.

The leading edge of the desk landed with a loud crunching sound on the hood's upturned head, shattering the animal's long needle-like teeth as it crushed its skull against the floor.

The hood's body jerked and spasmed beneath the two fallen desks, until at last it lay still. Dead.

Silence.

Then Holly heard a soft *bing!* followed by the grinding sound of the elevator doors closing again.

She knelt beside Selexin, looking quickly in every direction. 'Where's the other one?'

'I . . . I do not know,' Selexin was badly shaken. 'It could be anywhere.'

Now it was Holly who grabbed Selexin by the arm and pulled him to his knees. 'We missed the elevator,' she said, determined. 'Come on, we've got to get out of here.'

'But . . . but,' Selexin mumbled feebly.

'Come *on*. Let's move.'

'But my . . . my hat!' Selexin clawed at his bald head. 'I need my hat.'

Holly spun around quickly and saw the hat. The small white hemisphere was sitting on the floor, jutting out from behind a nearby upturned desk.

She crawled toward the fallen desk on her hands and

knees, rounded the upturned legs, and reached out to grab the hat . . .

Holly paused.

Then she froze.

Beside the hat stood two bony black forelegs—one with a bloodstained claw; one with no claw at all.

Her eyes lifted, rising up the forelegs, following them until she came face to face with the second hood.

The hood's jaws opened wide, salivating in evil anticipation, inches away from her face.

Selexin watched helplessly from the floor ten feet away. Too far.

Holly was still on all fours, almost nose-to-nose with the hood.

Totally defenceless.

The hood stepped forward and stood over the hat.

It was so close now that all Holly could see was its teeth. Its long, pointed, bloody teeth. She felt the warmth of its hot breath blowing on her face; smelled the foul odour of rotting flesh.

Holly shut her eyes and clenched her fists, waiting for the animal to strike, waiting for the end. Her terror was extreme.

Suddenly, the hood hissed fiercely and Holly wanted

to scream and then, as her horror hit fever pitch, she had the strange sensation of hearing her father's voice.

'*Initialise!*'

There was a sudden, glorious flare of white that shot through Holly's eyelids.

Then she heard the hood shriek in total, rabid agony and she opened her eyes and was instantly blinded by the small sphere of dazzling white light that had flared to life above Selexin's hat.

The hood's shrieking cut off abruptly and Holly heard her father's voice again.

'Cancel.'

The blinding white light vanished instantly and for a moment Holly saw nothing but kaleidoscopic spots of colour.

Then suddenly there were two strong arms wrapped around her, holding her tightly, and still blind, Holly's first thought was to break free.

But the grip was firm and gentle.

A hug.

Holly blinked twice as her eyesight slowly returned and she found herself in the warm embrace of her father.

Her muscles drooped with relief and she let her body fall limply into his.

Then she began to cry.

*

As he held his daughter tightly in his arms, Stephen Swain closed his eyes and sighed. Holly was safe, and they were back together again. He didn't want to let her go.

Still holding her, he turned to look at the remains of the hood.

The body had been cut perfectly in two—only the hind legs and the tail remained. The head, forelimbs and upper torso had simply disappeared, teleported to God-only-knew-where. Thick black blood oozed out from the exposed cross-section of the animal's torso.

Selexin limped to Swain's side and grimaced at the sight of the half-bodied hood.

'"Initialise". "Cancel",' Selexin laughed softly to himself. 'It is nice to know,' he said wryly to Swain, 'that you do not forget *everything* I tell you.'

Swain smiled sadly, still hugging Holly. 'Not everything.'

Holly looked up at her father. 'I knew you would come back.'

Swain said, 'Of course I came back, silly. You didn't think I'd leave you here all by yourself, did you?'

'Ah, ahem,' Selexin coughed, 'I beg your pardon but the young lady was certainly not *all* by herself.'

'Oh, excuse me.'

Holly said, 'He was very brave, Daddy. He helped me a lot.'

'He did, huh?' Swain looked at Selexin. 'That was very noble of him. I really should thank him.'

Selexin bowed modestly.

'Thanks,' Swain said softly to the little man.

Selexin, proud of his new-found hero status, shook it off. 'Oh, it was nothing. All part of the service, right?'

Swain laughed. 'Right.'

'I knew you'd come back. I knew it.' Holly nestled into Swain's arms. Then she looked up suddenly, made a mock-angry face, and adopted a severe adult tone. 'So where have you been all this time? How did you find us?'

Actually, in the end, finding Holly and Selexin had been rather lucky.

From the parking lot, Swain had run into the Stack and arrived at the small red door through which he had been bowled out by the hoods. When he found nothing there, not even a trace of Holly and Selexin, he was at a total loss.

And then, in the silence, he had heard the nearby elevator ping.

It must have just been sitting there on Sub-Level Two when somebody on another floor had pressed the call button.

Swain raced for the elevator and reached it just as the

doors were about to meet. He jumped inside and rode the lift to whichever floor the call had come from. It was better than nothing. And besides, who knew? Maybe Holly or Selexin had pressed the call button. Then again, it might not have been them, but by then Swain didn't care. It was a risk he had to take.

The elevator had opened onto the Third Floor and Swain had been confronted with the burning study hall.

He had ducked and crawled out of the lift on his hands and knees, trying to stay out of sight.

Then he had heard voices and the grunts of the hoods, and then the crash of a falling desk, and then another.

He jumped to his feet, and followed the noise, rounded a clump of desks and saw his daughter crouched on her hands and knees, nose-to-nose with one of the hoods.

Swain was too far away, and didn't know what to do, when he realised that the hood was standing over Selexin's white, egg-like hat.

And at that moment, a single word had leapt into his mind—'Initialise'.

'Can you get them?' Marshall asked the radio operator inside the NSA van.

'Negative, sir. There's no response from Commander Quaid or Agent Martinez.'

'Try again.'

'But, sir,' the operator insisted, 'all I'm getting is static. We can't even tell whether Commander Quaid has his radio turned *on*.'

> *Status Report: Station 4 reports detection of*
> *contaminant inside labyrinth.*
> *Awaiting confirmation.*

'Just keep trying,' Marshall said, 'and call me as soon as you pick up anything.'

Marshall climbed out of the van onto the parking lot ramp. He looked up at the electrified grille, at the crumpled lead cube at its base, at the surging blue grid of electricity.

What the hell had happened to Quaid?

*

In the study hall, Swain stood up, holding Holly in his arms. 'We better get going.'

Selexin was putting his white, dome-like hat back on. It was stained with the black blood of the hood. 'You are right,' he said. 'Bellos cannot be far away.'

'Bellos,' Swain thought aloud. 'It had to be.'

'What are you talking about?'

'Bellos is the other one,' Swain said. 'The only other contestant left.'

'There are only *two* contestants remaining in the Presidian?' Selexin asked.

'Yep,' Swain offered him the wristband.

Selexin perused it for a moment, then looked up at Swain. His face was grim. 'We have a serious problem.'

'What?'

'Look at this.' Selexin held Swain's wristband up to him. It read:

INITIALISED—2
STATUS REPORT: STATION 4 REPORTS
DETECTION OF
CONTAMINANT INSIDE LABYRINTH.
AWAITING CONFIRMATION.

'What the hell does that mean?' Swain said.

'It means,' Selexin said, 'that they have discovered the hood.'

'Which hood?' Swain asked. 'And who on earth are *they*?'

'The hood that you just killed using the teleport in my hat.'

'And *they*?'

'*They* are the officials watching at the other end of that teleport, who I imagine received quite a shock when half a hoodaya was teleported into their laps. They are in Station Four, the teleport station assigned to monitor the progress of contestant number four—you.'

'So what does the message mean?'

Selexin said, 'This contest is for seven contestants only. It is a fight to the death between the seven intelligent beings of the universe. Outside assistance is strictly forbidden. Hoods are like dogs. They are not intelligent beings. Wherefore, they do not compete in the Presidian. And they most surely do not live on Earth. So when the officials in Station Four received a hood teleported from the labyrinth on Earth, they immediately realised that the Presidian had been compromised, con-taminated by an outside agent.'

Swain was silent for a moment. Then he said, 'So what are they doing now?'

'They are awaiting confirmation.'

'What's confirmation?'

Selexin said, 'An official must go to Station Four and visually confirm the existence of the contaminant.'

'And what happens when it's confirmed?'

'I do not know. This has never happened before.'

'Can you guess?'

Selexin nodded slowly.

'Well?' Swain prompted.

The little man bit his lip. 'They will probably annul the Presidian.'

'You mean call it off?'

Selexin frowned. 'Not quite. What they will probably do—'

'Daddy . . .' Swain heard Holly's soft voice come from his chest. He was still holding her in his arms.

'In a minute, honey,' Swain said. Then to Selexin, 'What will they do?'

'I think they'll—'

'*Daddy!*' Holly whispered insistently.

'What is it, Holly?' Swain said.

'Daddy. *Someone's here . . .*' she spoke in such a low, hissing whisper that it took Swain a couple of seconds to realise what she had said.

He looked down at her. She was staring fearfully out over his shoulder.

Slowly, Stephen Swain looked behind him.

Across the wide room, he saw a body—bloodied and mutilated—hanging upside down from the ceiling, just inside the stairwell door.

And standing beside the body was Bellos.

Swain spun and saw the body next to Bellos swing around lazily. A wave of sadness shot through him as he saw the police uniform.

Hawkins.

Without a word, Bellos began to walk through the tangle of L-shaped desks toward them.

Toward them.

'Let's *go*!' Holly said loudly in his ear.

Swain moved laterally to his left, trying to keep as many desks as possible between him and Bellos.

Bellos did the same, moving in a peculiar, wide arc from left to right, threading his way calmly and quickly between the desks. He still had his white guide draped over his shoulder.

Swain stumbled away from the big man, toward the elevators, Holly in his arms, Selexin by his side.

'Nowhere to run!' Bellos boomed from across the study hall. 'Nowhere *to hide*!'

'They've found you out,' Swain called, walking back-

410

wards. 'They know you brought hoods into the contest. You cheated, and you got caught.'

Bellos continued to move forward in wide arcs, left and right. It was an odd movement, a movement that seemed to force them back. Back toward the—

'Their discovery will be of no help to you,' Bellos said.

Swain looked over his shoulder and saw the gaping black hole that was the left-hand elevator. The doors to the right one were closed.

Swain moved sideways until his back was pressed up against the call button panel.

'The Presidian is over, Bellos,' Swain said. 'You can't win anymore. They know you cheated.'

Behind his back, Swain's free hand searched for the call button, found it, pressed it.

'Perhaps they know,' Bellos said whimsically. 'Perhaps they don't. It does not matter now.'

'You have disgraced yourself!' Selexin blurted.

'And I don't *care*,' Bellos said defiantly. 'I did what I had to do to win. And even if they do find out about the hoodaya, I will still prove to them all that I have won this Presidian.'

'And how will you do that?' Selexin said.

Swain grimaced, knowing the answer.

'By being the only surviving contestant,' Bellos said.

Swain groaned.

Then he heard Holly's voice again. It was loud, close to his ear. 'Daddy, it's here.'

'What?'

'The elevator.' She pointed up at the numbered display above the elevator doors. The number 3 glowed yellow.

There was a soft *ping*.

The doors opened. The darkened interior of the elevator yawned before them.

'Inside,' Swain said quickly to Selexin. 'Now.'

Swain and Holly stepped back into the elevator as Selexin ran to the button panel and pressed a button.

Bellos didn't react quickly. In fact, he didn't react at all.

He just kept walking forward. Toward the elevator.

The doors began to close.

Bellos walked casually toward the lift.

As Swain watched, he got the impression that Bellos was in no hurry to get to them. It was as if he had all the time in the world.

As if he knew something that they did not. As if he had calculated . . .

But then the doors closed and they were swallowed by darkness and the elevator began its descent.

*

Two long cylindrical fluorescent light tubes lay on the floor of the lift—they were the tubes that Hawkins had removed from their sockets when Swain and his group had been hiding on the First Floor earlier that night.

Swain put one of the tubes back into its socket, bathing the elevator in a dull white glow.

'Well, that was easy,' Selexin said.

'Too easy,' Swain said.

'Why didn't he follow us, Daddy?' Holly said. 'Before, he chased us all over the place. *All* over the place.'

'I don't know, honey.'

'Well, we are away now,' Selexin said. 'And that is all that matters.'

'That's what worries me,' Swain said.

And then it happened.

Suddenly. Without warning.

A loud, heavy *thump!* on the roof of the elevator.

They all froze. And then slowly, very slowly, looked up at the ceiling.

Bellos had jumped down onto the roof of the elevator!

He must have jumped across from the open doors of the other elevator.

Swain realised his mistake immediately. 'God*damn* it!'

'What?' Selexin said.

'You'll be happy to know,' Swain said wryly, 'that we've just managed to trap ourselves.'

He cursed himself. He should have seen it. While they were running away from Bellos, he had been moving in those strange arcs, virtually guiding them to the elevators. When they thought they were escaping, they were actually going exactly where he wanted them to go. *Shit.*

Suddenly, the hatch in the roof opened.

Swain pulled Holly and Selexin to the rear corner of the lift.

Bellos' head appeared through the open hatch upside down, his long tapering horns pointing downward.

He smiled menacingly.

Then his head disappeared from view, back outside the lift. A moment later Bellos swung down through the hatch, landing on his feet.

Inside the lift.

Right in front of them.

'Nowhere to run now,' he sneered. 'Finally.'

Swain pushed Holly into the corner behind him. Selexin stood by his side. Bellos was standing in the opposite corner of the elevator, beside the button panel. He didn't have his guide with him anymore.

Swain saw the panel next to Bellos and wondered which button Selexin had pressed. He hoped the little man had pressed the next floor. Then they might be able to make a run for it.

He saw the illuminated button and closed his eyes in dismay.

SL-2 was glowing.

That was Sub-Level Two, the Stack. The bottom floor. They were in for a long ride.

'You pressed the *bottom* floor?' he whispered to Selexin in disbelief.

'To get as far away as possible,' Selexin whispered back. 'How was I supposed to know he would jump on top of the—'

'*Silence!*' Bellos boomed.

'Oh, shut up,' Swain said.

'Yes. And fuck you, too,' Selexin added.

Bellos cocked his head, amazed at this display of impertinence. His face tightened, angry.

He began to walk across the elevator.

It was then that Swain realised just how big Bellos was—he had to bend so that his horns wouldn't hit the ceiling. And he was built like a house, too. Swain eyed the golden breastplate on his chest. It was dazzling.

He also saw that Bellos had added several more trophies to his belt. He still had the Konda's breathing mask and the NYPD badge clipped to it, but now he had two more-recent additions: first—and most gruesomely—the severed head of a thin, stick-insect-like creature; and second—a more earthly object—a small canister of police-issue chemical Mace, still in its belt-pouch.

Swain froze at the sight of the Mace.

It was Hawkins' Mace.

It was Bellos' trophy from killing the young policeman.

Bellos caught Swain looking at his newly acquired trophy. He touched the small canister on his belt.

'A curious weapon,' he mused. 'As his dying act, your companion sprayed it into my eyes, but to no effect. You humans must truly be fragile beings if something so pathetic as this injures you.'

'You are a coward, Bellos,' Selexin spat.

Bellos rounded on him, took a step toward him, extended his arm toward the little man's head.

Selexin leaned back against the wall, trying to pull away.

Then, roughly, Swain swatted Bellos' arm away. 'Get away from him,' he said flatly.

Bellos pulled his arm back—away from Selexin—dutifully obeying Swain's command. And then suddenly he thrust his arm viciously forward, hitting Swain hard in the face.

Swain fell to the floor, clutching his jaw.

'And fuck you, too,' Bellos said with a sneer. 'Whatever that means.'

Then the big man moved quickly, grabbing Swain by the collar and hurling him into the far wall of the elevator.

Swain banged hard against the wall, fell to the floor again, wheezing.

Bellos strutted across the elevator, following him.

'Pathetic little man,' he said. 'How *dare* you touch me. My great-grandfather also killed a human once. In another Presidian, two thousand years ago. And this human cried, begged, pleaded for mercy.'

Bellos picked Swain up by the hair and threw him against the doors of the lift.

'Is that what you will do, little earth man? Cry for clemency? Beg me to be merciful?'

Swain was lying face down on the floor. He picked himself up slowly and sat with his back up against the doors. The cut on his lip had been reopened and now it was bleeding profusely.

'Well, little human?' Bellos jeered. 'Will you beg for your life?' He paused, and then turned to face Holly in the corner. 'Or perhaps, you would rather beg for hers?'

'Come over here,' Swain said evenly.

'What?' Bellos said.

'I said, *come over here.*'

'No,' Bellos smiled. 'I think I'd like to acquaint myself with this young lady first.' He stepped across the elevator, toward Holly.

Selexin took a step sideways, blocking him. 'No,' he said firmly.

It was a strange sight. Selexin—four feet tall, dressed completely in white—protecting Holly from Bellos—seven feet tall and clad entirely in black.

'Goodbye, tiny man,' Bellos said, delivering a heavy blow across Selexin's head, sending the little man crashing to the floor.

Bellos towered over Holly. 'Now . . .'

'I said,' a voice said in Bellos' ear, '*come over here.*'

Bellos turned to see Stephen Swain and a long white fluorescent light tube come rushing at his face.

Swain held the fluorescent tube like a baseball bat and he swung it hard.

The swing connected. The tube smashed against Bellos' face, sending glass shards flying everywhere, and showering the big man's face with a strange white powder that had been inside the fluorescent tube.

Bellos jolted slightly with the impact. But despite the spectacular explosion of the tube across his face, he remained unmoved—uninjured by the blow, save for the layer of powder on his jet-black face—and simply stared coldly down at Swain.

'Uh-oh,' Swain said.

Bellos hit him.

Hard.

Swain bounced into the elevator doors, just as the elevator stopped and the doors themselves opened. He stumbled backwards, out onto the floor of the Stack. Bellos stepped out of the lift after him, walked over to him, and picked him up by his shirt.

'Yes, yes,' Bellos said. 'Begged for mercy, that's what he did. And do you know what my great-grandfather did when this human begged?'

Swain didn't answer.

'He decapitated him,' Bellos moved his powder-covered face close to Swain's. 'Tore his arms from his body, too.' Bellos stroked his golden breastplate. 'And then he took this. A glorious trophy from such an inglorious creature.'

Swain looked at the breastplate more closely. Indeed, upon closer examination, it looked like . . . like the gilded armour of a Roman centurion.

A Roman centurion? Swain thought. *In a Presidian? Two thousand years ago? My God . . .*

Bellos raised Swain higher so that his sneakers were a full foot above the floor. He carried him over to the crumpled outer doors of the other elevator. When the Karanadon had climbed out of the broken elevator at the bottom of the shaft, it must simply have crashed through the outer doors to get out.

Bellos threw Swain through the open outer doors and he landed heavily on what was left of the roof of the destroyed elevator, resting at the base of the shaft. The roof was a good five feet below the floor level of the Stack.

Bellos leapt down onto the roof after him. 'Well, human?' he said. 'Do you beg?'

Swain coughed. 'Not in this life.'

'Then perhaps in the next,' Bellos said, picking him up again and hurling him into the concrete wall of the shaft. Swain hit the wall and fell to his knees, aching, coughing.

'Are you thinking of yourself now, little man?' Bellos said, circling Swain. 'Or are you thinking of what I will do when you are dead? Which is worse? Your death, or the prospect of what I will do to your little one *after* you are dead?'

Swain clenched his teeth, felt the warmth of his own blood in his mouth.

He had to do something.

He looked up and saw the other lift, hanging above them like a big square shadow in the blackness of the shaft. There was a dark gap beneath it. *Maybe . . .*

Bellos moved in close again—and suddenly Swain came to life, launching himself quickly forward, tackling the big man around the ankles, throwing Bellos off balance, sending them both falling toward the edge of the roof.

They fell.

Both of them.

Off the roof of the destroyed lift, out into the shaft *underneath* the working elevator.

The drop was about ten feet and Bellos landed heavily on the concrete base of the elevator shaft. Swain landed on top of him, the big man's body cushioning his fall.

Swain got to his feet immediately and looked around the base of the shaft.

Solid concrete walls on two sides—a series of counterweight cables on one of them. Opposite the counterweight cables was the battered side wall of the destroyed elevator, lying crumpled at the bottom of the shaft. On the fourth side of the shaft, however, Swain saw the most unexpected sight of all.

A pair of outer doors.

There was another floor down here.

The working elevator could come down.

And if it could, then . . .

'Holly! *Selexin!*' he called desperately. 'Are you still up there! If you are, go to the buttons! *Press anything below* SL-2!'

*

421

Inside the elevator, Selexin was still sprawled on the floor, bloodied and dazed. Holly was huddled in the corner.

Then strangely she heard her father's echoing voice and she blinked back to life. '—*anything below* SL-2*!*'

What?

She ran over to the button console and scanned the buttons there:

$$3 \qquad\qquad 2$$
$$1 \qquad\qquad G$$
$$\text{SL-1} \qquad \text{SL-2}$$

SL-2 was the lowest it went. There *was* nothing below SL-2!

What was he talking about?

Groggy, Bellos got slowly to his feet. The fall had hurt him.

Swain called up again. 'Anything below Sub-Level 2! Just press it!'

Holly's voice floated down the shaft. 'There isn't anything! There's nothing below that one!'

Christ, Swain thought. *I can see the doors. There has to be!*

He called again, 'Look below the buttons! Is there a

small door in the wall! A panel of some sort! Something like that! Anything like that!'

A few seconds.

Holly's voice. 'Yes. *I see it!* I see a little panel!'

Beside Swain, Bellos staggered against the side wall of the destroyed elevator. On the other side of the shaft, Swain saw the five or so counterweight cables running vertically up the concrete wall. They were taut and greased and they appeared to run all the way up the shaft, past the elevator hovering above them. 'Holly!' he called urgently. '*Open the panel!* If there's another button there, *just press it!*'

Holly opened the small white door set into the wall beneath the button console. Inside she saw several switches that looked like regular light switches.

Underneath them, though, was a mouldy green button, beside which was scrawled in white chalk the words: **ACCESS TO STORAGE BASEMENT**.

'I found one!' she called.

'*Press it!*'

Holly pressed the green button and immediately felt her stomach lurch.

The lift was going down.

*

The cables running up the wall of the shaft suddenly came to life, some going up, some going down—all moving too fast to tell—as the complex pulley system of counterweights burst into action.

Swain looked up as the elevator fourteen feet above him began to move.

Downward.

Toward them.

That was good. He'd needed to do something, to provide some sort of—

And then abruptly he was slammed onto the concrete floor. Bellos had thrown himself into him and both of them went sprawling to the ground.

Swain hit the floor hard and rolled quickly just as a big black fist came plunging down into the concrete right next to his head.

Bellos roared in pain, clutching his fist.

Swain leapt to his feet. He looked up at the slowly descending elevator. It was close. There wasn't much time.

You can't fight Bellos. You have to find a way out of—

Then suddenly Bellos was on his feet again and he launched himself at Swain, driving him back against the side wall of the destroyed elevator.

The moving elevator edged downward.

Twelve feet off the ground.

Bellos punched Swain in the stomach. He buckled over.

Eleven feet.

Bellos hit him again. Swain gagged. Bellos was just too damn big to fight.

Ten feet.

Bellos glanced up quickly at the descending elevator and then all around himself for an escape. He saw the rapidly moving counterweight cables by the wall. There seemed to be enough space there to stand . . .

Nine feet.

The bottom of the lift scraped Bellos' horns and he ducked.

Eight feet.

And Swain saw the speeding cables, too. Beside him, Bellos was crouching now, bent over at the waist, facing the other way, looking at the cables.

It was a chance.

Swain seized it.

He moved in quickly behind Bellos and kicked him hard in the back of one knee. Bellos dropped immediately, fell to his knees.

Seven feet.

Swain dived in front of Bellos, scrambled for the counterweight cables.

Got to get out.

Have to get out.

Going to die.

He was almost at the cables when suddenly—violently—a big black hand clasped his ankle. Bellos had his foot in a vice-like grip, and was *dragging* him away from the cables!

Six feet.

Swain broke out in a cold sweat.

Bellos was holding him tightly, pulling him backwards —so that now *Bellos* was closer to the counterweight cables.

There was nothing Swain could do! It was obvious Bellos was going to hold him until the last moment and then roll to safety near the cables, leaving Swain to be crushed underneath the elevator. There was no way out this time, no way to break Bellos' grasp. The elevator came slowly down.

It was then that Swain saw Bellos' trophy belt right next to his eyes—saw Hawkins' chemical Mace canister hanging from it.

The Mace . . .

But it hadn't worked for Hawkins before . . .

Five feet.

And then Swain saw the white powder on Bellos' face. The white powder from the fluorescent light tube that Swain had smashed across his face.

It was oxidised fluorine.

And fluorine added to Mace would make . . .

Don't think! No time. Just do it!

Swain wrenched the Mace canister clear of Bellos' belt and aimed it at Bellos' face.

But Bellos saw him move and in response, the big man lashed out at the Mace canister with his fist and hit it a glancing blow, snapping its spray nozzle clean off!

No! Swain's mind screamed. *Now he couldn't spray it!*

And then he saw another option.

Gritting his teeth with determination, Swain slid in close to Bellos' head and then, in one fluid movement, holding the Mace canister tightly in his fist, he banged the base of the canister down on the *point* of one of Bellos' horns—puncturing the canister in an instant.

Blinding chemical Mace sprayed downwards—out from the puncture hole in the base of the canister. Swain then whipped the canister up so that the spray jetted directly into Bellos' powdered face.

The chemical reaction was instantaneous.

The active ingredients of chemical Mace—chloroacetophenone and diluted sulphuric acid—combined with the oxidised fluorine immediately to create hydrofluoric acid, one of the most corrosive acids known to man.

Bellos roared in agony as bubbles of burning acid rippled across his face. He squeezed his eyes shut *and released Swain's ankle instantly.*

Four feet.

Swain was free!

But he wasn't finished yet.

As Bellos recoiled, Swain rolled onto his back and let fly with an upwardly directed kick.

The kick hit its mark—slamming into the underside of Bellos' jaw, causing the big man's head to jolt sharply upward.

The big man's head snapped up—and his sharp horns penetrated the *floor* of the descending elevator—and in a moment of pure terror Bellos realised what had happened.

He was stuck!

His horns were jammed into the floor of the descending elevator, and he didn't have enough room beneath it to manoeuvre himself out!

Three feet.

Swain was flat on his stomach now, crawling away from Bellos, across the base of the shaft.

Two feet.

And he could feel the bottom of the elevator touching his back. It was like crawling underneath a car.

He reached out for one of the speeding counter-weight cables running up the far wall. His hand closed around the cable.

Behind him, Bellos now lay on the ground, his neck bent upwards at an awkward angle, wrenching desperately at his horns. He let out a piercing high-pitched wail. '*Arrrrrrggghhhh!!!*'

One foot.

And Swain felt the cable yank on his arm and he was pulled into the air, his feet sliding out from under the elevator just as it hit the bottom with a resounding *boom!* and Bellos' hideous wail cut off abruptly and Swain flew up into the darkness of the shaft.

Swain swung to a sudden halt.

The counterweight cable stopped dead as the elevator came to rest at the base of the shaft.

Everything was silent.

There was no light, save for the weak yellow haze coming through the crumpled outer doors that led to the Stack.

Swain was hanging by his arms six feet above the roof of the working elevator, dangling against the wall. He looked down at the elevators.

It was a peculiar sight—both elevators, side by side, resting on the bottom of the shaft, one totally destroyed, the other just sitting there, silent.

Suddenly the hatch of the working elevator burst open and Swain's heart jumped. Bellos couldn't have . . .

Holly's head appeared through the hatch and Swain sighed with relief. Her head swung around anxiously, searching. Finally she saw him, hanging above her, swinging gently from the counterweight cables on the side of the shaft.

'Daddy!' Holly climbed out onto the roof of the elevator.

Swain let go of the cable and dropped down onto the roof beside her. She leapt into his arms and held him tightly.

'Daddy, I was so scared.'

'So was I, honey. Believe me, so was I.'

'Did I do the right thing? Did I press the right button?'

'You pressed the right button, all right,' Swain said. 'You were great.'

Holly nodded to herself, satisfied, and hugged him harder.

Selexin's head popped out through the hatch. He saw Swain and Holly and then looked around the dark, empty shaft.

'It's okay,' Swain said. 'Bellos is dead.'

'I, uh, gathered as much,' Selexin said.

Swain frowned. Selexin nodded back at the elevator's hatch. Swain looked down through it.

'Oh, yuck . . .'

Sticking up through the floor of the elevator were two high-pointed horns—Bellos' horns. Having pierced the underside of the lift, they now appeared *inside* it— unmoving, still—like the hood ornament of a Cadillac. The only remnant of Bellos.

'What happened?' Selexin asked.

'Crushed,' Swain said.

'*Crushed?*'

'Uh-huh.'

Selexin winced. 'Not a very nice way to die.'

Holly said, 'He wasn't a very nice kind of person.'

'This is true.'

At that moment Swain's wristband beeped softly.

Swain checked it to find that its rectangular display was now filled with scrolling lines of type:

PRESENCE OF CONTAMINANT CONFIRMED AT STATION 4.
* PRESIDIAN HAS BEEN COMPROMISED *
REPEAT.
* PRESIDIAN HAS BEEN COMPROMISED *
DECISION TO ABORT PENDING.

The screen flickered and a new line appeared:

INITIALISED—1
OFFICIALS AT EXIT TELEPORT REPORT ONE
CONTESTANT REMAINING INSIDE
LABYRINTH.
AWAITING INSTRUCTIONS.

There was a pause.

'What does that mean?' Swain asked.

'When only one contestant remains,' Selexin said,

'the Karanadon is awakened, if it is not already awake, and then—'

'And then the exit teleport is opened,' Swain said, remembering. 'And if you can avoid the Karanadon and get to the teleport, you win the Presidian.'

'Right,' Selexin said. 'Only now that Bellos has compromised the Presidian, the officials are deciding whether or not they should abandon the Presidian completely. Because if they do decide to abandon it, they will not open the exit teleport. And we will be left here, *with* the Karanadon. And as I wanted to tell you before, they will also probably . . .'

The wristband beeped loudly and Selexin immediately stopped speaking.

OFFICIALS AT EXIT TELEPORT BE ADVISED THAT A DECISION HAS BEEN MADE TO ABORT PRESIDIAN.
* DO NOT INITIALISE EXIT TELEPORT *
REPEAT.
* DO NOT INITIALISE EXIT TELEPORT *

'They're calling it off,' Swain said flatly.

Selexin didn't reply. He just stared at the wristband in disbelief.

Swain shook him gently. 'Did you see that? They're calling the whole thing off.'

433

Selexin said softly, 'Yes. I saw it.' He looked up at Swain. 'And I know what it means. It means that you and I are most certainly going to die.'

'What?' Swain said.

'*Die?*' Holly said.

'*You* will certainly die,' Selexin said to Swain, 'and without the exit teleport, I cannot leave this planet. And what do you think my chances of survival on Earth are?'

Swain knew the answer to that. The NSA were outside the library right now and they weren't here to borrow some books. Selexin didn't have a prayer outside the library. And now there was no way he could leave.

Swain said, 'So why do I have to die? Why is that so certain? There's no guarantee that the Karanadon will find us.' Now there was an alien that Swain would gladly give to the NSA.

'It is not the Karanadon that comprises your greatest threat,' Selexin said.

'Then what does?' Swain asked as his wristband beeped again, announcing another message:

* OFFICIAL SIGNAL *
PLEASE RECORD THAT DUE TO EXTRINSIC
INTERFERENCE IT HAS BEEN DECIDED THAT
THE SEVENTH PRESIDIAN WILL BE
ABORTED. GRATITUDE IS EXTENDED TO ALL
OFFICIALS IN ALL SYSTEMS FOR THEIR

**ASSISTANCE THROUGHOUT THIS CONTEST.
AN INQUIRY HAS BEEN INITIATED INTO THE
CAUSE OF THE CONTAMINATION OF THE
LABYRINTH.
* END OFFICIAL SIGNAL*
PRESIDIAN COMPLETE.
STANDBY FOR DE-ELECTRIFICATION.**

Swain said, 'De-electrification? Is that what I think it means?'

'Yes,' Selexin nodded. 'They will bring down the electric field surrounding the labyrinth.'

'When?'

'As soon as possible, I suppose.'

'What about the Karanadon?'

'I presume that they will simply leave it here.'

'Leave it here?' Swain said, incredulous. 'Do you have any idea what something like that would do in this city? When they cut the electricity around this building, that thing will be loose, and there will be no way to stop it.'

'It is not my decision,' Selexin said sadly, vacantly.

Swain knew that the little man had other things on his mind. Without the exit teleport, Selexin could not leave. They had survived the Presidian and yet he was stuck on Earth.

'Well,' Swain said, looking up at the dark elevator

shaft around him. 'It's not going to help us standing around here doing nothing. If they're going to pull the plug on the electricity, I suggest we find a place where we can get out when they do.'

Holding Holly, Swain stepped from the roof of the working lift onto the roof of the damaged one. Selexin didn't move. He just stood there sadly, deep in thought.

Swain and Holly climbed out through the crumpled outer doors into the Stack and looked back at Selexin.

'Selexin,' Swain said gently. 'We're not dead yet. Come on. Come with us.'

On top of the lift, in the darkness of the shaft, Selexin looked up at him, but said nothing.

'We have to get to an exit,' Swain said. 'So we can get out when the electricity is cut off.'

'Bellos.' Selexin said flatly, thinking.

'What?'

'Bellos knew of a way.'

'What are you talking about?' Swain said, checking the Stack behind him. 'Come on, we have to go.'

'He had to get the hoods out,' Selexin said. 'He said so himself.'

'Selexin, *what are you talking about*?'

Selexin explained. 'We were on another floor, I think it was number Two. Bellos was there, and he spoke to us briefly before the Rachnid arrived and they fought and we escaped. But at the time, I asked Bellos what he planned to do with the hoods if he won the Presidian, because I knew that if he left them here, they would certainly be discovered. What he told me was very strange. He said that the hoods would be long gone from the labyrinth by the time he went through the exit teleport.'

Swain watched Selexin intently, watched him thinking.

'But the only way he could do that,' Selexin said, almost to himself, 'was if he had a teleporter.'

'A teleporter?'

'A large chamber in which a teleportation field is created.

And as you are no doubt aware, there are no teleporters on Earth.'

Swain thought for a moment, a hazy picture beginning to form in his mind. A picture of a puzzle that hadn't yet been solved.

'Just how big is one of these teleporters?' he asked Selexin.

'Usually very large, and very heavy,' Selexin said. 'And technologically, extremely complex.'

It was now Swain who was lost in thought. The hazy picture in his mind was slowly becoming clearer.

And then it hit him.

'Bellos brought a teleporter with him,' he said flatly.

'We don't know that,' Selexin said.

'Yes, we do,' Swain reached into his pocket, pulled out a sheet of paper—Harold Quaid's list of energy surges at the State Library that night.

'What's that, Daddy?'

'It's a list.'

'Where did you get it?'

Swain turned to Selexin. 'I found it in the pocket of another mystery guest who happened to find his way into your Presidian.'

'What is it a list of?' Selexin asked.

'Take a look.' Swain held out the sheet of paper.

Selexin stepped from one elevator roof to the other and then climbed out into the Stack. He took the sheet and examined it.

'Something from Earth,' Selexin scanned the list. 'Detecting energy surges of unknown origin. What are these numbers on the left?'

'Times,' Swain said.

Selexin was silent for a moment. 'So what is it?' he asked.

'It's a list of every teleportation that has happened in this building since I was teleported here from my home in Connecticut at 6:03 this evening.'

'What?'

'And now I've figured it out,' Swain said. 'Thirteen

teleportations detected. Twelve in the library, one in Connecticut. Before, I could only account for eleven of the twelve surges that occurred in the library: namely, seven contestants with their guides, *plus* four hoods, equals eleven surges.'

'Uh-huh.'

'But I couldn't figure out the last surge,' Swain pointed to the bottom line of the sheet:

13. 18:46:00   N.Y.   Isolated energy surge/Source: **UNKNOWN**
                             Type: **UNKNOWN** / Dur: **0.00:34**

'Look at it. It's thirty-four seconds long—three times longer than any other surge. And look at when it occurred: 6:46 p.m. That's nearly *twenty-three minutes* after the surge before it. All of the others occurred *within* twenty minutes.'

Swain looked at Selexin. 'The last surge was a separate surge. And it was big. Very big. Something that took a long time to teleport—thirty-four seconds to teleport.'

'What are you saying?'

'I think Bellos had someone *teleport* a *teleporter* into the library so he could get the hoods out of here before he left.'

Selexin took it all in silently. He examined the list again. Finally he looked up at Swain. 'Then that means . . .'

'It means,' Swain said to Selexin, 'that somewhere in this building is a teleporter. A teleporter that we can use to get you home.'

Selexin was momentarily silent as it all sunk in.

'So what are we waiting for?' Holly said.

'Nothing now,' Swain said, grabbing Selexin's shoulder, starting to run. 'Let's find it while we still have time.'

James Marshall stood at the base of the ramp leading to the parking lot. He was watching the grid of blue electricity stretched across the metal grille when his radio operator came up to him.

'Sir?'

'What is it?' Marshall didn't turn around.

Status Check: 0:01:00 *to De-electrification.*
Standby.

'Sir, we're not even getting a signal now. Commander Quaid's radio is completely off the air.'

Marshall bit his lip. The night that had begun with so much promise was not panning out well at all. They had already lost two men inside the library, destroyed one Radiation Storage Unit, lost track of a bum who had been seen by the southern wall of the library, and now had a building that was burning itself to the ground. And for what? Marshall thought.

Jack shit, that's what.

They had nothing to show for their night's work. Not a single fucking thing.

And Marshall would be responsible. Too much was riding on this operation. Sigma Division had been given complete authority on this matter and they needed *something* to show for it.

Christ, not long before, the New York Fire Department had shown up in response to all the explosions and the NSA had held them back. The building was the source of a National Security Agency investigation, he'd said. Let it burn. But it's a National Register building. Let it burn. That wouldn't go down well with the bosses upstairs.

So now the situation was clear: if Marshall didn't get anything from this building, he would be the scapegoat. His career now depended on what they found inside that library.

They had to get *something*.

As it turned out, Swain, Holly and Selexin didn't have to run very far before they found the teleporter. In fact, they didn't even have to search beyond the Stack. But they almost missed it altogether. It was only Selexin's keen eye that had caught sight of a deviation in one of the long aisles of the Stack as they had been zigzagging their way toward the floor's central stairwell.

Status Check: 0:00:51 *to De-electrification.*

'It's so big,' Holly said in awe.

That was an understatement, Swain thought as he stood in the aisle and stared at the enormous machine.

It looked like a massive, high-tech, steel-sided telephone booth, with a glass door in its centre, and thick grey walls that almost reached to the ceiling. All of its edges had been rounded off to give it an elliptical shape and a big grey box sat on the floor beside it, connected to the teleporter by a thick black cord.

Surrounding the giant teleporter was a perfect sphere of emptiness that had been cut into the bookshelves and the ceiling around the big machine. The spherical hole in the air through which this machine had travelled had simply vaporised whatever had been standing here when it had arrived.

'That's a portable generator,' Selexin said, pointing to the grey box. 'Bellos had to bring one of those in order to operate the teleporter on Earth.'

Swain stared at the teleporter and at the bookshelves around it. They were right in the middle of the eastern section of the Stack, at least thirty yards from any entrance to the floor and surrounded by the towering floor-to-ceiling bookshelves. It was highly unlikely that anyone had been through here during the Presidian.

'Well hidden,' Swain observed.

'I do not think Bellos had much choice,' Selexin said.

'What do you mean?'

'Well, I have been thinking about this—about how Bellos teleported his hoods into the labyrinth. Do you remember that every time we saw him, Bellos always had his guide draped over his shoulder?'

'Yes.'

'Well, I kept wondering, *why did he need to immobilise his guide?* What I think happened was this,' Selexin said. 'On his home planet, Bellos steps inside the *official* teleporter with his guide. Once inside, the guide receives the co-ordinates of the labyrinth on the wristband, which he hasn't given to Bellos yet. Bellos then attacks the guide, beats him, steals the co-ordinates, and then reopens the teleporter and relays the co-ordinates to someone else.

'Then he and his guide are teleported to the labyrinth alone, while at the same time, at another teleporter nearby, the hoods are sent.

'Much later, they teleport this teleporter, but they only have co-ordinates that are rather general. The teleporter could have arrived *anywhere* inside the library. It was impossible for them to teleport it intentionally into a dark corner. But then, when you're teleporting some-thing into a *maze*, the odds are in your favour of teleporting it into a dark corner. A calculated risk, no doubt, but obviously one that Bellos was prepared to take.'

Status Check: 0:00:30 *to De-electrification.*

Next to Swain, Holly was staring up at the big grey machine. 'So what do we do now, Daddy?'

Swain frowned, looked back down the dark aisle behind him. In the distance he saw that some shelves were now on fire.

'We send Selexin home, honey,' he said. 'So he can tell the others what really happened, and so he can get away from here.'

'Oh,' Holly said, disappointed.

'That is right,' Selexin nodded slowly.

'Can't he stay, Daddy?' Holly said. 'He could live with us. Like in *E.T.*'

Selexin smiled sadly and reached up for the handle to the glass door of the teleporter. He said to Swain, 'When I came to the labyrinth, I thought about myself being assigned to guide the human contestant through the Presidian. And I was not happy at all. I thought you would not last a moment, and if you did not, I would not either. But having seen you, and the way you

445

defended your life and the life of your daughter, I know now just how mistaken I was.'

Swain nodded.

Selexin turned to Holly. 'I cannot stay here. Your world is not ready for me, just as I am not ready for it. Why, even the Presidian was not ready for your world.'

'Thank you,' Holly said, crying. 'Thank you for taking care of me.'

Then she leapt forward and threw her arms around Selexin and hugged him tightly. Selexin was momentarily taken aback, unprepared for this sudden display of affection. Slowly, he raised his arms and hugged Holly back.

'Take care of yourself,' he said, closing his eyes. 'And look after your father, the same way he looks after you. Goodbye, Holly.'

She released him and Selexin turned to Swain and extended his hand.

'You are a little too tall for me to hug,' Selexin said, smiling.

Status Check: 0:00:15 *to De-electrification.*

Swain took the little man's hand and shook it. 'Thank you, again,' he said seriously.

Selexin bowed. 'I did nothing that you yourself would not have done for her. Or for me. I was only there in your absence. And besides, thank *you*, for making me change my mind about you.'

He reached for the door to the teleporter. It opened with a soft, pneumatic *hiss*.

Swain put an arm on Holly's shoulder. 'Goodbye, Selexin,' he said. 'You'll be a hard memory to forget.'

'That is just as well, Mr Swain. Considering you have forgotten just about everything else I have told you tonight.'

Swain smiled sadly as Selexin stepped inside the teleporter.

'Don't forget to teleport this thing back once you get there,' he said, pointing at the teleporter.

'Do not worry. I will not,' Selexin said, closing the glass door behind him.

Swain stepped away from the teleporter and looked down at his wristband.

STATUS CHECK: 0:00:04 TO DE-ELECTRIFICATION.

'Oh, damn . . .' Swain said, realising. 'Oh, *damn*!'

Inside the teleporter, Selexin punched some buttons on the wall and then stepped up to the glass door.

A brilliant white light glowed to life behind him and the little man pressed his finger up against the glass.

'Goodbye,' he mouthed silently.

The dazzling white light inside the teleporter consumed Selexin and then, abruptly, there was a bright, instantaneous flash, and the inside of the teleporter was dark again.

And Selexin was gone.

Holly was wiping tears from her eyes as Swain looked at the wristband again.

STATUS CHECK: 0:00:01 TO DE-ELECTRIFICATION.
STANDBY.
DE-ELECTRIFICATION INITIALISED—

Swain grabbed Holly by the hand and immediately began to run desperately down the narrow aisle, toward the central stairwell. Holly didn't know what was happening, just ran with him anyway.

A loud beeping filled the air.

Swain knew exactly what was going on now—it was what Selexin had been trying to tell him before. He didn't even need to look at his wristband to confirm it.

The damn thing was beeping insistently again and as he heard it ringing in his ears, he realised what aborting the Presidian really meant.

The electrified field was down.

His wristband was no longer surrounded by the field.

It had reset itself to self-destruct.

And nothing could stop it. There was no other electric field on Earth to surround it with.

Swain looked down at the wristband as he hit the stairs on the fly. It read:

PRESIDIAN ABORTED.
DETONATION SEQUENCE INITIALISED.
* 14:54 *
AND COUNTING.

Jesus.

SIXTH MOVEMENT

30 November, 10:47 p.m.

Outside the library, Marshall was barking orders.

'*Move! Move! Move!* Get in there!' he yelled, oblivious to the falling rain all around him.

Moments earlier, the grid of crackling blue electricity had vanished to nothing and Marshall had been faced with a gaping hole in the metal grille of the parking lot. Now he had Sigma's SWAT team racing past him, charging into the car park.

'Higgs!' he called.

'Yes, sir!'

'I want a total media blackout on this matter from now on. You go straight to Levine and you tell him to call the networks and pull some strings. Get those cameras out of here. And get me a No-Fly Zone over this whole area. I don't want any choppers within a five-mile radius of this building. Now go!'

Higgs ran off, up the ramp.

Marshall put his hands on his hips and smiled in the rain.

They were in.

Swain and Holly climbed the stairs two at a time, rounding the banisters, hauling themselves up, breathing hard.

They stopped at the Ground Floor. Swain peered out through the fire door.

The Ground Floor lay before him—wide and dark and bare.

Empty.

Swain could just make out the First Floor mezzanine above. It was still dark there, too. No fires here. Not yet.

There was no-one here.

Wristband.

14:23

14:22

14:21

There was a light over by the Information Desk. Swain stepped cautiously out among the bookshelves, heading toward it. Holly followed nervously.

When he was ten yards away from the Information Desk, he said to her, 'Stay here.'

Swain edged closer to the desk. He peered over the desktop and suddenly turned away, wincing.

'What is it?' Holly whispered.

'Nothing,' he said, then added quickly, 'Don't come over here.'

He glanced over the desktop again and saw the grisly sight again. It was the bloodied and mangled body of a policewoman.

Hawkins' partner.

She had *literally* been torn limb from limb—her arms were simply *gone*, each one ending at the bicep as a ragged bony stump. Her uniform was covered in blood. Swain could just make out the long jagged tear in her shirt where Bellos had ripped off her badge.

And then he saw her Glock pistol on the floor—lying inches away from her desperately outstretched hand.

Swain had a thought: *maybe he could shoot his wrist-band off.*

No, the bullet would pass through his wrist. *Not* a good idea.

He bent down and picked up the policewoman's gun anyway. Protection.

And then, completely without warning, there came a sudden, crashing *whump!* from somewhere behind him.

Holly screamed and Swain snapped around instantly and saw—

—the Karanadon, crouched on one knee, slowly rising to its full height.

Right behind Holly!

It must have been up on the First Floor! It must have leapt down!

Without even thinking, Swain levelled his new found Glock at the beast and fired twice. Both shots missed by three yards. Hell, he'd never even fired a gun before.

Holly screamed through the gunfire, ran over to Swain.

Boom.

The Karanadon stepped forward.

Swain raised the pistol again. Fired. Missed. Two yards off this time. Getting closer.

Boom. Boom.

'Run!' Holly squealed. 'Run!'

'Not yet! I can hit it!' Swain called back, raising his voice above the beast's thunderous footsteps.

The Karanadon began to charge.

Boom. Boom. Boom.

'Okay, run!' he yelled.

Swain and Holly dashed for the bookshelves. The Karanadon was gaining. They rounded a corner and entered a narrow aisle, bookshelves on either side. Running hard, Swain looked over his shoulder.

And then, suddenly, his feet hit something—and he tripped—and went sprawling head-first to the ground. He hit the floor hard and the Glock went skittling off down the slick marble aisle.

Boom. Boom. Boom.

The floor all around him was shaking violently and Swain rolled onto his back to see what had tripped him.

It was a carcass. The ripped and torn carcass of the Konda—the grasshopper-like alien that the hoods had killed before, while Swain and the others had watched from the First Floor balcony.

Boom.

The floor rumbled a final time.

Silence. Save for the beeping of Swain's wristband.

Swain looked up and saw Holly standing on the other side of the carcass.

And behind her—right behind her—towering above the little girl, its massive frame silhouetting her body with total blackness, stood the dark shape of the Karanadon.

Holly didn't move a muscle.

The Karanadon was so close she could feel its hot breath on her neck.

'*Don't move*,' Swain whispered fiercely. 'Whatever you do, don't move.'

Holly didn't answer. She could feel her knees shaking. She knew that she wasn't going to move. Even if she'd wanted to, she couldn't. Beads of sweat began to appear on her forehead as she felt the Karanadon move slowly closer.

457

Its breath came in short, rapid spurts, as if it were breathing very, very quickly. As if it were—

Sniffing. It was sniffing her. *Smelling* her.

Slowly, the big beast's snout moved up her body.

Holly was terrified. She wanted to scream. She clenched her fists by her side and shut her eyes.

Suddenly, she felt a cold wetness touch her left ear. It was the Karanadon's nose, the tip of its dark, wrinkled snout. The nose was cold and wet, like a dog's.

She almost fainted.

Swain watched in horror as the Karanadon brushed the left side of his daughter's head.

It was taking its time. Moving slowly. Methodically. Intensifying their fear.

It had them.

Swain could hear the constant beeping of his wristband. How long to go? He didn't dare look—didn't dare take his eyes off the Karanadon. *Shit.*

He shifted his weight—and, oddly, felt a bulge in his pocket. It was the broken phone receiver. That wouldn't be much use here. Wait a second . . .

There was something else in his pocket . . .

The lighter.

Slowly, Swain reached into his pocket and pulled out Jim Wilson's Zippo lighter.

The Karanadon was sniffing Holly's ankles.

Holly just stood stock still, her eyes shut, her fists clenched.

Swain rolled the lighter over in his hand. If he could light something with it, the flames might momentarily distract the Karanadon.

But then, he recalled, the lighter hadn't worked in the stairwell before.

It had to work now.

Swain held the lighter up to the nearest bookshelf, up close to a dusty old hardcover.

Please work. Just once. Please work.

The Zippo flipped open with a loud metallic *calink!*

The Karanadon's head snapped up immediately and suddenly the beast was staring accusingly at Swain as if to say: 'And what do you think you're doing?'

Swain held the lighter closer to the dusty book but the Karanadon bounded quickly forward and in an instant Swain found himself slammed against the floor, face-down, the weight of an enormous black foot pressed hard against his back.

Holly screamed.

Swain was pushed down against the floor, his hands spread out in front of him, his face tilted sideways, one cheek flat against the cold marble floor. He struggled in vain against the weight of the Karanadon.

The beast roared loudly and Swain looked up to see

that he was still holding the lighter in his left hand. On his left wrist, he saw his wristband, beeping insistently. In a distant corner of his mind, he wondered how long they had before it exploded.

The Karanadon saw the lighter.

And Swain watched in horror as an enormous black claw slowly descended upon—and clasped around—his entire left forearm. It gripped his arm tightly. Squeezing it. Cutting off the bloodflow. Swain saw his veins pop up everywhere. His arm was about to snap in two—

And then the big creature banged his wrist hard against the floor.

Hard against the floor.

Swain roared in agony as his wrist hit the marble floor. There was a loud clunking sound, followed by a sharp burning pain that shot right through his forearm.

With the impact, his hand holding the lighter reflexively opened wide and the Zippo dropped to the floor.

Swain never noticed it.

And he had instantly forgotten about the burning pain in his forearm.

Now he was staring. Staring at his left wrist in total disbelief.

The wristband had hit the floor, too.

And the force of the impact had unclasped it. Now it just rested loosely around Swain's wrist, still beeping incessantly.

Only now it was unclasped.

Now it was off.

Swain saw the countdown.

12:20

12:19

12:18

And then suddenly he felt a claw clutch the back of his head and push it roughly against the floor. The weight on his back increased.

Time for the kill.

Swain saw the Zippo. On the floor. Within reach.

The Karanadon lowered its head.

Swain quickly grabbed the lighter and held it to the lowest shelf of the bookcase and then he shut his eyes and prayed to God that once, just once, Jim Wilson's stupid frigging lighter would work.

He flicked the cartwheel.

The lighter ignited for half a second, and that was all Swain needed.

A dust-covered book next to the Zippo burst instantly into flames, right in front of the Karanadon.

The big beast roared as the fire flared in front of its head, the bristled fur on its forehead catching alight. It pulled back instantly, releasing Swain, clutching desperately at its flaming brow.

Swain rolled immediately and in one swift movement, removed the wristband from his wrist, reached for the Karanadon's foot and clasped the band around one of the beast's enormous toe-claws.

The wristband clicked into place around the toe.

Clasped.

And then Swain was up. On his feet, running. He scooped up Holly, grabbed the Glock from the floor nearby and raced for the massive glass doors of the library's entrance. Behind him he could hear the wails and roars of the Karanadon.

He came to the doors, threw them open.

And saw about a dozen cars with revolving lights on their roofs parked out front. And men with rifles. Running toward him through the rain.

The National Security Agency.

'It's the police, Daddy. They're here to save us!'

Swain grabbed her hand and pulled her away from the doors, toward the stairwell.

'I don't think those policemen are here to help us, honey,' Swain said as they ran. 'Remember what happened to Eliot's house in *E.T.*? Remember how the bad guys put a big plastic bag around it?'

They were running hard. Almost at the stairwell now.

'Yeah.'

Swain said, 'Well, the people who did that are the same people who are outside the library now.'

'Oh.'

They came to the stairwell and started down the stairs.

Swain stopped.

He could hear voices . . . and shouts . . . and heavy footfalls coming from downstairs.

The NSA were already inside.

They must have come in through the parking lot.

'Quickly. Upstairs. Now.' Swain pulled Holly back up the stairwell.

They climbed the stairs.

And as they ran past the fire door leading to the Ground Floor, they heard the loud smashing sound of breaking glass, followed by more voices and shouts.

Swain shut the door behind him.

They were inside the photocopying room on the First Floor.

'Quickly,' he said to Holly, guiding her toward the Internet room, 'through there.'

They entered the Internet Facility of the New York State Library and Swain walked directly over to one of the windows on the far side.

It opened easily and he leaned out.

They were on the western side of the building. Beneath him, Swain could see the grassy park that surrounded the library. It was a fifteen-foot drop from the window to the grass down below.

He spun around and looked up at the wires hanging down from the ceiling.

'Daddy,' Holly said, 'what're we doing?'

'We're getting out,' Swain said, reaching up for the ceiling, yanking on some of the thick black wires.

'How?'

'Through the window.'

'Through *that* window?'

'Yep,' Swain yanked some more wires out from various other outlets. He began to tie them together, end to end.

'Oh,' Holly said.

Swain walked over to the open window again and with the butt of his gun, broke the glass. Then he tied the end of the length of wire around the window's now-exposed horizontal pane and knotted it tight.

He looked back to Holly.

'Come on,' he said, jamming the gun back into his waistband.

Holly stepped forward tentatively.

'Jump on my back and hold tight. I'll climb us both down to the ground.'

Just then, they heard shouts from inside the First Floor. Swain listened for a second. They sounded like directions, orders. Someone telling someone else what to do. The NSA were still searching. He wondered what had happened to the Karanadon. They mustn't have found it yet.

'Okay, let's go,' he said, helping Holly onto his back, piggyback style. She gripped him firmly.

Then he threw the length of wire out the window and began to climb out onto the ledge.

*

'*Sir!*' a static-ridden voice said.

James Marshall picked up his radio. He was now standing outside the main entrance to the library. The majestic glass doors in front of him were now shattered and broken, totally destroyed by the NSA's bold entry only minutes earlier.

It was the radio operator in the van.

'What is it?' Marshall said.

'*Sir, we have visual confirmation, I repeat, visual confirmation, of contact on two floors. One in the lower parking structure and one on the Ground Floor.*'

'Excellent,' Marshall said. 'Just tell everyone not to touch *anything* until I say so. Sterilisation procedures are in force. Anyone who comes within twenty feet of one of those organisms will be presumed to be contaminated and quarantined indefinitely.'

'*Roger that, sir.*'

'Keep me informed.'

Marshall switched the radio off.

He rubbed his hands together and looked up at the burning library above him. It was the building that would skyrocket his career.

'Excellent,' he said again.

Swain dropped to the grass and set Holly down beside him.

They were out.

At last.

It was raining more heavily now. Swain looked for an escape. They were near the south-west corner of the building. He remembered coming out of the subway before. Over on the *eastern* side of the library.

The subway.

Nobody would care if they saw him on the subway— his clothes ragged and torn, Holly's not much better. They would just be another bum and a kid living on the subway.

It was the way out, the way home.

If they could get past the NSA.

Swain pulled Holly eastward into the shelter of the southern wall of the library building, the rain pelting down around them. They passed the broken window at ground level that he had used to get inside before. Using the cover of the rain and the shadows of the oak trees in the night, Swain hoped they could get past the NSA undetected.

They came to the south-east corner.

Beyond the row of oaks, Swain could see the great white rotunda. And beyond the rotunda, the subway station.

Yellow police tape still stretched from tree to tree around the library, forming a wide perimeter. Swain saw a few NSA agents armed with M-16s stationed on that perimeter, their backs to the building, keeping the small crowd of helpless firefighters, local cops and late-night onlookers at bay. There weren't many NSA agents, just enough to secure the area. Swain guessed that most of the others were now inside the building itself.

'All right,' he said to Holly. 'You ready? It's time to go home.'

'Okay,' Holly said.

'Get ready to run.'

Swain waited for a second, peering around the corner of the building.

'All right, *now*!'

They dashed out from the building, across the open ground and into the treeline. They stopped beneath a big oak, catching their breath.

'Are we there yet?' Holly asked, breathless.

'Almost,' Swain said. He pointed to the rotunda. 'That's where we go next. Then on to the subway. You want me to carry you?'

'No, I'm okay.'

'Good. Ready?'

'Yes.'

'Then let's go.'

They ran again. Out from the treeline. Out into the open.

*

Boom.

Marshall felt the ground beneath him shudder.

He was still standing at the main entrance to the library. He looked inside, through the broken glass doors, to see what was causing the vibration.

Nothing. Darkness.

Boom.

Marshall frowned.

Boom. Boom. Boom.

Something was coming. Something big.

And then he saw it.

Motherfucker . . .

Marshall didn't wait for another look. He just turned and ran—down the steps, away from the entrance—a bare two seconds before the library's enormous doors were blasted from their hinges like a pair of matchsticks.

Swain and Holly were halfway to the rotunda when it happened.

A booming, thunderous roar echoed across the park behind them.

Swain stopped and spun. The pouring rain pelted down against his face. 'Oh no,' he said. 'Not again.'

The Karanadon was standing at the top of the steps of the main entrance. The huge glass doors of the library, now totally destroyed, lay in pieces in front of the enormous black beast. NSA agents were running in all directions to get away from it.

The Karanadon paid no attention to the people fleeing from it. In fact, it didn't even acknowledge their presence at all. It just stopped at the top of the steps and stood there, its head turning in a slow, wide arc.

Scanning the area.

Searching.

Searching for them.

And then it saw them. Exposed between the treeline and the big white rotunda, standing there in the pouring rain.

The huge beast roared loudly.

And then it leapt forward and with frightening speed, covered the distance between the library and the treeline in seconds. It bounded quickly forward, charging through the sleeting rain, its every step shaking the muddy earth beneath it.

Boom. Boom. Boom.

Swain and Holly ran for the rotunda. They reached it and climbed the steps, up onto the circular concrete stage.

The Karanadon hit the treeline and crashed through the branches of one of the giant oaks, charging toward the rotunda.

Then it stopped. Ten yards away. And watched them for several seconds.

They were trapped on the stage.

Marshall had his radio out.

'I'll give *you* fucking confirmation! The damn thing just charged out the front fucking doors! Get someone over here right now!'

The radio crackled back.

'I don't give a flying fuck what you're looking at! Get someone over here *now* and tell them to bring the biggest gun we've got!'

Swain led Holly over to the far side of the stage. He picked her up as the Karanadon moved slowly closer. The rain drummed loudly on the roof of the rotunda.

'Stay down,' Swain said, as he lowered Holly over the railing at the edge of the stage. She dropped lightly to the ground, six feet below.

The Karanadon reached the base of the rotunda. The pouring rain had wet its fur, slicking it down like a dog's. A running trickle of rainwater ran down a crease in its long black snout, dripped ominously off one of its huge canine teeth.

The big beast took a slow step up the stairs.

Swain moved in an arc around the circumference of the stage, away from Holly.

The Karanadon stepped up onto the stage.

It stared at Swain.

There was an endless, tense silence.

Swain drew his Glock.

The Karanadon growled in response. A low, angry growl.

Neither of them moved.

And then suddenly Swain made a break for the railing and the Karanadon bounded forward after him.

Swain reached the railing and had just started to vault over it when a giant black claw snatched his collar and snapped him backwards, and he landed in the centre of the concrete stage with a loud smack.

The Karanadon stood astride Stephen Swain and lowered its snout until it was face-to-face with him. It had his gun hand pinned to the stage beneath one of its massive hairy claws.

Swain tried in vain to turn away from its hideous fangs, its foul hot breath, its dark wrinkled snout, set in a perpetual sneer.

The Karanadon cocked its head slightly, seemingly daring him to escape.

It was then that Swain turned his head and saw the beast's hind foot step forward.

A wave of terror flooded through his body as he saw

the wristband that he had worn for the duration of the Presidian *right in front of his eyes.*

'Oh, *man* . . .' he said aloud.

The countdown was still ticking downward.

1:01

1:00

0:59

Only one minute to detonation.

Holy shit.

He began to wriggle and squirm, but the Karanadon held him down. It seemed totally unaware of the bomb attached to its foot.

Swain looked around the rotunda for an escape—at the white lattice handrail that circled the stage, at the six pillars supporting the dome-like roof. There was a small wooden box attached to the handrail, but its door was padlocked shut. In a detached corner of his mind, Swain wondered what the box was for.

There was nothing here. Absolutely nothing he could use.

He had finally run out of options.

Then suddenly, there came a voice.

'*Hello* . . . ?'

The Karanadon's head snapped up instantly, turned around.

Swain could still see the numbers counting down on the wristband inches away from his face.

0:48

0:47

0:46

'Hello? Yes. Over here.'

Swain recognised the voice.

It was Holly.

He looked up. She was standing over near the edge of the stage, the rain slanting down behind her like a curtain. The Karanadon swivelled to look at her—

—and abruptly something small smacked against the Karanadon's snout. It dropped to the ground next to Swain's head. It was a black school shoe. A girl's school shoe. Holly had thrown it at the Karanadon!

The big beast growled. A deep-chested rumble of pure, animal anger.

0:37

0:36

0:35

Then it slowly lifted its foot, moving toward Holly.

'Holly!' Swain yelled. 'Get out of here! It still has the wristband on and it'll blow in thirty seconds!'

Holly was momentarily startled. Then, in an instant, she understood and she began to run, leaping down the steps, vanishing from Swain's sight out into the park.

The Karanadon took one step forward in pursuit of her and then it stopped dead in its tracks.

And turned around.

0:30

0:29

0:28

It still hadn't released Swain's gun hand—still had it pinned down against the stage.

Swain struggled vainly against the giant creature's grip, but it was useless. The Karanadon was just too damn strong.

0:23

0:22

0:21

And then, just then, as he squirmed, something on the stage scraped against Swain's back.

Swain frowned—and saw that he had brushed up against a part of the stage that wasn't perfectly flush against the floor.

A small square of wood, sunken fractionally into the stage.

It was a trapdoor.

The same trapdoor that he had seen used in the summer pantomimes over previous years.

He was lying on top of it.

And then, realising, Swain's head snapped around— and his eyes fell on the small padlocked wooden box that he had seen attached to the lattice handrail before.

Now he knew what that box was for.

It housed the controls for the trapdoor.

0:18

0:17

The Karanadon stood over him, growling.

0:16

0:15

Even though his gun hand was still being held down by the beast, Swain's pistol was aimed roughly at the trapdoor's control box.

0:14

0:13

Swain fired. Hit the top corner of the box. The Karanadon roared.

0:12

0:11

He adjusted his aim. Fired again. This time the bullet hit the box closer to the padlock.

0:10

Third time's the charm . . . he thought, narrowing his eyes.

Blam!

Swain fired and . . . *shwack!* . . . the padlock snapped open, smashed by the bullet!

0:09

The control box's door swung open, revealing a large red lever inside. Simple operation: you pulled the lever down and the trapdoor on the stage dropped open.

0:08

Swain fired again, this time at the lever. Missed. He stole a glance up at the Karanadon—just in time to see one of its mighty black fists come rushing down at his face! Swain swung his head to the side, just as the gigantic black-clawed fist smashed into the stage *right next to his ear*, punching a hole clean through the trapdoor. The Karanadon raised its free claw again, for what would no doubt be the final blow.

0:07

Swain saw the big claw rise. He loosed several shots at the lever in rapid succession.

Blam! Blam! Blam! Blam!

Miss. Miss. Miss. Miss.

0:06

The Karanadon's claw reached the height of its back-swing. Its knuckles cracked loudly as it tightened into a fist.

'Goddamn it!' Swain shouted at himself. '*Focus!*'

The Karanadon's fist came rushing down—

Swain looked down the barrel of his gun—

—and suddenly the lever came into crystal-clear focus. 'Gotcha,' he said.

Blam.

The gun discharged and the bullet whistled through the air and this time . . .

. . . *crack!* . . .

. . . it *slammed* into the lever, severing it at its hinge

477

in an explosion of sparks, causing the whole lever mechanism to snap and fall and—

0:05

Whack!

Without warning, the trapdoor beneath Swain dropped away.

0:04

The Karanadon's fist hit nothing but air as it came rushing down, missing Swain's nose by centimetres as he dropped unexpectedly from beneath the massive beast, falling like a stone into the belly of the stage.

Swain landed with a dusty *thump* in darkness.

0:03

He saw the Karanadon on the stage above him, standing in a square of light, glaring down at him through the hole that only moments before had been the trapdoor.

Move!

He looked right and saw a vertical sliver of light in the darkness—a sliver of light that indicated the small wooden door that led out from underneath the stage.

0:02

Swain scrambled toward the little wooden door, firing his gun as he did so, pockmarking the door with holes, hoping to God he would hit the padlock on the other side.

0:01

And then he rammed into the door with his shoulder and it burst open before him and he flailed out into the pouring rain and landed clumsily on the wet grass that surrounded the stage.

0:00.

Cataclysm.

The explosion from the wristband—white-hot and blinding—blasted out horizontally, like a thousand-mile-an-hour ripple in a pond.

Swain scrambled on his hands and knees and pressed himself up against the concrete base of the stage as the white-hot wall of light expanded laterally— and spectacularly—above his head. He saw Holly on the ground over by the trees, her hands covering her ears.

The Karanadon simply disappeared as the brilliant white explosion shot outward from it, shattering all six of the pillars supporting the domed roof of the rotunda—reducing them to powder in an instant—and the massive white dome, without its supports, came crashing down onto the stage.

Behind Swain's back, the thick concrete base of the stage cracked under the weight of the explosion, but held.

White concrete dust and about a billion flakes of

paint fluttered in the air before the pouring rain broke them up, dispersing them.

Swain stood up slowly and stared at the rotunda, its huge domed roof now crumpled flat on its stage, the rain beating mercilessly down upon it.

There would be nothing left of the Karanadon, the explosion had been too big, too hot. The Karanadon was gone.

Swain hurried over to Holly and picked her up.

He saw NSA agents running toward them through the rain, and was about to break for it, when it happened.

Suddenly.

Unexpectedly.

Concurrent explosions—six of them—white-hot balls of light, bursting spectacularly from different sections of the library.

The biggest explosion came from the Third Floor. It seemed to be a combination of two separate explosions, twice the size of the other white fireballs that boomed out from the Ground and Second Floors of the library.

Glass blasted outwards from nearly every window of the New York State Library. People all around the building were diving for cover when suddenly an *underground* explosion—strangely, right where the underground parking lot was situated—dispatched a large oak tree clear from its roots, sending a gout of soil and grass flying into the rainsoaked sky.

Shrouded by a veil of slanting rain, the whole library was ablaze with fire now. Flames poured out from every window and as Stephen Swain led his daughter inconspicuously away from the pandemonium, he saw the Third Floor cave in on itself and crumble downwards, crushing the Second and First Floors.

The building's roof was still intact when the sixth and last explosion rocked the library and the strangest sight of all appeared.

An empty elevator—rocketing upward through the shaft—burst through the roof of the building and shot up into the sky, reaching the height of its parabolic arc and then falling, flying, crashing, back down onto the roof.

It was then that the roof itself caved in and the New York State Library—amid the sound of girders creaking and explosions multiplying and fires burning—collapsed in a blaze of glory and, despite the pouring rain, began to burn itself into oblivion.

James Marshall stared in dumbstruck awe at the fiery demise of the building that had promised him so much.

There had been nearly thirty agents inside that building when the explosions had gone off. None could have survived.

Marshall just stood there, watching the building burn. They would get nothing from this building. Just as they would get nothing from the rotunda. Marshall himself had seen the big black creature crash through the main entrance. And he had seen it explode.

A white-hot—micro-nuclear?—explosion like that would not leave much behind. Christ, it wouldn't leave *anything* behind.

Marshall put his hands in his pockets and walked back to his car. Phone calls had to be made. Explanations had to be given.

This night had been the closest they had ever come to contact. Perhaps the closest they would ever come.

And now? Now what did they have?

Nothing.

Stephen Swain sat on the subway train with his daughter asleep in his lap.

At every jolt of the train, they would tilt and sway with the other four passengers in their carriage. It was late and the near-empty train would get them to the outskirts of New York City. From there they would catch a cab—an expensive cab—back to Connecticut.

Back home.

Holly slept peacefully in Swain's lap, occasionally rolling over to make herself more comfortable.

Swain smiled sadly.

He had forgotten about the wristbands that all the contestants in the Presidian had to wear. When the electrified walls had disappeared, their wristbands—like his—must have also been set to detonate. So when the Karanadon had exploded with Swain's wristband, the other wristbands had gone off, too, *wherever* they happened to be—Reese's in the underground parking lot, Balthazar's on the Third Floor, and even Bellos', at the bottom of the elevator shaft.

Swain looked at his clothes—greasy, black, and in some places, bloody. Nobody on the train seemed to care.

He laughed softly to himself. Then he closed his eyes and leaned back into his seat as the train rumbled off through the tunnel toward home.

EPILOGUE

Workers on the New York Subway called it the Mole, an ordinary electric engine from a subway train that had been converted into a street-sweeper on rails.

Late at night, when subway services were at a minimum, the Mole would amble through the tunnels, its rotating forward sweepers scooping up any debris that might have fallen onto the tracks during the previous day. At the end of its run, all that debris would be tipped from the Mole into a furnace and destroyed.

Later that night, the Mole made its usual trip through the subway tunnel adjoining the State Library. And as it passed the Con Edison Booster Valve, the driver began to doze.

He never noticed the open doorway, never noticed the crumpled interior—packed solid with collapsed bricks and fragmented concrete.

487

And he never noticed the soft *clink-clink* of metal on metal that rattled underneath the Mole as it went past the Booster Valve.

The Mole ambled off down the tunnel, and all that remained in its wake was a pair of handcuffs, clasped to the track.

AN INTERVIEW WITH MATTHEW REILLY

THE WRITING OF *CONTEST*

What inspired you to write Contest?

There were two key inspirations for me to actually sit down and write *Contest*. First, the works of Michael Crichton. I still believe that Dr Crichton is the best storyteller in the world today. Not only are his stories original, they are also told at a cracking pace. Back in 1993, the year after I finished high school, my brother, Stephen, gave me a book and said, 'I'm told Steven Spielberg is going to make this into a movie, it's about a theme park built around genetically-engineered dinosaurs.' More than any other book I have read, *Jurassic Park* made me want to tell big action stories (especially stories with big scary 'animal' elements).

In terms of the *story*, the inspiration to write *Contest* came from my love of sports. I think there is drama in any kind of competition. All I did to turn that into a story was to make my contest the *ultimate* contest—if you win, you live; if you lose, you die.

Contest *originally appeared in late 1996 in self-published form. What are the differences—if any—between the self-published version and this one?*

In terms of the overall story, there are no differences. Structurally, it is exactly the same now as it was back in 1996. The differences come in the finer detail—in the *way* Swain does battle with the other contestants. The biggest alterations I made were in the 'final confrontation' scenes involving Swain and the three big villains of the book: Bellos, Reese and the Karanadon. In the original version of the book, these scenes were not as complex. Now they are bigger, badder and meaner.

The other big change was the addition of the Konda and the Rachnid. In the 1996 version, these two contestants weren't named or described. The reason for this was simple: when I originally wrote the book, I dreamed up six different alien species (Reese, Bellos, the Codex, Balthazar, the hoods and the Karanadon) and I just couldn't think up any more! But after a few years of thinking about *Contest*, I came up with these two extra species. So I put them in.

Apart from those, there are a lot of small changes, ranging from tightening the narrative in places to telling the reader how Swain's wife died, a piece of backstory that didn't appear in the self-published edition.

You mentioned that there are 'big scary animal elements' in your novels. Tell us about the various creatures in your books. Why are they there and why do you choose the ones you do?

I wish I could think of some loftier purpose, but the true reason for the big scary animal elements is very simple: they're there to eat people. I think there is nothing better in a book or movie than to see someone running from a big scary creature (think *Jurassic Park*, *Jaws*, or *Aliens*).

As for *why* I choose the creatures I choose, well, in *Ice Station*, for instance, I selected killer whales and elephant seals because I wanted the water to be a dangerous place— kind of like *Jaws*. The elephant seals were also the guardians, so to speak, of the underground cavern—making it a challenge to get there. In *Temple* I went one step further, and tried to make land *and* water dangerous places to be. There I used rapas (big, black, five-foot-tall cats which are the subject of myths in South America) and caimans (large crocodilians). I chose those animals because I wanted *Temple* to be darker and scarier than *Ice Station*.

As for *Contest*, well, as any Hollywood screenwriter will tell you, the best creatures of all are the ones you make up. For when you create an alien species, *there are absolutely no limits*. They can bleed acid (*Alien*), they can see via infra-red (*Predator*), or they can just be bigger, meaner and nastier than the biggest, meanest and nastiest Earth-based creatures.

Do you have the ending in your head when you start writing a new novel?

Ah, yes! This is Frequently Asked Question No. 1. Whenever I meet people and they discover I am an author, they always ask this question! The answer is: yes . . . usually.

The reason I say 'yes . . . *usually*' is because I feel that some flexibility is always required.

For example, the last line of *Temple* (which I won't give away, for those who haven't read it) was something that occurred to me halfway through writing the book. I love that line, and it's a great reason to remain flexible.

As for *Contest*, one question that nagged me all the way through the writing process was: *How the hell am I going to kill the Karanadon?* The answer—using Swain's wristband—came to me completely out of the blue. It just hit me. I started dancing around the house, pumping my fists in the air. It was so neat, so tidy, it saved Swain and yet it left no trace of the Karanadon. But neat as it appears in the book, it was not something I knew from the very start. Again, flexibility.

I see you have a new author photo for this book. Any reason for the change?

Yes—too much grief from my friends! Some took to calling me 'Mr Suave' because of the old photo! I kind of liked it, but it was getting a little dated (it was taken in 1997, before I had glasses). The new one looks more like the real me!

Any final words?

As always, I just hope you all enjoyed the book, and I hope to see you next time.

MR
Sydney
November 2000